MANIFEST OEDIPUS

AMERICA AT WAR

Liston Pope

MANTIS PRESS
New York
2009

Copyright © 2009 by Liston Pope
All Rights Reserved

Library of Congress Cataloging in Publication Data:

Liston Pope   1943–   Fiction
I. Vietnam War, Tet Offensive, RevDev hamlet
   Post-Traumatic Stress Disorder

   U.S. Presidential politics, Chicago Convention 1968
   U.S. Opposition politics, 'Sixties Era
   Anti-war activism, hippies,
   Berkeley 1967–68, People's Park

   Major League Baseball

   North Carolina, the Lumbee, Indigenous peoples

I. Title

Library of Congress Control Number: 2006906528

ISBN 0-9638900-9-3
ISBN 978-0-9638900-9-2

Distributed worldwide by Mantis Press, P.O. Box 237132
New York, N.Y. 10023

FIRST EDITION

ἡ ποικιλῳδὸς Σφὶγξ τὸ πρὸς ποσὶν σκοπεῖν
μεθέντας ἡμᾶς τἀφανῆ προσήγετο*

<hr />

*The Sphinx with its spangled (riddling) chants compelled us
To look to the present while neglecting the inscrutable (past).
Oedipus the King, lines 130–1.

MANIFEST OEDIPUS

Chapter One

I

1969

Now what's up with Jojo? What is wrong? Oh, don't tell me—not that again! At such a moment he goes into his mad act? Such an important game with first place riding, a key moment in the season: and now he decides to play the fool? No; he must be doing it on purpose.

Was he thinking about his wife again? Was he missing her: the woman who ran away while he was fighting for his country in Vietnam? Boy, forget her!

Oh, oh! From afar you could feel it coming over him, upstaging play on the field. What ever happened to the poor guy? Players in both dugouts, fans in the packed stands; the excited St. Louis stadium no less than millions following the play-by-play on TVs and radios—they knew. They sensed the disaster. They either loved it, laughing, taunting him, or shook their heads and asked themselves: Is this a night game or a nightmare?

Out at third base the League leader in four categories scuffed his cleats in the dust. But he lifted his head, losing concentration on home plate and the next pitch. His dark eyes rolled up ominously at the sky . . . Big, tallish, so strong and gifted, all his being a reflex for the playing of a game called baseball: the great athlete looked like a splendid wild stallion come to a halt on the infield grass after a long jaunt in the mountains. But there was something wrong with that stallion.

II

When Joey Gilbert stood in position awaiting the 2-2 pitch to the St. Louis hitter, he seemed to take all the light in the ballpark unto himself. It was the rubber game of the series, and now in late August the pennant race went along toward the drama of September. From here on in each game would be tense.

A step behind the bag and shaded toward the line for the righty pull hitter, Joey stared in but then shook his head a little as though at a buzzing insect. The banks of stadium lights shut out the night; they flooded the diamond and base paths, the wide green expanse of outfield. But tonight the lights had a way of highlighting Joey because no one knew what would happen next: because he was a third baseman with more on his mind than the game—crazy as he was after coming home from the war. He was like a ballplayer with a halo.

III

—Baw! cried the ump.

Full count.

Jojo gazed in from third, but his posture was strange: not bent forward, hands, glove spread like a mantis preying on infield chances. No; his body had a crick. And he seemed to listen—to what? Not the umpire, not infield chatter; not the groundswell of crowd noise, clamor of expectation, footstomping like murmurous thunder along an ocean floor . . . He stood almost straight but cricked slightly sideways. He listened. To what?

Outside the sold-out St. Louis park, all along the river for miles as far as the eye could see . . . there was a second crowd on hand tonight. Not baseball lovers, those—oh no. Not fans, but anti-fans;

and they picketed, marching slowly, a crowd so big it took nearly nine innings for them all to file past the ticket windows and the gates outside.

They chanted. From inside the park you could hear them. It sounded like an immense lamentation, a paean if you will: chanted by the chorus of the people. What is wrong here? What happened, America? Those voices raised in the night beside the great river winding through the nation's heartland—they seemed a lament for the loss of security, loss of faith in the country's mission. A bad, unwinnable war; social unrest at home, riots in the inner cities, chaos in the streets! What happened? What went wrong? Was it a plague? A plague in America of all places?

Through the evening of baseball the protest and demonstration wended its way in a circle extending for miles. And the chorus of the people pleaded for peace: for a restoration of the nation's lost health, and social well-being.

Joey Gilbert, the heroic soldier home from Vietnam, this star athlete whose season had been as erratic as it was fantastic, raised his head to listen. He looked like a cross between a hippie and the god of war. Really this 'Sixties Era was different; but shouldn't there be a limit to things? Land in turmoil, anarchy in the streets . . .

Full count on the St. Louis hitter. Joey awaited the payoff pitch, but he also sniffed; his nostrils twitched. Was it incense? Was the city filled with incense, as if to say: this is serious, this has to do with the gods? . . . Whiffs of tear gas drifted in from the goings-on outside the ballpark.

Out at third he seemed to ask the angry voices whose chants surged above the crowd noise, in the lull between pitches—why me? What does this have to do with me? Why tonight again? . . . For they followed him from park to park as the season geared up toward its final weeks, and the war went on raging in Southeast Asia. The activists and hippies chanted their slogans and made their speeches, and Joey Gilbert's brother was out there among them, one of the leaders.

Why me? The third baseman's posture seemed to say: why picket me? Can't you see I have enough on my hands? Do you think it's easy for me to play this game after the war unstrung my nerves? And with all the stories, the lies going around about my wife: sportswriters asking if this is the national pastime or a

soap opera. All this racket you are making brought on by a poor
madman trying to do his job and play third base . . . why, I didn't
make the war; it's not my fault; so what do you want from me?

It was like a curse on this land he had known since childhood
as a place to play baseball and strive to win and be the best. A
calm place, cordial, conservative—but now the curse seemed to
come looking for him, Joey, and single him out; it addressed itself
to him in the form of pickets and demonstrations against the war:
wherever he happened to be playing that evening.

—Baw . . . faw'!

Walked 'im. Bases loaded.

IV

Gilbert's quirks didn't go unnoticed. The St. Louis bench
watched closely. For them it was better than a stolen sign. All
were aware; all held their breath; what next? This lunatic brought
a new dimension to the game of baseball . . . Right now the New
York manager was in a state of shock, fearing a routine grounder,
a bunt to take advantage. Skipper cuffed the water cooler with a
gusto and muttered to himself:

—Here we go again!

The 2-1 delivery—

Joey shuddered. At any instant he might see things. Like an
anti-personnel mine his mind flared up; it flashed back to combat.
War images, ambush patrol, 30-klik hump between two ridgelines
. . .

High in the night sky a chopper blinked its red taillight and
sent out aerial images of the stadium nationwide. Bright, bright
green in a shower of light . . . From so high up the infield and
gold tan base paths, outfield grass with its combed sheen, crowd
color, players like specs whose destiny depended on hitting, chas-
ing, throwing an invisible ball—it was all a blur, a greenish mist
beneath banks of incandescent lights above the stands. And past
the stadium flowed the broad dark Mississippi in this stretch of
its journey toward New Orleans and the Gulf. And beside the
river up and down the quay the picketline moved like a caravan
of ants.

V

It was the home eighth.

Joey's thoughts drifted in and out of focus. Bases loaded. 3-1 New York lead.

Phthwoomph-woowoomph: engine drone with rotor beat. The helicopter thumped as the crowd noise went into its crescendo, and the St. Louis hitter stepped in. Fifty thousand fans footstomped, hooted, howled and sang out trying to distract the other guys. Jubilantly they booed in the seventh when Joey juggled a routine grounder to set up the lone St. Louis tally. Tasting blood, they jumped all over him. Ha ha ha! Go on outside and smoke dope with your brother and the other hippies. Ha ha ha! This game is for men, not potheads. They ragged him: a Vietnam vet breaking down mentally.

—Two gone! Two!

The New York shortstop, unheard in the din, held up index and pinkie for the outfielders. The batter stepped in. Play at any base.

The ace reliever came set. Kicks, delivers—

Swinguna'! Pop foul twisted back of first beyond the field boxes, into the stands.

Out on third Jojo tried to focus. He shook his head looking ruffled. Red taillight high in the sky, earsplitting chants, taunts, stomps, shrill whistles in the stands; firecrackers poppopped. There was a scuffle in the rightfield bleachers. A drunk set his hair on fire.

—Bench this clown!

—Naw, dance with the one that brungya'.

They moved in a wedge. Better bump Chingi from point. RTO Troupial, medic Tootie in center. Behind them the RevDev hamlet was an Armageddon scene: flashes, nourished gunfire, distant screams. No air-support as yet. Ahead of the squad, far out in the darkness, Truong Son's southernmost ridges sprawled in a mass beneath the stars.

Radio spluttered:

—Cheetah-six, over.

—Request numeric approximation, over.

—Dunno, Cheetah-six. Hold on.

Fifty thousand fans screamed, groaned. Joey saw visions.

Out across the zone it was a whirled confusion. Pop! pop! tatatata! Flare on the right: the field of fire hung with bright lights. Psst, explosion, psst, explosion. Rocket grenades: angle? The village was under attack. Sudden sharp crack, artillery, faint whistle; shells overhead. Orange tracers arced out gracefully. Punpun! Punpunpun! Tut! Tztut't! VC inside the wire! Past the claymores, concertina wire maze—sappers! Hold the squad in place? Strike for the ville, slowly, a closed wedge.

—Bawwah! cried Ump.

1-2 high: sailed above the letters.

On third Joey's eyes rolled. He peered up into the lights. Air support! Out of the night sky two Cobra gunships roared on the scene and drew .51 caliber, 37 mm ack-ack barrage fire.

Return to the doomed village?

—Bawwull thuhree! the ump swayed.

Instinct told him hold the squad in place. But Drawber was a dictator. Matter of duty. Retrace the outward swath?

—First Sergeant orders: most direct route!

Ump stretched and clicked his indicator. Count full, bases jammed, bottom of the eighth. Two down: off to the races. The runners led. The capacity crowd stood and hollered; they screamed, ululated as the righthanded reliever came set, kicked briskly, and the 3-2—

Suddenly, on his left in the wedge: an explosion. A man cried out, surprised. Sanger.

—Freeze! Nobody moves!

The runners flew. The hitter swung, and sent a high, high Baltimore chop toward third.

Joey's eyes fluttered . . . Entranced by the flashback he didn't pounce forward, glove 'er, throw. Instead he shouted:

—Squad in place! Hold positions!

A second explosion. Clement glanced right, stunned. Manito, the assistant gunner—puff! Triggered one. Up in smoke.

—I said don't move!

Boom! Boom—

Tootie scurried where Tommy Lerch lay on the ground.

—Help me! God! God! Help me!

Pandemonium. The one-hopper hung above the infield and bounced down, plup, a few feet before Joey to his right. But he stood frozen, his mind in the grip of war images. He stared and gestured wildly to himself while runners rounded the bases and the ball rolled slowly toward the bag.

Orange tracers arced out over a dreamlike slow-motion fire field lit by pastel streamers.

Grunts broke ranks and scrambled in panic. Plup! plup! A fourth, a fifth mine detonated. Fern shrieked, his voice cracking, and called for his ma. Jib Benson rushed toward him and—boom! With a cry he leapt up clownish and flopped back.

—Help me! Fern wailed. Oh God not now, not me! Will I die?

St. Louis runners rounded the base paths. Pop! Tatatatata. Flare! The third baseman watched the ball roll, roll and squib sideways toward the line.

Grunts cried out their horror in the smoke and smell of burnt metal and powder. Darkness, howls.

—I don't want to die!

Round third base the lead run raced home. Hysteria in the stands. The shortstop swore.

—Throw the ball!

Sanger writhed on the ground, burning. Tootie leaned over Chingi's gristle: shrapnel wounds. Troupial tripped a mine and ignited smoke grenades hooked on his web belt beneath the radio transmitter. His legs were engulfed in a purple shower.

—Mama!

—Freeze!

—Hit!

Blast after blast: more mines exploded.

Medic Tootie crouched low. He chicken-walked to where the man writhed.

Joey Gilbert gave a grisly laugh. The capacity crowd shrieked while a soldier halved at the waist pleaded feebly for his mother. On tiptoes, ever so nimbly, the RTO or radio operator, a short-timer—

Boom!

Troupial leapt, high up, fell back on his helmet. Neck jack-knifed. The radio flew in bits.

—Oh God, not me! Only four more days!

Burnt metal reek. Men were yelling in the smoke.

—Corpsman! I don't want to die!

To Joey's left the shortstop threw up his arms:

—Screwit.

The lead run scampered across. The stadium shook.

The medic trembled and mumbled a few words.

Joey bowed his head and stood strangely, bent sideways with a kind of crick, in shock. Plup! Pop-pop!

—I said nobody moves!

—Ma.

—Oh, no! Please . . .!

—Screwit.

VI

But the runners drew up: halted in their dash round the base paths. They whirled back and threw up their arms as the ball edged into foul territory an inch shy of the bag. After pausing it took a last half twist off the ridge of lime.

—Fow' baw'!! shouted the third base umpire.

What a genius that Joey Gilbert: no one, least of all his manager in a St. Vitas dance by the water cooler, had a notion to let the unplayable ball roll foul.

—Medic! Tootie!

Joey screamed, wild-eyed. An unearthly glow lit a field of limp dervishes sprawled here and there. There were moans, sobs, a few more words. There were pleas for help. Joey raised his mitt and shouted at a runner trotting back across the diamond:

—Nobody moves!

He darted forward and tackled him and held the grunt shaken by sobs against the ground. Now the stands went mad. Gilbert had jumped on a St. Louis runner and pinned him down against the infield grass. He yelled in his face:

—I said don't move!

Both dugouts emptied. In a rage of frustration the players grappled one another and threw punches. It was chaos on the field and in the stands. The donnybrook spread as more brawls erupted. Blood flowed. Police came in vans.

VII

That night the game could not be resumed. The final outs if not a 9-inning replay would have to be set for a later date by the League office. There were arrests of spectators who walloped cops: the contingents arriving in riot gear. But there were no player suspensions—not even the cause of it all, this amazing Joey Gilbert whose antics in St. Louis were only the latest in a season marred with such things. Wow! That man was a one-man band when it came to boosting box office receipts in an off year. For the country seemed to turn away from baseball: more focused on war in Vietnam and here at home, political demonstrations in the cities, hippies and Yippies, leftist radicals and Trotskyites and Marxist ideologues. The whole place was infested with outside agitators. Only Joey's act combined the two worlds and brought an extra dimension to baseball: a human note which kept people on the edge of their seats. He demonized the game.

Of course the nation's newspapers were full of it the next day. What was wrong? What happened to Joey Gilbert in Vietnam? And what was going on with America?

What had the poor fellow seen over there to make him so crazy now that he'd traded his jungle fatigues for a Major League baseball uniform? Where had he been, and what had he done? What was the talented athlete's problem?

One sportswriter asked how a man could hope to play baseball at all after a war had ruined his nerves. In an instant Joey goes from the superhuman lucidity and discipline of a great player to the murky mood of a psychotic.

Another asked: how does a nut lead the League in hitting, and ten minutes later have a popfly bounce off his forehead?

Reasons, causes, conjectures, guesses . . . And then came the rumors that went around to do with Joey's wife: a Native American woman from a North Carolina tribe. Not all of those tales were in good taste. For she ran away. She left her man, a war hero fighting for the country's ideals, in his moment of need. Did she really do that? Why?

Say! Is this our National Pastime or is it a tearjerker? And what about all the racket outside the St. Louis ballpark, all those protesters? Was that called for? Or was it downright unsportsmanlike?

VIII

The people asked: what went wrong over there, Joey? What is your problem? Is it a mystery? Yes, surely there's a mystery at work here, like a Sphinx's riddle. This was Joey's nickname for his wife: Sphinx.

Her real name was Carlyne. She was a humanities major at the college where they met. Once she told him the Sphinx was sent to ancient Thebes by Hera, the goddess of marriage—sent as a curse, part of the same Labdacides curse that fouled up Oedipus. The Sphinx was sent because Hera's precepts had been violated; the new reason and orderliness presided over by the later gods, as opposed to the old regime of Fates, the Furies, the old matriarchy, had been disregarded . . .

In a similar way across the United States, those turbulent days of the 'Sixties, our people old and young were trying to solve a riddle of their own. Just as the mythological monster with human head and lion's body carried off and devoured young men who failed to answer its question—so now many American boys were dying in a faroff war. Was it because we were failing to solve the riddle of history?

What went wrong? What had happened, somewhere in Vietnam, at a crossroads in Joey Gilbert's life?

How had he come to play third base like a man possessed? Was someone to blame? Was it due to his wife? Was Carlyne to blame? Why did she leave her man, and he so promising?

Yes, it must have concerned Carlyne: the beautiful young woman, the mysterious daughter of the Tuscarora. His strange behavior had its cause—in things which happened long before the night game in St. Louis when all hell broke loose.

At least two years prior to that we must look back, if not longer, a lot longer: to the origin of the curse! . . . But we'll begin with two years ago: in a small southern town in the Piedmont area of North Carolina. One autumn night . . .

Chapter Two

I

Many were surprised to put it mildly when Joey Gilbert failed to show up at a Minor League ballpark one afternoon, and it turned out he had gone to a recruitment station and enlisted in the United States Army. He said he hadn't done anything for his country, unlike other men in his family, and he wanted to go help out in Vietnam. Nobody was more surprised than the parent club front office in New York which knew nothing about it; or than his wife Carlyne who was presented with the new situation and never mind her feelings on the matter: never mind how such a decision might affect her. It was a stunning gesture, one of patriotism, idealism, spirit of sacrifice; although not widely known, not picked up by national media since at the time Joey was a prospect and not in the limelight. Also he refused interviews: a quiet ballplayer who said he would do what his uncle had done during World War II, what any man must do; only that, nothing more or less. Well, yes, at the time he might have tried to capitalize with a book contract, the whole shebang, but only on the coattails of his dad's fame; he was the great writer's son. But his own achievements which were in the offing then, and his unknown name, couldn't really bear such freight.

Away he went to basic training with a special course in counterinsurgency tactics at Puyallup in Washington State: artificial jungle terrain, anti-guerrilla warfare and enemy minefield simulation. Then Southeast Asia.

But in the hours before shipping out, on leave back in Durham with his wife for a weekend, he said to her:

—See you in Bangkok, okay? R & R. They'll cut me some slack halfway through the tour.

Carlyne stared into the darkness. She had a tear in her eye, and maybe it was the first time he had seen that. She stopped crying during her years at an orphanage in La Grange, across the state, after Judge Vick's kin got at her inheritance in the courts.

That night she looked at Joey and said:

—I wish you hadn't done this.

—Oh?

She had said so before but in her usual listless tone. Now she seemed to mean it, and this thrilled him. He would take those words and that tear in her eye away with him to Vietnam. Did she love him a little after all?

—Why did you do it?

—To serve.

He shrugged.

—I see: to serve. Why not ask my opinion?

—I didn't think you . . . minded.

—So you decide and that's it. You could have stayed with sports; you belong there, not ten thousand miles away in a jungle.

He wrinkled his nose:

—Sports are good for kids. Anyway you don't like baseball.

—I can take it or leave it. My husband playing for money is a little different.

Impatiently she brushed the tear; shook her head and looked away from him, into the predawn darkness.

He said low:

—Don't worry, I'll be back and we'll start again. First I've got a job to do over there.

Happy now for the first time in a long time, he gave a shrug, a Hollywood smile.

Carlyne shook her head on the pillow, blinked, choked a little:

—I'll miss you, Bub.

He thought she looked very beautiful then.

—If they do give me a week or ten days at Christmas, will you come? Will you fly out?

—Sure.

He took a deep breath.

—Well, now I'm myself again. Go get 'em, champ. We can write, and I'll phone. But look: if you get lonely then I want you to go to them at the Rock Castle. Just take the train and go live there. My little sister will love you so, and Dad. We all love you, Carlyne, so much.

She gave a small laugh and said:

—I can just see the likes of me in that town. What a creature.

—I asked my father about it, and he says it's fine. Don't worry at all; he'll take care of things. And you and Lemon can keep each other company: she's such a good guy and pretty much alone in that big house. She'll love it if you go live with them.

—Jo, I think your dad has enough to worry about without me getting into the act.

—Not at all. I mean it: go to the Rock Castle. You're a Gilbert. We're your family.

For a long moment at dawn he kissed her, caressed her, wished he never had to leave this paradise.

She pressed against him: stirred by his excitement.

—Oh, Jo, oh—

But then he drew away. He stood up. By the bed he hefted his duffel bag.

—Before you know it I'll be home. Then we'll start thinking about a family and kids, okay? But enough baseball: what do you think? We'll settle at the Rock Castle and revive Granddaddy's farm, like Dad wants. Okay? I always thought about doing that. Okay?

—Sure.

—How many kids you want? Eleven?

—No, thirteen.

—That's a deal! ... Well, bye, sweet baby. Goodbye, my darling.

He bowed to her again. He knelt by the bed and kissed her lips, her face in disarray. He nestled to her womanly breast a long moment.

—Bye now.

—Bye.

Joey kissed Carlyne's hand in the aura of dawn light. And then he stood up tall and went out closing the door quietly.

II

That morning a cicada sang before sunrise. In the first light the soldier went along toward Five Points in downtown Durham. He looked straight ahead like a man in a trance. His heart was beating quick as he walked on air strolling away from the woman he loved to go risk his life. Joey felt flushed with a new hope then and he thought: So she loves me? Wants me after all? I was no great shakes, neglecting her for baseball; didn't pick up on her needs. Insensitive jock I guess. But she seems willing to give me another chance. Amazing, my wife loves me.

And then Joey Gilbert grinned. That grin—it was metallic, a pro athlete's grin. He made his way toward the bus station feeling very full, ready for anything, cocky! She inspired him with a need to do good and sacrifice. It was patriotism he felt that morning: ready and willing to meet any challenge. Well, he thought, it is one thing to be a ballplayer but another to become a man.

Bright leaf scent embalmed the town where Joey and Carlyne had gone to college; where she was just finishing her B.A. a year behind him and thinking of a Master's degree. In the twilight a reddish star flickered high up over the tobacco factory's long brick wall with its dark smokestacks. Along East Main he breathed in the sweet pungent aroma of processed tobacco, caressing his wife in thought, and marched off toward the world's uncertain fringes.

Ah! the way he felt now . . . What a fine guy that Joey Gilbert is! So dedicated, such a loving husband and father someday. Joey, Joey, he's our man—if anybody can do it (save the world for democracy) *he* can! . . . He had spent his early years totally engrossed in sports. But unlike his brother Newell, a hippie, a rebel if there ever was one, Joey had a true-blue attitude toward America as toward his family and famous father whom he admired without reserves. Now Carlyne's love had come on strong to fortify the desire to serve. Oh! what a redblooded talented boy that Jojo! Go get 'em, kid! Hawn', you babe!

In the seamy Durham bus station, open all night, a few travellers sat in the waiting area.

Two prostitutes had taken a booth inside the greasy spoon just now opening for breakfast.

Joey went in too. He ordered a 3-egg omelette and settled in to wait for his first hop toward the faroff war.

III

Joey went to Vietnam.

And Carlyne? What did she do?

For a few more weeks she was busy with her classes and studies in the Women's Campus library. She kept on with the routine of a college senior, the flurry of work on term papers, cramming for exams. Then it was time to put on a cap and gown and go get her diploma at commencement exercises.

This was a stirring event for her. A reporter made the trip from Pembroke in Robeson County, down in the southeastern part of the state, land of the Lumbee Tribe. For Carlyne Gilbert was the first of her people to attend the elite southern university; and now she had completed her course of studies and was receiving a diploma with her name in gothic script, up on a stage before class members and the world.

But the ceremony was marred for Carlyne, who had a husband fighting in Vietnam, by impromptu chanting in the audience. They sat listening to an address in support of the war, but they called out:

Hell no! We won't go!
We won't fight for Texaco!

This was taken up like a groundswell in the Indoor Stadium. Probably it was organized beforehand by antiwar groups on campus with their posters, pickets, rallies and teach-ins through the academic year. Also, Carlyne didn't like it when students came naked to the ceremony; that is, bare-assed beneath their gowns. This was due to hippie elements like her brother-in-law who had nothing but scorn for such pomp and circumstance. And then, as Elgar's strains started up again, and the new graduates filed out led by a line of dignitaries: one female senior had the cheek to run ahead of the procession and flash her pink butt at the stonefaced university president and the cameras. That's for you, meatheads. Let the whole world watch and be put on notice.

Carlyne watched and frowned. She didn't like it. In those same moments her husband was risking his butt for an ideal in Vietnam. And she just got a letter from him about the wounding of G.I.s from his platoon in a place called Phu Bai.

Through the afternoon and evening she visited with sorority sisters, hugging her friends in the women's dorms, helping them pack, saying goodbye. Then she went home to her and Joey's off-campus apartment behind East Campus, and slept twelve hours.

Carlyne woke up to a warm summery day in Durham and asked herself: what now? What to do? There was nothing for her here, so she got on a bus and rode south past Fayetteville for a visit with her mother's people, Aunt Lovedy Locklear, Daystar Lowry and them. She stayed two weeks: paying calls and receiving congratulations. She was a star with her face on the front page of the local newspaper. Daystar and some of the men urged her to run for Miss Lumbee—beauty contests being such a big thing in Lumbee land;—maybe become the first 'Indian' Miss North Carolina. But Carlyne laughed at that idea. She wasn't into beauty contests.

She just went her way, eating too much rich food, dancing in the Long House with good old boys she remembered from childhood, and doing a peck of other things she used to do way back then: making preserves, going to quilting parties and the like. She enjoyed herself a lot; she put on weight, swam and fished in the pure cold tannin-brown Lumbee River just like when she was a girl and went down there for a visit with her mother from Judge Vick's in Kinston.

But it became clear she couldn't stay at Aunt Lovedy's and wait for Joey to come home. For one thing she grew a bit bored. Also, there were things to do and take care of in Durham after all, so in early July she went back there.

And now Carlyne was faced with a decision. Perhaps there was no need to think and think about it like she did. The question was this: should she draw on her husband's money—joint checking and savings accounts—to enroll in school and pay for tuition, books and the rest. There was plenty: the New York club had paid the bonus baby Joey Gilbert well. Without qualms she would use it to live, pay rent and buy groceries. But she meant to look for work at least part-time: maybe substitute teaching in a Durham grade school. As an undergraduate she majored in education; she fulfilled her education block requirements and now she could teach elementary school. But she planned to do more: what she wanted was to become a principal in Pembroke or nearby; if not there then out West on one of the reservations, a school administered by the Bureau of Indian Affairs. And for this she needed a Master's degree if not a doctorate.

But for some reason she could not persuade herself to use Jojo's money. Maybe because their marriage just hadn't jelled; she always had doubts about it; and maybe because she couldn't see how such career plans of her own might fit in with a Big League ballplayer's needs. Make no mistake: that's what he was. And when he came home from Vietnam, when this whim of his, so she called it, was over: then he'd go to baseball again and head on up. And then he'd expect her to be there by his side.

Well, she might choose to be somewhere else. Yes, she might. But not on his money, not at his financial expense at least: later on that could seem dishonest even if she paid it all back. So thought Carlyne then. In the case of her career and goals, her intellectual development, the third baseman did not pay the tab.

IV

In late July she went to the small southern town halfway across the state and paid a weekend visit on her in-laws.

Life at the Rock Castle was quite enjoyable after the long hot Durham days and nights with little to do but read. For some reason she had dallied about finding a job, and she couldn't spend her life rereading the Russian novels she liked. But the boredom of inactivity turned to a curious excitement, full days, new ideas, pleasures, in that quiet backwater where Joey had his origins on the paternal side. There was one factory; there was a dead up town like so many other places. And there was a lot of nature, Yadkin River, wide untilled Gilbert farmlands, birds and wildlife and sunlight. Oh, and the nights! They had a kind of romance in the country quietude, like a nest of gentlefolk.

Like everyone else she admired the famous writer who was
her father-in-law. For one thing she saw Emory through her husband's eyes, and Joey always worshipped his dad. No doubt Carlyne looked to Emory as a surrogate father: since Judge Vick died
when she was just coming to her girlhood; and then her mother
died too, one thing led to another, and she spent formative years
in a dark place, an orphanage where things went on. Oh, a man
like Emory Gilbert made things seem all right and gave you new
interest in life. Everything would be fine! After all her worries and
loneliness Carlyne felt herself step out into the sunlight.

Then there was Joey's younger brother. Newell was full of
cockeyed fun and pranks, humor, a goodnatured irony. At night
the grad student turned hippie and social critic liked to argue politics with a semiretired Army General named Maximilian Doan.
Doan was jingoism in the flesh, a living symbol of what Newell
despised. But the blond gentleman also had a twinkle in his steely
blue eye; he liked women to a fault, and he made Carlyne think
twice when he came in the room. But he did the same thing, turning on his middle-aged charm, with Joey's younger sister: the 13
year-old Lemon who laughed and called him Thanks-a-Million
behind his back, because he was so cheap.

Carlyne spent a rainy Saturday afternoon playing—that's right,
playing with dolls and puppets—in Lemon's room on the second
floor of the Rock Castle. And she seemed to breathe freely there:
as if she took the little quivery breaths of a child who calms down
after a crying spell.

Also there was Cindy, the Gilbert's maid: a black woman with
a kind way about her and attachment to the family. Carlyne felt at
home with Cindy Phillips at once. She went in the kitchen to help
her with the country cooking.

Then there was one other man on hand: a churchman named
Bishop Commynes. That man's piety, the way he stared at the
young voluptuous wife of Joey Gilbert as if seeing through her
. . . soul—this made Carlyne quiver another way. And she looked
down, then up again. She smiled at the retired minister and felt a
twinge of—what?

But mainly she felt at home with them: safe and accepted.
Among the Gilberts and their friends she was more alive, hap-
pier, than she had been in a long time. Now the bus trip back to
Durham would be a dreary ride.

Twice Emory brought up Joey's idea, urging that she come live with them while waiting out his year-long tour overseas. At the Rock Castle she could count the days until her husband came back home to her, and those days would pass more easily.

Yet a third time Emory said it: as the moment drew near for him to drive her to the old depot. And she thought how pleasant it would be: how lively to come here and spend the weeks and months with Lemon, Cindy, and the Gilbert menfolk.

And she accepted.

V

In those late summer days after Carlyne moved in, the Rock Castle was full of life. For her part she was just an easygoing, slow-moving, average southern woman who liked to sleep late after chatting about this and that on the front porch. She enjoyed helping Cindy, and she could spend two hours in a hot perfumed bath; in fact, she spent all the time she wanted in the guest bedroom's thick-carpeted bathroom with its oldfashioned tub and fixtures, and cosmetics table like a sort of small battlefield. Carlyne rested up and pampered herself. She looked forward to the days.

And Lemon was so happy with her. They played together like girls: parlor games; or dressing up in the grand old outfits of Wilhelmina, Emory's mother who died a few years before; cooking, going on eating sprees in the kitchen while Cindy looked on and shook her head. There were long walks out back across the fields to the river, or up town as night began to fall. But there the locals stared too much at Carlyne.

When Newell emerged from his binges of studying in the Rock Castle attic, then you better watch out. Why that boy might say anything and do anything. He danced the women around including Cindy whom he called 'comrade'; he romped with his dog Pyggy, a collie-husky getting too old for roughhousing but who loved her master so. But he was goodhearted, not impertinent, until the political argument started up again with General Doan and Emory after dinner. Then he went after Max Doan and time-honored American values with a glee; then he treated his father with an irony and used the famous writer's mannerisms against him in a way which was funny even if nobody got the point half the time. Newell was obscure; he was in his obscure period; and he liked to quote Hegel and even talk like Hegel, making fun of Emory who said he too owed a debt to the great German. The effect was strange and comical.

Oh, those were good times at the Rock Castle. There was high life in the laughter and chatter, the good rich meals and spirited conversation, the outings, little family projects, even rehearsals for an amateur theater production in the living room. Maybe it was a bit like the old plantation life; and that's what this antebellum mansion once was: a manor house with a large barn still standing today, and numerous outbuildings; important farm acreage exploited to the full in pre-Civil War decades when Europe wanted all the cheap cotton it could get from the South.

So much good life and laughter, flirting, desire for pleasure there were in those warm late summer days at the Rock Castle. Emory even thought of throwing a grand ball and lighting up the high-ceiling'd rooms like in the olden days when his father, P. Laster the banker, and socially minded Wilhelmina had their daughters to marry off; and the beaus came flocking in their buggies from as far off as Charlotte and Raleigh, even Charleston, and they were good boys and danced the night away.

But despite all the fun there were undercurrents.

For one thing there was TV footage from Vietnam on the nightly news which could take away one's appetite for supper. Joey was over there in the middle of it, and his letters home to Carlyne were a little like the news. They had taken a new tone not quite so gung-ho anymore, as the infantryman spent his days a different way from his lighthearted family. He was deep in it, head over heels in muck somewhere in the Central Highlands of Vietnam. And so the day came when Carlyne said she could not read the smudged letters anymore: penned in haste, in the darkness, since it was dangerous to turn on a penlight when they stopped for the night and laid out their mines so that VC would at least give warning when they came in past the squad's perimeter, and attacked in the night.

VI

Then, late one October night . . . It was the night when Emory Gilbert seemed to turn into his opposite, as Newell, or Hegel, would say.

Emory paused on the front stairway of the Rock Castle and asked himself just what he was doing there. Was it really him? Or was he dreaming? It seemed the gods took him up by the scruff and were shaking him around. He stood in a trance, and felt yanked down a few steps toward the dark front hall, but then pulled his body back up a step or two on the wide red-carpeted stairs of that stone mansion built by his ancestors. Emory Gilbert, who wrote 'literary classics in a national spirit' as one critic said, seemed to wrestle with more words. And the violence in him was such, in those instants, it drove him forward, it dragged him back; it was like an earthquake in his person. He was at the crossroads, and he didn't know which way to take. Half a century's repression of sexual passion was roiling up in him.

But he must think—the consequences!—before rushing in. He must think, think, before he did what none might ever undo or set right again.

And so the man of letters thought of an ancient myth: a boy named Chrysippus kidnapped and raped by a man who was the father of Oedipus. And this was how the curse began: the curse of the Labdacides which said the hero must kill his own father and marry his mother.

Emory Gilbert thought of this Chrysippus as he stood on the verge of—what act? Couldn't it have been done a gentler way: that personal renewal needed so by Laïus? Was physical possession necessary? After what seemed a lifelong abstinence—despite a lovely wife, Anne, and thirty years of family life—Emory felt he had to have such a sexual renewal, now, and nothing else mattered. This woman he must have: her, have her to live. And let the Furies do their worst. And then the sparagma, the disaster, if it must come to that. For he could not help himself: go on as he had been. He would hang himself first, and what was the good of that?

His heightened senses heard the night in this quiet southern town. Outside, a breeze rustled among the shrubs and tall oaks on the long sloping front lawn. Some night bird gave its call from out in the fields. Then, so close it plucked at his nerves, the staircase creaked beneath his weight as he drew back another step and said softly: this cannot be; never! But the old Rock Castle seemed to sigh and ask him: why not? why not?

For a long time, probably since childhood, he had not felt things so acutely, in the essence. Kitchen and pantry scents, the resiny back porch, hearth, roughhewn granite walls; his father's wainscoted den to the left off the front hall with its old leather armchair and cigar tinge; all this was in the pores of the old place. And such odors summed up the tragic sense he had of his passion. For in the first floor bedroom alongside the stairwell a young woman slept with no inkling of the things in his mind. She was happy to be here, unafraid, a guest in his house. And now Emory's heart beat so quick, so hard, he put a hand to his chest.

Why? said the staircase. Why not? . . . Cree-e-eak!

In small sounds and smells lurked an otherness as though he might never sleep in his own bed again, never rest easy, and talk calmly to a friend.

Now he stared downstairs into the shadows like a misty pool—dining room entry, then the den; front hall table where letters from Joey lay in their envelopes unopened. He took another step down, and . . . *cre-e-eak!*

Oh how he wanted to go back up to the master bedroom and sleep peacefully till morning. But up there if he backtracked was a kind of living death, without her; while before him was life, risk.

On the plush stairway with its banister, finials molded as gargoyles, Emory made an impressive figure. So big and talented: men like him were the remembered ones, the honor of their country centuries down the road. Never mind if they were scoundrels: Racine was deceitful and two-faced, envious, wicked even; he made his own people suffer, and like a great tree took away the sunlight from others who had the bad luck to be near him. But Racine wrote things which stimulate our lives today. Racine was a genius. And so was Emory Gilbert, standing there, a tall handsome man with a noble forehead, his temples graying with a grave dignity. No other person in this town ever inspired such awe. He was a national figure. Up North he made the grade: and this despite a decency he had, a liberal fair-mindedness, and good down-to-earth humor.

If you said to this man yesterday, an hour ago, he would set out to do what he had in mind, do this thing like a wildest fantasy: then he would have drawn up in his most imposing manner and said through his teeth: You lie!

VII

After his wife died Emory came South to live out his days in the town where he was born and grew up, and still had friends from childhood like Paul Commynes. In his loneliness he was drinking too much. After three decades of labors in New England, major works completed, he wanted to come home and seek peace amid nature and these old Gilbert farmlands: the scenes, friends and folkways so to say, from his boyhood.

Kindly to children, good with them like his banker father, he might start Newell or Lemon when they were little with a quarter in the morning; and through the day he made change with a few pennies interest until the two bits became a dollar by dinnertime.

Personable, brilliant at social gatherings, also modest in his way: he could steer a meeting on the right course with a few sure words. Often he waited coiled up for the right moment and then spoke to the point. Emory had a way with people in the small southern town.

He was an enlightened aristocrat, let's say on the Jeffersonian model, or like John Taylor of Caroline who was an old hero of his. He was also like a planter in some ways: style of life, interests, patriarchal airs. He came out for liberal causes and said his piece when he felt like it, yet he stirred little or no resentment around here. He stood by an underdog, a laid-off factory worker, an older person neglected or in trouble, a poor but worthy family in Skeeter Hawk, the poor section.

He cared deeply for his four children. But it was the eldest daughter Evelyne who died while in high school that he loved most. He called her Lady.

His late wife Anne was a fine woman (*Proverbs* 31, 10-31), and he mourned her until it began to affect his health.

It seems nature gave Emory Gilbert everything a man could desire, health, wealth, fame, good looks, a progressive outlook,

joy in things, and all of it crowned by the classic books he gave
to America. And, if that wasn't enough, he also had a fine sense
of honor imbibed long ago like mother's milk in this same noble
house along the town's main road.

VIII

Yet here he stood in the warm Indian summer night on the
verge of a terrible act. Day after day he had felt a mounting desire
for this young woman, for her flesh, until it was more than he
could stand. Newell liked to tease his dad; Newell always took
things too far. And so he would say after studying in the attic all
night:

—Oh ho! I think you are too horny, Sir! I think you want to interpenetrate with your opposite! The quantity of your lust would
like to become the quality of the act, as you set yourself on your
head! Try it out, Sir. Find a nice girl. Identity in non-identity is
great fun once you get the hang of it, as General Max Doan, that
amateur of young ladies, too young, can tell you: if the rumors
around town are true!

Well, Newell was a scamp. But he was also on the scent with
his remarks. Carlyne's arrival at the Rock Castle shook Emory up.
He held himself in check for as long as he could, but now he came
down the stairs toward the guest bedroom; and then recoiled in
horror from the very idea; but then lingered and was simply unable to go back upstairs. He was a man caught in fate's toils as
midnight passed. He must be insane to think of such a thing: as
though he no longer had a say in his own actions.

But there was one more thing. Yesterday morning a call came
from Washington, D.C., and this too had shaken him. Suddenly
there was a new chance to live and forget his grief for Anne; and
leave behind the alcohol problem. That phone call was a godsend.
The Democratic Party invited the noted author to come on board
as adviser and speech writer for the '68 Presidential Campaign.
He would go to D.C. and be in the inner circle with all this meant
for a high post in the future if they won.

The idea had the key Vietnam issue in view: that hot potato in
the Democrat's hands. Criticize the war and you're soft on com-

munism. But now Emory's son, the ballplayer, had gotten media play as a squad leader over there. A news segment showed the big lithe soldier as he patrolled near a place called Buon Me Thuot; it compared his tour at a time of NLF guerrilla upsurge to the wartime sacrifice of other athletes. This could give Joey's dad moral authority to address the treacherous issue. Emory's son put a pro sports career on the back burner for patriotic reasons. So it may have been Jojo who got him that call from Washington, and the exciting job.

The offer swept Emory off his feet. There was much merriment this evening when he dined with his two old friends, Commynes and Doan. Go to Washington, young man!

And so if he could hobnob with the President what couldn't he do and get away with it? Only renew himself: like Racine! Never mind at whose expense. Win! Success conquers all. Go forward, great man. Plunge in—as Bishop Commynes told him to do, in a toast. Nobody knocks a winner.

IX

And now, as he came down the stairway with its old totem-like balusters, a tremor ran the length of Emory's body. He felt hot and cold. He shivered with desire for the woman, and he feared.

Had she locked her door? He gave her a key for the guest bedroom: only he and she had it. Did she lock the door tonight? In his passion he asked himself if someone else could be in there with her now . . . Newell was awake and studying up in the attic. Max Doan slept over sometimes in a room kept ready for him on the third floor. Max had the run of the place.

Was she awaiting a visitor? after all the good fun and Cindy's sumptuous fare and the wine and champagne and cognac? There were glances across the dining room table, oblique and fleeting. Ah! ah! Did she want it too? Did she want a man to come to her tonight—*him*, Emory, whom she loved and revered? Ah! Go! Go on! Dare! Risk!

The sensualist hung there shivery with desire and anguish. He tried to control his nerves, those obstacles to life. Act? Don't act? What about telltale signs? Would there be clues? Would proof exist

if God help us it ever came to that? To be sure he had gone crazy
and was not responsible for his actions. Crazy with love for her, and
voluptuous lust. In a court of law would this be a crime? And if she
wanted it too? Was it adultery? Ever enforced in North Carolina?

She would not tell. Anyway Newell had already gone in to her.
See how she invites them, all the men? Well, she was like the notorious prostitute named Cherokee who used to work this small
southern town and almost got its first citizen P. Laster Gilbert, the
banker and man of probity, in a heap of trouble—did get him into
it, lifelong, with his wife.

In all Emory's nearly sixty years of life Carlyne was the first
woman who ever seemed to hold out to him this sense of completeness and new life and health. Could that be sick? No one.
Ever. Only her.

It will not come to light. If ever there was a man in this town
you could trust, respect, it is Emory Gilbert.

After all hadn't Joey left her and gone over there to fight because they could not make it together as a couple? . . . And the
way she looked at the great Emory Gilbert sometimes, as if she
. . .

But how would she react now? It was hard to say. Day to day
around the house she was quiet, even humble, and grateful to
be there living with them. But she was also strong and active,
and she had proud airs. She really didn't mind wearing her fine
breasts like a pair of heirlooms. Seen in profile she could take
your breath away.

Would Carlyne resist his entry? Would she begin to fight back?

The violence of Emory's emotions drove him down the steps
further, and dragged him back up. When he turned around toward his bedroom, then relief came flooding into his soul. But
the next instant he couldn't bear the idea of being all by himself.
What? All night alone in a solitary bed? His life missed?

He felt lost, drained of strength, unable to go out and meet the
challenge that lay before him. He sighed and hung there not in his
own power but caught up in the grip of his fate.

Then he felt infused with a vital force. Wasn't he the one?
Wasn't he the man of destiny? Didn't Oedipus do a similar thing?
And how that man came to suffer, but he had to do it! Ah, but he
didn't know.

Emory shuddered. Without her, safe, a death in life. With her

. . . Was this how it had to be? Taboo life versus a deadly conformism? Ruinous passion versus a rotten solitude?

Emory paused a few steps from the bottom. A wonderful time was before him: public life, governmental affairs. He would be a leader among leaders of the most powerful nation in history. Maybe a top post, an ambassadorship would be his if he played it right and his man won.

X

Down the steps he came and the old stairwell creaked like an animal caught in a trap.

Fate had its grip on his better self since the day he first laid eyes on Carlyne: when she and Joey drove north for their wedding.

And now he was bewitched. No choice? No free will? For the first time in his life—throw up the reins?

The girl wouldn't tell. And self-destruct? As for Jojo—if the boy did make it back alive and somehow found out—then deny. That's a lie! Are you calling me a liar?

A giant of a man, America's answer to the cultural figures of Europe, Emory Gilbert would outface reality, and justice, and the wide world. Go on. Try. For how to control this frenzied madness, this sexual ecstasy after a lifetime of toil and renunciation?

A few more steps . . . along the hall. Don't knock. Use your key. Is it open? Pry the door. A little further . . . and then in, yes, in, to her.

Can it be?

No.

Yes.

No!

Ah, he had an idea. Why not go back upstairs and get the brooch he meant to give his daughter-in-law? It was an ivory cameo of a tribal woman in profile with a proud feather erected from her headdress. The story went that Emory's father, P. Laster, had this brooch from a woman named Cherokee who came through town on a visit from year to year.

Yes, why not do that? Get the brooch, and then go in there, and give it to Carlyne.

Chapter Three

I

Moving along a ridge the thirteen men on ambush patrol tried to stay in position. They gazed out at the mountain range: southernmost Truong Bo where enemy swarmed as S-2's intelligence reports told them. On the slopes of Krong Ana valley a river meandered among glittery lakes and marshland. Joey Gilbert had the squad pause as it surfaced from jungle to this panorama of blue green ridges far across.

Sweat stung Emmet Bufillu's eyes: worse when he wiped them, blinked. Kevin Blair, a botany major in college, strayed from formation despite Joey's barked orders. What was going on with the squad leader? Why the sergeant's bark after he told them not to make a squeak?

The kid Blair saw this tramp over basaltic red earth plateaus intercalated with schist hills, Central Highlands sandstone and granite, as a field trip. They sent Blair to Vietnam for being such a high-pocketed nurd. But the boy seemed happy amid his rare plants and giant trees with Latin names. There was the Hopea odorata, as he told them, breaking the silence. There were Lagerstroemia tomentosa, also Dipterocarpus alatus and Xylia dolabriformus, Dalberia bariensis, Dhorea obtuse!

—That's deep, said Izard.

—Shut it.

The others glimpsed Joey because his tone was new. In the hellish mission he was their guide, and by his side the grunts felt like an elite corps. Hadn't he worn a Major League uniform during his cup of coffee in New York at season's end? The U.S. war effort might be a loser, filling up hell with the groans and complaints of its troops; but Joey Gilbert was a winner, a leader. And it shook them to see how he was acting, so distracted, into himself. What was wrong? No letter from his wife?

Blair pointed at a hillside: scarlet vong flowers common in the North but misplaced here.

Bufillu said:

—Transplanted by NVA with their Ho Chi Minh sandals.

Izard winced but not at mention of North Vietnamese Army. He picked a leech which had dripped down from foliage saturated with insects. The small sallow thing was good at getting under a grunt's collar, and biting in. Its saliva even stopped clotting, said Blair, with a boyish smile full of his bug-eyes. He was so wild about his snakes and leeches and insects he was starting to look like them.

In the afternoon there were deep shade masses, the forest darkness punctured by a sunlit burst, and the glare of crumpled palms. The squad leader bit off his words saying they would avoid any path made by Ede tribespeople and their elephants between the hamlets, in this hotter somewhat lower region now, in a thinning forest.

—Imperata cylindrica!

Blair blurted, telegraphing the squad's presence. He was excited by the change of landscape.

And so they toiled the long ridge, 40-lb. pack plus weapon, double ammo rations. The men clambered stone to stone, dacite and rhyolite, as the jungle canopy gave way to a glade shot through with fiery spears. The columns of insects sifted in the violent light.

Eucalyptus trees lined the next ridge, just wisps in the sun and mist, off to the right toward Cambodia. There were red daisies. Even the daisies, said Vane. Red. There were arborescent ferns, cicadas, palm and latania trees. An ape sent its sad modulated cry. Some undergrowth was crushed—broken by the passage of a wild buffalo? No one spoke.

Joey raised a hand as Skol, up on point, knelt. Skol gave a gesture palm up. From the ridge they saw a huge blue-misted mountain chain merged with the aqueous horizon.

II

Later it rained. A heavy, flat, lukewarm downpour drenched the trees and stirred the skein of clingy creepers like a jungle soup. For twenty minutes they hunched under ponchos. RTO Troupial bent over the tinny stitch of his radio blent with the pitter of rain. In a minute there would be sunlight as bright and piercing as a tribesman's spear.

—Six . . . Six.

Joey whispered in the transmitter. His squad was probing for enemy contact in a semicircular patrol. Rainwater purled over stones and the gnarled roots underfoot as he crouched by the multichannel radio and relayed coordinates in code. Company intelligence was reporting a sighting: VC local force battalion, 500 or more, where a Ranger platoon humped southwest over hilly terrain toward the border.

Suddenly the sun came pouring out with a vaporous glint on a big bamboo. The squad began moving forward again in an aroma of stagnant pond: the hardening mud where generations of bugs dried up and decomposed in a moment.

Someone muttered:

—God, where to now?

This time Bufillu hissed:

—Save it.

The reality clung and fastened onto them like lianas—or the unreality. Their nerves were strung tight just to keep going. Their thoughts drifted among missed family members, a high school sweetheart who had forgotten how to write, pleasures and comforts of home, Stateside. When was the next mail run?

—Man oh man now I ask you, said Vane. What the f-ing-f is this all about?

There was a loud bark. Not far. Stag's call? On the hauts plateaus the grunts went in the terrific heat and the glare. For now no breeze: even the trees seemed in a death grip. On all sides it was a struggle in the dripping jungle silence for space to grow and get free of the hosts of parasites. And all the while there was that fool Blair in raptures over his flamboyant trees and lavender willows. He loved the sudden iridescent splashes of color. He bowed to take a few notes over a veined and hairy, mottled and lacquered aspidistra enwound in a spider's uncanny gauze. All Indochina far and wide was just one exotic botanical garden—right, Kevin?

—Sssss . . .

Click, click. Drenched with sweat they made the quiet slow trek into nowhere. The thirteen were immersed in it deeper than Billy Ringwood's immersion-foot with its fetor of pus drainage. They were up to their necks in jungle and in the past month's mad brutality. Slidell was impaled by a punji stake not a football field from the cold landing zone where his first mission began. Then three more struck down like lightning: Jimmy Kossuth, Skiball, Milt Luna—medevac'd after an L-shaped ambush; they were all real bad, and gone, suddenly. Uncle Milty had that pregreased look: it is bigger than both of us, said Medic Artus, softly. The street kid Skiball gushed blood from his side with a look of hurt wonder; his features looked childish going into shock. One instant they moved ahead in a mindset of slovenly love among soldiers: as if this were Midway or Bataan, and they were the patriotic fathers and the uncles, those heroes who fought against the Japanese. But in the next instant there was sniper fire, or a trap ate up a troop waist down, pecked off his pecker! A sudden blaze of sun in the jungle penumbra took their breath away. And then at night came a numb sense, like an absurdity in the nerves. It was Stage I in the process of becoming a killer.

Morning came. After the first bloody combat there was a scab on a man's conscience. The march resumed. They went deeper into what felt like a landscape of death. It was The Nam.

Loseby, the E-4, and Horse Shue won their ticket home in Joey's first days with the platoon. That was during bridge duty outside Phu Bai. There was a rocket attack. Since then the third baseman had stayed alive and won blood stripes and become a squad leader.

The shit patrol went on. What capped the madness was what happened to Ben Bolt three days ago on the trail. Well Ben Bolt meant it when he said he didn't care anymore. But Joey had to care for them all: think and suffer like Jesus for the others. This he did even while carrying around anguish like 60 extra k's over Carlyne's silence and her failure to respond to his letters. What happened? Weren't the envelopes getting through? He thought they were, but he couldn't believe it. What was going on at the Rock Castle? Had she been unfaithful, and now turned away from him? Newell was there. Was it with him—*with his own brother?* No, that was unthinkable. Moreover this couldn't be happening to him. For he was Joey Gilbert, once and future Big Leaguer, always successful in what he did, always a winner ever since he was a boy. One way or another he would save the day again, but maybe not this mad fiasco in Vietnam.

III

On the beach at Nha Trang there had been a beer and steak standdown before this mission began. The grunts laughed and carried on making a list of prostitutional excellences, cultural differences so to speak, between cool dips in an emerald blue South China Sea. There were Chi-Bar, Bufillu, Blair, Izard, Vane, medic Artus, Ben Bolt, Tombigbee, Billy Ringwood from North Carolina where Jojo had family. They lounged in sunlight and drank their cups and enjoyed the day. Hey, it could be worse.

The afternoon was waning. They sprawled on the fine white sand as a warm sea breeze moved in the filao trees. A metallic sun glared off the broad leaved combretums. In the distance there was a peaceful bay shimmering in sunlight. Nha Trang was a fishing port, and, for the grunts that day, a little bit of paradise.

—The phoenix bird—said Kevin Blair—symbolizes marital fidelity.

Joey felt protective toward the botanist. Blair made him think of his brother Newell, also a pedant, outlandish in a different way. Joey loved his younger brother and admired him even while resenting the hippie's wayward behavior. Just as he once resented, if he thought about it, their mom's too obvious favoritism . . . He loved the mad guy, but now suspicion had entered in, and a shrill jealousy. This was all new for Joey and it unmanned him.

The learned grunt Blair lectured from his beach blanket:

—In Vietnam the phoenixes don't rise from the ashes. They are not mythic birds. They exist: black with a white spotted collarette at the tail, and wing center. They are rapacious.

—What's that? said Izard.

—They like to eat. And they hop from branch to branch of the ancient tung trees, in the summits. Red crest, clear yellow talons, haughty and large with a big curved beak, and immense tail: *coc!* they go, *coc! coc!* goes their guttural cry. Phoenix birds range wide for canari fruits and dates but come back at night to their perches among the tung. Tribesmen in the Central Highlands—

—Our trusty friends—said medic Artus, grinning.

—The Montagnards respect these birds for their conjugal fidelity.

—They don't write Dear-John letters to grunts in a world of hurt—said Vane.

—They don't go to the drive-in with Jody—said Ben Bolt.

—But get this! The male broods the eggs: two big ones, goose-like eggs, per hatch. There he is: can you believe it? The hardass sits the nest in a hollow among the oldest trees. Meanwhile the female brings food.

—Life of Reilly—said Izard, and swigged.

—Early retirement type thing, said Bufillu.

—I'm ready right now, said Tombigbee, the Indian from Tuba City.

Blair went on:

—With his plumage he feathers a bed for the young'uns. Seals it with his excrement.

—Ah, not a kiss? said Vane.

—Leaves a slot for his wife to slip in the food. Then later Papa teaches the kids to fly.

—Wish my dad taught me to fly—said Chi-Bar back from a swim.—I wouldn't land around here.

—Just think—said Ben Bolt, dreamy—one's very own Free-dom Bird.

—Taught me to dry my face first—said Kid Ringwood, a hick—then the private parts.

—The phoenix stays young, said Blair, because it gives of itself. And it moults each year and keeps changing.

With a grim interest Joey Gilbert listened to this tale of marital fidelity.

Troupial took a *Saigon Daily News* from his bag.

—Talk about faithful partners, he said. Read it and weep! 'A South Vietnamese country boy had a city girl for his fiancée. She lured him to a night aboard a sampan on the Perfume River in romantic Hué. They met in Saigon, but she came from the Imperial City, so she said; and they must go there to get the permission of her parents. First they would have some fun before betrothal, and then pay a visit to the folks at home. She persuaded him to bring along his money and valuables to impress them . . .'

—Uh oh, said big Tombigbee, the Navajo.

Joey gazed offshore at a black tanker gliding slowly in the emerald mist.

Troupial read on:

—'The young couple arrived late in Hué and went as planned to spend the night on a hotel sampan. The soldier, a sergeant in the ARVN, proved his virility coup after coup, as for the first time his girlfriend gave him all. Then the happy man drifted into a deep sleep and awoke in late morning to find himself alone and poorer by 70,000 piasters plus family heirlooms and jewelry. Welcome to Hué, City of the Dead.'

At the punchline Joey's head went down so brusquely, the others must have thought: poor dude. But if Joey Gilbert started to falter then how could they hope to make it through? For a moment after Troupial stopped reading it was like a silent chorus: who will save us from the fire-bearing plague god of Vietnam? Our wise leaders back home in the White House and Congress are supposed to help us out of this mess. But it appears the great nation is tottering and can't lift its head; there is no health Stateside, and nothing thrives; while here in-country the American boys die and are maimed everyday. And now our squad leader is down on his luck too. And what will we do? We are used to his leadership, his past service from one turning in the trail to the next. If he weakens then where will we be?

IV

They gorged the brief pleasures. They were stunned by such luxuries as cold beer and a swim in the sea—coming so close on the week's events.

For a moment they didn't talk. There was only the surf.

And then Ben Bolt gave a low sort of devilish chuckle, and said:

—Don't make a grain of difference to me if I buy the farm.

—So they say, said Izard, and guzzled.

—No, but I mean it. I'll tell you a story.

Now they had the proper glow on. No morbidity if you please!

Joey, dark eyed, unshaven with his black curly hair and leathery tan, said:

—Go on then.

—The date was May 17th, 1966.—Ben Bolt stared out at the water; he shook his head a little.—I went to a party in Manhattan. Reefer, coke, you know, music. Good vibes, guys and chicks; more came in when the sun went down. Well this one guy was pretty lit up, you know. Someone says: Hey whuz' up, Lukey? Snow? Snappers? Hey, we got it all. But the cat shakes it off, no, no, laughing: Got mine already, Clyde, way better. Lukey smirks, says: Head, baw'. What say? head? Shit yeah, Clyde boy, head says the kid, and select. The best! Sure, sure, we all laughed with our double-buzz on, you know. Heard it a few hundred times: not good ol' you-got-bread-I-got-head; but hot chick with a la-di-da, sequins and a pearl necklace, and Little Miss Ermine Cunt does it for free. Hello macho, goodbye truth. Sure you do, ha ha ha. But Lukey says: You want some too? It's not far, West 84th Street. Tell her Lucky Luke sent you.

—All comers type thing, said Bufillu.

Ben Bolt was speaking low. But his voice flew up:

—So . . . I turned away. I felt sort of on edge. Lukey was a handsome kid, like Ringwood here, but less refined. Somebody says: You know I do indeed want some head. What number over there, Luke? And he gives a broad grin because one person at least believes him, and says: Try 148 across from the schoolyard . . . Then I could only stare at him and feel the bottom drop out of my world. My heart was pounding, and I said: Apartment number? 2B, he says. As in bitch, says another. Well it was a stranger saying this, you know. Lukey was Clyde's friend, but he didn't know me from Adam. So I put down my drink, and split the scene.

After a swim the others moseyed up, like driftwood left by the tide. Uncle Milty, Skol the Pointman, Thingum (FNG-VIII): they were almost human again after a bad case of LZ jitterbugs, search routes in hell and operations to locate and destroy, with air support, invisible VC regiments. Even these shell-shockees mellowed out for a spell on a sunlit tropical beach.

The late afternoon was quiet. No din of rockets shook the distant mountains, Truong Son. There was no sudden confusion, the chaos of contact with VC regional forces, and frantic radio transmissions. Tonight no perimeter to set up.

But the grunts looked up. High in the blue sky seven Hueys flew in formation up the coast toward Da Nang.

—So? said Izard, sipping.

—So, you know, I had quit City College in my third year. I wanted to marry this girl I met in class: goodlooking, and figure better than good. Nice warm sort. She stayed in school while I kept my 2-S deferment by going part-time. Then I got a job as assistant technician at a Midtown TV studio. Some loot. Well, I liked marriage and she seemed happy after her days in class. So I thought: this is it, happy. And she had that you-know thing, you know, some women have.

—Most all 'em, said Thingum.

—It made me want to talk to her for a long time.

—All your life, said Joey, quiet.

—A lifer, said Izard.

—Enter Lucky Luke . . . type thing, said Bufillu.

—That's right, this gone cat he said 148 West 84th Street.

—2B, said Vane.

Blair nodded:

—Or not to be.

Joey grinned: hard, metallic. World Serious, the squad called him.

Ben Bolt gave a grimace, like it tasted sour, and looked away.

—Go on.

—So then I went there. I told her: I'm going for a walk now. As for you . . . it's time to leave. Get out. Git. I know what you've been doing, and when I come back in an hour, I don't want to see you.

—Nice, said Vane.

—No more? said Emmet Bufillu who was married. She didn't argue?

—She did not. I said something like: we never really knew each other.

—So you chucked her—said medic Artus—body and all.

—I chucked her. Goodbye.

Ben Bolt stood up shakily. He tossed his crushed beer can backhand on the hot sand, and trudged to the water for a dip.

—Wife sent 'im to The Nam—said Tombigbee, a curl to his lips.

Ben Bolt waded into the surf for a last swim.

Then at dusk they returned to rear base in Nha Trang. En route they saw a 6-by truck rumbling by, and it was a sight they didn't care for. Human ears were strung on the 6-by's radio antennae.

Back in the bush four days later Skol ducked, raising a hand, on point. Ben Bolt was a few steps behind; it's the rule: never break contact with the next man on small unit patrol.

From center Joey watched and felt himself seize up as Ben Bolt took a hit frontally, straight on, from an RPG. His head flew in red and yellow bits. Blood fountained from his shoulders still upright as skull, facial flesh, the whole mess that was Ben Bolt became a pink mist gleaming in sunlight. It was a few seconds before his legs buckled and he crumpled on the trail.

—Corpsman! cried someone.

—What corpsman, Joey said. Get down and stay down. Troupial, call with coordinates.

V

In quick encoded volleys over the transmitter Joey dealt with his captain and adjusted directives from fire support base to conditions along the trail. He was waking up again—getting used to her desertion. His system was trying to process the sense of loss, like a grief, though it didn't have time. In his life Joey Gilbert had never known anything like it. His mind seemed to take a deep dive and probe the potential for negativity and depression he had in his depths. Many young men and women go through such a time as they confront adult reality. But at the moment it was very dangerous because distracting in the midst of the ongoing crisis which was Vietnam.

After nearly six months, midway in the tour, he had developed a superb tradecraft. He was a soldier. Nicknamed World Serious by the men—when talking about him; but to his face it was Jo, or Joey G.—he applied his great eyesight, reflexes, power of concentration to this life as a line dog.

For two full weeks there was no letter from Carlyne. Why? She showed him such love before he left her in Durham. Was it possible she would 'change her perfume'? The mere thought crippled him and caused a lapse, now and again, which could be fatal.

He needed to know. He wanted the truth so he could know where he stood. Well she was the Sphinx. And when he was able to answer her riddle, and all went well, he felt like the luckiest man able to deal with life's fortunes and pains. Then he was the hero. But when he couldn't answer the Sphinx's riddle, as lately out here in the field; then he felt like all the other young men of Thebes destroyed because no god helped them and saw them through.

From his first day here it was a vision. Vietnam. He remembered ants on white columns in the bustle of Tan Son Nhut airport. Cherries, fresh grunts just in-country, newbies like himself gazed with awe at the dirty sweaty faces, dead-eyed above a bristly, lippy grin—a group of survivors homebound with a Guam stopover. They looked like they spent a night with Hanoi Hannah.

Then came replacement battalion compound with its cyclone wire, piled sandbags, artillery and helicopter roar. The oily chow heated over peanut cans was spiced with insect repellent.

He went to 'recondo' school at Nha Trang. And then his AO, area of operations, was no plum. There was bladelike elephant grass taller than a man where he went with 40-pound pack and bandoliers taped to his chest as armor.

He learned the early twilight at noon beneath a triple canopy, and the mountains in a purple haze as the sun set. He learned the pranks of grunts, hoots and splashes as they dunked one another during a risky swim at nightfall, naked, in a 2000-lb. bomb crater courtesy of B-52 which did a good business installing such swimming pools. Hey no matter if we detonate an explosive: just give us a few ghost-time moments as if it was R & R delights in Bangkok or Japan. A few boonierats forgot the fear that went with survival.

But one afternoon the pranks became shock and horror. Ambushed. And after combat a bone weariness came, and they were deeply shaken. And then did a grunt write a more urgent, more sexual letter back home to his wife or girlfriend. He jotted it, smudged with clay or blood, by last light in a foxhole.

The Viet Cong could be farmers by day, but they came out at night to use the countryside in other ways. It was all theirs after dark. But the next day there was more silence and soupy air, the claustrophobia of the jungle. Someone please tell me why I couldn't have an MI (military intelligence) desk job among the pogueys, the Saigon soldiers. Because yuh too stoopid, Thingum, ha ha ha! And O Jesus let her still love me a little after these needy letters I'm writing. I'm so afraid to lose her. Maybe she won't understand. But if this goes on much longer, I will go dinky-dow.

Night and day on patrol Joey G. hardly napped. He had a more than human alertness, and judgment like a great artist. But with Six's—their captain's—pat on the back after a kill he felt a strange unreality to this whole affair. His senses were on full alert as a numbness came over the rest of him. Still he was thinking and thinking; he was no fool, and a question kept asking itself. Are we here as liberators or bullies? Are we raping this land? Is that why not only my wife but Vietnam too is like a sphinx? I cannot answer her riddle and so nothing goes well here, no success, but only a plague.

He trudged with the others: hefty Bufillu, cool as a fool in a duel, and sensitive plant Blair; Kid Ringwood the semipro ball-player from a town in southeastern Carolina not far from where Carlyne's kinfolk lived, the Lumbee. Once she had taken Jojo for a picnic down there, during their brief courtship; and that was a day he would never forget. The Lumbee River ran a deep mauve from tree tannin but so clean and cool you could slake your thirst on a summer day.

Not only the newest kid, FNG-VIII, or Thingum, but the other dozen grunts looked with some awe on the bigtime athlete Joey G. who was their squad leader. Well hadn't he bounced a homerun off the rightfield scoreboard in New York last September for all to

see on TV? The man had a career in Major League baseball waiting for him, and it was unthinkable he wouldn't make it through
the tour—and themselves as well. But why was he so stern, more
and more into himself and distracted as the days went by? They
wished he wouldn't be so terse with them: like Col. Pricecroft out
here from base camp when the ringknocker was on a tour of inspection. If Joey was rude to the grunts it could affect their respect
for him, and the squad's performance. Instead of tending to business on the trail he seemed at moments to be plucking a trench
daisy: she loves me, the bitch, she loves me not . . .?

VI

They went in fear of the elusive Charlie. VC was unreal. The
enemy in fiber helmet and black pajamas toted his carbine or M-1
and didn't let you see him. That's a neat trick: when an unseen
enemy is beating you in the field. They imagined him with a hand
grenade dangling from his sash. Sometimes Sir Charles dug in
with his .51 caliber MGs ringed by claymore mines.

Once they were a gracious and gentle people these Vietnamese. But that was before savagery came to call, the French, now
the Americans, and turned the venerable mama- and papa-sans,
the virgin sister-sans, all the good citizens—said Izard, quite a
social scientist—into prostitutes, pimps, black marketeers.

—Hey!—Vane did a little dance.—Long live freedom and democracy, and a good fuck for a carton of Luckies.

The grunts feared the false step: Bouncing Betty's click. Please,
God, if I have to die then make it snappy—not castrated, of no further use to womanhood. For Miss Betty, the emasculating woman
par excellence, did not inflict miracle wounds which meant a
ticket home, pop smoke for a dust-off. No; she went for the prick,
and snipped it! Goodbye, walking tall; hello, wheelchair.

Joey had listened a few days before shipping overseas as an
NCO lectured on jungle warfare while caressing a rabbit. Calmly
amid talk about tactics and survival the NCO broke the rabbit's
neck, skinned it, then tossed the guts at them and walked out.

In a white termite colony on a porous tree trunk; in gruesome
stories, say an officer fragged with a CH (chlorine) gas grenade:

I'll court-martial every swinging duck of you! raged Pentagon East; in the very Halozone tablets taken against worms: the grunts caught a whiff of terror, and their vulnerability. It helped, but not enough, that they had a huge retaliatory power of F-4D Phantoms, A-4E Skyhawks, Skyraiders just an AN-PRT-4 radio call away: our guys.

Skol the wiry pointman, Bufillu the All-State tackle from Atmore, Alabama; medic Artus, RTO Troupial: they soothed their shaken nerves with revenge fantasies for Skiball, payback for Slidell skewered like lamb on a brochette. Give tit for tat for Loseby the E-4 greased, and Horse Shue, and Ben Bolt.

On they went, on and on, humping the quiet kliks through fern and bracken. Their flesh was chafed by the straps and gear. There was a scent of sandalwood in their nostrils.

A time came when the horrors and culture shock had a dampening effect on the gung-ho of grunts; on the idea of America's way of life threatened by communism, and here they were bringing light to darkness. No. This wasn't Iwo Jima. You could hoist the Stars and Stripes on a worthless hill after fighting all day and losing lives—and then what?

Why had they come here? They were infantrymen, but they were exposed like infants abandoned by their parents: sent away from home and left in a barren place to die.

An acid loyalty to squad, platoon, company, O'Deuce, 101st, but mainly squad: some of this remained. Less did, by the week. What politician's arrogance, what system's oldfashioned hubris made them come over here and fight and die for what seemed more and more like a lie?

Just cross off another day on the short-time calendar taped to my helmet. I want to go home.

VII

Night was falling. In the viscous creepers was an odor of rot. Grunts marched, and pleaded with the mosquitoes to bite. Falciparum malaria meant clean sheets in an air-conditioned field hospital, pink lemonade with ice. There would be a round-eyed nurse at bedside, and Doughnut Dollies in the a.m. Okay, sign me up!

—Here—said Jojo, low.—Home again.

He called in for Six's benediction on their perimeter. Then they set out their claymores for the night.

Now a black ant column moved through: long insects like wasps, with a stinger. Two weeks ago an ARVN guide joked that VC took the red ones and ranged them in battalions: 43rd VC local ant force, 500-strong; M-1s, rifle ants, MG ops, grenadiers, medic and RTO, dumb suck of an S-2 intelligence officer—all ants, red. The ARVN was having his fun with them, and he could do it because he was helpful.

Now Vane muttered:

—Zipperhead dink ants.

Izard:

—Slope jarheads.

—Slit your gizzard in the dark—said Artus—then it's *zzzt!* split the scene like millipedes.

Vane:

—I seen one little bugger wearing the equivalent of four Silver Stars, three Legions of Ant Merit with Combat 'V' for Valor, three distinguished Flying Ant Crosses, and a handful of Bronze Stars all pinned to his commie ant chest.

—Ant type thing, said Bufillu.

—No gab, said Joey.

Do not converse. Do not shoot the bull. Simply spoon your ham 'n motherfuckers.

—Say, said Izard, I heard a real rat was found in a can of C-rats.

Chi-Bar mumbled:

—VC eat rat. I read it in *Pacific Stars & Stripes*. Said it tastes like chicken.

—I ate dog once, said Izard, chewing. In Da Nang, only R & R billet where you don't have fun.

—Shh. Settle in.

—I'll take dog at Ramuntcho's in the Eden Building. That's in Saigon. I heard about it.

—Mm-good, said Thingum. Asahi beer and cockerspaniel.

—Charbroiled, said Skol. But cost you some jing.

Blair laughed:

—Disgoosting! as they say in French. Radio Operator Troupial, please call the ASPCA.

—Blair, you scholar grunt—said Vane and belched—cut me a

hus with the big words. On your wedding night she'll ask you for
an erection, and you'll give her a big word.
   —Antidisestablishmentarianism, said Blair.
   —What's that? said Kid Ringwood.
   —Something to suck on, said Izard.
   They talked. They spoke in murmurs. Couldn't help it.
   Joey didn't stop them. He was in his thoughts.
   Like a long march of prehistoric trees the Vietnam night came
on: like the tall kindly vung pine, and the Iri (banyan) haunted by
forest demons as A-Sao valley ethnics believed. Spidery branches
clutched at the ultramarine sky. Blue misted mountains were
turning to purple, then indigo, in the distance eastward.
   Another moment the men chatted: maybe too loud. The words
had a nervous edge. There was a sense of—what? in the moments
before darkness.
   —Now I mean it, said the squad leader. No more, silence, or—
   —Or what? said Izard.
   —I'll send you to Nam.

VIII

   Joey felt a touch of marsh fever as the vaporous air seeped in.
Night breathed in the lichen moss. It was two weeks, three days,
seventeen hours and twenty-seven minutes since the last letter
from Carlyne. Why? She had not written him: unless some loser at
base camp in Buon Me Thuot misrouted the pouch. That was possible; no dust-off, no resupply or mail call for the past 72 hours.
   In the moist earthen odors, in the dense humus at midnight
he breathed in the deep mysterious spirit of his Sphinx. His fingertips could feel the sheen of her jet black hair worn tight, the
long tresses swept up in a bun even in bed. He yearned to write
her a love letter and put his soul into the words in this instant
forbidden to penlights, matches, the tiny glow of a watch dial. He
yearned to tell her of his passion and kiss every niche and fold of
her flesh with words that would startle her—kiss her strange lake-
blue eyes and her proud eyebrows, and pure childlike temples,
full lips, sensuous cheeks, the warm hair. Oh he would lick her
chin and womanly neck to where her full breasts parted toward

the large, hard nipples erect like a penis and goosebumped under his tongue and the stubble of beard she'd never seen on him. He would suck her swart teats slick with hot saliva as her ribs shivered beneath his ticklish kisses, kisses on her taut stomach which hadn't carried a child, kisses to her hips which had a virile curve. He moaned and fondled her. He gave himself over like the strong male craving humiliation, and it was their secret: like a tiger turning to butter. Oh he was so eager to serve her in every way, and he would kiss her thighs, kiss her lovely rack, kiss, kiss her and then, O Carlyne . . . Jo . . . at last she couldn't hold back and he kissed her like a puppy at chow, slurp, slurp. My darling I love you beyond all the coordinates and azimuths: from the next embattled ridgeline to the stars. I love you so, my dearest darling, more than God and America, and more even than I hate this filthy war. I send you all my heart in a thought since Six forbids us to switch on a light out here in the bush at night . . . Non-hackers jeopardize the survival of a squad but I can hack 60 mm and 81 mm VC mortars and I can hack jungle ambush at fifteen meters and I can hack hell itself, in more combat than any glamorous Special Forces ever were, only we're just used as bait. I can hack the reality so different here from TV and movies shown to you at home so you won't know the way it *is*. But your silence, my darling, but the evil sick jealousy I begin to feel and my deep desire for you wounded and gangrened: this I cannot hack.

In Buon Me Thuot before this saddle-up he had written her about the grisly end of Ben Bolt. What a blunder that was: three stark pages almost unpunctuated like a terrible poem. Now that's immature—so she would say. And what could he do but feel repentant after shocking her? Well no wonder she was silent.

Yet he'd do it again so she'd know how he was suffering, and how he loved her. He was no phoenix bird of husbandly strength and devotion. He was more like a child missing its mother and feeling left out and jealous. Pretty soon he might go mad, but in the meantime she would understand and suffer a little too. Honey, your man could meet his end at any instant, a prime target with the radio man in the center, as the squad goes probing some ridge or other.

And then before the dust settled Six would bark: Saddle up!

Bufillu would have his blood stripes and be installed as squad leader.

Was there a hint of blame in Joey's last letter? Did he blame his wife on some level for this sorry fiasco?

IX

A gibbon screeched in a tree. VC sentinel? Or was it a harassment tactic to trouble a G.I.'s sleep? S-2 said there were enemy at battalion strength in the area. Joey's squad acted as bait as it went probing the folds of Annam cordillera: as it slogged jungle and cut underbrush and sought to make contact. Take the onslaught and ring up air support: the daisy cutters.

On a green towel he wiped his face spongy with sweat. It gave him a twinge when he thought of Carlyne's past: her mother a full-blooded Indian born near Lumberton. Was that woman like these Vietnamese: watching her tribal land get overrun by the whites? Again the gibbon sent its high call across the forest . . . Here, there it was Indian country; only here they didn't ride out in full regalia with a peace pipe. Here they were organized and faced better odds. And so after its rape the land became a mystery; you seemed to hear it whispering, plotting, stalking the invader. Its silence was like the Sphinx's with her riddle—Sphinx sent by an offended god to test the young men of a guiltridden city; and, when they didn't know the answer, they died.

Gently he jostled Vane's shoulder. In sleep the grunt was gritting his teeth with such a ferocity it could give away their position. No noise, no light after dark: thus Six. Tonight the kook Blair was on perimeter duty. Skol, the sly pointman, lay dug in at the forward position.

Seven more weeks, thought Joey, then R & R in Bangkok. At least he'd put in for it. And they knew he had earned it and deserved a break. Once approved: then call home and ask her to come out. She said she would: in Durham she promised. And then, when she came, walk hand in hand with her along Pat Pong which was the center of the world for lurid sex and prostitution, as the late Loseby said.

After rich Thai cuisine, drunk on the Thai beer which was better than Saigon *La Rue* or *Tiger Beer,* they strolled back to the hotel. She wore a straight black dress of fine material with a bit of dainty lace at the bosom. Her hair was done up, skin flushed a rich copper hue as it did sometimes, like Vietnamese women's. He felt a lewd and explosive desire for her; it was a tenderness like revenge. Oh wouldn't he just get down on his knees and bow his head to kiss her feet? She laughed and said: Third baseman, you still have a sunburnt neck. But now she also knelt, no longer so contemptuous, and put her self into a kiss until his lips bled. Aïe . . . She dug her fingernails into his curly nape with its boyish sunburn.

When he decided that day in Durham to enlist, he felt he had to up the ante, and play the patriotic hero for her sake: to keep her respect and save their marriage which wasn't working. He didn't talk to her about it. That wasn't Joey's way. All his life he was the star, every league he played in, but not as husband. In the marriage league he was no phenom; he choked in the clutch. But he hoped to revive her love by his sacrifice, by his belief in an ideal, in America. Did she the tribal daughter share such a love? Now he thought of Carlyne's response when he told her the big news. First her jaw dropped and she knit her brow. Then she laughed and said:

—What a foolish thing to do, Papi Jack!

X

At daybreak the grunts began to grope and stir in the silence. Click, click.

—Now gents—Six spluttered in the tinny radio—saddle up! Witty Six: gents for grunts.

Another day. How many more? Don't count 'em. Just hump. Hump it and lump it: hump like a pump in a sump. Probe the next ridge, and do not ask why. Take malaria pills, chew C-rats, mix cherry Kool-Aid in canteen, grow mustache, swear like a bear at the air, dig foxholes and mortar pits, clean weapon, play poker, get Dear John letter from My Beloved, have diarrhea, sleep at post (bad radio battery, Cap!), write home wish you were here, daydream gooey sex. Run night ambush. Find weapons and ammo cache: 82 mm mortar rounds, mortar tubes, tripods plus 75 mm recoilless rifle and rounds, Soviet SKSs and carbines, boocoop. Look for firefight. Hi there! Why it's Betty-More-Bounce-To-The-Ounce: care to dance? First the ten-foot punji pit, then Freedom

Bird not first-class, not a routine 365-day DEROS (go home) among the crisp majors and colonels, the prim Western steward-esses and then Travis AFB, wife, family—oh how sweet it is: I kiss the ground of my homeland—; no, not that way but as freight in a fart sack: remains unviewable.

Hey, baby, shake it. Concentrate on terrain and order of march. Skol, Izard: point squad. Bufillu, Tombigbee, Vane, Thingum: flank squad. Ringwood, Blair, Chi-Bar, FNG-IX: tail-end Charlie. Squad leader in center plus RTO Troupial and medic Artus.

Someone said:

—Where's Blair?

A twig snapped. Chi-Bar broke the quiet march. There was a sharp cry, eerie wings in the treetops, as Chi-Bar waved an arm. He called through the brush with a tremor in his voice:

—Blair's gone!

At sunrise the sharp rays came piercing through laterally. A metallic light stabbed the eyes as it glinted past Kevin Blair's tall silvery trees and the supple creeper grass looking azure in the new light: Blair's tram bau myrtle and wild soi leaves and his rau dua; his thorny mac co plants whose leaves fold when people or animals come near. Kevin was forever consulting his *Botanist's Guide To Southeast Asia* and other books which filled half his pack and added to the load. At night on perimeter he murmured the foreign words.

Chi-Bar cried out. A moment later Bronco, the aerial observer, alerted RTO Troupial: bombs, napalm, artillery on the next ridge-line south. Thud, thud: the G.I.'s boots could sensor the chain of explosions. Maybe an ambush awaited the squad just up ahead where two streams confluenced.

—Blair's AWOL? said Vane.

—No way, said Artus. Went to cull herbs, like he says.

—Pick red daisies, said Izard, spat.

—Shit call type of thing, said Bufillu.

—Who saw him last? asked Joey, frowning.

He glimpsed Chi-Bar, who was Blair's link on marches, and thought: My distraction caused this; didn't run a check last night thinking about my own problems ... Dammit, Carlyne, why don't you write?

The formation shrunk. The squad seemed to crumple on itself, pausing, staring around for Blair. All liked this rare college kid in the infantry. Is it your junior year abroad, Kevin? Or back to

nature? Joey cut him slack and looked after him on the trail: like
his brother Newell way back in Boy Scouts. Airy, as if he might
levitate in a minute, he was like a ballet dancer in jungle issue. He
was kind of zany but not a sissy as he took long gung-ho strides
from a gao tree to a camphor laurel and let the others bother with
guerrilla warfare. A short-timer's calendar was taped on his helmet, and maybe it jinxed him as he X'd off the last month of days.
He showed them photos of a cute fiancée and his homey folks
where they held their breath in a small town in western Virginia,
on the banks of the broad Shenandoah.

Joey Gilbert thought: my fault. And he felt anguish well up in
his gut, and flush his dirty neck. He was hot with anger—at himself and at Carlyne.

XI

Chi-Bar's eyes were wide. But then he shrugged.
Troupial said:
—Six on the hook.
—Beta-six . . . Two-five, over.
—Beta-six, over.
—Kevin Blair, Sir. Disappeared.
—Ten minute retrace. Then move. I need to see some bodies
today. Over.

At Blair's night position there was an ominous sign. Ringwood
found the small notebook Kevin jotted and sketched in.

Joey read the last entry:
—'Beside a persimmon tree like those at home I saw the cây
thi pointed out by our ARVN guide on patrol that day south of
Pleiku. Also I saw sau dong which has purple flower clusters in
springtime. Yesterday on the trail we passed loofah, that tropical
climber with white flowers and large fruits, and the sa cu that
leads out beyond treelines from forest to arable field in'

Then a sheet fell from the back flyleaf: a letter to his girl.

'I love you so much, honey, and never more
than right now as we penetrate deeper into
dangerous terrain in these last few weeks for

me here. I keep your sweet picture in my
breast pocket; it is a charm to bring me home
to you, a lover so filled with love after this
grim ordeal. Guys kid me when your letters come.
They say: well, Dr. Grunt Einstein, Sir, has Jody
gotten to her yet? But they are just jealous, my
Sweet Honey Cake, and I can afford to laugh at
them because our love has the solid properties.
Or let's say it is the first perpetual motion
machine.'

Joey folded the paper slowly and put the notebook in his
pocket. This wasn't a psych case, a breakdown under stress. Some
lost their wits under the strain and wandered out alone in the
darkness.

Troupial jiggled the radio and waited for Six who had his own
indications to request. Joey didn't want to move yet. It was too
soon to leave Blair behind.

In the abandoned foxhole they found the grunt's entrenchment
tool jabbed in the loamy soil.

That afternoon during the squad's R & R in Nha Trang, after
they listened to Ben Bolt's story, Kevin Blair sought a moment
alone with the leader.

—What would you do if your wife ever—you know—?

Joey gave a little laugh and said:

—I'd do the same thing you would.

—Sit down and cry?

Joey chuckled:

—Take it easy.

—Sometimes I think I don't deserve her. She's so good.

—Well in that case, troop, permission granted to think one stupid thing a day.

Later all the grunts were tipsy in a seaside café. Blair laughed
happily and lit up a Ruby Queen after his plate of shellfish. There
was a warm sea breeze. A phosphorescent moonlight played over
the broad-leaved banana clumps across the dirt road.

Now, as the men paused to wonder where he went, a breeze
was in the speckly shade. The bent grass glinted.

Then one other fact didn't help the jitters. A few steps from the
perimeter post lay a small object tossed there, or dropped. It was
Blair's penlight.

Chapter Four

I

The mood changed. Sullen after Blair's vanishing act, the grunts were forced to wait. They stood there between numbness and a stunned wonder. The heat was worse. Things seemed to pile up and suffocate them the moment they stopped going.

Six's ten minutes stretched out to an hour. And after a worthless search they were still, still in place. And it sweltered. They felt a burden worse than the gear in their rucksacks: C-rat provisions, poncho and liner used as bed; twenty 20-round 5.56 magazines snug in two ammo pouches, as action awaited them around the bend; fragmentation plus colored smoke or white phosphorous grenades; green plastic-cased claymore mine with fuse, detonation cord and detonator; one single-use light anti-tank weapon (LAW). Chi-Bar was sweating like a pig in his web gear and wide canvas belt with suspenders; but he was a skinny pig. Izard wore two bandoliers crossed over his chest: M-79 rounds, M-60 ammo belt. Canteens and first-aid packages dangled. And then there was the bazaar of the ground-pounder. Vane toted mosquito repellent, blue heat tablets, water purification tablets, camera, cigarettes, gun cleaner kit, E-tool. Forty pounds plus for the hard hump in 100-degree heat to Pork Chop Hill. And, would you believe it, LBJ wasn't even here humping with them.

—Little suckers—mumbled Thingum.—Come out and fight like men.

—That's likely, said Tombigbee.

Joey knelt among maps, flashlight, binoculars, compass.

Carefully medic Artus counted anti-malaria pills as the grunts stood around. They had shadows about their eyes and a growth of tangled beard. Facial pores oozed the slime and grime of The Nam. They waited for Six to say: go.

Strong friendships grew among them—always, in war; it was survival morale. Beyond the next ridge in a gray-blue haze all the patriotic glory seemed to recede. It wasn't for them. Could the Pentagon's anti-communism crusade stand the test over here and sanction so much madness and keep up their spirits? Could it hope to win? Right now the grunts had all they could do to worry about Blair and resent his escapades and pray to Six they didn't have to make another 100-yard radius search patrol ordered by Company Commander.

—Move out, said World Serious. Hump it.

They gave a sigh and put their legs in motion.

This probe, the platoon's forward advance with each squad used as a prong, was headed into a conflictual area SSW toward Ba Bien on the Cambodian border. One night in a Buon Me Thuot bar Joey and Bufillu heard the horror story of a Ranger (commando) platoon overrun in this sector by regular NVA.

Now it was midmorning. Heat and thirst. If that wasn't enough: poisonous centipedes. Hump. Jungle rot, sunburn. Lips, noses chapped and cracked. Humpty-hump. Hump it and bump it. Twisted ankle? Walk it off. Dehydration? Save your water.

Snap! whine—rifle fire across the valley. The squad leader looked through his binos at the next crest.

—Rest here.

What was the mission's significance? Vital. Control these Central Highlands, the strategic ray—slash-and-burn hillside regions where the ethnic tribes grew glutinous rice and corn: areas perfect for revolutionary bases—and you controlled South Vietnam, Cambodia, Laos. The French had failed: on this same joyless road. The U.S. were failing so far despite CIA-trained CIDG, Montagnard Civil Guard units.

Behind them the undulant rustle of a huge teak tree swept over Kevin Blair's blithe spirit and his botany studies amid war and his faithful phoenix bird. His squad left him behind—somewhere in the long bluish contours, the matt distance and the fierce silence.

The sun rose higher. Gear straps cut a grunt's flesh. There were angry itches, infected bites, exzema. Worse than enemy was an impersonal death among the treacherous vines and jungle growth. *Oh! God not me, not now!* Slidell had screamed, impaled, as others stood and watched. Oh! how a grunt began to hate Battalion Commander and Operations Officer for these saddle ups day after day and rarely a sign of slack from the hack and the flak.

II

Today's was an ass breaker, a hilly 9-klik hump.
—Move out. Pass it on.
—Move out . . . move out.
They spoke the hated words low. Rest was over. Now more heat, thirst, more deadly blahs jolted by fear at a crunched twig. Do not count on any bennies, beer and letters: not so far out here. Be glad there are salt tablets for the heat.

Pack straps burned. Nerves played tricks. Sudden crack, whine—assault rifle—where? O anopheles minimus, praised by Blair who knows: please come to me like a lover, I need your malarial sting! You are my ticket home—not Freedom Bird, but Freedom Mosquito.

The hours passed. Lost in the wilds of Indochina they emerged from the forest to another panorama. A lush blue of placid hills and valleys spread before them, far out, to the southwest. It was so blue and beautiful out there at the world's end.
—Keep on, said Jojo. Shh.
This hump. This oven. Glint and glare. Phew . . . down wind of Izard. In the hip pocket of his fatigues was a VC ear; or Vietnamese at any rate; and it didn't smell like lilac soap.

Through the morning they had moved with unsure steps. They came to an empty hut here and there like a haystack: the walls covered with coconut palm leaves soaked by rain.

The squad filed down a slope to a flat grassy plain. Six's orders were to stay away from Moï tribe hootches: those plaited bamboo dwellings bound by lianas. So far there were no Moï guards in sight: no men in military tunics and wearing loincloths, their long black hair done up in a bun.

Toward noon the jungle turned to woodland. The terrain grew level with long stretches of a coarse grass. There were clumps of deciduous trees. Then there was visibility so a bit of smalltalk was not amiss. Then would a grunt groan under his breath: O for an SOP job, O to be a rear base support poguey with plenty of jing to spend on the slanteyed gunnies and O-Club girls, leftovers from the Officers Club, and good kids all. God bless the rear echelon officer with his air-conditioned room, cold beer and dry bed, showers at all hours, steak and wine, boocoo free time for the Saigon floor shows. Why didn't my old lady take better care the night she conceived me by a street vendor in East Harlem: me, Chi-Bar, who was not destined for a student deferment and the thrill of being ROTC on campus; me, the kid from East 116th Street, who is getting an education and seeing the world here in the middle of nowhere. O for DEROS Day, O for rotation back to the known world, Kadena AFB in Okinawa and then on far across the Pacific to an enchanted place called Travis Airforce Base in Oakland, California, where it never rains; and then a 90-minute drive down Interstate 80 to San Francisco International Airport; and a sweet flight, military standby, for the last lap home. Manhood intact, prick not punji'd, balls and all still on call, not greased yeast (the Moï gourmets, Kevin Blair once told them, prized a certain maggot served in rich sauce on festive occasions); not lunch caught, not ranch bought. Not all sliced up by a homemade trap like Slidell; not blown to bits by an NVA anti-personnel mine; not a headless wonder like Ben Bolt up ahead there: where wiry Skol still led the way in the bright sun.

Men had died bloodily in this squad. But things did change a little when Joey Gilbert became the leader. The idea he played eighteen games in a Big League uniform helped to sustain them and lent some sort of confidence. Moody, tense, he didn't smile much. But then, at a sign, as the capable Skol raised a hand and danger could be up ahead: then came the steely grin, like a mask in combat. Now into the third week of his wife's silence Joey had a somber brow. But he lightened up and gave a hardass grin at the first sign of trouble, like he welcomed it.

Brief pause by a dry creek bed. He poked about for tracks. Looked at some thistle. Trail? Tunnel?

—Le's go.

9 K's. How many done? Hump. Move your rump, and do not slump. Torrential sun. Insects and other sounds. Routine, right? Quiet day, one more, count 'em. Zippo a leech with a toothpick. Daub sweat on olive drab towel. Thoughts wander: wife, Sphinx. Fantasize sex. Cold beer and a grilled t-bone at firebase. Oh ho! My girl, wait'll I get back home, and we're in bed. Prepare to be bare in the lair.

Shortly past noon they heard explosions in the middle distance. Alpha Company was catching some as it probed further south and drifted beyond the Highlands toward Loc Ninh.

In these stretches the stream beds led down into foothills. Still Skol and Izard saw no movement. No threat at present? The grunts thought of their buddy Blair somewhere back along the trail in the swarming heat and brilliant hush of the forest. Kevin was becoming enwound in the ancient silence, the vast sunbaked day of Asia. Blair MIA. Was he Kevin Kool-Aid by now? Then revenge time soon. Then fuckemup.

III

They broke the march and popped down in a patch of shade for lunch.

Later, in midafternoon, the terrain relaxed beneath their steps. Up ahead they could see the approaches to a village.

Six told them:

—Just move on through. Don't dally, it isn't Da Lat, not a resort. Early tomorrow I want you seven K's on the far side. You and Beta-3 intersect . . .

No seal and search this time. Last week this ville, named Xo Man, had been cordoned off for sick call, population control, i.d. paper check. Rice caches were confiscated along with VC-usable materials.

The huts squatted on their heels sunk in the sodden ground amid fruit trees and banana clumps. The dirt road went wriggling between trees and led to a well beside a kapok tree truncated by a bomb of some kind. So the place had seen action. Pigs and chickens snorted, pecked, scratched the ground. Vane raised his rifle sidearm when a water buffalo trotted out in front. Vane took aim at the glint of sun in its crescent horns. But Joey froze him with a look.

—Down boy.

Two kids knelt playing with bottle tops. An old peasant woman in black watered her garden. A child cried being lugged by a young girl across the dirt square. There was banh chay, a sticky rice cake, in the girl's free hand. Cái ông, the men, and cái ba, the women, gazed out from hootches of torchis, grass and straw cement. A few mangy unfed dogs were yapping in some garbage; one, a birdcage on four legs, skulked in the clayey shadow of a palm roof. The forest villagers had a creatural look, blank as an earthen floor; they went about seeing to the next meal, and the woe of their day.

But Xo Man was like a bennie to the G.I.'s bone tired after the miles of jungle.

Was it VC-controlled?

—Assume affirmative, said S-2. The L.L.D.B. is weak here.

Loc Loung Doc Beit was the Vietnamese version of the Montagnard Civilian Irregular Defense Groups. They were less than trustworthy, and Green Berets called them Lousy Little Dirty Bastards.

Xo Man.

—Move 'em through—said Joey with a nod at Bufillu.

From further in among the hootches they heard some tribal dance. A tom-tom was tuning up. For what? Goings-on after the sun set? With their music and rhythms the Vietnamese village, and Montagnard buôn, traders, sang of the war: the joy of small victories, the fierce grief of retreats. From these hamlets the VC chignon battalions, women fighters with their hair up, issued forth after dark to make quick work of a regional outpost manned by ARVN (Saigon Govt.) soldiers.

The drum dance was spirited despite the heat. But it paused.

Joey hung back. He was cautious, looking around as the big heat held the village in its grip. From a doorway, from behind a wattle fence the papa- and mama-sans watched the giants Bufillu and Tombigbee, one black, one red, stride two-abreast along the main dirt road through the humble ville. They went as if on stilts. The bandoliers, M-16 magazines and other gear seemed to cascade from their massive shoulders. The M-67 fragmentation grenades hung like green fruit from their belts.

—Look, said Ringwood.

A strange striped bird went flapping low over the hootches. It was black and yellow with a horned casque over its enormous bill. It was ominous.

In the dirt square a woman sold bitter tea in bowls on a bamboo counter. A second woman had sticky rice cakes and sweet potatoes roasted over open charcoals—her wares wrapped in banana leaf. Both hunched on their heels where a path came out from the maze of hootches. Was Blair in there somewhere, a prisoner?

The squad leader took in the scene with its items of interest. But he had to make himself stay awake; it was no easy task keeping his antennae on the alert. Last night once again it was the long dialogue with his wife. Why, Dear, why don't you write me? And so he had stayed in place mulling over his own worries and didn't make the extra effort to keep tabs on Blair. And then Blair was gone, poof! And the leader hadn't done his duty because he was in tête-à-tête with his jealousy. It was the same thing now: Joey so distracted, so weary without her support anymore. He kept on but he wasn't paying the usual close attention. Was Blair being held in a tunnel or dungeon just under their feet as the grunts moved uncautiously along? So be it. What could be done for him?

IV

Emmet Bufillu ambled up to the tea seller.

The woman had two brands. There was green tea. And she poured voy brewed from some wild plant which was bitter. Joey tried the voy once, sipping it slowly, and his thoughts were on Carlyne.

Now Bufillu lingered by the little table. Izard and Thingum were by his side having a look at tobacco packets for the water pipes. A few natives were on hand: an older man with wizened features, a mustache, yellow hat and old regime army jacket; his cheviot trousers were rolled to the knees. He looked sly. Then a woman came up with dishes to appetize a G.I.. There were boiled chameleon eggs, sliced banana flower, wild mangosteens, coac wine, chuon bark chewed for energy.

Chi-Bar, Vane, Billy Ringwood, FNG-IX or Meno, a kid just out of high school with boocoop acne—they were groovin' and glad to relax after the bush. They bantered the locals a little. This was not the Platoon of Death on zippo inspection. In the sweltering sun they had trekked to detect and get wrecked—gear plus weapon and double ammo rations. Behind them and up ahead again was the torrid forest dripping with a lambent mist. And always there was the fear of ambush or a lethal trap, psst! grunt does Houdini act sawed in half. Guess what, folks. Or a 122 mm rocket attack tosses up clods and grunts.

Here they tarried a minute, chatted, acted right suave for the fans. La dai! la dai! Their dozen Vietnamese words drew a laugh from the tea vendor who had a rustic charm, a sensuous note in her furtive eyes. Say, she wasn't so bad looking.

Bufillu handed Joey a cup filled with the bitter voy. But Tombigbee was not in sight; he had a habit of drifting quietly off by himself.

Then came a kind of vaudeville. A tiny grandma in the paper-thin pajama bottoms, black, shiny, with a cotton top and woven reed hat, came riding her rickety bicycle right at them across the square. She had a sack of charcoal on one shoulder, a bundle of sticks on the other, and honey locust bunched in her free hand. She was a sight. A fatty hen hung from the front handlebars.

It gave the grunts a start the way that old lady came tooling right at them. But Bufillu gave a chuckle:

—Allow me.

—Watch out, said Artus. She's got a bomb in her pajamas.

From deeper in the village came Buddhist bells. Joey was thinking: there's something strange here. He sized up the tea vendor. In the younger ones he glimpsed his wife minus half the flesh—same high cheekbones, and Oriental cast to the features. Her blood had roamed these distant valleys during the great prehistoric migrations. In the faroff ages of matriarchy she was one of the proud nomadic women who resisted submission to the man. The tea vendor caught Joey's eye; she held his dark unshaven gaze and almost smiled at him. Was it an invitation? She looked self-contained, hardbitten, alert.

Halfway across the square he waited on the others. In no hurry they were being disobedient to Six. So he said to RTO Troupial:

—Go tell them spread out. Don't linger in one spot. Five more minutes, then saddle.

But as he spoke Vane acted up. The grunt said he didn't like the tone of the tea vendor: some remark she made in her tribal dialect. Maybe she said he was cute; but Vane didn't hear it that way, and so he came on with his nerves stirred up by her voy. Also he was jumpy like the rest after Blair cut out; he was upset yet unable to get it in the open. So Vane reached forward, grabbed the woman's blouse, and yanked it, ripped it. Nine months through his tour by now, he had been three steps from Loseby maimed and medevac'd in the Phu Bai rocket attack; he saw Ben Bolt walk a few steps more after being blown away; he held Kossuth's hand after the ambush near Ban Don northwest of Buon Me Thuot. He watched Slidell get dusted off: Slidell stuck through by a punji stake. And now the sultry woman with her bilious tea and mute hate was laughing at them, so he thought, and it set him off. He ripped her blouse and struck her.

—Hey! No!

Before Joey could get there Vane upset her bamboo counter with its little bowls, teapots in a hempen nest. Bufillu was in ahead and grabbed the boy's wrist.

—Trouble, brother. Cool it.

It was a friendly village on the surface. At least no VC flags flew in full view of all: blue and red with a gold star. But the rash soldier spilled the sister's goods in the dust. A fool's move. Her yellow tea trickled away.

As Bufillu peered in the G.I.'s eyes all set to take on the world, Joey glanced back at a papa-san with a pointed beard and wisp of gray hair, a poor man's Ho Chi Minh, spitting betel.

Then a lively kid, bright-eyed, with a fake smile, came trotting by with his shoeshine box.

—Numbah one! Ha ha! G. I. one suckah!

The kid held up his middle finger.

—What's that? said Vane, turning, ready for more.

Bufillu laughed and said:

—Never mind. —Then to Jojo: —Six name this ville?

—Xo Man.

None of the natives looked angry exactly. The offended tea vendor screwed her eyes and whined at the military scrip Bufillu held out to her. She sniffed and wiped her eyes. Playacting, thought Joey; she wants a greenback.

A pig grunted. A water buffalo snored in the dusty patch behind a thatched hut. Women, old people looked on impassively

from the shadows and plaited bamboo. Life went on in Xo Man
as they worked a cassava garden outside the kitchen door, and
a snippy parrot chattered away in a bodhi tree. Here, there were
manioc stalks with leafy tops.

To Joey the life and activity in this village seemed staged somehow. It must be the men were main force NLF and away on a
mission? The few who dared to peer out from the low shadowy
hootches were their families?

—Time to move—said the squad leader.

V

Still in no hurry the G.I. patrol sauntered through the village
of Xo Man. They went past a banyan tree whick looked like organ
pipes but was lived in by demons—as Kevin Blair once said, citing
a popular superstition. They passed more hootches and tin shacks
abandoned behind the bamboo hedges. Where was everybody?
Relocated to a strategic hamlet, a RevDev project somewhere . . .?
A crow gave its hoarse caw in a kapok tree. Well, life was sparse in
these wartime hamlets where a few old people trod the dirt roads.
Mostly you saw grandmas yoked to baskets balanced on poles:
with their rice, breadfruit, grilled manioc tubercles, lê fruits, staple foods. Or, round a turn, it was like a picture postcard from
ancient Vietnam: a buffalo boy in his loincloth played a flute on
the far side of a lotus pond. At dusk a few kerosene lamps began
to flicker in the villages from ridge to ridge.

Now a toothy kid came along and called out to them in a high
voice, like it was a signal:

—Numbah ten G.I. Pfeuh!

—Shoo, little brat—said Vane who was trying to control
himself.

—Numbah ten G.I. lat!

The kid drew up even, but he kept his distance. He taunted
and called them a rat. They could crush him like an ant; or use
him as a target for C-rat cans. This was an arcade game the Americans played from APCs along the highways, and sometimes they
hurt the kids scrambling after their leavings.

In those moments Joey saw a wedge of wild geese flying south toward Mekong. High in the afternoon sky they flew above the scrawny ville, and he wished he was a goose too.

The boy trotted past with a grin and a gesture:

—Mah sistah! Gnuyet 'dat mean Moonright. She fuckee G.I. gooed.

Toothful, he waved. The boy moved his hand to say sister Moonlight had a shape like ... Carlyne. Tomorrow a young man's parents would come to present betel leaves and areca nuts and ask her to become their son's wife. But today there was work to do.

—Sistaah! We take sclip!

He pointed toward a hootch on the way from town. Joey shrugged. The others closed ranks: they wanted a look at Moonright, the hooker sister, who took military scrip.

A few more villagers were on the scene. They stood staring. Joey didn't like the feel of it, but he was too in his thoughts to keep rustling up the squad. A hawker called: sweet potatoes! bamboo shoots! A G.I. could really use bamboo shoots: how many ways?

Moonlight lived in the usual hut squatting on its heels. It was roofed with broad banana leaves. Inside: the frayed mat, bamboo stems piled for firewood, a dried fish pungent on the cereal air. Outside was a wild tamarind. Some bamboo spathes lay strewn to dry. Fur rippled on the roof: a rat which was edible too, quite tasty to the palate, said Blair.

Now the sister dressed for the occasion peered out shyly, and she was pretty. What's going on? thought Joey: can she be doing this? Playacting? Moonlight was a sight for sore eyes after five days and nights of jungle hump, cloudburst drenchings, fitful sleep on a poncho liner, and one man kidnapped. Vane, Izard, and FNG-IX (Meno) went to case out the gracious invitation of the sister-san.

And now a woman came by with crab soup. She cried in a high cutting tone:

—Banh troi! . . . banh duc!

Yet another had rice cakes, sticky and sugary, while she toted papaw fruit in a net over her shoulder.

The squad leader just let it happen as his thoughts, relaxed from the tense trail and fear of a booby trap beneath each step, spanned ten thousand miles to the small lazy southern town where his wife had gotten too cozy to write him a note saying they were a couple, and things were okay. Had she been unfaithful? Was she making love to his brother Newell? That could be, knowing him. Joey was deep in his thoughts, but he'd remember the scent of crab soup and wild tamarind, the sight of papaw in a grocery net, and the pretty sister's hut covered with banana leaves among the other trapezoidal roofs of Xo Man.

VI

Moonlight smiled coyly from her low front window hung with thatch. There was no vulgar fuckee talk from her. Vane calmed down. Izard turned back toward Joey with a high sign.

—Gio cha!

This was sausage: gio cha. It was a grunt's best friend because he got the runs and then drew field hospital duty for a day or two, maybe.

A boy skipped by with a wink. Twelve, thirteen years old. Joey had seen him back in the square: he was pals, it seemed, with Kid Pimp and Sister-San.

—Dollah shoeshine! G.I. numbah one dollah!

Now really. And the little twirp probably sneered at military scrip.

Joey glanced where Bufillu was having a chat across the way. One day in Da Nang when they were just in country Bufillu bet a dollar he could quaff the noodle soup called pho—sold in the street and eaten at breakfast time—and not puke. It proved delicious. And so Bufillu took some now through a hootch window beside Numbah One Sistah's where the shoeshine boy had also set up shop.

—Time to split, said Jojo. I mean it now!

But they paused.

—Hold on—said FNG-IX who didn't know any better.—Let them do it, you know.

Where was Tombigbee? No sign of the man jack for some time. Found his own girl in this port? Skol with his wiles had drifted off somewhere too.

Now up the dusty main road came the first tea vendor with a frown and one hand to her ripped blouse. Peekaboo, I see you.

Not a knockout like the debutante sister, but not bad either—a village woman unused to indignity from the likes of a Vane.

Suddenly the scene was so quiet. A child cried in a nearby hut. A cicada fiddled in its tree. The country boy Ringwood finger-licked a peach tin and crossed the dirt road into the sunlight. Sights, sounds, a few casual words. No takers for the dollar shoeshine; but for the sister-san, outstanding, one dollah.

Chi-Bar and medic Artus stood by watching a crumpled green-back emerge from Vane's fatigues. Same magic trick from a car-tridge loop in Izard's bandolier; and FNG-IX's helmet. Here, take it please. But no shoeshine needed for a date with first sister.

Quiet, peaceful here, off the trail.

Then—

Joey Gilbert with his hitter's vision saw it. Suddenly he was tense, but didn't know why yet.

The tea vendor turned back with a bow and a frown at Kid Ringwood. She went on her way with short steps but not too quick: head forward, smiling, looking pained and dutiful like a Chinese woman. Bufillu spooned the pho. In the window a woman had taken his piaster. And then? The shoeshine boy reached down and plucked a pencil stub from the box, and took off. Hm, he skipped away with a laugh and a twinkle beneath his arched eye-brows. He left his kit.

—Kid, your stuff! Hey, what the—

Vane bent his head in the hootch. The pretty sister with the fake satin bodice didn't take his dollar after all. She had gone. Where to? Was she back in the shadows with Izard who won the toss and elected to kick off? No, Izard waited calmly round the side while FNG-IX, the high school dropout not long from his gas pump in Salt Lake City: FNG-IX-Meno gave the grin of a yokel all Adam's apple and goober peas. Fun and games? Heyhey! A good time in the old town tonight.

No orders from Six: the squad was left to itself. So the men lounged and savored another moment before the humptydump. No tea vendor. Hm. No teenage whore. Hm. No kids, fruit and vegetable sellers; in fact, there was hardly a native to be seen. Where'd they go? Trap door exit?

Suddenly Bufillu gave a little leap. He dropped his soup and leapt back at the squad leader. Bufillu bounded ten yards with his arms flung wide like the football tackle he was. Gone dinky-dow? Joey never saw the big man move so fast, not in action, not in combat. The sidekick gave a wild cry and they both went sprawling—bruised by gear, rounds, grenades, webbing, the whole mess ground in the dust. It all happened so fast. There was no reaction time for Ringwood, Izard, FNG-IX standing just too close.

Vane went catapulting back—blinded by the fiery impact as the shoeshine box ignited and blew. The blast crumpled the nearest hootch and gashed tree trunks. But a few never knew. In an instant Billy Ringwood was turned into a human gristle. Izard, FNG-IX were blown so apart they ceased to exist. Joey saw it. In shock he watched. He pushed Bufillu off him. First he crawled, then made it to his knees; then called out for the RTO.

VII

—Sniper fire!

It came from the trees. It was around them: on them.

Joey stood dazed with a howl in his ears. Pta! pta! MAS-36 carbine from the French occupation: that's what it was. An instant later he knelt between two huts firing into a tree on the far side. Behind him there was a crazed laughter. There was horror among the men of his squad. Burnt thatch made a crisp acrid smell. More shots. Pta! pta! pta! A sniper fired down at them—from where? Angle? . . . Then Joey knew, and he got him. The sniper fell in stages, clinging as he came, like a monkey; and he was that light. Joey finished him.

On all sides confusion, chaos.

Then the squad leader went down a narrow lane. Stunned, his senses were reeling. The blast had staggered trees. Smoke filled the air and hid the ground.

Further on a grunt crouched to windmill a grenade in a hootch window. Then he stood and fired his M-16 into the lopsided hut, but Joey couldn't tell who it was.

Again he called for Troupial. The RTO had left his radio on the ground in the excitement.

Up ahead Chi-Bar, Thingum, Troupial ran about wildly and shot off volleys. Chi-Bar fired rounds at a pig covered with blood; it wobbled a few more steps and rolled over, squealing; its pink legs trembled.

The grunts were going from hut to hut. They emptied their guns and screamed: payback for Ben Bolt! This is for Kossuth, you chickenshit bastards! They torched a hootch after tossing in a grenade. This is for Skiball! Revenge, suckers! For Horse Shue!

—Dong lai! Dong lai!

They shrieked and swore. They whooped. What a victory it was. Submachineguns kept ranting and then a branch fell. Kill! Kill! Kill! Anything that moves! This is for Loseby the E-4! This is for every grunt messed up for life by Bouncing Betty! Ah! ah! So you say Milt Luna won't be going home at all? Remains unrecoverable? Smoke rose and seethed amid the trees fringed with gray. A dark cloud massed over the ville from the singed foliage. Kill! Kill! The surviving grunts caught up in the gale wind of violence laughed madly and raged as they looked for a target.

Chi-Bar touched his neck hit by a sniper bullet. Casually he fingered the flesh. Then Chi-Bar went to one knee and fell on his side.

Troupial had an old gray-headed woman lined up in front of a hut. This was the bicyclist with charcoal, wood sacks, a hen on her handlebar. He swore at the grandma-san and shook his gun at her. Features shrunken like a death's head under her white hair, she drew in her frail shoulders and waited.

Joey came up and turned the RTO roughly around.

—And the radio?

A ways further Thingum with his blond crewcut—a surfer from Huntington Beach not long out of boot camp—Thingum held high his knife and ran after a bristling chicken and screeched like the chicken.

—Come here, dear!

Artus the medic had left Bufillu's back burns and knelt over Chi-Bar.

But the cagey Skol had drifted by himself among the hootches on his own mission. Like a sleek panther he followed a girl in early teenage away from the scene. What a coincidence: it was Sister-San. It was the boy's pretty sister, Miss Dollah Fuckee who slipped away from her post as taker-on of all comers and none:

creating a diversion as she drew the G.I.s in a group and they hadn't realized what was happening until their ass was grass. Well, it was love at first sight. They never knew what hit them. But she had flitted off between hootches in her satin bodice—with a scared look since she knew the man was there on her tracks. One of them had not been that distracted and kept his eye on her despite the violence and the carnage.

Now Skoly-Skol overtook her and forced her to enter an empty hootch and shoved her against the wall. Bayonet fixed, he gave a grin. He cowed her with a thrust of the gun, poking Sister-San in the ribs, and forced her to kneel on the earthen floor before him. Skol grabbed a fistful of her silken hair and lifted back her face. The girl's rigid features were aquiver. Rapid breaths shook her slender body as she had to submit to him. Would it only be rape? Okay then? Did she think she might be allowed to get away after his buddies had been blown to bits?

Now the wiry pointman unzipped his fly and moved against the winsome Moonlight gone stiff, all alert and trying to survive, like a VC chignon battalion fighter. And she closed her eyes, her features strained and taut, as her cheek twitched and she waited for him to enter her . . . She gasped, not loud, clutching his sweaty jungle fatigues at the shoulder.

Outside it was mad minutes as the deafening rant went on. They showered the hootches and trees with semiautomatic fire. They were stunned in their depths and fired back wildly. Then in a lull, pta! pta! another VC sniper. A savage female scream rose on the air and died away. Smoke drifted up and dimmed the trees. There was more laughter as Thingum beside himself set a hootch on fire with delight. Ha ha! Ha-ha-ha! Take that, Xo Man. You don't live here no mo'.

Outside along the dusty lanes it was a world of hurt. But inside the twilit hootch where Skol did his business, there was a strange quiet. The girl gave a dry whimper beneath him. And she knew better than to try anything with this smart one, who kept his head and guarded his movements even in a sex act on top of her. Would she make it through this? First the rape, and then—? With a will Skol flew into his orgasm and drove home his hate. Hnnghhn, honey, hnnghhn, little honey . . . His breath buzzed in her ear as he held her down in the dirt. Skol's teeth gritted when he made love. Oh, Uncle Milt Luna, the pointman's one buddy

in the unit, looked very bad after that ambush on Dac Lac plateau: so bad when he was medevac'd up, up, and all the way.
Japan, home, and then to heaven: Luna's war ended, and his life.
Hunnghngh-hnnghnngh! The crafty pointman, hypersensitive to
any unfriendly hint, a VC booby trap; the superb bushman able
to stay on a course set by Six as he went hacking a path through
prickly underbrush for the squad to follow—Skol quivered on
top of her. He gave a sigh at the height of his pleasure.

On his sleeve next to a Combat Infantryman's Badge—silver
Kentucky rifle in a silver wreath on blue infantry background—
was a second patch which seemed to preside over his lovemaking. It was the Puking Buzzard.

VIII

—Six, Beta-5 . . . Six, Beta-5.

Mad minutes were on the march as a dust-off hovered with its
big blade swuffing not high above the trees. Rotor wash fanned
smoke and raised dust and dirt in a whirlwind; it tore sections of
roof from the hootches in flames. World Serious had his elbows
draped with red bunting, Ringwood's shredded flesh, as he carried a stump of the remains to the LZ being sniped. There was
blood, blood, and more blood. On all sides the hootches crackled
and hissed, sending up rivers of smoke. Faces grimed with soot
and pinkish flecks ran about under the roaring chopper. Joey's
eyes were bloodshot as he hung on in a state of shock. He watched
while the pilot tried to maneuver down in the dense smoke. The
helicopter came in and out of view up there amid the treetops; it
looked unreal as a modern god. Behind him the shooting kept on:
ratatatatata—pta! pta! Someone shouted:

—Can bo! Can bo!

Bufillu came through the fumes. A grim figure in his tattered fatigues, his broad back bubbled up with glistery welts, he glanced
back at the huts on fire. A roof spiralled up in a blaze. The walls of
plaited bamboo collapsed as smoke poured up. Smoke saved the
grunts from a merciless sniper fire.

Bufillu said:

—Fuck 'em up. Can bo.

Joey stood waiting. In his arms some of Billy Ringwood still twittered. Blood fell in flag-like sheets from the gashed abdomen. The entrails gaped open. Joey breathed in smoke laden with animal dung: Xo Man a pungent stew of burnt flesh and greenwood forest. He smelled the sweat of soft bodies unused to the humid tropics. He saw. He blinked. In those instants the grisly scene was fixed in his memory; or fixated, a death imprint. And he breathed deeply. He seemed to breathe out his innocence.

Then he watched the Medevac lurch back and rise up in a frantic clatter away from the field of carnage. The chopper cleared the trees. It veered out toward the northwest and a triage at Buon Me Thuot.

Behind him down the path there were more shots like an afterthought.

Get them together. Who was left? Where was Skol? And Tombigbee?

IX

Half in a daze he went looking.

Next thing he knew he gazed in the low entry of a hootch. He was thinking of Bufillu badly burned and Vane blinded; and now they flew through the air with the greatest of ease toward base camp. Plus what scraps and morsels the corpsman could gather like leftovers from a meal of death, Izard, Chi-Bar, Ringwood, FNG-IX, were now on the way to Graves Registration. This was a clapboard structure with a large mobile refrigeration unit well away from the air strip. Washed down and identified if possible, the limbs and assorted organs were grouped in a jigsaw and stored in the communal fridge. Later the honored dead would be embalmed in Da Nang or Saigon. Torn ragdoll of a Billy Ringwood, once a pretty smooth infielder, and the others would be labelled for shipment to wife or family Stateside. Try to get the labels on right!

Joey stared in the hootch. Numbed, overcome, he made out two, no, it was three slender bodies fragged and then riddled with bullets at close range. Then he saw the mother. Three Vietnamese

children were with their mother. Tightly they clutched one another. But the blood was enough: it glued them in a gory sculpture. Joey Gilbert loved children and thought they were beautiful.
So were these before their little bodies were gashed and gouged
beneath the shreds of clothing awash in blood. Ah, but these were
VC? VC kids? Or were they an ARVN family—friendlies, insofar
as anyone in Xo Man could be friendly: not told by the village
leaders and VC cadre about Operation Shoeshine?

There in the doorway in a strange posture, with a crick, stood
Skol. He waited for his squad leader to tell him what to do. Just
say it and Skol would do it if he could: a gifted soldier.

Quietly the flames snaked along the thatch overhang and blent
in a golden light as dusk came on. Well these didn't look much like
can bo, militants—the woman thirtyish but aged in an instant, her
features crimped in death, dull yet surprised. A girl was maybe
twelve; and Joey seemed to see his kid sister Lemon who wasn't
so different from this one with a listless arm lifted a bit and a look
of hurt wonder in her dark eyes.

He paused there as the others grouped behind him, Troupial,
Artus, Thingum, Skol, the survivors. In those moments there was
a kind of dull throb as if to say: well, what the fuck.

What else could be said?

Still he lingered, looking in. A shutter seemed to open in his
mind. He saw cassava roots on a table in there, and some bundled
pumpkin leaves. There was mountain rice in a tin. A rootstalk of
ginger.

Joey turned.

They followed. They went around the side, and away.

As the others trudged away Skol zipped his lighter and with
a smooth move, behind the back, put its small flame to the straw
of that hootch where a woman and her children made a piece of
ghastly sculpture.

X

The grunts wandered out of Xo Man. They headed as directed
southwest toward the platoon rendezvous with Beta-3, seven Ks
on the far side.

Six told them:

—Replacements will come at 0500.

Behind them the ville crackled and sent up more smoke to the dark gray cloud overhead. They still felt the heat on their backs. When a grunt turned for a last look, his grimy face glowed with the sorryass burg of Xo Man gone up in flames.

Up ahead on the dirt road a tall figure stood alone waiting for them. His lean jaunty form had an aura to it as daylight waned. At first it looked like a ghost out there along the road. Was it Blair?

They came up to him.

—Where you been hiding? said Troupial.

The man's lips parted and showed his teeth, but he didn't deign to speak. Far out across the plain spread a panorama to the ridgeline. A stark twilight was gathering. Southernmost Truong Son, the spinal column of Vietnam, went a mauve hue. It looked dramatic as the mountain range cast long purplish shadows out over Nam Bo plain.

A monkey screeched in the trees. It was with them from morning saddle-up to night settle-in and the jitters on perimeter. The sad cry of that gibbon spoke to their mood. Later it would pierce through the silent mist at nightfall and give them a shiver.

—No, man, now I mean it, said Troupial. We catch flak and you hightail it out. What do you call that?

Smoke and more smoke soared in deep gray billows over the trees. When those hootches burned they gave off a savage forestial smell.

In normal times Tombigbee, the Navajo from Tuba City, Arizona, didn't talk much. He was polite but he kept his own counsel and liked to stay alone. No #1 bud for Tombigbee, no partner. But now Troupial was glaring at him; and so he, the only calm one among them, had to say something.

Tombigbee said:

—Congratulations.

Thingum gushed:

—This time we got body count. Six'll put in for medals.

—Yep 'n paid in full—said medic Artus leaning to grab a leaf to wipe his bloody hands since his towel was a big gob of it.

Thingum urged Joey:

—Did you tell Six?

Over their heads the sky was going a deep purplish red. It was vivid: the evanescent glow of the tropical sunset. And somehow the massacre they just did was a magenta hue like the sky.

Big Tombigbee paused with his lips pursed. Why bother? If the boy didn't know then he couldn't tell him. But he said quietly to Troupial:

—Yes, tell Six we controlled a few families back there whose men are off fighting with our ARVN allies. Tell Six we greased some friendly elements who were not in the know: who weren't told to get out of sight before the bomb blew. Hey, with friends like us who needs enemies? Congratulations.

—You lie, said Troupial frowning. It's a VC ville. Right, Jo?

But the squad leader didn't answer. As so often lately he was in his thoughts, and Southeast Asia might sink into the mire for all he cared.

The six men moved along. Silent now. Click-click. In the open with a broken formation they had no heart for their own defense. The leader went in front but he didn't lead worth a crap in the spell that came after those mad minutes. Stunned, his mind on tea vendor and shoeshine boy, the old bicycle woman and pretty Sister-San who was not a whore but a decoy; on the horrible hootch with a bullet-riddled mother and her kids not VC or even VC sympathizers if Tombigbee was on the mark. Maybe she was a village outcast since her husband went away to join Saigon Government forces so he would be able to feed his family and maybe get ahead a little.

So it was. Local guerrilla forces had their monkey hunt, their G.I. turkey shoot—replete with cover fire from tree snipers, a VC cadre theater troop, a fountain-pen bomb to set off plastic explosive. In the nick of time the villagers had filed through slits in a bamboo clump to a tunnel. This was all well planned with precisely their platoon on its strategic Central Highlands mission in mind. And now watch: in a day, in a week the news spread among Muï hamlets and it was all the talk in the hu-tieu soup shops across the province. Massacre in Xo Man! G.I. baby killers! Vietnamese children slaughtered! Look at this Western-style freedom and democracy they're always telling us about. Right on, troops. Bravo, American boys. It is boocoo National Liberation Front PR coup. Boocoo, and boohoo, and (obscene gesture) to you.

XI

Night fell. Behind the remnant of squad members a lurid light flickered. Now it was a jungle mass: a darkness of matted vegetation. Branches jutted angrily at a carmine sky. Joey tried to think of his wife some more, but there were no new thoughts. The long ridges south toward Mekong were outlined against a green strip of horizon. Stars came out in the purple sky. The grunts marched a little more. They wanted distance from that village.

These months Carlyne had traipsed the land with him in the heat and the fever. He had embraced her mentally in the furnace of noon; he heard her voice in a wild lament from the summits, an animal's shriek or VC signal along their path. And now he tried to desire her despite everything in the shimmer and last light of the forest. My darling, all is forgiven only don't leave me. Oh the Asian look of her features and high cheekbones—lovelier than a Cham girl in tight-legged black satin slacks and loose fitting jacket of fine embroidered material. Three weeks and no letter: so he must go this joyless road alone. It was too much. Who could do it? His loneliness went flapping out to the dark confines of the Southeast Asian night on heavy wings.

Unfaithful to him? Okay, never mind. But gone? Gone out of his life forever? If so, then . . . defeat. Then death. For what did it matter if he was killed, or turned into a savage beast who ate children? He might walk down this road all the way to nowhere and lie down in the deep forest with no more thought for such a thing as a wife and return to his first primitive state. What's the big difference between himself and Ben Bolt, Loseby, now Billy Ringwood, Izard, Chi-Bar, the new kid FNG-IX, except he still felt pain and inflicted it? He was the living dead, and they were the dead dead.

Xo Man glowed behind them. It would be tomorrow or the next day before the fire went out.

Finally he said:

—Set-up time.

XII

Then they went through the motions of setting up a perimeter, laying out claymores, entrenching for the night. It was body-warmed C-rats: like it or lump it. Troupial called in. And Six, his voice sternly tender amid static, said:

—Troops, outstanding. I've spoken to Colonel Pricecroft about it, and you will get R & R for this. Hats off, grunts of the 2nd Battalion, 4th Infantry Division.

Apparently excitement had greeted the body count news back at base area in Buon Me Thuot. It was only marred by the usual concern over few or in this case no captured enemy weapons. Inflate a VC casualty tally? Okay. But someone on up the chain, perhaps the current brigade executive officer, in this case Daniel Pricecroft himself, must come up with a more believable figure. And then began the medal awards. Medals flew about like a flock of starlings toward winter. But more to the point was talk about a standdown worth the name—in Bangkok, Thailand, where the honeys were not VC eager to cook your gizzard on a skillet, and eat your manhood sautéed for breakfast.

Tomorrow early a motley FNG crew would fly in by chopper from Replacement in Da Nang. Then it was a big headache for the fire team leader, Jojo.

Grunts settled in with a sigh. From the tall trees rustling with a breeze came a cry. Monkey?

A meditative Thingum spooned his rations. He broke the silence.

—Look. Don't we have a job to do here? We're technicians, that's all. Mistakes are made.

Troupial chewed, swallowed:

—The big picture is: sat cong. Fuck communists.

Medic Artus said:

—Think Kevin'll check back in? I hope so.

Squad leader:

—No talk.

He knew and they knew the next day would not be a pleasant outing. As for Smoky Blair—they called him Smoky—he could be waiting for them just up ahead, round the bend, at the next turning of the trail. But there was probably no joyous reunion in store with the botany student. Sensitive Kevin, a nature lover, was the best kid on earth; but it was hard to like his chances after Xo Man.

This Nam was a dizzy place.

Chapter Five

I

Emory Gilbert paused before the drawn dining room table with the monogrammed service of his ancestors. He gave a last touch here and there to Cindy's place settings: the chased silverware, the plush napery folded carefully. Pendent lights of the crystal chandelier's upcurved arms sparkled in the long-stemmed wineglasses.

The host looked over the dinner table. For such an important man he had an eye for detail: a compulsiveness in little things. His son Newell liked to tease him and say he 'went berserk for the micro while the macro was out of control'. Why of course: that's how he had written several of the nation's best books.

Tonight he was not in tuxedo, but he did dress the part. His latest triumph called for a finely tailored blue suit of the most expensive cloth. Brow knit—Newell called him Zeus—he caught his own eye in the mirror with its classical urns and swags above the sideboard. Emory needed a minute to confirm he was such an attractive man; so he lingered and thought yes he was, remembering a verse from *Faust*. Yes, still handsome; there was a period of drinking too much, but it had ended.

This southern mansion was his habitat: the elegant dining room with its silver and glass wall sconces, silk shaded table lamps; an ornate candelabra on a bow-fronted side table. From the table he glanced at the high cheery windows open on a warmish evening in November.

Darkness had fallen in the small southern town. It came like a tide over the long sloping front lawn, the pleasant shrubs and secular oak trees. Half a mile away a train came rolling through the deserted center. The Southern Pacific trunk line clanked and chuffed along its elevated tracks past the low-eaved depot. In past decades many a hometown boy had hopped a boxcar up town and ridden west with his hopes and a restless energy. But during the Second World War the young men of this town, as in towns across America, had boarded a troop convoy and made the jaunt east to the big military base near the Carolina coast, or else Fayetteville. And from there they journeyed to the war theaters overseas, Coral Sea, El Alamein, Cassino and Anzio, the Marianas Islands, Normandy.

Now Emory thought of his own boy gone far away to a different kind of war. Night after night on network television there was terrible news footage.

Into the distant fields, forest and farmland, the train whistle blew and quavered in a hurry after the cluster of empty store-fronts and dusty furniture showrooms.

An instant longer Emory checked the seven place settings.

Then the doorbell rang.

II

—Hello, Max. Hello, Paul.

—Hail Caesar—General Doan laughed.—In your hour of power, ne vile velis!

—Incline to nothing base? I'll try.

—Nil sine numine—said the churchman Commynes.—Nothing, statesman, without the divine will.

—Heu, said Emory.

In the wide front entry of the Rock Castle the two guests stood side by side. They were in good form tonight: old friends on a lark after a life of hard work. But no two men could have been more unlike.

Both were successful like Emory, but there the similarity ended.

The military man was blond and blue-eyed, crewcutted, slender and in good shape. The pastor was dark eyed with dark wavy hair gray at the temples, and he tended a bit to the portly. Max Doan looked so fine and upright after his career as a soldier and then top government and corporate posts; he smiled and bowed charmingly even during arguments with Emory's hippie son. But Bishop Commynes was a deep one, a subtle man often in his moods; he had a direct line to God, and they debated the nature of faith and redemption. Whereas Max stuck to a few home truths, the goodness of America and her way of life, Paul seemed to nuance his simplest comments with a tone, a word unsaid. Paul came at you in coils for a casual hi on the street.

Emory's daughter, Lemon, had a nickname for everybody, and she called them Mr. Outside and Mr. Inside. Max was funny to look at and listen to, but the retired minister had the wit of Mephistopheles, sinister perhaps, yet it cast a new light on things and made you tingle.

Besides all this the two men were contradictory in themselves. For instance General Doan was a world-beater if there ever was one; he had been a lot of places and done a lot of things; yet he was modest, courteous. Why, he even called Newell 'sir' and laughed amiably while Newell Sir, or Sir Newell (twinkle in Doan's steely eyes) railed and gesticulated at the old soldier and termed him a Neo-Nazi.

As for Bishop Commynes: his depthless eyes showed such a sincere concern, as though a rich humanity glowed out from them warming all like the great hearth of God. At the same time he had a sense of his own salvation, and personal sanctity, like the heavy folds of an ecclesiastical robe. And this separated.

General Max Doan was an American type everyone knows well enough. Indeed you could see such a man any night on TV as a part of the Vietnam coverage: the 4-Star General giving his spiel for the media during the Five O'clock Follies, military press conference, at MACV headquarters in Saigon. Blond and blandly handsome he was springy on his feet at sixty with a starch to his crewcut and his humor. The semiretired Grl. Maximillian Doan was a big boy with a hand in the big game, high-level ties in Washington, career friends at the Pentagon. Currently he served as top adviser for military wargames and commuted to the West Coast every few weeks where he had seen Joey Gilbert the past summer. Max could at times be rather loud with his have-at-you remarks on faith in the nation and its leaders which he never questioned. On hot days he liked to dress like a colonial planter in khaki shorts and safari jacket, solar topee.

As for Bishop Commynes: he had been a prominent banker before becoming a minister; and now in retirement he was still a sort of split personality. His was a paternal interest, friendly, wise; but those dark eyes brooded, and his gaze fell away from nice everyday things. The saintly man seemed to glimpse a devil in your depths; and he had such a stare it could make you shudder. His face had a curious lunar note due to a slight disproportion in one cheekbone. Also he was stiff-necked; he had been shot many years ago when the banker rode out in his buggy to foreclose on a factory worker named Dewy Spivey. There was a folk ballad about that: part of the town's lore and legend. But for all his mystery, and a gaze that weighed your chances of eternal damnation, Paul Commynes was an attractive man and you would have liked him. Time had a way of going faster in his presence, which wasn't always the case in this small southern town.

III

Tonight the Protestant minister had on a dark suit with the usual clerical collar. But Max sported a light blue seersucker job that looked summery on this fall night in the South: just as he was past his own year's prime but still quick to see nature's bounty in the form of a female.

As Emory ushered them into the den where Cindy would bring cocktails on a tray, the gallant Max asked:

—Will Carlyne and Lemon be joining us for dinner?

—Carlyne wasn't feeling well earlier. Let me go knock at the guest bedroom.

Just then Emory's daughter came in. Sprightly girl, she moved with a lilt through the den entry. She reached up and touched a curious wooden arm, hung from the lintel, with a candle socket at the end: this could be swung down in front of a settle or chair for reading and writing in the old days.

Lemon gave a sidelong glance while curtsying to Pastor Com-

mynes. She was sort of bold for a kid and went among them fuss-
ily like she was getting up a game of Red Light. Nothing could
have been more pleasant, while her dad went to see about Carlyne, than the way pert chirpy Lemon, 13 years old, played hostess to the two middle-aged gentlemen—those two pissers, as
Newell called them, who beneath the fond often humorous manners were the two most self-important men alive.

A half hour later they sat at table. For a moment they spoke of
Joey since Carlyne hadn't come out from the guest bedroom yet.
Any talk of him might have upset her. She was so worried about
her husband, as Bishop Commynes noted, she couldn't read his
letters. There was a small pile of Jojo's envelopes out on the front
hall table. And they lay unopened, smudged, reddish, after coming from *Somewhere in the Central Highlands of Vietnam,* as they
were return-addressed instead of the usual Armed Forces or APO
address.

Then Max Doan changed the subject in that gung-ho tone of
his and brought up a news story run by the major networks yesterday. It told of how Emory Gilbert, the famed author, would be
going to the nation's capital to serve as adviser in the Democratic
presidential campaign.

—Morning sessions over breakfast!—Doan flourished his
fork.—Media positionings, and all the stirring rhetoric a future
President does make . . . Well, I can see it now: your exchanges
with our hardnose press corps. Watch out! They're lying in wait
to ambush you on Vietnam.

Emory shrugged:

—Mr. President has kept his head on the war. We'll sweep the
spring primaries.

—Ha!—Max was eloquent as he chewed.—There'll be mustard
on your face at the county fair. You'll shake the calloused hand of
your dear friend Labor at the factory gate. Then comes the endless round of functions, the hundred a plate fundraisers where
you introduce your candidate and drum up enthusiasm.—Doan's
voice went low as he cut into Cindy's roast.—Tense last-minute
decisions that can make or break. Brilliantly you skirt the sticky
issue of Vietnam. Then in Chicago next summer there will be
deals done in darkness: in the back rooms of our nation's destiny!
Well, you have spent your life among the classics, a bookman, but
now it is time for reality.

Emory laughed. He looked a decade younger. He was entering a second prime of life as he sat at the head of the table for this celebratory dinner with family and close friends. That afternoon he had gone for an interview at a local TV affiliate's studios: a segment to be aired by the nightly news.

Of those present only Emory from his seat at the head could see into the front hall. And now his eyes left Doan and fixed on a figure who paused there, in the shadows by the stairwell, and seemed unable to proceed. It was Carlyne.

She wore a straight black dress of barège material simply cut, severe, sensual over her figure with a brooch; it was her husband's favorite before he went away. Carlyne didn't have much in the way of feminine graces, and she didn't try. What she did have was a kind of womanly ruggedness, her features regular but roughhewn, forehead pure with fine arcing eyebrows. She was too busy with the inner struggle of the moment to try to charm.

She was a stunning young woman but with no use for the usual wiles, girlish whims, the latest in ladies' apparel. Maybe her vanity had been burned away during nine years of life, formative years, in an orphanage. But her Lumbee momma had given her something which would see her through this life. She had a raw and very strong appeal for the male; so much was clear; but by this late date—she was twenty—it left her cold.

In company she spoke little. She didn't mind listening, looking. Some mornings she was too thoughtful to say hello and went about with a distracted air. She never rambled or wasted many words; though she liked to play the winsome games of childhood upstairs in Lemon's room. And she talked about serious things, philosophy, politics, old stories of Gilbert family life, with Newell during walks they took together out back to the banks of the Yadkin River. Also she liked to gab happily with Cindy Phillips while helping her to get up lunch or dinner in the kitchen, or doing the dishes; but not lately.

Carlyne didn't show off; she didn't try to act any part or be the center of attention. She wasn't the type to put on airs. As for crying, showing emotion: it had been a long time since anyone saw her do that. Perhaps she seemed like a cold woman—right now Joey would have said so. But Joey was too busy with his own emotions to notice when she went a shade pale: when maybe something upset her, or pleased her; when maybe some inner travail was taking place.

No; she wasn't a woman who explained herself. She didn't talk about her feelings. She didn't show them either when the Gilbert men and their friends, Commynes and Doan, spoke of the ugly war where her husband was, and the body bags were being shipped back; or of the protests and banners raised these days and weeks in the nation's streets, like a plague in the land. In the same spirit voices were raised in Granddaddy's den; it was a little bit of the war staged here at home. But she had a sense they were arguing for her sake in some way, as if she were the spoils of that war.

Long ago in childhood Carlyne had lived and grown up in a large pleasant house like this one: Judge Vick's over in Eastern Carolina. It too had sunlit rooms, high cheery windows with sculpted lintels.

Now she stood in the dim front hall, in her dark outfit, like someone wondering if the sun would ever shine on her again.

IV

The host met her eyes. He gave her a little sign and drew her forward into the dining room, and that gathering of sympathetic guests.

They greeted her. Bishop Commynes said:

—That's a pretty brooch, Carlyne. Someone give it to you?

—An heirloom.

Serving herself she shared a glimpse with Cindy who sat in the seventh place near the swinging door to the kitchen, and across the table from Emory, as though sitting in for his late wife.

The brooch fastened her dress at the neck to the left. It showed a proud tribal woman wearing a feather as headdress. It was a focus of eyes and a conversation piece maybe because the rest of this young wife was so striking, like a soul going naked. Her deep blue eyes seemed to veil a story of desire and seduction told only to the old Hepplewhite mirror in the guest bedroom. Her fine brow and cheek, her sumptuous black hair had the susceptible note of an expectant mother; and her body the bit of extra weight, since at the Rock Castle she had her days to herself. There was a mystic hint to her sensuous figure: not for nothing had her husband nicknamed her Sphinx.

The view of Carlyne was not an inviting one somehow. And so the pastor's eye fell on the brooch.

She paused before eating—for lack of appetite? She stared at the autumn night outside, fallen, with a last purple tinge of sunset in the windows.

For a moment they watched her begin to eat. There was that about her—it wasn't her fault, she tried to play it down, but from the day she came among them in the Rock Castle the air had been heavy with sexuality.

Max Doan turned back to Emory. Max crooned:

—Good deal! You'll make a fancy advance man, I can tell you: a writer compared to Victor Hugo. They'll love it when you intro your product at a press conference: the President of the United States. Emory Gilbert gets in a few good words of his own. He says: instruments of power . . . Then comes talk about what our decent, sober, responsible Americans believe.

At this a voice came from down the hall:

—Here I am! Did you say decent, sober-minded?

It was the hippie, and he gave his chuckle.

The solemn features of Bishop Commynes seemed to light up at sight of him.

From the head of the table Emory shot a glance into the hall. Like a wild child with flowers in his hair Newell came wandering in from the fields into this formal setting. He hung there in the front hall looking truly amazing.

Seeing Max Doan among the guests he threw up a hand, dropped to one knee, and cried out:

—Everybody under your chairs, it's a Japanese air raid! Look! Silvery planes over the Matanikan jungles and coconut groves in the South Seas! The propellor arcs shimmer as they dip: Jap bombers, wave on wave. Shells burst!

Max sat with his back to him. But the big man turned for a look and gaped on purpose as if to say: I know I'm in for it this time but I'm not afraid because I have a big stick which can break your bones.

And so the General went on with his own show:

—Emory, you thought it would be a private breakfast, a parley among campaign honchos. Strategy and tactics; who are the key players? where do things stand with in-Party talks? But sooner or later a moment comes: now the great writer must give us his view on this issue. We are honored by his presence, but the time has come for him to participate. Maybe it is missed by you, Emory, this pause as the others try you out. Present your credentials. Now address the vital issues if you don't mind: national security, the war, the economy. But be careful, my liberal friend. This is your Toulon: snap to it, Nappy, but use discretion. Is there fuzziness? Ill-considered word? An unhelpful slant? That could alienate a sector of voters! And then—Max Doan thumped the table, and his voice went low—then kiss your career as a public figure goodbye. Go back to your books. Homer and Sophocles make better playmates than these committee men.

V

Newell came on. He was allured by the scent of Cindy's cooking, and didn't bother to dress for dinner. Or rather he did dress but like an actor for a part. For one thing he'd found a blindman's folding cane: maybe at the pawnshop of Bishop's brother up town where he liked to go and bug crazy old Jake Commynes. Now he touched his way forward in the dining room entry. He looked tattered as a vagrant, but also serious, intent on some mischief. Strange for a blind person: he had a large red book under his arm.

His father asked:

—Why the dark glasses?

Newell said nothing. Tick-tock, went the grandfather clock in the hall. It was embarrassing: no answer. And that was one of his hippie tricks: to let a question hang in the air.

So Lemon took it up. She loved her dad and felt sort of maternal toward him since Anne Gilbert died. Also there was a serious side to Newell's dark glasses which she alone knew perhaps.

—Nuper's blind, Dad. He studied 72 hours straight and fell asleep at his desk with his contact lenses in his eyes. Woke up and couldn't see.

Emory said:

—You'll damage your eyes permanently.

Bishop Commynes said:

—Say, I like your hairdo.

Newell's hair was long and scraggly with wildflowers and a few weedy stems.

Lemon pulled back the chair beside her:

—Park it here, Nuisance.

—Yes-yes! said Newell. I heard the noble Doan going on. Election polls, campaign momentum . . . pressure the grassroots politicians into one's camp. A worthy task!

The six others sat watching in their semiformal attire as Newell lifted a bare foot and seemed to pick at a splinter.

Emory turned crimson when his son stopped the show, upstaging Presidential Race '68.

Bishop said with a smile and a glint in his eye:

—Immature.

There was another moment's silence as Newell absorbed this remark. Again Lemon filled it:

—Newby, sit down and eat. You're really a scream.

She chirped and began to fuss over her brother, or bruvver as she called him.

Emory said to the table:

—It's true I haven't seen him in three days.

The contrast really was too much; though none of the older men, dressed for the downs, thought it funny. The hippie had on a pair of madras Bermuda shorts, baggy and rumpled, which hadn't been changed for months. He wore a faded tie-dye t-shirt a few sizes too small. On his person were a few burrs from romps through the fields with his dog.

Down he plopped the big red book shaking the table. He gave the hippie chuckle.

—Come, Cindy, come-come! Comrade! Slop it on unparcimoniously! Look here, you are a worker, I respect that. You produce the world's wealth so we parasites (I include myself), all the great writers, church and military men, politicians and prostitutes, circus clowns and dignitaries . . . to paraphrase Marx in the *Theories of Surplus Value,* so we can chow down at our ease.

Newell nodded to himself. Then a good burp for his fans.

Slurp, slurp. Dig in.

VI

Now they watched him eat.

Bishop said:

—Can't see it, but wolfs it down.

Doan:

—Hearty appetite for a person who just lost his eyesight.

Newell raised his free hand, like the Pope, and gave them a hippie benediction. With his mouth full he spoke:

—Doan the hawk conservative . . . Gilbert the left liberal, a beautiful soul . . . Commynes the saintly devil, whose thoughts are an airy dialectics turning into their opposite with each beat of his angel's wings! Not bad. As a deep connoisseur of *la chose politique,* with amazing innate spiritual powers, I have once again uttered a basic truth.

With this he gave not the chuckle but a few bars of opera, a roulade—so enchanted with himself as he shovelled Cindy's supper down his gullet.

Max Doan said with a laugh:

—And you're a radical.

—What?!—Newell dropped his fork.—Never, Sir! Do not call me that. Do you wish to duel? Must we imbrue? I am no radical, Sir.

—What then? said Max.

Newell's lips were like a locomotive slowing for a depot. He thought, and said:

—During the Paris Commune . . . you remember it, Sir? Your class drowned the workers in blood and blamed them for it. And the radicals were with you. They fled to Versailles with Thiers. They, Louis Blanc and his ilk, feared and hated the Commune.

—And you? said Doan. Inside Paris?

The hippie looked at Max but didn't answer. He chuckled and dug in some more.

Then the table fell silent as a train rumbled over the crossing up town. It moved past the old commercial sector and gave a whistle.

Emory glimpsed Carlyne who was looking at Newell. Did she have a thought for Joey then? Joey far away on patrol in the Central Highlands of Vietnam—and sun glared across the rice paddies as he went M-16 in hand, stunned by her silence?

Newell lifted his face from the steaming plate which fogged his dark glasses. He said to the three men who smiled at him:

—Finished, you and you . . . and you . . . finished society, and finished men.

—What does that mean? said Commynes with a glance at Emory.

—Let me eat in peace, gentlemen. And then, with my ability to process the perceptual world in instants and convert it to understanding . . . my intellectual speed in solving the knottiest problem . . . I will tell you. A man like me is not entitled to leave humanity in the dark. I must share my brilliant surmises!

He gave another operatic roulade, and munched away.

VII

After four undergrad years in New Haven and then a Masters in art history and curatorial, Newell had gone off his rocker. He said so himself: never in human history since man stood upright and engaged like it or not in political economy: never had there been such a case of ideological indigestion. For him the dialectical method was like a crystal ball; and he applied it to his little sister's place in world history when she got home from school and he just had to talk to somebody after days all by himself studying. In one hand the *Communist Manifesto,* in the other the *Grundrisse,* reading two books at once, he paid Lemon to spoon-feed him, and then tickle his feet. He took *The Permanent Revolution* on his jaunts by the river and kept *Left-Wing Communism: an Infantile Disorder* by his pillow. In the shower he sang The Internationale.

He was obsessed with organizing workers. Blear-eyed after his white night over the socialist classics he waited in the shrubs for the politically backward postman. That comrade had a southern drawl:

—How y'all doin' this mornin'?

Calmly he put the letters in the slot as Newell sprang out from the bushes and began to harangue. But he scratched his head; it was the craziest stuff a mailman ever heard.

—Listen to me now! You're a wage slave, and it's time you became class-conscious!

—Huh?

Newell agitated Cindy Phillips who was a gentle woman in her late sixties. She had served the Gilbert family for forty minus one years; and now Newell urged a work stoppage on her part. Together they would list her demands, print up flyers and posters, picket the Rock Castle. They would wheatpaste the Georgian living room with her 'Ten Domestic Demands and Seven Theses'. Let massa' cook his own meals! Guided by his profound analysis, his astounding capacity for fundamental insights, his knowledge of class conflict and ability to grasp the next Leninist link—they the workers, he and Cindy, would open up other fronts and handout leaflets up town outside the Chamber of Commerce. From there the forces of liberation would march to the four fast-food restaurants which were the de facto town center. And then onward into High Point and Greensboro: at every shopping mall from here to Myrtle Beach they would use their conspiratorial powers.

—Victory or death! he shouted at Cindy in the kitchen. We will win!

From her oven she stared back at this red devil. Then with a smile and little curtsy she offered him a slice of the mince pie she just baked.

—Huh? Extra whip-cream, dear. Commissars must eat!

The rich dessert dripped from the cadre's lips as he mapped out world revolution.

But above all Newell organized his little sister. After teasing the cute spunky Lemon throughout her childhood, all but blighting her joy in life with his bullying: now he indoctrinated her, and agitated her night and day. It was a mania equalled only, perhaps, by Lemon's 'reactionary' love of horses, her obsession with horses, horses. She also loved her mad brother, though not as deeply as she did Joey whom she liked to call Horse. But for the life of her she could not become a good Marxist, a 'consequential revolutionary . . . thinking dialectically' and able to experience, analyze, *change* reality.

At four in the afternoon he awoke from sleeping all day, punctually, and met Comrade Lemon coming home from school. He gave her the day's 'mot d'ordre'—a catchy slogan for the struggle of this small town's exploited, oppressed proletariat, peasantry, and dispossessed classes. With her help he put on agitprop events at the Rock Castle, and got ready to do some guerrilla theater up town. It would be relished by local police; their response would be priceless.

Now he called Lemon subcomandante before Emory's dinner guests, Comrade Doan, Comrade Commynes. Their father he called not Sir, as Joey did; not Pop anymore, or Old Man; no, he called him: Mister Liberal. He treated his father with a Trotsky-ist contempt for the possessing class—after having taken up residence, with free room and board, in this nest of gentry.

Well, Newell had a bad case of intellectual dyspepsia. Yet he gorged more *Eighteenth Brumaire,* more *Accumulation of Capital,* more of the *Cuaderni del carcere,* and more *History and Class Consciousness.* This stew he spewed in Cindy's or the good Max Doan's face and called it 'organizing for the victory'. All night he studied, night after night as the weeks went by; and then slept away the daylight hours, a deep rosy-cheeked sleep without a care in the world—while the masses of humanity's wage slaves toiled for a few crumbs from the plate of Capital.

But sometimes Newell grew disgusted with himself, all this passive life. He gave a great yawn and said: human, all too human! . . . And then he wouldn't let himself go to sleep, but worked during the day too. So his eyes were affected, and now he couldn't see, or not much.

He said to Lemon:

—Soon I'll have to get out of here. Soon I'll go on the open road, and ride the rods, like a Wobbly.

VIII

Emory Gilbert was no more charmed by his younger son's latest monomania, namely Revolution, than by the boy's rudeness, and utter disregard for the merest amenities. Also he didn't like the idea of leaving Newell together with Carlyne at the Rock Castle: without his chaperoning presence after he went away to begin his new public life in the nation's capital. It wasn't enough that Max Doan slept over some nights; or that Bishop Commynes had a key to the old place—master key except for the new lock on the guest bedroom downstairs.

Now at the head of the table Emory had one eye on carving the roast, the other on his son's antics.

The semiretired U.S. Army General Maximilian Doan also stared at the hippie, who was fully retired (so Newell said) until age 65 when he might go to work. Max was fond of Lemon; in fact, he had a sort of crush on her, and came a-courtin' in topee helmet, safari jacket, gartered nylon socks, planter's cane in hand. At table he told war stories for her sake—a Japanese air raid, silvery planes high in blue skies over the Matanikan jungles and coconut groves in the South Seas. Propellor arcs shimmered as they dipped. Dive bombers came wave on wave. Shells burst. Newell went to one knee by the dining room table and a hand to his brow, the other pointing up, cried out: It's the Japs!

Now Max stared at the hippie. Usually Newell wasn't easy to provoke; he had a long fuse and didn't grow hostile; he thrived on argument and had no beef with his rival—though Doan held up Joey's selfless enlistment, Joey's heroic service to the cause of freedom, as an example to the draft evader.

But Max turned away. For the moment he addressed his host:

—When the glamor and all the whirlwind ends, Emory, when your candidate has lost as you know he must because 1968 is a Republican year: then you can establish Gilbert & Associates, a consultant firm, and rake in the millions.

—Gilbert & Sons! said Newell.

Hippie chuckle. Merry and snide Newell liberated portions of the dishes Cindy and Lemon, those peace lovers, shoved in front of him.

—Your bookshelves will be lined with commissioned reports on current national trends—

—All lies, said Newell, fingering his greasy hair as he chewed. Bourgeois spin on things, false consciousness.

—. . . analyses of past elections . . .

—Our historians revising the past. I give you Freedom and Democracy, gentlemen. Vietnam burns. The people die like flies, but they are free.

Doan paused with a smile. He hadn't attended West Point forty years before; commanded a field artillery battalion in World War II with the rank of lieutenant colonel; led an airborne combat team in Korea, '51; in order to take a backseat to a hippie.

—You'll fly up to weekend meetings at the Metropolitan Club.

—Grandiose!—Newell hefted his fork.—Decide with your fellow plutocrats on new ways to swindle the wide world.

—You'll plan and advise on strategies—

—War crimes. Wall Street crimes. Same thing.

—No more liberal humanities, no more lofty classicism for you, Emory. The man of action requires poll samples, and statistical approaches to media manipulation.

—Military-industrial-media complex.

—The politically salable image.

—Hey, hey, LBJ! Long Binh Jail: you know they call it 'LBJ'. That's troop morale.

Bishop Commynes broke in to ask Newell:

—And your brother? Does Joey have low morale?

—Jojo obeys his coach. Always has. In this game it's Coach Lyndon of the Great Society team. Have you heard? Coach Westmoreland says life is cheap in Vietnam. An apt comment for a man engaged in taking it wholesale. There was a race riot at Long Binh Stockade, did you hear? I read about it.

Newell made a pithy statement; then pigged out some more, chug-chug, like a train. When was the last time the boy ate?

Doan said:

—I think you feel guilty, Newell. You're blaming your wonderful country for your own misconduct.

—In the old days I was an art student, a beautiful soul. I had not fallen to knowledge, and so I took pride in my unconscious America. In my heart I still pledged allegiance to the flag: like my brother Joey I admired so when we were kids in grammar school. But now I know. I grant you such knowledge is hard to digest. Yet such is the result of my profound studies which have nourished my extraordinary perspicacity. (Newell sang out with his mouth full: a sort of roulade, like a quick run of operatic notes.) You see I have engaged in such ruthless auto-critique: from now on I'll get it right the first time, and my predictions of the course of history will always prove true. (Roulade.) And so I give you Uncle Sam, gentlemen, world history's biggest bully.

He stood up and sat down with a smirk. Hippie chuckle. Not everything was such a joke, however: for instance his enrollment in a doctoral program with fees and tuition fully paid as stipulated by his grandmother's will; also his thesis on a period of art, the Flemish quattrocento and crazy Hugo van der Goes, of no interest to him except to keep his 2-S deferment.

Doan, red-faced with Cindy's rich cuisine, said:

—To the poorer countries we give hospitals, schools, millions in foreign aid yearly. USAID is a light to the world.

—You mean we maintain the comprador elite, the ruling oligarchies, all our Third World dictator friends. Them we give military aid to repress their people. 0.7% of our national budget is for humanitarian purposes; in reality it is 0.2% we give—but who benefits, as Washington tries to beat back the tide? Natives restless again? Crush the little buggers. Underdevelop them, so they won't become industrial and trade competitors. And meanwhile Third World children die from curable diseases, malnutrition and related causes: one child every three seconds, twelve million a year, thirty-five thousand a day, tick, tick. Well, hell with 'em, if that was God's plan. Let the mighty Western corporations take, take: steal the fabulous mineral and agricultural resources from those smaller countries where the children die. Steal the natural wealth legally; control Third World markets; turn the population, adults and children, into slaves at substarvation wages. Extort, exploit, dominate. Look, Ma, no hands: all done through economic penetration and political manipulation. Use military force as a last resort. Hey, that's life. After all what does our middle class, kept carefully ignorant by U.S. media controlled by the same corporations who do all that, or have it done: what does our well-fed bourgeoisie care about the fate of a lot of colored kids? Rationalize. Deny they exist. Or say those people over there make too many babies—plenty of mileage left in Malthus. But as for us we are good Christians, all good little brothers of Jesus who feel good about ourselves. Besides, we have a manifest destiny, right?

In a quiet tone Doan said:

—America is benevolent. It does have a special mission in history: to bring true freedom and democracy to a world falling into the hands of fanatics, extremists, communists and terrorists. Look, we did not ask for such a task. Now across America families must look on while their loved ones, like your brother Joey, pay a high price if not the highest so liberty may survive in the face ot totalitarianism. Many, many, Newell, are making the ultimate sacrifice, while you and I sit here enjoying ourselves. Many good men die, the best! so tyrants will not have time to get the nuclear weapons in their hands which will destroy us all. This Twentieth Century is the American Century: which means we are meeting our responsibilities to humanity. We are the leaders of the Free World.

We have the best system and the longest-lived government, but all around us a new Dark Ages threatens mankind. I mean communist dictatorship. So we will hold our heads high and carry the torch for freedom: no matter what it costs, no matter what it takes, and with or without a few deluded hippies.

Newell looked up from his plate, and said, into the silence:

—Hell's bells.

From the head of the table Emory, brow knit, deep-toned, said:

—You may disagree, but you'd better be respectful.

Dapper Max Doan wasn't daunted by flippancy. He went on in a measured tone:

—We work toward democracy methodically, in a realistic way, wherever we go. Yes, this is our destiny, and it is positive. Say what you like, Newell, a lot of leftist rant: America's great technological advances are being used generously to serve people, and help develop the smaller countries. For a hundred and fifty years we have been spreading civilization, enlightenment, Western progress, in every latitude. Yes, do-gooder America: the world's last and greatest hope. Respect the U.S.A.! You see the affronts and attacks on our way of life, which is the most abundant, the most honorable—filled with opportunity and a vital attraction for the poor, the hungry, the neglected masses of this earth yearning to be free! Who attacks us? Those who hate us! envy us! If our way is bad then why does most of the earth want a visa to come live here, and participate in the very great thing which is America? No, sir, you are wrong. We must hold the course for the sake of all humanity. And we must work for law and order so decent folk won't fall prey to communist propaganda—the Nazi-like lies of your friends, if you ever met one personally.

—Not yet.

Doan laughed:

—Then you know whereof you speak.

There was a moment's silence.

Newell, chewing, head down, said with a shrug:

—You'll have to learn the hard way, Mr. Doan. My words are only words; it takes more to teach you anything, so you fall to knowledge. You are smug, sir. You have your own words. But nothing can change the fact that the wide world hates America, an oppressor nation, more and more. We're the world's most destructive empire ever.

—Well—said Max with a laugh, eating heartily now, pleased with the debate—well they'd do it to us if they could. In the meantime they want to come here and partake of our benevolent America and its good things.

—And send some back home to their families—said the hippie.

IX

Bishop Commynes looked on. He turned to Emory, and the two shared a glimpse.

—Immature.

Carlyne rose from table—a bit slowly, in the sensuous black dress a bit tight on her, as she had put on some weight. On her way into the kitchen to help Cindy, she said:

—Dessert anyone?

Now Lemon tugged her brother's sleeve, the shrunken t-shirt, and let it snap back.

—You punk, she said. Why upset people?

Bishop Commynes said:

—Carlyne, why don't we take a snapshot for Joey? Call Cindy in: we'll do a group photograph.

—Upsetting times.—Newell mumbled, coming up for air.— Plague in the polis.

Carlyne went in the kitchen.

Commynes said low:

—His antics hurt you in town.

—I know.

—A time may come when you . . .

—I know, said Emory. He should leave.

—Or better maybe—

—What?

—If he becomes a danger to himself and others? Then—

When Newell lifted his eyes from the gruel to Max Doan's blond crewcut, the Four-Star General smiled. A moment later the hippie saw fit to bless Bishop Commynes, and mimic the man's piety, and whispers, with a snide comment to Lemon. Mincing grin, cheeks puffed, the Bishop seemed to live his life in a gold embroidered chasuble, and wave a censer at smelly neighbors: so Newell did now at his little sister, and the other sinners. For the office he shook a bell in the pontiff's direction:

—Ding, ding. Get high on incense. Civilization and all that jazz; I mean liturgy for the savages. (Hippie chuckle.) Wow. In this matter of world history I must wholeheartedly agree with myself. My judgment is profound. (Roulade.) At least Nazis picked on nations their own size. We destroy small nations to save them: I guess this makes us ideologically inferior to Hitler. Right on.

X

There was a silence which maybe boded no good for someone.

The men and the hippie settled into the den for after-dinner drinks. Again a long train rumbled through the deserted up town sector; it clattered over the crossing at the main intersection; it shook a few flakes of paint from those quaint rows of two-storey commercial buildings.

Emory paused as the modern angel passed. Then he turned to his son. He cleared his throat, and, in his doctoral tone, said:

—Newell, I'm afraid you must mend your ways; that is, if you wish to go on living with us here. I've been too lenient. I let you alone to run wild and now look at you. Look how you're dressed, like a tramp, while the rest of us made an effort to mark the special occasion. You're living off me yet you attack me in front of guests. You go up town and have arguments with strangers, and the offshoot is they all think you're a fool, and me too for letting you do it. Please tell me, son, I want to know. What's the meaning of this act you're putting on?

Newell lifted his dark glasses for a closer look at his father. Then he tapped around his feet a little with his blindman's baton. He said:

—I'm Teiresias, blind seer of Thebes, and I've got something to tell you, Oedipus. (Hippie chuckle.)

Bishop Commynes' dark eye twinkled at sight of the pagan:

—Have you studied the birds' omens? Have you read the entrails?

Max Doan laughed after the fine meal:

—Oh, Teiresias, you who know all: please tell us what can't be said. Save us. Save our country.

—A thankless task, said Newell. And I know it. But I go on opening my big mouth.

Bishop:

—Looks to me like the seer could use some psychological help.

Newell said to his father:

—Listen, I'll go upstairs and study, if you don't mind. Better for you, Sir, and better for me.

Emory:

—How can you study if you're blind? No, boy, out with it. What's on your mind? What is it you say you know? What are these home truths of yours? If you don't spit it out I'll call you disloyal.

—A traitor—said Max Doan with a raised eyebrow.

Carlyne appeared in the doorway. For a moment she hung there, waiting to say goodnight. She watched the show her brother-in-law was putting on; and, just as at table, listened to the men. She didn't speak. On one level: all their talk and arguing was like a war they were waging for the desirable woman.

Newell:

—No, Sir, what's the good? I don't want to upset people.

Emory:

—You come here to the Rock Castle and do exactly as you like; insult us; show off and play the jackass. It's enough to make me lose faith in you. Watch out, son, I'll get angry.

—Hypocrite, said Newell. Cast out the beam from your own eye.

Bishop:

—That doesn't sound like Teiresias.

—Well who wouldn't get piffed? said Emory. You've no respect for your family, for our nation and your brother at war—

—For God, said Bishop Commynes.

—Don't confuse the issue, Pastor . . . No; I'll hush up this time. The facts in this case will come to light by themselves when the moment arrives.

Maybe Newell stared at his father. With the dark glasses it was hard to tell.

—Disloyal! Emory plunged in. And lying too! All evening you've acted like a wise guy. Well, if there's something you need to say, then say it, or I'll call you not only a liar but a coward.

For a moment Newell looked at them, one by one, slowly. Then he opened the thick red folio-size book in his lap, and began to read:

—Gentlemen, my reading matter for dinner is not Marx, nor Chairman Mao's *Little Red Book*. No, it is a tome called Who's Whose in America. Read it, and weep. 'Maximilian Geffe Doan, army officer, former government official, business executive. Born 1907. Student, North Carolina State, 1926, B.S. (stands for bullshit); U.S. Military Academy, 1930; M.A. Harvard 1937; grad. Naval War College, 1948, Army War College, 1955; grad. hon. law degree, Tufts; LL.D. (hon.) U. Richmond. Commd. 2nd Lt. U.S. Army, 1941, advanced through grades to gen., 1962, staff officer Office Chief of Staff for Ops., 1951-53.'

The blond Max laughed, flushing with pleasure. His eyelids flitted like a coquette. It was a joy listening to his own Who's Who entry.

Bishop Commynes said:

—How can the blind seer read?

—Notice, said Newell, that military and government go together with business in this man's career, as in this society's. No wonder he's so successful. Throw in culture (Harvard) and the law degree, and you see how our institutions are no more than lackeys to the corporate system they serve.

Emory took this up:

—Our institutions aren't what's wrong. It's the ones who disrupt the social order and won't work patiently for peaceful change, reform. Frankly, I agree with Max in this, though we disagree on much else. Such people, Marxists and so-called radicals, anarchists, are not helping. Maybe they're the curse our country is suffering from.

Suddenly Newell rose to his feet and cried:

—Hoch lebe Vladimir Ilyich! да здравствует Советский Союз! Workers of the world, unite! You've nothing to lose but your chains! —He tossed his liqueur glass against the wall; and, as it shattered and fell with a tinkle, cried out:—Go reds, smash state! 毛泽东万岁！ 中华人民共和国万岁！

Then he sat back down, in the silence, and looked in the reference book again.

—Immature, said Bishop Commynes, and his wise dark eyes seemed to smolder.

Newell heard him, and said:

—True, immature. First crude attempts in a thousand year effort to build socialism. Do we have time? It's socialism or death. But for you, Reverend, the superstitious reactionary, there is no hope, and there will be no maturity.

Eyes wide, the hippie put back on his sunglasses.

—Good night, said Carlyne, turning from the den entry.

XI

Newell read:

—'Mil. asst. to Sec. of Army, 1954; dep. spl. asst. to Sec. and Dep. Sec. of Def., 1955–56; brigade comdr. 1st Inf. Div. U.S. Army, 1957; regtl. comdr., dep. comdt. U.S. Milit Acad. 1958–60; mil. asst. to asst. to Pres. for Nat. Security Affairs, 1961–62; dep. asst. to pres. NSC, 1963; vice chief of staff U.S. Army, 1963; comdr.-in-chief U.S. European Command, 1964; ret. 1965. Cnslt. Tact. Sch. of Counterinsurgency, Puyallup, Wash., 1965–present.'—Newell gave the hippie chuckle, and said:—There you have him: parasitus americanus. On his way up, up the chain of the U.S. military structure paid for by the people's labor, the huge governmental parasite on the back of our people: in more ways than one if we act up.

At this Max stretched his long legs, and chuckled. He ran a hand over his Teutonic crewcut, that never-setting sun; and, pointedly ignoring Newell, said to Emory:

—Red Chinese nuclear and missile capacity means one thing: we must act. The day will come when they take us hostage in Asia.

Newell answered him anyway:

—You can't win. Your pacification program in Vietnam is a failure. Imagine China. You cannot impose a solution by force on a hostile population.

—For years—Doan went on—we were nice. Persuade our enemies . . . a loser's strategy. They, at least, know morality has no place in this.

—Revolutionary morality, said Newell. ·

—We pour in more and more millions to develop the countryside.

Emory glanced right and left; said:

—The Revolutionary Development teams are doing well. They could succeed.

—Too much Vietnamese corruption, said Doan.

—Too much logic, said Newell. NLF controls the rural areas, or eighty percent.

Doan threw up his palms:

—You mean North Vietnamese! This is why Johnson must commit a million troops if we mean to wage war like we mean it: into the North, and China.

Emory pressed his lips and shook his head: the liberal between two poles. When it came to politics his ideas were like magnetic filings. So he mused:

—Defend freedom by sparking World War III? . . . Yet the communists are on the march over there, you're right, and we will intervene on an ever broader scale.

—Ha ha ha—Newell laughed as if it was his turn.—My papa the opportunist. Reforms haven't worked in Vietnam, the lure of the great PX; so the masses become more demanding and insistent. Their needs are urgent. Also they hate our vulgar, our violent arrogance, American hubris, the giant white foreigner. See the way Washington ignores the 1954 Geneva Accords, and sabotages free elections? What wonder: Uncle Ho defeats Uncle Sam hands down. And so the freedom-loving United States, fearing the masses, all those totalitarians, has to align itself and become co-conspirators with the worst most fascistic elements in Vietnam and around the globe, every Third World dictator. Far rightwingers of the world, unite! Save the Republic! . . .

Hippie chuckle.

XII

Emory looked ruffled.

Max stayed calm, and said:

—Inexact. The Vietnamese people want freedom. They are flocking to our banner.

Newell sneered:

—Oh, sure. Some two million Vietnamese refugees have fled from Washington's terrorism, a more massive bombardment than all the warring nations of World War II on one small country the size of New Mexico. There are scorched earth operations to deny enemy troops shelter, food, material support. But all the while communist agitprop units have a field day. Oh see these Western barbarians! They rain down Agent Orange from their planes: dioxin, the most deadly chemical agent known to man, a weapon of mass destruction. The Americans, those state-of-the-art savages, toxify the Central Highlands (where Joey's fighting your battles for you this very moment). See how the U.S. occupiers kill all life and make the mountains and valleys a barren waste for a thousand years? In the North U.S. planes have tried to level every hospital, school and factory built since 1954. They have dropped one hundred pounds of explosives per person across Vietnam, North and South, and twelve tons' worth per square mile.—And now Newell started mimicking his father; he nodded, shook his head, all flustered; oh yes, oh no! . . .; his bold stare was an insult.—Say! You there, Mr. Left Liberal, Opportunist Sir! Why cave in every single time at first sign of a real conflict in Congress? Wait! They'll call me a red! Oh! oh! Wring your hands, you coward. Goodbye to my brilliant career! Ooh! Save me! . . . Well, I understand the military man: he executes orders. But your kind, all you self-styled humanists, lovers of peace, you hem and haw while Agent Orange defoliates provinces and causes Vietnamese women to have molar pregnancies for many generations. That means, in case you don't know, grotesque fetuses, three-eyed babies good for the formaldehyde jars of future war museums.

—Leftist rant—said Doan with a grin for his friends.—The la-la land of hippie children. But it's a problem because it undermines our troops' heroic effort over there: our campaign against the real aggressor in Southeast Asia which is Sino-Soviet imperialism. While the other side undermines negotiations and places new and more extreme conditions—

—You mean *we* do, you hypocrite.—Newell raised his tone.— Last February's Johnson-Ho Chi Minh exchange of letters showed that! Even Westmoreland is on record as saying the NLF, not Hanoi and not Peking or Moscow, is the dominant force in South Vietnam's resistance. The day we withdraw our AID program, let alone the mighty invasion force: that puppet Saigon government will collapse in a heap under the economic pressure, and political instability. Admit it, General, all your collaborators are out-and-out scoundrels, disreputable intriguers on the take from square one and hated by the entire populace. The United States has no moral authority anymore. It only has big bucks.

—Malarky—Doan shrugged.—Just like everywhere else in the Third World: we foster an independent South Vietnam with a strong, democratic government sensitive to the Vietnamese people's nationalist aspirations.

—Oh hell. Just like Iran, Guatemala, The Congo, Brazil, Phillipines, Dominican Republic the other day: you depose any real nationalist who puts U.S. corporate interest in the country at risk. Then come the massacres of communists and everyone who ever spoke to a communist, or didn't even, but just got on a list. More millions die. It's genocide CIA-style; but our people are kept carefully unaware, of course, by our corporate media in whose interest such humanitarian activities are carried on.

Max Doan paused. He gave his own little chuckle, and said:

—We want stability for Vietnam. Security for its people. We want prosperity south of the 17th parallel. And we *will* deter communist aggression from the North, Hanoi, which began in 1959 to try and seize South Vietnam by force . . . Defense Secretary McNamara said it well: political change must not come from Hanoi's external aggression and military force. I also agree with our President when he says America must never become a bound and throttled giant which is easy prey to any yellow dwarf with a pocket knife.

—That's statesmanship, said Newell.

—He said it twenty years ago. But what did he say last November? The world has three billion people, we but two hundred million. Now you gush over your Utopian socialism at variance with any practical approach to human affairs. But what will you say when we, outnumbered fifteen to one, find the piranha hordes on our shores? What will you *do* when they come to take away the good things we enjoy? What then, eh? Tell me, Sir Hippie: shall we give away the store? They want what we have.

—Why yes—Newell took off his dark glasses, and his bright eyes went wide.—Why of course. Here we are cowering in fear: the haves. Our GNP is a third larger than all the European countries combined and three times as large as the USSR's. To defend ourselves from the vast hordes of have-nots there are our missiles and napalm factories and enough nuclear warheads stockpiled to blow up everything this side of the Milky Way. We have a thousand plus military bases around the world. We are the richest most powerful nation in history by far, but here we cringe in a cold sweat! We get the shakes because a tiny country twelve thousand miles away, after centuries of brutal military occupation by the bigger ones, says: alright already, that'll do. Now you get the hell out of here. Scram, Uncle Sam.

Hippie chuckle. Back on with the dark glasses, and visionary air. Blind seer Teiresias.

XIII

Emory cleared his throat, in effect demanding the floor, after his son's harangue:

—Western Civilization grew great on an inalienable faith. We are the enlightened forces in Vietnam, and we are waging a great crusade. 'Man belongs not to the state but to the creator', said a respected commentator, once, and not with impunity can any 'magistrate or political force' violate the supreme bond . . . We as Americans take such words very seriously. And we are sending good men, very good ones, like Joey Gilbert, the flower of our youth—a human and material treasure to withstand aggression wherever it may occur. When President Johnson says we must conclude an honorable peace and then withdraw, I believe he is being honest and sincere. Yes, I know of our President's sleepless nights while this tragic war rages . . . But as regards the Revolutionary Development hamlets, Newell, you are wrong. Once again your argument, with its ideological bias, misses the mark. Not long ago I read a CIA analyst's report, by someone who knows, that is, saying the RevDev program is working to a tee. It is trying to give the Vietnamese villagers a truly free choice between our way and the Viet Cong's. And it does that. The CIA expert called RevDev 'a genuine social revolution in the rural areas'. And so when Marshall Ky calls his government 100% social revolutionary, we should try to help him, that's all, not criticize time and again. Let's make things better on the ground for the average Vietnamese citizen. It is too easy, Newell, far too easy and naive, and dangerous, to play the armchair cynic and nay-say every good word not in perfect accord with your Leninism.

Max Doan said:

—If only our too free media wouldn't distort the big picture and turn young heads like Newell's here. Every evening it's more of the same gruesome combat footage. How does it get on air? Do our network producers okay this? Or is it part of a conspiracy to discredit our war effort?

Once again Newell chuckled. He said freshly to his father:

—Well, go to Washington, old man. Posture and make your bowwow speeches and show off. It's the world championship of hubris, Mr. President the big fool, Supreme Court justices See-no-evil, Hear-no-evil, and Speak-no-evil; and all that honest Congress bought and paid for by the corporations. Look how upright they all are on TV. I give you Washington, D.C., a world historic high school where overgrown children who never grew up morally, bad children too big to spank, decide things for the planet. Good night! Someday maybe America will wise up to their lies and throw them in the Potomac, but I doubt it. Maybe when it's too late.

Max Doan grinned at the hippie, and gave his own laugh:

—Ever been to the nation's capital yourself? Seen the monuments, have you?

—Immature, said Bishop Commynes engaging Newell, calmly, in a contest of stares.

But the boy only bowed his head and read, through dark glasses, the fine print of the Who's Who from Emory's shelves:

—'Pres., chief oper. officer, dir., U.S. Technics, Greensboro, N.C.; chmn. pres. Int'l Assoc. Inc.; bd. dirs. (eight major corporations). Author: Foreign Policy, a More Realistic View, 1962; A Question of Quest: the U.S. Abroad, 1964; Man's Memoir, 1966. Decorated D.S.C., Silver Star with oak leaf cluster; Legion of Merit with four oak leaf clusters; Air Medal with 19 oak leaf clusters; Army Commendation medal; Gallantry cross with palm; grand cross Order of Merit Fed. Repub. Germ.'—Then Newell closed the thick volume, with a thud, and said: —Ecce homo, what a man. Military-industrial-media complex under one skin, three-in-one, the father, son, holy ghost of Capitalism. Amen.

Hippie chuckle.

XIV

Carlyne lay in bed. Sleepless, she waited . . . Through the formal dinner and their chatter she had kept a gracious composure and even eaten some of Cindy's dinner despite waves of nausea that came and went. She knew all she had to do was sit there since those men were happy to be with her and cast glances at her; it didn't matter if she said a word. They were enchanted by her physical presence which made them feel young again: even if she was going wild inside all the while and trying not to show the state she was in. Now she had a piece of news that changed things and meant she couldn't stay too much longer in this Rock Castle where the good Max ogled her, and Bishop Commynes seemed to study her every move while she endured his look. Well, she would try to stay long enough to . . . yes, she would stay here if possible until Christmas.

Now she knew the truth. And so she had closed her eyes an instant in pain as she picked at Cindy's rich food. And that devil in a clerical collar, that man of darkness, watched her with his dark eyes so wise and kindly from across the table.

Pregnant. That's what it was. She felt guilt. She felt self-hate. She felt alone with her fate. Now the truth had latched on to her and gained a foothold; and it would grow day by day, minute by minute in her belly. In despair she foresaw a moment when she would have to destroy this truth, this new life which was her guilt incarnate—kill it and then herself. Meanwhile her breasts bloated even bigger . . .; it disfigured her. Even her body showed disgust at such a secret. Honor, beauty, gone. Decency, security, the normalcy she took for granted by his side: gone. Forever. These past few days her situation had hit home: how she rejected her husband in effect and sent him away—because she was already loving and dreaming about another man? Now when it was too late she yearned for Jojo's boyish shoulder; it was pure; she felt sorry she had hurt him and sent him away. After all he believed in her. Even his sexual need seemed attractive to her now; but too late, for she never hoped to see his face again.

In the morning she awoke at dawn and vomited. All day she went about feeling not right. And now there was no chance she could get the night's sleep she needed. For one thing she heard their voices through the wall since the den was next to the guest bedroom where she slept. Those voices didn't sound so courteous anymore; they were raised, and she could hear every word, as the liquor and evening's excesses took effect; and Doan and then Emory let themselves be provoked by Newell's sarcasm. Tonight it stunned her; it sent a sort of dark thrill along Carlyne's spine when Newell raised his voice too, and said:

—You're the impious ones who stink up the place. You're the criminals.

And then Emory:

—Aren't you ashamed to speak to me and my friends that way? Do you think it will go unpunished?

—Truth is mine. I shall have my say.

—And where did you learn such a 'truth'?

—You taught it to me, you and yours, and I have no choice but to say it.

—It is treasonous, said Doan.

—No, you're the traitor here.

—Say that again, said Emory. Once more: and see what happens.

—Okay: you're the traitors. Mr. Bishop the Saint here does it, but he doesn't know it. Shamelessly, without a clue, says seer Teiresias, you do the deed in darkness, damning yourselves and your own people even as you poison life with your wars, with the corporate pollution which has become your essence it seems. Business as usual while the planet dies and humanity's chances on it, says Teiresias.

—Not Teiresias—Emory boomed—but Newell Gilbert! And you really think you can get away with it?

—If truth has any strength.

—Irresponsible boy! Your mother and I slaved for you. But you really are blind—blind in spirit, blind to gratitude.

—Poor man. Someone tells you the truth for once in your grandiose comedy of a life, and you call him blind. Well the time will come, says the seer, when you'll get your own craw full of insults. Then we'll see if the insulter is insulted. Deed of darkness!

There was a pause. With bated breath Carlyne listened through the wall as her father-in-law said:

—You're the one who feeds on darkness, but you can't hurt those of us who see the light.

—Your fate isn't up to me. Apollo will see to it: that's his job.

Emory:

—Let someone succeed in what they're doing, art, science, statesmanship, and he'll never lack for envious detractors.

—If you're so good then why don't you stop this insane war? Oh Oedipus: answer the enigma of *this* Sphinx who is devouring our young people.

Max:

—We will do what we have to in Vietnam. Our ancestors built this great nation with their courage and the sweat of their backs. It is sacred. And we will protect it.

Newell:

—You're in power now. You have all the arms factories, selling 40% of the world's weapons, but you don't have the truth. And so I am telling it to you, because I am not your slave—I am Teiresias the blind seer of ancient Thebes, and Apollo's! But if I am blind, you're the ones who can't see. You are the blockheads, but you'll have to learn the hard way. It will take more than oracles. Look at you three: as flinty and unfeeling, if truth were told, as this Rock Castle—you care only for your own advantages, pleasure, comfort. Finished! as I said before: finished men, like this finished capitalist society which can only decline and putrify from now on! . . . I think you don't even know you are hurting your own people, the people you love most and who love and depend on you, no less than yourselves, by acting this way. How I know it? Why I'm so exalted? Because I know the curse of the oracle: the same curse of your parents and ancestors which advances on unseen steps to destroy your kind and your hubris and the arrogance of this land. And then what refuge, what bunker deep beneath the earth won't hear your cries of pain? What Mount Cithaeron won't resound with them? When the wide world knows your secret and just whom you've been in bed with all this time—namely the fat whore Capital who is your wife, and your daughter . . . then what? Ha ha ha! Like it or lump it! Insult me all you like and call me immature—your generation never matured, it grew rancid—you will see how it is. For I see, I see a retribution more terrible than any other falling on your heads and those of your class, O cohabitors with the whore named Capital. No man will ever have been crushed that way.

There was a silence: maybe ten seconds.

—The boy is mad, said Bishop Commynes.

Then Emory's voice quivered:

—Leave here, Newell. I mean now. Leave my house in the morning. Pack your things and evacuate the attic. Out.

Newell:

—You call me mad, but the day may come when I seem wise to an old whited sepulchre like yourself. And as for you . . . the famous nitwit whom nature chose to be my fond progenitor—I'll get out of your polluted house, don't worry. My eyes need a break from the studying, so I'll go hitchhike for awhile and hop a freight train west. I'll ride the rods, like a Wobbly, and talk to people across the fifty states, and try to learn from others. As for you, I'll say this: all your good luck and success, solving the Sphinx's riddle, will be the end of you. As Teiresias said to Oedipus, so I say: the same day will see your birth, and your death!

Emory:

—Very cute, with your obscurity, enigmas. Leave the room now, offensive boy, so I can talk with my friends in peace. And get out of my house tomorrow.

—Don't worry, I'll get out. But you can't! Wherever you go, Washington, D.C., or hell itself: you'll still be there, threatening and accusing others when it is yourself you should accuse. Oedipus didn't know the score: he was innocent and came to be revered later, a hero's grave. But that was a whole history ago; and you do know what's up, and do it despite the taboo . . . So you and I both know well enough who is the guilty one here. In your bestselling books you claim to reveal Man's darkest secrets. Yet you are a blind fool of instinct the moment it comes to real life, and the chips are down. No character. The liberal par excellence. Pfui! . . . Well, a fine pair of victims, if you will: Oedipus of fate, you of this system, its arrogance which is yours. You are the blindman who said he saw but didn't see at all. Father and brother to his own son! Father and husband to his daughter! Son and husband . . . to his mother! Good going, Pa! Way to go!

—You're raving! Get out I said!

—Sure thing. Out now. And you go in, in yourself, and think about it. And if what I say proves false, then say I know nothing about the art of prophesy.

XV

For a long time Carlyne couldn't sleep. She listened to their voices in the den. It's a war, she thought, as she lay in bed with a knot in her stomach: a war for the woman with herself as the spoils. Just as it was once a war between such men as these and her Croatan and Tuscarora ancestors: a war for the good, rich land of a place named—renamed—North Carolina. And the white man took the land . . . and then came the curse. Prosperity, and a curse. And the question became: what would happen next? How would the curse live out its life? What victims would it claim? . . . Oh, the Rock Castle was filled these evenings with a heavy sexual atmosphere . . . She knew . . . she knew there were rumors in town—
Carlyne drifted off.

She awoke with a start. Her heart pounded as she listened. Someone on the stairs? Cre-eak . . . Him? Tonight again? Never get enough . . . Leaves stirred in the autumn night outside her window. She heard a belated car pass by. Would he come in the room and wedge his way into her defenses as if he were plough-ing the land? Would he take her in a way her husband did not—paw, arouse her despite herself with his caresses? Oh, oh. Jo—
On the front hall table were those letters, soiled envelopes, like a warning. On a jungle trail, in a night camp Joey jotted: 'Central Highlands, Vietnam', or 'Somewhere in Vietnam', for effect, in-stead of his service address, APO San Francisco. His letters scared her: the combat descriptions, and then sexual language. Dense pages of wounds and a lurid desire. She couldn't read them. No more patriotism, no more idealism in this man's army: defend the homeland from future attack, defend loved ones back home. No; now it was a village in panic, women and children dying grue-somely, a land given over to terror, Joey given over . . . There was a shrill whistle; there were screams as incoming shells rained on a firebase. Or Central Highlands rain pattered down on his poncho as he wrote in the dark.

Alone, Carlyne listened. Footsteps? . . . Always her distance made Jojo desire her more, too much; not natural. When she drew away and seemed to stand outside their passion, he grew a bit strange. Then he seemed to want a toy lover, not a flesh and blood woman. And so she became a fetish. He came at her glancingly, and no longer went for the kill.

Men were a trip. After all what had a girl of her background done to have such importance in such a family? So she thought. She still had her mother's country girl spirit despite her degree from an elite university. She had her high cheekbones and olive skin. Yet here she was among southern gentry. Fair game. An easy mark.

Then she felt herself becoming a thing. She was her husband's projection. And this led to their estrangement: at first a subtle ambiguity as she gave herself, her selves to him in different ways, but more and more controlled. This stirred him up; it made him crazy for her. The only reality was his desire; it stood outside, and went wild. All this gave Carlyne an unreal sense of power. Had she earned it? Did she deserve it? A month into the young marriage she was cool toward her husband. Wan, bored with him, and irresistible. And he began to understand.

One day in Durham, without a word, he went to a recruitment station and joined the army. He did it, she knew, partly to impress her. Baseball just didn't get it; so he said no to a likely start at third base in April when the New York club opened its season. He turned down a Major League contract, glamor, luxury hotels, packed stadiums, headlines, celebrity. For what? For her sake? Joey didn't say. He never said.

When he left for Vietnam, after a weekend leave spent in ecstasy with her, Carlyne felt alone. Inadequate.

And now she was pregnant. By another.

She heard . . . slippers along the hallway? . . . Who? Was her lover coming to her again?

Chapter Six

I

In Saigon at Tan Son Nhut Airport the camouflaged hangars in rows, the bunkers, quonset huts, fences crowned by concertina wire appeared to unfurl in liquified heat off the runways toward the far perimeter. One jet and another at brief intervals screamed in low over the steamy land.

With a slow, contained movement Joey Gilbert took the Christian missionary magazine *Vietnam Today* from an end table and scanned it. 'War? Yes! Opportunities? Many times yes! In destruction's very presence, in waste and loss and conflict, the door to the tribesmen . . .' But he glanced up.

There was MG fire in a village. So close? Air base defense lines integrated blockhouses and watchtowers which were manned by Saigon regular battalions and had adjacent strategic hamlets on the outer side. Then there were beds of entangled barbed wire with minefields in between. And then came the runways, airport and military installations; there were garrison headquarters for American pilots and administrative personnel. Here in key areas, Joey knew, the enemy could only infiltrate if he had the most complicated operational movement based on detailed inside information.

For a moment the soldier stared out toward sheets of rippling air off the concrete. He ran a palm over his duffel bag. Inside, wrapped in brown paper with a skeegaw bow in the string, was a Christmas gift for his wife—one to remember. Soon now, in a few hours, he would give it to her.

II

In the wide terminal three line soldiers waited out the last hours of their tour amid canvas bags the worse for wear, flak jackets good for the trash, helmets with shorttime calendars and the usual pinups and badass stickers. The grunts grew quiet as Army Broadcast System played 'White Christmas' over a tinny transistor radio.

Weary but spruced up a little for the journey home, the group of line dogs weren't laughing and bantering. They had come here a year ago and made a descent into filth that wouldn't wash off, that was imprinted on their minds and was labeled like a fart sack with some names—like Izard, Chi-Bar, Ringwood, Vane, Blair—they didn't care to say.

Joey looked at them: one smoked a cigarette, one rubbed his eyes. One napped. Did a doubt about going home slip in this silence after a year of war, sort of like ice melting? Were they worried about the return to civil life—in a small town, in a job, an office? Had the wife been faithful and answered every letter? Would parents be interested in the precious details of the son's war experience? How to tell them, back home—about this? How, ever, to get it off one's chest?

There was a kind of inner vision which you needed for life to make sense. Was it blinded in a lightning instant back there along the trail? After combat, after blood and guts, sudden death of a buddy, the body count numbness—what return? Would this depression lift when they saw California's sunny shores? What of the hundred wonderful things a grunt daydreamed while out on the torrid land, in the hump between treeline and hill, and when they closed camp at night? Could life go bad? A descent into evil?

Now they took back a lot of hatred to America. High school sweetheart flew away with white wings aflutter from a G.I.'s screwball letter. Folks didn't know, as they waited in a hometown somewhere, their part in the tragedy. Yet.

—Watch my shit.

One stood, stretched, and went shakily back toward a magazine stand.

III

Joey gazed out where sun glared off a flattened beercan hootch among the perimeter shanties. He looked beyond and saw green rice paddies and the Truong Son ridges bathed in a blue haze.

Inside Tan Son Nhut terminal the three grunts were quiet as they began to thaw on the edges. He heard one mention ETS: Service Time Expiration. First Shirt (sergeant) gave him a reenlistment talk in the tour's final days. No, sir; it's time to go home now and throw war craft in the garbage. Let it be. Next!

Men came here to do a job and they did it. Technicians. There was no guilt. There were no regrets. Chalk this fiasco up to experience. Okay, there wouldn't be any parade; so go on home as a goat, Fred Merkle who missed second base. Blend in with the routine. Settle down: get a haircut and a job. Hey, 365 days and then—when Freedom Bird, black winged with a shipment of greased beliefs in the hold, flew up and away from this unreal place, this nightmare—then a wake-up.

Joey sat alone in his grunge, the caked filth. Unshaven, unslept for three days: he wanted Carlyne to see him this way. Do you love me? No? Then the hell witcha' 'cause you didn't write. (Slap.)

At nightfall he had hopped a resupply flight south of Gia Nghia along Dung River, where his platoon was operating this past week. Then before daybreak he boarded a lift-ship from base camp. Now he waited for the flight call. Is this me? Ten R & R days in Bangkok with the world's most gorgeous woman, who was his wife? In fact he couldn't believe this happy outcome to all his doubts about her. He was afraid she wouldn't come and wasn't counting even now on seeing her. Maybe pick up a whore in one of the hotels: if he could get it up in his depression.

Would Carlyne Gilbert be at the Airline Center inside Don Muang airport as agreed? If so, he wanted her to see him this way. Look, honey, at what your loving husband has become. He needed to punish her for the silent weeks when she shut him out. The instant she cabled yes to his letter and said she would book her flight to the Far East and their hotel reservations: then he couldn't help himself. He meant to make her pay a little. He felt hurt by her—beneath mental layers numbed by the war. He blamed her. Hadn't she sent him to Vietnam? Hadn't she said foo to baseball? Wasn't she unable to love her husband? Didn't she set him up for a fall? and so he fell, and it broke his spirit; though she alone, soon now, could kiss it and make it better. Carlyne was too stubborn! And it cost them a once in a lifetime success together, third base in New York, which was money, respect, an abundant family life. Because of her whims he had shut down the gold mine of his pro career. Why was she willing to throw their happiness out the window—did she love someone else? One of her classmates? Some boy on campus or back home with her kin in Pembroke, Lumbee like herself, someone she never mentioned? What, Carlyne? What was wrong? Well, now he wanted her to know just how dead he felt in his chest, like a jungle mist, after his days and weeks and months out there. Rub her nose, her lovely face in the guilt and muck run red with shed blood. Hate, baby. Hate, and annihilate.

Across the wide room over the grunts' portable radio came a popular song; it was that one about sunny California which made you feel so far from home and yearning to go back—don't tell my folks the state I'm in, what I've become . . . Joey sat there. He stared his 100-yard stare and waited for the call to go on board.

IV

A high ranker passed by: West Point class ring, dress khakis, dapper. The man looked like he was stepping out of a magazine ad.

Joey had seen the ringknocker before, Daniel Pricecroft, Chief of Staff at Division Headquarters. Now the officer eyed the grunt as if fishing for a salute. Oh hell, why didn't he wait for his flight in the VIP lounge? Him and his Silver Star.

—Soldier?

Pricecroft paused for a closer inspection of such outstanding dirtiness. He noted the blood stripes.

—. . .

—You could lose it—said the officer.

Joey looked away. He was thinking: I won't shave for her, comb my hair or wash, until we . . . But he turned his gaze to the colonel; shook his head once; croaked low:

—Infantry unit. On leave, Sir, meet my wife.

—I know about you.

The other glimpsed GILBERT over the breast pocket.

—Yes, Sir.

—Your dad's name is in the news. You should be proud: Presidential campaign adviser.

—Yes, Sir.

—I remember your homerun in New York.

—Yes, Sir.

Joey watched a plane taxi in. The liquid heat wreathed up from the runway. Not before we, she—

—Right, you're in the Highlands.—Pricecroft seemed to make a mental note and turned; but he looked back over his shoulder.— How much longer in your tour?

—I'm halfway.

—Well, good luck, soldier.

—Thank you, Sir.

V

It was two more hours before he boarded. Then he peered out at the guard towers as the airplane rolled and bumped its way into position and revved its jet engines and raced headlong into a glare. It took off; slung and veered over the Saigon boulevards lined with shade trees, Saigon's Jardins Botaniques, and Khanh Hoi Bridge, and the orange tile roofs that looked—as the passenger beside him said—like a French provincial city. A floating restaurant by the quay receded beyond the sunlit smoke of Newport Shipyards.

The plane gained altitude and sailed high above fumes curling from the sectors across Saigon River. Then Joey gazed further out to where sallow Mekong took in its hundred tributary streams and Delta canals spangled in the bright sunlight like

a huge school of fish. He could still see stilted houses on piles
whose wooden walls were leaved with water coconut; they were
roofed with sheet metal or thatch.

Paddy fields shimmered. Red rivers looked on fire in the brilliant light as they ferried soil deposits from Cambodia, Laos,
China. Small waterside hamlets seemed to cower behind their
bamboo fences; they were afraid of violence, G.I.s and VC, where
historic forces came in contact and threw off sparks. Skiffs, junks,
river patrol boats moved through the glittery labyrinth of Mekong and Bassac: where the war raged, and claimed its victims.

The air-conditioned plane gained altitude to the north and west.
Now from afar he studied the terraced rice fields set in the blue-
green land edged by treelines. This was his hell since last August.
Nearing the Parrot's Beak, VC base area hills where the war was
hot, he gazed down upon long defoliated tracts of forest blackened, pocked by yellow overlapping splotches which were bomb
craters. Everywhere there were craters of various sizes. Ten-mile
crater avenues showed the path of B-52 strikes that crisscrossed
a valley geometrically. Deep craters from delayed fuse bombs in-
terspersed with jagged napalm gashes to make a monstrous path:
like gypsy moths mad with hunger, here, there, as they ate their
way across a wooded area.

Joey saw small settlements among the Montagnard rice and
corn farmlands charred by phosphorous rockets from helicopter gunship patrols. The tiny structures were targeted by twenty
mike-mike (20 mm. cannon) fire: a hundred explosive shells
strafed per second down on bamboo dwellings, wells, garden
patches, and the peasants who lived there. During his months in-
country he had seen at eye level the 750-lb. bombs dropped on
fieldworkers bent to the task knee-deep in paddy fields; or the
gray reddish squares once their homes were dotted out by rocket
hits. He had seen the smoke streamers from burned off hootches.
Sometimes a door-gunner took target practice at a water buffalo
herd wallowing in a river.

He knew deadly defoliant poisons by the tens of millions of
liters were being sprayed down on Vietnam's future. How did
that tally with fighting to make it free? Well, the NLF bases had to
be flushed out, and war is war; but—Joey thought—if it was my
wife who would someday give birth to a three-eyed brain-dead
monster, I might feel differently.

Loc Ninh, Phuoc Binh, Gia Nghia. Ten thousand feet overhead he craned his neck for a glimpse way, way down—where his unit went in the torrid humidity thick with insects. Bufillu was his partner from the start in boot camp: shipped over on the same hotel flight from Oakland. Now Bufillu, back from treatment after Xo Man burns, was squad leader in Joey Gilbert's absence. With him, way down there, went Skol the pointman who was a shorttimer, yet Pricecroft and rear base declined to call him in. It was the same for Tombigbee in his tour's last twenty days. RTO Troupial and the medic Artus were also massacre survivors. And then there were replacement troops who went slogging their way toward a Yuletide stand-down in Da Nang (where you didn't have fun); and these missed their squad leader a lot. For he was a self-made specialist in bush warfare who also had their survival at heart. But now he had only his wife and Thailand's many pleasures in mind.

It didn't matter how many firefights they won, jungle ambushes they beat back; how much ground they took and then abandoned on orders from Six (less reversible the death and maiming that went into taking those positions). It did not matter how many such disastrous victories they achieved, how many seemingly senseless sacrifices they made even while they won every battle but not the war. For nothing could change the fact denied everyday and every way at MACV's Five O'clock Follies press conference in Saigon—to wit, that Viet Cong and their NVA comrades had mastery in the Central Highlands, in the Parrot's Beak, and southern Truong Son slopes, as soon as the sun went down.

And so there were no coordinated advances with a known objective, like in a winnable war; but only endless six- and ten-klik daily saddle-ups, the wrenching humps on ambush patrol, so-called suicide probes, used as feelers to make enemy contact. The boonierats were put out there to play cat-and-mouse with catastrophe. They were sent to do a thankless task by the bourgeois boys like Pricecroft back at firebase in Buon Me Thuot. There were no rational steps toward a realistic goal that Joey Gilbert could see; but only more mad scrambles for a nondescript hillside left to the enemy again the next day, or week, after heavy casualties. There were only inflated body counts with scant if any enemy weapons capture. The bureaucrats lied about it.

This was an idealist war—in Pricecroft's mind, and his superiors', safe in their Saigon offices; maybe in the American people's, a continent away beyond the sea. What did they know? More and more grunts fought their own private battle on the terrain of morale. They were no longer so easy to gull with 'big picture' talk; not after the things they had seen, the Ben Bolts. All in all it was a loser's mentality, a moral standoff at best. There was no real intent or hope to win anymore. Joey Gilbert the pro ballplayer knew something about winner's instinct, and this wasn't it. And from month to month U.S. soldiers fell by the thousands and saw their young lives run off in the sand.

A pretty air hostess handed him a tropical drink with chopped ice. It was beaded to the brim and had a palm tree swizzle stick. He took it and toasted the men, way, way down there, out the window. And then he sipped.

VI

The jet liner's shadow, like a marker on a military map, soared past the Parrot's Beak area and out over Cambodian territory. Now the Siam Gulf shimmered on the southern horizon.

In an hour he would see her—if she came. His heart skipped a beat—and if she didn't? He still couldn't believe his good luck and felt nervously expectant but also resigned, almost, to yoking his despair to a high-class Thai prostitute, and an opium pipe.

Down below, the bleached Pnomh Penh quarters sprawled along the riverbanks: where Mekong made its mighty bend through Southeast Asia.

He thought of Carlyne's moods, and her uncouth refusal when some notion of his didn't suit her. If she went away for an hour, for a day, she didn't feel she needed to explain. And he didn't ask. Strange flights of fancy, a girlish wildness at times; but the next moment solemn, maybe angry for no reason—her face had many aspects. There was a mystery which played in the veil of her elusive features. He had her the way men have their women, with a touching lust, a need to appease the virile gnaw; and then sentimental thanks came after as he left her to go play ball. But after all a stranger had shared his bed. She hadn't been keen on his thoughts and plans. And she didn't ask the rising baseball star for his autograph unless on a rent check.

—Love me at least enough—he told her one night as they lay side by side in the Double-A town—to tell me if I'm not doing right by you, if you don't feel happy.

She gave a little laugh and turned away.

—Good night.

With a strange poignancy out here he recalled certain words of hers: like in grief for a loved one, and you think of the same things over and over.

Now he gazed at the blue afternoon sky high above Battambang toward the Thai border, and his heart beat with an anguish. Would she be there? Ten days together? Was it possible to take a jet plane from hell straight into paradise? Oh, hand in hand they would stroll through a pagoda, exotic gardens, park, market . . . Go for a quiet boatride on the river. No war! No in-coming, and diving for your life.

But Carlyne sounded sad the day he confirmed their plans with her on the phone. That was the week before from the PTT in Buon Me Thuot.

—I've missed you, so much, he said.

—Sure, she said.

Joey checked his watch: 30 more minutes till they met inside Bangkok Airport. Would she show up? If not, for any reason, they had reservations at Victoria Hotel on Silom Road, in the city center.

VII

As the plane landed bumpily he made up his mind to withstand the empty days and then go back. At Visa Control they looked at his curly hair and air of a vagrant, and asked to see his money. The camouflage smear on his neck and hairline did not look like a welcome guest. It was a new thing from S-2, division intelligence: Bufillu and himself, Skol and Tombigbee rotated on search-and-destroy missions in the predawn hours. It was a cruel order for the big Navajo into his final weeks. Since Xo Man, and a rumor begun by Thingum, Six seemed to suspect Tombigbee. Sympathy for the enemy? Indians like him? Among the four grunts it was Gilbert who had a kind of gusto for the hunt, and the dangerous sorties late at night. It's the stinger—Bufillu said of their LURP actions—of the wasp in winter.

At last Joey got through Customs: where a G.I.'s duffel bag took on a totem value since it meant an expensive spree, and the Thai economy boom-boomed.

His heart pounded as he went through the peacetime airport. His sharp eyes were on the alert as he hunted for his wife. There was soft background music as if nothing bad had ever happened. There were boocoo Western tourists with their luggage. One of their children gave a spoiled whine before a boutique crammed with glittery gifts; so different from little Vietnamese kids. Joey was sort of stunned by all this yak-yak and chatter. He drew up twenty feet from the Airline Center and looked around. No sign of her.

His heart sank, and the depression began at once. Well, he should have known it: she shot him down again. Stood him up after he came all this way.

By the airline counter stood an older woman in a plain black dress. Her hair was fastened back by a lotus hairpin, and this gave him a little jolt. She looked like a VC 'chignon battalion' cadre he might meet along the trail late at night; but she was older, like one of their leaders, and more full-bodied than a usual Vietnamese woman. This one wasn't heavy, but she had size; also she was less pretty and fresh, girlish, than Carlyne. On her wrist was a jade bracelet; above her breast, a brooch.

She turned—brazen, he thought, a live-in Thai whore?—to stare at him. Maybe a Eurasian courtesan . . . Hm, Carlyne's not coming. Make my move now? . . . The grunt's heart was sinking in a punji pit as he took a step toward her, and another. But he faltered: not here, no show. Oh Carlyne! Will I strangle you with my bare hands when I get home?

No, he didn't want another woman. It sickened him. Alone, like Ben Bolt the walking corpse, for ten long days.

At the counter his voice trembled.

—Have you seen a young woman? Black hair, dark blue eyes. High cheekbones.

He gestured.

This older woman almost fitted the description. Lips parted she stared at him as if she couldn't believe the extent of his grunge. She wore no makeup at all. What struck him now was the way she wore her hair in a rooster-tail hairdo like a Vietnamese woman, and it was jet black and silky like theirs. But she was too bold. Most would have dropped their gaze when stared at the way he—

Then he frowned.

—You?

He turned full toward her. He saw now. Yes. On her breast was a brooch; it was a tribal woman in profile: ivory on brownish red enamel, gold rim, clasp and pin.

What had happened? Aged this way in a few months? Carlyne looked like a Lumbee woman, like her Aunt Lovedy, who worked hard with her hands. And there was this other thing: she had filled out as if . . . as if she had gotten married.

She waited quietly before him. She waited, and gave a little curtsy. In the first instants of surprise, before she composed a face, she had a determined air. Yes, her coming all the way here had been an act of will. There was a purpose—so he seemed to glimpse, staring at her: not love perhaps, not a deep joy to be with him; but a plan. Well, maybe she was just amazed by his outstanding grease and grime. She was so serious!

Joey held out his hand and felt ashamed by his thoughts of a minute ago. His caked fingernails were in line with his sweat-stained jungle fatigues. Why hadn't he at least washed his face on the plane? Why hadn't he rubbed off the red clay from his boots? Was he trying to insult her? Punish her for not writing? If he was clean he could have taken her tenderly in his arms, the arms of a soldier. But her cold statuary aspect, also something not good in her lake blue eyes, maybe jet lag, did not invite him to do that.

After a few seconds she looked down with a frown and moved, still without speaking, the few steps between them. She pressed herself against his chest, and bowed her head to his shoulder. What happened? He never saw Carlyne as someone in need of protection; but now she drew against him like a refuge while he stood with his eyes closed, and hands by his sides.

Then he did return her embrace though reluctant to touch her with his welted leathery hands, his forearms scratched by thorns, insect bites. He held her to his chest and breathed in the fine toney sheen of her hair. O the scent of her, O the spirit of Carlyne Gilbert née Locklear—it put a feeling into him that made him want to cry like a little boy. Here, here with him: he couldn't believe it. In his arms: his wife . . . The rapture flowed over in a tear on his stubbly cheek.

For a long moment they held one another in silence by the front desk at the Airline Center. A ground hostess looked at them. They gave a sense in the wide room ashuffle with tourists and porters and loud speaker messages—it was love's rare chance amid the envious bustle of time.

VIII

Arm in arm they went out into the glare and sunlit afternoon of an Asian city. Carlyne had hired a fulltime chauffeur cheaply for the ten days. And the comfortable hotel only cost a few dollars a night. A plate heaped with fish—Joey's favorite: prawns, fried crab claws, lobster, sliced raw fish with *gang pet* coconut curry, prikenoo peppers—three dollars. Along the parapeted roadway from the airport she told him of her day alone in the City of Angels: 'Krungthep' to two million people crowded alongside Menam Chao Phraya's banks where the Grand Palace rooftops gleamed. Into the maze of traffic they went, open cabs, cycles, three-wheeled scooter taxis.

In downtown Bangkok she seemed stronger to Jojo than before. She was on the alert. She had a mind of her own.

Inside their hotel room he said meekly:

—I'll go wash.

—Wait.

She took out packages from the drawers. She had gifts for him—luxurious Thai silks, a robe, a handsome suit, new shoes for him to wear; a few blouses of handwoven Chiengmai cotton. He had a gift for her too, but he didn't bring it out for her yet, and in fact he felt ashamed to.

Then, her fingers in the cartridge loops of his fatigues streaked with sweat and dirt and . . . Vietnam—the woman drew him to her.

—Let me wash off the war, he said.

—Not yet.

—But I have lice, if not worse. It's a wonder they let me pass Customs.

She ran a finger under his collar and said:

—What happened here?

—Never mind.

—It looks like a bad bite, she said. Teeth?

Again he glimpsed the new thing in her: a maternal instinct. In a word, in a gesture, in her touch at instants, she was like a mother to him.

—You've changed, he said.

—Have I?

Along his collarbone there were reddish-purple bruises, inflamed welts each with a tiny scab, like nail heads at the center. She ran a finger over them. They had a nasty air and needed to be looked at. But he didn't go to sick bay when his squad came in from the bush. He hadn't even told the corpsman.

—Let me wash up, he said. Then we'll rest.

—Wait a moment, she said. I've got the hots for swamp men, or don't you remember?

One Sunday in college they rode his motorcycle for a picnic by the Lumbee River down in Robeson County, and she told him a story. It was about the Civil War and Reconstruction Era in her hometown. The menfolk were forced to hide out in the marshlands of southeastern Carolina where they fought for their lives against the Home Guard, which was KKK of those days, and local law enforcement attacks on their families. Her ancestors led by a man named Henry Berry Lowry became swamp outlaws in order to resist the forced conscription, the unjust arrests, the lynch law of the whites who were using every means to grab the land.

IX

Now her kisses told another story and no less unexpected by him, no less strange. It was a dizzy swirl of kisses, and he could hardly believe his happiness. Not with Carlyne and not ever had he known anything of the kind: as she pecked at him in a sexual ecstasy, and returned his rapt kisses, and went so far as to lick . . . lick the unsightly necklace under his chin, the infected lesions which looked like a human bite. Their embraces had a fury as she nipped at his chapped lips until he tasted salt blood.

In the past she would lie there and let it happen, if she even did; and gradually she drew away from his advances, and had her way of playing hard to get in the same bed together. In fact, she didn't care to be gotten, and their young marriage just couldn't seem to jell. Carlyne drew back; she wrinkled her nose at his caresses, and their relationship sank into a rut. So Joey remembered. In those days his desire would come back so fast after the act: it was like drinking liquor which makes you thirsty. Or it was a hypnosis. Stronger subdues weaker in all species; often as not the stronger is female. Queen uses drone, and discards him.

Back then he was unable to solve her Sphinx riddle. And so, young man in a sulk, he clung to his need and felt dependent on the woman—become a part of her which she disdained. When something was wrong and things weren't going well between them; when he had somehow violated the sacred convention of marriage but couldn't for the life of him think how or why, insensitive jock: then Carlyne was the Sphinx who baffled him.

He remembered taking his pain to Emory on the phone one night and asking his dad for advice. And when he mentioned the Sphinx and said it was his nickname for Carlyne: then Emory the classical humanist went into a lecture on the meaning of the myth:

—Her question seems natural, straightforward: what goes on four legs in the morning, two at noon, three at night. But it has sexual depths, and these are treacherous as the young men of Thebes, who couldn't come up with the simple answer—Man—found out. One by one she 'shot them down' as you like to say. One account has her devouring them; in another she cast the inept lovers to their death from where she sat on the heights above the city.

—What sexual depths? said Joey.

—Well, she is asking how a man might embrace life the right way, fully, naturally, without denial. Does he know the mysteries of birth and regeneration: so he can please a woman and fulfill her and himself as the years and stages of life go by? The gods gave this instinctual knowledge to Oedipus—Oedipus the exile though he was coming home: the outsider not caught up in the social neuroses, which limit, and obscure the right answer to life, of his native city. And then he succeeded; he defeated her, or so he thought. There are no definitive victories.

—Where did the Sphinx come from?

—Good question! Oedipus' father, Laïus, had abducted and raped a boy, the son of King Pelops. So Pelops in a rage cursed Laïus, saying that Laïus would be killed by his son Oedipus who would then wed and bed Laïus' wife—Oedipus' mother in other words—Jocasta.

—What does Sphinx have to do with it?

—Ancient writers differ on this. It seems Hera sent the Sphinx, a creature with woman's head, lion's body, and wings, to ravage Thebes as punishment for Laïus' rape of the boy. Zeus's wife was goddess of marriage and custodian of family life . . .

Joey listened to his father long distance that night from the Minor League town, and shook his head. He could play third base, but as a lover he wasn't one of the lucky ones. He loved his wife body and soul yet he was such a klutz at it, all thumbs at that hot corner, that his life beside Carlyne grew strained.

Later things got so bad—he thought she didn't respect him—that he enlisted in the service and put in for combat duty in Vietnam. It was his way of trying to save the situation: both in the privacy of his marriage and in the great public world where the nation he loved was an all-star.

X

Now she had changed. Why? Was he a real man now? no longer a kid out at third, but a soldier facing death? What had he done to deserve this? Did war turn her on? Service to his country?

Suddenly here in Bangkok she was the passionate lover. Well, there were moments when she was motherly and related to the boy she knew in him. This felt strange, not quite right, but better than the strain, the estrangement of their life before.

Now he paused a moment, lifting on one elbow, in wonder at her behavior. Oh, he only wanted to take her in his arms and hold her close and sway to and fro like a palm tree in a tropical breeze. Stroke her, stroke her hair, her brow. Oh! Here in a small hotel far away from the war—in a nice room snug among the *klong* canals, the Buddhas at peace in their emerald shrines, where saffron robed monks intoned a chant in the ancient wats and the Khmer-style *prang* pagodas; here among the gold glazed tiles and the lacquer pavilions: he only wanted to love his wife and tell her so over and over. Ten days in this niche beneath the eaves.

—Don't think so much, Jojo.

She ran a hand through his tangled hair and his beard. She drew back, a finger to her lips, and didn't quite meet his eye.

—Come in the bathroom, she said. I'll wash you.

XI

Next day he woke up toward noon with a jolt. Where was she? Had she gone out? Not left him again?

She came at noontime from another round in the fancy shops. Packages, laughter. She brought him a beige-tan leisure suit with two brocaded white blouses—soft feminine apparel his hippie brother might like to wear; also plaited tan trousers, fine handkerchiefs, socks and underwear; a pair of fine leather sandals.

—You paid from our account? he said.

—The baseball money belongs to you, Jo. I haven't touched it.

—It's yours too.

Life in the bush, war with its frenzy and horrors, seemed to recede. After first combat came that numbing of the person, and then a gung-ho desire to fight and kill and get some back. Survival made it necessary to get desensitized; but now she was bringing him back to life, his hope, his faith; and he felt like the luckiest man alive. He was overwhelmed by his wife who looked and acted so different now, so responsive. Yet he couldn't quite let himself relax and enjoy every minute with her because he was still on the alert, and still—he couldn't help it—asking himself questions about her. How had she changed? Why did she seem distant and yet so giving, as if all this were an act, and she might have some ulterior motive . . .? He was in love. He was so relieved suddenly, almost happy. But he wasn't easy in his mind.

She made him slow down. She told him a few times she wasn't going anywhere, she was all his, and he should take his time. Where did this new maturity come from?

They lingered over their lovemaking day and night, night and day. But she shuddered once when he touched her.

—Jo?

In late afternoon he lay eyes closed on the bed. He breathed in her beloved presence and didn't want to think about anything.

—Yes, ma'am.

—Is the soil so red in Vietnam? Come here a minute.

On her knees she washed his jungle fatigues in the bathtub.

—We can send those out. You don't have to do that.

She wrung the cuffs and let them float beneath soap bubbles.

—I want to.

The green camouflage had its own sort of life. At the sight Joey gave a little wince.

—Oh, he said.

—What, Jojo?

—Nothing.

In his mind's eye he saw cassava roots on a table, some bundled pumpkin leaves. There was mountain rice in a tin, a rootstalk of ginger. He mumbled:

—They were humble.

Carlyne stared up at him as he gazed in the distance; and his cheek twitched, a facial tic she had noticed. What happened? A dream snatch while fully awake? Again the twitch, beneath his right eye: into his field of vision flashed the grunt Kevin Blair. In the brown sudsy margin of Dung River the grunt turned with wide white eyes . . . Why? They had at last stumbled on Blair, but he wasn't in the water.

Joey blinked. He shook his head.

—What? she said, and looked at him with her brow knit.

He gave a little laugh and shook it off. He went to his knees by her side on the cool bathroom tile, and hugged his wife.

XII

That night they dined in Dusit Thani rooftop nightclub with its view of the city, river and sunset, the lights.

He asked her how they were at home, and she said Newell had left the Rock Castle after an argument with Emory.

—Where'd the crazy guy go?

—West Coast. He's living in Berkeley in a hippie commune. Sometimes he calls and talks to Lemon.

—You know—Joey laughed—when you didn't write I thought maybe . . . you stopped loving me. I got so rotten jealous because I was afraid you and Newell . . .—He gestured.—I was so miserable, my darling, out there in the bush with that on my mind. It's embarrassing to talk about it.

—Never mind—she said, with the look of concern, the maternal note that was new between them.

—Anything else going on at home?

—Cindy wants to leave the Rock Castle too.

—Really? Why? She's been with us forever.

—Says she's getting old, and needs more time with her grandchildren.

—Hm. Cindy's been such a faithful servant. She always cared about us; I don't know how . . .

They drank white wine and danced. At midnight they came back in a spell to their room, and made love for a long time. Through the early hours they lay clutched in one another's arms, as he told her a few things about the war, but then broke off afraid to upset her. A few times he asked why she didn't write him, and she said his letters made her afraid. Then an hour later he asked her again: why did you stop writing? as if he didn't believe the reason she gave. Her silence had been such a betrayal, it scared him worse than the war. Why? Why, Carlyne, my darling . . .? Why, Sphinx—why didn't you support me, every day, and help me make it through? He couldn't get over her silence.

Daybreak blushed through the drawn blinds at their bodies joined yet again in an erotic trance, straining, trembling with lust.

The days passed by, and the nights. Joey didn't count. He sent time off to Vietnam on history's terrible errand. His wife was giving him a honeymoon ten times, a hundred times better than the first one. It was like a dream with some talk but more silence between the momentous events. They played like two children and laughed and said what came in their heads. In a few days he would be back in the field with his unit, but now he blessed her beloved presence.

Yet it made him wonder: had she said goodbye to the bad times? Forgotten the way he kept her cooped up all summer in an Iowa backwater while he played baseball and blamed her if he struck out twice or booted one at third? Back then he took her over his knee and spanked her one night when she made fun of his religion which was sports, and mocked all goofball jocks. Hard man: he put his flat hand to her shapely rump. He branded her and called her: baseball wife. Then he forced her to make love to him in a way—inspired by teammates' banter in a hotel lobby?— a way that was degrading to say the least. But now in Bangkok, a far cry from Iowa, she let herself go and went in for that same mad act, but done to him this time, Cupid's payback.

XIII

At night they ate more spicy food and drank heady wine brought by room service. She sat crosslegged on the bed: in the same black top as that spring day his senior year when they went on a picnic by the Lumbee River. Her black blouse was severe and sensual with lacework at the breast. He gazed on the wonder of her shoulders, incomparable neck, her full figure with the bit of extra weight. Bangkok twilight was in the window: the city slipped into its negligée. Joey ran a palm along Carlyne's strong back. In a mirror he glimpsed her pouty Shiva grin: Shiva the fertility god, also the god of destruction, in the Grand Palace museum that afternoon. She had a hieratic pose as she let him adore her. What was she thinking? Was it with joy she had made this trip across the Pacific? or with fear in her heart, and shame for some reason beneath her breast? He looked at her, and marvelled. An hour from Taipei, she said, it made her thrill when the plane dipped in a gale wind, and the copilot gave a tense order to stay seated.

Now she said:

—Tell me about the war. How'd your neck get scraped that way?

Joey reached over and opened the nightstand drawer. He took out a four-inch cubed package done neatly in brown paper and tied with a red string. The Christmas bow was crumpled. He took up the gift, light as a feather, and said:

—The war's in my letters. Read them.

In country he didn't fear the war so much, strung taut; he only feared she would leave him. But now suddenly he blinked—Billy

Ringwood, gristle—he saw the kid who played some ball down in Lenoir County, near the town of Carlyne's father, the circuit court judge. Split second: Ringwood dying before his eyes there in a Bangkok hotel room.

—I will—said Carlyne distantly.—But tell me. I want to hear.

—Why?—Joey, pale, shook off the vision.

—Wait.

She rose and took away the tray.

He watched her movements. Did love give her this fullness and grace, like an expectant mother? She went in the bathroom and then came out perfumed with her hair done up in the sensual 'rooster tail'. She had on another sheer nightgown. Why was she going all out for him night after night? Making up for lost time? Giving herself to her man, and giving it good, in case she never saw him again? She would have these nights to remember him by . . . Carlyne's deep sensuality seemed to shimmer like the aura outside the window. Seduction accomplished, Sir! But why the over-kill? He wasn't caring about her large moiré breasts right now; he only wanted to hold her close while the two of them drifted asleep, and tried to rest, but then anything could happen at 3 a.m. when they awoke . . . Or else at midmorning they'd wake up in the peaceful city and go for breakfast and a look at the sights. This enchantment made the Central Highlands seem a lifetime away.

Carlyne lit two candles on the dresser. She turned off the bed-stead light and took his curly head in her arms.

But she looked at the gift he had brought her. A souvenir of Vietnam? Not some horror she hoped. Stories came over the U.S. media about ears snipped off Viet Cong bodies and worn as trophies: strung on a belt like a key chain.

—Talk.

—About what?

—All the Vietnamese women you've had.

—Not one. Instead I keep a pet scorpion. Left it in the field with Bufillu.

—Who's Bufillu?

—Ah, see? If you'd read my letters . . . He's my partner since boot camp.

Hesitantly she said:

—Have you made any—have you killed someone?

—We and a couple others drew a special recon assignment. We rotate.

—And?

Why these questions? Did she want to hear about death? Redeeming herself—after she couldn't make it through his letters? Her large nipples went hard beneath his nibbles.

—We go out late at night past the perimeter.

—Perimeter?

—Our defense lines.

He wriggled down and curled by her ribs: snuggled his head, kissing in the crook of her thigh. Down there his voice went hoarse and low. He breathed roughly and got stuffy when the desire welled up again. His words were jerky, sort of childish, in the minutes before he became all hers. He liked to linger kissing her taut, swarthy belly grown a little bigger like her breasts.

—And?

She waited. She seemed impatient with his kisses. Don't think! What she wanted from him again, and again was not thinking— what was she afraid of?—but abandon.

He drew back his head and thought a moment. Tell her this? Confide in her?

—Well, at any instant we could die. And we know—

—Know what?

—It has an effect. Something comes over you. Adrenalin I guess . . . I almost dig it.

He kissed.

—Don't stop, she said.

—I'd rather kiss.

—Kiss, and talk.

—Alright then . . . At nightfall I take out a pocket mirror. I daub paint on my forehead, cheeks and neck.

—War paint.

—Oolooloo! . . . It's camouflage, you know, black and green.

—Go on.

—Our perimeter guards have settled in, out there by the wire.

He kissed her stomach with its bulge as she leaned forward over him. Her flesh was like a water balloon but covered with goosebumps. And he thought: she's not a girl anymore; good.

—Go on.

—You've changed, Carlyne.

—Out on perimeter . . .

—Huh? Oh, I almost forgot.

—Having fun down there.

—Yes, my darling . . . it is fun down here.

—So earn it, or I'll turn over. Talk.

—Past the perimeter I become two eyes, ready to stalk, and strike. Kill, no half measures in this, no mercy. So I think things to get me in a rage. I think: why doesn't she write me? And I call you names.

—Wait, hold on, you little pig. Not that yet, Mister Jo . . . tell your story. Call me names. I deserve them.

—No, it's just when I'm angry.

—Say them! Whore, bitch . . . right? I deserve what I get because I didn't write. I'm your wife the streetwalker, the whore. No, I said, don't start that . . . you can't talk and do that at the same time.

Sigh.

—I think all about how you don't love me, you coldhearted Sphinx, and how you sent me to Vietnam. I think what I'm going to do to you if I ever make it back home: you won't like it as much as an orgasm. A shivery rage comes over me made of jealousy and the . . . how to say this? The sexual aspect of war, the aggression in the nerves. Oh! Carlyne, I could forgive you anything if you just told the truth, if we had an honest bond, not a riddle. But you're a two-timing liar and a . . . a . . .

—Yes, I am.

—Are you?

—Just tell the tale please. Never mind the commentary. Then what happens?

—So I go out there thinking you don't write me, you take away my life, so I'll do the same. Not me? No love for me? Then none for you either, VC gook. All this is in my letters, but you don't read them.

—Some. Enough. Now I'm listening to you.

—Absolutely positutely?

—What's that? she laughed.

—Six, our captain, always says over the transmitter: absolute'—

—Okay, okay. Look, I brought the letters here with me. So we could read them together, and make you ashamed to write your wife such things. I'm the woman you care for: please remember that.

—You are.

He paused, as he panted beneath her with a pathetic lust, or comic. His head was spinning; he took the lace hem, a black silken material drawn tight, between his lips. Joey Gilbert moaned like a child with a tummy ache, and the candles flickered. From the Gulf of Thailand a warm breeze drifted across the city into their open window.

—Later I'll make you reread those things: stick your nose in them, like a puppy.

—Alright, I will.

—You're a bad boy!

—I know it.

—Go on now. Tell me about Mr. Bufillu.

XIV

—Faces painted, like two devils, we move out. At that hour you can feel the trees, and hear distant ridges, because you're moving into the zone where life is up for grabs. Beyond the perimeter there can't be a false step. If you trip a Claymore, bye bye. Make no noise, not a click-click; less than when a person slips in your room, in the wee hours when you're asleep, and—

—I'm a light sleeper.

—Are you? Bufillu and I unsheathe our knives.

—Oh.

She spoke low. She gave a small jolt.

He murmured:

—It's a humid night. Jungle odors. Mines, trip flares dot the ground out past our stations but we know the pattern. So we creep through the bush toward a treeline where ARVN intelligence has told us . . .

—Told you what?

Joey swallowed. His breath came in starts.

—Details were relayed by Delta-Six.

She grabbed his hair and yanked back his head. She drew a leg over his chest and mounted him, casually, with a laugh. Candlelight danced on the walls, on her black silk.

—Then what, bad boy?

—I can't recall just now.

—You'd better.

—(Slurp.) Where ARVN spotters reported movement the past twelve hours . . . there we . . . go.

—And?

—And what?

—You better keep your mind on business.

—I'm a little distracted just now.

—Alright then, playtime's over.

—No, no, don't do that. I'll tell you! In the distance we hear: thud, thud.

She whispered, like a hiss:

—What is it? Who goes there?

—VC cadre just fired his BAR. I try to tell how near, in what direction. Their units roam the area in small attack groups, also snipers. Have they heard us?

—Have they?

—No. More automatic fire: dat-dat-da. Next ridge, not our concern.

She straddled his shoulders. A hand to his forehead held his head down: halted his kisses.

—Then?

—I nudge Bufillu. Trail bends this way, to the left: where villagers send children with bowls of rice for the snipers.

—Then?

—We wait. We fish in the dark.

—Fishers of men.

She pinched his lips, and gave her little laugh. From the night table she took the strong Thai beer, the large bottle warm by now, and put it to his mouth making him drink. Liquid dribbled on his cheeks and neck.

—You're wetting the bed.

—What about Bufillu? How long do you wait there?

—An hour, maybe two. Midnight passes, shh, don't talk. Zip it.

—Sip this.

—Oh . . . We . . . we hear a twig, or—

—Or what?

—Back to back we sit by the path. Snap: ever so slight, pspt! Him? Twenty yards or so ahead. My spine tingles. These people speak the forest language, and their pspt! says a lot. There's a knife in your back before you can say ow.

Carlyne held down his head. Her eyes stared in his.

Joey ran his fingertips along her stomach and up, up over the deep cleavage. He touched her chin.

—Oh, he said.

—Well then?

—We have our own signals. Your play? My play? No doubt about it now: we have a visitor. Few more seconds to decide . . . I crouch low, knife in hand. I'm stripped down for this, sleek, no packs. Pspt! again. Small animal? Or an NVA division on the move? I tense. Okay, do this for the grunts whose wives went dead at the other end. Grunts no longer loved when they needed it, because she just didn't care what came off. Hey, stuff the poor boy in a fart sack and load 'im on a C-130 with the next batch. Till death do us part. Hubby's in transit home via Guam. Remains unviewable. Colonel Pricecroft has a telegram sent to the wife and parents, a lot of flowery language dear to brass. It reads: Your son fought valiantly and made the supreme sacrifice for those values we all cherish . . . Now let's give him a victory parade: three cars to the local cemetery. For the girlfriend, or wife, it may be a relief. A bittersweet occasion. See him to his final resting place, and then . . . go fuck a duck.

—Duck?

—For us a 'duck' is a draft dodger, like my brother.

—Tst . . . Go on. You and Bufillu.

—Now I'm waiting in the dark. Coiled up. Oh yes: hate is my mainspring. Here comes the target a few meters to my left. Night bird cries. Signal? Hush . . . There's a tree smell: Blair's *xa-nu* wounded by a shell. It oozes sap like blood.

—Who's Blair?

—Our botany student. Greased. His girlfriend loved him: judging by her letters. They weren't married yet . . . Now a dog's bark, or wild boar? Hm. Too purposeful I think. Crouch down, and wait by the trail. They travel late between guerrilla camps so this kill requires silence, that is, precision. It could be a lone scout, or a column, like mites.

On his back he touched her, and she arched back with a keen light in her eyes. The story was affecting Carlyne. She caught her breath—the way he . . . with his lips . . .

Suddenly Joey slipped from under, rose behind her, and caught her in his steel arms. He pinched her nape, so hard with two fingers, she cried out—before his hand clamped on her mouth.

—I leap out! he whispered. I thrust the knife in a short curve. He pinned her forward.

She gasped.

—Jo, oh—

—Into the flesh it goes, deep in. The blade goes in the soft skin.

—Oh! oh—she gurgled.

Stunned, in abandon, she let herself be yanked down, as he drove forward into her. Now he held her down by the neck, and she tried to catch her breath, drooling on the sheet.

—Past the bone—his voice quivered—chest high inside the VC's slight form, like a shadow. I shut the mouth with my free hand: dig my fingers in that bony jaw.

—No . . . no.

—I crush the jaw—but hardly a sound, a groan. Uhhh. Later for you baby. There's a warm liquid on my hand. There's a moan and a hiss at the lips, which comes from death, as the VC's dull weight goes limp in my arms. So light, couldn't weigh a hundred pounds. Is it a juvenile? They start young. The NLF trains 'em mind and body from the cradle. Children make effective guerrillas, good fighters, and spies too.

He rocked forward. He held the VC immobilized while giving a thrust, and another. His great strength showed her no mercy. To the depths he plunged the blade, and she cried:

—Please, Joey, you're hurting me too much! Please, what if . . . what if I'm pregnant . . . by you?

No stopping him now. She rode out his fury as they both made sexual pantings and moanings toward the climax. In his wildness he still spoke low into her ear:

—I kneel by the path . . . with that slight body in my arms. Blood drips on my forearm. Bufillu whispers: man, we got to move. Must be others! . . . Nope, I ain't going quite yet, I want a look at the face.

—Cut off . . . the ear? Christmas gift for your . . . oh! Jojo, it's too much.

Brutally he kept on, his whole body rigid. He kept the rhythm even as he spoke. Then with one hand he turned her head, and leered in her eye—said:

—This one has long hair.

—You're killing me. Oh! no, Jo—

—Don't worry, I don't cut off ears for trophies. Child's play. No, I want to see this corpse because—

—Finish, will you? And get off. I must be pregnant: you think your baby is enjoying the bumpy ride?

—I want to see this corpse. It's a woman.

For a spell Joey didn't speak. He let his wife gasp all she liked. He felt her feminine will go ripply beneath him. Rigid, he held back his throes, his climax, and unloosed her black hair done up in a tight bun. He let Carlyne's chignon flow forth on her shoulders which were like rocks in a forest stream. Now her face dripped sweat and spittle on his hand. Mounted from behind he draped the fleshy mass of her body which subsided and dissolved in a shiver but was getting no pleasure from this. Her legs spread wide in submission: that was it for resistance. A strong sadistic desire came over the grunt for this woman he knifed the way they taught him, a textbook kill.

—My stomach . . . I'll throw up, Jo, I mean it.

—Bufillu hisses: man, turn that off! I say no, I have to see.

—See, she said, but hurry.

—Damp odor. Blair's *xa-nu*. Blair greased, like tallow when we found him. I want to stamp this one's face on my brain: to blot out something else, Carlyne. There's a strand of black hair matted on the cheek, like you now. There's a silence, a silence. So I killed a woman. She stares at me: the Asian features. Young woman—a mother? . . . It's war. I touch her pouty lips gone sultry when she had to die fifty years too soon. There's twilight in her eyes. The spirit is dimmed in her, a worthless thing, a shadow on her high cheekbones. She has a final glance, like a thought of the man she loves, the earth, her cause . . . Bufillu says: switch it off. But then suddenly—

From his stiff pose Joey lurched back. He gave a jolt.

Carlyne hunched forward and tried to protect her stomach.

Joey flew weirdly out of control, non-sexual now, his violence in a paroxysm. His voice broke, as he ground his teeth in her ear.

—Little bitch stares straight ahead but she's only playing dead. See? the lynx eyes still in focus—she shrieks!

Carlyne gave a shriek.

—Don't—

—Snake! Eyes, mouth wide she strikes, she still attacks. Chignon battalion VC: don't count them out till there's flies in the mouth. I draw back but she fastens her teeth on my collarbone, ah! She bites deep. Maybe the jungle paint makes her miss the lifeline. She grabs at my knife and knocks it away. Bufillu jumps forward—she—holds fast, squeals her crazy speech—my fingers—find the knife drive it upward she clutches her hand falls away—

Joey shuddered. In his knife thrust he climaxed and expended himself and again, again, again, within her.

—Ah! ah! ah! Carlyne shouted when he drove deep in the inner folds for the lifeline.

—Her life—

For a wild moment Joey mauled her. He tried to get it all out finally.

—Ah-ah-h-h! she choked.

He glugglugged:

—Her war—her war—war—over.

XV

The two candles burned low on the dresser. After awhile one guttered with a fizz and flickered out. The other, tenuous, did a weaving dance blue at the base.

Her head rested on his left arm. So he reached round with his right and took the small package from the nightstand.

—Open it.

—Tomorrow.

—Now. Go ahead.

As Carlyne unwrapped her gift, she sniffed. Then she gave a whimper. Inside the small box was black hair with a sheen to it like hers. She put her fingertips to the soft texture. But it had a bad smell; there were rust colored blotches, the woman's dried blood.

Joey said:

—On the trail Bufillu was impatient. Man, let's go . . . With my knife I took the chignon from her scalp. I let her fall. In a hamlet, a guerrilla stronghold in the mountains, maybe a tunnel, a VC cadre looks out at the darkened cordillera. He doesn't know it, but he's a widower.

—Oh.

—Next day my cut gaped. Infected, and it needed a plastic surgeon. I said no when they wanted to send me to the field hospital in Tay Ninh.

—Brave boy.

—Not me. She was. A soldier.

With her fingers Carlyne flicked her Christmas present from the bed, and said:

—Thanks.

At dawn he lay calmly asleep. Bangkok, outside the window, was into its daily round.

Carlyne rose from bed, took the macabre gift in two fingers, and sniffed its odor. She sensed the distant war. She thought of a small country put to the sword because nothing was more precious to its people than freedom and independence. By first light she saw on the sheet a fine powder. Dried blood.

She took the guerrilla fighter's fine black hair in the bathroom, and her first impulse was to flush it down; then her second: to wash it clean and preserve it?

XVI

Joey awoke in late morning, alone, and gave a start.

At noon Carlyne came back from strolling the boulevards where she bought a gift for his sister Lemon.

They had lunch in the room and then went out together: walking toward Chao Phraya, the river on its wide greenish curve through the city. Men in business suits and military uniforms; monks in saffron robes come from their shade tree in a temple courtyard; tourists in loose florid garb: a motley crowd browsed the busy commercial sidewalks. People paused along the khlongs, sallow canals with reeds and lotus beds; they stood watching outboard water-taxis raise a white wake. A boat woman handled her one-oar dugout and sang an ancient chant. There were interminable kiosques filled with bright Western merchandise. There was the klak-klak! of traffic. There was the glare of sunlight.

Above it all rose a multi-tiered wat with curved gables, a pointed ornamental spire; it seemed a distant relative of the Rock Castle where Carlyne must return in three more days . . . In the timeless silence at Wat Arun the G.I. and his wife stood hand in hand; it was the Temple of Dawn with its massive tower and five-ton Buddha half in gold. But the real masterpiece was a statue two feet high: the Emerald Buddha in green jasper.

Then they saw a mural in natural colors: the *Ramayana*, Hindu epic in Sanskrit. They saw Rama, Vishnu's reincarnation, cast by trickery from his throne and driven into a fourteen-year exile with his wife Sita. But Sita abducted by a demon had to be rescued with Sugriva's help, Sugriva the monkey king, and his right wise monkey counselor, Humayun. Rama got his kingship back but lost his wife when her mother, the earth goddess, had to call her after gossips said she wasn't faithful. Even though Sita had proven her virtue, and also borne him twin sons, Rama shook his head and had her put away.

In late afternoon Joey and Carlyne walked through a crowded bazaar with cascades of clinquant, jewelry, curios, imported toiletries, silk and brocaded stuffs, liquor, lighters, cigarette cartons in pyramids. Further on was an immense slum district with its tin sheet huts and rotted plywood. Small children went naked amid the refuse, their bent legs rachitic, their abdomens distended. Flies stuck on the children's foreheads. The bad air had a latrine odor.

—What use? said their cabdriver shooing away beggars as Joey gave out his change.

In college Carlyne once heard how, in the great Asian cities, millions of children worked sixteen hours a day starting at age five in factories, sweatshops, brothels, businesses owned by Western capital, some by Japanese and 'free' Chinese; or local entrepreneurs after a 100%-plus profit. On a stroll down Sampeng Lane, near Yawarad, Bangkok's densely populated Chinatown, Carlyne made a remark. In the slum she had winced and clutched her side: maybe too much rich food? Now she frowned at the neglected children, and said quietly:

—Ho, Ho, Ho Chi Minh.

She was apolitical. She had never been to a demonstration in college. She finished her studies just when the new radicalism staged its first anti-war activities on campus: pickets, administration office sit-ins. But she shared her mother's background: summer visits as a girl to Aunt Lovedy and kinfolk in Robeson County; old stories about the mighty Tuscarora and the white man's coming—the whites' endless guile and violence to get more land. Aunt Lovedy's family was removed from their Pembroke farm to Fayetteville. There were Government blood tests to determine 'Indianness' . . . Carlyne remembered the racism used by whites to justify such injustice: the three school systems in Pembroke, the bus station's six bathrooms, the restaurants which served only whites. In the movie theater the 'lights' were in the best seats; then came the Indians; and Blacks were on the balcony. She was a light-skinned child, but she didn't always pass; she walked a sort of tightrope through her adolescent years, after her father, the special judge, lost his Kinston status. Now Carlyne, seeing the lot of Bangkok's slum children, thought of her people. Joey gave her a sidelong glance:

—What's with the Ho Chi Minh? Get it from Newell?

—No, the nightly news.

He said in a clipped tone:

—We fight and die for the folks back home. Glad they appreciate it.

His look then . . . She turned pale and for a moment walked slower, with a palm to her side. Again she winced with the stomach pain. He looked at her—at her navel bulging a little, at her breasts a bit bloated . . . For an instant, then, her features seemed to lose their composure. She walked slower, making some sort of effort with herself. It was strange to him. Then she put a hand to his arm, steadying herself:

—If you don't mind, Jo, I'll love the warrior, not the war.

XVII

Late that night he woke up because something was happening beside him on the bed. Was she crying? In their life together he had not seen her cry.

—Darling?

She gave small noises, breathing with difficulty, and holding her stomach.

—No—she said, strangely; ashamed to show him?

—Are you sick to your stomach?

She doubled over in a spasm of pain. But she made an effort and said:

—On the trail . . . you knifed her to death?

—Her or me.

—Young woman . . . whole life in front of her.

He said low:

—True. I'm sorry, my darling. It's the war.

Carlyne turned from him. Curiously, she buried her face in the pillow and groaned.

After a moment she turned back.

—You told me something about the war, Joey. How you made a kill. It was your secret, and you confided it to me. Now I'll confide in you, a mutual confidence.

—Please.

—Out there today I wanted so much, so much to tell you about something, Jo. I wanted to throw myself down on the pavement and grovel at your feet for all I'm worth, which isn't much, and ask your forgiveness. Like women in the old times I wanted to scratch my face and tear my hair.

—No need.

—With anguish, Jojo, with guilt. That's how much I wanted to tell you this and confide in you.

—Tell me what?

—You . . . how to tell you—?

Carlyne fell silent then. It was such a silence, as the seconds passed.

—What?

She said to him:

—You remember I went to an orphanage to live after my mother died?

—You told me.

—In La Grange.

—Yes.

—Well, I . . . Jo . . . I was raped there, at age twelve, by a staff member. I wasn't a virgin when I came to you. That's why I . . . why so many things. That's why I have such bad moods a lot of times, and make you unhappy. I don't mean to. I'm sorry, my darling, I'm sorry, I'm sorry, I'm so sorry.

By his side in the late night in Bangkok she began to cry as if it all wanted to come out of her. A whole lot, the past. But it couldn't.

Joey took her in his arms and held her a long time as dawn put a pink streak on the window sill.

Then they drifted off again, holding one another.

XVIII

Another day passed, and another night. Joey tried not to count the last hours.

Now they felt more like staying outside. They visited a few pagodas, also the Grand Palace compound, museums. They saw national treasures. Their guide took them to a back room where precious gems, rubies and sapphires had been smuggled in from Burma.

At sunset Joey put on his tan leisure suit. Carlyne's blue summer dress and pearl necklace highlighted her lake blue eyes. They dined and danced on the terrace of a luxury hotel among foreigners and affluent businessmen. There were the more elegant Thai prostitutes. One night on a visit to Phat Phong, Carlyne stared at B-girl hostesses and go-go dancers in the bars and rock 'n roll cafés where they sold themselves. Behind a glass partition at the Happy-Happy off Sukhum Vit a hundred young women herded in from the provinces watched TV and ate chocolate; they were nearly naked, painted up, all ages and sizes. They waited for their knight in shining armor. Brow knit, Carlyne looked at them. Then she had a strong Thai drink and got in the stag night spirit when two Siamese fighting fish, red-tailed and blue-finned with blackish scales, locked jaws in a glass jar and ripped away strips from each other until one, eye torn from its socket, gill shredded in the pink water, went belly up. This was at an after-hours club in Phet Buri, as men shouted and fisted wads of cash at the wire-like fish underfed to make them fierce, and tear at each other.

—Like our kisses, she said.

That night back in the hotel room she wanted none of his sweet tenderness. She made love to him with an edge; she bit him and whispered in his ear, taunting. Then he lay by her side and held her close. He played at peace though the moment drew near for return to the war.

They stayed awake all night and at daybreak took a boat from Chang landing to a river market where sampans cargoed exotic fruits and vegetables. Boats filled the river lined with low structures on stilts, sand barges, the moss-grown teak of the dockside piles. Myna birds and potted orchids, Chinese antiques and gems, pedigree puppies; it was all haggled over between sampans held in place by a housewife's oar.

Later, their last full day together, they rode an elephant and watched a cockfight. They visited yet another Buddhist wat: on the River of Kings.

That night they slept. They didn't make love but slept quietly side by side. It was as if all the quantity of emotion and physical passion and misunderstanding, between them, all the things that went into their relationship had turned at last into the quality of a marriage—the way friction at length makes fire; the way elements of springtime combine to make new life; or the way albumin produced the miracle of a live cell once upon a time. All the different things in Carlyne and Joey, her virile traits no less than the feminine, his passive and active drives as well, came together like opposites interpenetrating and made a new unity, a new identity of all the non-identity in their young lives and beings. This didn't mean they had sentimental dreams as they lay there together. It wasn't like a musical chord coming home. No; it was more like the dissonance of the possible for that man and woman in that moment of time.

XIX

When she awoke to a ray of sunlight across the quilted bedspread, he sat quietly and waited in his cleaned and pressed jungle fatigues. It felt like the time he went away from her in Durham, but different.

Neatly he had packed the new clothes, leisure suits, blouses, silk robe and sandals, and put the lot in her suitcase.

—Keep them for when I get back home.

—Sure. When you have road trips.

—I don't think I'll play baseball anymore, Carlyne.

—No?

—No. I want to be a farmer. I'd like to revive my granddaddy's farm.

—Alright then I'll be a farmer's wife.

—Dad was hoping Newell would lend a hand with that. Dream on. I'll do it.

At eleven o'clock inside the airport he gave her their leftover red 100-baht notes. Her flight to California departed at seven in the evening.

They waited at the gate before his embarcation. He held her in his arms as they rocked slightly.

—Two hundred and twenty-four.

—What?

—Days more. I like to call it half, halfway done with it. To lift my spirits.

—Don't count them.

—We've got a new guy named Wisembroder from an old whaler port on Cape Cod. He just started but he counts. He says: three hundred and farty-far.

She gave a small laugh and rested her head on his shoulder.

—I don't fear it in the same way now. These ten days we became a couple.

—Sure.

—If I die tomorrow I won't complain after what you've given me.

—Don't say that.

—Do you know what I'd like most?

—No.

—For you to get pregnant.

She raised her head. For an instant she gazed past him at the wide airport space ashuffle with passengers.

—Me too, she said, softly.

He thought a moment.

—My darling, you've given me back my hope. I almost don't want it: to call up the man, the sensitivity again underneath the war monster. Because now I have to go back to that . . .—He sighed.—That. And it's better if I don't feel too much. But if you hadn't come, I . . . I don't know what I would have done.

There was a tear in his eye—the big, sort of masterful man looking down at her.

—So no more baseball?

—Well, if you wanted it. For you . . . Now I'll probably even start thinking patriotic again. But naw . . . why not let's put Granddaddy's farm back in shape? They always said it was prime acreage, out there back of the Rock Castle down to the Yadkin. Don't you think we might have fun together? To make it a success?

—Okay, she said.

He rubbed his hands laughing boyishly:

—More fun than that cussedy old baseball which I got sick of anyway.

—Really?

—You by my side . . . farmer, father, bringing up children in decency . . . Do your homework!—He laughed.—Let the other boys make headlines and be great, I've had enough.

—Okay.

—Oh we'll have fun at it Carlyne, we'll have so much good ol' warm fun. You bet!

—Modest, quiet lives then—she said, thoughtful, in a falling tone.—Not a circus.

—That's right. No need to be sad over baseball. Forget about it.

He swayed slightly and held her. His eyes were closed same as when they met ten days ago in this Southeast Asian city like a dream.

Then he looked at her a moment at arm's length, so proudly, and proud of himself; he gave a smile quite unlike the metallic grin she had seen him give in that other life when he played third base.

—Seven more months. Then count on it: I'll be home.

—Home—she said, and her eye fell from his.

She stared at the letters, GILBERT, in black over his olive drab breast pocket.

Then he picked up his green duffel bag and hefted it on his shoulder. He bowed to kiss her hand.

He turned for a last fixed glimpse to take with him—a seven-month glimpse. In his dark eyes there was so much love.

Her lips moved to tell him—what? The words wouldn't come. Maybe she had no right to them?

Still he lingered an instant. He looked at her brooch, and fingered it.

—Here, she said. You gave me something; now let me give you a present. Take the brooch. Wear it on your fatigues, like a good luck charm, a talisman.

—No, Joey shook his head. I'd just lose it out there. You keep it.

Chapter Seven

I

High above Saigon which seemed expectant as the yearly Tet celebration got in gear, Emmet Bufillu waited for his partner gone to place an overseas call. Bufillu sat at a table of the Caravelle terrace bar while far down below a bright dragon danced past the Wild West and Papillon clubs along crowded Tu Do. The streets were gushing flowers—blossoms and festive branches of yellow *mai* apricot special to the country's one major holiday. Tet Nhat, the Lunar New Year was the first day of spring coming between the previous harvest and planting of new seeds.

In it all Bufillu sensed the crop cycles and seasons he knew as a boy on a farm in Atmore, Alabama, where his ancestors had drifted from Louisiana after the Civil War. Now he sipped his drink and felt an unusual mood. Why so sad? Because he was out of it here? This wasn't his to understand and enjoy? Was that why he felt a keen attraction for these Oriental women and wouldn't mind spending time with one tonight?

On holiday from the Central Highlands he sat quietly in his thoughts and let the war take a breather. It was strange. In this savage place, tonight at midnight across Vietnam, each family would seem to play a comedy and stage a goodbye ceremony for the tutelary genius, the last lunar year's spirit who was on the way to give a detailed account of the household's actions good and bad before the Jade Emperor enthroned up in heaven. Good idea! The poor folk in rural areas spent their savings on a lavish farewell dinner and provided 'mandarin' footwear for the spirit's journey, also a winged bonnet authorized solely for such hearth and 'stove' gods. There was even a legendary carp to serve as steed in the spectacular ride to the sky. Then, in Buon Me Thuot as elsewhere, came the customary visits. And the first over a family's threshold must take the blame for any bad luck which came down the pipe during the next year; for example, if the family was stampeded into a barbwired strategic hamlet.

At Tet each household put a plate of five fruits before the family altar: five fruits to represent the five elements of life, metal, wood, water, fire, and . . . hm, Bufillu forgot the fifth one told them by the ARVN guide on their way into Saigon that afternoon; and also show respect, somehow, for their ancestors. Wine was placed next to the fruits that were special to each region, let's see, milkfruit, mango, coconut, pineapple, tangerine—was that it? Did he have it right? These were kept during the days prior to Tet and then given out to family members later. The plate was to show gratitude to the wandering souls of the ancestors.

Now the grunt felt a kind of envy for all that homely ritual, and he wondered if he might not find some good Vietnamese woman to lie with before the night was over. 'Cause right now he felt kind of left out.

Bufillu sipped and raised a hand at his waiter being annoyed by a tipsy American construction engineer. But wasn't Emmet in a curious mood—almost like anguish? Why? Something was badgering him in his gut. And yet what could happen to him here in friendly Saigon where public vehicles had metal grills for VC hand grenades and every second passerby was probably a VC sympathizer? Well, calm yourself, brother. When a man gets shook up in the field, in the mad minutes after a catastrophe such as Xo Man, then he simply glints his bayonet grin and carries on. Right, soldier? Bear down, boy! said Colonel Pricecroft. Pathos won't help matters around here, or fear of death.

II

—Quack! quack!—the drunk American flapped his upper arms and showered spit on the Vietnamese waiter. —Get the technology outa' my f'ing cocktail. *Chao chi*, you motherf'ing duck, *chao an!*

The other stirred his ice like a French waiter; he was used to abuse in this Caravelle which headquartered the U.S. press corps, and he took the saliva in his face in stride. But Vietnamese detested Western mimickry of their high-pitched accent, and also any discourtesy. In the grapevine Bufillu heard tales: how in POW camps U.S. soldiers were told to believe what they pleased but 'here you must speak and act politely'.

Now a Saigon woman rose from her seat. Elegantly dressed, heavily made up, her eyes darted fire like the dragon lady Bufillu and Joey watched that afternoon in a crowded town square on the way here along Highway 20. When the dragon paused to cavort before a private home or a merchant's shop, it brought prosperity.

—You animer' Yankee!

—Whatsay? Hey! Dragon Lady, come have a drink on St. George. Xe-xe-xe. The way I see it, yer' kinda' cute.

His voice rose up in a squeak.

—Always shit othel peoper hrouse. Go shit own hrouse!

—Say! You don't say . . . Looky here, Dragon, I go where I damn it all please, see? Wanna' make somethin' of it? America owns this whole goddamned planet, and I'm glad!

—Please don't talk so loud, Sir—said the urbane bartender.

—Loud? I'm quiet! Hey, I'm the quiet American. Xe-xe-xe.

Witty guy. And the repartee went on: between a Western drunk in a tan summer suit and two Saigonese maybe not as 'puppet regime' as they were supposed to be. Well, the pedalo fleet, the bar girls and cyclo girls, thousand piastre per half hour prostitutes, shopkeepers, Europeanized hotel personnel, even Saigon street children with their hard Savoyard-like look: all were bent on getting hold of your 'funny money', military scrip; and all might be spies. Bufillu looked over the chic whore, but turned his eyes away. The white man's crudeness made him angry too, and depressed his holiday spirits. All day long he was trying to shake an uneasy sense he had: not with it. He was a G.I. but right now he wanted to be something else—as far from the military as he could get.

He gazed far down where treelined boulevards led out from the river and quayside activity with its ships and distant sounds. Ben Thanh market was this way, the Bui Phat slum district out there. He could see the long thoroughfare to Cholon, the Chinese night city filled with opium dens, dives, places to gamble. There were taxi girls with neon characters reflecting off their satiny bodies; they looked so fragile, and they were steel. Now back in Atmore his wife Nora, a patient steady woman, slept toward dawn a day ahead of him in the countdown; she was praying to have her husband home alive: oh God in the sky, bring him back to me still in one piece.

Saigon simmered and sent up long pale plumes of smoke. Crack-crack-crack! There were fireworks all over. The 'salutes' scared off the bad spirits. Crack-crack-crack! But fireworks could also attract the good spirits. A scent of cordite came wafting across the Caravelle terrace. Down below in the crowded streets there were shop owners vying to put on the most expensive display; that was how they guaranteed this year would be a rich one.

But Bufillu felt sad amid it all.

Was Joey able to reach his wife? She was the restless kind who don't help matters; nothing homey about her. A man has his life, and his wife. If neither is strak; if there is no profit or pleasure in it, then bonsoir, sweetie.

In late afternoon the dense and turbulent city was steamy. The tension of war turned toward something else.

III

Earlier that day on the road between villages in their jeep, the two G.I.s on leave listened to an ARVN guide describe Tet preparation in the countryside. They shielded their eyes from sheet glare off the flooded paddies: where peasantry had to put in seed and open sluice gates before they cooked up *banh chung* for Tet and wrapped it in *zong* leaves. In courtyards the pigs began to squeal, uh-oh; and the three soldiers could hear, as they stopped for tea on the way, the pounding sound as the glutinous rice was whitened. Teams in the fields pulled up bug-infested and stunted azolla plants; they had to remove the insects and respread the azolla amid their other festival chores. Traditionally a great deal got left to year's end when superstition took a hand and so you had to do it.

At Tet the people went to the pagodas to make their offerings and burn incense sticks. The ARVN guide told Joey and Bufillu all about it, and that man sure did know a lot. He was good to talk to, and he spoke of the kids going from house to house to wish a Happy New Year. Relatives came to visit and wish one another health and longevity, and good studies for the young ones. At Tet people returned to their native village and had a good visit with family members and old friends. Special dishes were prepared. There was cockfighting, and chess playing. There was swimming in the river, and the young men held wrestling matches. That was Tet, said the ARVN guide, and much more.

Then Saigon gave them a pleasant jolt after months of jungle in the Central Highlands. In Saigon it was boom time. You heard it in the street vendors' excited cries; in the streets swarming with bicycles, pedicabs, cycliles, pony carts, small blue and white Renault taxis, big black MAAG Chevvies, the wire-screened public buses. Look out! A water buffalo wandered into a frenzied intersection and it was guts galore . . . Everywhere was a dizzy business urgency as the Far Eastern city saw its affairs mushroom due to the U.S. occupation. Bars, hawkers, jaunty whores on platform heels gesturing at passing drivers in the broad daylight; Chinese women's trim slit skirts; the breezy tunics and pantaloons traditional to Vietnamese; the black marketeers and war profiteers alongside robed Buddhist bonzes and Cao Dai cultists; millionaires rubbing elbows with beggars in loin cloths; Chinese men in sharkskin suits, 'Choy boys' (debauched men), supplicants with joss sticks, grim opium smiles, strident cries and car horns, klaxons, firecrackers, backfires; —but there was no cannonade after days and nights of it in the distance. Saigon was a sea of faces and figures. The city was filled with car farts and a promise of sudden fortune from the Pointe des Blagueurs and Saigon Port wharves to the Dakao suburb and Gia Dinh.

But a pause came in the turbid air on the verge of impressive pyrotechnics to usher in the Year of the Monkey.

A woman in silk *ao dai* moved swiftly toward home and the three-tiered altar where she kept her rendezvous with her dead. Outside the Rex Theater a vendor briskly folded her portable lunch counter, noodle and crab soup, sugary rice cakes, manioc, sweet potatoes, fried *rô* fish, rice jello; and her movements, too, had an *entrain* to them. Outside The Brink, a downtown officers club bombed—how embarrassing—on Christmas Eve but now reopened for business, there was a kid hawking his newspapers, shouting through rotted teeth:

—Saigon Post! Vietnamese Guardian! 15 p.! Saigon Dai'ry News!

Tamarind, camphor, flamboyant and frangipani, gomenolier trees lined the wide streets in the quartiers aisés. There fragrant effusions mixed with the exotic restaurant smells. But septic odors were spreading from slums sprawled along the river where black rats gave rise to rumors of plague in wartime Saigon.

—If you choose the wrong hotel—said Top Drawber the new First-Shirt lifer in base camp: he was a meanspirited nitwit who tried to block their R & R spin in Saigon granted by Col. Price-croft—you'll wake up with a nest of baby rats under your pillow.

—Tooth fairy type thing, said Bufillu.

—Hey, said Joey, VC eat rat and praise the chicken taste.

—How do you know? said Top.

—They invited me to their goûter the other day.

—What's goûter? said the lifer.

—Maybe bonbons type thing—said Bufillu; and he chuckled trying to relieve tension which already existed between Joey Gilbert, who was the real leader, and Drawber who was a fool.

IV

Tall plane trees in double rows bordered the affluent boulevards and shaded the French colonial architecture of the 'plateau' quarter. Those were tan hued villas amid a tropical vegetation behind the broad gates and walls, shuttered windows, orange tile roofs of this city situated on a plain and surrounded by vast agricultural areas, rice paddies to the far horizon.

Tet 1968. A festive spirit moved in the pagodas, Truong-Thanh, the Indian pagoda of the Chettys, the Chinese pagodas of the Quai de Belgique and the rue Pierre.

In the hive-like Cholon industrial suburb veined by canals where junks and sampans glided, bamboo masts, a lucky-eye or bat wing painted on the prow; in rue des Marins, rue de Canton, rue de Paris, Canal des Poteries; in Dakao and Arroyo of the Avalanche; Chien Si Circle where U.S. Intelligence housed its analysts; Xa Loi Temple home to politically outspoken monks; Place Eugène Cuniac near the railroad station where food vendors sold roast sparrow, curried eel, ram's testicles, dog hotdogs; in Boulevard Charner soon to explode with fireworks and bright animal balloons, with citizenry in their finery among flower stalls of potted miniature orange plants, mums and gladiolus: —Tet was on the march. This year the festivities would be a winner.

After a preliminary ride around the city, the two soldiers on a spree dropped off the ARVN guide at a certain café and parked on a side street near Ba Son shipyard.

—I could almost get used to this, said Bufillu, and gave his easy laugh.

A breeze from the sunlit water tickled their sweaty necks and played in the shimmery leaves and quayside trees. They walked along Ton Duc Thang toward busy Tu Do Street and the Caravelle Hotel. Joey had to make a long distance call, and Emmet wanted to tell him: let it rest. But he thought: what's the use? Again Joey's wife had fallen silent, not writing him a word in weeks; and so there was the logical need to find out why and maybe tell the good woman a thing or two over the long distance telephone. This Joey would do and show he was boss, but there went the good holiday spirit down the drain.

At midafternoon a smoke trail rose from Saigon River's far bank. Hot over there, said their guide. No-go at night.

The months spent in the field had put their platoon through the meat grinder. But now word had come down: there was relief in sight. The deserving grunts would soon be transferred to patrol a Revolutionary Development (RevDev) hamlet. And this was a plum. So big Bufillu got up his best holiday spirit and hankered for famous Tu Do Street and Saigon night life and the wonder of Asian woman. Joey said he would join him in that activity if there was no satisfactory response from Carlyne. Usually as other grunts mulled over ad nauseum the joys of dating and sex, these two married men had less to say.

But now sensual pleasure was unfurling like a Tet banner in the Saigon air. Bufillu's five senses were astir, and he wanted action. Already in the villes by the roadside the grunts' nostrils had widened to scents of ripening vegetation, sweet cassava cooked over hot ashes, apricot and peach trees in blossom. Bufillu thought of springtime back home in Atmore, Alabama. There was a kick to the perfume of the joss sticks.

Now Joey's partner gazed out from the Caravelle terrace bar at a first hint of evening in the wings.

V

Into a second drink Bufillu waited and seemed to share his friend's apprehension. He didn't quite know why but some scent in the air gave him a little shudder. Hey, he shrugged, and sipped. Luck type thing.

His wife wrote him: once a week. That woman was like clockwork. But Joey's mysterious wife had hardly written a line since they enjoyed themselves so well during the R & R stint in Bangkok at Christmas. Well, Emmet thought he knew the difference between a good woman and a mystery. But what can you do? Some men like tickles, and some like prickles.

Through January Joey had scant leisure time to brood over it as squad activity went badly. Skol, the crafty point man, was shot through head and chest in a trail ambush. Three days later Oakleigh, a replacement troop, had to be medevac'd amid sniper fire. Oakleigh, unconscious on the stretcher, might wake up in Japan to darkness, blinded like Vane in Xo Man, but he would wake up at least. Skol the shorttimer was greased by the VC beast, and released. No more wake-ups.

New guys arrived: Gamecock whose mom was a Charleston socialite, of all things, or so he said. There was a skinny kid named Sanger: seems C-rats made him anorexic. Chingi, also called T-Bone, came from El Barrio in New York. A replacement medic named Tootie took over when Artus split the scene.

And then, as they worked on special assignment beyond their area in a desolate northern Mekong Delta sector adjoining the Plain of Reeds: then a new E-8 came on the scene, named Drawber, a lifer. He was an arrogant nitpicker who didn't try to understand The Nam. No way he would learn new tricks of the trade from men experienced in the bush like Joey. No humility at all! Mostly incompetence. He made the grunts angry and frustrated because this was no place to have your head on backwards—facing the past, Korea, which he always brought up.

In the field Joey Gilbert was the de facto leader. And even as he endured his wife's silence, strung tight and visibly depressed, he came through for the men. He helped them respond to danger and trail events with inspired courage, an improvised war craft; with infantry tactics not taught in the counterinsurgency school at Puyallup or anywhere else. You had to learn it on the spot. Squad members saw him as a kind of anti-Viet Cong and all but worshipped the ground he walked on—oops, not this rotten jungle carpet, in the Nam. World Serious, they called him, with respect though he kept on defending Top Drawber perversely, and carrying out the man's ass-backwards orders. Joey's brilliance shone to the offices and hallways at Division Headquarters where it eclipsed a dull First Sergeant limited by a Korean War mindset.

Bufillu guessed the platoon had Joey's record, and also December encounter with Colonel Pricecroft in Tan Son Nhut Airport, to thank for the softer RevDev hamlet assignment that was coming their way once Lunar New Year celebrations ended.

Better times were on the way, kids; though Top would probably find a way to wreck them too. But in the meantime take heart, lay a juicy fart, and don't upset the applecart. Sit back and relax a moment, and let the good times roll.

VI

Joey came from his overseas conversation.
—Let's go.
—What happened?

He looked stunned. Tottered, a little, on the way to the table. For weeks he had led them through the hell of the Parrot's Beak. Now a call to his wife, and his steps were unsteady.

—Tell you later. Come on.

—You spoke to her?

Joey glanced out across the city. Disgusted, he shook his head and said:

—No, not her.

—Stepped out, type thing.

—You could say that.

Joey gave a low laugh, but nothing was funny.

Bufillu rose:

—You talked to your father?

—No, Lemon. Little sister.

—And?

—Not here. She's not here, Joey. Well where then: walk up town? No, Jojo, I don't know. Nobody does. Oh, I said. Well, maybe Newell would if I called him. May be, Jujube (he imitated her voice): that's what she calls me at such a moment, Jujube. But I don't think so, she says, because Newby's been gone since November. And Carlyne? Oh, it was early January, just a few days after she came back from seeing you in Bangkok. That's when she went away. Early January? . . . Yes, Joker, first week in January.

Joey fell silent. He stared out high above Saigon into space.

—Then what? said Emmet.

—I asked her: no note? No address? Some college friend's name? Did she go to Durham? . . . I don't know, Jojo, she just went. I was in school. Carlyne didn't even say goodbye to us.

—That all? No forwarding address, not even a thank you note, type thing.

—My little sister started to cry. It's nighttime there; I guess I woke her up. Dad's in Washington. I asked about Newell gone to live in a hippie commune in the Berkeley Hills. Ah, no telephone. Lemon gave me the address.

He smoothed a bit of crumpled paper with his jotting: 2779 Hillgard.

—If she went out there, you'll find her.

Joey gnashed:

—With Newell? I don't think so. Lord, I hope not. —Stunned, he gazed out. —No.

Bufillu thought a moment and walked to the terrace edge. Now more often as dusk came on the fireworks poppopped in the streets. A large one, it seemed an enriched cherry bomb, sent a tremor through the hotel.

—Your brother's okay, you said, when he isn't screaming slogans against us and starting a riot.

—He likes to argue. He's a crazy guy always provoking Dad. They had a bad argument last fall over the war. So Newell walked out to the highway with his rucksack full of books. That's what Carlyne told me in Bangkok.

—But she stayed? said Bufillu.

—Until early January. She came to see me, acted like we were the Married Couple of the Year, all lovey-dovey, and then she took off.

—And ... she didn't give even a hint about it, in Bangkok? Something wrong at your Dad's place?

—Just 'my love' and 'my darling', let me wash you. Head on my shoulder, tears in her eyes. What an actress.

—Jujube—Emmet laughed softly—I don't think you know the whole story.

—She'd make a good VC, chignon, secrecy, the works.

—Naw. Just wait and have a little faith. You'll go home and find her.

—Find her where? Waiting for me in Durham? Then why doesn't she write? Why not tell me she was checking out of the Rock Castle?

Joey leaned back against the terrace rail. His wiry size, his big cat physique was outlined against Saigon settling in a gray gold haze. The city grew opaque as the day waned; it played hide-and-seek in the torrid fumes of its Cochin Chinese mystique, and Tet Mau Than getting ready to happen.

Buffilu sounded far away:

—Don't conclude, type thing. You and she ain't finished yet by a long shot. When you're playing third base in New York she'll come looking for you.

Joey's senses swam in a pain of abandonment. He felt like a child just then. He gave a shrug and laugh like a man.

—Sure, sure. Lemon said: don't fret, bruvver. She loves you. We all do.

—Still early in the game.

—But how will she live? Where will she go, and what will she do?

—You have a joint bank account, didn't you say? If she uses it, you'll know where she is.

—And that's just why she won't use it, die of hunger first, besides the fact that she's stubborn and proud and probably crazy into the bargain after being raped in an orphanage, so she told me.

—C'mon, partner, let's go see the sights. Try to calm your wits and enjoy this bit of huss Pricecroft cut us. It's Tet in Saigon halfway around the world from nowhere, and we're two G.I.s on a lark, type thing.

VII

Joey strolled up Tu Do toward the Cathedral in a daze. He couldn't get over what he suspected long before the call he just made. He grumbled to himself:

—Nobody tells me a thing. She didn't tell me. Dad never mentioned it. I'm the last to know my own fate, yet Lemon says: we love you, Jujube.

—They don't want to worry you. They don't want you distracted.

—How many more days in this madhouse? I've got to get home and give her a spanking she'll never forget. Why? Why does she act this way? Dammit, goddamn it! I've got to know why.

—Bet she's faithful to you, said Bufillu.

—That's some way to show it: leaves me high and dry. Remember Ringwood? He had a high school sweetheart too . . . Dear Billy, me 'n Jody, well, you know, we decided . . .

—Forget Ringwood.

—And Ben Bolt? Another true romance.

—Never mind Ben Bolt right now.

—My wife is gone and I can't do anything about it. How many more days in this shithole?

Bufillu was on the alert as his partner raved through clenched teeth. The two men like a pair of giants made quite a sight there in the center of Saigon nightlife on the threshold of Tet. They went along the sidewalk, one black, one white, and people stepped back to watch them pass. But Emmet scoped out the Tu Do strip joints and bars with blaring music. There were the *Melody, San Francisco, Rainbow,* boom-boom rooms where the neon flashed fast. An angular woman a third their size beckoned from a doorway. Bufillu stared at one who was round-eyed after cosmetic surgery.

—You take scrip, dear?

—No sclip, darrah onry.

Bufillu felt a tug, looked down at his feet, and gave a hop.

—Man! Look at that. Get back, you devil!

A human crab snatched at the big man's cuff.

There was a high wailing sound which came from down there on the sidewalk. It was uncanny as a few human crabs like a school of them pleaded and pincered, whined and puled:

—Gim'money!

More came. More showed up from nowhere and hoisted sideways toward the G.I.s. They were frail and shadowy gliding along the pavement, but they were also wiry, singleminded as machines with only this one function to fulfill: begging. Did they ever sleep? Have holes to go to?

The human crabs gathered and advanced pincers high: like crabs on the moonlit beach at Nha Trang. Each was a convoluted mass of flesh and bones. Each was bent, spindly, with poliomyelitic spine and legs—yet powerful. They had mechanical arms and moneymaniacal eyes in the middle of that tangle. They cried out in shrill whines even as they yanked pants, grasped ankles, demanded handouts.

Joey was in no mood and lashed out, kicking one. Shocked, they gave a chorus of pathetic howls, and backed off. It was a shared reflex: this man has no heart, so turn to the gentler black man. The G.I. tossed a few coins behind them and said bye bye with a laugh.

A block further on Bufillu took out a business card given him that afternoon by the ARVN guide.

Visit Madame La Caî's Fashionable Parlor. 20% Discount.

VIII

—Here it is. Let's do it.

Beyond a foyer they entered a wide poorly lit space which was sparsely furnished. It was unadorned except for a mildly pornographic calendar on the wall facing a Buddhist shrine. Deeper in the den was a sense of quiet but morose relaxation. The G.I.s' eyes adjusted to a scene as strange as the riptide just outside the door—a far opposite ambience yet somehow related.

A few flabby middle-aged men lay about in sarongs. They looked like lower echelon Thieu regime officials, also Saigonese businessmen grown prosperous in the boom. There were discreet civil servants. These and others lounged and hung around. Most were in vapid negligé.

Seven, eight opium addicts lay side by side in a partitioned space to the rear. There was a broad low platform used as communal bed with small wood boxes used for pillows. Legs draped here and there those smokers lay in an asexual disarray. They were cool. They were duly unstrung after the stressful day. They shared a same languorous repose: if you could call that sharing.

Opium. It was the premiere release from the wartime scramble. By day these gentlemen were the hounds of profit U.S.-style, at least some of them. They were exporter-importers and service sector agents and brokers; their nerves were groovy here despite the nightly artillery fire in the not too distant Truong Son foothills.

It was a kind of stale haze. The opium devotees listened to the siren song of self. Around the room it was a murmured amphigory with overtones of a blessed inner peace. A few cogs to the U.S. war effort, a foreign sales rep, a technical specialist in the field of providing 'security', a friendly AID office clerk with a wife and kids in-country—all subsided in a revery beside their pipes. They glubglubbed. They sucked.

—Our luck, said Bufillu, to find Danny-boy Pricecroft doing his thing in a dark corner. Back to the bush with you, type thing.

—Oho.

Joey shrugged. He glanced here and there: the shabby wood bowl affixed to a plastic tube. There was less pleasure in pipe preparation ever since Diem raided the *fumeries* and seized the finely carved, artistic 'works'. Now for the most part there was only the simple stone, needle, lamp. Some had bamboo pipes like an ancient wind instrument, or a recorder. Out came the jar of opium—if bad it was black as boot polish, if good yellowish, tawny, a viscous substance like glue. A glass cap protected the flame of the copper lamp. The opium ball, held on the needle, was heated over the spirit lamp until it boiled and took on blisters which foamed whitish in the shadowy room. The two G.I.s watched as the opium was rolled on the polished stone till it became a harder mass, pill-like. Then the morsel was pierced by the needle, like a bead, and placed in the aperture of the pipe bowl. The little pill of opium, heated over the lamp, gave its sickly sweet smell into the fumy room while a wick was burning slowly and floating in mustard oil beneath the glass cap. Men chatted awhile as their faces turned blue, looking cyanotic, dead to life, and their lips and mouths fell away in abandon from the pipe.

One patron, so gaunt with eyes fixed and sunken, all but starved as he lived for his addiction to the tune of thirty pipes per night. He drew in and held a good minute and then twitched in his extremities, ah . . .!

Another on his back with knees raised shook a little. He cursed low and lamented the bad stuff, the admixture, to his neighbor who was a Germanic type in skivvies.

—Thai trash. I'll go to Laos. There you can still find pure stuff.

A smoker grinned up, dimly, at big Bufillu:

—Opium . . . the people's religion.

—Let's go, said Joey.

—Hold on, why not try it out? Five pipes.

—Only make a beginner sick.

—Alright then, but I want a woman. I got it coming.

Bufillu shrugged and laughed.

A polyglot smalltalk filled the somber den. There were names: Ky, Westmoreland and McNamara, Bac Ho. There were places like the Tay Nguyen, a guerrilla paradise where cadre filed their teeth and dressed in loincloths. The G.I.s overheard bits and snatches as they lingered. Did you know Kim Phiar, the firebird, drops excrement on insurgent villages to show God's anger at communists? *Bay da, chong giay, ten lua:* these were killer traps with spiked rope, fire arrows and the like. Ranger companies (Americans) were called 'big noses'. Camp Davis was a Tan Son Nhut sector and Bach Dang a port. . . . In a slur a smoker mentioned the *dac cong*—elite, highly trained VC sappers who had proven their ability to infiltrate and blow up U.S. installations as well as military craft moored in Saigon Harbor . . . *Shum-shum* was a Vietnamese vodka brewed of rice. Daisy chains—grenades strung in series along a trail: a point man trips one, and goes up. Etc. The opium addicts tried to forget the war but it had a momentum in their minds. 'White tiger'—female principle, negative, filled with menaces; 'blue dragon'—male principle, positive, benign, said local sages. Hm! . . . And on and on: the low murmur of the smokeheads putting in time like it was eternity.

Bufillu laughed quietly. The scent had got in his nostrils, and he wanted to stay.

Joey browsed among the bleary conversations another instant. They liked to talk. Old tales, anecdotes, gossip. On the fringe in English a rapt smoker confessed his wife's infidelity since the opium made him impotent.

—What do I care? I've got something . . . more solid . . .—he gave a choirboy smile.—Je m'en fiche pas mal, si je n'arrive pas, tu sais.

Behind them the two soldiers heard the broken-souled murmur. Sighed words. Someone hiccupping. War nerves.

—Let's move.

IX

They went out into the mild twilight. Fireworks soared up, sputtered, poppop! poppop! hissed over the wharves and low steamy Thu Thiem sprawl, the nightly no-man's- or VC-land across the river. Cordite blent in with dinner and riverine scents, the city's slums: shacks of thatch and flattened beercans on a sludge of delta in the South China Sea. Saigon, city of sampans.

Bufillu glanced here and there as more fine women walked by in native tunics and pantaloons, in slit-skirts. A belated man-driven cart turned into Tu Do and went toward the river; it had jackfruit, mangosteen, pineapple, mandarin, in pyramids.

Night fell. Lanterns hung from the crimped windows on a side street too narrow for cars. The reddish shadows had a tremor. Near the Cathedral a flute sent up high notes like a butterfly. Along the quay a Chinese gong seemed to warn in a muffled tone.

—Wo, hold on—Bufillu peeped in. —Looks like good ones.

VC house? Here were no stained kimonos and permanent waves, falsies and faked interest in a G.I.'s family. Who's your favorite Hollywood star, G.I.? Here the bar girls didn't chatter a lot of trash and say over and over: You numbah one! Buy me Saigon tea? Sollyboutdat. You velly handsome. Saigon tea?

—And your wife? said Joey.

—Understands.

—Are you sure?

—Just get the breadwinner home intact. VD no problem, but watch out for VC.

On a dark lane off Tu Do three ARVN soldiers talked to a simply dressed woman. When their G.I. allies came strolling by, they grew quiet.

Bufillu muttered:

—Shit-coolers?

—Why take the chance? Christ—Joey winced—look at that.

Exquisite, gracious, a young woman smiled at them. This lane was on the fringe: beyond it was a dark maze of opium dens, brothels, gambling coveys. The ARVN drew aside with a nod for their U.S. Army counterparts. Go on in the bar, please do!

X

Inside was a dim pinkish aura with not a Westerner in view.

The chitchat in Vietnamese lapsed as Bufillu asked Mama-san what she had.

—La Rue.

—That all?

33 Bière Export.

So no imported. Bad sign.

From a cabinet she took Red Label.

—600 piasters.

Emmet handed her the bills.

Joey looked around, and he didn t like it. In Tu Do dives the women came up right away; they tried to coax you with a patent phrase in their mosquito voices. Not here. On Tu Do you felt a nervous edge to the bar girls: separated by the war from family, native village ethos, fiancé and normal friendships, they lived on the make from day to day. There was a whiff to it all, guilt or sadness, which even a G.I. picked up at instants. Tu Do hookers carried on, aimless, demoralized by life in the South Vietnamese capital under U.S. occupation. At the core they yearned for home though it might not be there anymore. There was shame; there was money frenzy; also a romantic notion, for some perhaps, of the heroine of Vietnamese literature, named Kiêw, who prostituted herself for love of family. Some sent loot back to their parents.

Here the lay of the land was different. It was quiet in this bar. Sort of severe, if not sinister. The two unarmed G.I.s in jungle fatigues were not ogled, approached, spoken to.

Toward the rear stood a table spread with fruit, sweetmeats and sticky rice, *banh Tet*. From the cornices hung red streamers with Chinese characters.

Bufillu clinked:

—Happy New Year, grunt.

—And to you, said Joey. But we should leave.

—Hold your horses, it's a ceasefire. Absolutely, positutely.

—But they don't like us.

XI

A red lantern glowed for Tet.

In back a door opened, and the same young woman came out: Kiêw in the flesh, whom they saw just now in the street. She had slipped into a high-necked *ao dai*.

There must be a rear entry. But was it conceivable this girl turned tricks? In the mind of any upright and redblooded American boy would be the idea: save her, rescue Kiêw from this hell, give her a husband and a clean productive life.

Joey remembered the jeep-ride in: the bamboo groves by the roadside; a peasant's large hat of plaited bamboo leaves; a heron in flight above a rice paddy. Despite the war's terrors this humble land with its grim and courageous people was bent on enjoying the Lunar New Year celebration. From hamlets set back in the bamboo thickets to broad Saigon streets lined with reddish barked tamarinds, camphor laurels, French villas nested among topiary shrubs: life in Vietnam would go on for another year.

Joey, beside his buddy, sipped the whiskey. Like in Xo Man that afternoon when his squad caught it: now he was thrown off his usual mistrust, watchfulness, by the call Stateside. Carlyne gone? Where? *Why?* What went on at the Rock Castle? Why so strange, Carlyne, such a strange woman? . . . Newell, my brother, if it was you messing with my wife . . . then I'll break your neck with my bare hands when I get home.

Outside in the shadows Tet fireworks had begun their celebratory rhythms. Loud detonations nearby; but for once it wasn't the war. Gone, Carlyne! . . . What did I do this time? I tried so hard in Bangkok, and I thought we did well, I felt we were happy . . . Firecrackers, skyrockets: Vietnam was a cancer patient dancing to a nickelodeon. The important thing is to have faith, so we told each other; but you haven't written me since our visit and I don't know *where you are* . . . Celebratory shots have a rhythm, but real ones have no rhythm. Oh, Carlyne, what did I do this time?

Mama-san barked an order.

—What's she saying? said Joey.

Bufillu sipped.

—She said hurry up and boomboom. Bet you the dude comes out with a grin.

—No, I think the dude uses the rear exit. But she's over there in the entry. Next?

—Fresh *ao dai,* type thing.

—If even. Look, Emmet, I don't like this. Let's split.

—We're okay. They just want to enjoy their Tet.

—Maybe okay, and maybe not.

—Look, what'd Kit Carson tell us on the road in? Their yearly blast has 'em paying off debts till the next. They've fought the foreign occupier for two thousand years, Chinese Han, Tang and Ming, French, Japanese, and last but not least our guy, Uncle Sam. You'd party your guts out too.

In the back alley bar the madame sat perched on her stool. A Far Eastern crooner sang a twangy romance. Then there were murmurs. There was a silken rustle. The grunt Bufillu eyeballed the beautiful *ao dai* profiled in the doorway, and she was direct about it, stare for stare. Well, she was dressed to kill with her small shapely breasts and her black silky hair reflecting the red Tet lantern. Took his breath away.

—She deserves a beau, said Bufillu.

—Don't worry, she has beaucoup. And this isn't the time or place for philanthropy.

Outside there was a terrific din. Blasts, like explosives. Were those fireworks? The walls shook. Joey perked up: it's toward Phan Dinh Phung, main north-south boulevard.

—Sounds like shots to me—he sat forward. —And not far.

At the next table a Vietnamese swigged his *ruou de* with a haggard air. A mesh fell on his forehead. A moment before Joey had thought: So you're gone, Carlyne? Then I don't care if I die tonight . . . But now he only thought: what's going on out there?

Nonchalantly Emmet stood up and went over to Kiêw. In his bulk he dwarfed the delicate woman.

—Com bick, she said. Combick!

The man laughed low, and his dark cheek glowed with light from a beer ad behind the bar.

—How much, honey? Do you know English?

He produced a roll of local currency. How's a cool 1000 p. sound for a half hour? Paw in the raw for a geegaw? as Thingum once said. No? She shook her head: dig deeper, G.I. So he did and—eureka, he drew out a crumpled ten dollar bill . . . With her dark eyes so intent and her lips pressed the VC deb didn't look quite so young.

Again there were explosions: they creased the wide night filled with festivities.

—Let's get out of here, said Joey.

But Bufillu had given her the money.

—Just be a sec'.

—Hell, get it done.

The red lantern trembled, and plaster dust sprinkled down. Mama-san stared at the outsized G.I., and the frail bar girl, and didn't budge.

Bufillu grinned round at his partner:

—I dedicate this to Uncle Ho.

—Look, Emmet, that doesn't sound like a child's rattle out there. Go on, go on.

No longer so gracious the prostitute brushed past the soldier and gestured him to follow.

—Finally—Bufillu laughed, moseying after her—I'll see a real VC, in the bush.

—She's a pretty one—Joey said and sipped his drink. —Ugh, shit-coolers, like kerosene.

XII

Well Kiêw was a cute kid from a distance. And now a second one came to pose in the doorway and this one looked over Joey, and looked: as though she were trying to hypnotize him, immobilize him with her bright *ao dai,* like animals in mating season. She would make him her own to play with as she liked, and then discard. And yes, her gaze got a rise out of him; she was goodlooking as the other, and he might have gone for her if only in revenge . . . But Carlyne's departure from the Rock Castle had stunned him, and he felt depressed, no sexual drive at all. He'd only waste his money if he followed her in back like Emmet.

So she came out and glided by him like a bamboo viper with her petite shimmery bulge, and tight slacks. But where to find a remedy and the right antivenin when such a woman stung? For her kind didn't go to the spy-infested light shows where her sisters went, *The Shack, Mimi's,* the country music blare in bars along Tu Do. They soaked their sensual bodies in pungent Western perfume, but this one gave off another scent, and it was less fetching. Call it eau de politique? Their made-up features were withered in the relentless sun of the war; they were a pearly seashell with its rainbow, and the real life and tenderness pecked out of them by gulls which mewed and scavenged in the back streets of Saigon. But this one's eyes had an onyx hardness, her cause.

In the back room Bufillu must be unbuttoning his drabs by now. Meanwhile Joey caught a small mustachioed man's eye in the entry. That one was not ARVN. Unsavory type . . . tense.

Lickety-split Bufillu would be going into his foreplay—to an accompaniment of gun rumblings in the suburbs, an ominous thunder in the distance. Boom! boom! Tet boomed. And the cot jumped under the big grunt and grumbled on its four stumps—not the 1000-p boom but the ten green Yankee-darrah boomboom. In the dark cubicle Emmet lay upon her and in a trice he was drained after delirium and drenched with sweat. She pushed him

up and off her and removed his limp hand from her breast. Done
deal.

—Okay, little woman.

Suddenly the night exploded in the narrow lane outside the
bar. It was pitch dark. Voices were raised: orders, cries. There
were flashes as feet whooshed past. And no more whores in view,
no bartender mama-san on her stool—it was like the ville that
day, Xo Man, when they took definitive flak.

A shot—poom! Second gunshot, loud shouts, from the room
in back!

Joey was jolted from the bad liquor and thoughts of his wife's
desertion. He lurched forward and scampered hands on knees
amid the flashes from outside. Three, four pistol shots thumped
and splintered the bar. At him? Missed him? Through the rear
door he did a jungle crawl; he looked for his partner. Maybe he
wouldn't mind dying tonight—five more months in-country
without Carlyne's love to sustain him . . . what for? Only not here:
not in this covey of VC. He glanced over his shoulder at the open
door as a flashlight probed the bar. After him? . . . Were there VC
commandos, barefoot, black pajamed, taking the Saigon streets?
How bad? Battalion scale infiltration? In any case it was a complete strategic surprise. How widespread were the sudden attacks? Coordinated across the city? the country? Everyone knew
NLF had no modern transport, and no logistics system as usually
understood. So the people, the Saigon population must have carried supplies, stashed arms and munitions in quantity; they safe-
housed and fed VC cadre?

—Emmet?

He heard a deep groan.

— Jo!

—Where are you?

—In here. Help me.

The big man lay alone on the cot. In his blood. He shivered.

—Hurt bad, Joe. Cain't move.

—I'll get you out.

—How? Caught a round and don't feel my legs.

More massive explosions barrelled and billowed across the
city. Rooftop fire creased the night air. So VC controlled the streets
with NVA on the outskirts? It was a battle for the airport, bridges,

police stations, communications centers? And if President Thieu fell tonight—?

—I'm scared. Just feel dead down there.

—I'll pick you up.

—I weigh too much. Oh-h-h!

Emmet Bufillu drifted unconscious as the tremendous din continued. Was it the Revolution?

XIII

Elite *dac cong* sappers carried on diversionary attacks at the U.S. Embassy, Presidential Palace and elsewhere; these were spectacular propaganda actions but done mainly to force U.S.-Saigon Command troop concentration. At the same time NLF forces were capturing priority munitions depots and distributing weapons to newly formed combat units of students, urban workers and youth, also Saigon army deserters. The NLF attacked and took over huge stores of light and heavy arms, ammunition, military vehicles and equipment, maintenance tools, tons of matériel. Near Tan Son Nhut Airport the Thanh Tay An arsenal alone provided five thousand guns for future battles.

Guerrilla units deployed for ambush patterns in the streets and set up permanent positions in various outskirts around airfields, major U.S. bases and military installations. In Saigon's 7th Ward VC attackers killed over a hundred G.I.s and burned an M-113 tank. At once in their communiqués the NLF identified its operatives by city district. The prime objective was a strategic entrenchment: the ability in future to hit U.S. bases by night and day from a permanent tunnel and trench complex. They would no longer be limited to attack and withdrawal before dawn when air support, bombing and strafing, became a factor.

Through a back exit Joey staggered and he was no longer distracted; now the horse was out of the barn door as in Xo Man. His great strength was wired by fear beneath Bufillu's 220 lbs. Pop! Barrabammm! Pop! Pop! Flames flickered in the street from an ARVN vehicle burst apart by an RPG. He waded out but ducked back: gray-blue pencil-flare rose eerily over downtown rooftops.

Orange tracers lined the Saigon night filled with smoke fumes.
And Bufillu's blood dripped and drooled from his spinal column
like a leaky spigot—from his fatigues sopped with clotting blood.
Pop! Boom-mm-m. Tinkle-tinkle, a C-4 charge shattered windows
in the next lane.

Artillery flashes rippled through the false daylight of the flares.
Joey strode on and tottered under the burden, doorway to doorway, on the way toward the river. Up ahead there were VC fighters
trotting through an intersection. The two uniformed G.I.s made
an easy target the instant they were seen, and the streets were
swarming with enemy. Deposit Bufillu in an entry? Come back
for him in the jeep? No, impossible. Then it was a POW camp in
the North for the troop or more probably a bullet in the head because Charlie didn't have time right now to think of prisoners.

Emmet's teeth chattered.

—Leave me, Bud. I'm done for.

—No, you're not. I won't leave you.

Fires raged in districts across the river and made a gray-gold
aura reflected in the dark water.

They came to the quay. Joey went on with Emmet over his
shoulder: the two of them outlined by flashes off smoke clouds
high above the wharves: toward the side street off Ba Son shipyard where they parked the jeep that afternoon. It seemed the
South Vietnamese capital, exempt till now from fullscale war, had
been overrun by communist forces. The pavement shook beneath
tanks and APCs moving through the quarters, as 1st and 25th Division troops, Saigon's defenders, went in a rush to redeploy on
a wider front and meet the enemy. But so stretched out and scat-
tered—they became a prey to attacks by VC mobile forces. Was
the United States Embassy in jeopardy? Even as Joey trudged and
almost lost his balance, tripping on a rut, he tallied the days he
must stay here. 143 more. Just survive this one and then 142 more,
142 plus a wake-up. Then ship home, in one piece. Then find her:
a reunion to remember. Clear up this mystery: the confusion . . .
But one step at a time: where did we leave the jeep? I'll find her
and strap her to a plow on Granddaddy's farm . . . She will bide
my will like an ox. Ah! There it is, still—fifty meters further on
the jeep waited with a glint in the darkness beneath the drift of
fumes . . . Get Bufillu installed, wipe my hands, and drive. Where

to? Field hospital. Where? Long Binh? 143, 142 . . . then forget this Vietnam sucker play forever.

XIV

He drove. Lights doused he flew into the gale wind toward Thong Nhut and the American Embassy. But he swerved; he ducked, suffocated by dust among an unclear troop movement as cavalry squadrons converged on defensive positions. The din of submachinegun fire, anti-tank rockets and fragmentation grenades, staccatto sniper fire echoed and reverberated on every side and flickered through the streets. One hand on Bufillu sprawled unconscious beside him, Joey steered with the other and sped beneath an armored helicopter which dipped low on recon. Machine gun fire, rockets, the deluge of automatic fire—it was deafening across the city.

Suddenly, by reflex, he veered when the chopper above them exploded in flames, its gas tank hit by a recoilless cannon, and nose-dived like a huge firefly.

Floor it now. This was a race to leave the citywide firefight before there were ambushes set up and roadblocks and the way became impassable.

Blood oozed from Bufillu's back where a bullet lodged in his spine. His head gave little bounces as the jeep stormed over ruts and potholes in its breakneck flight from Saigon.

Behind them the explosions roared and reroared across the city. Was the Embassy compound hit? Were the communications centers overrun? Bridges closed? Now eight-inch howitzers, tank guns, aircraft rockets led the way in a systematic pounding underway to fend off the all-out coordinated enemy offensive. From block to block there were residential areas reduced to rubble.

And then Joey stared up at a monstrous wall of fire as napalm cascaded like Niagara down on the densely populated quarters. People poured out howling through the streets in chaos. Now it was an infernal parade back the other way toward the downtown sectors. The jeep kept moving through an obstacle course always northward, out of the city. Would Saigon fall tonight? Would communist forces enter and surge down the main boulevards and into the Independence Palace?

And then they went on the outskirts in a pocket of strange calm and darkness. Behind them, in the rearview mirror, flashes shot up here, there into the sky. Smoke clouds massed and their undersides reflected the battle. The detonations thudded and echoed, bowling the horizon. Back there it was the apocalypse. The barrage fire and bright shocks quivered in the night sky.

Further on, along the road, they came to a tableau of terror. Out here was a weird silence; and in that silence an armored cavalry assault vehicle column stood motionless. It was ambushed by anti-tank rockets from the roadside, and now it smoldered. The lead ACAV loaded with mortar ammunition had been disintegrated by a command detonated mine. And then a furious annihilation went on. Dead troops lay strewn on the top decks by their machine gun mounts. Or else knocked off by rocket concussions they were flung on the ground where they still sprawled arms akimbo.

But the jeep bucked past and fishtailed a little to keep its grip on the road shoulder.

XV

Beside him Bufillu needed stabilizing and quickly—if it wasn't too late. He must have blood and intravenous fluids since he had bled profusely and soaked the shirt rolled in a bandage under his back. What chance would he have had at the airport under concerted attack? Who came first: a black infantryman, or the officers who were arriving wounded and worse at those logjammed medical facilities?

Joey peered into the night for a road sign. He saw not a soul as they passed by a strip village: a half mile of hootches in a row beneath the trees. There were no more groans now. Bufillu's life dripped quietly on to the metal floorboard. A few more minutes and it would be widowhood for a steady, faithful woman named Nora back in Atmore, Alabama.

Ah, road sign. Joey hit the light switch: Bien Hoa 7 K. Off. Highway 1 went north and east toward the coast. A sweet cereal odor came from the fields. Fragrances wafted from dikes and rice paddies . . . It was utter madness to ride at night through these dark stretches with their empty watchtowers, like monster insects, left here by the French. At any instant a mine might blow the jeep sky high. A VC sniper might strike: sharpshooter sent to hinder troop movement while his comrades struck at the capital. Invincible Viet Cong: ever ready to hate, fight, die if necessary for their tragic country. Cunning, resourceful, unafraid of a Cobra gunship, they crawled in their hole and waited another hour, a day, a century if they had to; and then came out again to take up where their fathers and grandfathers had left off. It was the long ·march forward inch by embattled inch toward total liberation. There was nothing more precious on earth, said their leader Ho Chi Minh, than freedom and independence.

But now tonight those stubborn fighters had come to a crossroads in their nation's destiny. They were making a qualitative leap in their long struggle for national liberation. And not only that. It seemed like a bifurcation in the route of world history as well. Now the victim, the smaller one, the true sons and daughters of Vietnam kept from their rights and political maturity across the centuries, had risen up. Like Oedipus at the crossroads of Delphi and Daulis they struck back at the tyrant's fury and sadistic arrogance. Tet '68 was a crossroads where the generations met for the test of force, and two epochs of humanity converged like ocean tides. Its forerunner had been a battle against the French colonialists at a place called Dien Bien Phu. No longer could the developed North count on taking the resources of small countries in the South with impunity and ease. For the great ascendant wave of the capitalist West was more and more a hindrance and negator of economic forces worldwide; and so a longer wave, greater in the long run and more sustainable, was rising up tonight to negate that negator.

All this caused Joey Gilbert driving along in the darkness north of Saigon to have a strange thought, an idea quite unlike him, a Newell-type take on things for a few instants. He was so excited: the old ideas and U.S. military frames of reference failed him and didn't seem to apply.—Ah! Could Carlyne hate what I'm doing here without saying so because it reminds her of what happened to her people, the indigenous tribes of North Carolina, long ago? Could she even have left the Rock Castle in early January without a word because of the story I told her: what I did to the female

cadre on the trail that night? Could politics have anything to do
with her contradictory behavior toward me and her going away?
Tonight I felt impotent and didn't want to touch a woman after
I got the news from home . . ., and now for the rest of Bufillu's
life, if there is a rest, he may not only feel but really be impotent,
paralyzed waist down. Might it, might all this come from being
on the wrong side of things? Are we fighting for the past in its
furious need to guarantee its rights against the future? Are we
all in bed with the world historic negator of new life forces and
of love? Are we outside the true human mainstream and being
used as pawns: lowly grunts with no real dignity being exposed
to death and worse by the masters of negation, deception, alien-
ation in Washington, D.C. —just as Oedipus was 'exposed' by his
violent father after an oracle said such a son would kill him; and
this was the curse of his family, the Labdacides; and it is the curse
of mankind as well, that, like it or not, life must go on? What
wonder then if a Joey Gilbert is impotent, and his true love leaves
him, their marriage unsustainable, if he is in bed with a negator
. . . Now tonight in Vietnam, as two mighty forces collided he and
his partner had wandered naively, like herded sheep sometimes,
into a Saigon crossroads—watch out!

And now, as he drove along in the darkness with sheet lightning in his rearview mirror—something flashed in his mind. It
was a vision of small things, a humble picture . . . yet it jolted him,
and seemed to blend in with the big thoughts of war and history
that were unlike him. Cassava roots on a table. Some bundled
pumpkin leaves. A rootstalk of ginger, and a tin of mountain rice.
A strange light, an energy came from the still life in a Xo Man
hootch, and it shook him. It was like a charge to last all his life.
And Joey thought: Am I going crazy?

XVI

Inside the army base slate-gray smoke billowed from the
ammo dump. It seems Charlie with AK assault rifle blasting had
come shrieking out of the night to body-bridge perimeter wire for
his fellow sappers. Before that a group of enemy combatants had

strolled free as you please through the main gate in 'borrowed' ARVN uniforms. And so the 199th Light Infantry assigned to guard the world's largest supply depot at Long Binh got caught with its pants down while frolicking amid a bevy of boomdee-boom girls, who were also VC, creating a diversion.

—Yes, soldier, yes—

Tonight the blond triage nurse had lost her perkiness. White top and slacks splotched with blood she glanced up from a Marine in a coma, whose skull was broken, and kept on applying a pressure bandage to the vertex of the bloody scalp. Beside her a surgeon held a Kelly clamp, but he was no less helpless as blood gushed from a second Marine's neck wound.

Now a new group burst in:

—Doc! Help!

—You gotta help us!

—It's bad, Doc!

Men squawked in panic even as they went through the motions of cardiac massage and mouth to mouth resuscitation. Their buddy stared up in wonder from a stretcher.

—Please help him.

—Is he dying?

The doctor had a glimpse and then pointed:

—That door.

The resuscitator drew up to spew out a mouthful of blood and vomit.

—Door?

—Graves registration, over there.

—No, Sir!

—Doc, no way! Chaddy just spoke to us.

—A few minutes ago!

—His last words. I haven't time.

Four more Marines came in with a stretcher caravan for the bunkered hospital compound in an uproar. Quickly the pert nurse looked at nerve, vessel, muscle damage; she glimpsed tissue viability, the patient's extremities, and physiological trauma effects; she hung I.V. fluids and blood for hypotensive patients. Medical staff ran here and there dealing with drivers and litter bearers: the local labor force also well infiltrated by VC.

They wheeled in Bufillu.

—It's my partner, he—

—Wait.

—Now, nurse.

In the harried mask her gaze was an apathy of blue eyes, and blond hair like sunlight in Southern California, where it never rains. Like everybody else she was a Stage III: movements mechanical by now, feeling dead inside. All the ideals and illusions, all the patriotism—made into a mockery by the war.

A doctor who seemed in charge swung open the treatment area door:

—I said no more dead bodies! Have a corpsman send them straight to Graves. Now I mean it! I wish this was a soap opera but it isn't!

The nurse bit her lip:

—We can't process the admissions.

A voice rang out:

—Hundred mgs Phenobarb!

—And I told you fug the civilians. Fug'em! I swear I'll court-martial anyone who takes the temp of a wounded civilian.

He went back in.

A Catholic priest moved about giving last rites to living and dead. There was blood on his cheek and blood on his sacramental fillet. He bent over a young soldier in shock whose thigh was torn apart, a shattered glob of gristle, ligament, gelatinous muscle, blood coagulated in a slab like jellied cranberry. The shredded lower leg hung from flesh and fascia in strips. A stump of the other leg lay to one side: severed above the boot.

—Seventy-five milligrams Demerol!

Medical equipment shelves, intravenous poles and bottles, bandages, first aid packages, cellophane wrapped butterflies and gear of every kind lined the triage area. In one corner a doctor sweated over closed cardiac massage, while a nurse ambubag-breathed the grunt who was dead at least for now.

XVII

At dawn after Bufillu's operation Joey went along the rows of medical cots which had men in traction, others merely malarial and heavy lidded, faces flushed with fever. They missed out on the Tet fun. A redheaded nurse bowed to suction a patient, and the blood splashed on her pus-colored skirt. By her side an infantryman vegetated, a pro forma admission: his bare torso was eaten by shrapnel, his eyes and brows bloated up, a horror, one arm a mass of crushed bones and blue flesh. What to do? Where to start?

A corpsman ran through from triage to an operating room or X-Ray Unit further in. The redheaded nurse looked upset and in a struggle to stay at it, remain functional; she emptied her suction bottle in a tin pail. Isopropyl alcohol tinged the odor from Graves Registration since the heavily sandbagged mobile refrigeration unit was so full it could only spill over corpses for all to see. There were heads burst open, truncated, for a good look at the brain. There were faces sheared away like a mask on a flange. There were bodies with the internal organs on full display. Somewhere a typewriter hunted and pecked to fill out death forms. Through the window by Bufillu's bed Joey watched a Marine hose down bodies by the light of the rising sun.

The big freezer generator purred and put a tremor in the walls. The night of war had worn itself down to a lull with the big guns intermittent now in the distance. Bare bloated bodies, eyes and lips tumefied, limbs fixed at rigid angles by rigor mortis and massive edema, a split tongue stuck far out; a shiny circus balloon scrotum with swollen penis erect and bold in death: —outside the window a masked graves detail used a nozzle to wash flies from mouth and nostrils, wounds. The refrigerator motor hummed. Joints snapped as two Marines slung a cadaver in a green plastic bag, fart sack, and zipped its zipper crisply, with a finality, amid the immense stench.

In another room the typewriter tapped its report on the honored dead—a taps without music.

XVIII

From hour to hour more came in delirous on their litters. It was too much really; it was way beyond the limit. The G.I.s groaned and coughed for air and dripped blood on the wooden floor. Wheeled past triage to a pre-op area they lay prone with their faces taped in an I.V. and chest-tube and EKG maze. They awaited their turn in the O.R.; or, if they just couldn't see their way to waiting that long, hey, they got a free ride home in a fart sack, tucked in for the night, zipped. Few knew much about it at this point as they lay there face up and looked mustered to death's attention on a stretcher. One wheezed and gurgled as he breathed through a trach.

Joey sat at Bufillu's bedside.

A few minutes before eight a.m. yet another unshaven doctor in scrubs walked the aisle between beds, under the reinforced roof, and noticed the grunt.

—Time to go, soldier.
—Who says?
—I do.
—And your name?
—I'm the ward master.
—Just tell me the deal and I'll leave.
—Shipment for Pfc. Bufillu soon as there's space.
—Where?
—Japan.
—Will he come back?
—No. His war has ended.
—Walk again?
—No.
—Never walk again?
—Never ever.

Joey nodded at his unconscious friend and turned to leave. For a moment he surveyed the long line of injured men, carts with medical supplies, equipment to dress and debride wounds. In this room some lay awake, eyes bright and anxious, as they tried to munch a dry breakfast. Hey, I'll see you Stateside, my man, unless a VC mortar plumps a direct hit and takes the rest of us out. Laugh, it's a laughing matter, this Nam of theirs. But tell me: that place in Oakland, DEROS delight? I was hoping to make it there all in one piece. Oh well . . . Black sutures shone on the inflamed wound flap. Pus and crud drained into a liter bottle. The Tet Offensive, oh yes it is, Six Sir. It seems 140 cities and towns have been attacked simultaneously, 37 of South Vietnam's 40 provincial capitals: an organized front six hundred miles long from the 17th Parallel to the Cau Mau peninsula. That's what I call organization. And it was done without modern transport or communications, with zero air power, but only backpacked supplies and an absolute secrecy, the surprise factor. A rat-pack NLF had stunned the most sophisticated military machine and technological apparatus in history. Such massive attack signifies: total popular support in urban and rural areas.

Joey paused by the cots. Now he had to go back out there, into it. Good times in Bangkok had lulled him to a happiness he couldn't really believe. But now that was over and he felt alert if deeply shaken like everybody else. After his walk to the river through streets gone out of kilter with Emmet on his back; then their wild jeep ride out into a dark silent plateau while the horizon was in flames behind them—he felt jolted. All this made him think: survive this, get home, seek *her*. Joey the seeker.

A wounded grunt mumbled from the fever:

—Yeah, Howie, I got to make it . . . You ever surf? Baby, watch me . . . pride of Malibu.

Trach tubes, respirators. Gurgle-gurgle, hum . . . Blood infiltrated the grunt's I.V. tube; he glanced down at his wrist and whimpered. Afraid of blood?

Every Saigon army zonal headquarters was hit hard, eight of eleven divisional headquarters, fifteen regimental headquarters, two U.S. Army field headquarters. Eighteen major targets were attacked in the capital: the American Embassy, joint U.S.-Saigon armed forces headquarters, South Vietnam naval headquarters. Saigon Radio was demolished. Forty-five airfields and eleven of fourteen major U.S. air bases were attacked. Many planes and helicopters were destroyed on the ground. It was said 200,000 U.S. troops in permanent position would be needed to secure Tan Son Nhut Airport alone from the 7-mile range of NLF rockets.

He'p me, honey, into my wheelchair . . . What a mess. Reddish brown Foley catheter. Pink urine bag hung from a bed. Hear the revved-up engines outside? Well I ain't got to go back into it. Say, you ain't Joey Gilbert? . . . Once I seen you clout one on TV, and I hearda' your dad, he was in the news a few days ago. Hell, that does me more good than a candy-striper! I thought on'y us hillbilly 'n factory workers' sons and city kids fought this filthy war fer' them filthy politicians safe in their golldarned 'zecutive suites in D.C. Didn't you, buddih'? Outside the window Motor Transport lurched by; it moved about the base fast. Well now I

call that sorta' poetic: war comes to Headquarters Battalion with
its fat fish and pogueys all in clover, the engineer corps, rear base
Riviera. Whoopty-do! Gott——dang!

U.S. First Cavalry (Airmobile) and Fourth Infantry Division,
173rd Airborne Brigade (half the mobile reserves) had to be re-
assigned, in pitch battle at this instant. Major roads were cut.
Strategic bridges were blown up. How many trucks and river-
craft were ruined? Military movement was shut down while the
skinny half-clad guerrillas held and strengthened their positions,
their trench and tunnel networks, strongholds, combat nests. In
Cholon, Saigon's vast Chinese sector, every rice warehouse was
seized and every center to husk and store rice occupied. The critical rice stocks were distributed among liberation forces and the
rural population in the event U.S. planes bombed storage centers
and tried to interdict foodstuffs.

In one bed a G.I. hung on. He had missile wounds with deep
chest and neck penetration. His neighbor gazed up at Joey and
said:

—Wish I had some apple pie à la mode.

So all the chatter in the media about military progress, increased popular support, light at the end of the tunnel—it was all
bunkem, a Pentagon myth. Here was more humiliation after the
Pueblo affair for the world's greatest power and super gendarme.
And there were mass ARVN desertions apparently; one unit even
took along its tanks. There was encompassment by new, closer
and better armed VC bases: heavy rocket and mortar barrages
on every key U.S. military installation; on munitions dumps and
petroleum reserves, communication and transmission centers,
air strips, radar technology and port infrastructure. All this took
years and billions of dollars to put in place. Much was ruined in
a few hours.

The war leapt from rural hide-and-seek into the cities. And
there would be no more safe areas for the Americans: rather, a
permanent VC presence on the Saigon outskirts, and the ability
to attack at will. Jungles, mountains, cities, everywhere it was
war; it was fullscale, to the death, as U.S. forces lost mobility and
strategic concentration: offensive capacity. The entire multibillion
dollar ultramodern infrastructure superimposed on Vietnam was
now fissured in its foundations. Logistical centers were in disarray. Air support for ambushed platoon and company sized forces

on the ground were suddenly decalibrated. All felt unsure, and it was. Materièl by the hundred-ton batches had been blown to bits and sent to the four winds.

When the NLF was staggered in turn, it went back to its bicycles and foot runners. But where could the gigantesque technological monster go—after it was dealt a blow unthinkable just one day ago? There was the official story of a U.S. retaliatory victory; there were lies and more of same by MACV brass at their Five O'clock Follies press conference.

Zip up the green bag, boys. *Disposition of remains: transferral to U.S. Naval Hospital in Da Nang for preparation and removal.* No, it don't rain too much in sunny California, that's a fact. So long to you, buster. Yay! That USO show at Christmas . . . that movie star's, you know . . . I mean her . . . whew! Now lemme' at 'dose gooks. Medcap. 'O' Club.

Yip!

Joey gave his partner a last nod, of respect, and walked out.

XIX

The air of the military base smelled like puke.

On his way beyond last armored defenses Joey slowed the jeep and stared at a sight by the roadside.

Perhaps a hundred enemy dead waited for the earth delvers. A gray cloud of flies hovered over all the putrid flesh. The bodies were frail and tattered: men and women stacked in mounds after they paid the full price since nothing is more precious than freedom and independence, which their people intended to win.

The U.S. soldier drove past in the jeep. It picked up speed.

Joey thought of the ARVN guide's stories the day before: of Tet and traditional celebrations. The chatty guide had mentioned a Tet or New Year's offensive that was launched way back in 1789 to drive out 200,000 troops of the Chinese emperor Ch'ien-lung. This was achieved by a leader named Nguyen Hue who shook his 'cotton shirt and red flag' in the face of Confucius for whom rebellion is the worst of all sins. That Tay-son Revolt, a great peasant uprising, was a source of pride for the Vietnamese. Nguyen Hue had led an epic struggle not only against the Chinese occupiers; he also defeated the Trinh lords in the north and the Nguyen lords in the south . . . Their ARVN guide seemed to know a lot about it.

This was the first day of spring. But a curtain had fallen over it: there would be no parades, feasts and festive dances, family get-togethers to start a hopeful New Year. The spotless house, the apricot and plum blossoms as symbols of regenerative nature; the budded *hoa moi* branches brought inside where they burst into bloom, and were good luck tokens, before mortars and rockets put on another kind of Tet ceremony—all that was now on hold if not spattered about in places where civilians were hit.

Ong Tao, the kitchen spirit, has flown up to give his annual report to the Jade Emperor, ruler of gods, in the sky. Ong Tao left pretty quick and forgot to get his 'lucky gifts', fruit, honey, cash wrapped in red rice paper; a paper fish to ride on the long journey: when he provided an account of Vietnam's household.

It seems some pickled vegetables, fried watermelon seeds, and *banh chung*—rice cake in banana leaves, sweet bean paste and pork in the center—went to waste this year. Greetings penned in ancient *chu nom* script for the sake of friends and neighbors went undelivered. Ritual visits were unpaid. Midnight firecrackers to shoo away the evil spirits were not heard.

The clear slate, the arguments put to rest, the paid off debts with a little money left for the children—all this took on new meaning at Tet 1968.

Chapter Eight

I

Everywhere and always life goes on affirming and negating.

Quantity converts to quality and vice versa.

The downtown Durham streets were filled with processed tobacco scent on a hot, hot afternoon toward the end of June. Inside a furnished room on Lamonde behind East Campus there was a gold band along the wall. Sunlight had been beating down through the day and turned the dreary room into an oven. No breeze stirred the cloying tobacco smell. Lint hung in a yellow column like an hourglass.

The afternoon wore on quietly. There were no voices outside the window. No passersby. Now and again a car came past.

Alone, panting like a wounded animal, the young woman in labor lay on her left side. Beneath her the sheet, bunched at the middle, was drenched with sweat and other fluids, a blood-tinged mucus which frightened her, discharged from her vagina. The baby was pushing on the neck of the uterus, opening the cervix.

When the pain came again, bending her in two, it was terrific after seventeen hours of contractions. Her face was twisted by the effort as she hung on grimly and tried to stay aware of what was happening to her. After it started, a few minutes before eleven last night, there were times when she could stand up and pace and try to forestall the griping pain. But the strong cramps came in her belly and back as her uterus tightened and relaxed to help open the cervix and push her child out through the birth canal.

Now they didn't leave her, and she cried out in a kind of wonder—ah! just how far can this go? Oh! oh! the pains outdid themselves—aaacchh, she coughed for breath, and then bit down hard on a twist of bedsheet by her head. Her body quivered and she thought: Push, push! . . . No, I don't want that baby out here, I'm scared if it comes out here! . . . Then she shook her head and mumbled a little to herself, talking out loud. But, at the height of it, for this time, her drum-taut features twitched and she gave a sob. When the pain became too much she couldn't help herself any longer. She lost her grip altogether and writhed on her back, on her side. She pushed, she pushed, she *pushed,* because push she must.

II

Did she lose consciousness? She reemerged. When the vice-grip let go of her pelvic region for a moment it was like bliss and she raised her head bathed in sweat, cautiously, and looked around. She was a stunned doe caught in a trap, in shock. Dehydrated to the danger point she reached for a pot of warm water on the night table, and splashed herself with it as the handle bumped the bedstead.

Quiet house. It was best if the landlady didn't know what was going on.

The room, with its double bed, dresser, small alcove, was torrid despite a fan. Carlyne looked at the alarm clock: nearly fourteen hours since her sac burst: the membrane surrounding the baby during pregnancy. Then fluid soaked the mattress beneath her abdomen. And this too scared her; though she knew what it was: she had spent time in East Campus library reading up on what was in store. Not once did she see a doctor or have an exam during her pregnancy because all this must be her secret, hers alone! And there must be no witness as to the timetable, no medical record anywhere. So she resolved. But she was also intelligent, and once thought of trying to become a doctor, a pediatrician to her people down in Pembroke. So she was able to read up, and prepare.

Within twelve to eighteen hours after the amniotic sac broke, the infant must come out; otherwise, she risked infection.

She wished there could have been a friend here to help her. Last weekend her neighbor, a grad student in economics, had gone off to summer haunts and pleasures, Myrtle beach and beyond, like other students in an exodus as the school year ended. So Lamonde with its nice old homes filled with student lodgers was empty now. There was no one around to assist the delivery, or call hospital emergency if she got in too bad trouble. Also she had no phone. Could she drag herself to the window if she had to, and shriek in panic down to the street and hope somebody nearby would hear and take pity? No, no; die first if she had to, but do this act in secret—like that other act when she wrecked her life. If she had to die, herself and this sorry child of adultery she bore in her big distended belly beneath her breasts a couple pounds heavier, lumpy and tender, tingling, throbbing, and ugly, the area around her nipples turned larger and darker—if she died then it didn't matter anyway. Sorry to make such a mess.

—Aïe! aïe! Will I really die? Get onto my feet somehow and drink, drink, slake this thirst!

There was a mirror on the night table but she was afraid to look at her red, red face. The tongue in her mouth was like a dry stick. Just breathing was no joke either: she took rasping jerky breaths which lifted her head from the pillow. And then she lay back and thought: yes, I know it, this is the end. Well, good for me. I deserve it.

III

The date of this child's conception was probably September 19, 1967; she was not likely to forget it. After a few weeks her body was changing; she missed a menstrual period; she had morning sickness as hormonal changes occurred: as the single cell of her baby became an embryo maybe a half inch long, weighing less than an ounce; and it developed a head and body, brain, eyes, inner ears, mouth, digestive system, arms, legs, and a new heart started to beat in Carlyne's breast.

As the fall days went along and the weather turned cooler

she often felt tired and needed more rest. This was due also to her mood. For who could tell the depths of her depression at the turn of events, and the way things had gone for her in the Rock Castle?

Then in December the baby began to kick inside her, as the embryo was now a fetus which could do things: turn its head, squint and frown, make a fist. Teeth, lips, genitals were beginning to develop; and so Carlyne had to urinate more often as the uterus enlarged and pressed on her bladder. Little things upset her then, even put her in a rage at men, life, herself; but she had to keep it all in and preserve appearances inside the Rock Castle. The one good thing was that morning sickness began at last to give her a break. But she could hardly stand living at the Gilbert place anymore and made up her mind to leave. First, however, she must go see her husband in Bangkok.

No words could express the misery and fear she took over there with her, and felt by his side during those ten days. For one thing, as the baby was completing itself inside her, eyelashes, fingernails, toenails as well as vocal cords and taste buds forming—Carlyne was beginning to look pregnant. How to hide this from Joey? With horror she saw a yellowish fluid, colostrum, ooze from her nipples, and what if he saw this? He was a big fool but not totally so. And when he looked at her enlarged breasts and the areola around them grown larger, darker? And there was even a strange dark line which ran down the center of her stomach: due she supposed to the pregnancy, if not some cancer or punishment for her sin.

Worst of all was the mental anguish because it was a lie, a lie, a lie that drove her to him in Thailand. Irrationally she wanted him to be the father after the fact, and she would try to play that comedy till the end. Also, now that she had lost him, as she believed—Carlyne began to know she loved him.

And so she went there despite her mental and physical pain and was able to make her husband happy in Bangkok. She hid the truth and shifted her veils with the skill of an Isis; she made it through the days, and all the lovemaking; though the baby was moving by now: it was the *quickening,* as her reading since then told her; and often at the worst moment she felt a fluttering of wings inside her, or like bubbles rising. But her pleasure with Joey was a desperate one, like a feast in time of plague. Lust before death.

Then she left him and came back. And she made her escape a few days later. In the first week of January she took a bus back across the state to Durham. She had to get away from that Rock Castle of despair: with its retired church bishop a little mad as he leered at her; and the gallant 4-Star General, Maximilian Doan, nicknamed Thanks-a-Million by Lemon because he was such a tightwad, besides having the hots for Lemon Gilbert in her early teenage. And then there was Emory Gilbert, Joey's dad, the famous author.

She left them without a word. Goodbye, take that at least. But she felt bad about Lemon and Cindy.

Then Carlyne came here to Durham: where she had been to college, and met and lived with her husband. She came to wait out the second and third trimester of her pregnancy; and then she'd see. She would not touch her husband's money because she had no right to it; also they could trace her that way; but she had a few hundred dollars of her own: saved from a college allowance left in trust by her father, Judge Vick.

The weeks of springtime went more smoothly. She read; she walked to Five Points, or visited the Gardens. She felt her baby active inside her, like a fluttering, as it woke and slept beneath the white greasy vernix coating that protected its skin.

She knew in March, the sixth month, her child could open and close its eyes, hear sounds, cough, hiccup. There were kicks high in her abdomen or low near her bladder. She had a sudden sharp pain in her groin, ligament pain, as uterus support structures were being stretched and caused her cramps. There were dark streaks, stretch marks on her abdomen, breasts, thighs. This hardly mattered: was she trying to please anyone? Inside her the baby had red wrinkled skin and moved more vigorously and often.

And often she was tired. As for her mood during this pregnancy—why talk about it? Her body was big. She had hemorrhoids. No indignity would be spared her; nor would lower back pains, shortness of breath as the uterus moved up and pressed against her breathing muscles, bowel irregularity. The baby—she knew from reading—could now hear sounds from outside.

And then it was the ninth month. If things were normal, the child would be fully developed by now at 6 to 8 lbs., and have smooth skin. The bones of the head were smooth and supple for delivery. The baby's head was turning down toward the cervical opening, and its feet were up under its mother's ribs.

Once again Carlyne needed to urinate often since the baby had dropped and pressed on her bladder. But she could breathe at least. Inside her the child might be two feet long. Soon, now, soon she would give birth, and this would be over, if all was normal. But she didn't know what would happen—she had such a shame in her, a shame the size and weight of a cannonball, she was afraid to see a doctor; afraid even to go for a visit down in Robeson County with her Lumbee kinfolk and her Aunt Lovedy.

IV

Now she had a sudden spasm: more nausea, dizziness . . . Did she faint? There was a gold light across the wide bright-leaf fields of her childhood . . . but here, as she came to her senses again, the baking streets of Durham were filled with sickly fumes of the tobacco factory. Carlyne couldn't breathe. Once more in the furnace heat she lost consciousness, and her mind swirled with images from her girlhood: summer vacations on an uncle's farm west of Lumberton; the long dusty farmlands where the Lumbee River (whites called it Lumber) flowed. She went by her mother's side. Oh, Momma . . . aïe! This pain! She surfaced to the pain. Was it preeclampsia? Then good night. The anguished thoughts surged in her mind, push! push now, push, girl! Was it edema, and blood pressure soars? Push! Albuminuria, decreased reflexes, headache, vision disorder like she just had? Oh! No one on earth cared if she lived or died; they cared about themselves after all, so what difference did it make? She recalled her reading as she might for a test: ah, ah, then came toxemia . . . Push, push! Thrust? Harder? Oh, eclampsia, convulsions, coma, death! Aïe! Please God this pain! Aïiiieee! She shivered the length of her body. It was time to die. Push, goddammit, push! Oh, oh—Aunt Lovedy had a cousin who died young, septicemia in childbirth; she lost consciousness one night and didn't wake up. Oh let it end, Lord, Lord. Let me and this child of shame die for the benefit of all. Remove this cup, I don't want it! Let me die like Aunt Lovedy's cousin but just get it over with. Push! . . . Oh-h-h.

A hundred times the first months she was on the verge of going to have the thing aborted. A dozen times she walked out the door with the idea of throwing herself under a train. But she couldn't do it—not from fear; it just wasn't in her nature. And did she think lovingly of boys' and girls' names? Yes, she let herself fantasize at times that all would be well. So would she call this child: Shame? No; she had a name for it if it was a girl.

V

Again the crazed suffering went away. Dazed, she looked around—too afraid, too cowed to maneuver her body against the big ache after eighteen hours on the rack. She was thirsty and exhausted. Now she raised her head but was unable to make out what was going on between her legs. What if the baby wanted to come out askew: shoulder first? Then a doctor was a must if she hoped to make it through, survive, with her child. But there would be no doctor—because the circumstances of this baby's conception were so terrible, nobody must know, ever, and no trail must be left that would help Joey find her. There could be no helper to heat water, provide clean linen, cloths for wiping, towels.

In the moment of relief she felt a new sensation: a vaginal pressure, stretched, unlike the spasmodic contractions. She levered up and tried to see. Had the head come out? On her back now, knees up, though less oxygen got to the baby that way, said her studies—Carlyne felt around. She reached down hesitantly and touched: the warm, soft, cauled occiput, the infant's crown.

So maybe the worst was over? The expanding cervix could cause more pain than the actual birthing . . .

The infant had crowned. Now what? It might wait there on the threshold for a long time, two, three hours, she knew. But what if it didn't move any further? What if it didn't come out? Then what would she do? If it was unable to breathe? Maybe asphyxiated? Again she panicked: like in the early morning hours when there was a dull sound, like a water-filled balloon bursting, and then the bloody fluid drenched her legs and the landlady's threadbare rug. Luckily Carlyne was on her feet at the time since this eased the pain . . . That scared her—the small thud, and then blood,

blood. But the bloody stream stopped brusquely, and then she felt better.

VI

When did the infant begin to breathe? Maybe never? Did breathing start while it was stuck there unable to move? Oh, Sir, won't you budge? What to do now? Carlyne fumbled under her: stimulate it? nudge it forward? Try to pull it out by the neck? Let's see: wasn't there advice on this in the obstetrics text she studied? She couldn't remember. And she couldn't really see or move very well to get hold of a facial mirror in the night table drawer. Why hadn't she thought of that? She couldn't afford oversights! Oh, God, do I need a C-section? Not long after her arrival in Durham she heard of a sorority sister, in Kappa Alpha Theta, who gave birth by Cesarean delivery.

Now she shook her head back and forth and the sweat dripped from her and she knew there was a grave danger of dehydration. She had a burning thirst. So she reached for the warm water on her bedstand, and, at the onset of hysteria perhaps, clutched it wrong and knocked the pot off so the water spilled on the floor with a bang. Good going. Now how to get up and fetch more? First have a look at the baby's crown and see the state of things down there. She hadn't thought to have a mirror handy because the sight of all this scared and repelled her and deep, deep down she didn't want to see this baby come out, no, she wanted it to stay inside and not come out here ever.

She tried to take her own pulse . . . so weak, so distant.

Then Carlyne laughed. Mildly hysterical between contractions she thought of a birthing manual's passage on the joy and sense of fulfillment mingled with wonder. How nice. A mother, whoopee. Ever since the start when her menstruation stopped and she had nausea and vomiting, then as the months went along and she could feel fetal movements and seemed to hear the fate in a prenatal heartbeat . . . she had not been living a proud experience 'integral to her nature', but, rather, she hated the whole thing and feared it and felt the life inside her give a shudder of pain in reply to her own.

It was certain now: caught in the obstructed muscles, the pinkish bulge like pads down there, a child was trying to get out but was being strangled by the too tight opening. Despite all the efforts of her stomach and loins to thrust it forward and expel it—a small blackish head or hand opening and shutting as if to grasp onto life was jutting forth from the vulva. Oh, please, please for my mother's sake and my own: let me come out!

VII

Ah! Then she gasped and threw up the reins. So violent were the renewed contractions that she gave up all resistance and plunged into the unknown horror a few moments away. Let this finish anyway and end her cursed existence. Still Carlyne tried to breathe slowly and deeply. But no, she could not; her breaths came in staccatto bursts. Feel pain, then push, pain, then push. She knew it was a deformity of some kind, or just vesicular tissue; it leered up at her from its flukish neck. Oh! how could this poor child hope to come out normal? Pain, ha! ha! ha! ha! push it, pain, push it down! Was she feeling the tiny body turn and seem to maneuver on the uterine verge? Her face was a tragic mask in the dusk of the furnished room, as she reached down with a groan and touched the head in movement sideways. Fluid flooded the bed and crumpled sheet in a reddish wash. Had she urinated all over herself and the baby? Could it drown? The head! She palmed, she palpated the tender emergent head. But it didn't cry! Oh, oh! Can't it breathe? Won't it cry? Shouldn't it wail out gamely like other newborn infants and stake its claim to the air? Wangh! Wangh! Wannngh! Why didn't it cry? Ha! ha! ha! ha! ha! She laughed wildly and shouted out in her spasm, the unthinkable pain. Ha! ha! ha! ha! Slap the godforsaken thing and *make* it take a breath? But the soft round ball just dangled from her, face down. She raised up, oh! oh! Don't let it drown, face hung down in the muck and mucus and blood! She struggled up and bent herself forward and tried to see. Ah! ah! I can't—the head stuck out shiny, blue in the penumbra, blue. It won't cry out or catch a breath! My dead baby! Oh, no, no! She shivered with fear and poked around down there and dabbled with sticky fingers.

Not pee but blood, clots, mucus inundated the sheet. She made a big effort to hoist up and turn her legs spread wide to a safer place. Already it had drowned. Yes. The poor, tiny defenseless nose and mouth dripped with gore and so couldn't get into their functions.

Aïeee! Aïeeeee! Push, push! She pushed down—no longer in her right mind, shaken about like a monstrous Raggedy Anne stuffed full of nerves; and nasty nature was oozing out at the seam. Die! Let us die! I'll sizzle in hell but please end these cramps and pangs! Suddenly the smell: now it seemed she had defecated and the stench must reek to the street. The bed was immersed in blood, fluids, clots like slices of raw liver, the horrific smell, feces. She leaned over the edge and vomited along her swollen pendulous breast and her arm. Through pregnancy her anxiety had built and built up until she dragged herself in the bathroom and threw up the day's overload of stress. Let me go! she cried, let me go! Now in her paroxysm she pushed and twisted and writhed, and she didn't care what happened. The infant squirmed and rotated to adjust its shoulders to her vagina; it turned its head toward the widest side to try and work its way.

Still there were no cries. There was no hint it lived, and breathed. Aïe! ha! ha! Let me out! Aïe! In the hundred degree heat of the furnished room like a pressure cooker, in the airless late afternoon, she screamed. Sickly sweet 'bacca scent floated through the Durham streets. And the swirl, and the whirl, and the distant images of her girlhood aswim in the cold, dark, clean Lumbee River on a hot, hot summer day, hey watch out there! Copperbelly moccasin'll killya'! . . . killya'! . . . *killya'!* ha! ha!

She lost consciousness.

VIII

There was a sense of being torn, ripped in two. Maybe it was a good thing Carlyne didn't have a mirror to hand and see the package of skin and bones hanging out of her, and her own features decomposed and animal-like with the pain, in such a wild abandonment only the suffering humanity seemed to remain. And down below among her pouches and rolls of fat, mucus on her thighs and pubic hair while a dark blood dripped on the sheet: the infant's head lolled out mouth open where it hung from the vulva.

Yes, maybe it was a good thing Carlyne was only semiconscious in these instants and didn't try to see and think: because her fingers were down there on their own, coaxing, applying pressure in the right places, all by instinct, like mothers for how many million years.

And then:

—*Ainnain'!*

The lint-filled column of light had drawn back over the sill. In the window there were leaves, boughs, an old oak tree across the street. The gold bar shrank back from the wall and scene inside.

For a moment there was silence. Then:

—*Ainnn 'hu-hu' ainnainnnnn 'hu'!*

Carlyne opened her eyes. The crisp whine of the newborn child came to her across a great space. For another moment she lay propped against the bedstead. But the baby's cries called out to her and calmed her a little. Now she had work to do, but she feared a first look at what was going on down there—carnage, she thought, red brown yellow, Joey Vietnam—down between her knees. But the baby once started kept on. It cried; it clicked, and seemed to choke and ask for help on her part, some needed response right now despite her howling pain and her panic.

She came to, and jolted forward: she wanted to get one matter straight at least. Check on it. With an elbow she levered herself and leaned forward, and gazed—on a parcel of wrinkled flesh which wasn't dry (some got born dry, shrivelled up, she knew, when the forebag burst too early). But it was blue among the wide blanching folds of its mother's flesh. Coming out along with it from the yawning circular cavity was a spitting excrement—plus the blood and fluids.

It was a girl. Scared by the blue-gray color Carlyne reached and took it in her spread fingers and turned it over. Wet, slippery. Be careful! Support the neck . . . It was a small sack of blood and nerves—a big head: too big—with parts looking so globular, dislocated, and fine skin so sensitive, she wondered if the body would hold together. The head was wide as the shoulders. A stick arm raised up to conduct the first notes of its symphony of life.

Carlyne patted. She stimulated her daughter anxiously when the blue tinge didn't turn to pink. Oh such a rush of love, such a

frantic care—now a brute pity guided the new mother's movements. She had feared to have a boy; that seemed even worse to
her; and so no masculine names came to mind that she liked. She
was in such a savage resentment against the male, not to say hate,
she didn't want to see a boy march out of her womb. Ah, a female; and maybe the fact saved her after all. This girl she would
name Rhoda after one of her ancestors: Rhoda the angry, Rhoda
the stubborn and daring one, in her will to survive . . . No; as a
few last griping pains came over her, not as horrendous now; as
she lay back a moment utterly exhausted—she might not have
tried to do her best for a boy child . . . O Rhoda Strong the stubborn—passionate woman of her race . . . No; she might have just
let it die away there on the bed before her, and herself as well . . .?
But no, Rhoda Strong Gilbert, you exist, a little bit of destiny on
the march now in your blue and pink uniform.

IX

But the tiny thing was choking badly. It stiffened in Carlyne's
fingers and turned purplish. So she patted the back some more.
Hm, that wasn't it . . . What else could she do? Ah! A greenish
substance caught her eye as she wiped off the face with a towel:
like flecks of pea soup around the mouth. She held the head and
shoulders in one large strong hand while she swabbed the green
brownish stuff away with the other. No good either! It was inside the mouth, oozing out! The child was being strangled by it,
had a spasm . . . Its windpipe was clogged up. Ah! meconium, it
was called meconium; that was in her reading. If the infant as-
pirates meconium into the lungs it can strangulate and die. This
was fetal waste matter and bile, mucus, 'desquamated'cells in the
mouth. Right away she had to clear it out! The umbilical cord allowed maybe a foot of play—Carlyne leaned to the face, sucked at
the small mouth and then drew back and spat forth a tarry mass
which was brown or blackish when not diluted by amniotic fluid.
And then again. With her own mouth she suctioned chaws of meconium which were obstructing her baby's airway.

Next thing! . . . Still connected to the child, she had to clamp
and tie off the umbilical cord. She had to cut it! But how? She

stared down at the membraneous chain luckily not lacerated, but entangled, knotted, and looped round the neck at delivery. A simple piece of string, a shoelace would serve the turn as it did for birthing mothers across the earth. But she had no string on hand, or laces since she always wore sandals. She had overlooked such basic needs because she was all alone and deeply depressed. When her life fell apart, one autumn night at the Rock Castle, she lost heart and didn't want to think about the future. Also, she was running low on money and didn't know what she would do in a few weeks: so her baby and she could eat and pay the landlady.

Carlyne was on her own. Maybe the birth ordeal saved her.

X

She straddled the edge of that bed like a morass and was able to walk, dizzily, to the window. She held the infant low by her spread legs, and could see how she was bleeding. This scared her and she almost fell. Again she thought: will I die? But there was no time for thinking since a tender helpless life needed her just now. The baby cried and clutched at air while she bowed to cradle it in the crook of her arm. Then with her free hand she yanked up the Venetian blinds.

But suddenly she began to pant and heave with a new onslaught of uterine contractions. Why? Why now? In her panic over what to do she placed her baby on the broad sill and began fumbling with the blinds' heavy twine to tie off. But then she bent forward and saw more blood gush onto the floor. This shocked her. Will I die?! . . . She gave a shiver and whined out loud:

—Cut the cord!

Cut it! But with what? Too distraught to see the danger of her baby balanced on its back across the second storey window sill, she looked around, behind her and found no tool. She hadn't thought to have a kitchen knife ready, let alone scissors sterilized over a flame. And now it was too late to go get them because she was attached with her frantic blue infant to the tight square knot she had tied in the twine. Aïe! With her teeth then! Bite into that human tissue with her teeth!

She leaned with a whimper and made to chomp down on the umbilical cord the child's side of the clamp. But just then the cord started to move! It was eerie. Of its own accord the tube slid slowly, slowly . . . What was it? Something else in the obstetrics text—but she forgot details. What? Well, here it came—it had to come out of her? Oh, oh it slithered like a snake from between her thighs. She turned to her bite into the cord—on the wrong side of the knot! If she bit there the child would bleed to death since nobody was on hand to help them.

But at the same instant she stared in horror as a large, dark red, rope-veined mass came bulging forth like a monstrous birth through her distended flesh. Carlyne shuddered as the grisly thing came out into the daylight. Again she pushed down. She tried to squat but could not—tied to the Venetian blinds. Her baby lay face up precariously on the window sill. It could fall out into the front yard. She pushed, she pushed: disgusted by yet one more hideous thing. At last it plopped before her like a ghastly pancake and hung from the twine; it too dripped blood from its frayed ragged ends onto the floor.

The placenta turned with a pearly hyaline sheen in the late afternoon light. A good hand's span in diameter, thick, disk shaped, it looked haggard and bad with a yellow-white ring of necrosis around the edge. The fetal organ seemed to grow old as its task came to an end. The underside was like chopped liver. The taut surface shone: where fetal vessels permeated the membrane. The cord stuck up in the middle from under pale bluish velamentum. Ah ha, now she remembered: the afterbirth. It hung there before her like a monstrous catcher's mitt made of guts.

Carlyne shook a little and returned to the repulsive cord. Her baby still lay on the sill. She leaned forward and made to bite in hard, but stopped herself with a shriek. Wrong side! Then she grunted and gnashed on her side of the clamp into that gelatinous sort of sausage with its two arteries and a vein; she spat out blood and mucoid tissue from her mouth. She bit, tugged, shredded the tough cord with her hands and teeth until finally it pulled apart.

But she gasped. The child lay free on the sill. Rhoda wobbled, helpless, right at the edge, all ready to fall off.

XI

In early evening the tobacco aroma filled the streets smelted by summer heat. Inside the furnished room on Lamonde the young mother, dead on her feet after twenty hours in labor, took a glance at this place where a hurricane had passed. Swampy bed, stained window shade, all sorts of things strewn on the streaked floor, blood, blood, blood—it was a still life of a paroxysm. Later on she would clean up and make order. For the moment she slumped in a corner with a bath towel rolled between her legs and another wrapped round the infant at her breast. Pink, fatty limbs could relax at last after so much pain and frenzy. Tiny fingers reached and touched things perceived as part of the new self: the breast. Eager lips sucked at a first ambrosial drip and had a taste of this sweet life of ours.

The woman sighed with her eyes closed. Carlyne's head rested against the wall. For a minute she let herself go and thought: what if my husband was here to see this wonder? What if he could be with us, we three together? What if Joey Gilbert stood here in this room marvelling at our skill, our courage which equals his, an athlete gone to fight in a war? But she winced and put away such ideas. She had no right to them—and thought of the true father's name; and her face changed from tender, contented, to a mask in the shadows. Brow knit, lips in a silent curse, she tried not to think, or cry.

Then she placed the child beside her for awhile, its little form set on a pillow. She stretched her sore limbs, her body one deep ache, across the floor. She closed her eyes.

Carlyne's features smoothed as she drifted off. Curled in a fetal position she slept—the sleep of the young.

On its own the infant was breathing—sort of navigating off-shore, in the shadows. Its features wrinkled; it gave a pink grimace. What a thing to come out here that crazy way into this chaos of a world.

Carlyne Gilbert and her hour-old daughter, Rhoda Strong, slept their restorative sleep in the silence, as night fell.

XII

Carlyne's first weeks living at the Rock Castle with Joey's people had been her happiest time perhaps after the day in April 1955 when her mother died. With Lemon Gilbert she played dolls again, and helped put on a puppet show.

Her father was the Honorable Fitzhugh Foster Vick from Kinston. When the Judge died in 1953, he left his women exposed to a campaign by the town's gentry against the dark enchantress, Carlyne's mom. That woman came where she wasn't wanted: a poacher from the land of the Lumbee in Robeson County.

Judge Vick loved her. He loved his homemaker the way Joey Gilbert would her daughter ten years later. As a special judge assigned to Superior Court circuit he had presided over the trial when Selva Locklear (Lockileer) lost her land due to a Lumberton jury. It was a 'tied mule', or 'hams in the corn crib' type of court action: White versus Indian land dispute to get hold of tribal acreage. The trial took place in early 1942 amid anti-Japanese hysteria following Pearl Harbor: when 110,000 Japanese-Americans were herded into concentration camps; and the U.S. Armed Forces upheld its Jim Crow system—segregated mess halls, separated Red Cross blood banks. Soldiers 'colored' like Carlyne's mother were stowed in ship holds, like slave voyages, but this time to go fight in the war against Fascism—and for corporate gains: the wartime situation so positive for business (10.8 billion profits in 1944 up from 6.4 billion in 1940) that company executives called for a permanent crisis with stringent controls, a freeze on workers' wages: and from this came anti-communism, the Cold War, also a great boon for capital. While Washington planners and diplomats maneuvered for postwar domination, President Roosevelt did not prioritize steps to save Jewish lives. Outsiders were scapegoated. It was the American way.

A Lumberton jury felt the same and left Selva Locklear's family on the street. There were no safeguards; it was racism. But Fitzhugh Vick took Selva to share his home in Kinston where she served as housekeeper and bore his only child.

They might have got married. The U.S. Government had declared as white, at least non-Indian and thus ineligible for Federal protection, her people's mix of Croatan, Hatteras, Catawba, Tuscarora, Cheraw, Siouxan ancestry. 'Lumbee' were rejected also, with a handshake, by the Cherokee nation.

Well, the Judge didn't need a course in anthropology to love a voluptuous woman. No; but he wanted to have his cake and eat it too. He enjoyed his social position in Kinston, his membership in the country club off Vernon Avenue. He had little taste for circuit rides and soon left his judgeship to settle in a semiretired law practice in town. He was a wealthy man from an old tobacco farming family, a descendant of plantation life. He still leased out prime Lenoir County tobacco land, and lived easy in the seigneurial house up on Park Avenue at the far end of Mc-Clwean—far end from Shine Street Cemetery. It has white pillars. Also, he and Selva with their bright young daughter liked to summer in a house by the sea near Morehead City.

XIII

But one afternoon the kindly judge in his sixties died. He had a heart attack on the golf course. The testamentary battles which followed, his kin contesting the will as an older sister led the charge, made clear what a happy pampered girl never cared to ask: her parents had not legally married. Judge Vick's sister in Martin County, plus the cousins, took away all but a bank account and a few shares of stock which were in Selva's name. In court they beat the Indian housemaid out of a fortune.

Twenty months later when Selva née Locklear rejoined her beloved husband under heaven's common law, a significant inheritance did perfect to the child. But this also was split up among others. The Department of Social Services stepped in, at the mother's death, and with local home court advantage easily defeated Lumbee relatives—Aunt Lovedy's—petition for guardianship. One day the eleven year-old daughter of wealth found herself alone in a Lenoir County orphanage while she was stunned with grief.

Carlyne didn't talk about those years. She never said much to Joey apart from the one revelation. Forget is the psyche's scar tissue. She didn't want to think of the mental and physical cruelty done to children at that place a few minutes off Route 70 in La Grange.

The ward administrator was a nun with gray eyes: who hated, maybe loved, in a sick way, the children in her care. She punished hard and arbitrarily. Her chief enforcer was a brutal woman named Carole: sweet as pie with superiors but a pitiless scourge to anyone who was weaker. Carole met her own twisted needs day after day and year upon year at the orphans' expense. With a perverse energy she and other staff broke those children and remade them in their own image: all appetite and lies. The institution took away self-respect and faith in life. Carole took away any little gifts or pleasures, and she hit the kids. Sister T., Carole: congratulations on inflicting pain, and mental torture, on orphaned boys and girls for a quarter century.

Meanwhile the administration falsified records and added up costs and ate what of Carlyne's inheritance had escaped the Judge's people plus their lawyers. A second guardianship petition by Pembroke relatives on her mother's side—*Yo' ar'n!* said Aunt Lovedy Locklear—also found no brief at Lenoir County Courthouse. But in the end one of her father's good intentions did stand up because it was extra-testamentary, and in an influential Durham friend's hands. This was Carlyne's scholarship to college. Intelligent, made alert and self-reliant by the abuse she had to take, she hit the books as an escape. Schoolwork helped her to survive. Back then no non-white had ever been admitted to the Woman's College in Durham reserved for daughters of the elite. Somehow despite her high cheekbones, and flesh a shade deeper, she was accepted. Helped by an influential ally she passed the color barrier and got in. Carlyne's hands had scrubbed, washed, swept, mopped, hauled, and fought from the first awful days after her mother's death to the moment of her release six years later. She had a blight where hope and dreams blossomed to a healthy girl's love. But she shrugged as she went among the young ladies and their finer graces, and had a laugh when the Kappas asked her to be their sorority sister.

XIV

One evening, not quite three weeks after giving birth, Carlyne stepped back from the dresser mirror. Her strong hips were still a bit on the slender side, but shapely; her figure was firm and young. At five feet eight inches her proud posture drew men's eyes when she went out for a walk. She felt very sore and not ready for any sexual activity even if there was love in it. But now she had no choice. Banks don't accept a good figure as collateral; though her breasts swollen with milk might bend a bank manager; at least if he had the county fair tastes of the average male. Yes; even more than before men stared at her on the street. They sensed her plight, her vulnerability, and dared.

Carlyne tossed out a tissue imprinted with lipstick and took a deep breath. She crossed the room to check on the child whose crib was in the alcove. Rhoda lay quiet for awhile after the nipple and a burp.

Outside, the sun beat down on the pavement and sooty redbrick factory. Clomp, clomp went her sandals to the rhythm of her will. Yes, yes, she would do this thing . . . Last night she cropped her black hair. Now she wore a dark blue silken top, tight bluejeans, makeup, perfume. She went into the seedy town. Hell, if only her milk didn't run through the brassiere and stain her blouse; if only she could meet some guy and make a quick buck without problems . . .

—Help you, miss?

Inside a pharmacy she browsed the aisle. Nervously, she glimpsed the clerk. She was hungry. She needed things for the child.

The scene at Five Points didn't look too promising. Fatty meat sizzled on a griddle. She looked over the rundown main intersection: Harvey's Restaurant, S.H. Kress 5 & 10, Young Men's Shop, Ellis Stone's. There was a store where you made your own candy in copper pots. Further along was the Criterion Theater where she once saw a movie with Joey during their courtship. But the department stores and nice scents used to stir her at Christmastime when she daydreamed about marriage and the modest yet godly man by her side through life . . . There were more dusty shops and outmoded displays. At a bus stop two older men nodded when she passed with her sandals, clomp, clomp, and her short hair, clomp, and her . . . hm!

Now check out the hotel lobbies. Was there a business convention in town? At the Washington Duke bar, or Jack Tar, the better hotels, they met in groups for happy hour. Those were expense account types with money to spend since it wasn't theirs. Have a drink or two then wend their way to his hotel room? That's how it was done? Or bring one back to Lamonde and shock the landlady? Hopefully not. But oh, if Joey made it home and came straight to Durham and found her like this . . . She felt self-pity well up and then shame as she walked those streets unchanged since World War II.

Well, she had her tryout in Bangkok. She made fake love with the best of them though it wasn't so fake. Lord, let him forget me . . . Let him come home and guess the truth and then let his anger and hurt turn to disgust. Forget me, Jo. Find another woman, will you?

And if her first customer was violent? What then? She ran a hand on the rim of her swollen breast.

XV

In midafternoon the hotel lobbies were empty. She knew better than to wait around. Students were gone for the summer, and the bus station made a sorry spectacle, hot, airless. A hooker in the coffee shop sized her up. A few people sat waiting for a 4:30 bus north to Richmond, Washington, New York. Carlyne wished she might take a bus and go anywhere at all, out west maybe, far away. She walked through glass doors on the street side, thinking: Am I clear? Do you get the message?

Outside the Melbourne, a cheap hotel back toward Five Points, she caught a man's eye. He didn't look too sure. Was it her skin tint? But he had a brazen stare on him. And he winked. Charmed, I'm sure.

—Hey there, little lady. Looking for someone?

—Could be.

Was he a tobacco worker? There was that odor beneath a dab

of cologne. He got off early and showered up? His black hair was combed back, and he wore a string tie. No beer on his breath.

Carlyne paused. She didn't like the sudden intimacy: as any woman knows, it can do strange things to men. Joey might sulk when he didn't get his way, but he wouldn't think of hitting her.

It was hot on the street.

—Your place or mine? he said.

She thought a moment about Rhoda alone. The baby could start crying, kicking, choking and then not be able to breathe. Carlyne stared at the John. Was he the ornery kind: once it's over then a scene?

—Better mine, she said.

—Nearby?

—Ten blocks.

—Where?

She glanced out toward Duke Street.

—Behind East Campus.

—Le's ride, he said.

In his car she gave a little laugh. It was to herself, but her lover asked:

—What's so funny?

—No. Nothing. Don't mind me.

She just remembered Joey's father once thinking out loud she might serve as his assistant, executive secretary, in Washington, D.C. Dressed in the finest business suits; gorgeous in a floor-length gown with priceless jewelry: Carlyne graced the halls of power by Emory Gilbert's side. She was the most powerful woman on Capitol Hill where her passage caused a stir. With sangfroid, with cold calculation, with an early abortion something like that might have happened after all. But she couldn't do it. She left. Good; it was better than anguish at the Rock Castle and living a lie. She went her way—and now some stiff punishment for what she had done.

—I need twenty dollars.

—Sho'nough, little lady.

—I mean first. Before bed.

—You shall have twenty dollars.

XVI

—Easy, she said.

A hand to his bare shoulder she tried to slow him up. A squirt of feeling oils the parts—but her throat rose at this act. The man didn't make a fuss about his needs. Maybe he didn't know what to do with her sort of grave tenderness—for a man far away, who wasn't him.

—Please be gentler.

But her kind word, the ripple in her tone only made him go harder. Any sign of weakness turned him on. It was assembly line love: only here he was the boss, and she, not he, must grunt over the quota.

For Carlyne it was not three weeks since childbirth, and so she squirmed with discomfort.

After the factory hooter sounded he drew up from her and asked:

—Any brew on ice?

—Sorry, but that does it for me.

—Aw, honey, come off it. Make overtime . . . ten bucks.

—Another day. You'll have to leave.

—But I jist got hyere.

—. . .

—Gimme' a l'il rest, we'll do 'er again. Don't worry, I'll pay. Fifteen . . . ha ha.

—No, sir. My daughter needs me now.

—Daughter?

—She's over there—Carlyne pointed—and I need to feed her.

—Hey, ain't that a kick! Streetwalker with brat. Feel free: jes' git me the beer.

He laughed low. He felt pretty fine and contented right now and he gave a polite little belch to prove it. Yes, he was spell-bound by this big-tittied l'il witch and he only half proved his-self that time and don't think he was in any rush to clear out. No, he warn't th'ough with her likes quite yet! Whew! Well them brown-skinned women like that; they can make love, oh yay. In his tone and in his drawled sort of laughter she heard an old, old note. Like them that took away her mother's land, and her own inheritance when the Judge died. Or at a Lumberton restaurant with her ma unable to get served: food not cooked yet, don't have no more o' that, no more o' this, ya' know. Now y'all run along: there's a fine restaurant fer' coloreds across the tracks . . . In the government officials' voices she heard that note when they came to administer the blood tests and remove Lumbee families to a tent in Fayetteville—one more bureaucratic ploy to steal their land. She had heard that ugly note when she was a child, down in the southeast part of the state; and then in college with its fine arts and liberal humanities. Say there, you aren't? . . . you know. Do you belong here?

There was the same sudden edge to his words—missy, this, that, come on over fer' a kiss. What? Aw, come off it, sexy squaw. You cain't pass here. I do what the hell I please where yer' likes'z concerned.

—Sorry, she said, softly. You've got to go.

XVII

She stood by the bed and faced him. Meanwhile Rhoda had woke up and begun to fret. Roused by tension in the room? or their guest's grunts when he made love: the child began casting up a scratchy whimper. Change my diaper, dear, I've got a rash on my rear. Help me, Mother, touch me, pick me up, hold me, feed me, you're all I've got! Yep, Rhody was worming her way into the act.

—I'm right comf'ible here, doncha' know. Kinder' settled in with my squaw . . . ha ha.

The man looked shabby in the afternoon light. After all he was a redneck beer drinker in his forties. In the mood he stretched across the bed and didn't want to budge. So the thing she feared most, before starting out on her new career, had now come to pass. This one was not a professional with a dab of savoir vivre; he was no affluent businessman, stay but pay. This one didn't know how to live from piss. Childish, he balked, and wouldn't go. Soon he'd begin bullying and try to get his way by force when you didn't cater to his whims. Make no mistake he would sock you, beat you, humiliate you on your knees. Love it! He had the mean streak of an alcoholic jittery for his nightly six-pack or three.

So far, real taken by her, he was playing it cute. At bedside he even kissed her hand; he wouldn't mind some gooey oral sex after the fact, if she was into it. Quite a feather in yer' headdress, l'il squaw!

Carlyne felt a dern fool sense of courtesy which almost made her give in.

—Well, for another twenty then. But not long, sir, a time limit.

—Oh, girl!

He laughed at her. It was a mistake to call him sir. Show no weakness! Now he fingered himself romantically: we had won a first victory, and we were about to see who was boss around here. After all what could she do: call the police?

Carlyne's eyes rolled up, and now her words had another tone:

—No, you better go. The child is hungry. She's crying.

—I cain't.

—Tomorrow I'll see you, if you like. Please leave now.

Mulish he shook his head:

—Don't mind if I do stay put. Feed 'er, then we'll romp. Little lady, you need a man.

That was bad. But a moment later when she still insisted he leave—the John got rude. Her words set him off, or maybe it was the shade of her skin, which put her beneath him. This was the thing she couldn't stand; and from upset, afraid of him, Carlyne was getting angry. But maybe it was just the quiver in her voice and the hint of her weakness, which set him off, and gave him the idea he could get away with anything in this situation. Wasn't he in here all alone with her? So who would know? He could beat her up bad and nobody would know. With his belt he could give her the lesson she had coming to her as another one of these up-pity women: just another dumb cunt wanting his money like the one he had to send alimony to each month or she would get a court order and have it taken from his paycheck . . . That one, his ex-wife, had him where she wanted him, by the balls; but this one was an alley cat who let things slide so bad she had to go out and sell herself on the street.

Well he couldn't let it pass. She was playing with him like they all do—playing hard to get as she dangled all that female bait in front of him and thought it gave her the last say. No way! She was only a whore in a sexy shift. And look at her now—breasts drib-bling milk down the front like a slob unable to take care of herself. Maybe she was a retarded broad anyway. Time to teach her a thing or two, if she kept on making it a tough go for him.

He leered and said:

—You cain't turn me on 'n off like a damned spigot. I'll take my money back. Give it hyere now.

—I need it.

Her upper lip had a tremor.

—Do yeh' really? Well I need what a man needs, and pronto.

Behind her the baby broke into a tinny wail. In the crib Rhoda worked her tiny pink fists and kicked.

—You see I have work to do.

Carlyne turned from him, shaken, with a look of disbelief.

—You shoulda' thought o' that 'afore. Little lady I ain't clearin' outa' hyere till you learn the ABCs o' how to treat a real man. You'll catch on the hard way mebbe'.

—Get out.

—When you give me back my cash. And not then neither, quite yet. You gotta' come up with the goods.

She took a step away from the bed and frowned down at him. Her eyes glared with a dark fire as she tried to stay in control of herself.

—You think I brought you here for fun, you idiot? I asked you nicely to go but now this time I mean it. Get out so I can feed my baby.

—Feed the brat, then me. And I ain't no idiot. You better mind yer' manners.

—No, sir. You go.

—You got enough for two. Ha ha ha! I like milk myself, though at my age it makes me feel a little bit crappy. Ha ha.

He gave a cackle: enjoying life now, in here all by himself with a knockout. Never had it so good.

—You're witty.

—And you're right high and mighty, for a whore. What bull-roar you got there on the wall, a college diploma? Had it faked.

He sneered up at the B.A. with its gothic script in a frame. Never mind her airs and her female fibs—he was good and aroused again by the lively exchange. Also he saw her hurt, and her fear. He was like a scavenger smelling blood.

She swung around exasperated from Rhoda's cries and said, shrill and jerky, choking on the words:

—Redneck, I said it nice. Now I'm telling you get the hell out of here.

Angrily he rose toward her and crossed over two, three brusque steps, and slapped her hard. Her head snapped sidewise but she caught herself, flushed, and held her ground. She let out a low animal sound, a snarl.

—Shit, he said in disgust. Fugya', bitch.

But the blow awoke her. There was no more constraint now. And the fear was gone. Nothing mattered—because suddenly she felt the ancient somber rage of her people, Tuscarora and Cheraw attacked, humiliated, driven from their farmlands into Robeson County's backwoods and swamps where they fought as outlaws and died one by one. They had turned at last in a cold despair for a last battle. Now she turned.

The John lashed out and tried to hit her again but this time with his hard fist. From summers of her girlhood spent in Pembroke, but above all from her years in an orphanage, she knew something about this. She ducked back and his fist missed her and he nearly fell. Then she slipped quickly past him round the bed and from the nightstand drawer took a pearl handled letter opener, a small stiletto Joey had given her to open his letters.

Now she swung back and the look in her eye halted the other's movement toward her. She held the knife poised toward him, and her hand didn't tremble, nor her lip. She had a sort of grin then, like Joey's hard grin, and different.

—You've got ten seconds to leave. Then you'll need a stretcher to take you away, an ambulance. One . . . two.

She looked ready and able to slice him and have done with her own bad life and her worries. Be sure now she wouldn't have minded. And be sure the good buddy sensed this too. A sad smirk played on his manly jaw dabbed with aftershave lotion for the sally to Five Points and maybe bus station where the action was. Slowly enough he reached back and grabbed for his trousers and things.

—Five . . . six.

Carlyne leaned toward him and took a step, and a step, because be sure she wanted to plunge the glinting knife between that racist's shoulder blades, and she didn't care what happened later.

He backed a step and began moving away from her, but coyly. Well maybe it wasn't worth it, you know, getting cozy with a whore. He mumbled:

—I'm just sorry I paid you my hardearned twenty dollars. You ain't worth shit nohow.

—Seven . . . eight.

She followed behind, leaving him room but also desperate as hell and all ready to swing out with the blade and spring at him and cut, cut. She hung on the verge as the rage took over her mind, the long hate. This sorryass woman hater carried hate around in his flannels just back from the cleaners. But she had hatred in the genes.

While he fumbled with the doorknob, she stood there waiting, and she would rather do it than not do it. Would he lurch back at her: attack?

—Crazy squaw.

And then it would be prison. Good: they fed you there. Then the electric chair in this racist state: blame the victim, the colored woman who cut the white man. Die, trash . . . Good, and to hell with all of you starting with the Gilberts. But then Rhody had to spend *her* life in an orphanage: childhood, girlhood years, as she herself had spent them. And there life, heart's blood, all human decency went down the drain. The bread of others has a bitter taste, but worse if it's moldy, putrid . . . But what would Joey have to say about all that if he ever made it home? She was a murderess who spawned another man's child—what man?

—Whore! You cunt! I'll be back, you everlovin' bitch! I hate you: do you hear? And I'll get you back!

The other gave an obscene gesture and slammed the door behind him—not shut but flinging it back open.

Carlyne said in a warble:

—Bring a gun, coward.

XVIII

Then she stood in a daze. In her fist was the knife glittery with late afternoon light from the window. She pressed it to her breast and gave a bad laugh.—Why, certainly, Senator, I commend your bold and principled initiative on the war issue. Let me give you a suggestion . . .—For a moment she paused in her thoughts and didn't hear the child's cries in the alcove—Why yes, Carlyne, we welcome ideas from a bright, I might say beautiful, woman, the companion of a great author. Since you came to Washington as Emory's . . . executive secretary, the brains behind the brains, shall we say, to take part in our historic campaign . . .—She was exquisitely dressed at the reception in the Rotunda. Her corsage with its jewels was the last word in elegance as she dazzled all alongside the famous writer, professor, lecturer turned political adviser to U.S. Presidents. The prominent older men flocking around her wore black tie . . . while her décolletage was the most influential since Madame de Pompadour.

Carlyne laughed, and it was a bitter laughter. But in the alcove Rhoda choked and was strangled with anguish, like her mom, for what she needed to live. Would it ever come? . . . Life under the great chandeliers of state—an aura lit the transfigured faces of power . . . Then the President stood before them, tall, thoughtful, bent slightly by his long ordeal: his sorrow over the war, and hard decision to bomb a smaller country back into the Stone Age . . . turn parts of Hanoi and Haiphong into rubble.—O Carlyne, I and my colleagues here feel a bipartisan grief for the heroic death of your husband on a battlefield of Freedom in Vietnam . . .—By now Rhody's cries had reached the limit, and seemed to snap, in a hiss.

Carlyne, her dry eyes with no tear but glinting like the knife, laughed with relief, and said:

—Alright!

XIX

Calmly she put down her weapon and crossed the room. The tiny girl flailed her stick arms where she lay in such a state. The shrivelled skin was turning purple. Sometimes Rhoda did that: gasped for breath like a crazy thing and changed color. Was there respiratory distress? Was it asthma? Once Carlyne lost her cool and started out for the hospital, but she thought better and came back when the attack went away. What she didn't want most of all—any sort of hospital or official records, any way to get at the true date of birth.

Rhoda shook her head and fought with the nipple crosswise. It took her a few more seconds to latch on. She screeched a last second of desperation as her lips fastened on and Carlyne pressed thumb and forefinger on the rim of her areola to express milk. Finally Rhoda fastened on, formed a seal, and sucked. Her mouth pumped.

The young mother sat down and closed her eyes by the crib.

—Poor kid—Carlyne said out loud.—If this goes on much longer I can't say I'll be here to take care of you. I could cry when I think what your life will be like living at the mercy of others. You won't go to the good schools, oh no, or be around polite society. Poor girl, who will ever marry you, once the true story is told, and the Gilbert shame gets out? You're a daughter of crime, of shame and betrayal, that's a fact. You'd better just go crawl in a hole somewhere and cry your eyes out, like a child of Oedipus ashamed of her parents . . . the real ones, that is, if the terrible fact ever comes to light.

Carlyne hummed. The full shiny globe tinted bluer by light from the window streamed with liquid. Oh she had milk. Behind the factory a lunch counter served the workers Brunswick stew and three vegetables plus all the hush puppies you could eat for 52¢.

Well, too bad, too bad her loving husband couldn't see them this way . . . if he wasn't lying dead beside a trail in the Central Highlands of Vietnam. And if he could . . . such a tender scene? . . . then worse. But now gravely President Johnson, with such humanity while people died in Vietnam by the tens of thousands: the President had a glimpse at her dramatic cleavage besprinkled with priceless jewels, and, in the best tradition of U.S. diplomacy, offered Joey Gilbert's wife and father standing before him side by side his most sincere condolences.

Chapter Nine

I

Short time.

Beyond the rutted road bordered by hibiscus hedge the land spread away in tiered sectors. There was stubblefield, then rice paddy. To the left there were long grassland tracts. A treeline showed its green wall to the grunts hour after hour. Further on north and eastward was a great forest—serried plaits of sierra along blue-vapored Truong Son, the Annamite Range.

The hamlet spread out among its terrains of ancestral tombs, some ornately sculpted with stone phoenixes, tall and grandiose, positioned so as to harmonize family fortune with the natural forces; others simple low mounds enclosed by piled stone in a backyard or manioc field. This was a frigging terrestrial paradise, as the grunt Clement said: an eden of papaw, guava, mangosteen, pomegranate, litchi fruit called eye of the dragon, flame trees, frangipani, white lily, banyan and lotus, high coconut palms beside soft needle pines. There was mulberry and sophora. There was a tall bo tree, our pipal, also called the sacred fig since by one of them Buddha attained enlightenment; it was like the banyan but without prop roots. There were cassia shrubs. There were plum trees. Sometimes the grunts dined not on C-rats but villagers' fare, exotically, and they made humorous attempts to mingle with the papa- and mama-sans.

Kids with a pure saffron skin skipped happily down the dirt pathways because there was more meat on their limbs since the Revolutionary Development program came to town. Gold-toothed semi-naked male inhabitants worked thigh deep day to day in the muddy fields but emerged clean as a whistle at night and neatly dressed; they met in a somewhat comic session to sort out RevDev affairs with their Western counterparts. But some, said the cultured Mister Quoc, among those same toilsome earthy peasants, could recite Nguyen Du's *Kiều* and had studied that national masterpiece. They knew *shih* verse from China's great T'ang poets, and had heard of Qu Yüan, the three Caos, Po Chü-i and even Li Shang-yin. They could reel off passages, said Quoc, from *Kiều* and loved to chant the Vietnamese epic while knee-deep in a rice paddy:

> *Mai sau dầu có bao giờ*
> *dốt lò huróng ay so tó phím này,*
> *trông ra ngon có lá cây,*
> *thấy hiu-hiu gió thì hay chi về.*

'Sometime if you ever tune this lute or light the incense in that thurible, look outside—you'll see a breeze move amid the leaves and grasses, and know that I've come home.'

II

A woman came from the maze of huts and garden plots, low striated walls overshadowed with a coconut tree or leathery jambosa. Her teeth black and lacquered, the woman grinned and bowed sideways. Her face had a way of gaping as she gave the grunts a droll prognathic smile: where a few of them hung out at the edge of the ville. She nodded and tried out her Lễ, traditional courtesy, on them: it was one of the five cardinal virtues.

—Pá-wé?

—Western movie? laughed medic Tootie. Tonight, dear, at six o'clock in the Communal House.

Tootie held up six fingers and rolled a hand forward. Carry on, dearie.

Joey Gilbert looked far out past crisscrossed hedgerows. He measured a slow lonely sampan's progress along a canal through the paddy.

The grunt Jib Benson, nicknamed Hole, blew his nose with aplomb between two fingers:

—90 cent a day plus mud and leeches. These V'etnam suckers fight for centuries, and why? Right to make 90 cent a day. Congrats, that's quite a contract you got.

—Hey, we bringin' 'em progress—said Troupial the short-timer RTO, puffing on his joint.

Tootie:

—Somebody should explain the facts of life to these good people.

Joey breathed in an alkaline scent of paddy mixed with grilled corn and cajeput flowers, spiced food back in the hamlet. After lunch the boy called Ha had taught him a poem in Vietnamese which started: *The lotus scent embalms the native land . . .* Lotus, lotus. There were lotus blossoms in vases and lotus leaves in tea, lotus seeds in rice; a concubine named Golden Lotus in one of the seven great novels of China, but Ha couldn't read a book like that yet, but Quoc did, at night. Lotus grows in mud, said Ha, smells so sweet.

Tommy Lerch gestured where a local named Dzui harrowed three ducks beyond the hedgerow. Try to get that name right: Dzui, Dzit, Dzeun, almost the same. Even their names: all alike!

—When I want comedy I watch TV, said Lerch. Better grease their tykey asses before they have a blast with ours.

—An astute observation, my good man—said the college dropout Clement.

Eastward the rice fields gave way to a fairly open plateau country dotted by fluffs of eucalyptus. That way lay Saigon, thought Gilbert the short-timer; that way the airport, jumping-off place for a new phase of life, and the end of this botch job. He could hardly wait: in just a few more days the big-ass Freedom Bird would go soaring over a great blue haze of Pacific Ocean toward the Land of the Free . . . Go on home, boy, and find that woman. She still loves you though you don't deserve it! She always wanted a farmer husband—go home and farm: don't buy the farm in Vietnam.

Past a treeline lay the next village bathed in mist with its gardens and fish ponds, its hovels huddled together plus some moats and earthen ramparts, if it was a strategic hamlet. Out that way it was a mere fifty miles to Saigon. He could walk it in two days if he had to. Yip! Aiyai, Sir, I'm gone. Not my party anymore. Hey!

The land went on beyond wide watery stretches silent in the late afternoon heat. There were pooled bomb craters which mirrored the oblique sunlight and seemed to explode a second time. Last night Hanoi Hannah thanked the G.I.s over Radio Hanoi for dropping 22 million gallons of a herbicide which would cause cancer and birth defects and organ dysfunctions for generations in Vietnam. Solly 'bout drat, Hannah, we had to flush out those bad boy VCs before they flushed us.

—Well—Simmer Jenkins worked his plug and summed it all up—they can have this piece of shit all for themselves, in perpetittity. Just count me out, Sarge, I don't like it! Yankee go home, and that's me.

The sampan inched along the horizon. Gold sail before sunset. A water buffalo found rice tasted better than grass and strayed out toward the paddy border. Get back there! you big shaggy-ass. Get a haircut and a job!

Joey squatted peasant fashion on his haunches, and gazed out. By the dusty road in stood a 150-foot banyan, man lookata' size of her: its trunk a collision of elephants.

—You know what? said Troupial. You know what the goddamn what?

—No, I doosn't, said Hole.

—Well then I'll tell yer' ignerant arse. It's like this. When the first Marines landed in Da Nang in '65 some gook honeys waded out and put lais round their necks.

—It was Diem's welcome for the heroic G.I.s, said Clement.

But nobody knew who Diem was, and nobody gave a fart either.

—You know—said Chingi, or T-Bone, Latino street kid—I don't feel like a hero.

—That a fact, said Hole, and spat.

III

The grunts cut themselves a huss from routine RevDev duties. Blah, dearie, I got a good oldfashioned case of the blahs . . .

but it beats the crud out of ambush patrol. You see the grunts were symbolic presences: soldiers with a heart, as they shuffled along in the dusty heat in this pocket of quietude. Oh yeah. They talked a lot of rot and bantered, fed, and slept but not too soundly. Nope. Now how much longer in this lallaland of gentle smiles and kowtows far from the boonies and 40-pound saddle-ups at dawn, 10 or 20 klik humps until dusk? The grunts lounged and traded pleasant repartee with the learned Clement and socialite Gamecock while north and west the manmade thunder rolled on and the war—155 mm, 57-recoilless cannon, B-26 sorties, DC-3 Puff the Magic Dragon, Huey Cobra attack helicopters with their 50 hosedown rounds per second, NVA 82 mm mortar rounds. The distant heavens shook to it. But here in RevDev heaven all was hunky-dory, my good man, and oh how I do enjoy a spot of tea with these hospitable villagers who are VC spies one and all.

In late afternoon the air thinned, and the blue mountain drew closer to the road.

An ARVN soldier also assigned to RevDev came walking out from the hamlet and casually joined them and lit up a cig. Joey nodded at Noup who was no boondock product but had a good family in Hué and passed for a man with connections and a prosperous future.

—Nui Ba Den—said Noup, and pointed.

—Please elucidate, my good man—said Clement the dropout from Temple who grew up in Philadelphia's Olney neighborhood.

—Nui Ba Den mean: Mount of Blide in Brack.

ARVN English was outstanding!

—Mean: beaucoup VC, said Tootie.

—Good luck to 'em—said the listless Troupial.—Not my affair. Clement:

—You wish top o' the morning and good tidings to our esteemed enemy.

—Yes I do—said Troup.

—I'll harass and interdict the whole female sex!—said Tommy Lerch also called Kid Marijuana.—Lemme' at 'em! Say, that Ha's ma is a looker.

Their gaze followed Noup's finger to where jungle slopes rose above rice cultivation systems in the distance. It was NVA haven all around, and so quiet. Clouds hovered like a lover's embrace above the ridges and peaks, Mount of the Bride in Black.

Noup waved his hand:

—Cambodge ovah' thell.—The eucalyptus wisps out that way were like the flag of Cambodia; they spoke of that strange land.—Me no go thell', ha ha.

IV

A few minutes later the grunts strolled at an easy pace through the berg they were sent to defend. This did beat the drastic days and weeks of hump-de-hump. Yes indeedy, this shellacked the seal and search operations which were so treacherous in the aftermath of Xo Man: when the squad was shattered and Joey Gilbert became the franchise who had to lead his motley crew of new guys through rotten missions under the sadist Drawber's orders from the rear. Top Drawber, Platoon Sergeant since the day Mark Robidou caught it too, said he blamed Xo Man on the men's non-strak attitude and mistakes. This was the honor the first shirt did his own dead such as Gizzard-Izard, Kid Ringwood and Chi-Bar, FNG-IX. Drawber called them a pajama platoon. What respect! Good going, Sir! They paid the highest price; they paid patriotism's top dollar; and all you can think to do is insult and discredit them? Will do, Sir! Of the thirteen grunts who formed the squad that day—Vane was blinded; pointman Skol and Cal-surfer Thingum were greased in an L-shaped ambush not long after; medic Artus had to be tied in restraints for dust-off as he railed in a madman's wild laughter: Heal thyself, doc! Drat Da Lat! Flak in Dac Lac! Ha ha ha! . . . Bufillu was carried off in a wheelchair: lost to the fair sex. Only Tombigbee the big Navajo had returned Stateside under his own locomotion, with a grunt: good, it's done. But Joey and Troupial were at least reprieved from Parrot's Beak patrols, and they couldn't believe their good luck even with Drawber's nagging and bad faith.

Just yesterday Colonel Pricecroft visited and watched his men help villagers plant vegetable gardens and mark off the orchards of the future. He saw them digging at a fish pond, constructing chicken coops and pigsties. How wholesome, really. These Nam folks never had it so good: what do you think? I hope they appreciate it—a regular Shangri-La! Even the magpies looked happy where they perched on the apricot and peach trees; and then circled, black-winged, chattery as if they sniffed a good meal on the burner while casting a glimpse past the tips of feathery bamboo. Everywhere were neat courtyards with few weeds. The people made their rattan basketry and grew orchids in coconut shells filled with coconut wood chips. There were civic patrols: the *dan ve* who went on rounds at night and manned posts out past the hedgerow. RevDev: it was truly the New Nam.

Further on the grunts walked over slippery moss. They lingered by a marshy pond covered with lotus. A buffalo boy played a few notes on his flute and called back to them: G.I., you numbah two! Why numbah two precisely? He held up three fingers . . . Go to school, kid. No playing hooky! The new RevDev school has books and supplies. We'll give you a pencil for your very own— with an eraser!

A village woman shuffled along the dirt road in her loose-fitted caraco and black slacks billowed by a sticky breeze. Her water buckets were yoked to a shoulder pole.

On the hamlet's east edge Joey gazed off at pale fleecy sky and distant mountains reflected in the rice fields. Tombigbee, he thought: the quiet scout, the stolid Navajo who had his own idea, and made a good LURP. Tombigbee had boarded a chopper six days ago for Tan Son Nhut; then the second leg to Kadena Airforce Base, Oki; and from there a big silvery Freedom Bird across the blue Pacific Ocean to Travis AFB, Oakland, mission accomplished, Sir! Process me *out*; and then a sweet hop to Tuba City, Arizona, si señor, The World, or the only one I care about. By now Tombigbee's Vietnam journey had ended; he made it back all in one piece, unlike Emmet Buffilu, and a few others.

V

Since Tet a sinking feeling had not left the squad leader. He did not need an oracle—his own intuition that is—to tell him something was wrong. It was wrong here in Vietnam, in the war effort. Yesterday Mr. Quoc told him with a chuckle that a few thousand people in a remote mountainous region were changing their surnames to 'Ho' in honor of the man they saw as the greatest leader in their nation's history. All those Ho's belonged to five ethnic tribes much courted by AID and CIA teams which had millions of dollars at their disposal for another sort of christening. The agents spent the money, but it didn't work. The Americans were losing not gaining ground.

Joey knew this and he didn't care. As a soldier he had become one of the living dead, a machine; he was in Stage IV of the process, which he might not come back from. No more feeling to it: no patriotic ideals and sanctions for the things he had done and seen in Vietnam. Now he was out of touch with the death, the grief deep down in him; but could it come back to haunt?

Since Tet he felt a shudder of dread not for a country which didn't want him as its savior, but for the one back there which sent him away. In the RevDev slack time he dwelt on his wife, and he didn't need an oracle to know something had gone wrong at home. His wife left his father's house without a word.

Here, in villages: the contagious corpses lay on the ground. Countless died as the fire birds swooped and rushed headlong from the shores of the Western god . . . Back in America too from what he heard it seemed life was in turmoil, the society sick. He sensed a similar impotence to the one he felt here, as though something went wrong at a crossroads sometime in the past: the meeting of two visions. And now there was plague in the land torn with conflict. Now America couldn't give birth to a child named Freedom despite its labors, despite more tens of billions spent.

What help? Who would set things right? Who would even tell the truth about it? The healer Apollo's immortal word: daughter of golden hope?

Since Tet Joey had room for only one idea in his head: get on home, go in search of her. Be a seeker, find out why. Why, Carlyne? Solve the Sphinx's riddle.

Was it Newell? Did the hippie pull another crazy stunt, but he went too far this time? Way too far. If he . . . with my wife, if he's guilty and afraid then just let him say so. He'll be banished from our family, but that's all. No scandal; we'll keep it among ourselves; and no violence. But he will be thrown out and disowned like the incestuous filth he is, if this is true. Let Newell get on with his hippie life as free as you please; but don't come around me anymore. I'm not that stupid; or if I am then you can call me the guilty one, I got what I deserved, let the curse fall on me . . . But one way or another I have to find out about this—for my sake, and for hers. And someone better find out and soon what is going on here in Vietnam; also what has gone wrong with our own country. If not, then all America's riches will be for nothing. Say goodbye to the good human harvest when the truth is not on your side.

VI

At times Joey had to make an effort with himself. His nerves were strained with a morbid jealousy. There was a tension in his tour's last few days even if the RevDev routine left little or nothing for its defense platoon to do. Top Drawber was a nit-picker first-class. In Drawber's mind the millions of determined little people were rising up in their conical hats and they made a tidal wave higher than the conical Mount of the Bride in Black, and it would sweep away our capitalist way of life, let alone this pet RevDev project. And Drawber's response: to criticize a spitshine, to have his whipping post Simmer Jenkins clean a latrine.

What also made Joey tense was that he didn't believe so many courteous nods along the pathways: when the villagers greeted the well-behaved grunts, their benefactors, out for a stroll before supper. Hey, meet and greet the San family. A normal grunt couldn't stomach the endless meetings, work committees and subcommittees for education, public health, economic affairs, defense: where the line dogs now sat as learned counselors. To be sure it was a sorry sight: the tight-lipped Simmer, the pair of street urchins Chingi and Manito, the pedantic Clement who called everybody my good man—there they were round a table in the Communal House talking over the program. What a scream. Mr. Quoc tried not to smile as he watched the grunts trade views through an interpreter with citizens Dzeun, Tu Sang, Dzit, Eay Tao. Well, a false note played in grunt-villager relations. You could hear it in the voice of Quoc's bright grandson, Ha. An angelic smile on his delicate features: Ha hung around G.I.s to improve his English which was already a prodigy for a village kid.

Beyond the bamboo hedges the greenish brown hectares seemed to atomize far out toward a shimmery horizon. In Vietnam the day was almost over. From flooded paddy fields the ancient land saturated with death had a way of beckoning the Western soldier. It winked at the occupier, and it was tricky.

Quoc, so friendly and urbane, now looked on stonefaced with a dozen or so mama- and papa-sans. There went the G.I.s alongside their large, glum, powerful athlete of a leader; they passed by with a goofy nod, a grin.

It had taken the Chinese nearly a thousand years to pass through Vietnam. But it might not take the grunts quite that long.

VII

None in the current group predated Joey's role as squad leader. For them his presence meant a continuity and a shoulder to lean on. They might not like his mean wiry style, hardly saying hi, while his last days ticked past and DEROS time drew near. But the mere view of the man helped them with anxiety, and they revered him at first sight. They feared the moment thirteen days away when he lifted off in a Skyhook and left them for Saigon. Grunts tried to steer clear of the lifer Top Drawber, nicknamed The Bulldog; instead, they looked for leadership to the clipped orders and aura of this Joey once natty not in the haberdashery of a boonierat but in a Major League uniform, and his name was known for a late season tear up from the Minors. Now they called him World Serious in rap sessions, but to his face it was: Sir.

The era of 'limited presence' had phased into that of 'troop buildup'. And so from military bases Stateside came replacement contingents all geared up for the great Anti-Communism Crusade. To be sure these were newbies. Proud of their country which was a mighty power for enlightenment, freedom and democracy—most new infantrymen didn't like longhaired hippies, street demonstrators and antiwar activists; they condemned race riots, the chaos in U.S. cities this long hot summer of '68. Well, now they were in for it. This was the Nam itself. So they didn't praise the draft evader who had escaped, or the pickets in front of Army recruitment headquarters, or a United States flag in flames. Deep, thorough, conclusive was the boot camp indoctrination against such de facto treason in the ranks. Those were Uncle Ho's little bastards; they were Marxist-Leninist agitators for world revolution and an end to church and family and America's manifest destiny. Pure, idealistic were these fresh grunts, FNGs, cherries sent over here to make the world a better place. Perhaps they had a crude vision of Vietnam as an affluent American suburb.

A few shorttimers in the platoon had changed their tune. They'd been around and they were sick of it. Since Tet you could hear—horrors!—a bit and a shred of anti-imperialist propaganda among the lowly grunts.

Tootie, Lerch, Fern, Sanger, Hole, Clement had entered the fray in post-Westmoreland days: in the Tet aftermath when President Johnson, himself now a Vietnam casualty, said no to the 'total Americanization' of Westie's request for 206,000 more reinforcement soldiers besides the 525,000 already on the ground; and LBJ kicked the General upstairs to Army Chief of Staff at the Pentagon. A lot of latecomers whose units were out there slogging shit might be likely to say: hey, they won't let us fight the war—why don't we just nuke the little buggers? But the RevDev platoon stuffed with bennies and grown fat on slack time could afford a more relaxed way of thinking. The grunts Tootie, Lerch, Fern, Sanger, Hole, Clement still cried down the communist bugaboo, if they bothered to give an opinion; but they had also seen a few things and maybe even learned something.

So had the softer more genteel Gamecock, Richard Danforth, who signed up one ardent afternoon in Charleston to his socialite mom's amusement. So had Chingi and Manito who came to the Nam as a kind of South Bronx rumble; also it was a job for the unemployed. The quiet Wade Jenkins, Simmer, hated Top Drawber too much to have a patriotic take on his unit's works and days. Simmer put in the time mainly by himself and didn't care much what the next guy was stewing over.

Joey Gilbert, the RTO Troupial, to an extent Wisembroder were in later stages of the experience. They said little and didn't think out loud like my good man Clement. Please spare me your philosophic views. Personal feelings got numbed pretty quick in combat, a buddy's bloody death, like Ben Bolt, Slidell, Loseby, Kossuth, Horse Shue, a lifetime ago. On the trail it wasn't hard to lose the drill sergeant's innocence. Then a grunt's jungle craft and kill skills had little to do with love of liberty. See that? Good guys are getting messed up, and for what? You say it's sweet to die for one's country? Well then I say give me a break. Why my ass?

Why must I do the dirty work? So ringknockers like Pricecroft can sip their apéritifs in the O-Club and Cercle Sportif? So the blue-suitors back home can make big bucks on government contracts? So factories can put out guns and all the other good things that go into a war? So our parents' tax dollars can flood this antediluvian land with bucks while the black market thrives, and gook profi-teers grabble after the rake-off? That's good work if you can get it. Quite pleased to pay, says the U.S.A., just see things my way . . . And meanwhile the poor peasantry and the ethnic minorities minus a few warlords and drug lords—all the real people in the maquis hate our gringo guts and pray to Buddha we'll lose heart and get the hell out. Scoot! Well that's the thanks we get, and maybe just maybe we deserve it. Any big fool can see they like their old graybeard Ho Chi Minh better than our diarrhetorical politicians ever running off about freedom and democracy.

Man, I don't know if this war is a kick anymore, and my nerves are shot! I worry more about Mom and Dad back home than where I fit into the big picture. Colonel P., with all respect to your rank, Sir, I think you may have been misled. No, the U.S. cannot play God, who is Uncle Sam's brother, and I am not Jesus as far as I know.

Sports fans: support us, but don't bore us to death with a lot of exalted drivel.

And yet the same tried and true catchwords had to sanction a soldier's acts, and give him strength to fight another day. Liberty, the Free World, the American way. But they wore thin. After di-saster came such a strange up-and-down you hardly knew your own name anymore; you were your service number. One sunny post-Xo Man afternoon there were brass, Pricecroft and others, whooshing through the bush with medals plus a pep talk for the heroic grunts. Affirmative, ay-ay, Sir! Oh there was no antidote for jungle blahs like a visit from those officers starched in their immaculate khaki, all our Tom Mixes of the rear. It rallied mo-rale truly. We slog jungle and sizzle while they sit in Saigon and swizzle. That's why all day long a still small voice was griping: you know you love it, sucker. A world of hurt! The objective was some worthless hill on a lost Central Highlands horizon, and it was madness for Six to issue such orders. Pay no heed, my good man, so goes it. Pledge allegiance, and do your bit. Since Day One some grunt or other has paid in full for his brave leader's fuck-ups. But you have to wonder how the Pricecrofts and all the other boy wonders can keep a straight face and manage such a trim, self-important air, in this hundred degree hell infested with VC and mosquitoes. Look like they just came from a Beacon Hill sitting room—no pain, no anguish for their strak lifer asses; only a phony thrill to their high patriotic cadences, as they rouse our morale with words of glory. For we are bringing hope and life to the victims of communism. We bring them the priceless gift of freedom, and we must not fail. And on and on as the grunts stand in a row like tenpins. And many a mother's son felt the need to believe the encouraging phrases—and couldn't, didn't, anymore. For underneath those fine formulations the grunts heard the headless drummer Ben Bolt as he beat out a tamtam on his drum of defeatism. Will I ever make it out of here alive?

Joey didn't like to think of Xo Man. That day as all too often he had let his thoughts wander back to the Rock Castle and then—a finger snap—and three G.I.s blasted to bits: the kid Ringwood turned to a bloody gristle . . . Izard . . . FNG . . . And then it was a rampage through the ville with torched hootches, a girl raped as Skoly-Skol sort of bragged later, but it was just more defeat and sadness. A pro-Saigon family was grenaded, and small children slaughtered. Was it us? You mean we did that? *Us?* No way! We are the bearers of peace and prosperity to this benighted people. The devil requisitions boots if ever I, a good hometown boy, ever did what you say. Say, shut up, you, I am not a baby killer! If you say so, you lie! . . . Now, now, big fella, calm down. Only kidding. Hey, you know, it was the thing to do: life is cheap in Vietnam, as the General informed the press at Five O'clock Follies in Saigon before he got cashiered. Seal and search, then line 'em up, like the penny arcade. Tatatatata! Hahahahaha! Don't think so much! . . . Don't justify, my good man—pacify.

Despite a few kinks in the rationale Joey's squad made it through another day in the war. For a shorttimer the mess and disillusion hardly counted. What did count was putting another X to the calendar on his helmet. Mr. Quoc, Tu Sang, Eay Tao don't really want us around here anyway. They on'ry want our darrahs.

But Drawber's ragging seemed to howl in their ears like a punji-trapped dog last night on the village outskirts.

VIII

RevDev was a plum assignment if only Top didn't stink it up with the smell of a lifer. He had an E-8's zeal for the petty stuff: an eye for detail that loved to land a grunt's ass, duly wiped with a banana leaf, in the wrong. Tightfisted with the bennies, a man's small pleasures like beer and mail call, Drawber gave out 'office hours' for any Uniform Code infraction. He was a stickler for military etiquette and pounced on a trifle quicker than Emily Post on a ramped knife. Sloppy grunts! Hefty, arrogant, mediocrity incarnate, he was less cocksure than his sergeant's bark sounded. He loved to hold Korea over their heads.

—That's right, puppies. We drove the commie bastards to the Manchurian border. And now look at you: bunch of country clubbers, slack non-hackers. Comedians! And compare your performance . . . Later on we drove them again and their Chink commie friends back north of the 38th parallel. That was under General MacArthur, a soldier. We weren't like you sissies afraid of a few mousetraps. In the hills of Central Korea we shed our American blood while talks went on in P'anmunjóm. But RTO Troupial here can't seem to grasp the concept: he says no to a piddling six-month re-up in his tour, and says no to serving his country, which needs him. Bravo, Troup! You're a real trooper. As for Gilbert he also turns a deaf ear to my inspired reenlistment talk and just wants to lie in a hammock and count the days. Well, we'll see if he gets a bedsore. And to the whole batch of you flabby non-hackers I say: you've come a long way since Korea, men.

Top sneered. Above all he didn't cotton to World Serious, who was a leader. And he gave the squad 60 lb. gear orders for no reason in this oasis—7 lb. steel pot at all times in case a coconut fell from one of the palm trees rustling in the breeze. Ouch!

So much went down during their last week in the bush before Col. Pricecroft rebilleted them and brought them in. Skol's replacement on point, Oakleigh, was sniped by a *sun van nang*, or crude VC ten thousand-purpose gun; it fires all bullets; and rubber thongs trigger the pin. Then Mosey Rink caught it—blown up waist down by a jungle bomb, an 'honest John'. Mosey wouldn't be carrying on and doing his Elvis the Pelvis bit again. Two more FNGs came in on an ARVN-34 and were gone so fast nobody learned their names. They were Cherry Kool-Aids, KIA when the squad ran into an L-shaped ambush one morning. The war gorged itself or it snacked on peanuts. The lucky ones were able to tenterhook their short time and then DEROS'd on home. But not all were lucky. Even a so-called gungi, a super-grunt hard to the core who knew no fear, and didn't get tired—if there was one—even a gungi would choose the pain in the ass Drawber to humping the bush.

Well, at first. But then? Within two weeks Marion Darby told off Topper to his pink face:

—Ah'll frag yo' staff-poguey ayass.

And he might have done it—some quiet night when the First Sergeant rasped an order between snores, and dreamt punitive details and special recon patrols, and insubordination court-martials with 5-year sentences not counted as service time. But the MPs came and handcuffed Marion Darby and took him away to Long Binh Stockade before the grunt could frag his superior officer.

IX

On a July afternoon Joey's platoon had received a cordial welcome from a Saigon Government cadre in the RevDev Administration—Rural Revolutionary Development—and a few locals. Mr. Quoc was the quiet gray-haired village elder; and he had a ten year-old grandson, Ha, with features so fine, like porcelain, you had to guess the sex. As usual the men set up camp along the perimeter; they did their thing and then went to get briefed on methods and objectives of this Ap Doi Moi, *New* New Life Hamlet. Technically they were serving as advisers for a revitalized version of the old strategic hamlet system which collapsed when the Diem regime fell.

Since 1959 forced relocation and 'population control measures' had been done in the countryside. The end of remote villages led the way to wholesale defoliation; it was quicker and easier for planes to spray dioxin on districts than for troops to destroy fields and houses by fire. Later U.S. artillery made the inhabitants flee vast free fire zones. So it was removal for the peasantry—then a strict U.S. policy to control and do away with 'people's war'.

The American program, which tried out a few names, was meant to take National Liberation Front organizers and fighters from the masses in the rural areas: the fish from the sea. Uprooted villagers were made to labor in a corvée and build dwellings, fortifications, wall yardage at the new concentration site. Burned off fields, skeletal hamlets, poisoned forest soon dotted the South Vietnam landscape and more so near the mountains.

In the early '60s around Kontum, Pleiku, Buon Me Thuot, the U.S. gave tribesmen many thousands of weapons—better ones than Government (ARVN) troops had in the area—and told them to fight the communists. But across the Central Highlands it was only NLF cadre who had worked and got results at the grassroots to uplift the living standard. This is why ethnic tribes gave many of those guns to the Viet Cong. When U.S. advisers paid young men 5000 piasters per month to serve in special units—as compared to 1500 for Saigon 'puppet' troops—the new tribal combat units did not seek contact and reacted in strange ways to firefights with the Red enemy. And then came a campaign to take back the weapons; there were arrests, there were executions. But this ended when a few of the U.S. advisers were 'eaten by tigers'.

One big blunder came on the heels of the next. More and more the occupiers put their faith in concentration camps. ARVN soldiers were posted at the gates of strategic hamlets to stop a mass return to ancestral villages. In order to poison tribal/Vietnamese relations, or else set one ethnic group against another, divide and conquer: the camp administrators gave out favors here and punishments there; they discriminated as they were told; yet most camp dwellers still tended to see only one enemy, and it was a foreign devil. The Americans, not the VC, had run them out of the forest and burned their homes and possessions and made them helpless. Shared misery brings solidarity. The National Liberation Front infiltrated the barbed wire hamlets and organized the struggle for better living conditions. The people had no liking for their 'new life' experiment: its perks and comforts which were handouts and meant to keep the good little children happy and the bad ones in line. What the people needed was to roam and hunt again and grow their rice freely and sing in the wind and bang their gongs—forbidden gongs since the Americans thought they were signals.

Sooner or later the NLF got control in each of these fake villages. It even dared to scrawl its slogans on the walls and front gate: 'Unite to Resist!' The U.S. overseers preached 'Divide and Rule' and turned to civil self-defense units as a control measure. From month to month the occupier had to get more repressive, and this was an old, old story in Vietnam. So the NLF came back with its own self-defense units which were based not on dollars, save my own skin the hell with yours, but on the tearing down of these glorified prisons; on the right of return to home villages, fields, ancestral cults; on a resistance to tax collectors and landlords' agents and their protectors.

What did it boot if the place was strategic, New Life, New New Life, or RevDev? A camp under any name stank the same; and it served mainly to rouse hatred and also political awareness. The families herded into them had lost their orchards, their bamboo groves, their family tombstones razed by bulldozers; so their hearts didn't go out to a campaign waged by Saigon plus USAID and U.S advisers to win hearts and minds. For the people knew the same thing went on all across the South; and the 'beneficiaries', namely themselves, were being used as human barriers against VC entry into the puppet military bases—for example where a ring of settlements made a first line of defense. And here as there it was the same: the human guinea pigs waited for their moment, and their chance. They wanted out. VC agitators told them how at Bien Hoa Airbase fifteen miles from Saigon a shoeshine boy, an old woman vendor, a youth press-ganged into ARVN, a prostitute on platform heels, brought out info on the layout and helped to make sketches. Then one night the NLF struck. A mortar barrage hit squadrons of B-57 bombers, Skyraiders, helicopters, a U-2 spy plane; it caught the pride of the U.S. fleet in South Vietnam with pants down.

Camp dwellers grinned and bowed by day at the foreign soldier, and then after dark helped to carry VC supplies, ready attack positions, dig trenches, cut camouflage, cart the wounded. Bien Hoa and other disasters brought a change to official thinking in Saigon, at MACV, and at the Pentagon back home. Only in a more positive and humanitarian way could Free World forces fight the communist rot in the villages of Vietnam. A new day had dawned. It was RevDev.

Joey Gilbert, Troupial, Wisembroder and company didn't know much of this history. And Colonel Pricecroft wasn't likely to send a team from Division Headquarters to clue them in. Follow orders, do your duty, big picture, type of thing. So the grunts could only feel what the real deal might be: in the sense of unease, in the lifeless smile or nod along a path in the ville, in the dead fish handshake of citizens Quoc, Dzeun, Dzit, Dzui; in the languid attempt at a grin by the boy Ha's pretty mom, named Mai.

Good luck trying to sort out friend from foe. In this godforsaken country the devil only knew.

X

A 'rural construction' team was made up of some sixty members. Over half of these did the propaganda work meant to halt VC gains in the ville. Psy-war and intelligence experts worked hand in hand with a census team. A dozen health and education workers led the self-help projects, gave out relief supplies, started up schools, and looked to people's aches and pains and the many cases of skin disease.

At chow one night buck private Jib Benson, our own 'Hole', overcame his phobia for social get-togethers developed while in the Army, and stood up to lead a RevDev cheer. With glee Hole sang out:

—Y'all gimme' a *W*.

Grunts stamped their feet and cried:

—Doub'yuh!

Top Drawber might not have affirmatived this somewhat unmilitary mode of behavior. At present Topper and 1st Lieutenant had guests from Division Headquarters to regale with an update on RevDev successes.

—I said y'all gimme' a *H* now!

—*H*, Hole-baby, *H!*

Outside the window it was dusk. The village settled in after the day of upbeat routine. There was quiet except for the raucous mess hall.

—Well then howsabout you gimme' a *A?*

—*A*, Hole! *A*, Hole!

—Damned straight, said Fern. A *A*.

Hole cried out:

—Whacha' got there?

—Not yet, you idiot—said Gamecock.

—*WHA*—! bawled the others. *WHA—WHA!*

The Hole had some goofball grin on his face as he glanced around. Whew! He scratched behind his ear, and seemed to reach back for the high hard one.

—Illiterate fool, said Clement.

—Wait, that ain't it—I know—

—He needs some RevDev hisself—said the hillbilly Fern.

—M . . . yeah. It's a *M*, boys!

There was a pause: in admiration of Hole's intellect. Then, like a crash of thunder:

—*M! M!* Yeah!

—Now whattaya' all got? Tell me.

—*WHAM!*

—Did you say *SPAM?*

—Hell no! We said *WHAM!* We got *WHAM!* Say *WHAM!*

—Wham-bam-thankya-ma'am!—tooted Tootie.

As one the squad, Troupial, Tommy Lerch, Gamecock, Manito, Chingi or T-Bone, Fern, Joey, Wisembroder, Sanger, Clement, Tootie, the glum Simmer Jenkins, stood up and hollered in a chorus:

—Win hearts and minds! Frigging *WHAM!*

Then they sat down, silent, and slurped chow, like thirteen puppies at The Last Supper.

A moment later Fern belched, gave a stretch, and said:

—Any, uh, slant-eyed honeys in this hyar', uh, RevDev 'spearmint?

Manito, looking to capitalize on Fern's monomania, lifted his fork:

—Wimp needs pimp?

Fern took a crumpled military scrip from a loop in his fatigues.

—I'll take Mai.

The boy Ha's mother: she was a looker and not too flat at all.

—That, my good man—said Clement—is what enthuses your likes.

—I called it, said Fern. First licks!

Joey pressed his lips and looked up. He said:

—You a pimp, Manito?

Night fell outside the windows of the Center where the G.I.'s took meals.

Gamecock gazed in space. The son of Charleston socialites didn't burp like the others; he eructated.

—'scayu-use me!

Slurp, slurp, keslurpety.

Simmer Jenkins rose first from the long table. He gave a shrug at nothing, and everything, and went outdoors to be by himself.

XI

Their task was to give perimeter defense in what was seen as a pacified zone—though not far from the hot areas of the Parrot's Beak and Cambodian border. Top's command center had red pins stuck in 544 unsure hamlets of 631 total. Luckily RevDev teams stayed away from red pins. Brass had the bright idea for once to do good works in those under control. Control? It took a Drawber wet behind his lifer's ears not to sense a VC whammy even on this model ville. One of a 59-member 'cadre team' fresh from a Civic Action course at Vung Tao on the coast said he could sniff communism in the air.

Everyday RevDevvers worked to upgrade infrastructure, repair roofs and walls, and win loyalty for the Saigon regime. The cadre weren't villagers themselves, but mostly students, town dwellers, who got the job because their middle-class parents knew some-one; it was known the Province Chief hired RevDev workers for a bribe or a favor owed. They wore black pajama-type uniforms to look like the VC who were so good at this game. 'Same tech-niques, but a true ideology' was the idea put in play; but it wasn't the same at all. RevDev cadre were careless and didn't mind loaf-ing in public. They had the usual bourgeois attitudes and looked down at a peasant and liked a manicure more than propaganda.

As a showcase in counterinsurgency the Ap Doi Moi was meant to stir Vietnam's peasantry from ages of silence and passive life. The people smiled when the bulgur wheat, aspirin, school books and other items got doled out. Cement came for building proj-ects. But when the day's meetings and activities were at an end, the RevDevees turned to the old ways. They fished for eels and ate wild yams; they drank rice wine and savored dog meat when they could get it; they spoke low at nightfall, squatting beneath the rotting thatch of hootches. Where the French failed and Diem after them with lavish incitement programs—did the Yankees have a chance?

At dusk the scent of hot onion soup beat hell out of a grunt's ham 'n lima c-rats. Local men sat in doorways after a meal of banana roots, boiled sycamore leaves, snails, wild grapes, plus the spam handout. Later they went to play the four-coins game in a den that was off limits for G.I.s. Wooden bells made a rustic sound on the water buffaloes' necks. A water mill creaked. Cicadas fiddled. The humble village was lulled toward sleep in the twilight.

But suddenly at 9 p.m. sharp an electric guitar section twanged out wildly and blasted the quiet night. Now it was time for RevDev propaganda tunes! Many families were in bed by dark; they were tired out and had their fill of RevDev. Forget it! Now they leapt from bed and danced out the door when a rock group blared, grated, moaned, strangled, and crashed its pastoral strains. It was *The Vampires,* and they were smash hits in Saigon; they found dollars in them there boonies as they went around giving concerts under Government contract. They took their fabulous show on the road and blasted this quiet ville outa' sight! For one thing *The Vampires* revamped old patriotic tunes—but not the usual nostalgiac thing about going home to one's native village. Next thing they gave out American candy to sleepy children who were trotted out by order of the Culture Committee. But to get the candy bars you had to sing along like you meant it.

Meanwhile on the hamlet's edge a cockfight got in progress. Cadres and grunts not on duty watched the referee light a joss stick as two owners faced off the ruffled cocks. Peck, jab. Clash of feathers. Wah! No, it's all bets off! One bird turned away before the joss stick burned to a stated length. But the next pair lurched and went at it like beasts. Haha! Blood spattered the feathers. This was more like it. A cloudy phlegm oozed from a pecked eye. Between rounds the owners sucked their cock's comb and blew water under the wings; then back at 'im. Attack. Slash an eye. Jerk, hack. Rip wattles. Tear at the other's hackles. Now the men looking on got excited, fisting cash. There was a break to stitch up gashes with a needle and thread. A feather was stuck down the bird's throat to sop blood. One angry owner took his near beaten cock's head in his mouth, bit it off, and then spat out a shiny red gob.

This act drew clapping and laughter. The next pair of birds darted
and pecked at irate eyes that went cloudy; or one bird burrowed
under its opponent's wings. Again, again the fighting cocks leapt,
fell back, bled all over the cockpit. And a few dozen men cried
out beside themselves and groaned in anguish and shook dong-
filled fists until the vanquished cock fell and quivered on its side,
gasping its last.

But if a G.I. asked a villager about it the next day, he was told
that a cockfight was a national pastime and was about moral and
even spiritual values. First that bestial act was one of purity: it
had no hypocrisy. Then, a fighting cock showed uprightness,
great endurance in pain, an ability to deal out while withstand-
ing the most disastrous blows. This was Vietnam. A fighting cock
symbolized the national character always being put to it, always
facing the *coup dur* with an inhuman steadfastness and integrity
and faith in the final victory. And, as the stages of the pitiless
fight wore on, as one cock pecked the other down bloodily to the
ground—there could be the most dramatic sudden reversals, but
no let up, no compromise. And how much went into the training
and the careful bringing along of a promising fighting cock! It
was like a prime contender in boxing. But above all, in these stag
affairs, the highest ideals of the national character were said to
be embodied in the most bestial performance imaginable—beast
and ideal, two far opposite extremes, actually did seem to take
the stage at one time and interpenetrate and find an uncanny expression, if you knew what was happening.

After midnight the war rolled its thunder down the mountain
slopes. From its purple repose Truong Son chain flashed and reflected the blasts. No sleep for me? said the war; then not you either. On a hill not quite so far off there was M-60 machinegun fire.
M-79 grenade launchers troubled the G.I.'s sleep. Joey awoke and
heard B-40 Chinese light bazookas, 40 mm mortar fire like a flock
of parrots squalling. And he wondered: could it come here?

Some gibbon apes gave a fluty chirrup in the night; they were
drawn close by spicy scents from dinner.

Far out across Nam Bo plain a B-52 air strike creased the night
of Vietnam.

The RevDev village drifted in and out of a fitful slumber. Along
deserted lanes between the silent hootches a PRC-25 radio blent
its thud-thud static with the sounds of distant battle.

XII

Another day passed. Joey's time wound down. He went from short to shorter, as the hours crawled like turtles across a hot highway; and the ville led a charmed life and drowsed out the sultry hours. Grunts lounged at their posts; they bitched about Drawber; they shot the breeze about good life they had left and meant to resume back home. As a rule they were rotated on the outer defenses, and this left boocoo leisure to sssss' joints of a superb Laotian marijuana. At night the men yawned in a darkness filled with faroff stars plus crickets and a few other sounds.

That afternoon Tommy Lerch gave a yawn and said:

—Pacify me, I don't mind.

Gamecock:

—So said Sally Ann to her Jody.

—Who 'dat Sarry Ann? asked the boy Ha.

Sanger laughed:

—It means any girl back home.

—Who 'dat Jody?

—He's a guy not sucker enough to wind up in Vietnam—said Clement the college dropout.—Jody's the one who got the girl.

—Oh.

Ha paused in thought.

—Pa-ci-fi-ca-tion, said Lerch. It beats the piss outa' *sat cong*-ification.

—Ha ha—Ha smiled sweetly—*sat cong* mean kirr' commie'lat.

A few PRU operatives in the hamlet—Provincial Recon Units—made no secret about former VC ties, and they had *sat cong* tattooed on their chests as punishment.

Each day the alert ten year-old, Ha, who was the grandson of Mr. Quoc, came to hang out on the perimeter. He was like a mascot. He didn't beg or say stupid things, the G.I.-numbah-one bit. He was well brought up by his attractive mom—a certain reserve lurked in Ha's playful words, as though beauty kept its secret. Also he had a gift for languages and picked up slang words which sent the men in stitches. They dug him.

—Beat piss outa'. Mean no good. Mean a dud.

—Quite the contrary, my good man.

His mother Mai had that thing about her, a sensuous hint when she walked in the village. There was speculation as to her man's absence; she went to RevDev events by Quoc's and her son's side. Ha was discreet beyond his years when a grunt asked him a question; but once he said his dad was in an ARVN unit sent after Tet up to I-Corps near Khe Sanh. Mai's smile seemed to suggest like a maquis Mona Lisa, and she nodded when she crossed Joey Gilbert's path. But don't be fooled—she had the mask of other villagers, such as Dzeun, Tu Sang, Dzit, Eay Tao, Au Co, Chi-Nguyet, Met, Kinh, Ngu, La Cai, Nit, an old man called Khiem, a bicyclist great grandmother named Kien who hauled the biggest bundles of sticks you ever saw along with a small girl named Little Pu. All of them, all greeted their friends the G.I.-Joes with a sort of grin, and half turned their eyes.

—Do your names mean something too? asked Clement.

Ha told them:

—Kien mean stlong, faithfur'.

Clement asked, but even he didn't pick up on it. For what has a grunt to do with linguistics? A grunt belches and says howdy-do on patrol after breakfast. A grunt lends his screwy grin to a meeting or show in the Communal House. A grunt chuckles at a cockfight the same way he takes the limp bony handshake, like birds served in sauce, of Dzeun or Dzui.

—Kinh mean othel' wu'ld, mean—hm.

—Mean hm? said Tootie.

The medic scowled as Ha opened the yellow and red book he had with him: TỰ-ĐIỂN VIỆT-ANH. When Ha looked up *kinh* in the dictionary, his pure features gave a wrinkle, like Tootie's. Ha could mimic a G.I., and it struck them each time, and made them laugh and say: Hey, what the . . .? Ha's eye found the place:

—D'dlead' . . .

—Enunciate, my good man.

—Dleaded seafirsh. *Kinh.*

Clement bowed to look too, and shrugged.

Ha shrugged like Clement.

—Dreaded sea fish—said Troupial with a laugh.—That's it alright.

Ha laughed and said:

—Dat's it arraht.

Clement and Tootie laughed. Fern laughed. Troupial laughed louder. Hole laughed.

Ha laughed happily, almost.

—Dleaded seafirsh. Ha ha ha!
They all laughed until it sort of got out of hand, and tears came.

Clement asked the boy:
—Tell me, my good man. All these cadres and such: just what do the people think they're here for? What do they accomplish?
—'comprish?
—Yeah, you know, achieve, get done.
—'chieve?
When Ha didn't want to answer right away, if in fact he could, he turned it into an English lesson.
Clement said:
—What do the cadre do?
—What do? Ah, make map, dlaw hamret. Take pitchall', V'etcong.
Ha sang out the word with a cute look.
Tootie said:
—Some of these cadre dudies ask a lot of stuff. I say put 'em in a crate like apples, and ship 'em off to Paolo Condor.
—What'door? said Manito. Paulie—?
—It's a pleasant resort area in the South China Sea—said Clement.—A vacation spot for communists. Just see your local AID travel agent.
—It's a tropical island paradise—said Troupial.—Five star, eh wot?
—Five-star tiger cages, my good man. Torture anyone? It was in the news Stateside.
The boy stared at Joey who sat off to one side. Ha looked at the leader's swart unshaven face. Joey didn't bicker with Ha like the others—what mean 'launchy' G.I.? Joey just nodded and treated kids as equals. And Joey didn't laugh, so Ha took the cue and didn't laugh around him.
For a moment Ha was silent and let the others talk. He gazed at Joey, and his eyes had a look to them, knowing. For the squad leader was a man apart. And Ha had seen him pick up and carry nine little kids at one time on a bet. It was fun to see village children dripping from the big G.I.'s shoulders, arms and hips that day, as he paraded through the main square and posed for a RevDev camera.

XIII

Short time.

Twelve days more for Joey Gilbert. Then a wake-up—and go home, begin the search.

The village went on with its quiet comings and goings as RevDev began to bear fruit in a new school, a clean well, a canal bridge in repair. And there was salt! No longer did one need to burn bamboo and reed roots to get a kind of salt, or use tannin from tree bark. No longer were stores of rice eked out by a seed manioc tuber. A few villagers still went in for 'magic medicine' to protect them from war; they made a powder out of bark ash and roasted bat dung which was a sure cure for 37 mm MGs and 57 mm recoilless cannons—guns captured by VC and turned around on their enemies, and RevDev collaborators.

At night on perimeter Lerch, Chingi, Gamecock could hear the long range guns and watch eerie tent flares, a slow-motion electric storm in the distance. The earth shook beneath them after an air strike a hundred hills away.

In the afternoon Mister Quoc spoke frankly to Joey and Troupial of the people's mixed feelings. The Americans brought wealth and technology to Vietnam and made men rich. But then a tank rolled its tracks over the rice fields. It was hard work to transplant rice. Or a crazy G.I. began to shoot pigs, chickens, carabao buffalo with his M-16 while shouting at them: Piggy, you numbah ten! Bomb craters made the roads a mess so villagers couldn't get their rice to market. One day a horror took place: U.S. bulldozers came and ruined ancestral tombs—for the fun of it! G.I.s laughing, whoopee! Many were the curses hurled at VC agent provocateurs, but the people also felt that Ong Tay, Mr. Westerner, must clean up his act if he wished to win hearts and minds. This term pacification dated back to the Chinese who held Annam for long centuries. Well now, can you drive families behind barbed wire, pen them up, and think they will thank you? In this candid moment Quoc also spoke of the people's hatred for defoliation:

—Planes come and spray the forest. Spray watermelons and tomatoes, which turn black. Our banana, papaya, coconut trees, so many ruined. Ground hard.

Sure the rice fields in VC zones must look to be poisoned. But defoliation also killed off the monkeys and gibbon. And farmers could no longer grow fruit and vegetables along the canals and roadside.

—You know VC make use of this. Woman give birth to devil, three eyes and seven fingers. Maybe look okay but no brain. One come out only flesh and blood vessels. Must bury right away. Medicine from sky is bad.

Joey nodded. In nearly twelve months no Vietnamese, not mama- and papa-san peasants any more than Tu Do bar girls and profiteers; not Noup and the other ARVN allies, guides, second-class grunts, all the war-oriented population—none talked to him this way on the sensitive things. He squinted out at a lone woman bowed over her paddy plot; and at the blue haze of mountains beyond, Truong Son cordillera which was Vietnam's spinal cord; and then at the humble woman working with the earth to earn her living.

—Why tell me? he said.

Ha's grandfather raised an eyebrow. His tan leisure suit and sparse graying hair went well with the smile in his eyes and bronze complexion. A cultured man, he must have ties beyond this poor rural village. But did he think the grunt Gilbert had any say about the way things were turning out?

In his mind Joey saw Quoc side by side with his own father at home. This one's past and family were part of a process dating from the dawn of time—the neolithic Phung Nguyen, and Bronze Age Dong Son civilizations. Quoc's life and spirit were deeply rooted in his people's history, its ancient tradition. Mister Quoc seemed full of secrets and shadings, but he also was solid. By contrast Joey's dad, Emory Gilbert, was a public figure. Emory had a kind of star-spangled persona that drifted on the modern surface: so glittery not with sunlight but with fame. Emory the brilliant liberal floated along bobbing and turning in the day's political and intellectual currents. Emory was a great success, and even Joey, his adoring son, knew he could be pretty vain; but Quoc hardly knew the meaning of success in that sense. Did it apply to Ho Chi Minh? In his fifties Emory was on the move again and very much in vogue, a creature of U.S. media. His snide younger son called him an Easter parade balloon, which was unfair. Mr. Quoc on the other hand lived not for photo ops but as a village elder with a quiet dignity, a respect from his people that went without saying.

Of course Emory had a shared past too; yet it seemed he had to recreate himself day after day in some new more spectacular way. Mr. Quoc *was* his people, in this ancient land, but Emory Gilbert was like a stark media image, all individualism risen to the ultra-competitive top, and pervasive network dominance—but brittle.

—I'm getting old now, said Quoc. You see, tired of war. Also, your . . . forgive me . . . your country is doing this . . . to us.

—Eleven more days, said Joey. I go home.

—Ah. —Quoc glanced away from the tall wiry soldier. —So . . . you go home.

—Yes. Good luck to you, Sir, and Mai and Ha, really.

In the fields the peasant woman stood up and stretched a moment. Joey thought of his own wife so deep in her work that way, with a pride in it. Hands to hips the woman took pause and stared in from the hot field at the two men who looked at her. Then she turned, bent forward again with her basket held to one side, and went on with the task.

XIV

When there were ten days and a wake-up left in the squad leader's tour of duty, a few things began to take place in the hamlet. Lerch's E-tool was stolen: now who would do that? Then it was a two-way radio from Troupial's gear, and medic Tootie lost a box of malaria pill phials, and Sanger couldn't find his boots. Top Drawber did not love it when two flashlights were lifted from his headquarters, and he said no slack time or bennies—and none of the ice cold beer sent in by Col. Pricecroft—until they were found. Top said the petty thefts had to do with grunts smoking reefer, and so he came down on the whole squad. Hard man, he also held back their mail. And then, as if that didn't put a cap on it, the sadist ordered as steady diet for one full week the ham 'n m-f-er C-rats so loathed by the men.

Stateside filled Da Nang and Bien Hoa warehouses with such items as were lost, but it was not a good thing when they went psst! into thin air. Drawber called in Mr. Quoc for a talk, but more gear went on its way the next day. And mistrust grew among the troops.

Lately the nights were too quiet for an area within earshot of heavy artillery exchanges. First Cav units with ARVN and air support were trying to repel VC-NVA incursions deep in this key stretch between the Tay Nguyen, Highlands, and Plain of Reeds sectors south of the Parrot's Beak. By day RevDev cadre and hootch dwellers went about their projects with a smile but after dark the hamlet lay in an uneasy silence. On Joey's ninth to last afternoon the astute Fern said:

—Some on 'em is plain VC gooks. I c'n tell a VC gook when I see one.

—You got many in West Virginia? said Sanger.

—Yup. Looks too happy, that'un. Up tuh somethin', he is.

—Well, yes—said Clement with a wink. —Give them an inch and they'll liberate Appalachia.

When Manito lifted his free hand to swat a cockroach, Noup cried:

—No!

—My good man—Clement chuckled—you stirred the pacifist yearnings of the ARVN.

—Nevah' kirr cockloach, said Noup. Bat ruck! Onet' pun time poo' student kirr loach. Loach say: I Buddha, hehrp pass bick exam. Hehrp. Bat ruck kirr loach!

—In a past incarnation—Clement shook his preppy head—I stamped out a roach, and it was the Enlightened One. Now Buddha uses these Viet Cong to get back at me. Well, next time VC sappers come in past the wire for us crying: Kill! kill! *sat phat! sat sinh!* —

—Sat trùng! —Noup giggled.—Kirr insect!

—Next time they try to avenge that Bhagavawaterbug I squashed in a past life, A.D. 1967 in North Philly, I'll lay down my M-16 and chant the Diamond Sutra. I'll preach the Dharma to those VC comrades. I'll tell them: hey, even Shakyamuni had to die, you know. Only our spirit belongs to us, but the rest goes its way at death. So much for materialism. Thus I must ask those gung-ho VC: why in such an all-fired hurry, comrades? Give it a rest! Anyway you may have my flesh and bones if you like, since I once did evil to a—Clement gestured grandly—O earthly illusion! Was it to a pest? Was it a god? Go on, gook person, do your worst! Wreak your Buddhist vengeance! You can blast these four elements apart, my temporary abode on earth, but they're not the real me. Shantih, my good man, shantih.

Noup, the ARVN cadre, stared at Clement who went on with his sutra. The grunts laughed at the college dropout in his exalted spiel; but Troupial looked sad: maybe thinking back on the botanist, Blair, who bought it. As for World Serious: he was deep in his RELAD dreams (Release from Active Duty) and paid no mind to my good man's chant of the cockroach karma.

—All these little bodhisattva Viet Congies running around—

—Body what? said Tootie.

—Bodhisattva, future Buddhas, self-sanctified ones. Though in this phase of eternity they are not perfectly pure yet, trying to kill us.

—Self what?—Sanger blinked.—Does that mean they jerk off?

—Please, my good man! They all stick around to help others on this sinful earth, by sending them from it: since desire for the luscious Mai, mother of Ha, bringeth such unhappiness.

The hillbilly Fern gaped at Clement:

—Garsh, I didn' think you knowed Vet'mese.

—Why stick around? you may ask. Why seek to save others and organize a lot of horny souls for nirvana's ranks, by offing them? Why stay away one minute from blissful nonexistence? Good question, my good man. I don't know why these bodhisattva VC still want to cock their guns so we grunts can transmigrate. Don't they feel envious? But there is no such dross in them: it is an act of saintly self-sacrifice on their part.

Sanger rang out:

—Mastur'grate, you say? Is that a Buddhist concept?

—Go straight to hell! Son, you must uphold the Four Noble Truths revealed to Buddha in the Great Enlightenment. Follow the Eightfold Path, and cease to desire Mai, I say, voluptuous daughter of Quoc!

—My good man, said Lerch, you can shove nirvana up your butthole.

—Renounce all sexual pleasure! said Clement.

—Does that inclue dipping my wickie? said Tootie.

—Forsake copulation! —Clement gave a broad grin.

—Do what? said Fern.

—Harm no creature alive!

—Somebody should convert Topper to Buddhism, said Lerch.

—The VCs may do it soon enough—said Gamecock, sauntering up.

—Right speech! No more swear words.
—Sheee-it! quoth Hole.
—Right conduct, right contemplation, right ecstasy!
—Ecstasy? said Tootie, and he picked his nose, and then ate it.
—To achieve selfless contemplation by a trance-like meditative state: this is the goal of the VC Buddha.
—Jagging off is my goal, said Sanger. It's quicker, easier, and more fun.
—And you achieve it, said Lerch.
—Twice a night, said The Sang.
—No matinee performance? said Tootie.
—Mortify your desire, my good man.
—That 'air'—said Fern—hain't suh 'aisy.

XV

Joey stood up and walked off a ways. Was he pissed at 'em for being such a bunch of grunges? Naw, he just wanted outa' this jernt . . . By himself he gazed at the mountains. What a beautiful country it was, so rich in nature . . . and how he hated it. Grunts called shorttimers like himself and Troupial the two-digit midgets when they talked over the squad leader's going away. Then there would be no more force such as Pricecroft's favorite, the star ballplayer, to offset this maniac Drawber's bad moods. Then it would be war chores galore, life as latrine duty; then came the day of recon patrol out beyond the stubble field. Go hump paddy and grassland to the distant treeline for no good reason. Insects, leeches, 60 lbs. of gear in the steam furnace heat; and it was dangerous, and of no use. All saw this and Joey too. All asked him with their eyes to extend six more months, and he felt a strange last-minute whim to do so. Would he miss these kids: the Pfc.'s he had helped train for the trail and broken in? It was hard not to feel sorry for guys left in this hell hole. Yes, he would miss the column he led, marching their tocuses through the forest. He wished they could all go home together.

But nothing could sway him from now on. For he had one idea in mind—or one question, as the final ti-ti time in-country went from nine days down to eight, and he turned his face Stateside.

When an AFRS disc jockey spun this or that tune, like the one about sunny California, he felt a kind of fear not like the one over here. Ah, did you say home? Me back there around all those clean upright family things I left behind? Hell, I'll just muck 'em up . . . And can I tell my people about this? No, they do not want to hear what I've seen here, and done. Why try to talk about it since I myself want to forget? Joey tried to focus on his wife's face, but her features escaped him. Dark blue eyes . . . Then Newell came to mind again, an obsession, and there was fear like a twang.

Eight more days and then a wake-up, oh yay. Fly far, far away across the Pacific Ocean from this shit. Let all Asia fall like dominoes if it wants to so bad . . . He saw the scene at Travis Airforce Base: stay in uniform as you process out and then on the street get splashed with red paint. Baby killer! Baby Killer! They shouted from a passing car. Well, he'd go up into the Berkeley Hills for a word with his brother. He'd go storming up there like it was the seven against Thebes, brother against brother, the two sons of Oedipus; and they kill one another at the seventh gate . . . He always loved his younger brother and admired him secretly even while resenting him; —but could he now love the seducer of his wife? Or would he yank him out of the house, that hippie commune, and kick him on down the hill and into San Francisco Bay?

Joey moved off by himself. He didn't care for their chatter just now. He gazed off at the mountains, and there was a jealous rage playing on his lean features. Had the woman poisoned his blood? his mind? . . . Even the First Sergeant, let alone grunts and the meek villagers, did not get too near World Serious. No, even Topper didn't mess too much with this one. Mainly Drawber wanted to see his last of Joey Gilbert.

Well, go on, boy. Go back home to your greased life, your dreams turned sour. Go home to frighten the people you love . . . Remains unviewable.

XVI

—*Oh my god oh my god!*
—Call Top!
—*God god god!*

—Where's Tootle? Tooot-i-ie!

It was too late for the medic.

At dawn Noup, ARVN scout seconded to the Combined Action Platoon, went with Sanger to take a turn on perimeter. In those instants a volley of shots rang out, then one, one, like an afterthought, out on the burr. Then there were Sanger's shouts. The troop bawled, hands to his face:

—*Oh, oh, oh! God, oh*—*!*

Gamecock, the refined grunt from Charleston where his mom kept a salon for well-to-do friends to talk books, art, gossip—Gamecock had now been to his last social function. He lay limp with a red spot on his temple. The pale blue eyes stared in space, and the southern accent was silenced. A neat job: his sandy hair was hardly mussed. By his side Wisembroder had got it too but messier. The jaw was cleaved by a bayonet thrust after he took a bullet in the neck. So it seemed. Close up. Wisembroder went about his duties with nary a word to the next guy. He nursed his stock of weed and didn't expend words on the meaning of life. Besides his speech quirks, his farty-far and crotchety hello of a morning, no one knew much about him. He had folks on Cape Cod, or was it Nantucket? And a wife? A sweetheart waiting for him? She would have a long wait . . . Well, in lieu of the person there was a service number. In war man is a cipher; only the idea counts.

Gamecock. Wisembroder. They lay there.

—Sappers did this, VC—said Sanger running up, breathless.

When Drawber got to the scene, he was quite irked that the enemy could waltz past a Claymore pattern and treat the wire like his own back fence.

—The enemy is within—said Joey, scanning the RevDev ville astir at first light: toward its day of constructive activities.

—Horse piss! —said Top quick to naysay any word by the squad leader. —Troupial, call for a dust-off, and I need two fart sacks.

The First Sergeant's tone was one of disgust. Look on these men who died by their own negligence: probably while asleep. Never happen in Korea . . . Top's response made Joey think of an assistant basketball coach at his college who had a phobia for any sign of weakness: when a player fell, was hurt, failed in some way no matter if small or large. Calmly he looked at the poor man's pug nose. The lifer badgered his line troops and made a none too brilliant career on their backs . . . Hell, seven more days: one little week of 24-hour days, then a wake-up. Leave this grim fiasco in Drawber's capable hands. But will Dad, Lemon, Cindy even know me? I'm not the same anymore: not a ballplayer. Who am I? And where did my wife go? Oh! Dad, why did you let her leave? Why didn't you keep her here, protect her, for my sake? . . . No, I'm not myself: does it show? Of course it does. I still love her, even more; and I—

The clever boy Ha and Mr. Quoc came along the path with Tommy Lerch. Quoc's eyes met Joey's. What can you do; they know all; they are everywhere, in a field headquarters and a Saigon ministry.

—Wham—said Lerch, softly.

—Check this out, said Sanger.

Wisembroder's helmet lay a dozen feet from the foxhole. They saw it as day broke. It lay there rim up like a dead horseshoe crab.

—Look, said Sanger.

There was a calendar taped on one side: the month of August 1968.

The day's date was X'd—in red, and not by him.

As for the grunt socialite Richard Danforth: he stared dully skyward past black coils of concertina wire in the instants before sunrise.

Suddenly Joey shot his gaze left. He winced—hit before he heard a shot: by a ray of sun bursting over the horizon eastward. Like an invading force the sunlight cleared the treeline and raced across the nacreous paddy surface.

XVII

There were the same village rhythms: hammers, files, saws, working away in the tense midafternoon. On the rim where thatched huts grouped beneath a grove of filao pines, the RevDevvers were hard at work digging a 10-meter pit for a communal privy. Was there ever such a mockery?

Next evening Joey went for dinner with Ha's family—minus Mai's absent husband. He had to bend his big frame to go in the low hootch. There was a nice pigsty on the veranda. Poultry had the run of the place. Plaited bamboo was used as walls for three small rooms. The kitchen had a larder and a hearth to prepare pig slush. All day long a hacked banana trunk was boiling in a cauldron to make puree.

Outside, a few cockchafers were stuck in spiderwebs along the thatch. Inside, it was a sooty earthen space, humble, but neat and well kept. The attractive Mai ground rice in a mortar while cassava roots baked and maize cobs grilled.

At night a tropical moon rose slowly amid the delicate trees. Through July the equatorial monsoons had blown: damp marine winds from sea to land. These blent with hot dry Lao winds from the west, like foehn winds, and blew on Truong Son's long slopes. The summer heat and humidity were hard to bear in the bush. At night monsoon mist made a flare shine eerily, like a cross on fire.

But tonight as Joey said goodbye at Mai's there was a clear bright August sky. A crescent moon outlined the clouds and dark mountain contours. Mr. Quoc, Ha, Mai stood in the low doorway gazing as the big U.S. soldier moved away.

Gamecock and Wisembroder didn't make it.

Now five more days, and one wake-up.

XVIII

In late morning Joey strolled past the Communal House where a RevDev cadre led her students in reciting a poem. Slender, with silken jet hair done up in a bun, the cadre waved shyly at the G.I. who smiled. The children all turned their heads to watch that Western giant pass.

Through the ville RevDev elements came and went in their black pajamas. They were making the sanitation trench, building a new wall, starting an outreach program for preventive health.

Joey paused a moment and moved on. Four days . . . 3,2,1 more of 'em . . . and a lift-off. Last day and then . . . wake up. The sound of a new water pump, puttputt, sher' . . . puttputt, sher' . . . went to the rhythm of his thoughts. In the gathering heat the children sang out General Tran Quang Khai's famous Thirteenth Century poem on the Mongol invader:

At Chuong Duong port with lances and pikes
We stopped them!
At Ham Tu channel we damned up
The barbarous flood.

Puttputt, sher' . . . puttputt. In high voices the kids chanted and stared at the slow-moving man. But then, like static in the serene lilt of the song—artillery eastward maybe a dozen kliks, not further. The thunder roared and rolled forth from some grotto in the mountains—NVA emplacement?

Long-range guns were in the children's song and the quiet village of palm and reed-woven hootches.

Let's deploy our best efforts to win
The livable peace.
Protect and preserve peace forever,
O beloved homeland.

XIX

Inside the command bunker Top Drawber and 2nd Lieutenant were planning an action in response to the perimeter deaths. They radioed Company Commander for approval to send out the squad of the two victims on a probe. Twelve troops would exit the hamlet, go out past the drainage ditch and, in a widening circle, try to draw fire. That way sniper positions could be located and an enemy detachment flushed out like quail. They must be hiding nearby. And then Command calls in air support if the two small-weapons fire teams can't handle it alone. Also, it was best to use Gilbert's squad, Top argued, since its leader had rare booniecraft after a year minus two days in-country. Might as well use it.

—A little work won't hurt the 11-B. —Drawber liked to call men by their m.o., job title. —It won't kill him to run one more mission. They're all going soft as 96-echoes (clerks) in this boudoir.

An hour later Wade Jenkins sat with Clement, Tootie, and pointman Chingi in their bunker.

—What boo'el-crap is it now? said Chingi.

—The good man justifies his lofty position—said Clement—at your and my expense.

They waited for Joey gone to fetch orders from 'Top Kick'.

—Way the lifer stay'ers at Jo 's ay'ess—said Chingi—he don' like it no'who when a grunt gits riss'pec'.

Simmer:

—Joey 'n my man Troupial shoat. Done theyz'.

Jenkins came out of his sullen silence. He'd about had enough. The fool Drawber had disgruntled him the past 48 hours. Deaths on the burr looked bad for Top, whose shtick was defense, and made him put on pressure all around. But it seemed ever since the RevDev transfer Simmer had been Top's main post to kick. Also, the bull's behavior had a racial note to it when he called Jenkins Mister Softee. So the grunt thought about it and then asked Joey: Should I protest? Lodge an official complaint? Well then: you must go by the chain of command, namely gripe to the man himself. Then the fox would look into what went down with the chickens, right? That's how the U.S. Army cleans its dirty laundry. Don't ask questions, soldier. Obey. For this reason you were duly brainwashed from the first day in basic. And the first rule drummed into your numb grunt's skull and then drilled to a well-oiled reflex every day thereafter until the day of discharge was: Thou shalt not jump the Chain of Command.

Amen.

—You cannot win with death, taxes, or your superior officer. Or snot—said medic Tootie, the squad's scientific consultant. —Go on, pick your nose until Doomsday: you'll never be done with it.

Thus said Tootie.

Drawber liked to cite Army Code chapter and verse. He knew what he needed of the Code, and he set the Great Seal to his bigotry. Top said early on he would straighten out Jenkins' shoulders; or, if not, then send his ass to Firebase Cody up on the DMZ. The lifer went after any personal weakness with a will; he did this in Army tradition's name. You grunts, remember the pride of past engagements, two glorious World Wars with Korea for the kicker—where Top got his famous wound.

—That wound—said Clement—was a gift of Ares god of war. The good man has a case of what is called 'command neurosis', but it doesn't matter. He's a hero with a wound.

One July afternoon Drawber marched Simmer Jenkins, Sanger and Gamecock out by the perimeter and ordered them to dig a grave. The platoon sergeant didn't look more teed off than usual; though for a week he had been at Jenkins and given him extra orders. In the humid heat Top kibbitzed and made a few remarks while the Spec-5 plus Sanger and Gamecock chopped with their entrenchment tools at the red earth. All three were dripping sweat.

—Go on—said Drawber. —Make it good and big. A mass grave is in order here.

Later, Simmer told Troupial:

—I felt damn tense. Didn' know what duh fool wannet'. He rip a peace symbol off muh neck an' den' de' udder two 'n toss 'em in duh grabe 'n say: bury 'dat shit.

In his way the First Shirt stood for twenty years' service to an ideal insulted in this man's Army by the term: lifer.

The night after the perimeter attack, at 2 a.m., some jerk lobbed a smoke bomb in the top sergeant's hootch. Was it a grunt fed up with Top's stuff and nonsense? Was it a VC agent among the RevDevvers trying to provoke discord? Now Drawber who was spiteful and petty on his better days—also a platoon liability since his poor tactical judgment in this situation far from Korea was rivalled only by his self-righteousness—now Drawber called the squad leader in for a talk. And the result, thought Simmer Jenkins, would probably be a suicide patrol with himself in the lead.

The plum known as RevDev had begun to rot on the vine. So Simmer sat in the silent bunker and nodded, deep in his anger, at a comment by the street kid Chingi. Then he said out loud for all to hear that if Joey brought back bad news about a dangerous mission, some cockeyed Drawber scheme to risk men's lives for no good reason: then his name was not Wade Jenkins if he would not go and frag that cracker's ass.

—Hey what they gonna' do? Send me tuh' Nam? Mebbih' Long Binh Stockade? Leas' I live that way.

Yip, Simmer would go and frag that racist asshole where he lay snoring up a storm on his bunk, before the sun rose.

XX

When the squad leader came back with news of a saddle-up at 2300 hours, Simmer just stared at him. Simmer was real long-jawed even before this piece of good news. And then he gave a sigh and got on his feet. He seemed to shake a little as he leaned and took his M-16.

Outside, in the dark, the grunt walked. During his time in-country he had strolled through dirt-poor villes after days out in the killer-grass, going waist-deep across paddy fields, with the silent threat of a treeline off to his right or left. Lonely hamlets were like a snapshot of the apocalypse; there was no movement but only a group of charred hootches with a skeleton stuck in the ground like a trophy. But now Simmer went along on a different kind of mission, and his steps had a bounce. He neared the fortified sector on the southern side where a wood watchtower jutted up in the night sky.

He passed rows of sandbags. In his nervous state he felt Top Drawber as a sort of neutral being. The man no longer mattered. Only accounts mattered. The man was no longer so hateful in these moments before the two of them settled accounts. Simmer felt no hate but only the wild spiel of his nerves like a paroxysmic jazz. He had the words in mind: a black life, a white life.

XXI

Inside the command bunker Top was staring at a terrain map. On a table lay two topographical sketches done by a local hand; they were smudged, primitive. But on the wall hung a cartographic tour de force; it was the entire corps in detail, dense with coordinates and tiny marker flags.

Top went over his plan of a late night probe. He was so deep in it he may have heard and not thought twice about a brief thud, thud, outside the closed door. Yes, a scuffle took place not twenty feet away from him, and he looked up—but then there was silence. It must have been a one-sided struggle, only one groan.

In fact it was over so fast—the grunt en route to blow his superior's brains out never knew what hit him. Joey Gilbert came like a cat out of the night and rapped him once with a service revolver. And Simmer fell.

XXII

It was a few minutes past eleven.

They went.

—Too quiet—said Manito, the assistant gunner, peering into darkness beyond the perimeter.

In close single file the men moved out. They distanced the wire and filed past the observation post where Gamecock and Wisembroder were greased.

—This RevDev ville—said Sanger too loud—is a sorryass piece of turd. It's as VC as the next berg.

—No contact? No action? —said Clement. —Yon grunt smoketh pot, is cocky and hard to manage. The good man Top says: go on a recon patrol.

—Shut up—Joey hissed, and he thought: two days. The idiot sends me out here with two . . . two days . . . two to go. Now get through this.

A twig snapped. Where? Them?

—Hey, give 'em color TVs in their shitpits—said Sanger from sheer nervousness. —A gook'll hate you either way.

—Topper is out of control, said Clement. I mean his oral sphincters—

—I said *shut* it. Shhh.

They went in a wedge. Joey led. He had bumped Chingi from point. RTO Troupial and medic Tootie were in the center. Behind them the hamlet seemed to huddle and try to hide; while ahead of them, out in the darkness, Truong Son's southernmost ridges sprawled in a mass under the stars. Noup, the scout, was with them.

Joey stepped slowly over the approaches: the strategic stretch beyond moat and earthen ramparts. His eyes honed in on a contour, a grass tuft; on clayey stubble field which was good for homemade mines. Now his LURP patrol gigs with Bufillu and Tombigbee were paying off. For now, tonight, World Serious had to play on a bad-hop infield. It had booby-trapped base paths. And home plate was a Pacific Ocean away.

He was in a strange mood: way up, in this mission's first moments, because using what he knew, and too he didn't have to think about her, and her. Into the homestretch on a calm, quiet islet of RevDev, his mind and body had been bogging down. Never in his life had he taken to the easy times. His digestion tightened. He slept off and on and bad dreams caught him offguard. This was true before Vietnam. But last night he dreamt of graves registration detail: on his dad's farm he tramped a bleak field where cauliflower rotted to a stench in late November. In one hand an M-1, in the other a glad bag, he went down the furrows and his boots squoodged an arm here, a leg, torso chunk, a pink face there; he saw Army dogtags planted in a row, like seeds in the reddish soil. Then back at base camp, in his dream, he smoked dope in a bare room beside the fart sack he was carrying: filled with cauliflower heads. It moved. The zipper went down, and a red, muddy hand came out.

By day Joey had flashes of such dream images. Lately he was unable to sleep soundly, and there were moments when he felt he might go dinky dow.

XXIII

Midnight. Now one more day. Make it through this day.

The squad went in the silence. There was no moon. In the dark each step risked to hit a trip-wire, trigger a punji pit beneath their feet. Last day; now the wake-up. Tomorrow early, if possible, catch a lift to Division Headquarters—and from there to Saigon, and wait out the last few hours.

Had Drawber gone mad to send a squad out here like this? Why not one or two grunts? Why not himself and Chingi, easier to maneuver? No, he must punish all for the smoke bomb on his bunk. And not a word to Pricecroft of course: that would look bad. What? You mean your men don't respect you? Well, Drawber's ill will and his petty envy would hurt him sooner or later. But where did the Army dig up such bullheaded bureaucrats: its functionaries so gung-ho to expose other people's lives on a whim?

Now Joey made his way with the nimble probe step. He had eleven months and thirty days of experience, and the idea was to cash it in. Okay: putter around and stall out here for five hours until dawn. Skol had had that skill: to put in time while trying to avoid contact. For all his tradecraft Skoly-Skol was greased in an ambush, his head and chest like a sieve dripping blood.

Now the point man stopped. He beckoned RTO.

—Cheeta-six . . . Junior.

In his earphone the two-way spluttered.

—Cheeta-six, over.

—Movement out front, over.

—Request numeric approximation, over.

—Dunno', Cheeta-six, wait up.

Suddenly there was a whirling sense. Confusion. Pop! pop! *Tatatatat!* On the right a flare went up. Suddenly the fire field was a tentage of bright lights. Psst! Explosion. Psst! Explosion.

—Rocket grenades right! Give me an angle!

—It's an attack on the village!

There was heavy machinegun fire. Thump, thump. There were mortar shells plus the sudden sharp crack of artillery—faint whistle, shells overhead. For a moment as tracers arced out from the hamlet Joey thought: night panic? Mad minutes? It was a joke as artillery pumped the countryside filled with enemy troop movement—in the grunts' minds.

But no joke if friendly fire, saturating the approaches, came this way. Leave it to Top—for confusion.

Now green VC tracers darted over, *sssss!* Flashes in series lit the perimeter. It seemed sappers had fixed satchel charges along the wire. And now every friendly M-16 opened fire as a first wave of enemy assault troops clambered through and fanned out. Artillery, mortar, MG and automatic fire, long bursts. Then— *punpunpunpunpun! Tut! tutut-t-t-tut!* Shorter bursts. NLF automatic weapons, single shots, rifle fire. It was them alright. VC inside the RevDev defenses. Enemy in the ville! Ha ha! Top wanted to get grunts killed by sending them out here? Instead he saved them. And who would save *him* now?

Joey knelt. He had to hold the squad in place. In the 155 mm artillery din, four shells at a go with pitter-pattering dirt clumps; in the whining scream of heavy mortars overhead; then again a heavier droned sort of trajectory—he tried to think what to do. First the attackers went for the blockhouse and watchtowers. They sent in bazookas on inner defense installations and moved to seize the radio room. Grimly Joey chuckled. Thank The Top after all? . . . But what to do?

Grunts had spent quiet days and weeks in a mum village filled with enemy grins. That's funny. And all the while VC cadre dug underground trenches and inched men and guns into position. Silently the other guy made ready to overrun this hamlet with its Western projects and hoards of materièl. Other sectors were stalemated so this place made a key link in north-south transport for VC and their NVA friends.

Troupial whispered:

—Let's stay put.

Joey was thinking. Within fifteen minutes VC would have their victory. Then shouts, whistles, bugle call, NLF flag raised over Top's headquarters. Two squads would be killed or taken prisoner: the remnants escorted north on the canal system as POWs. But if RevDev lines held longer—VC must pull back, fade into the night, before air support arrived.

—Cheeta-six—

More flashes, whistles. Once the three-tiered barbed wire fence was passed along with the drainage moat dug deep as a man and the ramparts: then VC medium weapons would move forward to fix up mortars and MGs on their base plates and tripods. All this was done in perfect order and timed to the split second since Dzit, Dzeun and Dzui, Mister Quoc and his angelic son, Ha, and maybe the ARVN Noup, had made reports on trenches, firepoints, arms depots, radio center, headquarters, the works. All was an open book, among family.

Joey sighed with disgust.

—Drawber wants us in now.

—Let the cocksucker defend himself, said Chingi.

—No, we've got to go.

—But no hurry, said Troup.

—No hurry, said Joey.

XXIV

Instinct no less than common sense told him to retrace the outward swath. But the first sergeant said come in by the most direct path. Pronto.

Chaos was the order of the day as VC gunners keyed on the tactical operations center and troop positions here and there in the village. The G.I.s were caught pants down when metal and fire began raining down from the other side. It was madness to go over ground held by the NLF above underground earthworks like a mini-Dien Bien Phu. It worked then, and it worked again.

But Joey knew and heard in his mind Drawber's charge: the squad leader avoided engagement by taking a roundabout way back to the ville under attack. Gilbert acted like a coward—thus Top; and court-martial was ever on the tip of that man's tongue. Well, Joey Gilbert had no bad mark on his tour so far, and he wouldn't give the stooge that satisfaction.

They struck for the village but slowly. They went step by step in a closed wedge. Joey on point tried to read the muzzle flash angles in the distance. Phwhooph! A projectile zoomed overhead. Now he guessed it was a diversionary operation while a large NVA contingent came on penetrating toward the southeast? Was this a Tet replay?

As the squad drew nearer and friendly danger was a factor, they must hunker down and wait. For when a pivotal emplacement fell, the allies fired wild barrages into the shadows.

Air support! Here they came! Streaking the night sky two Cobra gunships burst on the scene and drew ground fire. Now it was a mad light show. In the flash and flare their shark's teeth gaped helpless and were unable to coordinate above the intermingled lines as a .51-caliber flurry blent with 37 mm ack-ack bullets hurled into their path. Drawber might have the planes pulverize the entire sector where he stood finger to the trigger inside Tac-Op. But in the frenzied exchanges he would blow away grunts, ARVN, himself along with. Absolutely, and positutely.

By now villagers had scooted to a new bomb shelter on the northern edge: there *béton armé* was better than any hootch bunker. And not a blessed shell, Joey figured, would fall on the shelter; though the model agroville with its self-help projects and faces all smiles, its Drawberian desk wallahs cooking up a stellar report for Col. Pricecroft, had by now been turned into a mire dotted by 81 mm mortar pits. Tomorrow the size 14 rats and fire ants, scorpions and eight-inch centipedes would nose their way among the crumbled bunkers and deserted pathways. Spoils to the victors! No longer would the water pump, Pride of RevDev, go puttputt'sher ... No more the lilted songs and patriotic poems, the grammar lessons sung in unison by kids at the Communal House. And the new lights wouldn't flicker: lamps made of perfume bottles from the French occupation, at nightfall in the clusters of huts. And Mister Quoc, and handsome Mai, and Ha, Dzit and Dzeun, Tu Sang and Eay Tao, would not show up for the muster. No; they went with their VC friends into the safety of the forest. Comrades, mission accomplished.

XXV

Suddenly, on his left in the wedge, there was a closer explosion. A man gave a scream. It was Sanger.
—Freeze! Joey yelled. Stay where you are!
But there was a second explosion. How? Was it triggered by the first? Or remote controlled? Trip-wired? Clement looked right, stunned and deafened. By him Manito, the assistant gunner, seemed to go up in smoke, poof! a magic act.
—I said do not move! Dammit! Not one step!
A minefield. And this was why Joey did say no to Top's order to cloverleaf for snipers. Keep a close wedge and measure your steps. But they were caught anyway.
Boom-ahhh!
Tootie, the medic, bent and ran to where Tommy Lerch writhed on the ground and bawled:
—Help me! God! My—my! ... Help me someone! God—!
A fourth and then fifth mine went off as the grunts, lulled by RevDev and forgetting the trail lessons, broke ranks and scrambled in panic. Fern's voice was a high shriek, almost a whistle as he cried for his ma. Jib Benson couldn't stand that: he leapt forward to help his friend and then—boommmah! With a cry Hole

jumped about and then flopped back, like a limp dervish, nape first in the dirt.

—Help me! cried Fern. Oh god! Am I dying? Will I die?

Grunts shouted out their horror in the wafting smoke and the explosives smell, burnt metal, powder. First a bright flash then a vision: Chingi, his face a grimace, plopped up six feet like a circus clown and then down, dismembered by a mine. In the darkness now howls, shrill or guttural. Sanger lay on his back burning to death. He squirmed and sort of miaowed. With a penlight Tootie leaned over Chingi who had shrapnel, like ball bearings, in the chest. Chingi gurgled:

—I know . . . I know . . . Later for you . . . baby.

A purple aura enveloped the scene. The shorttimer Troupial tripped a mine and ignited smoke grenades (position markers) hooked on his web belt under the radio transmitter. In an instant his legs blew apart in a violet shower of bone and shredded tissue. But for another moment it was Fern who shouted loudest:

—I don't want to die! I don't want to die!

But each convulsive breath only pumped blood from Fern's truncated torso. And so his voice shivered, like an infant coming to rest, and his cries grew weaker. Fern's last moments had come as he drifted, drifted in shock, and puled like a child:

—Mama . . . Mama.

There was another explosion, and someone else screamed:

—Medic! Medic!

A purple glow enfolded the gashed bodies of grunts flung here and there. Held down by the great thumb of the war god they gave moans and sobs, broken words, broken shrieks, from their broken lives.

XXVI

For a good minute after the bombs began Joey stayed low at the point position. He was the only one who followed his order: do not move. He knelt looking and listening; and then he stirred from his pose on one knee like an on-deck hitter. With a clarity in the clutch he thought things over: density, breadth of the mine pattern, what way to flee the sector. He had heard no sniper fire. The enemy was busy at the ville.

—I can't see! —Sanger lingered. —I can't see!

Medic Tootie was spared so far as he moved among them and did what he could. Were there vital signs? The radio was kaput so no medevac. On their own now . . . Make a splint? Put on a bandage? What a joke. Tootie's fingers trembled as he shot morphine into them.

Then Joey lurched forward and stopped him. Arms around the corpsman in tears, he pinned him down and said low:

—Do you want to go home?

—Yes.

—Do you want to make it out of here?

—Yes.

He held the throbbing Tootie who was all out of dressings and first aid pouches now. They both knelt on the damp earth, as Joey in his mind called the roll: Chingi, gone, Tommy Lerch ditto. No sign of Manito. As for Troupial, the Xo Man veteran four days away from DEROS—so close, and so far.

Where was the Kit Carson scout, Noup? Ah, no sign of him. So the VC spy knew the mine pattern? Noup scooted!

Then Joey and Tootie stood up. With care they took a first step, a second. Joey led the way, glancing where mines had gone off—paths the grunts had taken as they ran about in panic. Joey paused a moment over the fallen: Jib Benson dead to the world. Sanger, Fern—no more morphine, buds. So long.

Simmer Jenkins lay wounded but alert. With him it was worse: torn, gorily, lengthwise. Simmer's guts were open to the night air, organs, viscera, as you saw when a flare lit the sky. The grunt cast a glimpse down at his own innards, then looked up at Joey, and said:

—Spaghetti 'n meatball C-rats.

—Shh, said Joey. Don't talk.

—Naw, I on'y got a minute, I'll spend it talking.

—We'll get you in.

Joey looked about. Get him in? How? Tootie sniffled at the sight of Simmer. At least cover him . . . Simmer looked his body over with wry eyes, and then said:

—You shoulda' let me waste that cracker.

Joey thought of Bufillu back home: the faithful wife, and the wheelchair for life. Which was better: this or that? And himself?

... He glanced around: no Manito. And Clement? What gave
with Clement?

—Just hang on. We'll get to the ville, and call for a dust-off. It
looks bad, but maybe no vital organ is hit. You could live.

Jenkins, eyes like purplish reflectors, gazed up:

—You go on home, Jo. It's your last day ... The Nam, what a
crazy place, right? Go on back to New York and play ball, Jo. Play
for us.

XXVII

Tootie patted Simmer's arm; then stood up looking like he had
ants in his pants.

Joey thought a moment, and said:

—Why don't you stay here with them?

—I don't want to!

—Let me risk it. You stay overnight; do not move. Then
tomorrow—

But a voice rose ... dreadful before death. It was to their left in
the wedge.

—Please help! Hel-l-lp me!

Joey urged:

—I may not make it to the village. You stay.

He gazed off at the flashes, more explosions, semiautomatic
fire like sparklers. By now a few Hu-18 single rotors hovered with
more troops to throw in—2nd Brigade special forces, 25th Infantry Division; but unable to land in the hot LZs. And there was
no leeway to hose down the landing zones and prep them with
air strikes before infantry went in. RevDev spies had charted LZs
with care no less than the command bunker and military installations and perimeter. All was known. And where did Charlie
get such outstanding information? In the same RevDev meetings
where USAID coordinators of the WHAM cadre thought they
were getting *their* updates: gleaning tips as to enemy numbers,
NLF-NVA movement, tactical and strategic objectives. All false,
on both sides! All a rigged deck. But one team was paying good
money for bad every time it turned around, and that wasn't Uncle
Ho's team.

—No, said Tootie. I'm going with you.

—Then I order you to stay here.

Behind them another grunt, maybe Sanger, still held on. Feebly he called:

—I wanna' go home!

At their feet Jenkins shuddered like a child when it stops crying.

They had lost all contact. The radio didn't work any more than did RTO Troupial: where his body lay burning in a purplish halo.

Joey thought of what Drawber said after Gamecock bought the farm. Outfit this man with a willy-peter bag. Top had the tone and twangy voice of a sports announcer. But what right by god let people like him make others do their fighting for them—always lying and lying, everyday and every way, about what a just cause it was, what freedom, what democracy? How did the Drawbers, who were menial servants, and all those above him ever get away with this: exposing the best young men of one generation and the next to the minefields of their wars of aggression?

Now strangely a grin came over Joey Gilbert's features, as he stood watching Hueys bob in and out of the billowing smoke and flashes above the ville. It was the pro athlete's metallic grin which meant he didn't give a hang except for the next play to be made. Risk injury? So what? Death? It was the price you could pay for a chance to play, and a shot.

XXVIII

He waited another moment before bolting. He gauged the scene. Tac-Air looked invalidated; there is no way to bomb, strafe, napalm when the enemy has you by the belt. And this time the standard joke didn't apply: S-5 (Civil Affairs Office) builds a village, and then S-3 (Operations Office) destroys it. It seems DH-10 Claymores beyond the wire had been a cold comfort when VC sappers shot up like jack-in-the-boxes from trap doors inside the perimeter defenses. Once a week the tunnel detection team, so-called exterminators from Division Headquarters, hit the ville and scoped it out like a bunch of laughing hyenas. They were outfitted with red smoke grenades and mechanized flamethrowers to shoot liquid napalm. But mainly they just eyeballed Ha's mom or another village woman standing hands on hips in her doorway looking at them. They poked about here and there like sore thumbs.

—It's an order, said Joey. Stay here and don't move.

But the medic was in a state at this idea. His shoulders shook as he wiped away a tear. In silence he watched the squad leader turn from him: the big wiry figure like a stalker profiled in the smoke and flicker of distant explosions. Then Joey was gone: his form woven in with the smoke-filled stubble field.

What a silence it was, for Tootie, amid the uproar. Even here nature had its small clicks and shivers . . . VC?! In a minute the medic would shit in his pants, as a grass tuft seemed to breathe, or a burnt fatigue cuff was mussed by a wisp of breeze. The young corpsman was surrounded by low mounds, dark, inert; these were the dead, his buddies a moment ago, in their deadness. One farted. One twitched in his extremities with a little sound. Someone moved an arm like a dangled goodbye, but didn't know it. There was a purple glow over the pathetic crackle of Troupial.

Tootie was by himself now in a terrain of ghosts. But suddenly a voice rang out. A grunt—was it the RTO being roasted slowly?—came to for a few seconds and stared up into the vibrant night; he cried out in a supreme nervous effort before slipping into a coma, as the blackness drew over. It was grisly as the lone voice laughed shrilly:

—I earned it now take me the fuck outa' here! Ha ha ha! Freedom Bir-r-rd! Here I come you fuckers! Ha ha ha! Free-e-e-e . . .!

Then it fell into a sort of rattle.

Silence. Eerie, amid the din in the distance.

The medic Tootie was alive, still in one piece, but unable to move an inch in safety. He might die of thirst before a helicopter came to lift him away from the minefield.

No one would find him out here. No one would know. He had no way to let them know: beyond shouting range. Tomorrow if he started yelling and waving his arms a VC sniper would probably find him first.

His only hope was Joey—not the worst of hopes because the squad leader did what he said. But in the big fear medic Tootie wasn't thinking about this.

Now head down he turned, in the darkness, ran a dozen yards after his leader . . . and tripped a mine.

XXIX

Joey made it through the maze of the minefield and set his path eastward. He went slantwise to the village across terrain which had shrubs and low uneven grass. Flames and smoke rose over RevDev. The smoke and underside of clouds made a light show to the rhythm of Spooky's hundred 7.62 mm rounds per second from three miniguns: Spooky often used this way in night combat. Half bent forward Joey ran along charged with his own fear and anger; he went from the others lying with their legs shredded like dynamited fish. In his mouth was a taste of betrayal as he heard it—pop! pop! VC mortar team, 60 and 81 mm; and then: ruhruhh! the 105 mm guns, as the heavyweight windmilled his arms in a futile maneuver for punching range. The skinny featherweight was laughing at the desperate roundhouse swing of the champion Uncle Sam.

Up ahead was an expanse of scrubland with a gully. He ran along as rounds ripped maybe a football field away through the scrub leaves. Not far off a shell navigated the air with a hiss. He crouched to listen—telling off fire angles and setting on a way in. Tomorrow was Day Zero: call in a dust-off for this soldier whose war is over.

Drawing nearer now he heard cries along the dirt lanes as the battle went hootch to hootch. Hell, why go there? To help? It was too late and why should anyone want to hold up this pasteboard ville with its phony reforms and its fake good will anyway? He and all the other U.S. forces had come here to negate communism—preserve a sphere of influence for capitalism—and that was all, if truth were told, if truth were ever told. But the problem was that communism was the living political force in the area, and it appealed to people like these poor ones. And so now the RevDev village was one more example like all across the Central Highlands of that great negator the United States being itself negated—because it was phony and wrong and had only its own economic interests at heart. So why should anyone, who knew, want to help prop it up anymore?

In the gully he paused to think things over. Tootie? He could make that call and give the medic's whereabouts from any phone . . . Joey hoisted up and sprang over the edge. He ran low. A shell screeched just overhead. Real close now. A warped sense took him over, kind of unreal, as, willless suddenly, he dove forward. His senses were blinded by a bright fire. His ears were deafened by a dull roar. He was smothered by a blast and sensed massive vectors across vast metal distances—in his mind. Bang! He was hit and went down.

Shock. Body in shock? There was a glaring light as he crumpled. There was a dizzy silence, so passive, all at once. His M-16 flew away raven-like into the night sky.

Joey tried to shout but only made a low babble. He was hit, yes. Badly? Where? Still he wanted to get up and move forward a few more Ben Bolt steps. Blue-gray flare. Pthwoooup!

With a hand he felt for his brain which was an amphitheater. Head, blood. Pssssst! His hard grin went soft. Thoughts dissolved. Now he flung out his arms and slumped to the earth.

Carlyne walked in black ahead of him down the aisle. Her bridal gown flowed like a dark river.

His face pressed to the earth, strange, no choice . . . as he clutched a postcard addressed to Aunt Lovedy for her, in Pembroke? which he kept in his breast pocket. My darling, I'm coming home to you. Could you meet me in Oakland?

He couldn't move, couldn't go, anymore.

To his left due east there were rice fields shimmering beneath a newly risen moon. That way . . . she was.

Relax, soldier. It's warm here. Moonlight over the paddy.

There were shots and exchanges all around him now. But he no longer heard them.

Chapter Ten

I

Democratic Convention 1968 was a week away.

Emory Gilbert, home to the Rock Castle for a brief rest, sat in his father P. Laster's old leather armchair in the den.

Outside, a quiet August night fell over the small southern town. But Emory, just in from the airport at Greensboro, was too excited to hear the evening settle in and smell its fragrance. For he was riding high with his success of the past nine months: in the spotlight of public life.

Now he closed his eyes and saw the Convention floor. Beneath an Olympian podium there would be a red, white and blue band playing a fanfare to power. Stomp! stomp! stomp! Across the vast hall the delegates thrust their placards up. That ecstatic foot-stomping was the political heart of the nation; it beat to the noble periods of the orator, namely himself, introducing his Presidential Candidate for the acceptance speech. Stomp! stomp! stomp! Emory Gilbert's voice and leonine image were transmitted to the fifty states and beyond.

As a special guest he went to the '64 Republican Convention in San Francisco. Now he seemed to watch the Illinois Senator's speech again—arms flung at the sky in diagonals like a wild baroque, yet no silver hair out of place. Politics are destiny, said Napoleon. And Emory could hear its faroff roar in the rapture caused by his words. Chicago's Convention Hall shook as he stunned America. Thus soughs an ocean in the conch shell of Man's ambition.

But just then he heard the still small voice of the telephone ringing.

II

Max Doan said:

—I need to see you.

—Alright.

—I mean now.

—Sure, why call? Just come by. But I don't have long. Early tomorrow I'm flying to Chicago.

—In a few minutes then.

Max's tone . . . It was something 'important'?

Emory's daughter, Lemon, liked to make fun of Max, but she also said he was too at home in the Rock Castle. Well, this was what Emory asked his friend for: to keep an eye on things. Yet Lemon said: 'Dad, it's not so good the way he likes to spend the night, and I've had Cindy stay over when she can. But she's leaving us soon . . . And any moment I half expect Thanks-a-Million to go on his knees and ask for my hand. Oh, wunderbar!'

Was this why Max needed to see him now?

III

The doorbell rang.

Emory went and opened. And he stood amazed at what he saw. It was the military man in dress khaki with visor'd cap and a broad chest full of medals: Silver Star with oak leaf cluster, Legion of Merit with two oak leaf clusters, Air Medal with twenty-one oak leaf clusters, Army Commendation medal, Purple Heart U.S., Gallantry Cross with palm, Distinguished Service Medal Department of Defense . . . There stood top U.S. Armed Forces brass Maximilian Doan with black leather briefcase in hand. Max posed, erect, and he was here for some official function. A marriage proposal to a 14 year-old? This time Don Quijote didn't send Sancho.

The soldier waited on the threshold as if for an order. West Point courtesy and correctness—and fond and foolish. The Four-Star General came to ask for the hand of a junior in high school.

—State visit? said Emory.

Max Doan spoke softly. The man had a pathos:

—May I come in, Sir?

—Please do.

Tall, blond, impressive: Max doffed the officer's cap and went past P. Laster's study into the Georgian living room. He looked like a southern beau as he sat composed, hands folded, on the damask'd sofa in that Queen Anne and mahogany Chippendale décor. He stared at a pair of wing chairs with cabriole legs, stretchers, loose cushions; then a primitive landscape by P. Laster Gilbert above the mantel. The Army General, in this tender moment, let his gaze go to the claw-and-ball work of a slant top secretary; then the smoothly turned and tapered legs, spoon feet and scalloped apron of an 18th Century lamp table. In the living room there was an antique map of the world; and a mezzotint, a botany print.

Emory waited for his good friend to begin.

IV

The Teutonic blue-eyed Doan gave a solemn look around. He unfolded his hands where they rested on the monogrammed briefcase across his long legs.

—I think you haven't heard.

—N-no, said Emory. Heard what?

—The media has the story.

Emory tensed. It was not about Lemon then? Emory sat in silence and breathed in the resinous scent of the stone mansion. The Gilbert generations had distilled their essence into its granite.

—What story?

Doan began to recite:

—I am here tonight on orders from the Army Chief of Staff. Sir, I come in the line of duty to inform you, with sadness as well as pride . . .

Emory knit his brow. On the front hall table lay the last letter from Joey to his wife. Scrawled on the envelope were the words: Please forward.

General Maximilian Doan opened his black case.

From an official envelope he took a letter, and read:

—Engaged in heroic action for the defense of Vinh Hiep village designated under the Republic of Vietnam Revolutionary Development Program . . .

Emory felt his senses fly up in a sort of vortex. It was the first instant of grief trauma, like a reflection of what he felt at his wife's death. Yet even as Max read, he was thinking: What tack should we take with Labor after all? Who would be a better head for the Women's Committee? And the discontented farmers . . . What to do about them? Amazing, the youthquake! . . . fourteen million new voters. Hot, steamy August weather in Chicago . . . what should I pack?

—Private First Class Joseph L. Gilbert upheld the highest traditions of United States Military service . . .

Professor Emory Gilbert: speech writer extraordinaire, campaign point man, kingmaker. Everyday there was a new angle, some masterful turn of phrase to out-bedevil the press corps. Time and again he was dramatic yet media prophylactic! Now get ready for Convention mania. In his mind's eye Emory glimpsed his faithful and steady wife Anne Gilbert (Proverbs 31:12, of course). Then he seemed to see a towering homerun bounce off the right centerfield scoreboard in New York—replayed on national television. Suddenly he wasn't himself; he felt all in movement as his thoughts swirled. Colonel Daniel Pricecroft . . . he heard the official envoy, his friend Doan, say. Democratic Party platform . . . Dizzy. Wake Lemon?

—At 0620 hours the enemy minefield, scoured for U.S. infantryman remains, revealed . . .

His younger daughter was asleep in her room upstairs. She had untroubled dreams: why wake her? Lemon always loved Jojo best; she worried about him, and couldn't watch the news footage from Vietnam.

—Nine soldiers of whom three, unidentifiable . . .

Phone Newell in California? Well, he'll call here soon enough. No; at a time like this Emory had one thing in mind. He wanted to see his oldest and closest friend, the most trusted, the confidant—Paul Commynes.

V

Max took a package wrapped neatly in brown paper from his briefcase. It was the deceased's papers and few personal effects left inside his bunker before the last sortie.

—Your son fell for the cause of freedom in Southeast Asia.

—Thanks.

—I'll stay with you.

—No, I . . . I thank you, but I need time by myself . . . to think.

—If you wish I'll spend the night upstairs.

—Thanks so for offering, Max. But that's okay. I'll be fine.

Alone in the study Emory unwrapped the few belongings left by his son in Vietnam. There was a packet of letters in twine: he dropped it on his blotter, like a hot object. There was a small Agenda 1967 filled with notes but not in Joey's handwriting: 'Sub-soil in evergreen tropical forest deep strata of feralitic soil without laterite layer. Five tiers of forest: A, 40–50 meters tall, Dipterocarpaceae, Leguminosae, Moraceae; A2, over 20 meters straight trunks, thick foliage families Caesalpiniaceae Mimocaceae, Papilionaceae . . .; A3, subcovered tier . . . plus young trees of two previous . . .; B, bush tier 2–8 meters, scattered, Rubiaceae, Apocynaceae, Rutacea . . . Euphorbiaceae families, also false wood trees Palmae, Bambusae, tall Scitaminaceae grasses . . .; and C shrubs under two meters, most Filicals, others Acanthaceae, Urticaceae, Araceae, Zinziberaceae, Liliaceae . . .'

He read. He leafed further. Beneath the final entry there was a reddish smudge on the paper: blood it was, not clay. Gently he placed the notebook beside Carlyne's letters, and then took out a second sheet from the official envelope. It was a document, photocopied:

UNIT: 2nd Battalion, 4th Infantry Division
NAME: Joseph Laster Gilbert
SEX: Male
RACE: Caucasion
STATUS: Regular, active
AVIATION: No
FILE OR SERVICE NUMBER: 9974087

RANK: Pfc.
BRANCH OF SERVICE: U.S. Army
DATE OF BIRTH: Dec. 9, 1942
AGE: 25 years, 8 months, 5 days
EYE COLOR: Brown
HAIR COLOR: Brown
COMPLEXION: Medium
HEIGHT: 74 inches

Emory paused. Here was big rough Joey, over six feet tall. But Newell was five-ten and weighed less; lighter complected. Someone once called Jojo the 'god-born'. Ah, it was Commynes who said this.

WEIGHT: 195 pounds
MARKS AND SCARS: S 1½ left forehead,
     vacc. upper left arm, right inguinal
     hernia scar, circ.
NEXT OF KIN: Father, Dr. Emory G.
PLACE OF DEATH: Vietnam
DATE OF DEATH: 14 August 1968
DISEASE OR CONDITION OF DEATH: Multiple
     wounds to head, chest, abdomen, neck
APPROXIMATE INTERVAL BETWEEN ONSET
     AND DEATH: Immediate
SUMMARY OF FACTS RELATED TO DEATH: While
     on field maneuver felled by exploded
     mine charge. Pronounced dead by medical
     officer 4th Medical Battalion. Remains:
     transferred to U.S. Naval Hospital in Da Nang
     for preparation and disposition
DATE SIGNED: 15 August 1968
SIGNATURE OF MEDICAL OFFICER

VI

For a long moment, after Max Doan went out, Emory sat with head bowed at his father's desk in the Rock Castle den. He sat there numbed in the first minutes of grief trauma.

He could still only think, *think,* about the upcoming Convention. What would his son's publicized death overseas mean for that? Could it be a key opening? A huge triumph as the ground-swell of public sympathy carried all before it . . .? Think of the *ovation* for the great writer who lost his son fighting for America.

When he stood up, he hardly knew where he was. But he did know one thing: he needed to go find his childhood friend.

And so, a moment later, he went out the front door and started on his way up town to see Paul Commynes.

VII

Emory Gilbert and Paul J. Commynes (J. for Jezreel = God sows) were two children of the Twentieth Century. There is a curious confusion as to the year of Commynes' birth. Old records say 1900, but he was in the same class at school, if he ever had time to go, as Emory born in 1905.

Paulie's mom was a dirt poor single parent in the Skeeter Hawk section of town: poor folk, and some called them something else. Over the warped doorstep he crawled and used the woods for an outhouse. With other backcountry boys he wore through his hand-loomed britches not fit for the new Graded School; and played a game of ball, and had a dip in the Yadkin. But mostly he worked for his mom, and stared up at all that Skeeter Hawk life that got pretty wild some nights.

Emory Gilbert, on the other hand, was born and grew up on this side of town among the antebellum mansions. He had all the good things a boy could want; though his mother Wilhelmina was so ambitious and drove him so, he might have liked Skeeter Hawk better at least for a fling now and again. His banker dad was said to: P. Laster had concubines, P. Laster was seen leaving his office up town, after hours, with a prostitute named Cherokee.

Paulie saw his own father here and there through boyhood, and didn't love him. But Emory's dad was the town's First Citizen: much loved for his Radio Sunday School which went on thirty years. Gravel-voiced, a little man with a big pink nose eroded by cigar fumes, P. Laster came to the bank each day perched, in his suit and necktie, on a red tractor. The man had a pretty big ambition for this one-factory town, and took it out—so they say—in gentleman farming and in lust. But he couldn't control his wife.

Emory and Paulie were friends. Together they ate rock candy and heard of the Rough Rider and a 59-second midair flight down on the coast over Kill Devil Hill by two bicycle makers. They talked over Henry Ford's story and read about the first cross country trip in a Packard. You bet! And what about John D. Rockefeller: the nation's first billionaire? Gee! . . . Also they saw a memorial dedicated to a famous Indian fighter who lived along Yadkin River: a folk hero set on driving the Red Man out of the Old North State.

Emory read a lot, but Paulie liked to go to the Country Store and listen to the men talk until it closed at dusk. They talked about machines: how an acre of wheat needed a few hours of labor, not sixty. The boy heard them discussing industrialism, its massive profits. Besides old Civil War stories he heard about steam to drive textile mill spindles and pneumatic drills delving the earth for coal; and how coal made steel; and then copper-wired electricity replaced steam.

Paulie also liked the place for its candy jars and things he couldn't have since his momma was laid off at the furniture factory and had little to give him except her ill temper. His pa still showed up sometimes, but the man was . . . well, why talk about it?

The boy stuck in the Country Store, and one noontime P. Laster Gilbert, the banker, came in and had a word with the owner. Presto! Plug o' licorish per day plus a meal for the kid—and two bits each Friday!—if he'd clean and sweep, lift boxes, run errands, jerk sodypop once he could reach up to the fountain. Now there's a P. Laster type idea for you: a liberal with his finger on the town's pulse.

So Paulie missed out on school. But he heard about inventors: Edison, Swift and the Chicago butcher's ice-cooled freight cars and warehouses. He heard how Duke tobacco processors put out a hundred thousand cigarettes in a session. Inside the general store the young'un had an eye on the fortune builders. The men spoke of Drew and Gould's million dollar bribery of a state legislature up North to get eight millions in 'watered' Erie Railroad stock legalized. It seemed P. Laster and the robber barons were Paul Commynes' surrogate fathers. Those were men to admire and grow up like.

Once, in the Rock Castle den, age twelve or so, Emory shared a bag of roasted peanuts with his friend who gobbled them. Paulie always gobbled. Then one slipped from the hungry kid's hand in between the armchair cushions; his fingers followed and touched coins, change, a lot of it, fallen from the grownups' pockets. Nickels, dimes, quarters even—real money in those days; it was loot to a kid with street instincts. The hunt was on, and Paulie led a mad scramble round the Rock Castle. All the chairs and sofas must be mined for loose change—amazing how much he got, over two dollars, and how little Emory, who was elbowed aside, as the guest from Skeeter Hawk laughed:
—Finders keepers, losers weepers!
Maybe a year later, at a summer camp off the Blue Ridge Parkway, the two friends slept on the same bunk. Through the chilly night a mute struggle went on for the single army blanket, plus room to turn and stretch. After awhile Emory ended up on a bench by a cold hearth in the mountain night.
Through their childhood going somewhere together Paulie tended to nudge his buddy and crowd him off the sidewalk. They made a picture: two good pals, the rich kid from the Rock Castle and the poor one from Skeeter Hawk. All summer long with Garnett Stonington and Tommy Tompkins they found time to fish, swim and have fun by the Yadkin, but Emory had to be nimble if he wanted a share of the sidewalk.
One day they came to a bridge, and P. Laster's son, in the boredom of those boyhood afternoons long ago, said:
—Wonder what fish you catch off here?
They got there and looked down: it was the new highway with motorists between Winston and Greensboro. Ha ha ha! That time Paulie laughed him right out of town; he knee-slapped about it for a week; and reported it with verve up town at the Country Store. He like about told every kid or adult he met what a fool

Emory Gilbert could be, but his friend let it pass, into some book or other as usual—off under a shade tree while the campaign to show him up went on. Emory didn't take such things to heart, but this one may have stung a little.

Oh yes: the bright son of P. Laster and Wilhelmina just loved books and ideas. Many a day you couldn't get him out of the house, or in warm weather away from his tree fort in that great oak on the Rock Castle front lawn where he sat reading some adventure story or boyhood classic.

For generations Emory's forbears, N.A. Gilbert and sons, had been toilers of the earth, farmers, and Indian fighters. Well, they weren't like the indigenous peoples, Carlyne's ancestors: at one with the land. No; they didn't live that side of life without reserves—didn't know Dionysus so to speak: Dionysus the rustic god, the productive, rich in vines; Dionysus god of the night, and the deep drinker; mountain wanderer, lover of mountain shade; garland wearer, clad in sheepskin, wood dweller, the golden horned; Dionysus the raw flesh eater, and soul disturber, and soul tearer; healer of sorrow, and the clamorous one, and seasonable . . .: to say a few of his hundred names.

The tribal farmers and hunters knew the god—under other names—because they loved the land and held it sacred. But the Europeans like Emory's people, the more advanced culture technologically, only used and exploited and exhausted this land and then maybe wondered why they themselves felt used, worn out, unhappy sometimes like P. Laster and Wilhelmina.

They were Puritans, those Gilberts—upright religious men who also went in for preaching and public speaking. They were men driven by a mission.

Old records tell the stations of their pilgrimage: 1708, passage to the New World, where old N.A. struck out south of Baltimore from the crowded eastern settlements. He and his kind were adventurers citing Bible versets while they cleared a field, clinched a good deal, tracked the Tuscarora through the Carolina swamps. N.A. & Company waged material struggles to get themselves rich; they had no time for Dionysus, vine clad, with the thyrsus.

Then early in this century P. Laster made it big. Well, he was always on the ball. P. Laster rose to Vice President of First National City Bank. Prudent to loan, slow to foreclose, he was known as fair-minded to all. Later he was a two-term mayor, a liberal, and friend to the deserving Negro. P. Laster became loved at least across the county for his Sunday school broadcasts.

Ah! They were worldly men, those Gilberts, ambitious as hell, obsessed with wealth. But they were also men of the Good Book; though they weren't known to spend time reading the *Institutes*. Their souls moved restlessly between the earthly crop and the return—ever since the first of their breed, the patriarch N.A., came to cultivate his faith on a tract of land out there by Polecat Creek a mile north from the railway depot where it now stands.

VIII

Paul Commynes' story was cut from the same cloth, but the pattern was different.

Oh, he lacked as Emory never did for penny candy, but he had his fill of rags to riches ethos: by the bellyful at age eleven. In his young brain the House of Morgan was a gigantic candy jar; its cinnamon sticks were rainbows wrapped in cellophane. Astor, Vanderbilt, Carnegie, Mellon, Frick, Armour, Stanford, Huntington, Cornell: these were the praiseworthy men, the philanthropists and university founders. They brought state and federal government, the courts, the Constitution itself to heel by their brisk-paced interests. Good for them, as long as they got away with it. They spoke with the soft voice of their corporations, and carried a big candy stick.

Now Paul and Emory might argue a little because one of them was thinking too much, and spoke of the sweat, toil, danger, duress, disease, poverty, death that underwrote such colossal private fortunes. Hadn't the Country Store idols stolen their billions from America's pocket? Were the field hands, and the factory workers and immigrants just so many commodities: men used as dirt cheap labor? Was the idea of a democracy to divide and conquer them and break their unions' backs?

While Paul was amassing his first small savings of capital, Emory was reading and thinking about the great railroad strikes of 1877 which had affected this trunk line town. The boy Emory was angry at Washington and Wall Street's chicanery; at the capitalist animals and the thieving politicians whose pockets were lined as wide as Union Pacific and Central Pacific joined together in the first transcontinental railway. Emory heard the other side of his best friend's daydreams of wealth: all about Labor's long calvary and the price people had to pay, the poor, the undernourished children, so a few could steal millions.

Paulie's life vision also gained scope, but it hardened too as he pledged allegiance each morning to a banker's career of probity. Taboo for him were such things as the Knights of Labor, the I.W.W. even worse. In his heart he scorned the struggle of workers for the eight-hour day and for livable work conditions. Do not mention to him the great bugaboo of socialism with its Henry George and Edward Bellamy, Joe Hill and Big Bill Haywood, Mother Mary Jones, Goldman and Berkman, populism, anarchism, Haymarket; not to mention that devil incarnate Karl Marx! No, no; Paul Commynes at age 12 and now at age 60 wanted to know nothing of muckrakers and sweatshops and the Triangle Shirtwaist blaze in March 1911 where 146 workers died, mostly women, because their employer locked the doors to keep them hard at it.

Such things annoyed Paulie even as a boy and cramped his style. Above all he detested do-gooders and didn't mind making fun at times of his liberal friend who hadn't grown up in Skeeter Hawk. Emory's kind were idealists who never would learn the score. Paul hated any idea of a limit to his chances: a restriction on his craving to make a fortune fast, and rectify what fate made amiss.

He and Emory argued. Emory was aghast at troops sent in to end strikes, and Government actions to uphold big money. Emory the precocious boy saw how bloodshed was legalized to save a Rockefeller and support bosses: how law and order was made by magnates. Emory Gilbert read and read again the names with an aura; it was Lawrence, Mass. in 1912; Paterson, N.J. in 1913; Ludlow, Colorado in 1914—massacres. Had a real Wobbly arrived in the flesh to describe at the Country Store how mill workers and mine workers, men, women, children were gunned down for the sake of Capital: Emory would have cried, and Paulie would have spit.

It warn't book larnin' ner' the Graded School that helped the future banker Commynes grow and develop. No, sir, it was admiration for P. Laster Gilbert because there went a successful man, gentlemen, there went status around here.

In the small southern town all were good Americans, good anti-communists, good anti-unionists though most worked at the furniture factory—with a grumble but glad to have a job. Everyone detested the godless Reds except Emory. Well, Paulie hardly knew the difference between a Molly Maguire and an all-day sucker, and he could care less. All he knew was his god P. Laster who was a man of means at age 30; and his mind went into a rapture of boyish veneration the moment he laid eyes on him.

IX

On a January day in 1919 an older man stopped Paulie along the main street and said:

—Don't have an overcoat?

—No, Sir.

From this day forward P. Laster became Paul Commynes' mentor. He remained so until his death in 1958. Besides a winter coat he got him a better job at the Chair Factory begun in 1904 by local businessmen with a public stock offer at $100 a share.

In 1905, sixty employees made 180 chairs a day, but soon the demand tripled plant size, as banks and businesses sprang up in town. By 1919 the Chair Factory had a central machine shop where Paul worked on equipment repairs and small parts production. There was a pad plant for upholstery, a veneer works.

At the time ten million men lay dead on Europe's battlefields, and another 20 million were doomed by disease and starvation in the aftermath of the First World War. Few asked why that was since the town had entered a boom period. After a decade the Chair Factory had its first million-dollar profit year. The ownership achieved its projected 'extreme growth pattern'; and, in the seven years young Paul Commynes worked there, it began the first nationwide sales force in the industry. It was also the first to market entire dining room suites and not specific pieces only. There was a full bedroom line. Hit them where they eat, and where they sleep.

X

What good friends Emory and Paulie became in their teenage years. They were the two inseparables; and up town you often saw them together—on a Friday night, say, or a weekend when Paulie had a little free time. They even went to church together; but it would be more correct to say Paulie (or Punchy: to use the Gilberts' nickname for him) came to the Rock Castle for breakfast of a Sunday morning, and then sat with Wilhelmina and her children up front at the Methodist Church.

How courteous he always was, how helpful to the family. And yet Wilhelmina never really liked him, never took him into her heart the way he wanted to be. But he could forgive her social airs, her fabled snobbishness; and his behavior with the wife of his idol was even more respectful, more attentive to her slightest word.

The two friends had left the time of childhood games and contests behind. They rarely went fishing and swimming in the river of a summer day—Paulie hard at work on two jobs now, and Emory at age 14 on the eve of going off to college. He was a smart'un.

Neither ever played much sports. But one day they found themselves in a pickup basketball game with some town kids at the playground. Before the other players Punchy started egging on P. Laster's softer son who wasn't much of an athlete. Neither was the kid from Skeeter Hawk, but he made up for it with elbows and knees, a roughness.

Now he baited his friend:

—Aw, c'mon, mix it up! Get a rebound! Gunner only knows how to shoot . . . Hit the boards!

A moment later Emory, who was provoked and out of control, raced in and lunged for a rebound, and the lights went out. He never knew what boy's elbow—as it jerked the ball sideways from another rebounder—had dealt the blow which broke his eyeglasses. Was it Paul's elbow? Emory fell nauseous on his hands and knees, and he was bleeding. Drops of blood were on his fingers.

That night he underwent surgery to take out tiny bits of glass from his right eye. All his life it ached after the day of intellectual

work. He said this put him in a rage and made him keep on in a
cold fury because he would not have any limits put on his development and literary output.

The devil does evil, but it turns out for the good ...
sometimes.

XI

The evening Emory was packing for college Paul came over
after work. Something prompted the young scholar headed for
university ahead of time to give his best friend an old coin collection. It was an heirloom but his to give. There was a purse full of
Confederate currency. There was a Spanish doubloon of gold and
well preserved though of less value since set in a brooch. There
were coins from faroff lands and times: worth who can say how
much. Was this a good gift from friend to friend?

Emory laughed:

—The Greeks warned against inappropriate gifts, I think
Socrates. But never mind.

At Thanksgiving that year the two young men were talking
outside Mrs. Commynes' new place financed by P. Laster—a long
way socially from Skeeter Hawk. They mulled over the future.
Wilhelmina wanted her brilliant son to become a church dignitary someday, but Emory was reading through Victor Hugo's
works and wanted to be a writer; he talked to Paul about 'classical humanism'. This latter on the other hand was less exalted, but
he knew his path. He was now P. Laster's errand boy and helper
up town at the First National: a kind of factotum for the menial
chores.

—I have equity in two things, he said. You know one.

—Do I?

—There's tobacco stock I bought: a good investment! And
there's the old coins you gave me.

—Good, said Emory. Enjoy them.

—I will! You know I had them appraised.

—Did you?

—I could sell them today for 1700 dollars, but I think they may
be worth much more.

—Gosh, that's a nest egg. Enough to get married!
—Or go in business.
Emory looked at his friend and gave a nod:
—Well then: make your bundle if that's what you want.
Paul sort of bucked then for some reason. He said:
—I just wanted you to know what you gave away.

XII

Emory Gilbert had started out on life's journey amid speculation as to what human domain he might reign supreme in. He
would not be a merchant banker, said Wilhelmina, no sir. She
doted on him so, and wanted him to be a great man, a plume
in the nation's cap and source of pride to his parents. So he took
his cue and moved on from the Rock Castle toward the higher
things in life. He left for college when just turned 15 and didn't
live at home again. Never. Was this because the old Gilbert place
had become unlivable—as Wilhelmina could not help learning
her husband's 'true nature' as a philanderer, and she began to
throw fits and make their home into a hell? For a long time all her
love and need to believe in someone had gone to her brilliant son
who won statewide academic prizes, in Latin and History, while
in high school.

At university he studied the humanities, but also sociology,
psychology, some economics. In four years he had one or two
teachers who didn't bore him. Above all he had a passion for recent U.S. history, and the Great War. What was the real story? the
truth behind the official version? What could be known, and what
conclusions drawn? Did history have laws? To what degree did
man's life depend on economics? The dismal science, it seemed
to Emory, was the one most subjective, contradictory, prone to
coverup.

In hard times the war had begun: a sluggish business climate,
farm prices falling, high unemployment, heavy industries under-
producing. On a pretext President Wilson broke his neutrality
pledge; and so America spurred on by a massive propaganda
drive, the Committee on Public Information, the National Civic
Foundation, the Alliance for Labor and Democracy led by Gom-

pers, all the usual jingoism, entered the war and fed her young men down the maw of wartime Prosperity. Emory recalled how Paul Commynes thrilled to J.P. Morgan acting as the Allies' agent and selling war supplies and goods made in America to the tune of two billion. But in college Emory scandalized people by deploring it, and saying the war was all about the world's weaker nations being made to open their doors since U.S. and European domestic markets—and poorly paid workers—couldn't hope to keep pace with industrial production. War and business were in a 'fateful union' to conquer foreign markets, and resources, and never mind who got hurt and brought to their knees in the process.

Emory read about how in 1917 the liberal Wilson had signed the Espionage Act. This was to jail activists, speakers, writers opposed to mass slaughter: where the industrialized nations fought over spheres of influence in Asia, Africa, and the Middle East; where the big ones were divvying up the little ones and making colonies and resetting boundaries. Great War—great interests at stake. And so overnight America mushroomed with pro-war vigilante groups, state-level commissions for the public safety; Liberty Bonds and loyalty tests. Why? asked Emory the undergrad. Was the New World afraid its Manifest Destiny covered up a historic illegitimacy? In time the Government would sentence 165 Wobblies to prison terms. Fifteen of that socialist party's leaders got 20 years; and thirty-three, 10 years. What was the charge? Conspiracy to sabotage the military draft and agitate for desertion. A thousand others led by Debs took their convictions to prison with them while the flags waved and the bands played.

In college Emory carried on parallel studies. He stuck with the course curriculum and made straight A's. That was easy for him—what recall! What a memory and what an essayist at that age: able to muster so much material and present it clearly. But he also loved to ferret in the library and study the not so nice underside of our U.S. society and its history. Then he went on and on about it in the dorm and bored his Phi frat brothers almost to death—as if it all had to do with him and them. For instance, he read about how an American Protective League set up by the Justice Department sicked 100,000 paid informers on six hundred U.S. cities, and these turned up three million 'documented cases of official disloyalty' among the American people. Draft evaders were in the neighborhood of 300,000; and conscientious objectors,

70,000. About fifty thousand U.S. soldiers died in the First World War—only.

In college Emory Gilbert was a rare bird. A big man on campus, in his way, who made perfect grades, he was also developing a social conscience.

XIII

Meanwhile P. Laster Gilbert's other son, or protégé, was working long hours at two jobs. Paulie saved, and daydreamed of meeting Morgan. Not only did the Wall Street titan make loans to the Allies, after Wilson lifted the ban on private bank loans, and thereby reap unheard-of profits; J.P.'s procurements also wooed U.S. finance to bed with belligerent British interests, and so drew down the curtain on neutrality. Oh, that was a banner crop of futures, in Flanders fields.

A few years later after the war ended Paul gave up factory work which only fattened the other fellow. Thanks to a P. Laster loan he made his down payment on a Model-T Ford and cranked up a taxi and errand service.

While others spent time on sports, parties, the chase after girls (right into a strapped marriage, the chaser caught, and unable to amass capital), Paul Commynes gave himself up to financial gain. At the wheel of his Model-T he thought long and hard about its maker. Ford's methods had such meaning for the proselyte: cut costs, and save, save every second of every day. Gain control. Control raw materials, in Henry Ford's case, and also means of distribution. Mass produce for sale at a cheaper price. Adapt the conveyor belt, the assembly line to cars more affordable than the Pierce Arrow and the Welsh Tourer. Speed up, and stretch out. The sequentially stationed furnaces and lathes, the tight line production system, the repetition, repetition, repetition of a single task for each pair of hands; it all meant one thing, and Paul Commynes knew it—get every last cent out of the other man. Maximum efficiency meant maximum profit. Suck the marrow out of each man-hour! Oh, Ford knew of the abuse involved, and he raised wages to a sensational five dollars per eight hour day. Hearing of this Commynes sneered no less than the Wall Street

Journal at a 'misapplication of Biblical and spiritual principles
. . .' Let the worker count off Tin Lizzies like sheep until he falls
asleep forever; that was the way. And to hell with trade unionism,
which was devil's work, and strikes.

But the greatest lesson was to scrap idealism.

At first the pacifist Ford called the war a conspiracy of international bankers. But then, after his idealistic peace mission failed
ridiculously, and the U.S. joined in the war, he ran with the pack
in munitions production, tanks, trucks, airplane motors and—to
show his die-hard pacifist convictions—helmets for America's
youth used as cannon fodder. Also he made ambulances to haul
their maimed bodies away.

Paul gave a laugh at all that and rubbed his hands because he
knew it was the right idea. Those ambulances were on the road
to success.

XIV

From the scrap heap Paul got four Ford jalopies and began
the town's first car rental operation. The young men came to
rent them, Lindy Hoppers and anti-Anti Saloon Leaguers who
had a date with the Jazz Age flappers. Sheiks and Shebas needed
struggle-buggies. They roared down the road like the decade of
the 'Twenties toward a head-on collision. They wracked 'em up,
and Commynes had his one failure in business. But he was also
getting the speculator's most cherished asset: financial vision.

At this time P. Laster Gilbert was foreclosing on a lot of home
mortgages, taking away what he gave in so friendly a manner. He
handed on a few such properties, sorry affairs in Skeeter Hawk
and other backward sections—tenant farmers, the factory low-
end, black families, immigrants—to his charge Paul Commynes.

He taught him how to cast the bait, and jerk the hook. But the
town's First Citizen, a Mason, Rotary founder, radio personality,
didn't pass on to Paul a sympathy at least in word for the victim.
Gently P. Laster reeled in the mortgager, a hardship case disabled
by a factory accident, or fired after a fight with an abusive foreman. P. Laster was like a father to the poor planner, the sick child's
parent, the man sunk in a moonshine cask and unable to make

payments. P. Laster had respect for the common man's problems; and he held out some hope when a client flapped on the deck of foreclosure, bankruptcy, ruin.

XV

While Paul with P. Laster's guidance was learning to make good deals—Emory fell in love. There was laughter and a scent of jasmine on a springtime afternoon. Anne was a precious yet lively thing in her silks and flounces, beaded lace, an aigretted bonnet from Paris. The young lovers walked the same fragrant pathways where Joey courted Carlyne thirty years later. Then Emory Gilbert's soul breathed deep among the magnolia trees, Women's Campus fragrant with lilacs and jasmine as commencement drew near. Anne liked to dance and have fun. She listened to jazz.

In a Phi Delt brother's jalopy they drove out for fountain sodas at White's Drugstore in Mebane. What kicks! Emory was a man to admire, oh yessiree. And Anne was such a good kid, relaxed and laughing as life passed pleasurably; her cute nose wasn't bent out of shape with stress like a Wilhelmina. She had no clue of the dark and demonic, the guilt-stricken regions, like her beau's mother; so it seemed; instead, she had a depth of concern and tenderness, like a quiet river. Later, as a couple, they would discover the dark side together, but not as Emory's parents in the small southern town. Up North, yes, they would pass through the valley of the shadow of Eastern Establishment: in an Ivy League setting that was conformist and narrow-minded for all its pretensions with one-upmanship a high art.

Anne Gilbert was a fragile determined woman. After the flapper faded, her beauty took on a moral cast. She became Joey Gilbert's mother.

XVI

Commynes Home Mortgage & Insurance Agency opened for business in the year of grace 1928 and grew quickly. In June of '29 it changed its name to *Friendly Insurance & Real Estate.* Ads in the county newspapers listed its financial services: 'Need a friend? We lend!' On the local radio station there was a catchy jingle: 'Have a ball, and fear no fall. Call Paul!'

But fall they did when the 'Twenties wild spree ended. And it was Paul who had a ball and grew rich from such a fall.

When Emory was just starting out, not long after marriage, he worked briefly as a banker; and later on he would portray the 1929 crash and its causes in one of his books. He showed how systemic factors led to the Great Crash. There were shaky corporate and bank institution structures, and dangerous foreign trade policies. There was a national income skewed to the richest five percent. Might a simple graph, if ever once made public, have caused America to take pause and know itself? No. The vast apparatus moved on its way and said hell with the people's real needs. So finally the mainspring of the economy, corporate profit, coiled too tight, snapped. So went the thinking of Emory the literary man, the illustrator. The machine gnashed its teeth, chewed on itself and spit its guts in a huge fit. There were five thousand bank closures overnight, and countless businesses went down. The work force was unemployed by a third as over half the country's productive goods ground to a halt, fell silent, after a decade of frenzy. That idealist Henry Ford, that humanitarian, blamed the workingman and called him lazy; Ford said there is work to do here, but these shirkers won't do it unless you put their noses to the grindstone. And so the great man laid off 75 thousand more of the lazybones. Homes were foreclosed and people went to Hoovervilles. They starved while an odor of rot rose from glutted warehouses and comestible tonnage stinking with unsalability. People froze to death and children grew ill from exposure while clothing sat in bales since it wouldn't bring a profit. In those days Capital seemed to take off all its fine apparel of fetishism, and the mystery was revealed, and then Capital went in its birthday suit for all to see. Horrors!

In the Midwest, in the Southwest, bank foreclosures hit the farmers hard. Crops turned to dust, as a locust plague of tractors took over the land for big business. In calamity was a bonanza— for the banks.

Locally, Friendly Paul knew the Great Depression was a sound investor's coup. Families in the back neighborhoods were bartering chickens, if they had them, for fatback. They gave a butchered goat for a pork shoulder. They went looking for wild berries and hickory nuts, creasy greens and spearmint leaves by the creeks.

Paul Commynes rubbed his hands. He was the Grim Repossessor. P. Laster Gilbert liked to leave a way out for his victims; he was the benevolent landlord. But Paul pounced.

The nation was in turmoil as infantry, cavalry, machinegunners, tanks lined the streets of Washington and beat down hungry First World War veterans and their wives and children.

All the while Friendly Paul made hay on his defaulting clients. And he yelled at them like his idol Ford. Sloth! Prodigality! If they played for time, and tried to stay out of his way, not home when he came to call: then he didn't act nice like P. Laster. He doled out abuse. Harsh words for hard times. He called in the police and had his prey evicted—laid off factory men, haggard women with underfed kids in rags. These were the friendly inhabitants of Friendly Paul's back street paradise. Presto, he pocketed their property and equity. Next!

XVII

One day he told a man:

—I tried to help you, but your kind never save, nor plan.

A shrug. He turned away from yet another family gone under. Dewy Spivey, redfaced, stammered a few words, but it was too late. He stood beside his wife, and small daughter hung on her sunken chest. The boy by their side might have reminded Commynes of such a hayseed of a kid he knew once, unkempt, untaught, as he stood there squinting in the sunlight—a kid with no shoes on his feet, and no pa neither, in Skeeter Hawk. But Mr. Friendly didn't care about that now.

—They'll rehire me. Give us time.

Commynes gave a glance at the sky:

—Crunch comes, and the sonuvabitches blame me.

Brusquely Dewy Spivey turned and went inside the house, as the repossessor cranked up his buggy. A first round of buckshot sent sparks off the car's metal frame, and punctured a tire. A pellet from the second blast, as Spivey's wife stood shrieking, caught the banker in the neck and by some miracle didn't stop the airway or paralyze him for life. But it did touch a nerve. A week later Paul came out of the hospital looking a little like a seized piston. His shoulders were a bit hunched. And he had a stare on him—set in stone. Through the years, but more in the tense times as big deals were done, his old injury acted up. What the hell: that's life! He said the pain was a hint from God, goading him on to succeed in his mission.

Dewy Spivey got off light with a 9-year term in the Central Prison in Raleigh. When Spivey's wife broke down emotionally, the kids had to be placed in a Charlotte orphanage. But she had time to teach their seven year-old son to hate, hate the banker in town who did this to them.

XVIII

Emory wrote his first book: a fictionalized biography.

During lunch hour at the bank, at night and on weekends he read for it and made notes and sketches. It was about the life and ambition of a powerful man in the South. He warmed to the topic, and his language began to sing. He was a writer.

The narrative turned a corner and became charged with life, reality, also American mythos. Innocence turned to a ruthless cynicism. There was glamor, there was eros.

What composing this was—what progressions. The sordid backstage it revealed! The rise to political influence; the few types of seduction scenes! And the way themes repeated through beginning, middle and end; the way major and lesser moments were handled like a Chinese scroll unfolding its near, middle and far distances, in a series of masterful relationships! In Emory's first great effort there was lucidity along with a mysterious grandeur: the compact and loose harmonies of a landscape scroll. All this took the breath away. The characters in this young author's first book lived naturally on contrast—but also on a fine gradation. Above all, plot came first, and made the narrative march. Character took on its contours from the plot. And such a plot—it was like a loom on which to configure the national life. And, in some curious way, maybe in the tone: the fathers—to use a Biblical phrase—seemed to speak through the sons.

The young writer worked in a fury. He knew he had hooked into an American epic; he could feel the great theme sporting on the end of his line, beneath the surface, and then see it jump and writhe up in a bright spume of words, images.

But, in the end, under an editor's watchful eye at one of the big publishing houses, the startling book had to be toned down a good bit. At that level it had to run a gauntlet of lawyers.

Emory cut such a figure back then: as a firebrand on the New Deal's left wing, with a lot of radical ideas. It was 1934. West Coast longshoremen had just struck to protest slave market shape-ups at sunrise. Teamsters paralyzed Minneapolis—so farmers transported and sold their produce directly to the people. When strikers controlled the city, the police attacked and killed two. In fall of '34 nearly half a million textile workers walked off the job in twenty states from Massachusetts to Alabama. A violent cotton mill strike in Gastonia, North Carolina, cost a few lives. In middle-class America there was a Red Scare feeling, communism at the gates, fear of socioeconomic upheaval.

Emory Gilbert won a major literary award. His first book went through many printings. He was famous.

And then he and his wife went North.

Soon he was a tenured professor.

XIX

The 'Thirties and 'Forties also saw the rise of Paul Commynes. He married. He bought a degree from a community college. There was one major deal after the next, as a section of town was developed jointly by Commynes' *United Commercial* and the big boy,

First National City, where P. Laster Gilbert was vice-president in charge.

The kid from Skeeter Hawk became many times a millionaire. In later years what praise was lavished on him statewide! At a banquet in Winston-Salem in his honor the MC lauded the career of this young hawker on the main street there by Red Douglas's drugstore; and now the kid owned the street. Well, this was so many thanks to his mentor, P. Laster ever there for him, since the faroff days when he stood by the side of an abandoned mother.

Along the way he caught breaks. Paul was let in the Masons which meant more financial opportunities. Even fallout from the Dewy Spivey affair helped his career and strengthened his hold in town. There was a front-page newspaper article about Paul and his support for a National Recovery Act proposed by the new President, labor's friend, who won a landslide victory over the stodgy Hoover.

Why did Paul Commynes favor such a bill?

1933 New Deal measures fixed prices and wages and brought competition back in control. Realized by the National Manufacturers Association, Chamber of Commerce and other major corporate alliances, the reform legislation benefited big business and consolidated power for the great industrial combines. A new marriage of Capital and Government was being celebrated as FDR gave the big corporations control on a silver platter.

Quick on the uptake as always Commynes got his real estate concern chosen to oversee Federal Housing Administration (FHA) loans in his area, and jockeyed his own appointment on the U.S. Building and Loan League's national council.

He had come a long way since the days he rode out to feud with mortgage defaulters, and repo a pitiful mess of pottage from the Dewy Spiveys to fill the glass cases of his brother Jake's pawnshop—*Jake's Hideaway.* Paul, the man of probity, learned his lesson from a bullet in the neck. Let others do the dirty work.

Jokes still went around town about it. Paul Commynes had come out of the hospital looking so strange, like a devil! And so now there were leases countersigned by Satan. There were the retiree communities of Vampire Realty. Residential Development Corp., a Commynes firm, had as motto: 'Ring our bell, and live swell'. And the townsfolk added: in hell.

XX

In those days a ballad went around town. It was penned by some anonymous bard and didn't appear in print anywhere: just part of the everyday life of the people.

THE DEVIL AND DEWY SPIVEY

Dewy Spivey went down to the Mortgage & Loan,
    said hello to the Devil there.
The Devil told Dewy to pull up a chair,
    —Let's talk about your home.
      Dewy Spivey, Dewy Spivey,
      let's talk about your home.

The Devil said time to sign and seal,
    leasehold, chattel, hypothec,
lien, antichresis, what the heck!
    Dewy's soul went into this deal.
      Dewy Spivey, Dewy Spivey,
      your whole soul went into the deal.

What happens next we cannot tell,
    spring rains, fall frost, winter storm.
—Sir, I got to keep my family warm,
    if I keep them warm in hell.
      Dewy Spivey, Dewy Spivey,
      keep 'em right warm in hell.

Dewy Spivey went down to the Mortgage & Loan,
    said the factory sent him away,
Depression can't wait for the NRA . . .
    Begged the Devil: Sir, please postpone!
      Dewy Spivey, Dewy Spivey
      begged the Devil to postpone.

Then the Devil drove out to Skeeter Hawk;
    said: my man you don't live here no mo';

now abandon these premises, pack up, go,
    ain't no use t' snivel, nor talk.
        Dewy Spivey, Dewy Spivey,
        ain't no use t' snivel, nor talk.

Dewy picked up his gun, pumped a blast on the run,
    installment, gage, equity, hypothec!
Pouah! shot that soul-greedy Devil plum in the neck,
    but the Devil bled green just for fun.
        Dewy Spivey, Dewy Spivey,
        the devil bleeds green and has fun.

What happens next no man can tell,
    spring showers, fall leaves, winter snows.
After foreclosure comes——the Devil only knows:
    Dewy kept his loved ones warm in hell.
        Dewy Spivey, Dewy Spivey,
        you kept them warm in hell.

XXI

Commynes' *Family Managerial* gave birth to 17 loan companies in the Piedmont area; and, even more than his car dealership, *Home Motors,* and the two banks he founded, *Family Industrial* and *United Commercial* (conversion approved by the State Bank Commission in 1950: the industrial bank took on a fuller schedule of commercial services), the small loan operations served to build his fortune. Soon new regulatory laws obliged him to sell them off, and avoid ties between fully owned subsidiaries and his bank concerns.

In time he organized, bought up, repossessed, got by hook or crook a dozen other companies: insurance, fuel, furniture veneer and upholstery, construction, an interstate truck line. Upstart competitor of *First National City*—just across the main street in a neoclassical structure among the up town cluster alive and vital in those days—Commynes' *Family Industrial* had a liberal loan policy and took on individual and business applicants seen by *National* head Gilbert as too big a risk.

Paul crossed the street so often to confer with his mentor: the townspeople said he kept his own money over there, and only a sucker deposited cash at *Family Industrial*. Many wondered at the old bank's support for the newer arrival denied its charter by the regulatory agencies. Why did P. Laster stand by that man? The town talked about some mysterious bond between the two bankers.

Through the 'Forties and the war Paul Commynes' home-grown empire outlived the rumors and just kept on thriving and getting bigger. Too young for the First World War and too old for the Second, he did well in wartime. His seed prospered while others died overseas to cut down these Nazis which U.S. corporations had helped to build up. Half a million Americans died, and twenty to thirty million Russians since—as Emory wrote his childhood friend in a letter—Roosevelt and the U.S. ruling class wanted Germany to crush the Soviet Union and so waited a long time before opening the second front.

In the boom period of the 'Fifties, Paul was on the threshold of a new career—Democratic politics. He was touted as next mayor to take over for P. Laster now on in years and more tempted by radio Sunday school than bank and civic administration. Or Paul Commynes could have waltzed to the State Senate.

But first the rich man tried his hand at some philanthropy. Tightfisted, as hard a bargainer as brother Jake behind the pawnshop counter, he had a soft spot for the town he owed his riches. So he said on TV. And now here he forgave a debt, there wrote off the last payments on a home mortgage . . .

Whatsoever he doeth shall prosper; and such noble deeds found their way into the newspapers he had helped for thirty years with his ads. Why, this good man had given a corner lot in Skeeter Hawk for a new Baptist church. And forget the tax deduction: it wasn't much. Prosper thou, and build the house.

And lo! There were outdoor toilets. Sanit-Johns courtesy of *United Commercial*. A few were at North State Mall.

XXII

Paul Commynes was one of the richest men in the state. He had fame. He had influence.

Then tragedy struck. In the day of prosperity the destroyer comes.

United Commercial got construction and zoning permits to develop a stretch on the scenic riverbank west of town. His wife Claire wanted this, and they took the best acreage for a summer home. At forty Paul had married the socialite daughter of George Worthington, a Greensboro attorney and Democratic Party pillar.

So on a sunlit July afternoon in 1953 Claire Commynes crossed the wide green lawn bordered by tall oak and elm trees toward the dock where they kept a skiff used to fish and take spins on the Yadkin. In the boat she put down a hamper filled with good things, wine, pâté, fresh baked apple pie. She stepped forward to switch on the ignition, and————

Paul was still in the house with a phone call. He felt the impact.

—Good God, what is that?

In a panic he ran across the lawn. By the riverbank he saw—what? A ways downstream there was a trail of . . . There were fumes. Débris. Like a skein of . . .

There was a silence in those moments. It never left him. Leaves rustled.

Later the motor was hauled from the river bottom. An ignition spark had ignited vapors in the motor compartment—said the press report.

Then came grief. It changed him. So lonely when he went to the bank, he was almost unable to do business. But the next instant he felt an unknown lightness. A new faith came like sun through clouds. Believe His prophets, so shall ye prosper.

Great God's house builded with stones, timber laid in the walls—and their work goeth fast on, and prospereth in their hands.

XXIII

Up North Emory was at the forefront of a political trend. Year by year he produced his literary works, and they are property of the nation; no need to go into them here. But he was also a sort of activist as, in pre-McCarthy Era struggles, the Left courted the national writer. They pushed the fiery liberal and wanted him to join, and come out for socialism. Well! This was dangerous terrain. Anti-communist Congressional committees would soon begin ruining careers. Spies everywhere: including the world's most famous cartoonist, ratting on his friends in Hollywood.

Besides a Taft-Hartley provision to expose communists, the McCarran Act attacked leftist organizations. Over a hundred CPUSA leaders were arrested and accused of conspiracy, under the 1940 Smith Act, to overthrow the U.S. Government. Well, they criticized it.

In March 1947 President Truman issued an executive order against 'infiltration of disloyal persons', and this led to a Red hysteria, and witch hunts. Between then and December of '52 the Government investigated six and a half million people through informers and secret evidence, without judge and jury. Did it find one Red spy?

The U.S. media true to form painted Bolshevism all over federal, state and local institutions. Many, many lost their jobs in cases of 'questionable loyalty'. For as Emory knew and said in print: only national unity, through fear, could militarize the budget and confront anti-imperialist liberation forces across Asia, Africa and Latin America, the colonial world.

So Truman demanded loyalty oaths and anti-communist legislation, and Joe McCarthy held high his dossiers and lists of 'communistically inclined liberals'. And who knows how many lives were affected? The witch hunters burned Thomas Jefferson's works. And the same Presidential candidate Emory Gilbert was now working for in 1968—back then introduced an amendment to declare the Communist Party illegal. No 'half patriot' he.

In 1950 the Republicans passed an Internal Security Act, and then Emory's liberal candidate out-baited the Red-baiters by proposing detention centers for suspected subversives. Then there were lists: such as the Bakuninist terrorists of the Chopin Cultural Center, and the Cervantes Fraternal Society, and Nature Friends of America, and The Committee on Negro Arts.

Then came the Rosenberg trial in summer of 1950. A young couple got electrocuted on false testimony for their beliefs.

Emory Gilbert got the message. When a nonentity made a name by red-baiting the great writer, it was time to draw back from politics. And the day would arrive when Emory red-baited a co-worker in the field of letters, tossing off a cover story for a fashionable magazine, for money.

He also wrote more big books. And he was a professor. He toured as a lecturer. But his activist career was over.

As his university president—Lemon Gilbert's godfather—said to him: Emory, which side are you on?

XXIV

Way back when the poor kid from Skeeter Hawk never had time for school.

Now he did.

All his life envy for his best friend was a sort of torment: P. Laster's son given every opportunity for studies, experience, ambition toward a higher goal. And then this best friend really did it: he staged a success bigger than anything this jerkwater hometown ever dreamed.

Alright then: why not Paulie's turn now? Then thou shalt make the way prosperous! Why not Paul Commynes as a student in theological seminary? Joyful in the day of prosperity. Earn a Masters of Divinity at the university where Emory held forth. Be united again with his childhood friend.

And so Midas revolted by gold, disabused with his earthly share, turned asset liquidation into the golden sands of Pactolus. It was a deal agented by faith, he believed, for the God of heaven will prosper us.

Paul made one last plunge into the murky waters of bank conversions, mergers and consolidations. He dealt *United Commercial* to the highest bidder. And then he came to rest on the far shore.

But even across the deep river, in campgrounds, he was dripping lucre. Prosperous in pleasure of the Lord—he glanced back at his fabulous rise in high finance.

One final deal!

Before going North to study he built North State Mall which opened the way to the national chains, and all but ended the old town life and sense of community. Up town became a ghost town.

He dedicated that last real estate project to his wife Claire's beloved memory. 'They shall prosper that love thee' (Psalms 122, 6) ran an ad for the new North State Mall.

XXV

In his fifties the multimillionaire sat among divinity students. God's sunlight lit the classroom blinds of an autumn afternoon.

Nights in the quiet of his carrel in the library he read Plotinus, Bossuet, Niebuhr. There was such a silence after the decades of business.

Organ harmonies like a tide of faith over the colonial campus; the rare uplift in a sermon; the poetry of compline and vespers— all stirred his soul.

He heard deep words along the colonnaded walkways between the student houses. Here he sang childhood's hymns and read old prayers of a cold December evening when lanterns reflected on the snow like the candles of votive offerings.

Paul woke to a joyous carillon on a sunlit Easter morn. In a flock the students went to chapel and heard of the living Christ's death on the cross.

XXVI

After his ordination into the Christian ministry, Paul Commynes served as pastor in a small parish in western Carolina for just over a year. Then, meteoric in this as in business, he was voted by Southeastern Jurisdictional to be a bishop. Did he buy it? 'Thy money perish with thee'—said Peter to Simon Magus.

A mysterious thing happened to Bishop Commynes during his years administering a conference.

Maybe he went crazy. Maybe he just saw a devil. Had some sort of devil's epiphany. Whether the breakdown was spiritual or psychological, it was real, and he resigned at once. He left his bishopric and came back home to the small southern town. It was like a deep regression, like a stage of some greater grief—after what dark experience he had as a churchman, what sick conversion?

Back home he found Emory, his childhood friend who had also returned after his wife's death: when he gave himself to liquor.

And, in his new state, Paul hated him on sight, and said nothing. Maybe he always hated him. Always did it, but didn't know it.

Hate is a weak word to express the depth and complexity of what Paul Commynes, after his Satanic conversion, felt for Emory Gilbert. It was a corrosive envy.

And he thought of the departed P. Laster, his mentor, who made him.

And he thought of one night P. Laster went for a ride to the lively Skeeter Hawk; it was a night at the end of last century. And P. Laster drove his buggy across the train tracks in the small southern town, and sired a bastard with the white trash Martha Commynes. And when Martha baptized her son by the name of Paul, then Paul Laster Gilbert suddenly became P. Laster, the future First Citizen. This was in the first year of P. Laster's marriage to Wilhelmina.

And now Paulie wanted to get at Emory, hurt him—ruin him, this son spoiled rotten who had all good things, while he Paulie didn't have a father, at least one he could call Pa.

Retribution. For a long time he was looking for a way to do it. But he didn't know it.

And now he would avenge his mother and her broken marriage. Now he would get revenge for half a century of P. Laster's filthy hypocrisy while he Paulie was left holding the bag—of gratitude!

Brother hate. It was Holy Writ. And perhaps Paul's mind had begun to go, and falter, under the heavy cross of such a monomania.

Vengeance is mine, and thou shalt know the hand of the living God.

It tingled in his loins: this power to hurt a man he envied with all his might. A shiver ran down his spine. And the grisly hatred hinted at a mental illness long in the works.

Yet a little while saith the Lord. Vengeance is mine, and I shall repay. Vengeance mine! Vengeance, mine! Ha ha ha ha ha ha ha! Oh fornicators! Sinners! Get thee hence, reprobates! Ha ha ha ha ha!

XXVII

—What is happening to us? said Emory. Is history turning against the American people?

They sat in the darkness of P. Laster's old executive suite in the bank building. There was a pinkish glow from a neon sign, POLICE, outside the window, across a wide back lot.

Facing Emory Gilbert sat Bishop Commynes. And, in the dark room, he was strange. His features looked in some kind of throes, as though trying to give birth to a truth. Would he start talking in tongues again? He did that sometimes. Now he gave a low chuckle, and said:

—The oracle . . . has good news.

—Good news? My son is dead tonight.

—I tell you good. Though the truth of the matter is bad. So bad, perhaps, it should be kept a secret. What do you think?

—No, say it openly. Is it about me? I stand on my record.

Bishop gave a little grin.

—Do you?

—I'd gladly die in the line of duty. I serve the American people.

That grin was a smirk, a chuckle.

—Apollo says the land has a curse on it, which it nourishes . . . If the contamination is not cut out; if the sin isn't purged soon, there'll be no cure.

—What sin? How purge? You're talking in riddles.

In his stunned mood Emory played along with Paul's mystification. From week to week his childhood friend grew more bizarre.

—The sinner must die, or go away. Sin hangs over the state like a blood curse.

Emory Gilbert grew pale. He said:

—Whose sin?

—Once—Bishop gave a little wave—this was God's chosen country. Now ... Doan is wrong. Our Manifest Destiny has perished at the crossroads where sin meets righteousness, and strikes.

—Vietnam is our crossroads?

—The death of righteousness must be avenged, the sinner punished, in public!

Paul's eyes went wide.

—Where is the sinner?

—Here, at home. If we look, we'll find. If we deny, then—

—Where was the crime committed?

—At the crossroads.

—Did anyone see? Does someone know?

Commynes' voice was mystery itself in those moments.

—One knows. There is one who can tell the story.

—Do you have a clue who did it? One clue could lead to others. Is it about money as usual?

—That and sex ... power.

—If the situation is as you say, and a curse ... or a contamination threatens to poison all of us, I don't see how we could let it be, and not look to it. A Congressional committee ...

Commynes murmured:

—People look to business as usual. Who has time to ask Sphinx-like questions.

He gave a laugh beyond sadness. Emory said:

—But I will. By helping our people I help myself too. This is why I'll ask such questions and clear up, from the beginning, this mess we've got ourselves into. I plan to speak up at the Chicago Convention next week, and tell the truth on national TV, to our people!

—Will you?

Chapter Eleven

I

In Quang Ninh Province the dawn approached in the air veiled pink and blue sifted with humidity from the sea. Twilight gleamed where silent figures moved in line rifles high on the Bach Dang River margin.

At daybreak here and there remnant shadows with low craggy hills behind them crept the Cam Pha outskirts.

Two women dressed in black and yoked with baskets crossed the single plank over a canal deep in the southern plains where the sun shot its first ray over long fronds onto the still sallow water.

The dark blue riverine sea runs aslant at Nha Trang. Birds chirp in the gao trees; a frog croaks amid combretum shrubs by the shore. Whose cry comes from the conical tipped filao?

Password?

Trieng. Phoenix.

In Hué ancient imperial city an older man in latania hat paused beneath the royal poincianas. From his banana leaf tobacco packet he rolled a 'caterpillar nest' cigarette and seemed to study lotus by the Citadel entry.

The man glanced around and invoked his protective deity in these days of lull after combat raged in Hué six months ago.

It was time to start—where the woman guerrilla lay buried at the foot of Ngu Dinh, so they had told him.

On Mount Tuc Dup along the An Giang hills pockmarked with caves and grooved with ravines the early silence fumed beneath a cloud of smoke and pulverized rock.

Pains were to be endured and sickness and want like fruit trees out there jutting charred, barren.

Women birthed monsters. War fires rushed life on life like birds' wild flight at the god of sunset.

In a Mekong hamlet near Long-Xuyen after the elementary school was hit the children writhed in their playground like silkworms dropped on a griddle.

What was it? White phosphorus fastened itself onto their flesh.

Now the technological monster in its desperation was using chemical, biological and incendiary weapons in civilian areas. In their shake and bake missions U.S. forces saw white phosphorus as a potent psychological weapon to drive VC enemy out of their lairs. As an improvised form of napalm it had a ghastly effect and was praised to the skies as a psy.-tool of warfare apt to demoralize the enemy.

Unlike napalm which left Vietnamese villagers with burns all over their bodies—this white phosphorus was burning the children's flesh slowly, slowly down to the bone.

Seven and eight year-olds felt the effects of phosphorus on fire in their skin. It was an intimate 1000° centigrade heat as scattered phosphorus particles went on consuming themselves and deepened burn wounds by degrees.

But the screams and squirming of the children weakened as the chemical compounds made a chemical wound like an acid drawing water from the cells. There are no words for the pain of this process which broke the register of the nervous system. The children stayed conscious. There was an organic toxicity as the white phosphorus blocked off all blood circulation with the burn area.

For a few seconds the children had thought it was raining as chemicals dropped down on them. Then their skin began to bubble, melt, waste away. At first they tried pitifully to scrape off the horror of oxidizing phosphorus with their little frantic hands.

They fell, kicked, convulsed, screaming, and then lay still with their eyes wide. There was no way to cauterize the slow, horrible melting into the nervous system and blood stream.

No enemy were smoked out. No psy.-effect was obtained.

Only a few dozen children and three teachers were incinerated slowly.

And then it was quiet.

The B-52 bombers returned to base.

The NLF scouts slept in nylon hammocks tied to ankle-thick cornflower tree trunks.

There were explosions in the plain. There was gunfire.

Regional liberation troops ate rice rations and settled to a few hours of rest.

No lovers in straw hats canoed the Lake of Sighs at Da Lat where the blue water glittered within its border of soft slopes and tall trees stirred to a midsummer breeze.

In the 'white belt' of no-man's-land the thorny mac co plants fold their leaves when people come near—the mac co which signals the presence of Mister Keo an ogre feared by children.

A 20 thousand ton ship unloaded armaments and matèriel crates in Da Nang's deepwater port as three soldiers named Twang, Drawl, and Stutter watched fish glide in the green limpid water and talked over their visit to the Marble Hills and exotic Ngu Hanh grottoes south of the city.

There was no sound of water in bamboo pipes and no parrots chattered in the tall parashorea trees called *sho*. This village perished too quickly for tears.

There was no orange blossom fragrance but only death contagious in the streets.

Elsewhere survivors implored at the altar where wives and mothers sobbed in concert.

What night leaves day achieves.

Daughter of the god gaze down and defend us.

In Saigon at midmorning a slight gray-headed man in tan leisure suit went in a stilted waterside structure on Thi Nghe River.

Who heard the low voices like invocations?

Who noticed when a few minutes later he came out?

Under the tall bo tree also called pipal or the sacred fig like a banyan without prop roots Buddha was enlightened but we must go to the cassia and sophora and the plum and with our eyes we must follow the swift swallows of spring and the summer cuckoos beneath the moon and plane trees mixing jade and gold in the autumn courtyard and we must wait, wait as time turns our grief to steel and winter moves toward spring.

II

Inside Tan Son Nhut air terminal a soldier waited out the last hours of his tour. In outstandingly dirty combat fatigues, left arm in a sling, he sat and stared dark-eyed in the designated area. On the end table beside him lay a glossy *Pacific Stars & Stripes* with its headlines of victories and upbeat reports on the war. An officer in neat khaki crossed over and paused to look at this line dog assigned for some reason to his own flight Stateside. He saw the blotches of filth, mud and bloodstains. He didn't like it when the grunt wouldn't stand and give a salute to his superior.

—Soldier, why haven't you showered?

—. . .

—One year not enough for you? Care for more?

He glimpsed the infantryman's nametag and raised an eyebrow.

—'*Passengers may proceed to board World Airways flight number 39 non-stop for Travis Airforce Base, California.*'

The soldier stood up with no pack to heft and moved past the officer. He gazed beyond the wide glass-enclosed space at heat fumes bannering up from the runways. Through the door he strode and then took a long deep whiff of the hostile air. His first day in-country came to mind and the hop from Okinawa. At each station on their way over here the excited newbies saw haggard burnt-out men DEROSing from the 365 day tour. Their long-gone stare seemed to look on a dying planet—stand back, no close objects, few people, if you please. We've spent a year in a nightmare, one year lost, but not only.

Over an oil streak he moved toward shirtsleeved civilians

waiting in line to board. The hot late morning was quiet but for a rumble of aviation far out toward the hazy mountains. On the perimeter a lonely watchtower looked over into the first green sunbaked village on the road to Cu Chi. Inside it two ARVN guards sat in the heat and humidity.

Across the asphalt taxi area the grunt walked. And then he too waited to embark. First went the civilians of some delegation with a diplomatic component. Then went some officers ironed into their uniforms and natty with the visored caps and attaché cases. On his way now he turned for a last glimpse and a last deep breath of that air—same thick cereal scent like a gruel of dung and tragedy that greeted him a year ago.

But he peered out at the watchtower he had trudged past the previous afternoon as a G.I. off on his own in The Nam, AWOL as hell, his boots and fatigues and wild curly hair splotched an insane reddish-brown. Wounded, fallen unconscious in a field and detached from his unit he came to and got on his feet. He was free of a RevDev hamlet overrun by the enemy and put to flames. Wasn't he? The massive rant of the attacks and VC swarming inside the perimeter as sapper body blows in close put a hold on calls for air support: the mad minutes of defense ended then with what sounded like mop-up shots behind him as he went on his way. And then began five days of dead reckoning, a flight into the unknown of dense sub-humid tropical forest losing its elevation beyond Dong Xoai on the southern edge of the Highlands. A G.I. on his own, unheard of, he wandered into a former Diem military post later used to concentrate population with a Refugee Reception Center alongside; there was an air strip; there was a ghostly lean-to where a human skeleton lay jawbones wide to the silent shriek of the wind. He picked up a helmet and splashed out the rainwater with a few tadpoles. Over these ruined hills like a cradle of Montagnard tribes there were other vestiges of U.S.-Saigon army passage. After a battle the tigers and crocodiles came out to feed on dead flesh and after them came a team of monkeys at play among the tin cans.

Then the second day the grunt crossed an elephant grass plain with a network of canals. He slogged waist deep in streams over the ancient alluvium and basaltic red earth of the undulated peneplains of South Vietnam. For seventy-two hours he avoided all roads always going south and east by sun and stars until toward

the third evening he came out along Highway 20 near the crossroads for Bien Hoa. This he knew. Now he was on his way as he
left the other life behind.

In Saigon back among the fold they looked at him and said
his story better be good because that RevDev ville hadn't fallen:
which is to say it was retaken, what was left of it, the next day,
and communist forces withdrew.

He stared past them and mumbled a few words about medic
Tootie who might still be stranded in the minefield.

III

Onto the metal steps he went with his boots leaving the ground
of Vietnam.

From the door a stewardess peered down at him and then
turned her gaze. Maybe there were problems on these flights,
psych cases.

Beside her a crewman who must have had his Wheaties that
morning said:

—Come on board, soldier!

Then he paused feeling faint and shot a glance back at the terminal. For a moment he seemed to ask something of the row of
quonset huts, a C-130 in resupply while two mechanics stood
by and chatted; the warehouses, the munitions dumps and repair sheds of Tan Son Nhut. There was a converted DC-3 Spooky
parked to one side. There was the shimmer of corrugated metal
and hot asphalt.

The others waited on him.

Then he turned away from this place where he died a few days
ago and left behind an old life like a snakeskin. But was there a
new?

Inside the plane he wrinkled his nose at a toothpaste scent.
It was air-conditioned. In Southeast Asia the air swarmed with
life and death; but what was this detergent smell? It was like the
smile of the stewardess when she said hello now.

One year and five days. The last hours were so filled with red
tape and desk soldiers he nearly lost control and went for one.

Clear me at once and let me go home! Right now: contact Daniel
Pricecroft, Chief of Staff at Division Headquarters.

A call put through, and the wheels started to turn. One year,
five days, and a wake-up. And now it was over.

Was it?

IV

Seat belts were fastened. A few civilians chattered on about
their junket and experiences in-country. Quite contented. The jet
engines raced. The grunt by himself stared out the sunlit window
as the passenger plane went in motion and rolled with a bump
toward an outer runway and position for takeoff. It went along
parallel to the terminal and then wheeled round as the engines
revved up and up. His gut sank. His stomach was doing tricks.
His thoughts flew way across a haze of blue ocean and seemed to
fall off in a void. At last he was on his way from the battlefields of
Southeast Asia back to the World.

And so the Freedom Bird picked up speed and flapped down
the runway and then lifted off—tilted up—and gained altitude
above the fields and began its turn in a wide arc northward and
toward the coast.

In the window seat he craned his neck to gaze down at the
broad deepwater estuary that flowed away in a sunlit glitter the
80 kliks from Saigon to Vung Tao and the sea. He stared further
down to where village clusters dotted coastal plains north of the
Mekong Delta and saw the glare of paddy fields and long tracts
bordered by treelines and forest. And then farther back as the
plane cruised in its wide swing toward the coast there was Truong Son the great mountain range and spine of Vietnam with its
contours in an aqueous mist.

For a minute there was this simple sense of physical separation
as he thought of others who had never known it: Ben Bolt, Loseby
the E-4, Skiball, men who died, Mosey Rink, Slidell, Horse Shue,
who died, Kid Ringwood, Izard, Thingum, Chi-Bar, Vane, Meno,
Troupial, Skol, died, Oakleigh Lerch Gamecock Sanger Manito
Fern Chingi Jib Benson Clement—they were greased before their
tour ended, and the officer Robidou. There was a thought for

medic Artus gone mad and Emmet Bufillu wheeled around Atmore, Alabama, for the rest of his life. And then there was that
other whose name slipped his mind: the botanist's notebook was
left with personal effects back in the RevDev ville.

Now the sandstone buildings and salient orange tile roofs of
the capital lay behind in the distance. Out there was Saigon with
its French provincial air and tree-shaded boulevards, its ugly red
brick Cathedral and the Independence Palace looking a little nervous behind a high spiked gate. The steamy industrialized river
wended its way south among the hundred Mekong tributaries in
the afternoon sun. The plane levelled off in its long veer eastward
toward the coast.

Far down now there were two-bit villes trying to keep to themselves off a slick of road, each tucked in its tuft of bamboo. But
way back there toward Cambodia was Manito the assistant gunner—puff! up in smoke like a magician's act. And Manito and how
many others were lost in the mountains and the blue mist and by
now his remains were a jungle humus, unviewable. Far, far back
there in the past Mister Quoc and his bright grandson Ha and the
RevDev villagers who were also VC had gone on to their next stop
in the war and they did not wait around to say bye bye.

While in transient officers barracks at Tan Son Nhut as his
clearance pended he heard news. There were in fact joint VC-
NVA operations to engage a First U.S. Infantry Division battalion
at Bu Dop on the Central Highlands' southern limits. So his own
last battle had been diversionary.

NVA forces had overrun a Saigon-manned post at Dak Son and
strategic hamlets administration center. Then the NLF followed
up with frontal attacks across Phuoc Long Province and hit U.S.
command posts, a Special Forces camp. Rear echelon staff had
looked at the lone survivor, this grunt in his filth named Gilbert,
and said with a grin he should give a briefing to press corps at the
Five O'clock Follies later that day.

Down below the pattern of blue-green rice fields and yellow
canal system neared the coastline. The airplane's shadow was a
big dark bird of omen across the land as it shot past the dunes and
pure line of sand where surf rolled in over the sandbars. There
was Cam Ranh Bay, and then came the emerald offshore waters. It
was another time in history when U.S. soldiers headed home this
way from the white beaches of Guadalcanal and Bataan, Midway

and Leyte, the Pacific theater. When World War II ended the winners went to hometowns and families in another mood. But this time the orders had been unfulfillable.

He wasn't looking to be met in Oakland.

A year ago he came over here with the idea he had found his life and thinking of a career in the service. But he rose up from that field a few days ago not as a finder but a seeker. Back there at the crossroads of Vietnam where three roads met, past, present, and future: it seemed all the old life died. And now he was on his way home in quest of a new one.

Joey Gilbert craned his neck to watch as the coastal plains receded far behind him and became a blue-green blur merged with South China Sea.

Then slowly he turned away and stared at the seat in front of him and thought: so. So it is.

His brow was knit. He had a knot in his stomach. He didn't nod at the stewardess or blink when she brought him a drink. She had a poise as if she had worked the hotel flights from Vietnam before and seen the eerie gaze of the ones lucky enough to be coming home. This time it was a talkative group and mostly non-military, so there was no strained silence on takeoff, and no cheer went up with a sigh and a deep breath as they lifted away. She moved past him with her tray along the aisle.

And he thought: it is over.

Is it?

V

Joey closed his eyes. An hour later or maybe two he squinted out the window: where an ocean river of sunlight flowed far out into the glare of southern horizon. Midafternoon was past as they moved through a time zone over the blue Pacific. From the chaos of enemy attack and then flight across a landscape of bomb crater pools shimmering in moonlight he had come to this smooth and tranquil hum among blessed islets of clouds, here and there, across the sky.

But it was coming back. Smudged with the blood of Sanger and Jenkins though himself only stunned unconscious, he had risen and walked away and fallen again with dizzy exhaustion on the edge of a forest. Over his shoulder he saw air support flea-hopping between beleaguered posts as it hardly observed lines and made swift kill-all destroy-all strikes. After awhile he had paused to rest but then before dawn set out and made his way alone out there.

It was strange to go with no orders from Six and no coordinates or co-grunts to look out for. He went on by himself: a lost patrol. He knew how to do it.

Upon arrival in Saigon he found himself listed KIA in lieu maybe of Manito shredded by a mine. A surprise awaited his father if they already mailed that mangled mess in a casket State-side. For here sat Emory's son more or less alive and wafted high above the golden Pacific in the late afternoon sunlight.

He closed his eyes. Sleep crept up on him like a VC and so he only dozed and had the safety catch of his nerves in off position. He awoke to a dinner tray on the empty seat beside him and a long band of reddish gold sunset lining a cloud in the window.

When the stewardess came by, he asked her in a croak:

—No stop in Okinawa?

—No.

—Where to then?

—Travis Airforce Base.

Righto, he forgot. There would be no layover. It was non-stop to California and then discharge for him.

He stared at her strangely with a question in his dark eyes.

Yes, she had seen them before. She knew the hundred-yard stare of the boonierat sprung from his mission in the jungle.

—Do you need anything? May I reheat your meal?

He shook his head no and looked away out the window. It struck him how in a few minutes the same red cloud with a gold lining had changed its shape and color; it was the same cloud but different now. Was life like that? Was the young gung-ho patriot who came to Vietnam a year ago still recognizable in the human wreck who was coming home today? His reflection in the airplane window looked like his opposite: like a disaffected hippie with bleary eyes and a beard . . . his hippie brother Newell in Berkeley whom he was on his way to see. It was sure that the old life died the other night, and now a new one for the same person and yet not the same was about to begin.

VI

Through the long night of the flight home he thought about his wife. He remembered their months of life in a trailer during his summer in the Minors, and the sort of line between them from the beginning. What was it? Why had she quit all at once and gone away without a word? . . . But suddenly he felt dizzy and waved a hand before his face.

Rotor wash stung his cheek as he stood in the whirlwind of the hot Xo Man LZ where Izard and Ringwood were lifted off after the shoeshine bomb. A blind Vane cried out and flailed his arms:

—*I can't see! Oh God! Help me, I can't see!*

—*Hold on . . . alright . . . hold on!*

Joey's voice fraught with terror rang out over the engine hum and a few casual voices of passengers unable to sleep.

The air hostess came to him.

—Can I bring you an aspirin?

He gasped up at her and his face and neck were bathed in sweat. His skin prickled. His eyes were wide.

—How about a hot washcloth? she said.

In an instant the images vanished.

He soared through the night sky high over the ocean.

Joey slumped down in his seat, took a deep breath, and thought of the time he was first aware of Carlyne. It was in the days when all his life had to do with baseball. She sat by herself on the grassy bank above the first base dugout; and she was one of a kind there, darker, more stern than the daughters of southern gentry who strolled the campus walkways among the hyacinths, camelias and Lenten roses. From third base he saw the gray skirt and white blouse of a schoolgirl, and he thought: she couldn't care for me. Then she got up, turned her back on the game, and took a path through the tall pines back to campus. That evening he went to look for her in the Women's College Library.

VII

There's a country road runs down in the southeastern part of the state among farmlands and pocosin swamps not too far from the coast. Along that road in Robeson County near the site of an old Indian village called Scuffletown a dirt path turns in among the trees. The grunt Billy Ringwood came from down this way; a small town, Shoe Heel, but now it's Maxton, in the valley of the Lumber or Lumbee. It's a fair piece from Central Highlands in Nam, but not in some ways maybe. The King of England's land grants to white settlers went against indigenous 'set-aside' claims deeded not tribally but to a few names. It's mostly farm country but prime: cotton and corn, soybeans, squash, horticultural crops. A velvet tobacco smell blends in with a salt tinge from the Carolina coast. Here the people hold on to their land if they can, and go to weddings and funerals together and keep strong ties of kinship and clan. Theirs was a lost dialect of the Eastern Siouxan language family, and Carlyne had echoes of it from her mother; it was a pure tone, and sounded more natural, but apart. Joey's eyes narrowed when she said swanny for swear, I swanny; or called him pappy sack, a boy child; said malahack for foul it up, and pure arnt for sure have, sure do: you pure arnt made a mess. A bog was a pot of chicken and rice, a juvember a slingshot. Jubous meant strange, and a booger was a ghost or a 'haint'. Pixture, plaskit, she might say, though a college grad. And in those rare moments when she dug his act, she called him: Mister Joey.

So to the country road Carlyne led him one Sunday in May and down a dirt path through the trees to the river where she played as a child. Another thing was: she talked around things and didn't come straight to the point. She didn't go at once into her ancestors who were land clearers and soil tillers in Ashpole Swamp, Long Swamp, Back Swamp, long before these were deeded and dotted with towns and hummed with new roads, machines, commerce. But that was part of why she brought him here: to talk about men and women of long ago and their struggles not to lose the land. It was treason to pawn or exchange this land into alien hands.

Yes, that's why she led him down here on his motorcycle into the woods. Far from campus with its English gothic and red-brick Jeffersonian architecture, she said: Meet my family the trees and the rocks, the plants and animals and people who share one spirit and sacred past. Meet our river why don't you: our ancestor. She came here on an instinct she had from her mother Selva and the other Locklears: from Aunt Lovedy whom they went to one weekend the fall after their marriage when she showed her big Joey off to the Oxendines, Jacobs, Brooks, Dials, Lowrys, all kin with a similar phenotype range in the high cheekbones and deep blue Hatteras tribe eyes. Their traits were mingled in the mists of early European settlement here when Walter Raleigh's lost colonists came to a place later called Roanoke Island.

In the late 1500s it was a small village amid the seaspray where tidal rivers flowed into the great virgin continent. But the lost colonists weren't making it so they sent home their governor John White to show off 'Indian' artifacts and the first potatoes the Old World ever ate, and ask for help. Three years later he came back and found a lone voice in the boundless silence: the word Croatan was etched on a stockade post. No one knows whether those settlers, the second English colony in the Western world, had joined forces with the Croatans. But Aunt Lovedy, Selva and others had a look to them and old ways which may have hinted at union with the lost island colony.

Later on Carlyne's people were driven from the best land and hunted down even in the Lumber Valley swamps spurned by whites for the more fertile Piedmont areas . . .

Joey sat eyes closed thinking of their visit to the river. Long time since he did this, if at all. Now after Vietnam he began to see what his wife told him through other eyes.

VIII

She spread their picnic that warm day in May when birds chirped and insects buzzed.

—We call this river Lumbee. My mother grew up in a housen along its banks. I came here to play as a gyirl.

—It's dark.

The deep auburn current flowed past in silence beneath the tall pine, cypress, live oak.

—Dark but pure. You can drink it. She starts out by Southern
Pines and known as Drowning Creek up there. The water flows
shallow in some parts but dark even then from the tree tannin. But
a few yards further on it'll gash you into the earth and show its
power. Looks slow, don't it, but she flows right quick underneath.
The water rattlers and cottonmouths'll sting ya', and pit vipers
have fangs with special membranes to strike underwater. Oh, a
lot of folk drowned roun' hyere, lots o' 'em. For a good ways she
snakes through these swamps and woodlands, then on down in
South Carolina she's the Pee Dee (Pee Dee's same as Yadkin north
o' hyere) and then flows to the coast.

That afternoon by the river she told him of her origins and
her people's past. He thought it was strange and wouldn't have
minded talking about something else, like baseball, or courtin'.
But she kept on, and seemed to see a solemn importance in this
moment of their relationship. Was she testing him—with all the
talk of bad white men and the Red tribes they victimized so long
ago that he wondered what it could all have to do with today.
As she got into the story he at least knew his role to sit still and
listen as if it was for his own good. And then sure enough it all
got pretty interesting; though it made him uneasy too . . . Carlyne
spoke with such an intentness.

She told him how most of the old tribal life was gone in North
Carolina by 1800 besides a few Catawbas and Cherokees in the
Appalachians. The ancient languages once heard around council
fires had died on the elders' lips until only names of villages and
rivers were left. She told him the old tale of a settlement no one
could get to at Rainbow's End where her ancestors danced and
sang at the Scuffletown Inn. But three things, gunpowder, liquor,
and smallpox, put an end to the Red Man's free life on the land.
Those three things killed off so many, so many.

From defeat of the mighty Tuscaroras at their fort system No-
horoco in 1713 to the Civil War 150 years later the native peoples lost all they had at the hands of the Europeans. There were
Scottish Highlanders and Huguenot settlers who would become
southern racists of today. An 1835 state constitution said no citi-
zenship for non-slave Blacks and free persons of color or mixed
blood; and thus the law shut out the Scuffletonians with their
darker skin. White supremacy was made into a system like South

Africa later: as the violent whites grabbed the land and worked slaves into the ground growing cotton for Europe's textile industry. The white liar and robber took property for recovery of fake debts. They trumped up a hog theft and used the same tied-mule trick as with Carlyne's mother. My mark on 'im! You stole 'im! Greedily the whites used the racist courts to rob fertile land often held in common, fee simple, no metes and bounds, untitled. But some there were who said no.

Some would not accept the white man's rulings. Some still had pride in their race despite the Indian Removal Act of 1830, and the forced labor camps during the Civil War, and the Cherokee Trail of Tears, and all the white man's false promises and broken promises and treaties and all the abuse and massacres of the Red Man and U.S. Government strategy as always to pit tribe against tribe and Black versus Black and so divide and conquer. But many men and women fought back.

All this Carlyne told Joey as they sat on a picnic blanket that day by the quiet river. And he folded his hands and heard her words and wondered why she was telling him this stuff.

Some of the men who were her ancestors, she said, would lie out in the jungle-like woods and swamps to get away from breastwork construction crews in Wilmington. In the swamplands there was yellow fever. But the men went waist-deep in water and weren't dressed warmly enough for winter as they gathered sod and rafted timber. They had lost their lands and civil rights to end up in a death camp where they ate light and labored heavy sixteen hours a day for the racist who took all and pride too. So a bunch of the boys headed by the Lowrys, Carlyne's kin back then, got up a group to resist and the leader Henry Berry Lowry killed a wealthy slave holder and then a brutal conscription officer named Harris: a man who was quick to ship Scuffletown bucks to the work sites of Lower Cape Fear and also as the local liquor dealer to debauch their wives and daughters. Harris ambushed and shot dead young Jarman Lowry whom he mistook for a rival lover and then he led a Home Guard detachment to arrest Wesley and Allen Lowry who were the boy's brothers and likely avengers. They were on furlough from the labor camp so Harris took them to Moss Neck depot for a train back to Wilmington, so he said, but then murdered both on the way there when 'they tried to escape' though handcuffed. Later on Henry Berry's men got Harris in their sites and the man's riddled body fell dead from the buggy as his horse made a dash for corral.

During summer visits to Pembroke as a girl Carlyne heard her Aunt Lovedy's stories from the 7-year war of the swamps. The menfolk with Henry Berry Lowry in the lead had to hide out and take to the forest. There were gunfights. There were attacks, ambushes, turkey blinds. Henry Berry made raids on the plantations and then gave food to the poor. The men staged an attack at the County Courthouse in order to seize guns. Pretty soon the Home Guard started to search area farms for stashes of guerrilla loot and weapons. The Home Guard killed two more Lowrys, Henry Berry's father and brother, and put his mother Mary through a mock execution.

*

*　　*

*

—All that's so long ago, said Joey.

—It's long ago, but it counts.

—What kind of sandwiches did you bring? Hand me one, and pour me a cup of milk, okay? Let's eat and take a nap and maybe then a swim instead of talking.

—You can eat, said Carlyne. But you must also listen. If you care about me and want to spend your life with me like you say you do, then these are things you need to know. It's important who I am, Joey, and the truth about it . . . I don't want you saying down the line you didn't know who I was, and if you did you'd never have married a squaw, an 'Indian'. So listen to me please.

In May 1865 a week after Appomattox a man cried historic words from the County Courthouse door in Lumberton. The slaves were now free. But a labor contract system took slavery's place, and it was bad too. And the Ku Klux Klan began to form up like a new Confederate Home Guard, a police for property. The Conservative state government went back to the Black Codes before the war and this meant Blacks and Scuffletonians were left out in the cold: not slaves and not free.

The North gave all the power to the same enemy it had just

defeated, the Confederates, but not to the Black and Indian allies who fought and died for the Union cause.

Hector Oxendine was shot to death by whites because Oxendine had led General Sherman's troops to the Carlisle plantation and got them fresh horses.

Right away the so-called Indians and the Blacks became the New South's mudsills like in prewar days.

—Over here was the white man's great plantation, said Carlyne. Over there the infested swamp. And we were in between.

Back then her people lived in log cabins and shanties. And she showed Joey one the day they went to visit Aunt Lovedy. It was up a cow lane and past a thicket in a field half cleared of old pine and post oak. In the hut there would be the yellow wife with a baby at her breast while her other kids played on the swamp edges and picked up ticks. Maybe her husband was at work as $6/month ditcher on one of the white farms. From her girlhood Carlyne remembered those pine board cabins with a funnel or smoke-hole chimney; clay chinks but no windows: only peepholes to look out for intruders. There was a well dug in the ground surrounded by cypress gum and some curb to keep chillen from drownin'. Now Carlyne told her beau of the sawed half-barrels outside the chimney to run off lye from wood ashes and make soap. A poor fice dog all ribcage and droopy snout went nosing about the acre of puny corn, potatoes, rice.

Henry Berry Lowry's family were mechanics and carpenters and lived better in a spacious log cabin. And so when the leader got married he wanted a ceremony at his mother's house and then an enfare or wedding banquet. For his bride he chose Rhoda Strong who was a pretty 16 year-old with large dark mournful eyes and long lashes, a light complexion and a very well developed figure; so goes the story. Rhoda smoked a pipe, used snuff, and late in life after their epic together was ended she said her husband Henry was the handsomest man she ever saw.

The day they were married the Home Guard came and arrested the bridegroom in front of a couple hundred invited guests. It almost got violent. Then in court the rebel treated his accusers with a proud contempt and wouldn't answer questions or cross-examine witnesses brought against him. Then his bride Rhoda smuggled a file into his Whiteville prison cell and he made the first escape ever from that jail and went back to Scuffletown and then the swamps.

Friends and kin joined him. There were Rhoda's brothers Andrew and Boss Strong. Boss only 14 would become the leader's
closest friend and most trusted lieutenant. There were also Henry's
brothers Stephen and Thomas and first cousins Calvin and Henderson Oxendine. There was John Dial, an apprentice blacksmith;
also two Blacks, one a skilled mason and plasterer named George
Applewhite and the other known as Shoemaker John. And then
there was a white youth, a Buckskin Scot named McLauchlin.

Group members had to risk leaving the woods to earn a day's
pay, and they took their guns to church on Sunday. As an outlaw
band they raided and robbed the houses of planters who were
their enemies and had hurt their families. Many local people
turned not to the local police or State militia when they looked for
justice but to the Lowry band.

A black woman who was a former slave, and had all but two of
her teeth knocked out by the master, said:

—Henry Berry's only payin' 'em back. With him better days is
comin'!

As the weeks went past and the months there were more raids,
skirmishes, dramatic actions on the part of the Lowry band. And
then they came out of the forest for a rich meal with Rhoda and
the other wives, and later Henry Berry showed off his talents as a
fiddler. One time the leader gave himself up in hopes of a normal
life with his wife and infant daughter, but soon he went to the
jailer with a pistol and bowie knife, and told him:

—Open the door and step aside. Enough of this: you haven't
treated me as promised when I agreed to come here.

Once again he went into the swamps and was never seen again
in Lumberton.

When the militia captured Applewhite, the former slave, and
Henry Berry's brother Stephen, the judge sentenced them to hang.
Rhoda walked eighty miles to Wilmington, and at the jail she
turned some heads. Like her descendant Carlyne a century later
she passed for white, and was able to slip her menfolk an axe,
chisel and file on twine through the prison window. Then the two
men along with Lowryists Calvin and Henderson Oxendine, also
in jail there, got out a hole cut in the third floor wall and shimmied on blanket strips forty feet to the ground. In the moonlight
they went northward into the tall piney woods and swamplands

of southeastern Carolina. Like fish in the sea they made their way and got back to Scuffletown.

Into Lowry ranks came a spy named Saunders saying he would teach them how to read. It was a legal crime in those days to teach dark-skinned people how to read and write. But the spy was found out and shot.

The KKK began a campaign of murder and arson in a dozen Piedmont counties, but the forces of order didn't bother them and kept on trying to get at the Lowrys. Henry Berry's men seemed to pop up from beneath the earth and staged more bold raids on plantations and stores. They gave away booty to the needy.

Militia went after them. KKK took revenge against the Indians. When a racist named Taylor put Andrew Strong and Make Sanderson—also with the Lowrys—in front of a firing squad, Henry Berry executed Taylor. There were more swamp battles and retaliation raids. 1871 was the height of Lowry operations. A bank robbery 500 miles away staged by Frank and Jesse James and Cole Younger was said to be by Henry Berry Lowry. From week to week there were bloody shootouts, arrests, escapes, and corn given to the poor folk in Scuffletown.

Rhoda was locked up along with the wives of Steve Lowry, Andrew Strong and George Applewhite. At the river that same mid-July evening two militia detachments heard voices upstream toward Harper's Ferry, N.C. Round the bend came a lone oarsman and, silent on the twilit Lumbee, he glided closer. Eighteen men began to fire their guns at Henry Berry Lowry, but he slipped over the side and used the canoe to protect his body from their volleys and still came forward. He didn't turn back but swam ahead and shot back from the water. A militiaman fell wounded. Then a second. And, as their ammunition ran low, the captain had his troops retreat from Wire Grass Landing.

The Wilmington *Morning Star* said Rhoda's arrest had aroused the lion in Henry Berry's nature. He was a man of few words, and his response caused a panic.

—Release my wife or some women of Burnt Swamp Township shall come to the swamp with me.

On July 18th a westbound train set the wives free at the Indian village of Red Bank.

Local men who didn't want to fight the Lowrys hid out in order to avoid being recruited.

```
            *
       *        *
            *
```

On the picnic blanket the thirdbaseman gave a yawn and said:
—I'm so sleepy, honey. Let's go for a swim.
Carlyne shook her head with a wry look and said:
—It's almost done.
—You mean there's more?
—A little more, yes. Why? Don't you want to hear it?
—Of course I do. Go on.
She looked away—across the dark reddish stream. She pressed
her lips: a bit unhappy with his lack of support. But he asked her
again to finish the story, and said he meant it.

Henry Berry, heavily armed and somber, didn't say much. But
his actions told a fact of this country. The Indian, the Black, or
poor white whose land was taken away, had only himself to rely
on. This racist conservative society and its courts would not help
him.

The Lowrys couldn't have won. They were far too isolated.
Also they were worn down by swamp hardship and partisan
warfare: seven years of lying out amid the mosquitoes. So the out-
lawed men asked for amnesty and a return to normal life. They
invited the enemy to come and talk and treated a General Gor-
man with courtesy so he later wrote: They bear little resemblance
to desperados. But the State Legislature would not hear of peace
with the Lowrys.

Well then, said Henry Berry's men, they would leave the U.S. if
they were let go. But if not then they would die game. The young
Buckskin, McLauchlin, had been shot dead by a traitor the past
December as he slept alone beside a campfire. Only one Lowry
band member ever stood trial and hung: that was Henderson Oxendine caught in February 1871 in a trap laid for Applewhite. Oxendine was also Carlyne's ancestor, and he walked head up to his
death with a firm step. But he paused to sing a hymn: *And yet shall
I delay . . .* A large crowd perched on every housetop and tree limb
watched it all and saw him go calmly up the scaffold on a day in
early springtime. They gave an aaah! when the trap fell, and the
handsome young man dangled and twitched.

In March '72 Boss Strong died by a bounty hunter's bullet while he was playing his harmonica.

One July morning of that year Tom Lowry walked into a turkey blind at Holly Swamp ford on his way to a political meeting at Union Chapel. Mortally wounded he ran back into the swamp, Spencer rifle in hand, but fell too weak to pull the trigger.

Only George Applewhite among the rebels lived on after the swamp war. He had been badly injured and twice reported shot to death. 'Hit in the mouth with two bullets, he spat them out.' But Applewhite was able to escape to Georgia. Rearrested in 1875 he was granted immunity under an Amnesty Act passed by Conservatives for the Ku Klux Klan. And he went back to his work as a skilled bricklayer.

Now only two were left. In their isolation they made risky forays out of the swamp. Andrew Strong died on Christmas day, 1872, the back of his head blown away by a store clerk's shotgun. After that Steve Lowry hung on to a lonely backwoods life for over a year. He was a strong man grown thin and pale as he lived on roots. But then he died too, his body riddled by three young whites after the reward. He put down his gun to pluck a banjo and sing at a wagon train party one February night.

And the leader? Where was Henry Berry Lowry? No one knew.

In February 1872 he left the scene. Some said he shot himself by accident. Others said he went from Robeson County to the far Northwest where as a Modoc chieftain he fought U.S. troops along the California-Oregon border.

Who knows? No one does—to this day.

But for Carlyne's people he was the man, the fighter, who stood up. A hundred years ago he burst out of Whiteville Prison as a golden Scuffletonian youth with manacles on his hands and went to his beautiful bride Rhoda. As late as the 1930s his people said he still lived, forever rebellious and therefore free, a heroic man among them.

Henry Berry led a resistance struggle in a state where the KKK head also chaired the Conservative (later called Democratic) Party's executive committee. The U.S. Government left the Ku Klux Klan alone but set out to slaughter the Plains Indians and anyone else who wouldn't toe the line.

But as always with a Henry Berry Lowry: it was political isolation which ended his struggle.

*

*   *

*

—So you see—Carlyne stood up from the picnic blanket and
stretched—that's how it was, and is . . . When my father died, his
relatives said in court my mother had bewitched him. Well, they
wanted the money. But I'm not bewitching anybody, and if I tell
you all this, Joey, it's so you'll know you came here today with an
Indian girl from the swamps, whose parents never married. I'm
not a southern belle with fair skin and dainty hands.—Carlyne
took a deep breath.—In the old days Catawba tribe threw themselves into this river when they got sick with smallpox.

She stood over him. She looked at him, and he thought this too
had a strangeness.

Then she held out her hand to her fiancé to go in for a swim,
and he took it.

Now eyes closed in the jet plane flying through the night, on
his way home from the war, Joey remembered the story she told
him by the Lumbee River that afternoon. He seemed to hear it
with other ears—not further away or madder than Vietnam.
Those were his wife's people.

IX

Toward dawn Joey opened his eyes and leaned to look far down
at the ocean. And then, off in the distance, he saw the sunlit land,
America. Trimmed with white surf a hundred miles of coastline
curved into the Pacific and the morning mist.

Somewhere in the plane a cassette player was turned up. Often
over Armed Forces radio, and that day in Saigon with Bufillu at
a bar called Soul Kitchen Café, he heard the song about how it
doesn't rain in California. Now he stared down at the coast and
thought of baked roads and hootches huddling among bamboo

groves, and the glare of rice paddies. He smelled rotten thatch where wizened mama- and papa-sans glanced up in silence from some eternal task while the G.I.'s moved through their ville. The flute boy rode his loping water buffalo on the edge of a lotus pond. A barefoot kid dodged a C-rat can and then ran after it by the roadside south of Pleiku. It seemed to Joey just a moment ago he was fighting for his life in a hamlet not far from the Cambodian border at zero hour of his tour.

—*In approximately ten minutes we arrive at Travis Airforce Base, Oakland.*

X

He sipped his coffee and gazed down at the Bay and bald ridges around San Francisco which were a bleached mauve. Cars went along the roads not afraid to trip mines. It was smooth down there in peacetime, but he didn't believe this peace, and felt a twinge of mistrust.

The plane coasted down past the Berkeley Hills where Newell rented a house with his friends the hippies and anti-war activists. It was time to go find his younger brother and ask him a few questions. It was time to begin the search. Once he was Joey Gilbert the ballplayer; then Joey the soldier. Now he was Joey the seeker, Joey-Oedipus, after the truth no matter how bad. Brother, what happened? Where is she? But he had a foretaste of fear.

Working its wing flaps like talons the 707 revved and glided down over the housetops and the land. In it came, lower, lower, on down just above the ground—and then it touched. The wheels touched down as it torqued way up and slowed before it let go and rolled a ways and then turned to taxi. He peered out at a C-130 which awaited takeoff in the asphalt glare off a runway strip.

And then the door opened on California and another day Stateside. Joey paused and glanced back at the stewardess. What if Carlyne stood out there waiting to take him in her arms like in Bangkok? What if there were newsmen and camera crews, and his dad had come with her to meet him and someone waved a flag and called: Good job, soldier! There would be joy and tears and payback for that world of hurt where he spent a year.

Outside, he smelled the sweet American air laced with jet exhaust. He'd heard hippies flung red paint from pails on G.I.s beyond the gate at Travis and cried out: You murderer! you baby killer! you fascist warmonger! They screamed at you and spit and threw eggs. Baby burner! And there were Vets for Peace, and G.I.s for Peace, deserters. They came to agitate among the soldiers in uniform for military standby at San Francisco International. But radical hippies were said to jump before burial details and deface the coffins of grunts while they shouted: Flipped out, man!

So he heard while in The Nam.

Down the metal steps he came not too sure on his feet. And his boot touched the ground and he looked around.

There were a few MPs in ponchos and beyond them some cyclone wire fence. A few steps ahead a troop looked too crisp and too much the desk soldier for his PVN campaign ribbon plus blue-silver CIB (Combat Infantryman's Badge) and other fruit salad from the Army Surplus Store; but he put on a show and kneeled to kiss paydirt.

Joey didn't kneel. Around him there were big hugs and a lot of broad smiles, the cheery voices of civilians. But he saw no sign of his wife nor would he since nobody had an address to notify Carlyne about his arrival. Or maybe they did know and his father, Newell, even Lemon lied about it to hide what had happened at the Rock Castle, and why she left.

XI

Inside the terminal he walked down a long wide corridor. On the walls were insignias of units deployed in Vietnam. Also there were signs to welcome the G.I.s home and thank them.

A uniformed woman in customs frowned up at him. She took a glimpse at the bloodshot eyes, the glum tunnel stare. Another one strung out on drugs? But cocaine and reefer didn't make him smell that way, and turn his fatigues into such a sight.

—Soldier, you better shower and shave before you go out there. Did you lose your ditty bag?

—I lost it.

She looked at him, nodded.

—Any items to declare?

—No.

Close search had become standard procedure for grunts coming home. But this one with his blood stripes and long tangled hair, also his really exceptional dirtiness, looked almost beyond military protocol.

Then a strange thing happened. He grinned. He gave her a soldier of fortune type grin, steely, like a what-the-hell look after combat and buddies greased. And she read the name over his breast pocket and said:

—Go on, Mr. Gilbert.

She gestured him through.

And Joey thought: maybe if I'd taken Carlyne's brooch that day in Bangkok, she'd have come here to get it back.

XII

Outside, as he boarded a bus for Oakland Army Terminal, a car horn sent him to one knee. Safety off? The sound jolted him.

Then along the safe geometric streets of America he felt a fear unknown in The Nam. After a year's nightmare he awoke to what looked like a lot of smug people going about their day. Were they mocking him? They went on their way as though nothing could hope to compare with their routine.

It was The World.

A farce.

An E-2 glad-handed along the aisle in his clean fatigues as the bus entered a big military complex beneath the Bay Bridge.

Joey proceeded to the separation building where a basketball court had a table for each step in the out-process. What if Carlyne was hurt? he thought. In trouble? He recalled an August day a lifetime ago when he said to her:

—We're going to New York. They want to try me at third.

She said:

—You go.

—No, my darling, I need you with me.

Counters, card tables, folding chairs in rows. Pressed uniforms, faces, questions, paper, more paper.

—Name and number, soldier?

—No, she said. You go along to your famous Big Leagues. I want a college degree, and my senior year starts next week.

The placid clerk was not too impressed by this hardass with his layers of dirt. He snapped his fingers:

—Please sit.

There were boyish tears that day he told her the great news. So long ago.

Joey stared as the other rose to talk with a supervisor, and the two looked over his papers. Pricecroft's signature was on the document. Still his mind wandered: a call to the registrar and they would have granted her permission for a late return. Critical moment, then, now . . . go it alone, boy.

He waited by the desk to process out.

XIII

For an hour he filled out forms. They photocopied the medical reports he brought from Saigon and waived his physical exam.

Later a clerk handed him a check:

—Retroactive pay, plus accrued leave.

—My wife didn't get it?

—I really don't know about that, Sir, but I could begin an inquiry if you'd like to furnish us with certain affidavits such as the social security cards of both parties plus birth certificates and your marriage license. Here, let me bring you the form to fill out in triplicate plus the instructions booklet. Within 72 hours if you'd care to wait we might be able to ascertain whether your wife—

—Forget it.

As he made his way to the exit he was handed a voucher for a meal. To one side there was a group being held overnight for more tests, lectures on readjustment to civilian life—'From Free Fire Zone to Twilight Zone'—and a seminar on how to clean up one's language. But he had come in alone as a special case and so he slipped through the grid. Behind him a voice seemed to laugh off Vietnam as a bad job. Hand over my back pay, man, fork it over. I'm history.

Joey went in the john to wash his face, and stared in the mirror. Was it him? He didn't know himself after a year of combat high, his nerves strained to the limit for weeks at a time. One year he slept lightly, in fits and starts, when he did. He knew the fear of a grunt's first firefights, shock, then grief over lost buddies. Then came a sort of erotic readiness for Charlie who was just up the trail—and he wanted to kill. After that it didn't take long to go over the line: he was hardcore, he was battle tested, numbed. The idea of death no longer exercised him so. From the fear, pain, sadness, traumatic shock of the early days in-country he had gone in denial; and this you needed, to make it through. Forget about it! Just gain the skills and strength and stamina if you still feel like living. And then—do as the Romans. Creature of reflexes.

But the numbness was starting to leave him. Last night in the airplane he felt like a piece of ice melting. Now the anaesthesia began to wear off.

In the mirror he didn't see himself in the deep eyes and scraggly beard, the greasy tangle of black hair. He had left his innocence and illusions and his old self back there in the war, like an old coat. All the cocky boyhood in him, the gifted third baseman, was burned away in Vietnam.

For a moment he stared at the mask of tragedy in the mirror. And he seemed to hear sounds coming to him from across the ocean. Those were the moans and windy howls blared by Division loudspeakers so enemy cadre couldn't get to sleep in the daytime and would be less alert by night. Unable to rest in death the wandering VC souls drew out their shrieks which were kind of comic too like an old horror movie.

And so it was. Nobody came to meet Joey Gilbert.

XIV

Into his ragged wallet he folded the discharge papers and looked for the way out. On he went through the last of the exit doors—and took his first few steps still in jungle issue out into the humdrum midafternoon.

But he gave a glance back and knew he should have gone to barracks behind the terminal and gotten some sleep. In the shadow of the Bay Bridge he trudged along feeling dead on his feet. They had hustled him in the processing while others took their sweet time, mulled about, gabbed. Behind him the G.I.s signed vouchers and then drifted away toward a good sleep so they could wake up with a better sense of things. Then they went for the steak and eggs they had dreamed of for a year.

Well, he didn't want to stand in the line and get himself billeted. He wanted to go. He wanted to start.

It was strange without his gun. He looked around. You didn't need that here. Did you?

Should he call home? Maybe he'd better call the Rock Castle.

This idea made him pause. He stood still on the sidewalk and looked around some more.

He saw movement. There were cars, a few people on foot. There was the arc of a white gull over a choppy San Francisco Bay. There was a plane high in the sky with a glint of sun as it lofted out past the Golden Gate for a flight back across the Pacific. Out there, out that way beyond the great bridge five thousand miles across the water was where real life went on. That was The World, not this.

Here the buildings and people had something of the unreal about them. A dog yapped. Blue sky, a few clouds; the choppy Bay water was a deep blue, like Carlyne's eyes. Alcatraz. Sharks.

He walked.

Beside him a car slowed down. It pulled over.

—Hey there! Mars Bar!

—Ha ha ha!

Teenagers.

—Gad zooks! Golly gee!

—Say there, G.I. Joe! How 'bout a ride to Jack London Square? There's a barbecue going on, and you're the meat!

—Ha ha ha!

—Mars Bar!

They laughed some more. No red paint: kids on a joyride.

Crazy laughter. He blinked as they peeled rubber and pulled out into the fast lane.

His stomach gave a flutter.

No gun.

And then he went along toward Berkeley. And he thought: why, my darling, why did you take our happiness, the love we might have shared this day, and throw it in the trash?

Chapter Twelve

I

At the top of Hillgard Street in the Berkeley Hills there were voices and laughter like people having a round-the-clock party.

A young woman in beach halter and short-shorts strayed from the house and wandered a ways on her own in a daze. But she met the soldier coming up the hill and latched onto the arm of his olive drab fatigues and said:

—Are you ready to take the test?

He gave a little jolt and looked at her. He croaked:

—What test?

—The acid test, silly.—She looked him over and whistled between her teeth.—Say, that's a far-out costume.

The soldier looked at her hands to see if she had a gun.

Then he said:

—Newell Gilbert live here?

She must have passed the acid test—the way she gave a chuckle and put a finger in his tangled hair. Up and down she stared at the combat fatigues tucked in his crudded jungle boots, and gave his stomach a little pat.

—Nude what? ... Dunno', kiddo. All flavors in this crash pad.—She sort of chanted.—Wear beads, smoke dope, grow hair, take off bra. (Chuckle.) Shock adult. Act weird.

—You don't know Newell?

She liked to touch. She played with the toy soldier, taking his dog tag in her fingers to read it.

—Gimme this, I want it.

—No. He's my brother. This is his address.

—Gimme-gimme. I'll give you something too!

—No. You haven't seen him?

She frowned.

—Shucks, Daddy, you're no fun . . . Brother? You can try the rear bedroom upstairs, but knock first.

The girl gave her toneless laughter, a hippie cluck.

—You show me.

She led him up a flight of outside steps to a second-storey foyer and kitchen.

II

In the living room entry he stood and his nerves didn't like the swirl and speed of strobe lights.

An older man in a Gandhi cap was talking low to a teenage girl seated on his lap.

—So we take a vow of sexual abstinence, and the name we have for it is brahmacharya.

She listened to him, head bowed by his, and then said:

—Oh? That's nice. I love the way you're so serious, Nicky. Wanna' fuck?

—Sure. Give me a few minutes.

—Where'll we do it?

—Here is okay.

—Sitting here in front of everybody? Far out!

—Or we can go out back in the woods if you'd like.

—I think you're cute!

The new one, toy soldier, looked them over. The lights spun round on the living room walls like a dizzying flight through space.

There was music by Eve of Destruction but turned low.

What looked and sounded like a grad student, granny glasses and beard, was talking to three chicks on their nightly lookout for a few hundred mikes: LSD micrograms. He gave them the egghead's mating call, and they dug it:

—Vulgar materialism begat the religious boom. And Wilson's Law, what is good for GM is good, begor', for the country, begat the mean and meager Eisenhower Era conservatism . . .

Two bikers in black leather came from an inner room. They both had gold eye teeth. One held out his hand and said:

—Put 'er here, Americal.

—It's a patriot, said the second. I'll buy that.

But the man in uniform was uptight and outa' sight. He looked at the hand held out to him, then the girl by his side, and said:

—What about Newell?

Grad student droned on:

—I-Like-Ike signifies the repose of conscience . . . Private property being the holy of holies we must dread all such deviates as the communist and the beatnik. Okay if our son becomes a juvenile delinquent, so long as he doesn't think.

—Oh.

—Oh.

—Ever see 'Hallelujah the Hills'?

—No.

—No.

One of the bikers said:

—Just get back, big man? Those Vet Congies make it hot for you over there?

—Looks like it—said the other, and made a fist, grinning.

III

There were more voices and laughter in the hall.

Inside the living room Granny Glasses went on with his talk about the 1950s, Ike and Adlai, the politics of fatigue. In the armchair Brahmacharya and his date were doing it, with her jeans and panties pulled down on her knees; but they went at it so slow and easy it may have been nirvana. Now however he was telling her all about psychosis as seer, drug tourism, and the systematic deregulation of the senses.

The flickering walls rode to the rhythm of the music. For a moment the soldier put a hand on his escort's shoulder, looked in her eyes, and said again:

—Where is Newell?

But one of the Hell's Angels pointed a ringed finger at him:

—Now don't touch the little lady.

The soldier ignored this. The girl in her beach halter smiled. Then her petals seemed to perk up as across the room the man himself stood in cutoff bluejeans with a fringe, loose black t-shirt, sandals. Newell Gilbert stood there with—what was that around his neck? Some sort of amulet? A snakeskin? Well, he looked a bit worn out whether by free love or else history's contradictions: SDS versus Progressive Labor, Vietnamese children napalmed in the Age of Aquarius, hip gurus and a lot of potheads in the Nth white night of an induced ecstasy. That couldn't be too good for your health.

The grunt from the jungle stared across the room, and there was a bad thing in his eye.

Newell was the host looking over tonight's motley crew plus a few leftovers from yesterday and a week ago. Now and again the house on Hillgard needed a good airing out, but a few of these drifting souls had no place to go; at least nowhere to scrounge good dope and a snack from the fridge. So the scene could get tense when he started to shoo them out saying his landlady was coming from Lake Tahoe.

The grad student looked at the big soldier who was so full of grunge from head to toe he didn't belong here. With a chuckle Granny Glasses said:

—O Freedom and Democracy, the crimes committed in your name.

But the host had a jolt gazing at his new guest. Newell's face was like sun and clouds, as his brow knit, and he looked hard. Then he gave a big whoop and went into a bent-knee Indian dance which surprised even Brahmacharya and his Kasturbai who were not easily surprised: not even by their climax if it was ever going to come during nirvana. Newell went on his knees and threw up his hands:

—O you up there! That's right: you, God, I said you! O nonexistent one, impostor! Though I won't even deign *not* to believe in you since atheism is religion too: now I give praise and cry hallelujah!

And he began singing the Doxology in a deep voice:

Praise God from whom all blessings flow,
Praise Him all creatures here below,
Praise Him with all the heavenly host (sic!),
Praise father, son, and Holy Ghost!

All paused to listen as he sang out dissonantly over the rock music. And then he laughed loudly. Tears welled in his eyes. He flung his arms wide and took a hop, skip, and jump across the living room. Gingerly he touched his brother's arm to see if it was real, and said:

—*You're* not the Holy Ghost, are you?

Grad Student said:

—Not a ghost, but Freud's ghost symptom. Ghosts come to haunt us from our repressed affectivity; that is, from some old trauma of childhood which our ego just couldn't accept, and digest. Thus the Devil is humanity's ghost: spawned by a reality which is just too much.

The hippie leaned and hugged his brother the soldier. But it was a fraternal embrace the other didn't return. Joey Gilbert showed no emotion. He only endured it, hands by his side, and looked glumly at this younger brother who had been on his mind since last November when his wife stopped writing.

—Where's Carlyne? he said.

Newell drew back with his eyes sparkling. A tear fell on his cheek.

—What? I don't know, Jojo. Lemon told me she left the Rock Castle, but nobody knows where. Gee, gee: it's so wonderful to see you. I'll never criticize the system again!

—You know.

At the cold tone Newell blinked. He paused; then said:

—Have you called Lemon?

—No.

—Well, I will in a minute. She hasn't stopped crying since Dad told her the news. But look at you, look at you. Made it back after all. But you smell bad, buddyroll, and seems like you're still over there in Vietnam. What a fighter, what a man: I hate the war but I love the warrior . . . I'd like to see the look on our father's face when he learns you came home safe and sound! Ha ha ha! I salute you, Vietnam vet! C'mon, everybody, let's give the hero of a hundred battles a parade here and now.

And so Newell rousted 'em all out and led them around the house singing and chanting slogans in honor of the heroic grunt who was his older brother. But it wasn't so easy in the case of Brahmacharya and Company; no, but they'd better snap out of it, and revert to the reality principle, as Grad Stud also advised: they'd better join the vulgar crowd and march if they wished 2779 Hillgard to be their paradise. Brahmacharya in Gandhi cap and his teenage consort with panties down paraded through the kitchen and bedrooms and back into the living room; they brought up the rear.

Then Newell made a speech which was duly anti-imperialist. He agitated them; though what tendency can compete with LSD? Nobody in the commune ever saw him look so excited, so happy as tonight.

But Joey home from the war just stood there and waited for his parade to end. One instant he glared and looked upset about something; the next he was glum as a bum in the scum. Really he was coiled up tight as could be, so it appeared, and ready to snap. He had a facial tic which fluttered by his left eye.

IV

Night was falling over the Berkeley Hills. In the bedroom window the twilight drew a magic aura over the Bay with its deep gold and red reflections. Stony Alcatraz had a warm glimmer to it. Stars came out, and electric lights were spreading east to Alameda while in the sky westward there was a spectacular sunset in tiers above the Pacific.

A flower girl lay sprawled on Newell's bed without a stitch of clothing or a care in the world.

—She's a Summer of Love girl. Showed up here a few days ago. At first I thought the FBI had my number, sending a spy up here with such big tits. I guess no spy ever got so zonked on a combo of Mexican mushrooms, peyote buttons we get at ten dollars a hundred from an address in Laredo, morning glory seeds and Benzedrine all blended in a milkshake of Romilar cough syrup.

At the look Joey gave her Newell laughed, gave her butt a slap, and, when she didn't budge, tossed a robe over her flesh aglow with sunset from the window.

The room was neat: desk with telephone, a portable typewriter, folders, small piles of paper and writing materials set in order. There were bookshelves; a card table with newspapers, political magazines and reviews. There was a shortwave radio.

Joey's features worked a little as he said:

—I thought I might find my wife here.

There was a silence, a duel of eyes.

Newell looked away, trying to relieve the tension:

—Welcome to the counterculture. We're cultural dissidents.

—Beethoven type thing—Joey looked at him, thinking.

—Not exactly. We dig The Diggers more.

—Diggers?

—Street Theater. We dress up as Green Berets and beat a Vietnamese family to death outside the Federal Building. We have it planned for activists to pass by, so there's a lot of screaming, and then the dead get up off the pavement and make speeches.

—. . .

—A crowd gathers. We try to shame apathetic Americans, but it isn't easy to win the hearts and minds of Federal employees. Mainly I guess we draw spectators from the security and intelligence services.

Joey looked bone tired but he didn't sit on the chair Newell pushed toward him. Clearly he didn't feel well.

—Would you take your act to Chinatown?

—Touché. No, we perform by royal command at the Civic Center after a practice gig in full dress by Sather Gate. That's our Schubert. But here on campus the make-believe Green Berets leave their victims to chase after a few heckler acidheads, like Abbot and Costello. Over there it's real screams from the crowd. And real not Keystone cops come on the scene with sirens. Then we try to mix with the crowd and avoid arrest so the show can go on.

A mote stirred in Joey's dark eyes. The tic on his cheek twitched, and he said:

—What fun.

V

The phone rang. Newell picked it up, and his voice went low, but he mostly listened. When the call went on, he handed his brother a few sheets of paper from his desk, and smiled. He said, a hand over the receiver:

—This'll be a minute. I just wrote an article. Tell me what you think.

Joey glanced at a few lines.

HO, HO, HO CHI MINH

By 1900 at age 10 Ho Chi Minh (then Nguyen Tat Thanh) had made his decision. And then he fought seventy years for his country and for socialism.

Ho was a brilliant student who came from a rural background. His father was a buffalo boy (and the son of a concubine) who rose to the doctorship and was a scholarly patriot. But he said no to the mandarinate, court honors and privileges, and yes to a life roaming the countryside working as a healer, storyteller, and scribe among the people.

Early on the future Ho worked as a secondary school teacher. But he had a subject in mind which was beyond the day's lesson. And it wasn't his paycheck. So students were sad one day when he went away without a word from Duc Thanh school in Saigon where he was teaching Chinese characters, French, and the *quoc ngu* romanization of Vietnamese.

Ho spent thirty years as an emigrant, a sailor, a wanderer. He worked as a cook's helper, and they called him Ba. He learned languages. He was an alert political tourist in the French colonies and the United States. Ho toiled at a hundred menial tasks. He was a gardener. He cleared and tended an orchard. In Le Havre he was a domestic servant. He was a dishwasher and snow sweeper in London where he shoveled snow until exhaustion in a freezing courtyard. He was a boiler tender dragging heavy loads up and down steps from a ship's boiler. He was a chauffeur de locomotive. He was a kitchen boy and then pastry cook whose

meteoric rise was due to the renowned French chef
Escoffier at London's Carlton Hotel.

Newell's call ended, and he turned to his brother who handed
him back the article.

—Where were we? Oh, the counterculture ... What you see
here is the permanent pot party. Watch out, you could be arrested
at any minute and taken to jail. We have a place in the heart of
enlightened Berkeley police officers; though they are less kindly
toward us since they got a taste of the people's anger during Free
Speech Movement street clashes a few years ago ... So here in
this commune you have a preserve of hippies. In the woods out
back there are deer, and the skunks scavenge. But in here we give
shelter to a wide range of herbifumous species. Don't get excited,
brother. Pay no mind to the young women who take off their panties, who speak freely, drop acid, smoke grass, eat speed, ingest psi-
losybin, take acid tests, read the Tibetan Book of the Dead, quote
I Ching at dawn after an all-night orgy, adhere to International
Federation for Internal Freedom (IFFIF), proselyte for Pranksters,
guide their lives wisely by astrology, embody Chakras, tour esoteric systems of yoga and Sufism, admire the cognoscenti, protest
they will never go back to their draggy dads, and in principle give
you what you want for the asking.

—How exciting, said Joey. And you? Are you on drugs right
now?

—No. Just in a minor political crisis at BPC.

—BPC?

—Berkeley Peace Committee to Stop the War in Vietnam and
Bring Home the Troops.

—I see. And this girl lying on your bed?

—Don't underestimate her. She's a budding intellectual.

—That so. What's her field?

—Well, for starters, in her more lucid moments she may read
The Barb where my Ho Chi Minh article is headed; or *The Oracle*
which I write for also, or Liberation News Service. In fact she reads
what I tell her to, and proofreads too: all my works. For a break
from the heavy stuff she listens to KMPX hip music pre-orgies,
and she may cry out amazed: Bring the *in*-in in! Mainly she likes
to wear beads, an Indian headband and granny glasses, and go
about the place lewd as a nude in a snood. She won't shave; she is
the organic woman, anti-permed, stringy tressed, and stoned.

—Does she ever wear clothes?

—Oh, she might, if there's a concert at the Fillmore or Avalon Ballroom across the Bay; or to go hobnob with the Haight-Ashbury supra weirdos and jive on their vibes, their god force. But it's easier to stick around here and sip a toddy of LSD-spiked Kool Aid. That's enough god force for any normal person.

—Hm—said Joey, looking around.—She's a hippie.

—She is! Her thing is seed catalogues, the speed of eternity, super organic mescaline, apologies owed to earth, active and passive kundalini, Tantra as the quintessential copulation. For her Zen Buddhism beats the hully-gully anyday or the mashed potatoes! In her selfness she embodies the nature and destiny of a freak.

Newell fell silent. Thinking of his phonecall?

Out the window dusk floated in like a tide over the comfortable split-level homes and patios shaded by trees above the Berkeley campus. Joey gazed out beyond the Campanile and far across San Francisco Bay going a deeper blue as night fell. Beyond the water the city spread on its mauve hills toward San Mateo, the airport, Route 1 down along the coast.

Joey had so much in him, questions for his brother, emotions—it was hard to get started. Now he plunged in.

—Look . . . I came here to talk about my wife. I need to ask you a few things, and you . . . need to answer.

—Sure.

—What happened at the Rock Castle? Why did she stop writing me last fall when you were there? Was she unhappy? Why did she—

But just as he got going a head popped in the bedroom door. It was a hippie who had a pair of women's panties round his neck.

—Someone out here to see you.

—Later.

—He says it's important.

—Okay, in a moment. So is this.

—He says it's an emergency.

Newell gave a sigh and said to Joey:

—Hell, I better go see. It's more of this BPC business. In crisis. While I'm out there don't you waste time. Never waste time! I'll only be a few minutes, and you can read this.

Again he handed his brother *Ho, Ho, Ho Chi Minh*, but Joey pushed it away.

—I'll pass.
—Ah. No guts?
Hippie chuckle.

VI

Joey waited.

His eyes rolled up as he began falling asleep on the chair. But then he jolted awake and rubbed his face. He didn't want to sleep. Not yet. Also, he was half afraid of his dreams: the dreadful images when he drifted off for a moment on the plane.

So he reached and picked up Newell's article from the desk. He forced himself to read. No guts?

Then Ho Chi Minh became a Paris bohemian and commercial
artist. He earned his money retouching photographs,
and learned how to lacquer and paint antiquities. Also
he was a political journalist and founder/editor of
Le Paria where his articles (as Nguyen Ai Quoc, Nguyen
the Patriot) stirred his countrymen far and near. At
Le Paria he was the treasurer, the distributor, the
proofreader; he did thirty tasks. In Paris he wrote
stories and a play called *Bamboo Dragon* which was banned
by the French Government. Like his father Ho was a
raconteur, also a poet and playwright.

During this time he started the Ligue des Colonies.
How many other organizations would he begin in his life?
He was an untiring propagandist. He was a Communist
Party militant in France, the first foreign member of
the French Parti Socialiste; as well as in the Soviet
Union, and then China. In China he worked as a street
vendor selling tobacco and cigarettes to survive. He
left the USSR for China the year Lenin died.

Then he served as secretary to Borodin who was Soviet
head of a Comintern aid mission in Canton (1924) where Ho
set up and directed a school called l'Association des
Jeunes Camarades Révolutionnaires de Vietnam for some 200
cadres. This he did with Pham Van Dong. At the time he

also founded l'Association des Peuples Opprimés de l'Asie
Orientale.

Ho went back to Vietnam in April 1927 when Chiang
Kai-shek was massacring communist allies in Shanghai.
Returning home Ho and his comrades began twenty hard years
of organizational work to prepare the armed struggle for
liberation of their homeland. It was Ho Chi Minh the
masterful tactician, the strategist of victory, Ho the
unifier of divergent tendencies and forces.

But then came more exile. In Thailand he was Ho the
educator once again. In Siam he set up schools, always
organizing, propagandizing; and this helped the quarrels
and compulsive gambling among his compatriots become more
rare.

Then he was arrested and jailed in Hong Kong as a
detainee in Chiang Kai-shek's prison. They drove him on
50-kilometer walks in leg irons between thirteen Kwangsi
Province districts. And all the while he was fed a handful
of rice and had to survive the winter cold without a coat
and went shod in 'Ho Chi Minh sandals'. The future
President of Vietnam endured hunger, sickness, the
abuse of jailors, the cangues. All the time he was
his optimistic self, humorous, a memorable diarist in
his collection of 115 T'ang quatrains in classical
Chinese called *The Prison Diary* which is a thing of
beauty. He translated *l'Histoire du parti Bolshévique*
from a Chinese translation with one finger on his
portable typewriter.

He was emaciated. He was exhausted. His coal-like
depthless eyes (all noted his eyes) were aglow in his
kind avuncular face above a wisp of grayish beard. He
went delirious with fever and infested with fleas and
scabies. Uncle Ho's thin strong fingers trembled yet
the next day he was calm and clear and once again furiously
gentle but terrible in his obstinacy against the impossible
odds. Often his eyesight suffered, and he had
rheumatism . . .

Newell sort of burst in the bedroom door. He looked upset,
shaking his head. Seated at his desk he glanced around. What was
to be done? Phone? Write a note? He picked up a pen and pad of

note paper. Now he had forgotten his older brother's problems. But in his excitement he turned to him.

—Do you know what those jerk-offs want to do? I can't believe it! The problem is BPC's doors are open to anyone off the street. It's a solidarity group: not a Leninist core sworn to secrecy. Our group has new recruits every week, younger activists filled with zeal wanting to stage events, picket lines, guerrilla theater like I said in downtown San Francisco. Take it to the streets! Okay, they have a do-gooder energy, but such good intentions pave the way to hell. The old guard activists know this, and don't like it. By old I mean in their late twenties: veterans of the May 1960 anti-HUAC (that's House Un-American Activities Committee) demo when student blood flowed on the marble steps of San Francisco City Hall and the New Left had its birth. Some came to us from SNCC/CORE voter registration drives in the South; they're Civil Rights demonstrators, Freedom Riders, Greensboro Sitters-In. Many ideas, many backgrounds: Freedom School teachers, Freedom Summer '64 organizers; a white Mississippi Freedom Democratic Party delegate to the '64 Atlantic City Convention where LBJ showed us his dark underside, his betrayal. We get new members from all over: the Beat milieu, the East Village in New York, L.A.'s Venice subsociety, North Beach colonists from across the Bay. Nuclear test protesters, draft card burners, an SDS co-founder and Port Huron Statement signer; a May 2nd Movement Against the Vietnam War graduate . . . you name it! And that's good. But it makes us open to spies, snoopers. Our lists disappear, members' names and addresses, outreach and media contacts. We're legal, aboveboard, a cinch to infiltrate by agent provocateurs.

Joey squirmed in his seat a little listening to the spiel.

—Look, I didn't come here today from Vietnam to get an update on the anti-war movement.

But Newell couldn't believe what he had just heard, so he put his hands to his head, and looked out the window. He went on as though he didn't hear a word of what his brother said.

—You see there are these struggles going on. Out there big things are happening. There are clouds of leaflets, long picket lines, spirited marches, and what rallies! Hell no, we won't go! We won't fight for Texaco! We've had college administration building sit-ins, and marathon panel discussions, and teach-ins against this unjust, this genocidal war, Joey. On April 27th mas-

sive demonstrations took place across the country with 200,000
being addressed by Martin Luther King in New York. And do you
know what he said? (Newell's voice went deep as he imitated
the orator.) He said: The United States is the greatest purveyor
of violence in the world today . . . And then not long after he was
dead, the great leader killed by the CIA and military intelligence,
if the truth were told, because he started talking that day in Central Park about foreign policy issues. On the same day 30 thousand gathered in San Francisco. And Chicago police broke up a
crowd of seven thousand savagely without the slightest provocation; that was a diplomatic signal by Mayor Daley to Democratic
Convention protesters in August. But on the inside, in the groups,
there is fighting and turmoil. The Student Mobilization Committee (SMC) has adopted a motion to exclude all non-independents:
that means CPUSA, SWP and YSA, PL, communists and socialists
but also radical pacifists, SANE, tendency activists. SMC said it
was to relieve tensions in the office, but it increased them, like a
split! In May and June the effect was that we, BPC, got bigger as
former SMC members were trying to spread their views and re-
cruit cadre from a fresh base. Our older BPC activists were against
free entry, but it was partly my fault, so worn down by media
work, press agent work, outreach calls, midnight wheatpasting
sorties and all the rest: me 'n other young firebrands won the argument. You see the older ones get burned out, and don't act; we
call them autumn leaves. So our events committee really did need
new blood, new impetus. I and others pushed for open membership, and we got it. But we've also got a big mess on our hands
now, and it's dangerous!

VII

Joey looked very unhappy where he sat waiting for the lecture to end. Just like his brother. And at last it did seem to lull a
moment; and he was working his lips to get back to the issue of
Carlyne. Right now he meant to get to the bottom of things, and
he didn't care what it took.

But again the bedroom door opened! This time it wasn't the
hippie with women's panties round his neck. This time it was

what looked like a ten year-old with a mustache, who wore a
Che Guevara t-shirt, and whose face beamed as he leaned in and
said:
—Newell, I've got to see you.
—Not now, Springer.
—Now. This is serious, and we can't wait while they're getting
ready to have us hauled in front of a Grand Jury.
—Tst . . . Okay, okay. Sorry, Jojo, I'll just be a moment. C'mon
Springer, what's happened now?
They went out.
Joey stood up so frustrated he was ready to hurt someone.
On the bed Summer of Love drew the bathrobe closer around
her as the fresh Bay breeze wafted in the window. She stirred.
She rose on an elbow and felt about her bleary-eyed. She said in
a slur:
—My peyote . . .?—Miss Yippie 1968 turned on her back and
stared up seeming to invite him. She gave a sigh and stretched—
Far out!—but then closed her eyes and began to snore.
So he sat down again to wait. On the chair he sort of dug in;
though he didn't mean to spend the night here. What he wanted
was to walk down into Berkeley and get a bus to the airport. He
needed to be on his way: out of this madhouse full of hippies,
marijuana fumes, strobe lights and spooky music.
He shook his head. His eye fell on *Ho, Ho, Ho Chi Minh*, the
sheets of typing paper on Newell's desk.
What could he do? He'd fall asleep if he didn't do something.

Uncle Ho was the committee man filled with gaiety.
He said to a meeting of Party leadership: Now let's
gaily proceed to today's study of our Marxist
dialectics.
He was the joyous and dedicated founder of seminal
revolutionary organizations: Thanh-nien in 1926; Parti
communiste indochinois in 1930 from different Tonkin,
Annam and Cochinchina groups; Viet Minh in 1941 (a 35-man
army at the outset commanded by Giap); the Lao Dong in
1951.
He served on the International Bureau of the Communist
International. Then the next week or month he was
hiding out in the mountains, huddling for warmth in a
Kuomintang prison. His one aim in life was the independence

of his nation, the freedom and well-being of his people,
the world's liberation from the long nightmare of capital
and corporate domination.

With Mao's Eighth Route Army in 1938 he made the Long
March from Tsian to Yenan. In China he became a political
commissar and revolutionary leader in Cao Bang Province.

In 1944–45 he directed movement in the liberated zones
versus the Japanese aggressor.

He made no declamatory orations. Ho was not on a
leadership trip. He was always simplicity itself, sincerity,
frankness, frugality. He had inhuman determination combined
with courage and the most magnificent human capacity. He
was an internationalist, a consequential revolutionary,
fighting for victory until the end.

And then one day, September 2nd, 1945, he was the liberator
and proclaimer of Vietnamese independence after he led the
August Revolution and the general insurrection and seizure
of power. *'All men are created equal,'* he reminded the world.
*'All are endowed by their Creator with certain inalienable
rights.'* And he drove it home: *'All earth's peoples
are equal from birth. All have a right to life,
freedom, happiness.'* But for this Independence Day speech
he didn't have a proper suit to wear.

VIII

Joey read. In his exhausted state he hardly saw the words, but
he sort of heard them drop into his subconscious, with a clunk.

Suddenly Newell burst in again. It jolted Joey upright on his
chair where he sat holding the papers, his head drooping on his
chest after a week without a real night's sleep, only naps.

—Do you know what they're thinking of doing? Do you know
what these exalted blockheads actually want to do?! Oh, make no
mistake, it's a standard operation; you can read all about it in *Covert Action.* State and Federal coordinate with our local Red Squad
to send trained infiltrators into the open, legal, wet-behind-the-
ears Berkeley Peace Committee! Like taking candy from a baby.
Not one but a few agents show up. Different cover, of course, and
styles; but all have a progressive speak. Maybe less sectarian, a

breath of fresh air; not all. They come in quietly or noisy, work effectively or not at all. This or that one creates a diversion while his partner fulfills tasks quite well, thank you, and takes time building up trust. Oh, the gung-ho spies are resolute fighters for social justice, and they give the sluggish group a new lease on life. One could be the African-American whose longterm cover is construction worker: deferential toward leaders and seems impressed if you've been on the radio. Perhaps one is the postgrad student in philosophy whose story nobody bothered to check out of course. Cruelly some call her Sea Biscuit because her face is long, toothy, a case of acromegaly. Now it seems she has been waging a slander campaign, pitting male members against each other. And there are more new recruits: a grade school teacher in an ultraleft posture; a Sauselito architect with an expensive car used on late night wheatpaste forays when we dot the town with posters. There is a RYM-II renegade, that's Revolutionary Youth Movement, with an out-Mao-Mao strategy he would adopt to the U.S. Also there's a new Progressive Laborite among us who is looking for a base . . . Spies? Who are the spies? And these newcomers being fresh and energetic they are likely to staff the office where they take phone calls, open mail; photocopy membership lists if they wish, and outreach names and numbers, group contacts, fundraiser and media lists. Come right on board! And now what are they trying to do with the BPC? It's unbelievable! In what does their wonderful propaganda action consist? On Monday, August 26th, the day the Democratic Convention opens in Chicago, a commando will set out armed with packets of the firecracker brand-named Atom Pearl. It's a beebee sized pellet which detonates loud as a 'Chinese' when stepped on. And what will they do with them? Toss them like Johnny Appleseed in doorways and inside executive suites if possible at a Federal office complex in downtown San Francisco. So it's like a minefield here, there, underfoot as a chain reaction goes on. Care to dance, you bureaucrats? The civil servants are jolted from Government business as usual—a Vietnam-like situation. Tiptoe through the Claymore mines and get blown at least symbolically apart. There will be screams. There will be shock as someone has a heart attack. There will be mass hysteria. During the waking nightmare some quiet G-11 pulls out his .38-special and begins to fire on anything that moves. And then more explosions down the close hallways, and more, as it is havoc. A few hundred people are hurled from their routine into a vortex of fear. I can see it now, and hear it! On all sides the staccatto shots send people to their knees in a daze. There are foot and leg burns and injuries from the potent bomblets, and facial disfigurement and worse if you fall on one. Somebody is blinded. And this is how America's liberators, the constructors of a new capital-free society, put their message across? Thanks to a few Government spies trying to discredit our love and vital activity against the Vietnam war. And then comes an anonymous tip. Or a BPC phonecall claims responsibility for the action. And FBI investigators come to Berkeley Peace Committee headquarters on Telegraph. There are arrests. There is national media coverage: U.S. TERRORISTS INDICTED ON THIRTY FELONY COUNTS. Then it's the grand jury. Then those not in on it, who never had a say in the affair's adoption or planning, must tell *all* they know of BPC and the Anti-War Movement or else go to jail for contempt of court. Keep it shut, refuse to inform on your comrades, and His Honor jails you for that Grand Jury's duration or longer if he wants. So it's an FBI-led provocation aimed at getting intelligence and also exploding BPC, an effective group, from within. And I'm learning about it tonight, right now, Joey, as we sit here. They want to destroy our grassroots organization and blow it apart with an Atom Pearl! They want no real opposition to the genocidal U.S. global policy being carried out in our era not only in Vietnam but across the Third World. And the corporate media of course with its boards linked to CIA and to highest Government echelons will broadcast the news far and wide. Bravo, BPC! Bravo, spies, and naive activists! Also in this way infiltrators get training for future work: if the war ever comes home, and there is Revolution. Then such deep-cover agents as instigated this Atom Pearl mess will be in place already—some still in the Bay area since they were never found out by their victims, the sincere activists, who are in jail for the long term. For the intelligence services know they must have their scouts and informers in place early on, during let's say Phase I of the struggle, which is surface calm. In Phase II, social unrest, it is harder to gain entry. Stage III, Revolution, makes it very difficult for a spy to penetrate key leadership circles. And so the snoop stays on at BPC if possible: he administers the ruins of a group made safe and pleasantly moribund by now. The Grand Jury gave it a frontal lobotomy. Now there is not much activism: no events committee except in name. No worldwide socialist press is called out to a Union Square rally. There is a quiet office where the phone seldom rings. And now a spy represents BPC in Bay Area coalitions, as his own activities broaden. At a big San Francisco demo which is militant so that many thousands want to sit down in the middle of Market Street, the spy is able to veto this tactic . . .—Newell paused for breath a moment, then said more softly:—So you see, Jojo, it's a war here too. It's a war where you've just been for a year, and I'm so glad, so very glad you made it back in one piece from all the fighting and dying over there. And it's a war here at home also, yes, an ugly one. The war at home.

IX

—Sounds like fun—said Joey, trying to keep his eyes open.
Newell fell silent. He was thinking. Then he said:
—I'll have to go out after awhile.
Evening drifted a deeper blue across the choppy Bay waters. Above Golden Gate the sky glowed its moment of most spectacular color and then dimmed tier on tier the way an escalator enmeshes. San Francisco undressed the organdy sunset and lay back amid its hills in a necklace of lights. With tender arms twilight enfolded the Sacramento Valley and far out there Yosemite and the Sierra, the Cathedral Range, the flats and mesas of Nevada's desert. Joey gazed down at cars headed east on Route 580 and he thought: Chicago; talk to my dad; him at least I can believe . . . then we'll see.
Newell gave a shrug.
—Fun, you say? It's no more fun than that World War II hero Max Doan has up the coast here in Puyallup where he rehearses real massacres . . . By the way, Jojo: are you on your way to the Rock Castle?
—Yes.
—Good. When you get there, please ask Papa-san not to sell our sister into slavery for the sake of his new political career.
—What?
—I only know what Lemon told me by phone. It seems the great writer might really be thinking of a marriage between his teenage daughter and Maximilian Doan, also known as Thanks-a-Million. I'm sure their honeymoon will be a romantic trip down

the river: our tender younger sister, who loves us and sticks up for us, side by side with the much-decorated 4-Star General, who moonlights as a pedophile.

—I don't believe you. Dad wouldn't do that.

—Why of course. You believed men like him, our principled liberals, when they sent you to Vietnam. Was it like they told you over there? Did you see the world, and fight for an ideal: for freedom and democracy? Say: where are your medals?

—I lost them.

—In Vietnam?

—In a minefield with my squad.

—Hm, I better feel your pulse. I guess you'd rather lose your life than your medals.

—I died and got up again.

Newell reached and held his brother's forearm. But Joey tensed and drew it away.

—We've started a Vietnam Vets Against the War chapter. It meets at a G.I. café off Telegraph. Would you go there tomorrow with me?

—No.—Joey's tone was clipped.—I'm looking for my wife now. Have you seen her?

—Sorry, I haven't.

Again they fell silent.

The soldier stared at the hippie, who looked away.

For some reason a tear was in Newell's eye. He shook his head a little.

—Call Lemon after awhile: use this phone. Or tomorrow; a bit late now with the time difference . . . It's like a miracle: you made it. You came home, though not like Max Doan with the Statue of Liberty saluting a heroic entry into New York Harbor while the Free World cheered and confetti poured down like manna at Broad and Wall. Fondly at the dinner table in the Rock castle he recalls that moment for Lemon's sake.

—That so?

—The Free World cheered, big hypocrite, after it produced a Hitler costing 50 million lives to defeat. And now it has given us an empire worth a hundred Hitlers, but who will put an end to this one?

—Not the Berkeley Peace Committee, it seems.

Newell chuckled. He nodded at the Summer of Love girl whose eyes were slit as she slept.

—The corporate men will send our boys to fight and die in more wars: always the same crusade, for profits, whether the enemy is communism, terrorism; it smells the same by any name. Bring the Third World to its knees and keep it there: no competitors, if you please! Extract the resources: gimme the oil! Dominate markets. Get dirt cheap labor. Sustain economic 'soundness' at home by a permanent wartime demand; that is, huge Government contracts for a trillion dollar war to wreck a country the size of New Mexico. But watch out! When the Cold War has exhausted and buried the Soviet Union, which it is doing, then our imperialist heel on the unindustrialized countries will make Hitler look benign. I'm referring to the campaign Washington will carry on across Asia, Africa and Latin America. It's an old one, but it will reach new heights. Then you'll see what Manifest Destiny is all about: with its superior race of Thanks-a-Millions.

Joey eyed the hippie's Viet Cong-style black t-shirt. Now he wasn't as sleepy, getting stirred up by his brother's words. And he said again, low, like a warning:

—That so.

—Onward Christian soldiers. Not suffer the children . . . but make them suffer. Right on. You and I, Jojo, are living our lives under militarized state capitalism: where a Dean Rusk, or our father's Presidential candidate, the old liberal, frighten an ignorant public into craven conformism with more sermons on the communists and the terrorists. Our American way of life is threatened! Each evening there is more gory footage in the news while 70% of our tax dollars go not to clean slums, educate, provide medical care, but to pay for wars of aggression to guarantee oil supplies and natural resources. Please don't get me wrong, Jojo: I admire my brother, but I hate this U.S. war against the people of the world. I hate it when our silent majority is so eager to swallow Doan's patriotic pills!

In silence, lips pressed tight, Joey looked at his younger brother. Life was always too easy for Newell: like this naked girl at his beck and call. He was irresponsible, as Dad often said.

Coiled tight inside Joey was afraid of his anger: the moment when he couldn't control himself any longer. And he was sick of listening to people who thought they knew. Newell's chitchat was exalted, but it was still just words.

And so the soldier waited. His curt tone should have been a sign: knock off the propaganda. Get down to facts—about my wife. It was time to leave this menagerie and go look for her.

X

There was a contest of eyes. Newell frowned, and looked down.

Now, as in the past, he tried to disarm with a smile, a friendly tap.

—Jojo, you look like a Skinner rat.

—Come again?

—You fly five thousand miles to get away from war, and what do you find? More war.

For a moment they fell silent. Night stirred and rustled outside the window. The beat went on in the living room.

The hippie's face said he couldn't get over the change in his brother. Haggard, overgrown like some thing from the jungle, filthy and rank, Joey Gilbert would never play third base again in a jam-packed stadium. He was a star athlete and a war hero, but he looked like a human ruins who'd be lucky if he found a job.

A sense of mistrust had come in the room. For once Newell seemed at a loss for words.

But the silence was a painful one between brothers. So he went on not so sure of himself:

—I tell you, Jo, this madness, the mass graves and tonnage of human and material waste and body bags and stench of State Department lies: it's all about one thing.

—You don't say.

Joey waited. His gaze was fixed, his brow knit. He flexed the fingers of his hand still fitted to an M-16. He glared, and his leathery cheek fluttered with the tic.

—One thing. It doesn't matter if they're pouring our taxes into a RevDev hamlet, or the CIA-AID's Phoenix Program to kill off—

—Phoenix?

At the word Joey straightened, and stared sort of wildly. In a flashback he saw Blair beer in hand on the sunny beach at Nha Trang. And Blair laughed: *'It symbolizes marital fidelity. The male broods the eggs while the female forages for food. Called trieng by Vietnamese tribesmen, the phoenix—'*

—Phoenix? Joey blurted.

He was hearing voices. He heard the grunt's eerie mumble in the drumbeat surf of the South China Sea. *'Long ago in the time before tung trees existed, the birds met and elected as their king a peacock. But a small honey bird spoke up and said; I do not vote for the brilliant but brainless and greedy peacock. The phoenix flies high and far and eats only pure forest fruits, and even humans or at least those who are winged with a common cause hold our phoenix sacred.'*

Newell stared at him as he breathed in starts.

—Are you okay? Maybe you need to lie down.

But Joey with a glimpse of the flower girl waved this off.

—No.

Newell paused. Then he kept on a little more if only to gloss over his brother's strangeness.

—The Seventh Fleet prowls the coast and rains shells on villages, trying to 'empty the sea' of VC supporters . . . When our troops go on a sadistic orgy of killing, and helicopter gunners pinpoint families in hootches . . . and dive bombers wipe out residential districts in Hué . . . it's only about one thing.

Joey looked sick. He croaked:

—And what would that be?

Newell shrugged.

—The private property of the rich.

XI

The hippie activist said one thing, and the Vietnam vet heard another.

And now a last tenuous defense gave way in Joey Gilbert, and he buckled under the inhuman tension and his long sleepless ordeal. A screw came loose, and he lost control. And so in slow motion, warily, the killer moved forward and seized the enemy by the throat. His large, powerful, scratched and calloused hands shook and squeezed the victim and he growled:

—Where's my wife? Where'd she go, ratfucker?

—Juju'—

—I know you fucked Carlyne!

Maybe he had wanted to do this for a long time: throttle his brother.

Newell gurgled:

—You . . . and I, Jojo . . . belong to an oppressor race!

—Coward, draft dodger—Joey's teeth gnashed.—I accuse you! While I was away fighting your wars for you . . . you had her! I know you . . . motherfucker!

Newell writhed and fought the death grip on his windpipe. He coughed, spluttered. Desperately, eyes bulging, he grabbed at the powerful arms. Veins bulged blue as the two brothers stood forehead to forehead glaring in one another's eyes.

With a grunt, a curse the wild contest went on. Joey's cheek quivered, but Newell's was turning blue as he tried to jerk back, held in a vice.

He gasped:

—She loves you still . . . We, we all love you! . . . So glad, Jo . . . you uh-h-h . . . made it back.

And then the soldier's eyes rolled up. Rubber legged he let go his grip and tottered sideways.

Newell choked and coughed. He threw wide his arms and kept his brother upright and moved him toward a chair.

—That'll do!—he spit out.—Alright then I'll tell you!

Joey looked away and threw out his arms in a faint.

XII

Voices drifted from the street below. People were still coming up here for the nightly happening: folkniks, more acid heads with their beads and amulets, with flowers or feathers in their hair, a marijuana pipe strung on a neck chain. The house reeked of incense in case Berkeley Police Farce crashed the party at 2779 Hillgard.

During the scuffle Summer of Love opened her drugged eyes and remarked:

—Far out.

Now she slept.

Newell sat on the floor and felt his Adam's apple with two fingers. Then he said to himself with, incredibly, the hippie chuckle:

—Citizens! Anacharsis! Ami du peuple! I now learn I'm accused by this man and it's terrible! If my own brother thinks I've wronged him in word or deed then I don't care if I live or die, which I almost just did. Because it's awful, awful, worse than any insult, to be called a traitor by someone you love. Jojo, what happened to you in that Nam of yours? Did you go crazy? How could you even think such a thing?!

Joey was coming to. His words were scary and disconnected.

—What are you doing here? he mumbled. You've got some nerve to come here after you snaked my wife. Do you think you're talking to a coward? Some nut like you? Did you think I wouldn't see through both of you when I got back, or know how to take care of it? I know you just wanted Carlyne, and you got her, and drove her to despair, and she left!

—Listen, Jojo—

—No, you rascal, I grant you can talk rings around me, but you're my enemy now.

—Please listen.

—Don't tell me you didn't do it!

—How arrogant you are . . . if you weren't mad.

—You think you can screw your own brother's wife and get away with it?

—If I did it! But I tell you no, no, and no.

—You were there under the same roof, in close quarters with her when she stopped writing me. I know your ways.

—My ways? What ways?

—You know perfectly well what ways . . . You were there. Tell me what happened!

—N-no . . . I won't. And if I don't know something I'd rather not say it.

—What's that? You'll say or else pay, in a minute. When I get my wind. When I go to Dad, and ask him, what will he say? He'll say it was you.

—I wouldn't be surprised. But let me ask you something.

—What, you little scamp? And say it was my fault no doubt.

—Tell me, Jojo: are you married to my sister?

—Your sister-in-law, I'm sorry to say.

—You're a couple. You love each other.

—So I thought.

—And if she's my sister, Jojo, can't I love her too *in my way* and love to talk with her? Don't I have my part, as long as it's pure, and good, like she is?

—I don't know what you're getting at but I'll never believe you.

—I just mean why would I do such a thing? Why would I want to live in fear after I ruined her life and yours and my own into the bargain? I may be immature as that devil Commynes says but I'm not a scoundrel. She's your wife and I congratulate you and leave her all to you, but I still have a right to be her friend and yours if you don't mind . . . Look, you better talk to Doan or somebody else who has such penchants. I don't have them. Please, be my guest, go ask the oracle at Delphi, namely your own heart, since the human heart is the only oracle. See if it says I seduced your wife, Joey, like a wizard. But do not find me guilty without the slightest proof . . . only your suspicions! I don't like it! The good ones are seen as bad and the bad ones as good! You throw away a brother and friend who loves you truly: why, you might as well throw away your own life, what is most precious to you. And yet only time can make things clear. Only time can show a man is just, but you can see evil for what it is in a day.

—I can't just let it pass. Someone has done this to me. Us.

—So what do you want to do? Strangle me on a hunch?

—If you did it, I don't care if you do die.

—Such hate, Jojo, such hate. And maybe you should save it for yourself. Maybe you're the one to blame.

—How so, you rascal?

—I say there's a curse on all of us, Americans. Capital is our curse, and it would make you do away with your own father . . . Capitalism is the plague in the land, and it won't go away, you're right, until we cry out who is responsible. Who raped Carlyne? And this is like saying: who raped the land, causing the curse? And you, U.S. soldier, only carry on that curse when you go off to rape Vietnam, or some other smaller country for its beauty and life force like Carlyne's, its vital resources.

—I don't know what all that means, unless that you're bats. I think you are, Newell.

—No, you're the one talking a lot of nonsense. Go to bed! I'll take the girl out of here. See if you can sleep off Vietnam, the curse!

—I don't talk nonsense when it's about my wife, my own interests.

—And what about my interests then? You think I like to hear I'm a scamp, a rascal, a traitor?

—You're a traitor.

—And if you're wrong? If you, patriot, are the traitor?

—You always were disobedient.

—That's not disobedience when the orders are bad.

Joey stared at his younger brother. He stared, deeply, a long moment, and then bowed his head, and said:

—O my country, my country.

Newell didn't bow his head. He said:

—It's my country too.

XIII

Then there was silence. Maybe five minutes of it.

The soldier sat forward with bowed head in hands.

The hippie looked out the window. He gazed at the girl, and around the room. It seemed he needed to leave, but not until he got his brother settled in.

At last Newell spoke, softly:

—I think our father may be on TV across the fifty states as we speak.

Joey, red-eyed, stared up, blinked.

—He is?

—He's supposed to give a speech: sock a roundtripper as the Democratic Convention opens tonight. Well, he can speak in public. He'll have more impact in half an hour than Granddaddy did in thirty years of Sunday school on the radio. Emory Gilbert needs limelight and network media the way a lizard needs sun. And now here his martyred son shows up and spoils it.

Newell gave a chuckle: just one, like a cluck, because his neck was throbbing.

—Spoil it? said Joey.

—Ah you don't know. Your death was kind of timely for our father. He's the dad of a true-blue Vietnam hero. So they put the great man up first with his moral authority as the pa of Joey Gilbert. Your death lends a cachet of principle to the Demo'rats. (Chuckle.) That's almost funny.

—I didn't die.

—No, you didn't!—Newell laughed more happily as he massaged his swollen throat turning black and blue.—I guess they still don't know it. Bit of a mix-up, eh what?

Joey sort of bucked, and said:

—You sound so cyncial.

Again Newell laughed, but it hurt to laugh.

—Sure, I'm cynical.

—You should have more respect for Dad.

—Respect? Respect for the ancient Gilbert can of worms. Give me a can opener. Truth comes out of the mouths of hippies.

—What truth?

—What truth? What truth? . . . I say whip the fellow.

—Whip our father?

—That's right. Then the flabby liberal might learn something finally.

—Learn what?

—The effect of his words and actions on others.

—What actions?

—His actions . . . his principled actions. You name it: to the Indians, slaves, Third World.

—Emory never did anything to the Indians.

—Oh no? Well his, our ancestors did. I tell you it's the plague, the plague of Capital. First the rape, says the myth, then the curse, and then the plague, on you and me, and all of us.

Newell blushed and looked away.

Joey's head seemed to go down by notches. But he said:

—You go on and on.

—That's true. U.S. history is a broken record.

—Same old refrain.

—Boring, I admit it, Vietnam gobbledygook.

—And false! I don't see what our father has to do with—

—Vietnam? Give or take some high-minded verbiage, he says yes to the system that brought us there. Him and all the other famous men, Kennedy in the lead, by the way, when it comes to

Vietnam: they all sell their souls to get in print and on TV. Or they give their birthright as free citizens with dignity for a mess of pottage ... as that devil of a devil Commynes would put it. Watch out for him,

Dizzy with fatigue Joey shrugged:

—I don't even know him. You're way beyond me now, like you're raving.

—Am I? Do you know that when Standard and Poore's decertifies stocks of a Third World economy, then panic ensues and financial chaos; and Western banks move in and buy up the small defenseless country's patrimony, its oil reserves and raw materials, real cheap. Do you know that, Jojo? Long ago Marx predicted this globalization: poor Marx who is dead and buried of course, deluded from start to finish as any investment banker will tell you, those geniuses. But the Invisible Hand lives, oh yes: the banker's Jesus redeeming all sins. And the children die like flies from hunger and curable diseases in those same countries stripped of their riches. The Invisible Hand whisks the genocided children to its Invisible Paradise.

Newell chuckled and fell silent again. It seemed in economics he sought a diversion—as if on the verge of telling his brother something he could regret, a word too much.

—On and on—said the big soldier seated by the bed, and yawned, and closed his eyes.

XIV

For Joey Gilbert sleep would not come. A long time he lay fidgety in his itchy fatigues with his boots still on. Through the wall came music specific to the 'Sixties, an angry song with the word *paranoia* ... When his senses began drifting off, his mind jolted back to Hindu chants beyond the wall. In Nam too he knew of the touchie-feelie and total sensory impact, LSD values; but there such fads went around with less idea of a Truth Quest, Zen, and communal sacraments. There grunts flipped their lid because they were afraid.

Joey lay alone in the wide night of America, and it was here that he felt afraid. His nerves were out of their proper element, humping the Highlands among his squad. At nightfall his nerves reverted to the LURP of Rung Sat forest.

Now he lay on his brother's bed and heard chatter from the street below, something about the anti-renaissance of the kundalini . . . and swami, and tantra turn-on . . . Waiting for sleep he named the grunts of his unit like sheep—Bufillu, Vane, Chi-Bar, medic Artus, RTO Troupial, Ringwood, Izard . . . now all gone, blown away to the maimed ward in Japan, if not dead. But by now the luckier ones from his platoon were back home, or in wheelchair heaven at the VA.

As he drifted off there was a toneless chuckle, over and over, so close. He looked to see—Skol the point man, greased, and the chuckle was an electric jolt, waking him an instant. But now sleep had him in its grip, as they hiked kliks southward from Buon Me Thuot. An insect clung to his gun hand, and it grinned at him. It was a camel cricket from summers he spent as a boy in the small southern town. One lived and had its weird web in the hollow trunk of the great old oak before the Rock Castle front porch.

Some villagers came from market day at the provincial capital. Their teeth were black with betel.

By the roadside scarecrow mama- and papa-sans laughed:

—Xe-xe-xe.

It was the breeze rattling their straw.

One said to the grunts passing by:

—My good ant.

Chi-Bar pirouetted through the dirt square. Chi-Bar spun one leg up in a saut de basque.

—No! no!—Joey tried to cry out.

There was a knell of Buddhist bells. From a big pot into a tiny cup Slidell poured the bitter *voy* tea. He had a punji stake in his chest. There was a heart drawn around it with lipstick.

—Sky-Six knows—said Izard coming out of Moon'right's shack.—Sky-Six, amen.

A long furry rat wriggled out . . . out . . . out . . . like a clown's handkerchief from the can of ham 'n motherfuckers Kossuth was finger-licking.

—Shoeshine G.I. one dollah.

—Mm-mm, good!

On haunches by his shoeshine box the doll-like Ha, Mister Quoc's grandson, gave a hippie chuckle.

—Come hill' numbah zirrion to zirrionth powah!

Joey looked up at wild geese flying south in a wedge in the afternoon sky.

Moon'right leaned from her window. Her breasts were exposed. High, cutting voice:

—Next fuckyducky G.I.!

Pain. Jealousy. Desire for her.

—Banh troi! Ban duc!

It was coming.

There was a scent of crab soup and wild tamarind. There was a grocery net with papaw.

It was coming: in an oversized postcard with views of Phat-An pagoda, Da Kao marketplace, the Pink Pussycat in Vung Tao . . .

—Wait . . . not yet, my darling.

From a doorway a woman blew him a kiss. There was a camel cricket in the lace of her black negligée: where its furry legs struggled to get free.

In her arms there were mangled children staring out from the darkness of the hootch with wide eyes.

Cassava roots on a table. What about them? They seemed to make the problem clear. What problem? At a key moment—it was coming!—a sprig of ginger looked filled with hate, like a revelation . . . Bundled pumpkin leaves—separate, so painfully apart from his own hate which was taught him. Cassava, ginger, pumpkin leaves: in this key instant marking a stage of his life's journey . . . toward what mastery of nature? For good? For evil? Mountain rice in a tin—so humble, it gave him such pain, worse than that for Carlyne! How to live, knowing this? Cassava, rice, ginger, pumpkin leaves summed up the experience: *what was it about them?*

He woke up.

XV

Past midnight. Beyond the wall the beat went on: the Zonked Yellow Screamers. Still in his nightmare he reached for the lamp switch. Then he rose, went in the bathroom and palmed water in his face. Time to go find a place in the darkness, trees and underbrush—curl up and wait for the dawn. He couldn't stay in here.

He went out and looked around for Newell. In the kitchen a pimply teenager lit his joint with a ten dollar bill. A longhair in dark glasses pleaded with him:

—Do not do this thing!

—I've got an idea. Let's freak out and call it a freak-in.

Chuckle.

Then Joey stood in the living room entry. The others did their thing and paid no mind to the blear-eyed G.I. in jungle fatigues. Maybe he made them feel like playactor weirdos. One look at that guy and you felt normal (perish the thought) all too normal beneath the strange outfits and goings-on.

From behind someone tapped his shoulder. It was a female with green sunken eyes in bloodshot sockets, sutured cheeks and vampire fangs, a large nose wart with hairs. He lurched back startled.

—Kiss the fairy princess!

In the space reeling with strobe lights Joey held on. The pundit in Gandhi cap sucked joint where he sat in lotus position entwined by Flower Child. Stone stoned they gazed in one another's eyes and said deep words about the chastity vow and ahimsa. She shivered a little.

By the far wall Hell's Angel in black leather with gold eyeteeth shook ponytailed Granny Glasses whose collar he fisted. The grad student's eyeglasses hopped on his nose as he kept up a monotone in a drugged whine:

—Pish. Paris this past May was history repeating as farce. France met its destiny when the Paris Commune let its class enemy off the ropes and got duly butchered, 30 thousand workers at least, Marx said 60. The best elements. As for the Germans they stood around in Alexanderplatz, wasn't it? while their moment passed them by. So much for Europe.

—Don't talk shit—said the sadistic biker shaking him.—Big words give me a headache.

In the doorway Joey stared at them darkly. His nightmare put him in a tragic mood, as the adrenalin, his war anaesthesia, began to wane. He knew there were no Bouncing Betties in the hallway, and no VC took up L-shaped ambush positions in the pantry. But his nervous system was shot—and refrazzled by the whirling lights, the rhythmic blare of music, and hippie laughter.

Joey had a last question to ask his brother and then he would get out of here. But it seemed Newell wasn't back from dealing with the crisis at Peace Committee headquarters down the hill on Telegraph.

XVI

Here and there the acid heads popped up like mushrooms. It was all sort of surreal as they sat cross-legged and saw visions and dug their stupor. Soft voices trailed off.

—Like, wow.

—Wowwy.

—Double wowwy.

—Wow spelled backwards is . . . wow.

Just the fumes were enough. Trip out! Speed, LSD, hashish and marijuana, Hawaiian rose wood seeds, hallucinatory cactus buds. It was back to nature with head and body drugs and natural and artificial psychedelics and synthetic stimulants. Through the open window when the blast of rock music paused there were strains wafted from an all-night Hindu chant party. A group held hands in the backyard and sang until they dropped. It was a potpourri of heroin, opium, barbiturates, alcohol, tranq's. Even skunks in from the woods to scavenge this last house on Hillgard fell over themselves and tripped on their tails and stank up the place for the fun of it after a whiff or two. The garbage was filled with vials, joints, you name it.

The light show sped on across walls and ceiling. The strobe kaleidoscope turned faster, faster as it swept over the yoga lovers Gandhi Cap and Kasturbai like a pair of catatonics in no hurry to orgasm. Joss sticks, tantra sex, trips and trip masters, hippie colonies and tribal culture, Reichian breathing, thought transfer, secret esoteric orders translated into body language, levitation, the transcendental touchie-feelie—let the multilevel awareness of visionary viscera glow. Switch into No-Mind. Grass vibrations. Better dead than a non-acid head.

XVII

Unheard went the sensitive grad student's whimper in burly biker's mitts; it seemed things could go badly for the boy. But just then as the Hell's Angel cursed and slapped the cheek of the studious Hippie whose eyeglasses went flying—just then the G.I. lurched to his left and glanced at the sky with a cry. *The chopper hurtling down over the hot LZ bumped out of control amid the treetops. Instants after catastrophe the RTO worked frantically to contact Six as grunts ran about screaming and firing wildly and waving their arms. On the fringe Tombigbee turned his back on that and strode off with a light step. Grunts cried out and shot off M-16 volleys pointblank into the hootches . . . not a villager in sight and no tea vendor with her wares and grin and no shoeshine boy or lovely sister-san or mama- and papa-san in the doorways but only a few women and children of men gone to the ARVN, friendlies. The dust-off roared in. Shots cries, rotor wash. Thatch bristled up and flew into the trees.*

—Sniper!

—Bring 'em in; move it!

The G.I. shouted in the hallway.

The biker turned from his slapping with a cackle at the psycho.

Enemy fire! A red bundle was caught on a bough; part of shredded Izard. Medevac whooshed and backed jerkily up and away.

—Torch 'em! This ville didn't exist!

Flames vaulted over the hootches. Pigs, chickens, children; if it moves, shoot the little fucker.

—No! No!

Suddenly all was silent. Light show off, loud music doused. Only a clip, clip, flesh on flesh. The G.I. had crossed the room and broken the biker's jaw with his fist. Second biker came up from behind, but his growl was a mistake. Next instant blood drooled from his lips, and he slumped down. The G.I. stood over them with an arm raised to direct traffic and shouted:

—Troupial, call in! Medic! Artus, where are you?

Girl in beach halter and short-shorts was crying to one side. The first biker puked supper, blood and spittle from his broken jaw and gave a groan. But his buddy still moved so the grunt took a knife from his hip pocket and said:

—Guess I'll just slit Gooky-gook's throat!

XVIII

In a jiffy Pundit and Miss Groupie, Beach Halter and Women's Panties, Pimply Teenager, Longhair, others quit their lotus position and fanned out toward the exit. Only Summer of Love didn't stir where she lay coiled up naked on a corner of the living room rug; she blinked her groggy eyes at the excitement and said:

—Far out.

The chorus of mystic chants droned on toward oblivion. From the backyard it flowed up into a silence as Joey held knife in thumb and index ready to cut soft flesh—like the chignon battalion fighter's that night on the trail.

—Kill—he mumbled—kill, kill. Six needs body count.

So quiet now—no more screams, desperate yells, roar and swoosh of helicopter rotors. There was only a kind of signal tone in his ears as he put blade to throat and gritted his teeth. He pressed the biker's flesh with the tip. Second biker bowed and spat blood on the rug.

The steel point went in the skin drawing a thin line on the neck.

Just then Newell, back from his BPC meeting, came in the room.

With a glimpse at what was happening he leapt forward and threw a body block at his brother.

—Are you mad!

They toppled on the floor. Joey gasped because of his hurt shoulder. Newell grabbed for the haft of the knife. They fought and rolled, and the soldier who was stronger and bigger got on top.

He hissed:

—Gooks!

—There are no gooks . . . here. There's everything else . . . but no gooks!

The hippie kept his grip on the G.I.'s wrist while his free arm flailed to slap him back to his senses.

Joey cried out:

—They're all around me now!

Hands darted at close range. Joey had the knife on his injured side, but he sought a hold with his good arm to shush up the commie and crush his skull. Then a hack with his elbow and that would be it.

But a tremor passed over his body. He seemed to wake up, and he stared down at the other. Ah! . . . He didn't let go at once: didn't get up because what he saw now was what had tortured him for months. So Joey said:

—Now tell me where she went, or I'll kill us both and end this bullshit.

—Ask Dad.

—What?

—Go on to Chicago. Ask him.

—You draft dodger, you coward. After your rotten betrayal . . . don't even say our father's name. I gave my all so you could stay home and have a fine time with a bunch of weirdos.

—Not so fine.

—You fucked my wife. Admit it!

—Never, Jojo. Never.

—All your talk about justice, but look what you did. Call yourselves revolutionaries, but that Atom Pearl business sums you up. Trying to stir up trouble while the real trouble is far away, and you're not sorry. Babies.

In his present position, on the floor with a knife to his throat, Newell theorized:

—Sure, sure, we're immature, like Pastor Commynes says. But this activism, our sectarian Left, our Labor Movement pinching pennies, is the quantity that will become quality when the time is ripe. Friction makes a spark. And in the meantime Uncle Ho wrote us a letter saying our movement is saving a million lives.

—To hell with your Uncle Ho. And shut up for once!

—No, Joey, I won't shut up. I wouldn't have hurt you and Carlyne for the world. Yes, she and I took walks in the fields, and we talked a lot, about life, about you. Why didn't you talk with her a little more? But no, your favorite subject was baseball. So who's immature? And as for our country, as you call it . . . it will grow up if it ever does when we decide to fight for a just one, for a USSA, for socialism, and stop fighting for Texaco and beating up on the little ones. But as for the Commynes and the Doans I think they never will mature, the unfallen sinners unconscious of their sins, finished men in a finished system, naive beasts!

—You—Joey spit to one side—you're no damn good. Dad always said it.

—Did he? I call that funny. Well then think over one thing, Joey, if you have room for it in your jock's brain.

—I wouldn't insult me right now if I were you.

—Maybe your wife didn't relish the bed of a caveman.

—Ah! You think you can say anything.

—And you think you can do anything.

Joey still on top rapped his brother's head against the floorboard, once, and ground his teeth.

But then he let up again as he had in the bedroom. A lost look came in his eyes since he had no more stomach for this.

As the sampler of freaks gaped at them from the living room entry Newell scampered to his feet and worked his head in its socket and said:

—You drove her away, Joey, with your narrow ways and your jealousy. You call me cowardly. What shall I call you? Deep down you always mistrusted people for the flimsiest reasons. Me you envied. Oh yes. I was Mom's favorite? Well tell me: did *you* take the brunt of Dad's unfairness? Were you the lightning rod for his temper, his irrationality? Were you? No, you were not. My dad, right or wrong, and it was all hunky-dory. You were a conformist back then, and you were one when it came to carrying on U.S. war crimes in Vietnam. You conformed while I took the heat! And yet you're the soul of bravery but I'm a coward.

XIX

Newell fell silent.

The weirdos of 2779 Hillgard clicked approval. There was hippie applause from the doorway where the sundry acid heads, Beat epigones, questers after empyrealism versus imperialism, clicked fingers at this Diggers skit like a kind of family guerrilla theater.

Late at night the drugged gathering gave a sort of laughter while the two bikers, broken jaw and slit throat, took themselves off—hobbling onto the stairs out from the kitchen.

Joey said again but quietly:

—I know you seduced my wife.

—Haw! haw! haw!

In the living room entry the dozen heads laughed at the one-liner.

—No, sir.

—Say what you like. I know you.

—Do you? Maybe the day will come when you know how Dad's generation, how the System said thanks for your efforts in Vietnam, or on a baseball diamond for that matter if you decide to play again. War medals or a World Series ring—here, chump, take your Mickey Mouse watch and scram.

At this there were boos, catcalls, whistles from the safe distance of the doorway.

—He's an existentialist.

—Such cynicism, tut-tut.

—Is that really Joey Gilbert? I thought he died the other day.

—Me too. It was in the papers.

—Say, is Un-American spelled with a big U, or a big A?

Newell said:

—Like Dad and his friends, like America itself, you don't see the beam in your own eye. And that beam is being used today to pound the poor suffering world. Well, we are raised this way: to blame the other, and be it a brother or a sister, or a child starving to death while the mighty corporations rape his or her country of its riches.

—On and on.

—I can't help it.

—If you were anyone else but my brother I'd brain you.

—Right on, slam a roundtripper, send all the godless commies to a mass grave.

—What repartee! said Brahmacharya.

—What zeugma!—said Granny Glasses coming out of it, after rough treatment by First Biker.—It's a literary device used by the pothead Pope.

—You don't know where you've come from, Jojo, much less where you're headed. So used to your high horse! Sock it to 'em jock, or baddest motherfucker in the valley. You fear no evil, but only the devil in your uptight outa' sight self. Well, yet a little while. Insult me all you like, but the day could come when you look around and only I the irresponsible hippie am standing behind you. Unless barricades separate us. Me and also tender-hearted Lemon, she loves you so. But as for your wife, the woman named Carlyne, she got fed up with the Gilbert sickness, namely smug bourgeois selfishness and snobbery. And she left. She went her way. So there. Put that in your peace pipe and smoke it.

Sniggers.

Granny Glasses said:

—Put that in your marijuana pipe and . . . pfff-pffsssffft!

More finger clicking, like a squall of geese, with tonsilitis.

XX

With two hands the ruffled host tried to reset his head in place. He looked a bit groggy after the concussion. Newell rubbed his neck bruised in their first scuffle, in the bedroom, and rubbed the discolored Adam's apple. He worked his arms and did a hurdy-gurdy to test his limbs for fractures, and said:

—What a night!

But the soldier put hand to forehead.

—Feel sick. Can't stay here.

Newell smacked a bloody lip:

—Sunrise before long.

Alone among the weirdos—besides fetal Summer of Love—a Zen meditator had not fled the room but sat legs crossed in an armchair by the dark window. He stroked his goatee and gave a gesture amid hashish smoke spirals. His words were slurred:

—But for you as per the dialectics of self and objectivity your birth mediated your death and your death your birth . . .

Joey looked around.

—I shouldn't have come here.

—No? Where then?

—I don't know.

—Well, go to bed. Get some rest. I can't tell you where Carlyne went, as it happens; and I didn't, repeat, did not do what you said. You're out of line there, brother, but I love and forgive you. Now go sleep it off. And tomorrow . . . your journey's next stage. Dig it.

XXI

So he slipped outside into the hills. Crouched in the dense
woods above Hillgard Street he awaited daybreak. Twigs snapped
as some deer passed shadowy in single file. Once he drifted off
but awoke when a ferreter sniffed by his ear. And then a predawn
breeze went in the summits, as he still tried to get some shuteye.

Toward midmorning he came in. He went up the outside stairs
and found a sign posted on the door: QUARANTINE—KEEP
OUT! At the kitchen table Newell sat rubbing his swollen lip, jaw,
neck, while he studied one of his thick books.

Joey looked calmer and said:

—Sorry about last night.

—Don't mention it, old man. How about some breakfast?

They ate in silence. Newell read and sipped coffee. They shared
a sense of shame, like the emotional hangover after old family
quarrels.

Joey stretched and gave a yawn.

—Time to saddle up.

—Stick around. You can rest and take a hot bath.

—Nope, got to go.

—Why the rush?

—Hot date with my girl.

—Hm.

—My wife may have left me, but like you say maybe she needs
me. You think Dad could know something?

Newell shrugged.

—Ask him.

Joey rose.

—I'll phone him now in Chicago. What hotel? Or should I call
Lemon for the number?

—I guess the Conrad Hilton with the other honchos. But forget
it, no phonecalls. The Chicago communication workers chose this
moment, the Democratic Convention, to go out on strike.

—Hold on, I'll try anyway. Can I use the phone in the
bedroom?

He called information for the number and tried to get through
to Chicago, but Newell was right.

Standing up from the desk Joey's eye fell on the few pages of
'Ho, Ho, Ho Chi Minh'. Last night he hadn't finished reading it.
His eyes rolled up. No guts?
He sat down another minute.

And then he was Président de la République.
But the French came and drove his socialist
government from Hanoi.
     So Ho in his sixties was a maquisard once again.
And this was after how many name changes, jobs,
prisons, grave bouts of illness, condemnations to
death?
     How many pseudonyms had he used? He wrote articles
as P.C. Lin for *Notre Voix*, a legal Party organ in
Hanoi. When reported dead in a Hong Kong prison in
1931, of advanced TB, he rose from the grave as
Linov, or Lin, in Russia in '33; and later as Vuong,
a teacher again, at a revolutionary school in China.
Then reported killed by the Kuomintang he founded
l'Armée de propagande de libération de Vietnam.
     And how many other names did he take? He was 'le
viellard de Tan Trao', le Père Chin, Oncle Chin, Tau Chin
as a revolutionary organizer in Siam, an
educator and founder of schools for children of
Vietnamese nationals. That was when he journeyed on
foot across Thailand.
     In 1937–38 in Yunnan they called him Tran; in 1940,
in the Vietnam zone de résistance where he built
insurrectional bases, formed cadres, wrote propaganda
brochures, they called him Thu.
     In China the communist cadres had known and revered
him as Ho Quang. And in July, 1942, they began to call
him Ho Chi Minh. There he went disguised as a blind man
with a baton, and coughed all the time and spit up
blood. Arrested, he wrote his prison poems on newspaper
margins with boiled rice scum; and sent them to his
comrades, and told them: Never mind about me.
     They called him 'le Vénérable' while he was in the
maquis, Pac Bo, as he fled the French; and: 'le Vénérable
de Nghe An'.
     He slept on dry leaves. He had snakes, centipedes,
every sort of insect and rodent for roommates.

Nationalist, statesman, master propagandist, practical
revolutionary, strategist, guide, Marxist: he never wasted
a single second in seventy springtimes of struggle to
deliver his people. And not only them, not only the
Vietnamese—but all people, yes, even the oppressors must
be freed; even the U.S. taxpayers supporting their fiendish
CIA and military apparatus. Even the imperialist
occupiers, the American hordes, Uncle Ho's last enemy,
must be made to understand. Even they could be
made free by the Truth.

And now, today, Ho moves on the horizon of world
history with calm strides. He keeps up the long
campaign to free this Earth of the foreign devil.

In every place and situation where he found himself,
he would teach literacy and political theory. He would
organize. He would inspire love of country and devotion
to the cause of workers worldwide.

He lived and taught by example. Gaiety, sincerity,
affection, delicacy of word and gesture, a true democratic
spirit not the usual bourgeois hoax; an inhuman tenacity
in the fight for socialism: so planet Earth can survive
the mighty tribe of titanic Western corporations who are
polluting it to death—all this was Ho Chi Minh.

Make no mistake. It is the economic and social planning
of socialism, or else death, for poor abused planet
Earth.

Socialism—or death!

Ho, Ho, Ho Chi Minh.

He makes Western politicians look like what they are: a band
of crude and selfish hacks.

Well then: who wouldn't want an uncle like that? He was
tender and principled. He was tender toward the weak, and
principled during the hard times for principles: when you
pay a high price for them.

He was a man: intent to live and die if necessary for
others, for people, for all people, for humanity. He was
a handsome man, Uncle Ho, and a good one.

But with age his features became more than handsome.

Yes, this was a man, a complete one—for once!

Bác Hồ.

XXII

Back in the kitchen Joey said:

—Could I telegram Dad? Say I'm coming?

—You can hitchhike faster.

—Then I'll fly there military standby.

—Okay, but don't think they'll let you near the delegates. Or our illustrious progenitor. Not the way you look! Go take a bath, Jojo.

—Not yet. They'll have to let me see him: I'm a war veteran.

—Ha ha—oops, sorry. Listen, I helped to organize it, and I know Chicago may explode. Our movement has weak ties to unions and the urban proletariat. It is hard to see how here the student phase would lead to workers taking the lead like in China. That's when it gets more serious. As for our farm workers, our 'backward peasantry', what to say of them? So we on the Left fringe try to provoke a little and touch the nerve of Law and Order. And the good Dicky Daley has his orders. In these days a lot of Trots will make the Windy City a bit windier. The tendencies will be there: from left Democrats and Women's Strike for Peace and local SANE chapters busy with the Gene McCarthy campaign . . . to a half million Festival of Life yippies—maybe a few thousand is more like it—who will camp out, smoke dope, feel hope, dance till they're dizzy and run wild like a pack of cocker spaniels remembering they were once wolves through the streets fuming with tear gas and bristling with bayonets. You'll have SMC and SDS contingents and LSD brigadistas and more than one liberal feeling betrayed by the system and now flipped to the ultraleft. There will be self-styled guerrilla fighters who will one day turn Establishment toadies at first opportunity. And there will be plenty of cops too posing as anarchists and the like; and they will break store windows and dabble in arson so the network media can have a field day discrediting our Movement and the sincere elements and their message to America. But many, many I'm afraid who are in the vital center of the spectrum, that is the moderate groups who speak to the mainstream, also many pacifists may shy away from Chicago as a scene of violence and a political liability. Too red! McCarthy forces have called off all plans for activities outside the Convention. The beautiful soul McCarthy has told his people not to demonstrate. So in Chicago you won't find burning tires and workers meeting in the streets, not big excited crowds come to hear Trotsky in the Cirque Moderne. You won't see the people fraternizing with police and soldiers like Saint Petersburg 1917. No. We are nowhere near such polarization here, I mean politically. Economically yes, we may be getting there; though this juggernaut isn't given to qualitative leaps. But what you will find in Chicago is a lot of lean and hungry Left diehards: all of them ill-fated by history, and, in a tiff with Mayor Daley's thugs, ill-pated.

—So it may get out of control?

—I'd say a good chance. There are five to six thousand National Guardsmen on the guest list, and they like to addle the brains of longhaired protesters. News reports also have 6000 U.S. Army troops plus 101st Airborne units on call in the suburbs. They have flamethrowers, bazookas, tanks. Add in a thousand or so of our noble FBI agents. And let's not forget the various other federal and state agencies, and, as I said before, beaucoup agents provocateurs.

Joey thought hard. Lips pressed he shook his head.

—You've changed, Newell. I know you want to help, it's your nature; and I've always admired you for that. But now . . . you sound sort of cynical.

—Righto. I spend my life looking at the reality and trying to gain a foothold to fight these war criminals from the President on down, or up; I risk my skin, my health to fight them, even if it's in a small way, but I'm cynical. Those who conform to the official story of the butchery that's going on in Vietnam, those who deny and say it's all A-okay, all a question of freedom and democracy of course, not of empire and spheres of influence and above all economics—they're not cynical.

—What I mean is . . . maybe there's something to what you say, Newell, but you don't have the secret of making things seem positive and hopeful, the way Dad does. I admire him so.

—You and Emory always did hit it off.

—In the end it was the one idea that helped me over there: the fact that our father is a great man, who will take care of things.

—Correcto.

—I guess I needed to believe there was a person, come what may, I could rely on.

—He's that alright.

—My wife might run out on me when things got tough, but Dad cared if I lived or died.

—So he did! Dear old Dad . . . He had a stake, so to say, in your well-being.

—I'm hoping he'll want me to take up farming now, and get the Gilbert acreage going again. I sort of feel like doing it, but first I have to find Carlyne.

—Oh, I know he'll be glad to help you find her, and take her back to the Rock Castle.

—She trusts him implicitly just like I do. It'd be just Dad's way to take us under his wing.

—Hear hear. Let's hear it for principle.

—When we were kids you got on Dad's nerves. He was always so tired coming home from the office.

—I got on his nerves, but he never got on mine. Jumping all over me for a trifle.

—You were a crazy guy.

—Still am!

—But he didn't take it the wrong way. By and large I think he really did right by us. Back then and now too.

—Emory Gilbert is a saint.

—See that, Newell? You're cynical. No, he's not a saint, but he's there for us in a pinch.

—Truer than you know. Ouch!

—And good to Mom. Not unfaithful once.

—You can say that again.

—He was a good father to us.

—Heck yeah.

—Stood up for his sons.

—Stood up, and in.

—What?

—Nothing, Jojo. Don't mind me.

Newell touched his neck which was painfully swollen. His face just went crimson and now his brother looked at him.

—I can tell you don't agree with me. Well, I guess some things never change. But I just can't see why you run him down so much.—Joey nodded, thinking.—Dad is such a good guy.

—Amen.

—He was a good provider, wasn't he? Sent you to Yale.

—God, country, Yale. Hard act to follow.

—I know deep down you feel grateful to him the way I do.

—Why sure. When he's down and out I'll invite him to come live in our hippie commune at 2779 Hillgard.

—You say he's making a speech at the Convention? And on national TV? Wow, we can all feel very proud of him, Lemon, you and I—

—Carlyne.

—I know she loves and respects him as a second father.

—Bingo.

—Once she told me so. That's why it's so hard for me to see why she left us. And without a word! Who was she mad at? Me I guess . . . as always.

—No, Jojo, not you. I know from our walks by the river and the good talks we had that she loves you deeply. But it's just not easy. The child in us gets married, but it's a man's league. If you can compare marriage to a game of ball.

XXIII

Toward noontime Joey shook his younger brother's hand, and said:

—Sorry about last night. I had no call—

—Forget it.

—How did things go with your group and the special meeting?

—Rotten. Or let's say: high farce. Now there'll be a split, if it stays afloat as BPC.

—What if it doesn't?

—Then go off with the better elements and start a new one. At least I begin to know a thing or two about it. Just for this high farce of a Chicago Convention you should hear the stuff I've done, the work I put in. Phone-banked at the Peace Committee office; did a few flyers and a poster to hand out and wheatpaste on Telegraph and around town. I got rally and teach-in permits and soothed U. Cal. authorities so they'd rent us Sproul Hall Auditorium; helped arrange a dozen buses to Chicago; staffed the office; wrote an article for the New York Guardian besides the thumbnail sketch of Ho; argued hard with comrades over theoretical issues until late at night. I even cleaned the latrines: good practice for cleaning the Augean stables of America, someday.

—You're quite a guy.

—Just a mild-mannered hippie. Another poor cynic who's waiting, waiting, and still doesn't know what to do.

—Well, I admire you, Newell. Always did. That's why it hurts so much when I think maybe you betrayed me.

—Let it go. I didn't.

—Okay, okay.

For a moment they looked in each other's eyes.

Then Newell said:

—Be careful in Chicago, Jojo. All the firepower is on one side.

—Don't worry about me.

Newell gave a little laugh, not quite a hippie chuckle; but then groaned with a hand to his black and blue throat.

—I mean don't underestimate the Chicago cops, and their esteemed boss Richard J. Daley, who is no prince of peace. You see those boys haven't tuned into LSD and had their consciousness expanded. They haven't had sensitivity training, so they don't wear a flower on their helmet. Reichian breathing exercises and thought transfers, R.D. Laing's theories are not the standard manual of the Chicago Police Force. Incredible as it may seem, they wouldn't know Marcuse from Al Capone. At this late date Ricky-Dicky-Daley's karma has not had the spiritual levitation of a good lick of acid. The touchie-feelie is not part of his repertoire.

XXIV

Joey started out down the hill. He wanted to walk because the sun shone warmly and birds, not VC listening posts, chirped in the trees. It was a sunny California day. He gazed at sunlit vines on a trellis. In someone's kitchen a symphony played on the radio.

He went along. Yesterday it was the Freedom Bird, and today The World. But which was the world, and which a dream? Far down past the Berkeley Hills a gold swath sparkled across choppy San Francisco Bay waters. In the distance spread the reddish-tan hills of the city. To his right, out there, was the Golden Gate and the chilly whitecapped Pacific beyond. And then, over there, way over, the madness went on—a dream?

In town more hippies gaped at Joey's jungle fatigues and combat boots stained with the red earth of Vietnam. One whistled through his teeth and said:

—Hey there, it's Westie's child.

The whistle went up then wilted when the soldier turned to look.

—Hey you! What's your sign? The goat?

A blond girl flapped into his space. She startled him. She waved a book in his face.

—Have you read *I Ching?*

Boldly she took his game arm. Her voice had a sassy lilt.

—You're my hero! I have so much to give you—you poor dear thing you!

Her nipples jiggled petite beneath a wrinkled blouse. But she was nervous.

—You look so tired. Well, take this—

Abruptly she spat at the name, Gilbert, above his chest pocket. For a few seconds he watched her trot back to her friends who were laughing.

—My dollar, I won!

Giggles. Laughter.

—Hey, muscleman! How's a' go? How's that there Oedipal complex?

—Ha ha ha!

He went on past cafés where summer students read books and chatted, sipping espresso coffee. He thought of the Saigon café where Emmet Bufillu lost the use of his legs.

Two cinemas showed foreign films. A poster announced a rock concert. There was a rally and march to protest the war. There was a teach-in at San Francisco State.

Organic Life Manifesto. Fact sheet on new age liberation. Zen Buddhist guru hypes seed catalogues. Course in coed hypnosis. Meditation all stages: it's the neurological revolution. Kids, your destiny is up to you. Send away now for super-organic mescaline.

He passed the G.I. coffee house his brother had asked him to go to. From inside came guitar chords of a folk song:

Drop your gun little boy
It ain't a toy little boy
Turn and run little boy
Get on home

He heard murmurs behind him:
—Man, it's the psychedelic Olympiad. Infinity yard crash . . .
Hippie chuckle.

XXV

Inside San Francisco International Airport he waited for a flight
to Chicago. He thought over things his brother told him.

Then Joey dug in his hip pocket for a crumpled leaflet picked
up as he tramped from the RevDev hamlet in to Saigon. It was
U.S. propaganda in Vietnamese. He had seen them before. A Kit
Carson scout once told him what it said: Everyday we find the
enemy's base camps and tunnels and destroy them. Hear the
planes? Hear the bombs? Those are the sounds of death, your
death, unless you rally with us now to survive.

He thought of what happened last night in Berkeley. It did
seem his brother wanted to help, and see him back with his wife
on Dad's farm, if that's what he wanted. Newell sounded sincere,
though you never knew with him.

So his younger brother cared about him and was trying to be of
use? whether or not those two ever slept together . . .?

Yet there was a lingering sense Newell only made things worse.
Somehow he aroused suspicions more, and made the mystery of
Carlyne's disappearance even more mysterious—with a new hint
to it . . . not clear at all, and not nice. How was that? What did the
boy say, and what did it mean?

Joey didn't know. He couldn't quite recall the precise words
that led to such an impression. But he meant to find out.

He was the seeker now, and he had to know.

Chapter Thirteen

I

In late afternoon at O'Hare Airport the flux of arrivals was dammed up and congested beside a long line of empty taxis. There was a cabdrivers strike. The cabbies stood chatting as they picketed and held up signs.

From the terminal a Yippie emerged with a placard: VOTE PIG IN '68! Solo he sang out anti-war slogans and looked around for a like-minded soul or TV camera. But none in the crowd took up the refrain.

—*End the war!* he cried.

But they turned with impatience from the lone voice. Where was a taxi willing to take their fare?

—*Free Huey!*—yelled the Yippie.

In these hours O'Hare was a bit like Tan Son Nhut in Saigon. Its city was under siege.

—*Legalize pot!*—cried the Yippie.—*Disarm the fuzz!*

In a big mess made worse by August heat the well-dressed people waited; they swarmed around hotel mini-buses, and paid high rates when a gypsy dared to cross the picket line.

Just then a G.I. made his way through the crowd. He strode along in his own world. Dressed in filthy fatigues the soldier didn't care to mingle with people and moved off by himself for the 15-mile trek to the Loop.

II

At lakeside the luxury hotels and apartment towers rose high above street level shops decked out for the Democratic Convention. There was a plush sheen to it all. The maroon and gold carpets spread away in hotel lobbies stirring with liveried desk staff, bellhops, porters. The baroque ceilings glittered like a coffin interior and seemed to contain a blithe world menaced by barbaric hordes—a Hippite and Yippite invasion just across the street.

—*Off Pigs!*

Through the city were chants and slogans. At all hours songs, yelps, yawks and squawks came from nymphs and hamadryads gamboling, some naked, in the flowery gardens and copses of Grant Park.

—*Off undies!*

—*Down with tear gas! Up with snuff!*

In the background as slogans were bawled from bullhorns, there were militant speeches hurled at the high lakefront facade and the five-star hotels. The angry words echoed into the wide rumorous stir of America's second city on the verge.

Just then a multi-lighted van came slowly up Michigan Avenue. On its side was the logo of a tourist agency. A loudspeaker got in its two cents while vying with world revolutionaries across the way:

—*'Hub of railroads, airlines, highways! Our matrix of industrial suburbs sprawls two hundred square miles across the Indiana border! Chicago has vast factories for farm machinery, railroad cars and supplies, electronics, food industries, printers, furniture, clothing! . . .'*

This was audible blocks away where a man in combat fatigues with a beard and long hair asked a passerby:

—Where's the Convention Center?

—You won't get close to it.

The pedestrian eyed him. Soldier? Acidhead? Or both?

—I need to see someone in the Amphitheater.

—Good luck, Bud.

—And the Hilton Hotel?

—On Michigan, soldier. Go that way, north.

Three hippie types came walking by. One carried a sign—STORM FORT DALEY! One said:

—He was creamed.
—Dead for real?
—Real dead. A Sioux Indian too.
—That does it—the third hippie said, and then he cried out at the top of his lungs, eyes bulging, pointblank at the big G.I. going the other way:—*Off pigs! End war!*
G.I. jumped back.
Hippie with sign said:
—Where'd it happen?
—Over in Old Town near Lincoln Park.
—Oof. A Sioux you say.
—*Clean pollution! Free necessities!*

III

Mostly the downtown streets were empty. This was eerie with such a sense of energy in the air. It was a quiet of vast crowds not far off and big things on the march.

Along the lakefront the G.I. strode past high-rise apartment houses. Elegant show windows on the sidewalk had a vulnerable look.

Then under a barrage of stares he went in the Hilton and asked at the desk:
—Is Emory Gilbert here?
The snappy clerk looked at this one wandered in from the streets in tumult just beyond their gold-trimmed entry with its fringed awning of maroon; and turned to check the register.
—He's not here, Sir.
—Emory is my father.
The desk clerk went to an inner office and came back out with an older man.
—Yes?
—I need to see my dad, Professor Gilbert.
The assistant manager looked at the tangled hair and beard, like a satyr. He had a glimpse of the tunnel stare and lean features which showed a haggard exhaustion. This gave him pause. But then he saw GILBERT stamped in black letters on the olive drab.

He too scanned the guest list with its names of VIP, and then shook his head.

—I'm sorry, Sir, but he isn't here.

IV

Outside on the sidewalk Joey trudged along. The way they looked at him in that gaudy hotel lobby—like he was his father's assassin . . .! And everywhere since his arrival at Travis thirty hours ago there was a sort of ugly tinge on things. There was hate. Now he felt like he might break down; his nerves were strained to the limit when he stepped off the plane. But now he felt so angry, and offended. Would he have to punch out the next passerby? Now it seemed any joker might challenge his manhood—so insecure he was, and out of sync. At instants his mind slipped back to his unit in the field, and he had the warm chunky ooze of Simmer Jenkins' intestines on his palm; Simmer blinked as the RevDev village in flames shone in his eyes. And Joey blinked in the aura from Grant Park. He had an urge to re-up and go back to Vietnam and get himself out of this worse mess here at home. No, no; it was over. You could go there far across the Pacific but you'd only find Top Drawber doing his thing or some other deadbeat lifer with a squad of new faces that looked like they had egg on them. Forget it. Forget about them, and their Nam. Finished.

But what chance did he have to find Carlyne in this chaos? Once, in hunkered-down daydreams of this very instant when he would be home again, he went in a peaceful landscape by the side of his loving wife. He was a farmer, and he was good at it. The Rock Castle had a warm hearth with Carlyne seeing to things. Oh, it was a good life: children, busy days, and the most wonderful nights . . . But right now his stomach was doing tricks as on every side there came new jolts startling him so he might fly out of control. Chicago was worse than Da Nang. Joey Gilbert felt . . . less than a person, somehow, as he strode along at wit's end; he felt not just physically dirty, but also dirty in his person, and defiled to the depths by what he had done and taken part in over there.

He wanted to see his father and then leave here. Regressed, in culture shock, he longed to rest his head on his dad's broad

shoulder. There was still one person at least he could trust. A boyish feeling swept over him, the old sense of family security, and
love for Emory.

Things were different now. Baseball had ended: that he knew.
Yet he yearned for that distant time, and wondered if he was still
a part of this dream world. Because what did they know about
it, all these innocents at home? Far, far off were the childhood
days when his father's strength and wisdom gave a framework
and a faith, and could seem to right a boy's wrongs. In war quick
enough the effect wore off. Home to America . . . What was going
on here? . . . Newell and his friends called it Shamerica, but they
always went too far.

Joey went along across the street from the park. He was afraid.
Any loud jolt from the unruly crowd or the police, and then watch
out. The Viet Cong couldn't defeat him but he might do it himself
if startled by some hippie or a cop. And he had no gun. He went
naked without his M-16. But he hung on and didn't leave Chicago
at once since he wanted to hug his dad—then he'd feel safe from
the wild scene in the shadowy park. So many weirdos! They all
came out of their lair for this show: subculture idlers like those
he saw in the Berkeley cafés, smug pseudo-intellectuals, Beatniks
like ostriches in their beards. What did they know? What did his
bookish brother know? They freaked out each night—and then
what?

The country had changed so much since he went away. In
The Nam and then back home: life was a war. Those who said it
wasn't were liars.

What about his brother? Was Newell lying when he said Carlyne still loved him? and he would find her and things would be
alright? There was a sense that guy was hiding something, yes, he
hadn't told him all the facts. Something after all had happened;
she went away without a word; and so you just couldn't hide it
no matter how hard you tried.

Why did everybody lie? At O'Hare Airport the mini-bus chauf-
feurs lied when they made people pay too much to ride a few
miles. The hotel clerks with their cold stare lied when he asked
them to ring his VIP father's room. Hippies and Yippies lied with
their anti-war salvos across the avenue. Utopia was a lie. Hey!
What did they care? You're only young once: gimme' that good
ol' time anarchy, and tomorrow I'll grow up and join the Stock

Exchange. And never mind if a Sioux Indian was in the wrong place at the wrong time; he wasn't the first. From Tan Son Nhut to Travis Airforce Base to this hot night in Chicago it seemed America was lying and betraying its own. What about it? He, Joey Gilbert, went off and fought for his country and gave all he had and what was his reward? Back home the good people stared at him like a madman. In his bone tired state they saw a drug addict, if not a psychopath. In his quivering cheek, and the bloodshot eyes where his rage still smoldered, they saw a baby killer.

All, all lied. But his dad wouldn't lie.

In the Berkeley Hills and now here he looked for trees and a spot to stretch out and be alone. On the edge of Grant Park he went to his knees. In his eardrums there was a high whistle, swish—boom!—enemy shells incoming . . .! But no—it was that truck again touting the tourist sites, and lit up very bright with a lot of lights.

—'Chicago . . . city of boulevards, elevated railways, urban thoroughfares. It spreads southward past the world's foremost steel production complex: in 1968 over 25 million tons projected, surpassing France. Steel . . . poured and beaten, twisted, shaped and fashioned into tractors, trucks, freight cars, heavy equipment. South the city runs, in the smog and swelter this hot August evening, on across the ethnic neighborhoods, the Black Belt grown to thirty percent of the urban population. And, north from Chicago River in a wide sweep westward there are Italians Poles Irish Germans Scandinavians Jews Croats Czechs Lithuanians Greeks Chinese . . .'

For a moment Joey Gilbert went to his knees on the pavement hearing the amplified voice giving instructions from a dust-off chopper as it swooshed and groaned above the white-hot LZ of Xo Man. There were screams. He felt panic and knew nothing better than to get in among the trees and take cover and hide.

So he crossed the street to be alone before he couldn't help himself anymore, and hurt someone, like the two bikers the night before, but Newell jumped in to keep him from going all the way.

Tomorrow he would walk south and get out of this town on the verge of who knew what. He'd try to make it through the night of violence, a riot, and then go away from here to look for his wife as long and far as need be. He was seeking, he was seeking. But he also felt a fear before the fact and a shying away from what he might find and a desire to deny, deny it. He knew that if he looked long and hard and well enough, hiring the right detective agency, he would someday find Carlyne. And he was afraid of that day. And part of him wanted to get away from it and go his way and leave her to her fate.

Right now he didn't have the strength in him to go much further. He had to rest awhile, and then find his father.

V

The soldier lay down on the dewy grass. Through the trees he saw upper storeys of the long Conrad Hilton facade. Maybe those lit up rooms were the front-runner's campaign headquarters where Emory Gilbert went when not out at the Amphitheater.

Joey's stomach fluttered as he heard the thousands gathered at a park band shell. They chanted:

—*Dump the Hump!*

—*Join us! Join us! Join us!*

—*Humphrey Dumphrey straddled an issue—*

—*Humpster Dumpster had a great fall!*

Joey wanted to stay still, but he sat up. Across the park in a field he could see helmets glinting and military gear. He saw what looked like the grills of jeeps and—was it portable barbed wire fences?

—*End the war!*

—*Make wu-u-u-uv . . . not war!*

—*Humanize prisons!*

—*Beat back blackjacks! mace! electric prods!*

—*Off pigs!*

There was a groundwell of slogans. There were more chants and more. The high-pitched strident speeches of activists and student leaders echoed off the lakefront towers.

—*Open media! End corporate censorship!*

—Hi there, soldier.

A group came near him, shadows, in the wood.

—Why, if it isn't a bonafide grunt from The Nam! Look, guys.

—On your feet, troop. Time for latrine duty. Ha ha ha.

Hippie chuckles.

They stood over him gazing down.

—You're in my light, he said.

—Private Boondock, Sir! Reporting for duty!

—This is the real McKoy jungle warrior type thing!

—Type thing?—Joey blinked up at them.

—Well then, there, now.

Suddenly one erupted with all his might:

—*Dump Hump!*

Then a chuckle.

Joey gave a shiver. He got up, looking at them.

The park was filled with chanting.

—*Return to the land!*

—*We demand a program to recognize the simple reality around us!*

One of the hippies said:

—I think this freedom fighter belongs on the speaker's list. You did indeed grease gooks?

Chuckle.

Joey stood and waited.

—C'mon, follow us. I know the Program Committee folks. We'll get you before a mike!

From the band shell came a high voice, twangy:

—*Eighty percent of the primary votes went to peace candidates, yet the peace plank got defeated 1,567¾ to 1,041¼, a sixty-forty margin. Tell me now what does that mean?*

The adolescent voice soared out into the offshore darkness of Lake Michigan.

—No, said the soldier.

—*Finish the American Revolution!*

—*Hippies, Yippies and Flippies of the world, unite!*

—Are you wacko, Jocko? Miss your shot to be on TV?

—Make speech, get famous! Follow us!

—I said no. Go along.

—*You have nothing to lose but your amulet chains!*

—*Comrades! The old-boy network controls this rigged Democratic Convention! They are all a bunch of slimy weasels! They dance to the same old corporate jig; it's genocide in Vietnam brought to us by the transnational sponsors. How many more undeveloped countries across Asia, Africa and Latin America have to be bled white before the long dark night of U.S. imperialism comes to an end? Tell me, comrades! How much longer before it's over, and there can be a chance for peace with justice? Tell me!*

—*Long live the Youth International Party! Yip, yip—*

—*Hourra-a-a-ayyy!*

—*Come one and come all! See His Honor The Pig officially nominated for President of the United States! Come one, come all! Come to Tricky Dick Daley's office at the Civic Center! Pig for President!*

VI

Now police and Guardsmen surrounded the thousands of demonstrators. They were showing force and meant at all costs to stop any marching on the Amphitheater.

There was violence in the air and Joey Gilbert stood wondering what to do. Could he spend the night here? Could he wait around for this madness to end? It was worse on his nerves than a Central Highlands firebase. No perimeter here.

Tensed for combat he went toward the park exit and saw movement around the band shell. Maybe it was a teenager who climbed the flagpole in an effort to snatch down the U.S. flag. But a group of men looking older, huskier than most hippies, did the job and were putting up a piece of tattered red cloth in its place. As though on cue the police charged in a wedge and raised their billy clubs and began to flail, thrash, pound about them wildly. They bulled their way forward and the big crowd fanned back in panic. The band shell speaker cried out shrilly:

—*Respect this legal rally!*

Joey stood and watched in a trance. He had no gun, and no side to fight on.

—*Do you see how the city machinery refuses to let us have our peaceful rally?*

Pockets of demonstrators were warding off the onslaught. Some had nail-spiked slats from park benches, and they tried to strike back.

—Peace now! Peace now!

—*See how these legal goons treat us! What's the difference between them and Brown Shirts?*

It was like a beach at high tide as a larger wave of uniforms and helmets charged in upon the area. An activist shouted for calm through a bullhorn, but a gas-masked figure came at him from behind and clubbed him to the ground.

—Look! Look at your law and order! Daley you hypocrite!
—The whole world is watching! The whole world is watching!
   Joey's eyes began to burn in the fog of tear gas sprayed from converted flamethrowers. The poison cloud spread over the green acres of Grant Park.
—Hell no! We won't go! We won't fight for Texaco!
—Off these pigs!
   From the massive crowd chants overlapped with an urgent staccatto effect. In the darkness blood was flowing. The slogans rose up and seemed to break in midair as hundreds ran toward an unguarded bridge onto Michigan Avenue. The panicked crowd was like a rapids plunging round the dark uniformed phalanxes of police. Here, there, the human river eddied and rippled past the crunch and the onslaught of billy clubs and cops and Guardsmen whose semiautomatic rifle butts rammed and knocked people down.
—Make certain that if they shed our blood it will be—
—Pigs! Pigs!
—Om-m-m-m-m—
   Drawn along in the gale wind Joey Gilbert moved toward the bridges and pedestrian overpasses back into the city.
—Join us!
—Peace now!
—Join us!
—Out now! Out now!
—They use tear gas against us but we'll make sure they use it against local voters as well!
—Dance the pig jig!
—Pig jig! Pig jig!
—Dance, dance, dance, dance, dance!
—Om-m-m-m-m—
   Sadness, anguish, a sense of futility gripped Joey as he bobbed with the flow. And then sprung past a barrier of Guardsmen and police the crowd surged in a headlong rush out onto the avenue. In the bloody twilight was a reek of tear gas filling the Loop, and Joey's mind flashed back to the night of Tet when he moved through the Saigon streets with Emmet Bufillu slung over his shoulder. Now he would like to see his partner again and talk with someone who understood.
   On Balbo Drive before the Hilton a few thousand stood crammed in the intersection like a herd at the stockyards. There

was a pause as they waited there. The halt lingered on. Then all at once unprovoked the blue-helmeted police lurched forward and pounded down with a jubilant sadism on the penned activists and shot off more tear gas and chemical mace into the air.

Joey Gilbert stood watching as the beaten and wounded got thrown in police vans like so much meat and hauled away. And now down the block he saw that same van again with its loud-speaker touting the wonders of Chicago. It was so brightly lit it seemed on fire, going along in a blaze of mist. But it wasn't sent here by a travel agency with a sense of irony; rather, it must have been the intelligence services roaming through the streets on re-con all day. For now suddenly the van was used to spew tear gas at the crowd even as it went on with its Chamber of Commerce spiel:

—'*Chicago! City of the 1871 Great Fire, and 1886 Haymarket Square Riot! It is a haven to banks with La Salle Street financial center. It has tightfisted bosses and hardfisted trade unions. Also there are the Gold Coast hotels and State Street shops and boutiques and Randolph Street theaters. Chicago has sensitivity to art and music with our Art Institute and Civic Opera. The city has its cultural veneer not only importing the Great Tradition, but also a rough homegrown provincialism perhaps more to the point. You could fill a library with books written by and about Chicago . . .!*'

VII

Amid an Old Chicago décor inside the Haymarket Inn, Emory Gilbert sat like a hero relaxing after his exploits. He was the liter-ary lion, and he was the man of the hour in the nation's politics. He sat there so handsome, brilliant, fêted among the other celebri-ties, movie stars, performers, fashionable writers in town for the show; also Democratic delegates. The archi-famous man whiffed euphoria even in the tear gas seeping from the streets in tumult, and tinge of a Yippie stink bomb set off in the Hilton lobby earlier. For success overrode everything else: all his personal and political doubts and the war not going well in Vietnam and all the death over there including his older son's. What did it matter who won or lost the Presidency and who won or lost in general? For his star had risen higher than ever, and he had played this historic moment like a past master at media exposure. While keeping his liberal integrity intact he cast a spell on people across the spectrum. All the mess and fuss of the Convention, the lack of laundry service due to a bus strike and the very slow elevators and the dead telephone lines did not put a dint in his great victory. It seemed his Party colleagues hardly knew how to say hi to the masterful man who was in grief for his elder son and yet riding the crest of success like a tidal wave carrying all before it. But where would it crash down?

Women were fawning on him. Every gorgeous or merely delightful woman he met seemed to hear some sort of siren song. Emory Gilbert had the exuberance of youth, the genius of a classic author's full maturity, and the charm of a patriarch. Nature chose to give this man everything, and society ratified the choice.

And so he sat there on a throne in the Haymarket Inn. And camera flashes went off here, there, around his table. And he thought what a crowning blow it would be—what good *pun*—if the buxom young waitress would come to his room upstairs later on: that one, in her Gay 'Nineties costume with its breathtaking décolletage.

After President Johnson bowed out of the race, Emory signed on with the Vice President's campaign, and it was a smooth transition. The two liberals suited each other. The great writer applied his talents to tricky issues; and first to the worst one, the scuttler, which was Vietnam. For a clear and principled position on the war was like political suicide on this level. And so Emory Gilbert rose to the task and wrote speeches and spoke so well he mesmerized the press and most of the public and no one seemed to mind. It was just such fun to listen to him. As usual he was compared to Victor Hugo; but one commentator said his name in the same sentence with the Prophet Muhammad.

Round the seam of conscience he could embroider with such a subtlety: the Devil must go to meeting in such an outfit. The key moments in each speech were a tour de force of literary style. He could retreat with a fanfare; and all were so pleased when he lived to fight another day. Everyday there were media opportunities. Weekly there were his stirring articles for the national magazines (not Reader's Digest where the Republican frontrunner had executive editor status). It was an ecstatic daily round: campaign review over breakfast, then hop to a fairground rally somewhere; taped in-studio television segments; then yet another press conference with its pitfalls and uncanny evasions like a Houdini. They practiced their Vietnam responses over and over—with laughter, and the Emory verve—in flight between venues. Then later on after a dress dinner there was another speech or maybe a guest booking on a talk show.

At all hours of the day and night the campaign went on. There were constant phone calls: terse, abrupt, no nonsense, every second counts. The North Carolina state campaign manager needed clarification so he came to Emory: there was some wrinkle or shift in the southern strategy. There was a question about 'bound imperatives', or voter reassurance on the eve of the Convention. Now pressure was mounting and Dixie constituents needed some cajolement; they wanted consultation rights, a say in post-Convention targets. And so the telephone rang, rang. Now it was a regional director; next a command post wanted some 'never split the Party' and 'national consensus' rhetoric. A masterful mix of Gilbertian wordplay and Open-sesame formulae was needed to lull all doubts.

Now Party morale was what counted. When one of six regional financial chiefs sought a tactical directive on fundraisers and -spenders, he called Emory. And it worked. They were in Seventh Heaven just to be on the phone with Emory Gilbert whose writings were translated in all languages and read to the four corners of the earth, a one-man Babel. Plus they knew he had immediate access to the Candidate; while the personal aides, the executive secretary and others in the pyramid might block them and cause a disastrous delay of five minutes.

This man, this prince of American letters was a genial phrase-maker, a magician of public opinion, and a seer. And all this made him a kind of wild card. If anyone knew the answer to the Sphinx's riddle, it was Emory. And so at any moment he could get in a word to the Candidate whose body was controlled by the Campaign Executive Director literally to the split second. The speech writers and the idea corps which had a liberal guru, a conservative guru, specialists in foreign affairs and finance and the urban crisis and farm sector: all these were overseen and coordinated by Emory. All these dialled his number round the clock.

One or two weekends he went to the Rock Castle as he had to relax and take a breather from the whistlestop speeches, meetings, luncheons, receptions, dinners, media events, talk shows, the whirlwind in weeks before he boarded a flight to the Wild West show in Chicago.

Left liberal forces had made breakthroughs in the spring primaries. Young voters, anti-war activists, issue oriented groups had tried to fashion new patterns for future U.S. Presidential politics. The Southeast Asian conflict came home to spark divisive activities within the Democratic Party. There were attacks on old boy exclusivity in the top control echelons. There were even challenges to the incumbent President. Pressure from the Left and the so-called Youth Candidate with his peacenik legions stirred an uneasiness not only in the Democratic favorite who got angry and cried for more stringent rules of engagement, and parameters to limit debate. A divided house falls, he said. If you didn't stay within certain boundaries and limit certain freedoms then it was the communists who would gain ground at the Free World's expense.

There was one label, one brand of discreditation which the prime contender feared above all others: to be called a communist, to be termed soft on communism. That's where the Republicans had liberal Democrats by the balls for all time. So you had better go on tiptoes when you started criticizing this system. Procommunist! Old Joe McCarthy pointed his finger and destroyed careers. Ah, so you liberals want a halt to the war? You want more programs for the poor? You want more support for education and healthcare? Well then, I as a good oldfashioned conservative who can be trusted call you a closet commissar! Watch out: I'll make your good name go poof!

Long before this Presidential campaign Emory's man had made betrayal after labor aristocracy betrayal of the rank and file workers' interests and been able to turn his fibs into a pro-Union media image. Labor's friend got the big labor endorsements like a vacuum cleaner of hope and votes from Maine to California. And even then he was selling out the common man. Well, Emory knew this was likely since the man came from the usual corporate power base while playing his opposition role in the prescripted comedy.

Emory knew this but he didn't care because Presidential politics was so much fun! He was having a ball as the apple of the nation's eye. So it didn't matter when his candidate's backroom fury hurled a curse at the grassroots activists—on a personal level Emory felt sympathetic to them—and swore grossly at those windmill tilters, amateurs willing to split the vote with their Third Party menace, and give Nixon a leg up gratis. Ah ha! Then you'll see a war! Then bring on Cambodia, Laos, China—if Nixon wins.

It was a tragic mistake to create this newly liberated space in bigtime politics for the hordes of irresponsible hippies. Those same hippies made up a national security threat though they may not know it.

Thus the Party standard-bearer since LBJ's abdication was an anti-communist liberal who ranted off camera against the young and the do-gooders, all these so-called people of conscience less liable to end an unwinnable war than erode the Democratic voter base and ensure a Republican victory.

In his heart Emory Gilbert did not share this fear of the younger generation: all the idealists bound for the crossroads in Chicago where they would pave the way to hell with their good intentions. That is, he did and he didn't. He had always loved the younger insurgent forces in U.S. society, and his books appealed to them greatly. In normal times they were his base. He was soft on youth and exuberance and idealism and the idea of noble striving for change. But there was an undertow of fear in him too; yes, there was . . . a deep unreasoning fear of the young and of what they might do if given a chance: if they knew their power and the situation. This new fear had been a twinge in his mood since . . . let's see, maybe since about a year ago. When his son Joey died in Vietnam, it seemed to go away. Oh well: maybe he was getting whimsical as old age came on.

End the war! shouted the hippies and radicals, who kept far away traditionally from city halls and state capitals across the land. Bring home the troops! cried the young while marching beneath red NLF and hammer-and-sickle banners through the free and democratic streets of America.

But the older generation told them: If you don't love the Land of the Free, then leave it. Get the hell out! Go join your comrade Mao Tse Tung and see if you like his company better. See if you don't come to yearn for a Jefferson and a Lincoln. And in this taunt, as Election Day grew closer, the liberal's voice had to chime in with the arch-conservative's.

Still the protesters shouted:

—Our tax dollars by the tens of billions are so much blood money to wage your unjust imperialist wars! In our name you genocide a tiny nation of people fighting heroically for their independence. But why not use those billions to clear slums here? And begin America's real education? Construct houses, not torch hootches! Why not fight a just war on poverty at home and sub-par schools and violations in our institutions of civil rights! Why not share our great wealth through better government programs? Why use Uncle Sam's vast plutocratic power to enslave and murder the Third World?

And Emory Gilbert believed this too. But now he had to say something else, and he didn't mind. The rewards were so tremendous: did he even think twice about it?

So let them bleat for all they were worth in the streets of Chicago. Let the young go up against the police lines in the violent sunlight and the dark of night. The politicians heard them physically, maybe electorally, so to speak; but the idea was to win.

For Emory such conflict gave a sense of his two sons face to face across the family barricades; and he feared it on another deeper level. But in times like these you just had to live with all your being and get some good fun out of life while the getting was still good.

VIII

And then a pinnacle was reached when he stood up high on the podium to address the Convention. And the nation held its breath to hear his every word—the nation maybe looking for a savior from this plague of the 'Sixties, and so it gazed up at the great orator instead of looking to itself.

And then Emory Gilbert's distinguished features were beamed to every home in the United States of America. For he had solved the riddle of success, that Sphinx of the spangled odes, and he knew how to capitalize on his magnificent triumph. Not for him to trouble his head over old mistakes and misdeeds. Up there he socked it to the voting public of the fifty states, and their delegates sent to choose a Presidential Candidate here in the Amphitheater;

and to Chicago as well stunned to its depths by the day's events. For even as he spoke there were chants in the distance; all knew police had clashed with the Yippies at their Lincoln Park camp-in; and skirmishes had occurred in Old Town as forces of order patrolled the city and made sweeps among the demonstrators.

The response to Emory's great speech was like a rumor of history in a conch shell. There was a surf-like thunder not of political protests and bleated anti-war slogans but of something else. Thirteen times the rapturous cheers and applause stopped him. The Convention floor's variegated glitter so vast yet compact was showered with bright beams from the rafters. And what a multitude it was of campaign posters and banners, larger than life photos of the Democratic nominees plus favorite sons; and all had cavorted, all pranced and danced and thump-thumped up and down to the full swell and cadence of his elocution with its rising and falling magisterial periods. His grandiose act transfixed the national network camera crews, which wasn't easy, amid the tulip field of microphones. Governors, U.S. Senators and Congressmen, political bosses, kingmaker chairmen from the corporate boards, sundry dignitaries, high-level contacts old and new crucial to the future of the Grand Old Party and an aspiring bigwig's place in it: they came, they heard, they admired him, Emory Gilbert. Lovely women gushed and shed a tear. Some wept at his stirring words. Never, never—or almost—had such a sonorous oratory served to avoid any clear and forthright position on the day's key issue.

His speech hadn't said a word on the Party platform. That wasn't his job. Did he have an anti-war stance? Your guess is as good as mine. Principled commitment to world peace as in his books? You figure it out. Emotion and literary genius were what sustained his glorious discourse. He would electrify the country on his Candidate's behalf, and this he did. From personal ambition he would upstage every other address and even upstage the Candidate himself. And so he strode the high podium like a titanic intellect, and delivered one of our era's great speeches. And it was success.

His timely words as father to war hero Joey Gilbert fallen for freedom on the western edge of Vietnam's Iron Triangle had carried the day. His magniloquent grief won not only the Democratic Convention but also the nation at large. This didn't mean they would all vote Democrat. Oh no. What it did mean was a lot of puffed up pride. Emory Gilbert's rhetorical furor of passion and pathos and patriotism made palpable at the operatic climax was above all an argument for U.S. greatness in this American Century. And all believed—or almost. The nation's hubris was reflected in the man's.

Yes, he made a masterpiece as enchanting in its ambiguity as the smile of Mona Lisa. He compromised no one. In essence he said nothing, but he filled that wide hall with his personality like a red, white and blue rainbow in a shower of light. Someone might have asked as an afterthought: what did he say? Or: how did he do that? Genius makes us believe the unbelievable, said Aristotle: Hector running from Achilles round the wall of Troy.

Soon enough, in November, the sheer ego of it could deflate like stale air from a flat tire. But for now Emory Gilbert felt swept away like everyone else by his brilliant success.

As he sat in the Haymarket Inn enjoying himself and wondering what further adventures were in store, the day of glamor, the Convention roar and hubbub wafted him up, up and away from reality on mighty pinions. Even he had to smile at such a deal of vanity: at the prima donna preening in the heart of man.

His plea to the voters using his dead son's testament drafted in blood from the jungles of Southeast Asia was a skillful thing. It navigated the Scylla and Charybdis of warmongery on the conservative Right and extremist cant on the radical Left. At one pole there were hawk Republicans cast as hardline reactionaries. At the other were dove street protesters calling for Utopia now: all the youth brigade which was forever beyond the pale. In the center he, Emory Gilbert, stood for Reason and moderation, like another great liberal long ago, his hero, the economist and enlightened plantation owner John Taylor of Caroline. Taylor argued with a lone voice in the Republic's early decades against the Founding Fathers, Jefferson included, who urged an expansionist course. Taylor said an empire may thrive within its borders and forgo the risk and human cost of imperialist war.

—'Now will you call Joey Gilbert soft on communism and say he did not love America simply because he wanted peace with dignity and an honorable settlement in Vietnam? Didn't he hate the devastation and waste but love our high ideals and our cherished democracy even more passionately because they must be fought for so darned hard and the ultimate sacrifice may in fact be required?'

The emotional groundswell rose to a tumultuous footstomping applause. Emory was not reading. He poured forth his phrases of amazement like lava from the inmost center.

—*'Oh, never did my son question whether this terrible war must end. Is there anyone among us who would like it and would profit if the catastrophe went on a day longer than the world historically inevitable? Go ask the Pentagon and the military planners. Go ask the political strategists with their Third Force ideas or maybe a Marshall Tito for Vietnam. Go ask our President with his programs for social renewal and his Great Society thwarted by a costly involvement halfway around the globe. And then go ask the victimized women and children, if you can, and don't forget to include America's mothers too. Yes, go see what they may have to say.'*

It was a euphoric flight over somber regions as Joey Gilbert's father gestured and shook a righteous fist in the mighty face of world history.

—*'So you see the old McCarthyist soft-on-communism slander fails to impress me. For I am a man in grief over the loss of his patriotic son. Never, but never, beg the question of whether this war should end. Only find out how to do it! Seek defensible terms. Look for the feasible diplomatic modalities. And then go on, Mr. President. Go ahead, Mr. Next-President! Please achieve peace!'*

He raised a proud V for the victory of universal brotherhood over all our wars and differences. And there are no words for the fervor of the awakened land applauding his sonorous sermon. Don't you see, America? Yes, you do, for it is all so clear.

At the grand climax all sides, Mr. President, the Vice President, Democratic National Committee members and delegates from the fifty great states, attendant dignitaries—down to Convention ushers; Cabinet and Department heads down to the radical brigades listening to this much-awaited speech over a transistor radio: every stripe of Leftist marching thousands abreast through the turbulent streets; all including the hardbitten Chicago Mayor and local political machinery and Chicago's not overly idealistic police force; even the nation's Republicans, who voted their pockets not a lot of misguided ideals, stared into TV sets and felt themselves transfigured beyond self-interested limits, if not a sheer creatural ignorance—all, all, every faith, every persuasion responded from the heart and clapped in a rapture and shed tears and shrieked forth adoration at the peacemaker's plea for an end to this intercontinental madness.

IX

—Refill, Sir?

The breasty young waitress hovered over him with her drink tray. She was thrilled to serve. What would he like? She waited for a signal. And as she bowed over him he said to her:

—What are you doing later? Could I see you?

Oh! How he longed for a surprise—some novelty to launch him and his lovely partner into the realm of ecstasy. Now her nearness made him yearn to lose himself utterly, submit, and become a thing of—what? Some sort of absolute sex that went beyond, O way beyond . . .? This eminently successful man had waited a lifetime to have his fling, and now he savored such an embarrassment of riches.

Propriety and common sense had him safely arrayed by Didi Fuschia's side: the dignified executive secretary had become a fixture of late, and she was far from sans charms. Didi was no slouch for a woman her age. But erotic tastes such as Emory's were slow to rouse by the handsome woman in her forties. For she did not have the . . . let's say, the fantasy of demonic excess? Stately in her sequined evening gown, she had southern savoir vivre, and might have made him a savvy wife to tour the world's 5-star hotels in his later age.

—Sir? Another refill?

—Yes, Dear. So when you get off at . . .?

He met her eye.

A well-known cartoonist leaned from the next table.

—Don't let me pry, but . . . don't you have another boy besides the athlete?

Emory gazed at the fashionable artist's cocktail glass: the beaded amber brim, and balled swill stick. In these days and nights the temptation to drink was strong at instants, but he couldn't do it.

His son's death certificate came to mind. A detail was off; it didn't jibe? He had passed over it at the first stunned glance, but now it came up like a message in a crystal ball.

Circ.

Emory winced. Circ. That single syllable seemed to dispel all the florid language and memorable phrasings of his speech. He felt a pang. Circ . . . He pushed down a sense of dread, down, out of his thoughts.

Now the pacifist chants from Grant Park echoed high off the hotel facade. They sounded distanced from this quaint Old Chicago décor with its tinkling piano. They seemed laden with destiny. Out there in the streets the nation's children made a tragic chorus, all the lost Joeys and the crazy Newells just beginning to learn what price they might have to pay for their ideals.

Emory thought of a phone call which got through to him an hour ago in his room. The phone rang. Hello? No response. Swoosh, a wide sort of silence, long distance. The receiver breathed. Again: hello? . . . The caller hung up.

It was strange. In these hours a key campaign call didn't get through since Chicago's telephone and communications workers were out on strike. In an atmosphere of subversive slogans, leaflets, tear gas, billy clubs, people thrown by police into Lincoln Park pond, MOBE and Yippie marshalls told to fuck off by movement toughs and self-styled enragés when trying to contain the ranks and keep order; in this left-wing stridency with its Security Force provocateurs, the city was as if demonized. There was much riding on it, a nation's destiny, yet you couldn't place a call. Many cried conspiracy.

In-house calls for last-minute jockeying were doable, but difficult. The Party's factional quilt work, and the candidates' personal staff members: the serious planners had to vie with guests for an open line, even as a fierce battle raged for delegate control. But few calls came in from outside and even less long distance.

So who was it? Emory had stared down at the receiver. He didn't know why, but the rare ring in this silent hour after so much excitement had given him a twinge. Was it the President calling to condole and praise? Why was there no voice at the other end, but only silence?

The telephone had rung, and now into his jubilant mood a doubt intruded.

Circ.

X

That morning after a brief sleep he had drafted a model for his candidate's acceptance speech. Another masterwork of lofty rhetoric. He handled the no-win issue of unilateral troop withdrawal from South Vietnam with an open-endedness that hoped to get votes. Trust us.

As ever the frontrunner was timid on major issues and unable to break away from LBJ's Southeast Asia policy. The majority plank for all its 10-point farm program, 8-point program for education, eighty-four point program for law and order, etc., inspired no one and didn't even tell their campaign apart from Nixon and the Republicans. For instance: *'We reject as unacceptable a unilateral withdrawal. We may stop all bombardment of North Vietnam when this action will not endanger the lives of our soldiers'.*

From venue to venue through the eventful day of August 28th, 1968, the mad and subtle war went on: the fight over an 'open Convention'; the inner Party insurgency of academics, labor leaders, progressive clergy, all the more Left elements up in arms against old-line backroom politicians such as Emory's candidate. They fought against the usual Convention of Party bosses, and delegate brokerage by the abstruse 'unit rule'. In the International Room at the Conrad Hilton and then on the Convention floor Emory watched the new anti-war forces agitate Rules and Credentials Committees and provoke open floor fights over Convention ground rules. As an important player he put in his word and helped parry any threat to their old guard candidacy while a dozen more disputes went to the floor like floodwater on a dam. But at key moments, tired from his white night and preoccupied by this and that, he grew distracted in battle.

Now in Haymarket Inn the pretty receptionist touched his arm:

—Sir, you have a phone call.

—Lines are restored?

—No, but it's there for you.

—Oh.

She smiled:

—They got through.

—Take the party's name, and tell me yours.

—Linda.

—Good, Linda, go see who it is.

She curtsied, young, prim. She too was well developed. She paused, turning away, so he could look at her.

—Yes, Sir. I'll be right back.

Everyone felt jittery. That morning over breakfast he found his Candidate in a stew about the chaos outside and Chicago under siege. If the Presidential nomination must be accepted against such a backdrop: then wasn't it a worldwide embarrassment? It wouldn't inspire voters: that's for sure.

Out by the stockyards Convention Hall was a fortress with a one-mile security zone: the Amphitheater ringed by chain-link fences topped with triple barbed wire strands. All manholes on the approaches were sealed against bomb throwers. Two hundred firemen were poised and ready on arson assignment. There was a catwalk high above the hall where Security Service agents and special police kept a lookout with binoculars, walkie-talkies, rifles. Such an ominous landscape did not bolster voter confidence.

The mood was the same inside luxury hotels where men and women debated a decision meant to get the world's greatest nation back on track. The stockaded Convention ambience lent an embattled sense not apt to sustain euphoria in these delegates with their chitchat and their provincial dress. Bad news items drifted in. The Mayor had ordered 20,000 National Guardsmen into the city after refusal of permits for the Yippies' Festival of Life. Dick Daley was playing hardball. Last April he responded to the King assassination riots with a shoot-to-kill policy, and he now denounced 'hoodlums and communists'. What else is new? But meanwhile Yippies threatened to smoke-bomb the Democratic Convention, and smuggle LSD into the delegates' punch.

Fumes drifted over the swelter of Chicago. The midsummer heat wafted a stockyard stench from Convention Hall out across the steamy neighborhoods. Something was rotten in Czechago, said the activists, as Soviet tanks grumbled their way in these hours through Prague.

Nevertheless the Candidate's distress didn't reflect itself in his top adviser Gilbert's composed features. Emory's every glance met a stare of fascination often mixed with a frank envy. The wide world seemed to gape his way, like a barmaid's voluptuous cleavage. In the stockyard stink no less than the high-powered perfume of wealthy and elegant women, he smelled his own heady success. A smile, a coy nod, and they took aim at the author, orator, grieved father, widower. Here, there, he sniffed at pleasure his for the taking. Probably he wanted either his waitress or the pert Haymarket Inn receptionist in his room tonight. He couldn't decide which . . . Both?

Tomorrow at a televised breakfast by the Candidate's side he must appear fresh and confident though played out after a night of passionate caresses. Well what couldn't the make-up team do with their cosmetics? The revamped older man looked young as he basked in the nation's gaze.

So go for it. Politics and sex always were bedfellows. Was there ever a randier town than our nation's capital? Where else did you ask a postman—as Emory once did—where some steak and eggs might be had for breakfast, and get directed to a striptease joint off Dupont Circle?

No doubt all that power made for such a charged atmosphere. The Kennedy years turned 1600 Pennsylvania Avenue into a sex motel.

XI

—Hark!—said a writer in town for a New York magazine.—Is it the Light Brigade?

Nervous energy erupted in bursts of laughter through the wide bar sprayed and perfumed to offset stink bomb odor. Two TV cameras went among the convivial groups and lit on well-known faces and newsworthy names among the celebs of this in-crowd. But the voices and laughter, the swirl of sights and sounds took on a self-conscious note as, outside in the street, there were shouts and cries.

Nearby a loudspeaker mounted on a van went past as it had all day reciting facts and figures about the city for the sake of all these visitors.

—'Chicago was once a frontier town where explorers, fur traders, missionaries paused to rest before going on their way west into the Great Central Plains. But Chicago is now a steelworks, an ironworks. It is an urban immensity of woodframe and redbrick and concrete two-family

houses for its toiling inhabitants. The more affluent middle-class Protes-
tant sectors have spread out to their northern suburbs and greener more
spacious neighborhoods and better schools . . .'

Emory heard the cries and the van, but he was deep in thought
for a moment. Ah! Circ. for circumcized—on Joey's death certificate. But he wasn't circumcized. Anne didn't want it: a barbarous
rite, a vestige. So a weary doctor's oversight: a typo in the heat of
action at one of the field hospitals over there? Calm down, man,
why such jitters suddenly?

Now past the wide plate glass people fled like ghosts from an
enchanter as their forms enwound in the thicker smoke gusts. Inside amid the period décor the noise level was lowered. The chatter had a more sober accent.

—Look!—The magazine writer raised his voice which was
slightly slurred.—Look, you want to argue? Okay, let's argue! We
count for one tiny planet in a zillion of 'em . . . all suspended in
outer space . . . pitiful! Outer space, inner space . . . same thing.
And meanwhile a few billion tiny creatures swarm and zigzag
their way through the days over earth's funny surface. Well, good
for us. But why get our noses all bent out of joint over a mere trifle
called life? I don't get it. Money and sex and this ratrace are way
overrated, if you ask me. We're all doomed anyway by our own
bad habits, so why get so excited? Uncle! I'd cry. Uncle! Except
. . . except there's the small matter of the children. On TV we're
seeing Vietnamese kids with their backs on fire. Boys and girls
napalmed: they look like roasted marshmallows. Whoopsy daisy!
Must be some mistake. The good ol' U.S. of A. couldn't do such a
thing. Could it? Hungry and in pain they die like flies from diseases you could cure worldwide for the price of a Wall Streeter's
luncheon tabs. Aw, what the heck, those kids are only tomorrow's
commies. They'd only grow up and make too many babies. Let
'em croak and make room for the rest of us. Right, Emory?

The wild sounds and tumult outside lent a strange note to these
pink jovial masks, fancy outfits, jewelry, the portly bonhomie of
successful middle-aged men. Did you hear the latest joke about
Spiro Agnew? Or what about the gossipy tidbit from Miami, the
Rocky and Nixon frolics? It seems one or two of these Young Republicans and YAF (Youth for American Freedom) aren't what
they're cracked up to be.

Brow creased, Emory listened as the young receptionist leaned
over him, like a cornucopia, to whisper in his ear. Didi and the

elegant dames at the Amphitheater didn't stir him up this way. There was a kind of boyish charm, a plea in the great writer's Olympian gaze and brow. He looked up as she patted his shoulder. He said:

—Just come and knock when you get off.

—Yes.

—You've got the room number?

—Yes.

—This war—said a Hollywood actor with blue eyes wide at the world's injustice—it's too much really.

People were streaming past the long glass enclosure. They stared in eerily at the festive scene: at the elite, the overfed, the half-drunk dignitaries.

An acrid scent filled the Hilton interior. Haymarket Inn was close to what was happening right now on television.

—Goddamned delegates!—cried an irate voice, muffled, beyond the glass.—They have to act!

The riot was loud and many-voiced as it roiled into view. The happy party inside grew quiet. An angry ocean silenced the chit-chat of kingfishers along a beach.

Screams, shouts and curses rose as terrified demonstrators came in view and lunged past the aquarium glass and glanced in wild-eyed with their features distorted.

—*Kill! Kill! Kill!*

There were police in dark uniforms, gas masks. Arms raised the cops thrashed and flailed and pounded down—swimmers between crests.

Swept up in hysteria the protesters lurched past shrieking. A bunch got wedged against the hotel. Then more were penned in, like livestock grown conscious of the horror. The glass wall began bulging in, in, inward under the pressure.

—*Hey! Hey! LBJ!*—

—*Pigs! Pigs! Pigs! Pigs!*

—*How many kids did you grill today?*

Inside Haymarket Inn the elegant guests began a retreat only to become trapped and jumbled toward the exit. They were stunned by the mad rush and crush outside. Media stars and public figures made a curious scene if anyone bothered to notice just then. The lifelong illusion of a personal salvation through fame seemed to shatter, for a moment at least, as the immaculate plate glass bulged and smudged. Body sweat spumed this hot August night.

Someone's blood turned the Haymarket logo to a green tinted smear by the interior light.

—*Join us! Join us! Join—uhh-h . . .!*

—*Kill! Kill! Kill! Kill!*

—*The whole world is watching! The whole world is watching!*

Havoc and craven faces blotched the glass. Tear gas misted the scene as people bent forward and spewed on one another, a chain reaction of retching. Women screamed. There were howls in a chorus and crazed grimaces of pain and more chants. From inside the TV crews leapt at this photo opportunity. Real violence! A bonanza, a scoop—it out-commodifies the commodities.

—*Free Huey!*

—*Peace now! Peace now!*

—Ow you, oof!

—Let go, motherfucker! Get away from me!

Emory Gilbert's adrenalin was pumping like the rest. For a moment he even forgot about his success and sexual obsessions: his fetishes. Just outside there were vulgar cries and the most insane brutality as contorted features pressed and beat against the heavy glass. To Emory just then it seemed a glass partition was screening civilized America and its everyday affairs from the savagery in its subconscious where some sort of terrible beast, namely its past, lurked. But the invisible shield was being strained to the limit. In a minute it would shatter.

—*Out now! Out now!*

And then, smudged with pink blood, the long Haymarket Inn vitrine sagged and caved under the weight of Chicago police and demonstrators stung from behind by billy club blows like gadflies.

—*Off pigs! Off pigs!*

—*The whole world is watching!*

—*Turn on! Tune in! Drop out!*

It steamed tear gas and mace. Emory stared as a big intricate spider web glinted red across the glass. Click, click—and it fissured. Then came a sickening—cra-a-a-ack-k-k-k!

XII

Television lights glared grotesquely as the gheet glass cracked in long jagged sections. Bright blood spurted from an activist impaled and hung up as police swung their clubs and swore and yelled at the Yippies and anti-war elements.

—*Sieg Heil! Sieg Heil!*
—*Hey! Hey! LBJ!*
—*Hitler! Moussolini! And Washington, D.C.!*

A tear gas canister popped and gushed. A moment ago the celebrities were imbibing and smiling as they enjoyed the spectacle from a safe distance. Then it added to their limelight. But now began a mad scramble for cover.

Yet Emory Gilbert stayed put as though caught in the coils of that spider web. Pale and stonefaced he sat still as the glass rampart jutted inward and snapped its angular wedges. He felt panic rising in a groundswell, but unlike the others he didn't move because something he saw had him riveted in place. As if appalled by chaos he gave a shudder of dread which was all his own, and seemed ancient as tragedy. But it had nothing to do with the Chicago riot of 1968.

For a figure appeared in the riven plate glass bulging and splintering inward but not yet collapsed. There was a kind of apparition calm amidst the madness; it was like a ghost.

Bigger than the others, one fighter showed a composure and a killer's self-possession as his eyes glowed darkly beneath a black tangle of hair. With one hand he grabbed a policeman's blackjack on the fly and bent it back and the uniform attacker fell away holding his shoulder. That one figure was cool despite the police violence which mauled protesters in a sort of group St. Vitas dance. Cops grunted laying about them. Hippies and Yippies squealed and kept up buffeted chants. It was a chorus. But the strange lone figure fended here and there with his great strength. He was in combat fatigues but no National Guardsmen. He was in his element.

Then the plate glass disintegrated. There were cries. Blood spattered. People howled, pleaded. Some fell on the shards of glass. Got trampled.

More blue-helmeted police came on stepping over the fallen and the injured, like pontoons. They beat and pummeled and conked skulls as they barged inside. Then rabidly and utterly beside themselves they attacked hotel guests, middle-aged men and women of the most respectable: delegates, gentle folk dressed for the Convention festivities.

—*Shame! Shame! Shame!*

—*Peace now! Out now!*

The political chants seemed to animate the forces of Law and Order as they rode to hounds among the tables and place settings and the swell Haymarket Inn scenery.

—*Off pigs! Off pigs!*

—*Free Huey!*

XIII

It was a recognition scene for Emory Gilbert, and with a reversal; but he didn't see this immediately. At first he had a sense of his nerves flying out of control in the instant before a calamity. On his dignified features a tremor flitted as he saw a hard stare, the dark eye of a hunter, on him. And then he knew it was his son. But all the boyhood and baseball were baked from that lean implacable face by the sun of Vietnam and the war. And then Emory had a sense of slipping and losing his hold; he felt it as he plunged from a high peak and fell down, down toward some dim unknown place where life could know defeat. And for an instant he had a smell of self worse than any Yippie stink bomb.

Here was his son Joey come home in the flesh, and all in one piece. Joey Gilbert was here in Chicago: not KIA as reported, circ.!, not dead at all. And Emory was denying, already denying, but he looked across and saw his son—the better half of Oedipus—who was seeking, seeking. And he seemed to see an opposite force in his life's dialectic, a force from his being's underside, and it charged him with life—or was it death, after a day of so much success? But just as Joey-seeker had another need which was not to find, so Emory denying had a deep desire to have his secret revealed and out in the open for all to see. Deep in him in that instant was an urge not to suppress a truth which was causing him such pain, though he tried to deny that too, and which was blighting his life on a basic level and his relationship with himself. He had to deny but he yearned to be set free. Sooner or later wouldn't the truth be known about what happened at the Rock Castle—that bad thing like a rape, like the white man taking what he wanted from the Indian, namely the best North Carolina land . . .? The famous liberal needed with a vengeance to deny this, but have it made manifest too; and then be reprieved from the life-blighting truth and its painful restraint. It was such a charge of life in that instant of recognition. To Emory it felt like he only then began to know himself.

But in that moment another instinct came, and it was generous. The father snapped to as tears filled his eyes. He felt pity. He loved and pitied his son. So he rose with an arm outstretched and took a step forward, and amazement painted his face a livid hue.

The soldier's dark eyes gazed and gazed back ten thousand miles beyond the grave on things they had seen. But Emory thought those eyes peered into his inmost soul. Ah! Has he seen Newell in Berkeley? Has he talked to him? Is the cat out of the bag? This idea was like a brink; and, dizzy for an instant, he nearly fainted. Then an image was in his mind's eye: a beautiful dark-skinned woman in a black nightgown rose forward in bed to meet her brutal lover.

—*Shame! Shame! Shame!*
—*Shamerica! Shamerica!*
—*The whole world is watching! The whole world is watching!*
—*Hey! Hey! LBJ! How many children did you kill today?*

XIV

There were more screams, jeers, slogans. A pianist played a few more bars of mocking honky-tonk, and then slammed his fist down on the keys.

Father and son stood ten yards apart as the vitreous sheet of glass buckled and broke like an ocean wave.

—Dad! Is that you? Dad! Oh, Dad—!

Joey waded in from the jungle. His features came alive when he saw Emory there before him—his own father in the flesh! Oh, oh, he moved forward and took his arms.

—Jo—

—Do you see me? I'm home!

The older man stood and stared as if struck dumb.

Amid tear gas and chants, screamed curses, catcalls, the whoof-thud of police clubs as people flung up their arms and jumped away, or else went down under the crunch of a blow—Joey shook his father gently.

—It's me, I'm here.

—I see.

He bored his gaze into Emory and said oblivious now to the rest:

—Tell me where she went, Dad? What happened? Why did she leave us? I've got to know, I can't live without my wife. You had Anne and I have Carlyne. Do you understand? Just tell me the plain truth, Pop, I can take it. I've got to know! What did I do? Did I do something wrong? In Bangkok? It seemed so good for us over there . . . But if it wasn't me then what went on at the Rock Castle? Did somebody try to hurt Carlyne? Is that why she went away?

XV

They took the elevator.

Emory, pale as a sheet, gave a gesture and said:

—Calm down.

—I can't, Dad, until I find out what it's about.

Emory shot his elder son an oblique glance.

—Just don't fly off the handle as your brother always does. Don't get excited and lash out . . . you'll regret it later. And don't believe everything you hear.

—Hear? . . . My wife is gone and it's the end of me if I don't find her. If anyone hurt her—

—Things are bad all around, Joey. Don't make them worse by accusing people.

—I didn't come home to accuse . . . do anything bad. But if Newell . . . or anyone—

—The way you look now: so full of hate. If you could see yourself . . . your own worst enemy.

Now Emory breathed a sigh of relief as the elevator reached his floor. What a scare! It's a wonder he didn't have a heart attack. But Joey didn't know anything and only suspected his brother. The bad moment past, Emory rallied.

—Where is she, Dad?

XVI

Inside Emory's suite they talked.

—We all make mistakes, son. Maybe you did too with Carlyne . . . Unity is so vital now: our nation is in trouble, America needs us, and this is more important than personal quarrels.

—Dad, I feel different about all that now than when I went away. I just want my wife back. What went on at the Rock Castle? Why did she leave? Do you know anything?

—I don't.

—But you must have some idea.

—Really no. Why would I? Newell was more likely . . .

Joey gave a little jolt:

—Look, just tell me, in the open. Did she and Newell . . .?

—I can't conjecture what they . . . talked about. Why not ask him? Have you seen him? He might know where she went: they stayed in contact.

—I saw him, and he doesn't know either. So he says.

—So you did have a chance to chat.

—I spent last night in Berkeley. To me it doesn't seem like he . . .

Joey's words trailed off as he stared at his father. He questioned him with his eyes. What with the violence downstairs a strangeness to their exchange in the elevator could have passed unnoticed, but it lingered. And Emory still had a curious manner: speaking with a kind of will amid belabored breaths. He avoided his son's eye, which sought his. He stared past him. He was holding on.

—What . . . what did the irresponsible Newell tell you?

—He doesn't know where she went.

—And you believe him.

—I don't know what to believe. You know that guy. He's kind of mad and talks in riddles and plays the seer.

—Well, he should have an idea about it because they used to talk by the hour. They enjoyed each other's company and took long walks across the fields to the river.

Joey looked at his father, and shook his head:

—I just want to find her. I don't know what went wrong at the Rock Castle with Newell or anyone else, and I don't care anymore. All I know is I can't live worth a damn without Carlyne.

Joey pressed his lips, shook his head, bowed.

—She left you, son. Who knows why? Maybe some redneck insulted her in public up town. You know how they do . . . if it's an Indian they call her Squaw and whatnot. Like the woman named Cherokee in Granddaddy's day: there were a lot of rumors about how she, a prostitute, used to visit town business leaders in the upper offices of the First National City building.

—It drives me crazy when I think my wife . . .

—Each of us has a destiny, Joey. Call it God or Apollo or any name you like. It is there waiting for us at the crossroads of time; there's no escape. The truth is you may just have to forget Carlyne.

—And do what?

—Why not revive the farm? Go live at the Rock Castle and become one of the state's important growers.

Joey gave a strange low laugh. He said in a soft voice:

—If I find her, we'll work your farm for you. If not, then . . . I don't know what will happen with me.

—Then you—

—Maybe Cindy Phillips knows something. I'll go ask her soon as I get there. I hear she doesn't work for us anymore. Why is that, Dad?

—She's getting old. Wanted more time for her grandchildren.

Joey ground his teeth:

—I feel like strangling with my bare hands whoever did this to us.

Again Emory went very pale. Despite himself he said with a tremor:

—You made it home.

XVII

They fell silent. Both stared in space. Joey glanced at the door beside them as if ready to leave. His gnarled combat boot with its red muddy splotches made a spark on the plush carpet.

Emory blinked. Not the lovely young receptionist but an offended husband, the wild beast of Borneo, was in this hotel room alone with him. Physical courage was not Emory Gilbert's forte. Face to face with a LURP, a killer: he had a lingering fear Joey knew something despite what he said and had found out the truth from Newell and would suddenly turn on him and point the finger at him or worse. Emory loved his two sons, in his way, but at this moment he hated them. The way Jojo was staring at him! . . . So Newell had told him after all? And Joey only awaited his moment to . . .? Then ruin, ruin, ruin for the great Emory Gilbert and for his fame and place in posterity as the truth got out to the world. Then the son's revenge, blood, a swift death for the betrayer . . . There was a surge of panic, and he strove to control himself at all costs and avoid a strained gesture, a telltale word. He must pull himself together and act naturally. To cover up an inward shudder he fumbled with the keys to the executive suite as if he meant to go out again.

—Dad, when was it? When did Carlyne go away?

—What?

—When did she leave the Rock Castle?

—It was . . . I think February.

—February?

—Yes, that's when it was.

—Where did she go? I mean which direction?

—I don't know.

—How did she travel then? By train from High Point? By bus?

—I wasn't there, Jojo. I was in Washington.

XVIII

Again a silence came over them: such a silence, for a full minute. Then Joey came out of it with a sigh and glance at the ceiling as if looking up there for help.

Then he went in the bathroom; and, when he came out again, looked a little calmer. He had even washed his face: a sort of nod to his dad?

—I'll hit the road, he said.

—Now?

—Forgive me, Sir, but I . . . I just need to get on my way. That's how it is. There's nothing for me to do here.

—Well, it's near my bedtime too—said Emory with a glimpse at the door.—Long day for me and I've got a strategy session at six in the morning.

—Suddenly . . . without a word Carlyne flies away? She vanishes into thin air after we were so happy in Bangkok, so close to one another.

—I guess she just took a notion, Jo. For weeks I worried about her. Felt personally responsible. Still do at times. I feel badly because I was her host and she was a guest in our house. Often I blame myself for her disappearance.

—You did what you could for us.

—I'm sorry about it, Jojo, sincerely. You entrusted your wife to me, and I let you both down. But you see I myself had to leave, so busy in those weeks with the nation's business, the campaign trail. I couldn't stay at the Rock Castle no matter how much I wanted to help. No, I couldn't think about family and private life. I had to ride out into the great world and serve. This isn't a time for personal pleasures, Jo. Now it is about renunciation of self, and that is the key to human grandeur. Goethe said: Geniessen macht gemein. I know you understand this, son, and will forgive me?

Touched by his own eloquence, and the poet's deep words, Emory nodded gravely. He looked away with emotion.

—Sure, Dad. I do.

—Caught up in the whirlwind of public life I had no time for Carlyne. So maybe she felt neglected. Maybe she no longer—

—What?

Emory paused.

—Felt comfortable with us.

—Why?

—I don't know.

Silence. Then Joey said:

—I was wrong to blame Newell without any proof. But I'm not ruling anything out.

—For one thing I . . . I could tell she didn't take to our town. All eyes followed her the moment she stepped out the door. Or so she thought.

Joey looked down and gave a little groan. Their talk about Carlyne hurt him and made him more and more anxious. Why? As a boy, and always before he went away to war, he liked so much being with his father. But now he just wanted to leave this fancy hotel suite.

—The day of Tet when I phoned home from Saigon: Lemon told me my wife used to staff your office up town.

—Last fall she did.

—You worked together?

—Yes.

—On the third floor in the bank building? Granddaddy's old headquarters?

Emory tensed. Was this an interrogation? He nodded.

—Yes, she took calls and did some dictation. Her secretarial skills were a bit rough, but helpful. For a few weeks she eased the heavy burden I was under: dealing with mail, keeping the place neat and clean. Carlyne was helpful. Then I went to Washington where the Party needed me: I had office space and an executive secretary named Didi Fuschia.

Joey shook his head. His brow was knit.

—In Thailand one night I asked her if she felt like an intruder at the Rock Castle.

—Well, I hope not, Jojo. I tried to make your wife feel welcome and give her a safe haven till you got home. All of us, Lemon and Cindy, Max Doan and Paul Commynes, those true friends: we bent over backwards to make Carlyne feel wanted, and loved. And her stay with us came off without a hitch. I've asked myself why she left us. And I don't know.

—Over there she told me you were all good to her, Dad. But why then? What drove her away? I repeat, and ask myself, again and again: why?

—In Bangkok she didn't criticize us? Say our hospitality left something to be desired?

—Not at all.

—Say we treated her with less than the utmost respect and care?

—She loves you like a father.

Emory gazed away, in space. He said weightily:

—Son, I wouldn't take the tragic view of this.

Joey fairly whined:

—But did she seem sad? Did some bozo bother or hurt her? I'll kill him!

—N-not that I heard of, Jojo. You can be sure I'd have put an end to it at once. But you know a woman like Carlyne will never lack admirers. And . . . the situation . . . Her nature makes her secretive.

Again Joey groaned, and sort of bucked.

—What went on then? In Thailand we had ten days like paradise, holding hands, seeing the sights. We had such kisses and words and promises. Tell me: did she look happy? sad? indifferent when she got home from Bangkok? Over there we made a loving couple for the first time, and the next thing I hear she's gone off and left no trace. No more letters. Gone, out of my life!

XIX

Grimly Joey nodded, shook his head, nodded again. He didn't know why but this conversation was tearing him up and he wanted to get out of here and hit the road. He came here to his father for a helping hand—and found anguish. Tensely he turned toward the door. He didn't know if he could take it anymore.

—Dad, I'll go in a moment. And I'll find her. I know she still loves me.

—Good luck to you, son. All the best, really.

—I don't know why, but over there it seemed she was afraid of me. Like she was a fallen woman or something, a lowlife who didn't deserve to be at my side. Though she has a university degree, and she's my wife.

Emory said:

—You never know, Jojo. You can't tell what people will do, or
. . . turn into. Max Doan once brought home a stray from the city
pound. Belgian shepherd, big, strong, fine looking thing with
sleek black fur. One night as guests left a dinner party at his home,
up there on the Heights, that dog got excited and bit a chunk out
of Max's forearm, as he bowed holding it back on the front walk.
Severed an artery; the gash needed many stitches. But do you see
my point, Jo? Carlyne may have a dark past too: maybe mistreated
by a former master. She was in an orphanage. Her ancestors were
Cheraw Indians who lived out by the swamps.

—Don't compare my wife to a dog.

Joey stared at his father. Then he raised a fist, gritting his teeth,
and looked at the door.

—Sorry, son. I didn't mean it that way.

—For months, in-country, I thought: Newell, you rascal, I'll
wring your goddamned neck. So the first thing after Travis and
discharge I went to Berkeley and had a chat with my little brother;
insofar as you can chat with a fanatic. And I asked him pointblank: Mister, did you . . .? And he answered: no. And now I don't
think it was him that . . . Crazy guy like always, but not *that.*

—Crazy, you say?

—Well he raves on about politics: you know the way. It was always something. On his bed there was a teenage girl naked with
flowers in her hair. But I don't think he messed with my wife.

—Glad to hear you believe him.

—I don't care what she's done, Dad. Now I'll go see her people
in Pembroke. Then Durham: I'll ask around the Women's College.
Maybe someone has seen her. If so I'll find her. We'll start again.
Never mind past sins.

—Alright, son, go ahead, look for Carlyne. But get ready for . . .
for a setback, if it must be, maybe a bad one. Has she fallen? If so,
she will lie, she will cheat and steal. She'll tell you any old cock-
and-bull story about how she got corrupted and led astray; how
she was used and abused. And yet . . . Jojo, people seek and find
their own level—Emory gave a sigh.—You may just have to get
over her. Then a day will come when you see more clearly.

—No, Dad, I can't. And I don't care what she did, if anything. I
know she isn't bad, like you seem to be saying. It makes me think
you know something and won't tell me.

XX

Emory Gilbert looked in his son's distraught eyes, and shook his head. Casually he glimpsed his wristwatch, then the door, and gave a shrug.

—In the end she betrayed you; that's what I know. She went away without a word, and it's no good. Take my advice and let her go, Jojo.

—What do you mean by no good? So she did it with my brother? Or a Max Doan?

—I didn't say that.

—But you . . . You thought it.

—As the saying goes: two kinds of women on this earth. One will drive you wild and then let you down, if you're crazy enough to love her; she will give herself free and easy to the first comer. No way to account for her actions past or future; she excites, she lies, you pay the price. Don't be surprised when she prowls about attracting the village mastiffs like a bitch in heat! She has that magnetism in the eyes, gestures, in her words and voice and voluptuous figure. Well, why cast aspersions at a force of nature? Why wonder at it, and lose sleep? The instant I laid eyes on Carlyne: when you brought her north after college; no, even before, I think the night you called me from Durham with your news: I knew, Jojo. Why this mad rush? Ah, she's got her hooks into him. No, no, I'm sorry, but a world lies between your mother and the girl you married. By the one's side we live and grow in a trustful marriage; we build a future together day by day. With the other you adventure and learn, you experience, renew yourself like the ancients in their orgies and biannual festivals; you walk on the wild side, you taste wild fruit. But beware! Beneath that beautiful icing there's a wormy devil at work, oh yes, and with a pitchfork! And behind all your anguish and self-doubt there could be a whore, my friend: produced by society's contradictions, if you will, and common enough. No need to call it her fault; there may have been little free will sharing the blame; one or two were turned into commodities long before this.

In wonder Joey stared at his father. There was such a vulgar note to it all—to be coming out of the mouth of a great writer. But also Emory's tone now, the nervous rapidity of his words: ah! so she had her effect on him too, on this noble man so intent on serving humanity, as he always said. Something deep gave a kind of click in Joey, and he blinked.

—Please don't say unkind things about my wife.

—Oh I know how much you love her, but a good marriage takes work, education, and . . . yes, I'll say it, a proper background, good breeding. The happy and productive couple puts a diadem on Western Civilization's head. Your past and Carlyne's are not the same.

—Over there—Joey lowered his eyes; his facial muscles looked ready to snap. With a dry sob he brushed the rotten words to one side since they came from the only person he still trusted. He was breathing in small jerks and almost couldn't breathe. For a moment he tottered, his eyes rolled upward, but he kept on:—Over there in Bangkok she asked me what I'd do if she slept with someone else.

He looked at his father. This time Emory's eyes held.

—What you'd do?

—So now I ask you, Dad. Do you have any proof? Anything real against her? If so, please tell me.

—Did you ever meet her kin?

—Yes, in Pembroke. I met her Aunt Loveday and them, one called Daystar.

—Many times?

—Once.

—Ah, it was a ceremony, a show.

—Hardly. They live in trailers. Humble folk.

—Did she tell you about her past?

—She doesn't talk about herself. But her people, yes, Lumbee they're called now. And the La Grange home. Some.

—But I mean her childhood, her parents.

—A little.

—Jojo—said Emory with concern—did Carlyne come to you a virgin?

Joey stared off. The question had a brutal sound. With anyone else he wouldn't have let it pass. But how much more of this could he take? The tic on his cheek fluttered as, softly, he replied:

—I thought so . . . the way she talked once at a picnic by the river down there. But . . . no.

He dropped his gaze.

—So she confessed that?

—Yes.

—And when did she—?

—At her orphanage.

—And with—?

—A counselor.

—Ah.

—It was against her will.

—At what age?

—Thirteen.

—An early start.

—Dad—

—And others, Jojo? Were there others?

—What?

—Did she sleep with others?

—Maybe. I don't know.

—How many do you suppose, Jo?

—Dad, don't.

—Did she tell you about others?

—No.

—She didn't name them?

—No, of course not.

—And during your time together: did you always know where she went?

—To school. Finishing her degree.

—But did she ever go off somewhere without a word?

—Sure, she went out. Who doesn't?

—And when you played in the Minor Leagues? Did she come watch your games?

—She didn't like them. She hates baseball.

—What did she do?

—Stayed in the trailer and read.

—Read? Read what?

—Russian novels. How sinful.

—All day long?

—I think so. I don't know. Why?

—Was she alone?

—Y-yes, as far as I know.

—Only Tolstoy and Dostoyevsky for company.

—She likes Turgenev better. Dad—

—You never knew her to leave without saying goodbye? For hours at a stretch?

—Please—

—And she never came back ... how to say it? ... distracted? Maybe dishevelled, skirt or blouse rumpled? Cool to your attentions?

—Stop.

—Couldn't you tell, Jojo? When you made love to her—you know—

—Dad!—Joey shivered with fear and disgust—I said stop it unless you have some real proof!

—This is for your own good. Couldn't you tell if she—?

—I'd better leave.

Emory looked so excited: in a kind of trance after days and nights of frantic activity. Like Joey he was churning subconscious: the two of them half-mad as they stood facing one another. But he came to his senses brusquely and held fire.

They stayed that way, in silence, a long moment.

For an instant Emory Gilbert felt a powerful impulse.

A call rose up from his depths to throw himself at his son's feet and confess, confess! Free himself of the whole hideous business: tell the terrible truth, regardless of what it cost him.

But the fear overrode; it was just too big. And why upset the applecart on this day of success like an apotheosis—a day like few men ever knew, and which wasn't over! For in a moment yet more success would come rolling through the door in the person of a lovely young career woman very impressed and ready to do his bidding.

No, he must stay the course begun a year ago: on the night he came down the wide Rock Castle stairway in a frenzy to possess a woman who was not meant to be his, not free to return his caresses, not for him.

XXI

—Your war has ended. Get on with your life, boy. Find a sweet honest girl and forget about the past. Run our farm, if you like, as partner.

—To hell with the farm ... I want Carlyne.

Emory's voice went low:

—Then I must tell you, and try to save you. A political associate of mine, in Durham, told me she plies her trade at the bus station there. It is first come, first serve.

—He saw her? He knew who she was?

—From a reception she and I attended in Greensboro last fall. He couldn't believe his eyes, but Carlyne Gilbert was any man's who had the cash.

—I'll go find out.

—She's a poor sick woman, Jojo. She'll say anything at this point, accuse anyone, blame her fate on God the Father. Don't believe her. She takes her psychotic fantasies for reality . . . It would be best, and by far the best, to leave her be.

XXII

—*Stop the war!*

—*Out now! Out now!*

The cries rose from the street.

—*Ho! Ho! Ho Chi Minh!*

—*Sieg Heil! Sieg Heil!*

—*Stop the bloodshed! Peace now!*

A siren cut through the Chicago night. There was a shrill whistle. Down below the voices cried out but distant like a muffled drum.

The phone rang. Emory went to the end table and picked it up.

—Hello?

No response. In-house? No; again the silent whoosh of a long distance call. It took more than influence to put through a phone call. The Vice President had a Secret Service security phone, but all others had to ring the switchboard.

—Hello?

A low provocative laughter came over the airwaves.

Emory paled. Was it a crank? Was it an intriguer—political intimidation? He knew he was seen by many as a dangerous liberal: cooling his act for the nonce, but a potential critic of the first order, a voice and what a voice.

So another mysterious call broke the communications blockade. But how? Was it intentional? A wrong number?

That laughter shook him. Only the devil got through on these overtapped and squealy phone lines.

Joey stood lost in thought. He was so exhausted—asleep on his feet? He came from the jungles of Southeast Asia to this plush suite high in a skyscraper. Still in camouflage, with a hard armored look to his features, he looked just landed from Mars.

Emory hung up. He crossed the room and from the window looked out over Michigan Avenue at the dark trees, Grant Park controlled by National Guard. His gaze soared away toward Lake Shore Drive.

Chants rose on the night air. Down there the thousands of demonstrators thought they could change the world with their decibel level. The cops herded them north into Congress Street.

—*Stop the war! Bring home the troops!*

—*Hey! Hey! L-B-J!*

—*Ho! Ho! Ho! Ho! Ho!*

But above it all came the sound of a powerful loudspeaker. It was the same truck with bright lights which roamed the city's streets like a barker for the tourist trade. But then it turned into a thrower of tear gas canisters.

—'. . . *Chicago with its Union Stockyards to the south in a cloud of stink from the animal slaughter, bloodrot and entrails . . . Chicago hog butcher of the world, tool maker, and wheat stacker . . . the nation's freight handler. Chicago city of gangsters and illegal pleasures, mythic brawlers, Chicago of the burly shoulders and calloused hands . . .'*

Chapter Fourteen

I

Joey walked.

In the hotel room he had fainted and, on waking in the pre-dawn silence, found himself sprawled on a couch. He sat up rubbing sleep from his eyes and then went out quietly.

Now he walked along empty streets under the twilit sky at sunrise. He took Michigan Avenue out of the city.

Past 35th Street on the right stood Comiskey Park. He looked at it, like a huge toy, and images of boyhood came in his mind—the leaky wadding of his first fielder's mitt, the baseball cards he flipped in the schoolyard: it's a leaner, I win! He thought of short-cuts along the brook in Spring Glen after his day at the Grammar School; and autographed baseballs that went lopsided when you used them; and riding his bicycle as a boy: how he and his friends attached a playing card with a clothespin to the frame so it would sound like a motor in the spokes. There was a late summer excitement in the radio announcer's keen voice and then a one-game playoff for the Pennant.

For a moment Joey Gilbert stood there before the silent stadium, feeling nostalgia, and then walked on.

By Washington Park a siren ululated as Chicago sent out troops for the new day's street clashes, and protesters singing 'We Shall Overcome'.

So he quickened his steps: like Vietnamese when they fled before the armored cavalry's entry into a ville.

Walk, walk. Highway 57, Kankakee . . . And then he heard the birds, their chirp-chirp in the dawn trees.

The sun poured forth its long rays. A pearly glitter spread across meadows and fields where the shadows were in retreat.

II

Why so sad? No need! He would find her, yes—and suddenly he felt hope in the glorious daybreak of America. He glanced behind him and saw Chicago, still too close for his liking. He seemed to see the pug jaw and entrenched look of his father's old-boy Candidate. Like a wild beast in a three-piece suit the 'Warrior of Joy' came out of the Party machinery's back room as Convention scenes were mixed with street fighting on TV. The peace candidate, the fresh 'Youth Candidate' had no chance to win Presidential nomination in the world's oldest Party. Delegates got brokered wholesale despite a few challenges to old-line Party corruption, and end of the 'unit rule' by roll call . . .

A warm southerly breeze stirred from the river. It was the big Mississippi out there across the fields. Joey's gut rumbled with hunger.

Still right behind him there was Chicago and the war—too close. See how in public life and private the old usurps the new? See how the past gets its bloody hands on the present? Long, long ago this story began, Joey thought, as he walked along. Did the Puritans who came here in ships decide the future when they made war against the tribes, and drove out the land's true children in a whirlwind?

Sunlight shot forth from an aspen grove. Warm rays caressed the delicate poplar trunks and green-gold leaves. Why? Why did it happen that way? Was it land greed? Or their hearts were not pious but criminal? Joey thought of the stories we heard in grade school: how the Indians helped the pilgrims through those first rough winters. They taught them how to survive. Then what was their thanks?

Now bees buzzed busily among the roadside flowers as Joey Gilbert made his way. The bees, the birds, the soft breeze were a hopeful chorus as he strode on past with long strides. He had a ways to go. And he thought: Was it our arrogance that caused the fall of America? Hubris? What curse haunts the nation and waits, waits to avenge a crime long ago, as though foretold in prophetic stone?

In the summer heat there were midges pillared over an outgrown limb by the road shoulder. They were feeding.

Joey walked. He tried to figure out his sense of guilt, of bloody hands, like a Sphinx's riddle.

III

A truck driver took him into a small town south of Urbana where he went in a greasy spoon. Here's what he ate: three eggs over light, double order of bacon, two pancakes soaked in syrup and butter, side o' hash browns, toast with marmelade, glazed doughnut, orange juice, coffee, toothpick; slice of lemon meringue pie for the road. Those were sweet, bland things he missed while overseas, in the bush. But he threw up by the curb a mile down the road.

He paused along the main street to look at shopwindows, in the land of the great PX, and think what he might buy Carlyne. He saw townsfolk looking bland like his breakfast—so overweight compared to Vietnamese villagers.

They watched him pass by. Old and young stared at the big, wiry G.I., lean, hairy, strolling through town without a duffel bag. They knew his kind from combat footage of Tet and Hué City and Khe Sanh on the nightly news.

He walked out into the countryside. With a yearning he felt the purity of nature as he never had before: as if it could cleanse the layers of filth he had on him.

In these hours he felt such a guilt and a gut-wrenching suspicion. In Berkeley his brother had wanted to help and give encouragement, but the effect was to make things worse and increase that suspicion. And why had his father's attempts to calm him

down stirred such an anguish? He only wanted to get away from
Emory and out of Chicago as soon as he could.

Both tried to help and make things better, but they had the opposite effect.

Along the road he hiked hour after hour and kept thumb out
with his back to the cars. So nobody pulled over. The tall peaceful trees bordering the highway on both sides with a faint breeze
in the summits; the August heat and blue languid sky sent his
thoughts back to baseball and boyhood days. The serenity of nature soothed his mind, and he had a rare moment of philosophiz-
ing: there must be laws in the sky which would work better than
those we have here if we could only know them . . .

Joey strode south into the vast noontime of America, and the
signs read Humboldt, Mattoon, Aetna where he stopped in a luncheonette after his easy hump on the road shoulder.

—Menu, sir?

Rangy, and strange, he stood in the homey place with its fan
and soda fountain, pie and cake racks, counter with stools, a few
tables. The young waitress met his dark stare; she saw the black
curly hair grown over his nape, and seemed to dream a moment.
Well, he wasn't a boy any longer on a hitch back to college in the
last days of summer. And he wasn't a ballplayer anymore. But he
still liked a root beer float, and the baddest LURP in the valley
blew bubbles in his ice cream soda glass. Then he licked the foam
and bent the two straws inside, and stood up with a burp.

IV

The day wore on as he trekked and got a few short hops.

Nature gave way to business routes with their bright billboards.
Ads littered the roads. Around Effingham, Salem, Centralia, it
was a mishmash of national chains. Was it like this before he went
away? . . . The open road was one long display of fast food auto
parts furniture gallery warehouse carpets electronic appliances
pools TV & Radio real estate hardware drugs motel storage auto-
mobile showroom gas self-service trailers shoes liquor cigarettes
plywoods Baby's World adult movies discount store musical in-

struments news center plants gardens sprinklers wholesale outlet office supplies ice cream model homes Bibles religious goods repairs everything must go fast food fast food fast food.

V

—Where?

—Alabama.

—So far!—The driver laughed peering across the front seat at him.—I'll take you to Cairo.

In her early thirties, she was a buyer for a Chicago department store. He was a soldier back from the war.

It was nightfall when they slowed in the waterside town where the Mississippi and Ohio River come together.

—I'll make dinner. You wash up.

After they ate he dozed off on the couch. Gently she shook his shoulder: he startled awake.

She drew back with a frown, then a smile.

—Undress in the bedroom if you like, and shower.

—I'm afraid my wife . . .

He gestured.

—She'd know?

—No, but I would.

—Lucky girl. No wonder she's faithful. Waiting for you at home.

He lowered his gaze:

—I'll clear out if you want.

She laughed.

—Hold your horses. I'll bring sheets for the sofa, but have a wash.

—Naw.

—Don't you itch?

—I'm used to it.

Before daybreak he rose and went out.

VI

In Western Kentucky he walked and hitched the local roads south: 51 through Bardwell, Crutchfield . . . into Tennessee.

—Ride, soldier?

Down here he hardly had to ask. A farmer stopped for him in midafternoon on Idlewild's main street where for lunch he had a triple-decker with the works plus strawberry float, extra whipped cream. Candy bars for the road.

—Thanks.

—Ahll' tekyu' furz' Jacksn.

In the farm truck a day game came over the radio. Pirates in St. Louis.

—Where yih' headed, soldier? T' home?

—Hope so.

—Where yih fum?

Joey told him and then listened to the radio and watched tall trees go by. It was a clear hot August afternoon. Home half of the fourth in St. Louis.

—Cards in first place? he asked.

—Yop. Deetrought in the Murkn.

—So people still like baseball?

—Sheee.

South of Jackson he walked ten miles far as Pinson then caught a ride into Eastview where he went in a restaurant and ordered most of the menu. As night fell Joey crossed the state line into Mississippi on foot. It was quiet out there. The traffic thinned to a few cars and trucks along this Route 45 stretch between Jackson and Corinth. A long van passed on the twilit highway with a whine of tires. Nobody would stop for him now.

So he left the road and went down a bank. He crossed some grassland to a treeline. The horizon was a reddish gold as he went in the forest and set up camp. He took off his boots to mute the crunch of pine needles, and moved among the trees with ears and nostrils honed. His steps were alert for traps. His sharp eyes pierced the gloaming. Dig a foxhole? Defensible perimeter? No entrenchment tool, Sir. Flat rock? Slat of bark?

Into the early hours he sat against a tree trunk and kept watch. He heard sounds. He thought: I'm back, but contaminated, like a death taint. Rub me the wrong way and I could hurt you, slug a cop. Why me? Why did I make it and not . . .?

The watches of the night passed. He sat against a tree somewhere. Later sleep came to relieve him from his post. But for a long time, late at night in the Mississippi wilds by a highway where long vans whined into the distance, he bowed his head on his arms and wanted to cry for the men in his unit.

VII

Toward dawn there were raindrops dripping down his neck. In the first light he got up and walked into Corinth where a diner had buckwheat cakes.

On the highway he went along south toward Booneville and always south. Between Tupelo and Amory he crossed Tombigbee River and thought of the Navajo who got back from his tour to reservation life in Tuba City.

Joey caught short rides on Route 45—Aberdeen, Columbus, Meridian—and walked through the sultry overcast day. That evening found him in Chunchula where he asked at a gas station for directions.

VIII

In late morning he came to Atmore, Alabama, on foot after a hop from Mobile to the turnoff for Perdido.

He looked in a phone book and then asked on the sidewalk:

—You know Emmet Bufillu?

—Ah know 'im.

—Can you tell me where he lives?

—They place offna' Freemanville Pike.

—How far?

—Three-faw mahl.

Then he walked a dirt road down an incline through the trees. He came to a cabin with a front porch and, quietly, took the front steps and peered in. A heavyset black man snoozed with his head tilted in a wheelchair. Midday light sifted with lint past a window curtain into the dim interior. In the next room a woman stood in a white blouse and straight skirt despite the heat. She worked at the counter. About the place there were trees hung with Spanish moss. There was the cereal scent of fields beneath the August sun.

The soldier knocked softly on the screen door.

The woman turned and said in a low voice:

—Yes?

—I'm Joey Gilbert. We served together over there. Should I come back later?

She looked at him, and a tear was in her eye. So Bufillu had told her. This one listened when the man tried to get it out. She opened the door:

—I know you.

She put a hand on her husband's shoulder. Bufillu looked softer, bulkier where he dozed in the light of the room like a cupboard.

On the wall a clock ticked, ticked.

—Emmet?

He gave a little shiver in the shoulders. He lifted his head, opening his eyes on her; then saw the visitor, and a low laugh, like slow waves, was going through him.

Joey stepped forward, leaned, and embraced his partner of a hundred battles in the Central Highlands of Vietnam.

IX

—Had your old ass televised with a piece on your dad in Chicago. They showed that opposite field homer you hit off the scoreboard in New York. They like to replay it like Mays' catch on Vic Wertz. Here is World Serious Gilbert, sports fans. Had him dead as lead, but he's back!

Bufillu was happy. The way his wife looked at him! Maybe it was some time since he laughed.

Awhile later Joey stared down at smothered chicken, black-eyed peas and stewed cabbage, honeyed yams, cornpone and hush puppies. It was the good stuff set before them by a woman with a sense of occasion.

—You'll play. Sure you will. Rest up a spell.

—Naw. Since Travis I feel strung out, you know: can't get into it. Can't find my coordinates and relax. I'm afraid of bad dreams if I fall asleep. And at a pin's drop my mind goes haywire.

—You too.

—Movement! Up ahead there! Incoming! Skol! . . . No, sir. I'm not worth shit here. I'd almost go back.

Bufillu laughed low:

—Me three. But I got no say in it. Ambush patrol kinda' hard for a paraplegic.

Joey had a lump in his throat, but he took a bite. He picked at the rich spread and shook his head:

—Welcome home. They took me and trained me and made me good for one thing. Now I'm crazy as hell. How could I play third base when my nerves are shot? On a dime I feel like I'll hurt some of these good civilized folk.

—They're more violent than we are.

—That's an affirmative. I know it's childish, but I keep feeling people want to trick or hurt me. I think my brother and my dad know more about my wife than I do: like they called her a nickname but I stand on ceremony. Well, what the hell, if I can't find her then I'll go to the woods and live in a cabin. Buy a piano and read Plutarch's *Lives.*

—She'll find you.

—Will she? What if she does? Hello, Honey, or should I say Frankenstein?

—Shit—said Bufillu, looking down.

For a moment they sat in silence. Each took a bite of the rich food. Outside the window birds chirped in the bright afternoon. It felt like Sunday dinner.

—Partner, they treat you okay at least?

—I guess. Some don't get diddly out of the VA. Come home sick from the toxic chemicals and want to sue the Government. Good luck. Go peddle it elsewhere. We catch hell, we fight for their rich white asses, 'scuse, and they don't want to hear it. That hurts: ingratitude, tricksters. Say what? I gave 'em my life in Southeast Asia but I still don't sit next to them. Bus, school, movie theater, lunch counter, water fountain, toilets round Atmore: law or no law, they separate. And the big fools call me boy. If a man wants his rights he's got to fight here in these streets and the devil take The Nam.—Bufillu paused for breath and made himself chew a little and swallow.—Nora, bring this soldier a cold beer, would you? I think we both want to drink, not eat. You know he came a long way from Bang Me Thwap to Freemansville and he worked up a thirst. Oh, man, it feels so drat good to see your bad ass and talk a spell. It's hard as hell to get this stuff out. She's heard her fill of it.

—My brother, my dad didn't ask. They think they know.

—Why not stick around? Stay a week. I know what: you live here with us, and we'll build a cabin out back with a piano. Then you can eat this way everyday. Be alone for weeks if you want.

—I could hunt the woods.

—Sure! Hey, anybody seen Joey? Nope, ain' seed de po' dude letlih' . . . ha ha! Chreee', you know, I still hain' digested all dat mess yet 'bout Mistuh Peedee 'n ol' Izar' 'n Ringworm 'n de res', Thingum 'n all, short-time Vane and Slidell and Ben Bolt and Mosey Rink and Skiball. What a mess! Kid Ringwood played some ball over in your state there, used to say.

—He played.

—I think about them, how they died. All day to sit here and think. What a life. They bought the farm cash down, but I sit here month after month paying the mortgage. Sit and stew in my juice. A lot of anger about how I got used. Thattaway, troop, sick 'em! Grease Charlie before he greases you. Hey, that's life. But is it? I learned the hard way, too late. Now an organizer came by here one afternoon with a northern accent like yours and he told me to ride my wheelchair right up to the polls and vote proudly 'cause this is my country too. Well I laughed in his smiley face and waved him away.

—I get dreams.

—Do you? Me too. Nightmares. I could go crazy. That other one, I always dis'member his name, maybe I don't want to. College kid used to converse with the birds in Latin, talking about the trees.

—I know.

—Or Loseby's sour puss when he said with a bow to Miss Bouncing Betty: Dear, care to fox trot? Is this the Cotillion? Whap! Ow! Stepped on my foot, clumsy! Or I see Slidell's ugly mug when the punji slit up his ribs. Gee, that tickles. Well, where the hell . . . ah, it was bridge duty that day in Phu Bai, remember? Horse Shue bought his ticket on the Freedom Bird at freight rate. (Sigh.) I wish somebody could please tell me why we were sent to Vietnam. Can you?

—No.

—Honey—Bufillu hardly raised his voice between rooms—please bring the troop another beer.

—No, really, I—

—What the hell. I got a lifetime to wonder why. But didn't those buggers in D.C. just set us up? I think they did! Processed and shipped us like so much beef.

—Ground chuck.

Bufillu shook his head and swayed a bit in the wheelchair.

—Booooelshit! But the nuttiest thing of all is a mood comes over me and I think: hey, I'd like to go back someday. Just a visit, type thing.

X

Time flew once they got started. In a minute it was evening. And through the trees out beyond the long fields the sun set in a red pool.

Emmet's wife brought a tray on the porch, gin and ice shaker, two glasses. The two men sat in the darkness slapping mosquitoes and listening to bugs dive through the quiet summer night. Mimosa round the house gave a feathery rustle.

—Seems a lifetime ago.

—A week.

—Crap'll never end.

—Just began.

—Times when I feel like I need help with it.

—Hell.

In a big rush so much had happened and it filled a man with rage. The whole thing was damned unfair. Now they stared at the dark trees and heard the woman's breath like a placid sea breeze asleep inside. Their minds were buzzing with Tu Do pedicabs and ships on Saigon River and the Majestic Hotel lobby and a lot of voices they wouldn't hear again. Officers, villagers, Hanoi Hannah, Truong Son range blue in the night.

—Go lie down awhile.

—I can't sleep.

—Me neither.

There were so many things, all the details—first hours in country, three weeks of bridge duty before assignment to a Central
Highlands probe unit. It was FNG time for two naive boonierats
saddled with gear for a thirty-klik hump from ridge to ridge. If
Six gave the order then that was that: time to take your shit for
the day, or sacrifice your life for America. Hop to. And then came
stand-down time at Nha Trang with Chi-Bar and Milt Luna beer
in one hand prime steak in the other: goofy smiles, white sands,
emerald South China Sea. There was Ben Bolt's story that day:
You want head? said a partygoer; then I'll tell you the address, *it's
yours.* And they saw the headless trunk of Ben Bolt stalk forward
three, four stiff steps and fall . . .

In the hot night fifty miles from Pensacola and the Gulf it made
them shiver to think of Blair, the botany major, that morning before Xo Man. And a few hours later they walked into the hamlet. Boom, a massacre. And Emmet Bufillu saved Joey Gilbert's
life and got his back burned. Barroomalooom! Christ. Welts still
there: he could feel 'em. And Tombigbee waited on the road out
of town, and said: Good work, men, those were friendlies you
greased. And a ways down the road they came on the botany student—but why talk about it? . . . Xo Man, pardner.

Then past mid tour there was the jeep foray into Saigon for
Tet as Six gave them 48 hours of reward. Big market and busy
streets after months in the bush. And Joey's call Stateside and
the Caravelle terrace high above the South Vietnamese capital.
Opium den. Tet night. VC brothel: Bufillu in his one weak moment, he said, lost the ability to walk and feel waist down. Joey
saved Emmet's life, turn about fair play, but for what? Well it's the
thought that counts, pardner.

They remembered FNGs and trail snipers and VC attacks at
the perimeter. Stubborn men those Viet Cong. Respect for the
little buggers. Then Bufillu's time in Japan and trip home. Then
RevDev, Top Drawber. A troop's brains like shad roe on Joey's
boots, in the minefield . . . Joey's AWOL flight from out near the
Cambodian border into Saigon.

Their words slurred.

—Can bo.

—Fuckemup!

ARVN woman in the hootch: in her blood, with her children.

One moved a sticklike arm, vaguely; the pain wasn't quite over, of a brief little life.

Cassava roots on a table. Mountain rice in a tin. Sprig of ginger, bundled pumpkin leaves.

—I see them. Keep coming back: sort of alive, glowing at me, trying to tell me a thing or two. I can't get over it: wake up at night and there they are, I feel alone in the universe.

—Torched 'em.

—Ball game.

Medic Artus laughed wildly as he got dusted off strapped to a stretcher: heal thyself! And Manito E-4 Loseby villages rivers Donmai Vaicos mountains Vietnamese courtesy tank warfare Wisembroder on the burr. Temples pagodas eastern cordillera diarrhea gooners 118° afternoons draw fire from next ridgeline ring-knockers Pricecroft leeches mosquitoes (slap) Skol's death. Oakleigh his replacement spiders green tracers Mark Robidou Noup Mister Quoc Ha Mai ambush at two streams junction. Tu Sang Dzit Dzeun Dzui Eay Tao Bronco aerial observer non-hackers Tiger Beer on the Romeo Third Herd body counts bodies. Gungi. Farty-far O-Club Brink Oki jing. Sau fruit. *Fires burn in the mountains South wind perfume of sandalwood* . . . Bai Nui . . . ox-drawn cart from provincial market . . . filed teeth montagnard loincloths . . . hu tien shops . . . . . . torch 'em . . . . . . torch . . . . . . kid's tiny arm . . . . grasps . . . . 'buff, what the . . . .

Toward dawn they fell silent.

XI

In early afternoon the soldier sat up on the creaky cot, rubbed his face, and looked around. The small house or bungalow was quiet. Across the front room his partner napped in the wheelchair. Joey splashed his face at the sink and then ate a covered plate left out for him.

He paused to scrawl a few words with the Rock Castle address and then stood by the screen door when the big man stretched and bellowed a yawn. Mentally Joey was riding the highways north and east past Blue Ridge into Carolina.

Bufillu blinked and knew. He held out a meaty hand:

—Brother, good to see you.

—Likewise.

—Yeah, we needed to talk. I do hurt—he laughed and patted his chest—since I came back. Happy-go-lucky guy, All-State
tackle. Never thought I'd have to live it out like this. Can't hardly
talk about it. Did I depress you?

—Naw.

—Yeah I keep the thing inside, sort of choke on it. Maybe I
need help with it, type of thing.

There was a tremor in Bufillu's voice.

—With what?

—Oh . . . That woman you know, my wife, she's straight. She's
sound as an oak. A stick, as we say down here. Gone up the road
to get groceries for our supper. She gives me nothing but kindness, and the necessary, day and night. And she's got courage.
Most of 'em may not know it, or have it, but in the long run a man
loves that most in a woman: balls. Anyway it's half the battle,
cooped up in here.

Joey said:

—Sure.

Bufillu looked shook up.

—But . . . I got this sneaky thing in me, and . . . it's hard, I cain't
stand it.

Joey glanced from his friend out at the sunbaked trees, road
and dust. It was hot here, like a pressure cooker when there was
no breeze from the Gulf. In a minute, on the move, he'd have
relief.

Emmet's voice went a deeper tone:

—Sit here day in, day out, think of one thing.

—What's that?

—Not even these—he glimpsed his atrophied legs—healthy,
vigorous I'd still . . . I would . . .

He threw up a palm. Features screwed like a mask, he choked
over a word which wouldn't come out. There was fear in the si-
esta heat, in the sunlight outside the door.

—You'd?

—At times I hate . . . not the VC so much who did this to me
. . . as her. If there was no her, and no love . . . then free and easy,
I'd know my way.

The big man shook his head.

—Go on—said Joey, a squad leader again.

—I want to kill myself. End this. Yep. For her sake so she can start over. It's not too late.

—Fine idea.

—I'll grease my tykey ass! Got a .45 in there. Just gimme time, matter of days.

—Right on. I know your wife will agree. Why not do it on her birthday?

Bufillu bleated:

—No damn body can live like this! I won't stand for it! I tell you it's too blasted much! I'm afraid to fall asleep at night and disgusted to wake up. Rotten dreams! Can't even think of love like a man. And no kids, no children and grandchildren for us. Absolutely, positutely. Nam, you motherfucker! You stick in my craw! Week after week, month after month, carrying it around inside me. I tell you I can't stand it anymore! I lost my goddamned manhood, and for what? For what high shitass ideal did we zippo hootches? Goddamn Nam hits below the belt and now my whole life is turned into a sorry joke. And so I hate, you know, I hate the livelong day, and I see things too. My wife closes a cabinet and I almost jump outa' my wits. And I feel guilty, not only a victim but guilty about . . . what I did. And about her too and unable to make her happy anymore. And so I cry out, inside not out loud: help! Help me! I just can't make it anymore. Help! Help!

Bufillu frowned and bowed his head. The big shoulders shook. And he started crying, like a child.

XII

—I'm sorry, man. I put all this personal stuff on you. I'm too selfish! Go along, Jo, go on and find your wife.

—You been to see somebody about this?

Bufillu laughed low:

—You mean in Mobile? At the VA? Gov'ment fat cats: don't see it nohow. They just want us gone, out of the picture. We're losers: didn't you know that?

—How will your wife live?

—Well, that's it. There'll be insurance, and my pension to tide her over.

—Oh.

The paraplegic squirmed in anguish:

—I don't want to hurt her. I want to help her.

—You can't commit suicide and not hurt your wife.

—But there's no other way.

—Have you told her your idea? Have you talked it over?

—Huh? God, you can't do that.

—Why not? Oh, I see: you're like Six, you don't hold debates.

Bufillu's hard, quiet style once bolstered a squad. Now his voice flew up in a whine:

—Tell her that? Ha ha!

With a sigh Joey looked out the window. A woman walked along the dirt road with a grocery bag under each arm. The stark light cast its shadow beneath her steps.

—Here she comes. Tell her now, if you've got it in you.

—I . . . I still think of the day out there . . . over and over.

—What day?

—In the village.

—And?

—What I done, and what I shoulda' done.

—Shoulda'? What's shoulda'?

—Tombigbee walked away.

—Good for Tombigbee. Then what?

Bufillu gazed up at the squad leader through glazed eyes. His voice jerked with emotion:

—I saved you at least.

Joey nodded. And, as Nora's steps creaked on the front porch, said:

—So you did. Now we're going to tell her, sport.

XIII

He stayed another night. But after breakfast the next morning he said goodbye to Pfc. Bufillu. There was a look in his wife's eyes, as she shook Joey's hand, and then hugged him.

In the doorway he turned and stared back a moment.

—Thanks.

—Jo, any old time.

—I'll call you. Let you know when I find Carlyne.

—Okay. Y'all come back. Pay us a visit.

—Or you two come to my dad's farm. That would be good.

Bufillu laughed.

—Ha ha! That's a good one. You mean New York, don't you?
Nora never seen them bright lights.

—Naw—Joey shook his head—I'm done with that. A farmer
now, if I can find Carlyne.

—Sure, sure. Mild mannered sodbuster. Say, you know what?
Over there maybe we . . . maybe there was some reason.

—I no longer believe it.

—Me neither. But I mean to learn . . . the hard way, so that
someday . . . I can't explain it, type thing.

Joey thought about this a moment, and grinned. For an instant
he gave the hard intent grin of his baseball days, and then turned
away.

—So long, FNG-III.

—Hey, goodbye, brother.

Mrs. Bufillu looked at him wistfully as he ducked and went
out. Then the two of them were watching from the window when
he wheeled to wave back from the torrid sunlight.

They saw him walk on down the road toward his few miles'
jaunt to Highway 65 on the way to Greenville, Montgomery, Atlanta, then on through South Carolina.

XIV

In Pembroke, where Carlyne's people lived, the cluster of
stores needed paint pretty bad and had the air of a Wild West
movie set. Junctioned at the nation's longest stretch of straight
railroad track, the town sat amid farm country bordered by forest
and swamplands. The heat beat down on the wood structures,
and nothing moved unless it had to.

The train still stopped here: same old cars that brought bodies
of Robeson boys, many Cherokee, back from World War II. Today

as back then the mail bag hung on a pole by the low-eaved depot. Queen City Bus Line stopped at the drugstore on its way from Charlotte to Wilmington and the Carolina Coast.

There were a few high cheekboned women in frumpy dress, cover-uppish despite the heat of late summer. They mulled round the shed-like up town. Gray hazel eyes and coal-black hair in a head scarf or bandana: the Lumbee women stared at the stranger. Was he a Lowry? an Oxendine? Locklear or Dial? The Lumbee comes home when he can: from points north like Baltimore, or from the war. Thinks of home.

XV

Joey asked the way and walked out to 710 intersection over the bridge and past the old cemetery in the fields. There you see the Oxendines and Brooks, Deese, Cummings, Chavis and Jacobs in Lumbee family plots. All around is corn acreage, tobacco, soya, hay in big round bales. He went on down a dirt road through a thicket of trees a ways out there behind Burnt Swamp Baptist.

The trailer sat under pine and hickory trees. Barefoot kids stopped running around to look at the tall unshaven man in camouflage with mud-stained boots. Out back was a domain of cages filled with squeaks, squawks, flutters, barks, snorts. A few lean dogs went snooping about in a mist of fleas. At the trailer he knocked. A woman said:

—Ain't got no taxes!

It was Aunt Lovedy.

—Ma'am, I'm Joey. I'm Carlyne's husband. Have you seen her?

Lovedy stared at him a few seconds. And she had a frown, but it seemed she didn't mean to. Then she opened the door and hung on the verge of a hug—but with a look at him thought better about it.

—Why, Joey Gibbet! Ah, ah, ah! Rest my weary soul. Come in, yurker, I'll cut on the light. Li'l yurkers mummock up the place . . . chauld to have me a visitor. Come, Jo, come in, boy—yo' ar'n! Cup o' ellick?

—Huh?

Right off she had to send for the kin, a bate of 'em, as she said, everwho. Them cooters slicked spiders 'n fixed chicken bog 'n paysta, cracklins, middlin' meat 'n hog jowls 'n deep fried bream 'n pumpkin seed fish from the river; collards, corn and squash dishes; pone o' oven fresh lightbread and biscuits; grits, slab o' whiteside, plenty cayenne pepper and homemade butter and molasses. Then sweetnins.

Lovedy was in such a flurry she hardly had time to talk to him.

—Aunt, did you see Carlyne this year?

—Yeah, she were here in the spring.

—Was she! And how did she look? Was she happy? Was she unhappy?

—Happy enough I guess.

—But did she have enough money? She just ran away from my father's house without a word, and I don't know why.

Seemed like Aunt Lovedy didn't want to get into it. He saw she looked thoughtful at moments as if she knew something he didn't know: something she didn't want to tell him.

—Pleas'suh! No pearly servins fer Lynne's Jo—him hongry! Some'un get'm a tower.

There was plenty of talk. At table the talk flowed, but it was about Carlyne's mother and Vick, the judge, who was not a bad white but should of married her.

—Selva Locklear she born with a veil, she'n see all kind of haints (ghosts) in her day. And her husband were one on'm.

—Ma'am, where was Carlyne living when you saw her?

—Well, Jo, when she came here in January she was just visitin'. Mentioned Durham . . . maybe not sure yet.

—January! She came here in January? . . . Why, Aunt, why did she leave the Rock Castle?

—Oh, I don't know 'bout that, Jo. Have to ask her.

But Aunt Lovedy's look then seemed to tell another story. The tear in her eye was not only for faroff years when Selva and her daughter came home to Pembroke in the summer and also spent a week with kin in Lumberton; and oh Carlyne was such a bright girl with her lake blue eyes. But later, after Selva died, she had the case in court and was taken away from her own. Then there were hard years for a child in the La Grange orphanage. But she made it to college, and she was quite the coed: had her picture in the Lumberton papers. She was the first Lumbee to go to that school.

And Selva so proud of her if she'd lived: to see Carlyne married to a Major League baseball player.

—I hope 'm clare, said Lovedy, I hep'd fotch up the poor creeter, and say now she sorry in the world? Gaumed up? Munked? Sech a jubous l'il cooter, I swanny, pyert yurker, sharp'un. Pure arnt miss her since the shake, damn skippy. You too, pappy sack?

—But was she okay, Lovedy? Was she meaning to work when you saw her, or what?

—She didn't say about work.

—What was she doing? What were her plans? She went away from my dad's house, and I don't know why, or where.

The look Aunt Lovedy gave him then—Joey could only guess what it meant, but it wasn't good.

—Don't know, Jo.

—Did she talk about me? Us? I saw her not long before you did, in Bangkok, and then . . . January, you say, January! But my dad said she left the Rock Castle in February . . . Now why? Which is it?

Joey looked at her. His mind was in a swirl, but Lovedy just gave it another flurry of Lumbee talk which he couldn't catch. A dozen friendly faces, Daystar and the others, smiled at him. 'Yo' ar'n!' So it didn't seem like his fault: not for them at least. But he, an honorary son of the Lumbee, had a time trying to decipher what they said.

—Them kyarn Kinston folk so in the pines, they indexed 'er'nhertence everhow, orta' notta' donit. Get shet o' the sow cat, gyarb! Selva'n me loved the cooter. We sat on'm pizer while she run barefoot among the young'uns, ol' pine board housen over'n Scuffletown yearsgo. Wail, Selva's haint cyum tahther night toten everwho in 'a woodses 'n pocosins, swanny, hyar out back, ol' gyps howl! Headnes solum, liketa die!

The kinfolk looked on smiling and having a right good old time as they told their stories. Joey looked at them, thoughtful. Yes, she had been here 'since the shake'; but maybe it hurt to see her mother's folks, and she didn't stay. January . . . already in January and Emory had said February . . . Well, she didn't stay here and wait for her husband to come home. Why not? What was she afraid of? Maybe there was just nothing for her to do here. So she went out on her own. To Durham? To find work? She had their bank book for the joint account: she could take out all the money she wanted. Had she? No—she was so stubborn. At least not when he saw her in Bangkok, and probably not after she got home either and ran away from the Rock Castle for some reason nobody seemed to know. Or maybe all knew it except him, the poor husband. Maybe he was the last one to know, and find a key to this mystery.

XVI

Early next morning he walked out of Aunt Lovedy's trailer after the wisp-haired old woman's hug and her goodbye.

—Whew! You need a bath, pappy jack.

—I'll go swim in the river.

—Well y'all bring my niece over here.

—If I can find her, Aunt, I will.

—I want to see her again hope 'm clare 'fore I join'm haints in'a woodses yonder.

She told him the way to the country road where Carlyne and he went the day they came here on his motorcycle from college. It's 1½ miles south of Wagram, the Riverton swimming hole. Fine thing as a kid, said Daystar, to swim in the cool dark water. But look out—current's swift in places, deep down.

After the hike Joey peeled his filthy fatigues and slid like a lizard down the ditchbank clumped with wild blackberries. He went in the pure cold water; took a swallow, gargled, spumed like a fountain. He recalled her taunts that day: how there were rattlers with a deadly stinger in the tail, sort of pasty color on top . . . and pit vipers. Cotton mouth or copperbelly mocassins'll bite ya', watch out! Quietly the tannin-brown Lumbee flowed on, and he swam across it as they had that day during their courtship when she took his hand and led him in the pure, cold stream. On the far bank he stretched and blinked in warm sunlight and listened to martins swarming the river for their breakfast of bugs.

The water ran strong beneath canopied branches of the cypress, the pine and live oak. From Drowning Creek up round Samarcand, Eagle Springs, Emery in Moore County, the river made its way southwestward, swift and treacherous in places as it got in stride and became Pee Dee on its way past the old plantations and the alligators to empty in ocean waters off the South Carolina coast.

Here they had courted together, and here that afternoon she had seemed to test his depths. She told him of the Lumbee summers of her girlhood: how she helped kill and dress hogs and pulled fodder and shucked corn and cropped tobacco in July and August, a hot job, and drove to market with the farm produce; how she held up a lantern for adults to cut, split, stack wood with the crosscut saws. There were powwows in the long house and barn raisings and quilting parties. And here by this stream she told him of her people's history: the Croatan struggles, and Henry Berry Lowry's swamp campaign, and his wife named Rhoda Strong who was the queen of Scuffletown.

Joey felt such a sadness, the pang of his loss, when he thought back on that day spent here by the river at close of his college career. They were happy together . . . High above the treetops a lone cloud drifted. For awhile he lay back and studied the blue serenity of the summer sky. Then he rose on an elbow to gaze at tropical ferns along the silent current. He felt clean and refreshed from his night's sleep and this swim in the river. His war was over now . . . but was it?

He stayed there by the river for a few hours till the heat of midmorning was beating down. There was a gold light, a hue of tobacco fields inland from the Carolina coastline, and the Lumbee current was a deep reddish-brown like a woman's hair. He seemed to see his girlish fiancée before him with her blouse drenched through and her hair fallen in heavy tresses on her shoulder.

Upstream some kids fished from a flat-bottom juniper boat the way they did a hundred years ago in the time of Henry Berry.

XVII

At Pembroke depot he caught the 1:20 train and in late afternoon walked the main street of Kinston where Carlyne grew up. There were more squat trade buildings with frittered moldings side by side with a Jeffersonian pile here and there, bank, town hall and courthouse. Downtown life had died like his father's town across the state except for a few lawyers' shingles.

The southern town baked in the dog day heat.

And Judge Vick's old place? Up there on Park Avenue: the white affair with columns and a balcony above the front entry. Tall trees, long green slope of a lawn, like a plantation manor—can't miss it. Far end of McLwean from Shine Street Cemetery where the Judge has a headstone; but his earthly remains were over in the next county.

Hon. Fitzhugh Foster Vick
1887–1953

She wouldn't have come back here.

He moved on: down Vernon Avenue past the outskirts and highway bypass. Joey walked past tobacco fields beneath the stars. He had night in his nostrils and the bright leaf aroma from Carlyne's childhood.

At the La Grange turnoff he looked for a place to lie down a few hours.

Route 70 West went through Goldsboro on its way toward Durham.

XVIII

Along the campus walkways a few students lingered in shirt sleeves as a wild man in combat fatigues strode by. Then his boots crunched under tall pines on the path to the baseball diamond. He looked out from the grassy bank where she sat that day he first laid eyes on her.

Play ball again? No way. But he heard the crack of a bat and a roar like music from childhood. The radio announcer was an excited boy too as pennant fever took over the nation. He heard the noisy stands and taunts and clapping hands. Hawn' you babe! Fire 'er in there 'atta kid thatta' way you sweet righthanduh! At the game in St. Louis he heard over the radio the other day, hitchhiking, there were vendors in the aisles and an airplane high in the afternoon sky with its bit of distant thunder. C'mon, ya' bumyuh! Clumsy oaf-yuh!

Joey looked over the grass and base paths of his college action.

There was a tall hedge barrier round the outfield: 330 in left, 410 in straightaway center. There was a scoreboard down the line in right.

Play again? Let her find you, said Bufillu.

How? Nerves shot.

He vaulted the low brick divider and walked out past the on-deck circle, first base line, pitcher's mound to his post at third.

Joey spit on his rough palm. He shook out his fingers and wrists and scuffed the dust a little; sort of rocked on his muscular back and legs, side to side; squinted; bent forward for the next pitch.

XIX

Then he trudged the downtown streets and looked for a clue, a trace of her. She wasn't in view, but her spirit haunted the hot, hot Durham evening with its tobacco factory scent along East Main to Five Points even seedier now with its Harvey's Restaurant, S.H. Kress 5 & 10, Criterion Theater.

Then next day outside the College Shoppe near East Campus he ran into a sorority sister of Carlyne's now a teacher in grade school.

She looked at him: the grime.

—Yes, I saw her.

—You did? When?

—It was . . . mid-May I guess.

—And? Tell me—

—We said hi.

—But what else? Was she back to her studies? Was she in grad school?

—N-no. Joey, what's it about? What gave with you two?

—She went away. She was at my dad's house waiting till I came back from the war. But she left there without a word. It's a mystery.

—A mystery? With an infant child on her hands?

—What?!

Joey was like a gun going off. He gaped at his wife's friend.

—She . . . she was pregnant, big—

—In May?

—Must've given birth by now.

—Carlyne with child and I didn't know . . . Was she okay? Was she alone? Did she have enough money? Was she working?

—The day I met her along Gregson she looked okay. She was alone. I don't think working.

—Then how did she live? What were her plans? I mean what was she doing?

—I don't know, Joey. We didn't talk but a minute.

—Where was she living?

—She did tell me that: over there on Lamonde behind East Campus.

—What number: do you know?

—In the big place students rent rooms in, next to the duplex.

XX

A child! So Carlyne had a child from the time together in Bangkok—*their* child! Big in May? 4½ months, midterm? Well, possible, he guessed . . . A baby: that sealed it. Oh! he didn't blame her for anything; he only wanted to serve her! Now he would start to farm his dad's acreage after all, and that was a feasible plan. Those dark-loamed fields from the Rock Castle out to the river had lain fallow for decades and so now they should produce well.

But was that why she left? Because she was pregnant? She didn't want to get in the way of others? . . . No, that didn't sound right: if she left in January. Why then?

After the sorority sister went her way he stood in a daze and wondered what to do. Go to Lamonde: maybe she's still there. Ah! Why was he standing around dawdling?

So to Lamonde Avenue behind East Campus he ran, ran.

The landlady was on the porch sweeping.

—Ma'am, have you seen Carlyne Gilbert?

—Who? Nobody by that name here.

He described her. And the landlady said to him:

—You a customer?

He stood a moment blinking in the bright sunshine, and then said:

—I'm her husband.

She looked him over.

—If that's so then I don't know what kind of husband: leaving a woman to have her baby all by herself.

—So she had it! I was away in Vietnam, Ma'am, but I'm back now. When did she have the baby? When? It must have been early.

—June.

—In June! In June?! That couldn't be.

—That could be, said the landlady, and a few other things besides.

—Well is she here? Did she step out?

—No, she's not here anymore.

—Where'd she go? Do you know?

—No.

—Look, I'll pay if you can tell me where she went. I've got money.

He showed her.

—I wish I could tell you. I need money what with taxes and repairs on this old place. But I don't know.

—Well when did she leave?

—In mid-July.

—Was she alone?

—Y-yes.

—Did she owe you anything then?

The woman paused, and said:

—Two months' rent.

XXI

—Now what? Now where? June!!! . . . No, that can't be. But it *is*. So something did happen at the Rock Castle. Let's see: that puts it . . . nine months before, back in September. Yes, she was with them by then. Wait, could it have been us . . . before I shipped for Vietnam? Then ten months, overdue . . .? It depends on the date: could be less than ten. So I need to know the exact date . . . hm, County Clerk's! And then to the hospital to find out if it was overdue, or else premature, from Bangkok! . . . But so premature?

If she was alone, unhappy, broke, under stress . . . oh! oh! My wife in despair.

He stood on the street talking to himself.

Then he turned and started walking toward Five Points. He went briskly, but this time he didn't run.

The County Health Department is on Main Street by the old Courthouse, the county seat. There he asked for a photocopy of his child's birth certificate.

—Name?

The clerk, a blondish woman who looked like she spent her life in curlers, stared up at the big man in combat fatigues.

—I don't know. Gilbert.

—You don't know?

—No, I don't know the first name, but it's my child, and my wife Carlyne Gilbert's. Maybe you could look up Gilbert, and Locklear, her maiden name.

—When was the child born?

—Recent birth: in June.

—So . . . June of this year?

—Yes.

Ten minutes later she was able to tell him: no child on record by the name of Gilbert or Locklear born in June 1968.

—You're sure?

—I am, Sir. But why not ask your wife about it? Are you separated?

—Yes . . . no . . . I don't know.

—Well then while you're at it you can ask that too.

—But . . . for the date, Ma'am . . . would there be a way to falsify it?

The fortyish clerk looked a bit like a potted hydrangea, not watered enough.

—Why do that?

She turned back to her papers.

At another desk sat a second employee: a younger man all eyes for the soldier in dirty fatigues. He had ants in his pants to get a word in. From across the room he said:

—A mother must show proof of pregnancy.

—I see. What sort?

The woman clerk frowned, but the other said:

—Her affadavit, signature, is enough. She has to show proof of residency in Durham County at the time, and her intent to stay

here. Any piece of mail with her name on it will do, or a statement
from a neighbor or landlady. Uh—

—Uh?

—Well you should bring a 'person in attendance' at the birth,
but in practice we take Mommy's word.

Joey looked around. Was this a help? He wanted to get back
out there: on the trail.

—Her word.

—No problem. Up to a year she can come in. And it's okay if
she makes a mistake: the Court won't see it as an illegality.

—I don't understand. So a birth certificate could be faked.
Maybe it's invalid?

—In what sense?

—If the date is wrong.

—As I said, we don't do any verification. We like for them to
bring in somebody, a witness, and most mothers do. But if she
doesn't then it won't raise a red enough flag for us to go out and
investigate.

—I see.

Joey looked down.

The clerk shrugged:

—She just comes in and says: ten months ago I had a baby. She
can be off by two, three, even five months. We issue a birth certificate and file it with the County Registrar of Deeds. Our copy we
destroy after a couple years, but Vital Records, the estate office in
Raleigh and center for such things, also gets a copy. So it's in two
permanent places.

—But shouldn't she have to bring in the child? You can tell
how old it is.

—Never mind shoulds. This is bureaucracy.

—Then if she chooses not to come in at all, said Joey, so be it.
That's all there is to it, right? Nobody can make her.

—Sure. But down the line it could be a problem. Even pretty
soon.

The office staff stared at him. What was he up to?

—So she can lie if she wants and finesse a few months.

—Sure.

—Who would know the actual birthdate?

—Well, the doctor who has details of her pregnancy. OB-GYN
at the hospital.

Hydrangea shook her head at all this.

—Maternity ward? said Joey.
—That's it: where she gave birth.
—What if she had the baby on her own?
—Then look at the doctor's observations when she came to clinic: the child's weight on a given date . . . like that.
—What hospital, do you think?
—Durham County General probably. If the birth was in town.
The talkative clerk liked this chat. It beat routine.
—Would they show the father the child's records?
—I think so. With your i.d. They have no hard and fast rules about that: I know after ten years they may destroy folders to make space.
—So they might let me look.
—Yes, if you can prove fatherhood.

XXII

Joey walked the three miles out Duke Street: there by the Stadium where he once played a few games. Off Roxboro he went along in the hospital's shadow, and his heart was pounding. Why? Carlyne hadn't gotten a birth certificate for the child. Was she trying to hide something? Hide the birth itself?

He went in Durham County General and asked to talk with an administrator. He told the duty officer who he was, Emory Gilbert's son, and gave a reason why he wanted to see his child's folder from Medical Records.

After a 90-minute wait he had the thin chart of Rhoda Strong Gilbert, b. June 19, 1968, in his hand. He read: *'August 7, 1968: Baby girl brought by mother to Pediatrics Emergency. Symptoms respiratory distress. Weight: 5.1 kg. Height: 51 cm. Admitted PICU.'*

They had kept Rhoda 24 hours in Pediatrics Intensive Care and then moved her to the Pediatrics Ward. Discharge: 8/10.

In panic when the asthmatic child turned blue gasping for air, Carlyne had come in and told a triage nurse the true birthdate.

XXIII

Was she still around here? Had she left the area?

He went to see the landlady again, but she just shook her head and said she had told him all she knew.

For three days Joey walked around town: Five Points to the campus and back again. Hotel lobbies, old haunts; the Blue Light, a social club on the outskirts of Durham. No sign of her. There was nothing more he could do here.

It was time to take a bus across the state to the Rock Castle. Hire a detective agency to look into it, and find her.

At the bus station he bought his ticket. What a place it was, smudged, dingy, unpainted for decades. And his wife had come here to sell herself, said a friend of Emory's.

Now by the public telephone a prostitute glanced from her call to the big soldier in fatigues.

In the luncheonette he got a bite to eat. On a stool down the counter an older man turned, looked at Joey, and said to the soda jerk:

—Look at him!

—What, Pops?

—It's the Gilbert kid, the third baseman. I'd know him any-whore. Thought he died in Vietnam.

—That's him?

The older man sipped his coffee with the unsure fingers of the alcoholic. He stared.

—Anywhore. Even with all that hair . . . It's the only time this town went in for college baseball. He outdrew the Bulls. Best hit-ter you ever seed. Don't never guess, right Jo? Wait on the curve. ol' pea looks like a grapefruit to 'im, same as Williams. And he was a Ted Williams type hitter, big corkscrew hitch 'n all, but righthand side. Splendid Splinter also missed great years off to war: honor o' our country.

—Williams?

—Yeah, you dummy. Last player to hit over .400. Same lean face and big build . . . even looks a little like the Pride of Fenway, doncha' Jo? Damn, I'd know you anyol'whore!

—Gotcha', Pops—the soda jerk smirked as he poured a lump of ice cream from a milk shake tumbler.

—Jo! Hey, Jo, how many them gooks you waste over there in Vietnam? Mess of 'em, I reckon. Look at you, yup! Honor o' our country. Hey, TV say you croaked, whatcha' doin' round hyore? Well I'll tell you what: can I buy you a beer for old times sake?

—No.

—You gonna play again? Give 'em hell! I'll tell you what: you're the best hitter I ever seed. Yup!

With his fork Joey soaked the white bread with turkey gravy and made a mash of wax beans. He remembered rising at dawn from Carlyne's side: the day he walked here dressed neatly in his uniform, shoes spitshined, duffel bag strak over his shoulder, for the first leg of the journey to Southeast Asia.

XXIV

As the bus rolled along Highway 85 he fell asleep and had a dream. Underground tunnel. He moved forward. In one hand was a Polish K-54 pistol, the kind used by VC officers; in the other, a flamethrower. What stared up at him from under the ancient, the death-saturated earth? The dull red laterite clay had a glow and was full of faces. But a guide led him on past rice stores, a workshop for arms repair, a medical clinic with a room for surgical operations. It was a second Vietnam underground where VC guerrillas slept in hammocks made of U.S. parachute nylon with a pair of Ho Chi Minh sandals beneath each one. The enemy grinned when the tunnel rat thrust his flamethrower at their greenish crimped faces . . . Further in was a danger zone. He hefted the weapon: compressed air, droplets ignited by gasoline, spewed liquid napalm from a nozzle. He moved on. Darkness. Then a red door: Carlyne's room on Lamonde. Open it and know. He held up the flamethrower and drew near. But fear came over him. Blood rose in his neck. The enemy was inside. He heard the soft babble of a child and the mother's laughter. Flamethrower leveled he made to open the red door and carbonize them.

He jolted awake.

—Ten minute rest stop!

They were in Greensboro.

He was drenched in sweat. It was the horror again.

XXV

Out on the bypass the express bus let him off in the dewy night air with its scent of summer visits here as a boy. Along the train tracks he walked past furniture factory plants with their smokestacks and reservoir tanks, the long aluminum conduits and vents shining by a night light, the back lots where shipments passed over a lading platform.

These were the last steps of his long voyage back from Vietnam. But his mind wasn't back yet. And he was not home; the Rock Castle was not his home, it was a place to rest.

Going along, he thought: Carlyne didn't go in for a birth certificate . . . the child called Rhoda Strong cannot be my child at normal term, which will be mid-September . . . then came asthma attacks and Carlyne panicked and gave the true date when she went into the hospital . . . sooner or later a birth certificate will become a must: let's see if she gives the same birthdate. *5.1 kg.*

In the silent town without a soul there was an older man standing by himself across from P. Laster's bank building. The man's posture had an odd note to it, stiff-necked in a clerical collar, as he gazed darkly.

—Welcome home, soldier.

Joey nodded.

Then nearing the Rock Castle his heart pounded. What if his wife heard about his arrival and came here also? What joy there would be if she was waiting for him. And never mind what the landlady in Durham said. It didn't matter! He forgave her, and that was why he felt such happiness at sight of her, and why he took her in his arms, and oh! oh! oh! he loved her more than life itself, and it was better than confetti.

But the old Gilbert place did not put out a hand to him, and give such hope. A great mass of granite in the ominous shadows, it was set back from the road amid the tall oaks yet towered and seemed to lean forward. Joey gazed up at the high gables and roof angles and turret to one side; he saw the balustrade with its crenelation in the upper storeys, above a front porch lined with exotic plants in a wood trough between pillars of the romanesque arches. The flowers must be a touch of his zany little sister, Lemon. A spire over the conical turret pierced a gold ball high up there.

No, this wasn't his home, but the place had a sense of destiny to it. The dim ponderous casements brooded, like the strange man up town just now. The gloaming of stone seemed to hover over the front walkway and long slope of lawn to the old main road below.

On Joey's right as he came up the walk was a hoary oak so big a good-sized cedar runnered up from the root. The shaggy bark whiskered by poison oak vines was hemmed round a large hole in the trunk where he and Newell had their tree fort as boys.

Leaves rustled in the silence at ten p.m. Joey tried the front door; it wasn't locked.

—Anybody home?

In the front hall panneled waist-high with gilt-edged coffers there was the scent of Granddaddy's den. It was a resinous smell blent with old leather and pipe tobacco. Beneath his feet were the same parqueted floor and soft rugs. The balusters of the wide carpeted stairs were tipped with totem-like finials above the mahogany handrails.

All this he remembered in an instant. Intimate. Then he looked down at the front hall table with its two Roman busts in black marble. He turned on the lamp and saw one of P. Laster's primitive oil paintings: cows on a commons before the local Methodist church. And, in the lamplight beside a letter holder and a few magazines, there was his last envelope addressed to Carlyne.

XXVI

Suddenly a scream came from the shadowy landing.

Joey dove into the den. He did a combat crawl—startled back in Vietnam—and positioned himself.

—Jojo! What are you doing here?!

Lemon Gilbert shrieked and took the stairs four at a bound using the antique baluster as a pogo stick.

—Joeykins, you are dead! You big fool!

She flew in the den and threw herself at him and began to cry.

—Don't give me the voodoo hex, ghost! Don't howl at midnight and give me the evil eye! Oh, Joji! Is it you? Is it really you, Bones?

She wept over him, and her frail shoulders shook.

He stood up and took his little sister in his arms.

—That's me, a ghost.

Lemon cried and laughed and called him pet names. She hugged him tight while tears streaked her cheeks. She was a kid when he went away, but she had turned a corner since then. In bluejeans and one of Joey's old madras shirts from college days, she drew back and grabbed his breast pocket and shook him.

—You couldn't call first, Jody? Say, you stink pretty bad. Can't you smell it? Please go in the powder room and freshen up. Or better yet: I'll go draw you a bubble bath and get out the scrub brush. Peee-you!

Joey took a deep breath.

—Newell said he'd phone you. I saw him in Berkeley, and Dad in Chicago. Both too busy.

—The skunks. And now I get scared out of my wits. Fig Newton never has time for his rotten little sister. He's going to save the world, you know.

She bowed her curly head on his broad shoulder and sniffled and gave a small laughter as she tickled his ribs. For two weeks she had been numb with grief.

—Dad either, eh?

—Nobody! Oh, oh. For all I knew my cussèd big bruvver bit the dust.—She bumped her head on his shoulder and slugged his chest with her forearm and hugged him and cried.—You . . . you Joji, you bad boy . . . you guy!

—Our post got overrun, he said. There was no hope so I took off on my own. I went AWOL. My tour was over no matter what. So I guess they reported me with the others.

—Dead. And look at you.

—Mistook my remains for someone else.

—My own Jomo a doornail. Drat, Joji, that hurt too much.

Lemon bit her lip and stamped her foot.

—So you see I was killed in action. Well, not yet.

—Have you had supper at least? Cindy left some corn pone and blackeyed peas in the fridge. Let's see.

—I thought Cindy left us.

—Yes, mostly. But she still keeps an eye on things, on 'a cause I'm one of her grandkids too, she says.

—Oh.

—Geezus, Giuseppe, what a shock. I could've had a heart attack before my time. Say there, you smell like shit!

XXVII

She led him in the guest bedroom beneath the stairwell.

—Carlyne stayed in here?

—Yes, Sir.

—Have you heard from her?

—No, Job. She split the scene. Voilà.

—Didn't say why?

—Never gave a hint. But so sad, so down, her last days here. She took off when Dad was away, and I was in school.

—Never one phone call?

Lemon worked in the bathroom which was a plush affair with its old fixtures. She set out towels and sprinkled scent as the water foamed up.

—I'll bring clean clothes. Leave those in a pile, phew!

—Don't throw them away.

But Lemon's mood changed. A scowl came over her pretty features.

—Oh, Yoyo, do you know what Dad is thinking of doing? It's barbaric; it's the act of a madman, not my Daddykins! He has such fame and power but does it make him happy? Something's gone wrong with the poor boy, and he doesn't care if he ruins the lives of his own children.

Joey went a shade pale.

—He what?

—It's a pitiful sight when a grown man lies in his bib, Joji. Sometimes it seems Emory-board has the conscience of a five year-old. No offense to five year-olds. He's changed a lot since you went away. Now he just makes up the rules as he goes along.

—You sound like Newell.

—If you saw Dad when he comes out of the den after one of Bishop Commynes' visits . . . His eyes are wild, like he was being tortured.

—Why?

—And then the fond sexagenarian who is my admirer, Maximilian Doan, saunters in free as you please and tries to court me. I call him Thanks-a-Million, or Thanks-a-Mill, because he's so cheap. Oh, he's dapper in his khaki planter's outfit, his topee helmet and suspenders. And he brings me a bouquet, twelve pink roses. Cool! Robbing the cradle. Lemon Gilbert, jailbait. But the worst is he has Dad's blessing. So the heat is on.

—For a June wedding?

—I don't blame Cindy for wanting to get away. I'll say ta-ta as soon as it's time for college. But I also love Dad and feel so sorry for him. Poor Emeritus: something's happened and it isn't good. The moment he gets home from his jaunts, his two good friends are all over him. I'm afraid he'll start drinking again.

—Why all over him?

—You tell me. The devil only knows.

—Commynes is the man I saw up town just now? Alone?

—He just stands in one spot staring for hours.

—Stiff-necked, dressed in black? With a turnaround collar?

—That's him, the tick. Oh, Joji, he does such a job on our dear old Daddio. He's got the goods on him, so it seems, and he whips him right up! I can see how it is when they come out of the den. But Dad still calls him his best friend, his childhood buddy, and Paulie. Then the man with his saintly airs goes out and haunts the empty streets up town all night. And at dawn you'll find him kneeling before the Satan cult altar in his home, the Colonel's House once famed as a brothel. He conjures as the sun comes up, and so on. Cindy says the whole town talks about it. But you know there's no lack of good oldtime religion around here, and it'll dress up in black and call itself a bishop.

XXVIII

—Strange.

—So durned glad, Joltin' Joe, so glad you made it back! You're even all in one piece, if not quite spic 'n span.

Lemon frowned and smiled. Shaken by a sob she lay her curly head on his chest.

—Now, now. Take it easy, kid.

—Oh, Jody, if only I didn't feel so sorry for him.

—Do you know if Carlyne left a savings book here?

—I haven't seen one. Maybe with Dad: call him. The bank sends mail for Mr. and Mrs. Joseph L. Gilbert. Why not phone them?

An hour later Joey got out of the tub. He meant to go in the kitchen for a plate of Cindy's food, but a drowsiness came over him. On the soft mattress he lay back, closed his eyes, and drifted asleep.

The soldier was back from the battlefield, and he slept.

Chapter Fifteen

I

—In ancient Greece, Laïus, son of the deceased Theban King Labdakos, kidnapped a boy whom he desired at the sacred Nemean Games. It was a violent act, and it was not needed for him to enjoy the boy's favors. He might have paid court to the youth and won his trust; and the boy's father, King Pelops, would probably have given his blessing to their union. That love, that passion could have flourished and become a positive force for life, with or without possession, if Laïus had gone about it in a caring and sensitive way. But no; the Theban king—whom a number of ancient Greek writers called the first homosexual—could not wait and so committed an act of violence.

'This is mythology. And, as myths do, it shows the human imagination working to know, understand, give symbolic expression to the facts and reality of our life here on earth. It has a profound meaning with relevance to our work as psychiatrists. What is this meaning?

'The rape of the boy Chrysippus is the rape of the land. It is any rape: any instance of man's arrogant violence, man's hubris which leads to the curse, and the oracle's formulation of the curse, and the plague which is atè, namely punishment for the rape, which must be expiated, sooner or later.

'Pelops, the father of Chrysippus, flew in a rage at Laïus' act. This is the same Pelops whose evil father King Tantalus had killed and served him up in a stew to the gods, testing their claim to know all. But at the gods' request one of the Fates saved Pelops—who learned his lesson the hard way and didn't like violence.

'So Pelops in a fury, after his son was kidnapped and raped, laid a curse on Laïus' family, on the Labdacide line. This is the curse of the Labdacides. If Laïus had a son then that son would grow up to kill his father, Laïus, and marry his own mother, the wife of Laïus.

'When a Delphic oracle made the curse known, Laïus tried to leave his wife alone in bed as might be imagined. He was afraid. But one night Fate played a hand with the aid of his wife Jocasta's charms.

'Jocasta gave birth to a son, Oedipus. And the father exposed him, sent him away with the idea he was being put out to die. This was in propitiatory sacrifice to Hera, Zeus's spouse, goddess of marriage, who was angry at the boy Chrysippus' rape; also at the invention, say some Greek sources, of pederasty. Hera did not accept Laïus' sacrifice. The gods aren't likely to be pleased by a lie. And so she sent the Sphinx to ravage the city, Thebes, killing all who couldn't answer a riddle. The answer was simply: Man. But the riddle, despite its simple form, was really the most profound question. Who is given the chance to live and fight for what is positive in life, other people, if he is true and refuses to lie? Answer: Man.

'Now today, colleagues in the field of psychiatry, I ask you. Is there an adequate and realistic vision of America which does not begin with the rape of the land? Is the genocide of the indigenous tribes a dead issue for us? Or does it still affect our society, our relationships, our psychopathological studies today?

'And, as we send our sons to Vietnam, exposing them as Laïus did Oedipus on Mount Cithaeron; are we still raping, not negotiating in a positive spirit for the good of all concerned—still raping with our tax dollars spent on an evil war; with our conformism in open or silent support of that war; with our denial and cover-up as regards the effects of U.S. invasion and occupation of Vietnam not only on the people there but also on our sons coming home with symptoms of Post-Traumatic Stress Disorder, PTSD, which all but a very few of my colleagues in psychiatry say does not exist . . .?

'We can deny PTSD and rewrite history all we want. But the rape was committed, and *is*. The curse lives on. Plague is in America—moral plague, affecting our mores and psychology as a nation and all our works and days. I'm afraid this plague won't go away until we learn, no matter how hard the way, and start doing something about it.'

II

Dr. Lydia Falliere put down her pen and pushed away the paper she would read at a conference in ten days. Between patients she gazed out her office window across Central Park. Springtime came a bit late this year but with a force of what felt like tenderness. The magnolias and cherry trees in blossom dotted the warm greens. There would be azaleas, peonies, lilacs, wisteria so sweet. The May day made her dream, and her heart was curiously astir.

She thought of her girlhood and school years. She sensed that since then there had been too much acquisitiveness, competition, success ethos, like a socialized war. This was in the environment; though psychoanalysis tended to avoid socio-historical factors as untreatable. It was a science wanting to limit itself to subjective categories—instinct or cathexis, guilt, reaction formation, defense, displacement symptom. She wasn't a revolutionary; but only, like the homeopath, trying to ally herself with the healthy elements in a patient's psyche. This bright May morning and springtime must do the rest.

Her Fifth Avenue office was wainscoted and stylish just as she was: a successful doctor in her late thirties. There were long shelves with collected works which gave a sense of intellectual life in its prime. Besides her great grandfather Pierre Janet the fine series of books were by Charcot, Breuer, R. v. Krafft-Ebing, a whole shelf for Freud, many by Jung, Adler, Ferenczi, other Freud disciples. There were monographs by Binswanger, Bleuler, Sachs, Eitingon, Rank, Anna Freud, Reik, Reich, Brill, Lévy-Bruhl, Lacan.

Lydia turned to her wide oakwood desk, good for a writer, and put some note cards in a manila folder. On a metal cart alongside there were library books and research materials mustered for the subject at hand. Among the titles were: *PTSD: Cardinal Diagnostic*

Features; 'Normal Versus Abnormal Reactions of Mental Health Professionals to War, Violent Death, and Horror'; *Comorbidity Theory.* There were also: *PTSD: Differential Diagnosis;* 'Four Major Themes of Post-Traumatic Stress Disorder'; *Freud and Breuer's Talking-Cure: an Inquiry into Abreactional Modalities.* And other medical texts, studies and articles had a lot of bookmarks and paper clips in the pages.

The materials came from a few libraries but mostly the East Side hospital where she headed the psychiatric group between lectures at New York University and her private practice.

III

Pulse tone; the intercom.
—Yes?
—Your eleven o'clock, Doctor.
—Just hold him two minutes.

She looked around. Why was she a little nervous? Tallish, elegant, reserved like a diplomat, she ran a hand through her short dark hair and smoothed her business suit. Why was there a wistful note, playing like a flute, amid the intentness of her features? It was eighteen months since her divorce—with its stress, and effects on her daughter and two boys . . . Lydia turned again to the sunlit window where the gossamer Park ended at Midtown a dozen blocks south. For a year and a half she felt she had less to give; so she gave more: to patients, to her children when she was at home; to her studies and writing. Despite the neediness and sense of loss she was working longer and better than before.

She felt she had fallen, but it was a lucky fall. It got her ready to begin again, and live better.

Now she had a little laugh at their normal adult phallic-genitality—glance at Freud & Cie.—for it was overrated, a good compromise at best, a rotten one often. Maybe a vital creative nature will tend to struggle against that compartmentalization of everyday life. Maybe the point was to live orality (passion, sensibility) and anality (discipline, ambition) as fully as possible. Both Apollo and Dionysus vie for sway in our love relations, our vocational striving; in our struggle for justice, micro and macro, which we all need to wage. Life is struggle. Happiness is struggle for a good cause. Justice is not a mere adjustment ... Say the phallic-genital (reason, balance) is in step with a society's contradictions—does it conform and take the line of least resistance? Does it give in for the basics? Doesn't a true maturity posit and pursue goals beyond the self, the family? Doesn't it try to change things and come in conflict with established norms?

She laughed at herself:

—Heretic!

Lydia Falliere laughed. For a moment she felt ... what? She didn't know what she felt. An anticipation.

Her ex-husband was a corporate executive. He wasn't the worst, and far from it. But he walked away from their Scarsdale home where her mother lived too. He went to live in Gramercy Park. And then came the liberal agreement. He left her.

Lydia took a deep breath and turned away from the sunlit window high above the trees. Along a wall were framed certificates, honorary degrees, Chevalier (not Officier) de la Légion d'Honneur. Over the leather couch hung a Boudin landscape in oils with its crimson patch like a signature. That painting was a holiday; and her mood had a similar je-ne-sais-quoi, blue sea, sunny beach, rowboats, love in a red stroke of the brush.

She had treated athletes before.

But why did the office visit of this baseball player bring her a ... springy sense?

IV

An oak wood door led to the consultation room. She went in and closed it behind her.

—Send him in.

For a moment she thought: take off my jacket? She was an impressive woman, nearly six feet in high heels, poised, very direct. She wore a stylish suit, a beige blouse with brocade.

The patient came in. He was taller than herself. Big, lean, hard-eyed and -jawed, a tiger.

—Hello, she said.

He gave her a grunt, sort of upbeat hup, between players, and looked around a little.

A smile of inquiry lit Lydia's brow as she moved to shake his hand. It was a limp fish. He stared at her forehead. He had that rock hard air of high-level competition and, no doubt, the daily ordeal. She knew them: the way they dismissed the non-jock, the outsider, but were polite about it with a cocky humor.

He came to her in jeans and a gray t-shirt sweaty from his run through the Park. Lydia met that bony gaze as her own features took on a connoisseur's look.

The fashionable psychiatrist gave a curtsy and nodded him not to the couch but an armchair. And she thought: he has character, he is handsome but . . . no lady's man.

Then silence.

V

In the tasteful space he stared past her at the half-drawn blinds. Was he claustrophobic? There was an unease to his cocky act, itchy, as if just in from the wilds. He twiddled his thumbs a bit and waited for her to start.

Almost to a man her co-workers in the field of psychiatry spoke of Post-Traumatic Stress diagnosis with skepticism. And they were hostile. Why? The major networks and newspapers, the corporate media had a way of trivializing the Vietnam vet's experience. World War II veterans with their memories of the Pacific Theater called Vietnam vets self-pitiers. Oh, don't talk about the odds. What are you saying? The United States could lose a war? That idea is unpatriotic and a gift to the communists. And so it was that her profession joined in the chorus of denial. It was a policy of non-diagnosis and non-treatment with no mention of PTSD in the DSM (Diagnostic and Statistical Manual of Mental Disorders). And meanwhile the most bizarre and dysfunctional clinical situations were cropping up under their noses.

Now the new patient peered past her with his eyes squinted. Lydia was very calm. She would be neutral in this duel. But she felt like her heart had received a charge. It seemed, hm . . . like a door had opened. No strong emotion bowled her over as it once did with her husband. But . . . something . . . Then she thought like a doctor again: more and more come back to us like this even as medical science backs away from Stress Disorder, and labels it neatly: Adult Life Adjustment Reaction. Well, yet a little while, and we will see. Go get 'em, Galileo: it's time to prove the common view is wrong.

With a serious look, and a soft voice, Lydia Falliere said:

—What can I do for you?

—Not a thing, Doc.

—Come again?

—Goose egg. Zip.

Silence.

Twiddle . . . twaddle.

But she was gracious. She said:

—I'm at your service, really.

—Well . . .

His voice had a lonely note: she heard it, like a bugle far in the distance. It sounded as though he hadn't enjoyed talking with someone for a long time.

—Sir?

—One thing you might do. But not you.

—Go on.

—Doctor, I need a referral.

—Okay.

—I need the name of a topflight detective agency. I've been dealing with the katzenjammer kids; now I need the best, and trustworthy.

—I see.

She thought a moment.

He said:

—But above all don't simply get me the number. Ask me some deep questions so you can pad your fee. And hey maybe I'm an interesting case.

She raised an eyebrow. Was he a mean one? . . . A great athlete might inspire her sympathy, but she didn't feel called on to admire. They were conformists to the core since they were given no leeway to think for themselves and speak out. On that level you were so in vogue, like a god to the children of America. So serve the system and keep it shut. One false step, a political opinion that went against the grain, and you could kiss your career good-

bye and your dreams and hopes and hard work since boyhood. A
spirit of inquiry didn't mix with pro sports. Beatniks weren't paid
fortunes to play ball. By now there were twenty million kids who
wanted to grow up just like Joey Gilbert (!) and they spent key
years on a playground where they didn't become Joey or themselves either. It was too bad they never saw her patient the long
and lanky Boston lefthander grovel in a seclusion room: please
don't leave me alone! The corporate media turned out its idols
from year to year: a pretty face or body was the latest hot commodity. But never a word of insight did it serve. Never a: know
thyself, America. And here we were killing millions of people in
Southeast Asia, and dropping 80 million liters of toxic chemicals
on the small nation of Vietnam, and half of it was one called Agent
Orange which caused cancer and was affecting the G.I.s too. Hey,
no guilt, America; it's a sporting contest. America the superstar.
We are beyond good and evil.

But the one in her office was not so naive: not a farm boy. He
spoke quietly. It seemed his mind had its own daily workout:
on a Universal apparatus of the psyche. She knew the story of
his death in a paddy field near the Cambodian border and then
resurrection as a Major Leaguer with a difference—a basket case
with a no-cut contract. Lo, the twists of fate: he had taken hold
of the nation's imagination. She met his dad once on the lecture
circuit; and now in spare moments she was reading one of Emory
Gilbert's literary classics.

Joey was uneasy. He wanted to go out.

He rose with a yawn:

—I'm cured, Doc. Send them your bill.

She looked at him: la belle indifférence. Still she paused in
thought, and then said:

—Hold on.

From her desk she took an address book and jotted a number.

VI

As Lydia handed him the memo she was thinking: control issues. Trauma induces systemic denial. Later the patient revisits
the event, the repressed material, and frees emotions beyond his

control. The psychiatrist's job is to help relate and work through such emotions using control strategies. It is like a loan of ego.

More and more Vietnam vets were coming home to find, some tragically, the old beliefs were gone. And so the usual control mechanisms didn't work anymore. Their therapists passed over the facts and did not care to reevaluate. Lydia read one case about a psychiatrist who told his patient, a combatant in Hué City: Look, you'll have to grow up, period. Just erase the war from your mind. Tell yourself Nam never happened, and then all your paranoia, bad dreams, psychosomatic symptoms and self-doubt will vanish, presto. And the result of the consultation? It was there in the patient's chart—suicide, a few days later. The doctor hadn't wished to talk about Vietnam, and so the soldier fell silent too. He grew up, but the time bomb in him was ticking. Now it was predicted there would be as many suicides among returnees as there were deaths in combat over there.

But this PTSD victim came from a well-known family and had backing and financial means. He went not to the VA, not to an apathetic perhaps hostile U.S. Government bureaucracy, but to Lydia Falliere. A Major League club told her to treat Joey Gilbert and give him back his mental health so he would stop having such lapses on the field.

—With my children I went to watch your game yesterday.

He shrugged.

—Oh? You like it?

—First Big League game I ever went to.—She laughed—Once in a blue moon I get to watch my two sons play a game. But I just wanted a look at it before we met.

—Slumming in the owner's box.

—I went for myself—She put a finger to her temple and laughed again.—Too much work.

—Well—he held up the detective's number, and made to go.— Thanks, I'll call them.

Lydia nodded. She thought: he must begin, not I.

—Won't you tell me a word about last night?

—What about it?

—On third base.

But Joey was cavalier. He gave a gesture:

—Naw, you can read the sportswriters. They're wise men, they know it all.

—All about you?

He turned from her:

—I'll tell the front office we had a wholesome hour together.

She smiled:

—Not too wholesome!

He went out. In twenty minutes he hadn't loosened up. His face was set: a mask.

Go play.

VII

She knew about him months before his club called.

A decorated soldier gone AWOL was named in a KIA report and then came back to life in Major League pinstripes. How did he do that? It gave him stellar media and box office appeal.

A front page article in January—WILL JOEY GILBERT PLAY THIRD BASE AGAIN?—caught her eye, and then she found herself skimming the sports pages. She could tell you the names of other athletes who died in battle: Eddie Grant and Hobey Baker in World War I, Elmer Gedeon, Nile Kinnick, John Pinder, Harry O'Neill, Al Blozis, and Jack Lummus, in World War II.

This past winter Joey spent in the southern town where his Scottish forbears settled as Eighteenth Century farmers. With a collie-husky dog he roamed the woods and streams. On snowy nights he was out there. For days he traipsed and didn't come in. After sundown the people saw his campfire far out in the Gilbert farmlands, the long fields by the Yadkin River. His tall, lonely figure showed up on the back roads or stood in thought by an unharvested cauliflower plot which had rotted and sent up a stench when the temperature rose above freezing. The winds of December clicked in the frozen grasses where deer bounded to a halt and put their front teeth to the stalks of dried out corn.

Off by himself this soldier replayed the war and tried to deal with a fear he could not shake. He hunted and took fish from the river. Decay and death, a specter of suicide went with him in the gray Carolina landscape. He was trying to survive the only way he knew. Forget pro ball.

With the dog he left the Rock Castle confines and went out to live in the wooded twilight. Cold and hunger relieved his mental anguish. He said he had eaten rat one day in the Central Highlands, not knowing what it was; a grunt played a joke on him. Dog meat was the featured dish in a Buon Me Thuot hotel. Now he fed on venison, or any small animal would do, or a root. For he didn't take pleasure in Cindy's rich country cooking. And soft life at the Rock Castle stuck in his craw.

The press went to find Joey Gilbert in the woods. His dad Emory was still in the news despite Richard Nixon's victory in November.

In two well-marked jeeps the reporters took their cameras along farm roads looking for this soldier still at war. They had generators, bright lights and reflector screens, booms, high-bias mikes. They rode out to the river and called to their man with a loudspeaker, like Viet Cong in the savannah grass—jungle warfare on some hill in the Parrot's Beak.

Then, gun in hand, like his wife's ancestors hounded into the swamps of southeastern Carolina, he came out and said:

—Get the hell out of here.

The network crew was delighted. They talked to him as snow fell in the background.

—Will you play ball again?

—No. And I told you to scram. Do you think I don't mean it?

—Just a few questions, Sir. We'll go.

Bearded, wild, he made an obscene gesture at them. He bit off the words:

—I gave my sanity to your Far East police action. I was a victim twice.

—Twice?

—Over there following bad orders, on ambush patrol with nickle and dime support. And back here called a nut, a baby killer. Do you get me? I'll never forgive you for saying I hurt a child.

Snow fell through the bare trees on Joey Gilbert's hair and eyebrows. He blinked.

—What do you eat out here?

—Rat, so watch out.

Laughter.

—Only a few more weeks till spring camp. Third base anyone? Won't you go to Florida for a tryout?

Joey Gilbert showed his teeth in a growl. Away from the campfire it was cold; he shivered in his flak jacket.

—Poor Tom—said a cameraman.—Tom's a-cold!

Sniggers.

—I gave all and now get blamed. Goddamn you. I'm expected to go through that and then come home and make the best of it. Smile for the camera: smile and slave for the same lying system that sent me there, and made me go through that. Make my way, get ahead, smile, nod approval, yes Sarge, a yes man. Well, I won't.

A newscaster in a camel's hair coat said:

—Mr. Gilbert, tell us what it's like to—

—Carlyne!—The grunt shook his gun at them and shouted.—Carlyne, do you hear me? I want you back, you're my wife! I need you . . . As for you, ass-lickers, scram, diddy. You I don't need, so truck out and take your contempt with you. Now!

He fired off an M-16 burst over their heads. Then in the silence, as they scampered back, he laughed low.

—Call me a self-pitier? You don't know shit about it, bunch of baboons. And you will be courteous.

This interview was aired nationally. Somehow it may have led to the New York General Manager's brainchild of a contract offer. Was the nation going political? Would it be another bad year at the gate? Then go with the flow and give them something different. On deck: the mad third baseman looking for his wife. Soap Opera Series. Yes you can go home again, if there's money in it.

VIII

Lydia Falliere knew the withdrawal symptoms of the warrior: his need to retreat and lick wounds. Many vets suffered from hyperalertness, intense irritability; a kind of somatopsychical programming. The everyday stimuli of civilian life could trigger a war response. So a Joey Gilbert took his anxiety into the woods and dealt with it on his own. The trained killer didn't want to hurt anyone else.

How much depended on inherited factors? Infancy, childhood setbacks and reaction formation, predispose: they may form the basis for a later traumatic event to prove pathogenic. Not rarely the psychoanalytic patient's earliest memories are like a war *en famille.* What sudden shifts, what vendettas: a caveman life of the subconscious. By comparison a real war might seem like peace: say a counterpoise to the post-womb violence when an infant has no defenses. In peacetime ambush lurks behind the routine; so it seems. Such emotional energy expended, day in and day out, to hold up under the pressure—thus depression. On all sides there is normal society with its well-adjusted snipers.

IX

A few weeks before the new U.S. President threw out the first ball of the 1969 season, the front office of Joey Gilbert's parent club issued a press release. The talented third baseman had signed a no-cut one year contract.

By then the snow had melted from the Davidson County woods. A new vegetation spread its green hues over the fields, and leaves were back on the trees. Yadkin swelled between its banks those first warm days. The woodland Grace and her sister nymphs unrobed to lead the new year in the dance.

While on rounds one day Lydia watched a news segment in the common room of a mental ward. It was TV footage: the soldier crossed a field with his assault rifle held high in two hands. There was a luminescence of birds swarming in the twilight. Next a baseball stadium applauded a long homerun bounced off the right-centerfield scoreboard in New York. All this dazzled. He would be a box office draw.

So Joey signed. What a sight he was when he joined the team on its swing north from the Grapefruit League. Man alive! Talk about out of shape! He had red eyes from lack of sleep and rickety steps like a wino and he said not a jot. On third it was a scream! His throws sailed high over first into the stands. The manager shouted: For crying out loud! The team laughed in a chorus. At third base today, ladies and germs, the eighth hitter in the New York lineup, pride of the Bowery Bums: Joltin' Joe Jigger o' Gin! Big boned and bearded, he had lint in his long hair plus a pink ribbon his little sister sent him for luck. In his high pockets were worms, snails and puppy dog tails. National Pastime: welcome to the 'Sixties.

—Look, it's the Piltdown Man.

—Jojo the psycho—said the trainer.

Like a thumb out of joint Gilbert came that first day to the club-house. He wore a rusty t-shirt from his college days with faded bluejeans tucked in his combat boots. For the fun of it he sucked a hayseed and held a Louisville slugger, with cleats and mitt on the end, over his shoulder.

—Brought his own equipment—said one of the coaches.

Same fielder's glove from before he went away, if not American Legion ball: a cracked A-2000 with thongs redone (by Lemon) between the fingers. At first impact the web flapped back, and all laughed. No amount of neat's foot oil could limber up this corpse exhumed for a dance.

Of course his timing and reflexes were shot to hell. So it was ridiculous when he stabbed at a routine grounder or dropped a pop-up. Plunk went a line drive off the big ape's shin.

—Hawn' you kid! yelled a teammate, and spit brown.

—Playing third base for New York today: Rip . . . Van Winkle!

—Or is it Von McDaniel? Forgot how.

Coffin dust not diamond dust puffed from that glove of another era when he did manage to catch a ball. And then he looked solemnly at that old horsehide like it had a mystery. He held it up in his thumb and index and studied it. A sports columnist wrote the next day:

—Alas, poor New Yorick.

But suddenly the former LURP flung it stiff-armed like a grenade toward the dugout. And he hit the dirt with a yell so wild, a few hot prospects fell to their knees as well. But the madman didn't give a grin. He got up slowly, looking out of it. Was he epileptic?

Joey gawked. His teammates preened at their warm-up catches in foul territory.

A bevy of photographers only had eyes for the ugly duckling.

Those first days back in a baseball uniform he went through his paces like a ghost. Batter up, Count Dracula. He had deep rings under his eyes. He fell all over himself charging a bunt. Pitiful. He'd forgot what to do in a 5-4-3 double play situation; never mind backhanding a short-hop behind the bag. Was he a big athlete paid a few grand per hour to play? Or a hippie pothead?

The other players gave him a wide berth. So did manager and coaches since his contract had special language about disciplining. For instance, he was not to be barked at; he could wear ear-plugs if he wanted; and he had the right to read a book while sitting on the bench. Let the baby have his bottle!

It seemed the shell-shocked veteran had no use for a baseball, and he was fed up to here. But a strong agent had got the client's way on most points. And so Joey Gilbert reported. And he was an affront to the conservative code of Major League baseball.

For a few weeks he turned his team into a laughingstock. One headline read:

GET HIP, HIGHPOCKETS!

X

But it wasn't all that funny. No one laughed in his face after he beat up a stadium security guard. It's true the fellow asked for it; and two, three short punches hushed him up. Don't provoke this lunatic who knew more about guns than baseball. You do not bicker with a maniac trained to kill. Look at him: the high-cut baseball socks rolled on his ankles; a shoelace untied; t-shirt crooked under his jersey; fly open; belt hangs down like a bent prick; he is unshaven; he is blear-eyed from insomnia.

Alone in a corner of the dugout Joey sat surly and withdrawn. In the clubhouse he thumbed his nose at protocol. Stardom, seniority meant a locker room pecking order. He ignored it. He didn't care about the privileges of a future Hall of Famer who was once his childhood hero. What did a baseball player weigh beside the papa-san staring with the wisdom of the ages from a dirt-poor hootch in a village across the Pacific? Carlyne was right to call ballplayers a lot of harebrained jocks—what did they ever talk about?

It seemed even the bleachers grew bored when they came alive and stamped their feet chanting: Joey! Joey! Joey! The high moment of the game was when he jogged shakily out to the left field bullpen before the first pitch.

He was like the prophet who, set on a scale by two angels, out-weighed all the League.

At the season's opener he scandalized everyone from the League President to the ball girl by not saluting during the National Anthem. Really this was too much. His contract had a special clause which set him apart in such matters, but they hadn't expected anything like this: an unpatriotic gesture from a decorated war hero. And to top it off he did read a book on the bench. What book? Instead of charting pitches, he read psychology. Jinx 'em!

From his back pocket he took out an all-day sucker, carefully removed the red wrapper, and started to lick it. On the bench! But there could be no fine, not even a wrist slap. It was the Big League 'Sixties. Now don't get excited!

One night in Philadelphia there was an unassisted triple play. It was a suicide squeeze: the third baseman charged, dove, snared the popped bunt—ouuut!—lunged and put the tag on runner from third while getting spiked in head; he fell back unconscious but held onto the ball—ouuuut!—while the go-ahead run on second tagged up and, rounding third by now, saw the New York catcher unable to free the ball gripped in the coldcocked third sacker's glove. So the lead run got waved round for the headlong dash home. It was Eddie Stanky scoring from first on a single. The runner slud in just as the catcher wrenched his teammate's arm from its socket and swiped the tag for him—ouuuuut! Score it: 5-5-5. Side retired. But would you believe it? 30 thousand fans missed this thrilling play because they were watching Joey Gilbert eat a pastrami special with extra melted cheeze, sliced tomato and onion, hold mayo, but don't skimp on mustard and potato stix. This he smuggled into the dugout for a late inning snack.

In the twelfth inning of a nail biter he blew bubbles in his root beer float through a straw gone soggy like the long legs he stretched to the dugout steps while burping like the call of the last of the great awks. If he yawned and stretched it was newsworthy. From his peaked cap he took a hayseed sent in a letter by his little sister, put it to his lips, and closed his eyes for a nap. On the New York bench there was a man snoring. He said he didn't like baseball. And it seemed the big crowd didn't either, but only came out to watch a player gone off the deep end; a morbid third baseman, a Beatnik!

The New York manager who was uptight and outa' sight on his better days, let alone with Sigmund Freud on the roster, sent Joey Gilbert to bullpen duty in perpetuity. The fans hated that. Out there was like Siberia. The crowd got on Skip pretty bad about it.

XI

SATAN SIGNS PRO PACT

This was the cover story of a Sunday magazine in late April. The media demonized the weird third baseman and made capital of his kinks. *'The devil is the most versatile utility infielder since Sibby Sisty of the Boston Braves . . .'* So ran the lead sentence. The witty piece with comic photos skimmed over the ballplayer's war record and his disability. It was light reading meant to stick on a label; it cast blame at his pranks in an upbeat style: a good piece for middle class readers at brunch. But it also caught Dr. Lydia Falliere's eye, and she clipped the article for a folder: Prototypical PTSD Cases (mostly from the two world wars). She had known other Joeys with their display of unconcern: la belle indifférence.

He was having his fling in the sports and business world. Yet he was serious. He didn't like to be made fun of, but what could the man expect? Before the game he made a mockery of infield practice, and a sportswriter coined the phrase: 'Miltown to Evers to Chance'. Pop that ol' sleeping pill! He wasn't clowning around, but he just didn't care. And so his act charmed the capacity crowd.

They came to watch pregame warm-ups. They grooved on Joey Gilbert's capers at third base, and his goofy look, hayseed in mouth, as he took his cuts in the cage. It was a mighty whoosh as his big bat fanned air. Out at third a low liner plunked off his ankle, and he cried: ouch! He rubbed it, hopping around. A routine grounder tied him in knots and the stands shook with laughter. They laughed, they cheered, they stomped their feet in cadence because they wanted him to play. Out of your tent, Achilles! They loved to see him carry on and act mad. And they were different too—hardly your common baseball audience, beer-guzzler vulgaris all set to light hair on fire and insult a rightfielder's mother.

One night—it was during a Midwest tour—the managers exchanged lineup cards at home plate. The band played: that song from our childhood seemed to waft into the night, like a flag. A deep voice read off the visitors' batting order over the p.a. And then fully half the crowd got up and filed toward the exits in protest before a pitch was thrown. Steeerike! cried the Ump, as the ballpark went out on strike.

Picket lines formed up at the gates. Sports fans of the world, unite!

Their signs on poles and posters had a new sports consciousness. For they knew even the screwballer's five straight strikeouts of murderer's row; even back-to-back no-hitters; even an outfielder slamming time and again into the wall; even daggers glared by old diamond foes, even a pitching staff trading their wives, even the glorious exploits of a Solly Hemus—all of it was so much boredom when compared to the human dimension at work in Joey Gilbert.

He was like that other special player who crossed a line. For Joey was The Thinker: where he sat fist to chin in the bullpen. Joey was baseball gone subjective, and trying for insight. So what if you struck out, or knocked the ball out of sight. It wasn't whether you won or lost; it was whether your dopamine was activated by the beauty of life, the lure of the night.

—Love, not baseball!—they chanted.

The National Pastime must become a happening. Those nine innings were the rites of a communal sacrament.

Oh! How they wanted Joey to get in the game. How they razzed Skipper's tight ass, and the New York General Manager's. From coast to coast now it was: 'Play Joey! Play Joey!' as the fans in their millions rode the crest of an ascending movement and seemed close to insurrection.

Play Joey! Free Huey!

XII

Not his no-cut contract perhaps, since there could be loopholes; but 'the customer is always right' kept this dangerous madman up with the club. Fans from the days of Cap Anson and the Miller Huggins era joined anti-social elements and neurasthenic recluses never before caught dead at a ballpark, magna rerum perturbatione impendente. Let it all hang out! And so it did, and gate receipts soared. Joey-mania was on the march. It was a brand spanking new commercial angle. It was human. Only the anti-commercial was commercial in these days of a 'Sixties nonconformism bad for baseball. It was a time of contempt for the mainstream, of disaffection with the system. The world had gone to the dogs of higher culture, and the cultivation of finer tastes, such as smoking grass.

Also, sports looked shallow when seen after the carnage on the nightly news. There were bombers over Vietnam, student strikes at home, slums torched to a cry of: Burn, baby, burn!

Joey Gilbert's sneer hit the cover of a national magazine. Joey-Cain became a 'Sixties ikon. Red banners flooded the gates and checkered the grandstands. Let him play! Calls overwhelmed the front office switchboard.

—You gotta' give this guy his shot!

—It's fair play, uh, the American way.

—Look you! The regular third baseman left his stinger in that unassisted triple play. He hasn't been the same with his bruised rotator cuff. Now we want the Gilber and we want him now.

—*What do you want?*

—*Gilber!*

—*When do you want it?*

—*Now!*

—*Boycott baseball!*

—*Fans strike! Fans strike!*

And somewhere in the crowd:

—*Bring the troops home! Bring the war home!*

There were hysterical letters to the editor.

If Joey was on the bench then it seemed America too was on the bench—its people, that is, not seeing any action when it came to the matter of their own destiny, which was political. In Joey's exclusion they felt their own: from real decision-making as to the great issues of the day.

For a few games all the excitement and thrills took place outside the park. The bleachers were a desert. The glum New York manager was hung in effigy from a mezzanine railing: the front office had to hire a bodyguard for Tight-Ass after there were threats to his well-being.

A fan screamed:

—Ya' big crumbbum ya'. I'll cut your dick off!

Here, there, a lonely voice taunted from the empty stands.

—That's right, you Sir! You Pharisee!

—Hey, baby! Stand up and siddown!

Before one game a woman in an evening gown ran out past the coach's box, kicking up lime, as if she got the sign to steal home in her high heals. She gave the matinee idol two dozen red roses. She bared her breast for Joey Gilbert to autograph in lipstick.

—I'll be your wife! she cried. Forget that other one!

—No, ma'am. I still love her.

The nation heard those words. It loved him for them.

Had America gone mad? Casting a misfit like Joey Gilbert as its darling?

XIII

So it went through the early season. A strange thing. Not Home Run Baker, and not Hack Wilson—but eccentricity, sentiment. In the stadiums were heard masochistic catcalls. Fans grew depressed en masse and had withdrawal symptoms. Suddenly a senior umpire was unable to make calls—like Buridan's ass, wrote an egghead the next day;—but stood at home plate debating with himself and reciting *Hamlet.*

Play-by-play announcers became introverted. They showed manic-depressive traits.

Fans began to resist the usual crude media manipulation.

Certain time-honored American values—such as a brainless pigheadedness based on shallow assumptions—were turned on their heads.

In fact, all across the land things were turning into their opposites. Right and left opposites were interpenetrating, and negations were being negated.

The National Pastime became a dialectical contradiction in the flesh of Joey Gilbert whose identity was a non-identity! How about that!

And so it was that ballparks around the League took thought of America's nature and destiny, and by extension Mankind's. Study groups formed up in the stands.

Joey was a micro-seeker after his wife. And America was becoming a macro-seeker after the facts of its own reality.

All in all it was a bizarre state of affairs. In those days a baseball park was like a fallen paradise.

Once peanuts and crackerjacks were munched happily between

cheers and razzings. Now there was a tormented crunch, crunch, as shells fell onto a thick treatise spread across a fan's knees.

Clap hands to encourage a hitter or pitcher? Hell no. The dwindling crowd inside the park formed into groups for 'criticism and self-criticism', and said it was chauvinistic to root for the home team. They were so deep in a collective effort to grasp the contradictions of U.S. society, they didn't pay much attention to what was happening.

Now and again some fool cried out beside himself:

—Hey! Yuh' mudduh wears uh leash, yuh big dodo yuh!

—We wanna' pitchuh not a glass uh . . . uh . . . LSD!

—Big banana!

That year thanks in part to Joey Gilbert the baseball fever was more like an overheated brain. Fans were sick unto death of right- or left-opportunist pitchers, umpires posing above the fray, adventurist pinch hitters, and aggressive double-play combinations.

—Sign-stealing infiltrator! Snoop!

—Curveballing deviationist!

—Contradictory manager! Expropriator of surplus value!

With so much ideology in and around the ballparks, and on the airwaves of America, it went almost unseen when the man behind it all began to run around a bit more and feel his oats. He seemed to get some fun out of it, and so he did his outfield sprints in a better mood.

Joey still had the great arm; it was a gun, but his pegs ended up in the next county. Now at practice he tried harder for the sheer physical pleasure of it: as an outlet from the boredom and morbid thoughts. He shook out the mothballs, and had a flash now and again of the old cocky glamor. His throws were more accurate. He ran faster, as a coach bawled after him:

—Shake a leg there! *Hot!* diggety.

One day Joey raised his head, among these overgrown boys with an intellectual horizon like a backstop, and began to carry himself less slovenly. Not that he cared a hoot for the pitcher's duel in progress, which was a beauty. But one day he did show up clean-shaven with his long curly hair stuffed under his cap.

What was going on? From day to day he changed. His uniform was on straight and he looked like a normal jock. Strong-jawed, he had the graceful brawn of the big athlete.

They stared at the ex-soldier, the war casualty, the nut, as he stood in front of a clubhouse mirror. Never since he joined the club had anyone seen him smile. And he didn't smile now. His features didn't soften at all. They grew harder. He wore the hard metallic grin he once had out at third, and he took it to Vietnam and put it through the crucible of war.

XIV

And then one afternoon the basepaths were hosed down and the outfield grass was sparkling in the bright May sunlight. And his name flowed forth, its syllables rippling in the breeze, like the folds of a banner. It poured out into a stunned silence from the loudspeaker system in the high rightfield scoreboard. There was no applause at first.

—*The eighth hitter, at the third base position, Joey Gilbert. Batting ninth, on the mound today . . .*

Excitement spread, as a news bulletin went out to the five boroughs, and the nation. Protesters hugged and backslapped at the turnstiles. There was joy. It was a victory, as they talked a blue streak and shook hands, vowing to carry forth the struggle to final victory. Comrade sports fan!

Now there were pretty bad traffic jams. In the lonely crowd of our expressways there were drivers getting out to do a dance on their hoods.

Commuting Wall Streeters forgot all about money and stock options; they rolled down car windows and sang 'Take Me Out to the Ballgame' in a rapturous chorus.

Jams and tie-ups got so bad on the City's main arteries that many simply switched off ignitions and sat listening to the play-by-play.

Battery go dead in the seventh inning? No problem! The joy will be such, when Joey pokes the winning homerun, it will jump-start our cars.

And they sat pounding the steering wheel not in a rage, for once, but in ecstasy as they bleated forth cheers like broken sobs:

—Play, Joey, you babe!

—Go get 'em, you kid!

—Lambaste that sucker! Send 'er for a ride!

—Oh you sweet kid! Oh you baby boy!

—Sock it with the rocket in your pocket!

Rubbernecked to the horizon in every direction, the Metropolitan Area was one great mass of motorized humanity. No more road rage: toot! toot! toot! move it, you asshole! But rather: root-a-toot-toot for the home team, which is the family of Man. Hurrah! You fool! Who cares what team wins? Don't be so narrow! If Joey plays, then we all win.

Rabidly ambitious executives jumped from limousines not for a fistfight with a fellow motorist but to do a jig.

—Yip!

—Honghh, you boy!

—For it's one, two, three decades and *yer' ouuuuut!* at the old ballgame of antisocial careerism. Free! Gentlemen, let's hang around. Forget profits! Be free and spree with me. Ah! Baseball, you honey. What a relief after my generation's life of quiet desperation. Play ball, Mighty Joe Young! Batter u-u-up! I've spent Dark Ages in this corporate Mudville, and I got a right to live a little. To hell with sound investments! The devil take stocks and bonds. I'm no longer a slave in the stocks, and my life force knows no bonds! Up next, in the on-deck circle, Life! If human beings don't win it's a shame! Over the fence with 'er, Casey. Transcend! I'm going out to the ballgame, and I don't care if I never come back to this slimy bourgeois existence I've been dragging out for a few hundred years! Ha!

XV

To see Joey Gilbert come out of the home dugout and take his position at third base—oh! . . . it was like Lazarus rising up as Tony Lazzeri. Calmly he walked, he didn't trot, past a third base coach struck by the look of him.

At the bag Joey scooped up a grounder tossed by the first baseman. He worked his body and arms a bit, getting loose, while his dark eyes scanned the grandstands in hopes it seemed he might spot a supportive fan.

The park and the world greeted him, but he didn't see his wife.

A sigh like a groundswell went round the stadium filled to over-flow. Did he hear, take note, care? He was poised, his face a blank, as he waited for the first pitch of the game. Now his chest and legs looked made for the clean uniform.

And now the people rose from their seats to greet the soldier back from the war. There were no cheers. At first it was a scat-tered applause for the veteran of a hundred battles in Vietnam. Over there the empire's reach was exceeding its grasp; but that wasn't Joey G.'s fault; he had risked and not spared himself, and he made it back to grasp a Reach baseball.

The other players stared at him. And now they, both teams, clapped hands and took off their caps to this strange man who could change overnight. It was one thing to hit, catch and throw a hardball, and another to face death everyday and inflict it, and get reported KIA, and come home and go back to baseball. Was he in his own league?

Joey didn't look at anybody. He stood out at third, and his dark eyes smoldered. It was passion: a man who cared more about his wife who was maybe alone and in despair than about being out here today.

When the applause stopped, and for the ten thousandth time since childhood the people hailed the twilight's last gleaming, maybe not so proudly—Joey's hands stayed by his sides. Today he would not remove his cap or salute the flag; and this gave the praise of his courage a bitter aftertaste.

But it was the 'Sixties. So a new wave of cheering rose up for a man who in the stubbornness of principle did not say yes to that flag of disaster.

The song ended. But this time no *rrrarrarahhh*, like the eternal deep in a seashell, followed the final bars and the 'home of the brave'. No; there was only a tense silence. What would he do on the field and at the plate in the first game of his comeback?

XVI

He led off the home third and was fooled so badly he could not hope to foul tip the Big League slider. Whiffed on four pitches.

Then he was able to corral a sharp grounder with his shin, like a goalie, and launched his throw high over first into the box seats. Awarded two bases the runner scored on a passed ball. Cincinnati 1, New York 0. It was an unearned run, but the manager didn't rant and kick the water cooler. The pitcher was upset and glanced at third from the mound. Joey stood in his thoughts.

In the fifth with two men on he had a good cut but again struck out. Curve low and away. Squelched a rally. Then there was a second fielding error as he let a grounder play him, bobbled, threw off line. Yet not a blink on his part; no scuff of the cleats. He was trying. He was getting into it a little more, and seemed to have his own idea. So he shook out his glove, and cast an eagle-eyed glance at the spectators.

Then it was the visitors' sixth. And he astounded the stadium. With men on second and third the lefthanded cleanup hitter nubbed a shallow pop, a dying quail behind third base. It was in shortstop territory but they had him shaded toward second for the pull-hitting lefty. The ball hooked and fizzled toward the line; it had double all over it. Like a parachutist Joey lunged backward into a crouching sprint and as his lithe body twisted, distended and went airborne—he dove and backhanded the ball blindly. In a fluid movement he wheeled like a standup slide in reverse and threw a perfect strike to second doubling the runner.

Cincinnati 1, New York 0.

There was silence. There was amazement.

But two innings later the crowd seemed to erupt in retrospect. A fastball sailed running the count to 3-1 on New York's seventh batter. The on-deck circle was empty. Are they pinch-hitting for Joey Gilbert? This manager is an imbecile! I'll kill him! All at once 50 thousand baseball addicts stamped their feet like mad and ranted:

—*Jo-ey! Jo-ey! Jo-ey!*

Ball four. Take your base. Two down and one on, bottom of the eighth.

The stands were in a crescendo of cheers and whistles.

If Joey Gilbert didn't get his licks there would be a baseball riot, like one of those South American countries where sports violence filled the hospitals, and morgues. We'll tear up this jernt!

There was a meeting in the first base dugout. TV cameras zoomed on Joey Gilbert and then the coaches in conference with the manager. Joey went up to them and said something. Was he arguing? He said more words in a few seconds than he had since coming to them. What pitcher or hitter balks at the hook?

The Major League ballpark shook like a bandbox under the stamp-stamp-stamp of feet. Watch out! The sports fans were in an ugly mood, and it could come tumbling down. Hey, let's lynch this dimwitted manager from the flagpole and be done with him. Don't make the bonehead play of taking out our darling!

But they grew quiet again as the warrior stepped out of the dugout. He came plodding toward the plate. 36-inch toothpick in one hand he leaned to heft a rosin bag with the other and rubbed 'er up and tossed 'er back.

Joey Gilbert stepped up.

He didn't dig in like a normal slugger. Didn't rake cleats, tap plate, thumb sweat, pump timber, sway torso. Didn't spit, flex, measure swing, jut massive chaw at pitcher; limber wrists on bat handle; grimace with one-run ballgame pressure; seem to say: this is man's work. No. If this one was an idol, deified by TV and reified by total paid attendance, then you'd never have known it.

Naw. Joey just waited with the bat on his shoulder. He stared out.

For a moment there was an eerie calm. Then—

—*Steeee'!*

Phew, what a wicked pitch. Did Joey bat an eyelash? Step in the bucket? Call for time, Ump? Did he raise a hand, back out of the box, tap cleats, put dust to sweaty palms? Did he spit photogenically? Squint? Blow nose through two fingers? Flick a lunger from his nostril? Did he touch crotch, finger cup, transfer chaw, spew brown like a locust?

Did he even check signs, touch cap, snort, blink?

No.

Nope. He waited. He was no longer the walking dead, but he wasn't in tiptop shape.

—*Steeeee'!*

A groan went through the stands. Was he out of it?

Now waste a pitch. Ride a high hard one in on his snout.

Catch-up run took a lead off first. Two gone, home eighth. The crowd was on the edge of its seat. In came the 0-2—

Ball one. Sharp curve off the plate. He didn't fish.

The Cincy ace took his time on the mound. He rubbed up the

ball. He doffed cap, wiped brow, tugged peak, fidgeted, looked in, shook off a sign, toed the rubber.

Here goes. He sets, eyes runner, rocks and kicks, the pitch—

Watch out! Low-bridged 'im. The 100-mph beanball rode in, kerrr-whap! The eighth hitter was down: flat on his back. Pretty good reflexes for a man who doesn't know where he is half the time.

But why all the fuss over this stiff unable in three trips to foul tip the ball?

XVII

On rounds at the hospital Lydia Falliere paused by a radio as the New York third baseman stood in for the 2-2. The whole city listened since the game wasn't televised.

She didn't know Joey Gilbert then: only news stories about his return, his winter in the Carolina woods. Now an associate by her side, a PTSD non-believer in line with most of the medical profession, tried to kid her:

—PTSD doesn't exist, so you'll have to invent it.

She said, as the Cincinnati catcher went out to the mound:

—The oracle said to Laïus, King of Thebes: Your son will kill you and marry your wife. So Laïus tied the child's feet and had him left out on Mount Cithaeron to die. Did he?

—N-no.

—And you can try to send away the truth, and deny it, for now.

The other laughed.

By this time Lydia was alerted to the plight of many soldiers coming back as basket cases from Vietnam, and she had one in her care. She was reading case histories of traumatic stress from World War II. She toured their hell intellectually and looked for patterns in the nightmares and dream-work. She knew former combatants had intrusive mental images: gore and death scenes popped in their minds even while awake. Cued by environmental stimulii a war veteran might relive past events as if they were vitally present.

Now as the Cincinnati ace shook off a sign Lydia asked herself how a brushback pitch might affect an ex-infantryman's startle response. His emotional state was one of generalized anxiety, an 'autonomic lability' even without the packed stands, and pressure to get a hit. For starters PTSD meant mental anguish which was often displaced somatically. Also it could mean a superhuman strength and clarity to confront danger—this amid an overlapped time sense, a kind of panoramic memory.

Most men, not all, might try to avoid a situation that was like the original trauma and the source of such acute symptoms: hyperalertness, cognitive dysfunction, survival guilt. But not Joey Gilbert. Why? What drove him? Was he using Major League baseball to try and find his wife? . . . That's love, thought Lydia.

Now a stadium full of fans sounded no less unstable than Joey when their silence broke into a riot of cheers and beseeching. They waited on the 2-2 pitch. They cried out his name; it was like mass hysteria as the park became a huge B-ward, seclusion room, for 50 thousand sporting schizophrenics.

XVIII

After the knockdown pitch he didn't bother to brush off the dust. Slowly he got up and stood motionless with the bat on his shoulder. He waited. Only his eyes showed a sign of life.

And the 2-2 . . . a hair outside! A slider slid off the trim. In the dugout the Cincy manager threw up his arms. Why the setup pitches? Why run it full on a sure strikeout? Drag out the count on this hitless wonder? Now that was fine—to walk the go-ahead run and put the equalizer in scoring position for a pinch-hitter.

The New York play-by-play announcer fell silent a moment in the suspense.

Then he called it:

—Count full, two outs. The runner takes his lead off first, he'll fly. Look out! Throw over nearly caught 'im off: leaning the wrong way. Cincy first baseman fakes a throw, tags the runner behind him. Now lobs the ball back to the hill. Tall righthander wipes his brow on 'iz sleeve; he has a three-hit shutout so far, Cincinnati one run, New York none through seven and two-thirds. Again he takes his sign. Comes set, nods. Runner at first into his lead, crouches, swings arms, half step from the grass after the near pick-off. And now the kick . . . delivery . . . *It's a line shot down the third base line, it's*———?———??———*foul!* (Wrrraaaoooaaaaaaaaah-h . . .) Good night! The cut he had on that boy! Joey Gilbert ripped 'er and sent a line shot down into the left field corner. Made you catch your breath the way that ball went on and on. All afternoon he hardly bats an eyelash, and then: whoomph! Uncoils the big hitch in his swing and explodes. He hung a clothesline from home plate out to the leftfield fence! All at once Joey Gilbert is a tiger and looks at home out there. Shot reflexes, you say? I beg to differ. A moment ago he hit the dirt nimbly enough, thank you. Seems it woke him up. Earlier in the count he didn't budge a muscle at the All-Star hurler's wicked dipsy-doo. But he jumped all over the last one, and it was not a Rip Sewall ephus pitch! Hey, don't count the Cincy flamethrower out just yet. How many late-inning jams he's got shut of since his first rookie start way back in '56 . . .? Now he steps off the rubber, takes off his cap, wipes brow on sleeve. He rubs up the ball and has a look around. Well, this two-time Cy Younger is one tough cookie. He's a veteran feared and respected around the League. Sure as death and taxes he'll reach back for a little extra this next pitch. Payoff pitch, two down, bottom of the eighth. Hey, you don't have a trophy cabinet the size of my garage and not bear down when it counts. Now he peers in for the sign. This one will not be Eddie Lopat junk. He comes set, nods back the runner on first. Steps off the rubber again as Gilbert just stares out at the mound. Lumber on his shoulder, like a statue. We do know blood flows in his veins after that drive he pulled a foot or two foul. Frankenstein is alive and well. He made contact and what a swipe he had . . . but got around a bit too quick. Well, let's see him do it again, says the Old Wizard. Calmly now, as if he was the only sane individual in the park, Joey waits on the 3-2. There he is: the soldier and leader of men. It looks like he's still a ballplayer . . . Big righthander in his set position; glimpses first, home, checks the runner over his shoulder again. And here's the payoff pitch, it's on the way . . . Oh! oh! There's a long, high drive toward deep right centerfield, it is high, it is deep, it is way back! Back . . . back goes the rightfielder nearing the wall. He times his leap and———and———does he have a play? He leaps, he . . . has he made a circus catch? Holy moly thar' she blows! Going, going, and it is gone!! Oh! oh! you can kiss that baby goodbye! Man oh man! I mean for a loopy-loop he knocked that sweet babyroll! Joey Gilbert has just slammed a two-run blast over the fence in right-center. He put that ball in orbit, sports fans! Outa' the ballpark she flew and into the night. Oh, pardner! Pass me my ammonium carbonate, if you please!

—*Oooooaaaaaaaaahrrrrraraaaaarahhhhh!*

Pandemonium. The stadium risen to its feet shook its fists and bawled itself hoarse while the batter trotted out his four-bagger and the Cincinnati pitcher gazed into space. Over the dugout steps came the manager as laughs and cheers went up at the man's deflated air despite a pot belly.

—*Raaaaraaaghhhhraraaaaahhh!*

Pausing on her rounds Lydia Falliere listened to the roar over the radio, and she felt stirred by a baseball game.

The New York announcer was swooning in the microphone:

—Oh, doctor!

XIX

Then they played him. His glove was erratic, and he could still be embarrassed at the plate. Some days he looked unrested, distracted, sort of half-baked. But then came late innings and the other side to his Jekyll-and-Hyde act. He got the club in a hole and then pulled it out. When he played, they tended to win. And as always the young nation honored its tribal fetish, which was: The Winner. His strikeouts stymying rallies, his errors and mental lapses on the field, were like a fall from grace. His bases-loaded triple up the alley in left center, and his backhanded stab at third to stave off disaster, were like salvation.

After a six-week sag since April the team went on a tear and won twelve straight. The veterans produced well. The three youngish starters of the mound corps began to settle down, and the bullpen drew on this momentum and had good luck. By June 10th the players were coming to an upbeat clubhouse. Even backup personnel seemed happy, riding the bench of League leadership.

But as Joey honed his old skills, as he hit his stride playing everyday, the sad lapses and errors went on. Dr. Falliere thought he looked so withdrawn: in a dissociative trance at moments. A sacrifice bunt went for an RBI double when, his mind on some faroff landscape of the war, he didn't charge and make the play but just let the ball roll toward him for precious seconds. This behavior she dubbed, in her first PTSD article for a medical journal, as: 'autonomically dysphoric'. The traumatic event in combat might leave a 'death imprint' on the psyche. Then came numbness which went with the denial (of a thing too much to handle). You could will to forget, but in so doing you denied a side of life, and this affected other sides. Her doctor colleagues might go along with the denial—and the nation, too, when Vietnam or future wars presented inadmissible catastrophes to the national conscience.

Suddenly one day the third baseman went berserk over—what? No one, not even the New York manager, that depth psychologist, knew what it was about. There wasn't any call for such an outburst—such a hot corner tantrum.

—You!—The home plate umpire jerked an arm at Joey.—Out!

When their idol was ejected, the crowd walked out too.

—His feelings! You jerk! You hurt Joey's feelings!

—You must show more understanding, Ump, and forgive!

—Respect the player's personhood!

These days the crowd shouted out profound remarks instead of catcalls. Well, they were in touch with their anger. From the stands they asked Ump deep questions and tried to psychoanalyze him. It was obvious he needed help.

One fan stood up and, at the top of his lungs, offered a diagnosis. Clearly the home plate umpire had a borderline psychosis with traits of pathological narcissism.

Someone tried to ask the Ump how *he* felt about the situation. It must be painful to have *his* tender sensibilities offended.

But before the umpire could reply, and vent his frustration, the place went wild. Both dugouts emptied. There was a free-for-all in the stands and a donnybrook on the field. The whole stadium 'abreacted'. Deep comments, attempts to empathize, were mixed in with fistfights, all-out brawls, bottles being thrown. In a moment someone could pull out a gun and blaze away even as he asked clinical questions and probed his victim's psyche and fixation at the anal stage.

Was this a war, or a group therapy session?

Down on the field Joey Gilbert rode out the waves of violence as ten men came on to try and pin him down.

When it was over: four players had been carried off to the emergency ward along with some forty spectators. As the parade of stretchers made for the gates, a band behind home plate struck up 'Take Me Out At the Ballgame', and everyone sang along with a sense of catharsis.

Dr. Falliere had to see such illogical moods and lack of self-restraint in part as decompensation due to his wife's absence.

But what would happen next? Was it time to call for the men in the white coats? Straitjacket and forcible injection?

One thing was sure: the New York manager would have to be committed pretty soon, if not Joey Gilbert.

The Commissioner of Baseball announced a month's suspension for the crazy third baseman. But it had to be rescinded. The man might as well sign our National Pastime's death warrant, as ban Joey.

XX

Then Gilbert spoke to the media in defiance of a gag order.
Question:
—Do you see your comeback as a patriotic thing?
—I fought in Vietnam. If you don't like it, then go (bleep) a duck.
Question:
—You've received the President's Citation. Do you care to comment?
—Let that bag of bones go fight the next one.
Follow-up:
—You mean you wouldn't defend your country?
—If they want me for another of their wars, they'll have to burn the woods and sift the ashes.
Question:
—Why did you throw a tantrum yesterday? Out of a clear blue sky?
His gaze drifted. He bent his arms forward, putting on a show for the press. For the image had come again in a dream last night.
—Napalm—he said, eerily, into the microphone.—This is how they walk when they're on fire. They go slow. They don't run.

—You cursed out an umpire because of napalm?

—. . .

A reporter asked:

—You miss signs. Blow routine plays. You're constantly scanning the stands. Are you the first ballplayer who ever came out to watch the spectators?

Joey shrugged.

Another asked:

—Your coaches hope and pray no fielding chance will come your way. Why all thumbs, Joey?

He grinned. He gave them the cocky mask of the pro athlete, but not exactly. From one day to the next now he pounded out a gamer, and made amazing plays at third. By the bag he raked his spikes like an E-tool and dug in against a sapper attack . . . Since his actions spoke, he did as he liked. And what he did now was turn his back on the press.

The masses paid to see him play. So the manager kicked the water cooler and popped a blood pressure pill between innings and crossed himself. Meanwhile the League in its dignity looked critically at the psycho jock who was not 'one of theirs'; although gate receipts, in such hard times, when people couldn't even forget reality at a baseball game, *were* theirs. And so they laid off Joltin' Joey, who was such a hot commodity. For they were not so out of their minds as to kill the goose that lays the golden eggs, and I don't mean goose eggs.

XXI

—What happened?

They sat in Lydia Falliere's office. He had come back to her. Joey Gilbert was the man who comes back.

—When?

—Last night. What got into you?

He smirked. A small laugh got out of him.

—You saw?

—The grand finale.

Silence. Lydia waited. On a personal level she liked to have him here in her office. She smiled, more girlish than professional, and she thought: Beware . . . boundaries. But what she felt was: him . . . him.

For a long moment the ballplayer knit his brow and brooded where he sprawled across an armchair.

She hadn't given her own psychoanalysis three years in order to flub the countertransference. A therapist's skill and equilibrium try to offer a live object, at issue, for the patient's parental love-hate transference. The care-giver must be steady and sure so the patient's repressed instinct, material, will come forth and unbind old graveclothes, say the winding-sheets of neurosis. Then treatment may proceed; but not if the psychiatrist's needs get into the act. Oh, she could see the bright be-careful signs on the borders of their therapeutic terrain. What Lydia could not see at the moment was why a deep, tender, human love shouldn't be better than an office visit.

Words from a Chinese poem, cited in a theoretical journal, came to mind this warm day in late spring:

> *Rare the good player,*
> *rarer still the good listener.*
> *Udumbara tree's flower*
> *is seen once in this world.*

The hour passed in a sort of vortex. Yes, she loved a patient. And, yes, she could not approve. If she loved science, if she loved vocational ethics, she would serve Joey better.

In the quiet office as she sat waiting for him to reply, she thought of Freud's mortality theory. A metabolism bred its own death. But it was in the contest of opposites, in the dynamism of contradiction—when hope wasn't taken away—that life thrived.

XXII

—So what was it?
—It . . . was my wife.
—In the ninth inning?
—She might see me and come to me.

—You mean see how you need her?

—Maybe.

—There's been no word from the detective agency?

The psychiatrist waited. From his own needs he must fill this silence. Not she from hers. At every turn there were issues of trust, and control.

—No.

—What were you thinking about her?

—I was just needing, and thinking. Please, Carlyne, come home.

—And if she did you'd be okay?

—Then I could focus. Then no more lapses on the field. I think so.

Lydia gave a nod. Her features flushed just a touch. From a none too safe distance she heard a siren song: ths song of her own desire. So overworked, so lonely at moments, now she thought: bind me fast to the mast of principle, but let me listen.

Silence.

—So you feel if your wife came back . . .

—I don't know.

He gestured.

He looked at Lydia as though he had never seen her—didn't know what he was doing here.

Careful . . . take it step by step, a delicate control. At his own pace the patient gropes, amid shadows of repressed material, to get at the traumatic past. He seeks to relive the event or period of life in question: where the fixation is, like a stagnant pool—where the flowers of reaction-formation evil grow. He seeks a new and conscious relation to those old events his ego could not accept. For he still needs to work through them, and it doesn't matter how long after the fact.

Finally he must face the facts, but he is afraid. He fears himself. His defenses and his denials have served a purpose since he cannot know such outrage and such suppressed rage and still hope to act responsibly. Someone is going to be hurt . . .

So it is with care and patience that the analyst begins to dig and open the grave where such pathology lies buried alive. But this can only be done in so far as the transference with its testy approach-avoidance and its pretexts, its proofs of trust, has been made to work for and not against.

A shared strength is needed to control the situation.

And so it is no time for the therapist's own needs—a counter-transference gone awry.

Respect defenses. Do not uncover until patient and doctor have agreed on how to maintain control within limits.

Together, and clearly, decide on control strategies.

In these preparatory sessions she must play it safe, and not go out on a limb.

Love's limb.

XXIII

Joey blinked. He looked at her but sought to shy away.

—I don't know what you mean.

—You lapse in concentration due to your wife's absence. That's the reason, no other?

—Righto.

Restless in the armchair he was all set to get out of there.

In a jam the sports hero likes to trivialize. It works.

Gently she said:

—When that happens out on third, then you feel . . . her? No other image or idea intrudes?

He shook his head—in a boyish tone, unlike him, said:

—Leave me alone.

She knew he might not return after this visit. So she risked. She took the plunge.

—She left you, Joey. She went away. Now what do you feel? Anger? Guilt?

—. . .

He looked away in pain.

—Let's try this. Focus on a side issue. Last night a routine ground ball bounced past you. A double play was turned into two unearned runs, and you blew the game. Now your team is out of the League lead.

—Well, I put 'em there.

—I know. But it was so unlike you: in the late innings that way. Now tell me one other thing, less painful maybe than Carlyne, on your mind at that instant: when the easy play got away from you.

—My father.

—Your father? Why?

Suddenly Joey's rugged features had such a . . . such a glow. He looked like a ten year-old; it was the affect of a child.

—Well, he always seems so, you know, so educated, so good. He's like you. And yet—

—Yet?

—No.

Joey shrugged.

There was a pause. But, all at once, it was filled with emotion.

—You love him.

—Sure!

—Is that what you thought on third base last night? That you love your father?

He turned toward her, with a kind of sigh, and seemed to reach up.

—I'll tell you . . . a story.

—Okay.

—But why bother you with it, Doctor? You don't need a lot of fuss.

She gave a warm laugh.

—My stock in trade.

—What do you care about a dumb third baseman?

—Tst. Tell me the story.

Again he sighed and looked up at her. It was a charm: Joey Gilbert so boyishly unsure.

—Well, he said, okay. You asked for it.

—I did. Now give it.

XXIV

—I have a younger sister named Lemon.

—Lemon as in tea?

—Well it's Elizabeth Mona. I guess my brother made it Lemon, since she cost him just a bit of our mom's favoritism. She's real nice, the best kid on earth, never selfish, or jealous. You know, I think I'm *her* favorite.

—Mine too.

Lydia nodded. This was his first sign of openness in three visits, and she felt so grateful!

—She just turned seventeen, real pretty. Supposed to go to college in the fall: same one I went to, down South. And now, would you believe it—Joey shook his head—Dad wants to get her married.

—Arranged marriage?

—Not only that. It's to a man in his sixties. Someone she makes fun of.

—A pungent Lemon.

—When he comes around the house and lolls his tongue out at her, she sings the song about a hound dog. His first name is Maximilian, so she calls him Thanks-a-Million 'cause he's such a penny pincher.

—Ouch. Not just pennies.

—How can I sit back and watch my dad sell his daughter into slavery? My brother, Newell, says it's for political reasons.

—Political?

—Emory's team lost the Presidential election last November, but his star goes on rising. Maybe he's still thinking about Washington ties, and Max Doan has them. The man is a West Pointer and World War II veteran of Guadalcanal and Sicily; he rose through the grades to General and has held various high posts, Deputy Secretary of Defense, others. Now he's helping to work out counterinsurgency strategies in Washington State: for Vietnam and the other Vietnams we may have to fight. His kind never die, they simply redeploy. He's the eternal Eagle Scout, his blond crewcut lined with silver. And now it seems such a proud life sees its dessert in my little sister.

After a pause Lydia said:

—Seven courses, then a sweet. What does your sister say?

—Been upset for months. Think about it! . . . I remember a hot summer day in the South. Not a leaf stirring. Here I come along the main street from the ball field, a kid who's thirsty and wants a soda. Ain't got a thin dime on me. You know the way.

—Many a time.

—Now here comes that jaunty man, Doan, looking so dapper. Safari helmet, cutoff khakis, suspenders. I squint up at him: Hey,

Mister, you got a quarter you could loan me? I'll pay you back! I'm dyin' for a raspberry soder up here't d'sody fount. Please? . . . Doan chuckles like this is a little joke between him and me. And passes by. I look after him, at his high nylon socks held with garters. Thanks-a-Million! No wonder he bores Lemon more than the Andrews Sisters, with his career and all his honors. He's a tightwad! So it gets me, Doctor, and I wish those two big bruisers, Dad and Max, would leave my kid sis' alone and let her get on with her life. But they won't. Emory keeps insisting. And little by little Lemon gets used to it, I guess. She gives in.

—She'll marry him?

—Could.

—Why? Is she afraid?

—Lemon afraid? Of nothing! She grew up around me 'n Newell, Gilbert ape-men. She's a spunky tomboy. Never asked for our help in the playground though she knew she could . . . No; it's because she loves our father. Doesn't want to let him down.

—Let him down!

XXV

When the patient had gone, Lydia jotted notes in one of her PTSD notebooks:

> *The traumatic event is swaddled in guilt. It may not any more than an infant say why it feels pain. There is reference to a violent dysformative experience—in a hint, a casual aside. This could pass by the interviewer.*

> *Fears (control loss, damaged integrity or credibility) find shy often symbolic expression in presented material. The words (interview protocol, therapeutic method) link up and lead to trauma-related material.*

> *Avoidance.*

> *Three cardinal features of diagnosis; 1) trauma history; 2) trauma reexperience; 3) avoidance phenomena. Avoidance is related via 'sprung dialectics' of pathology to the original (sic) trauma.*

Birth trauma, grief early or late, loss whether parent, spouse, lover, job, friend, comrade, child—life's milestones and systemic stressors may pale by comparison with the shock of traumatic stress which is so unexpected. But to what degree do they provide a predisposition, or, say, an arena?

Then Lydia charted their hour. As it drew to a close she had looked for a hopeful summation. This is a ground rule: gauge time for a positive closure. Do not exceed the sixty minutes.

For the first time she opened up with him, showing her wisdom:

—Our world may go out of kilter: not as we wish it, anymore, and need it. So we try out new ways to make it okay again. If your father is picking on his daughter and wants to take away her free will, then he must be hurting inside about something. I think maybe quite a lot. Something has gone wrong.

—Like what?

—You'd have to ask him.

—I don't think he'd tell me. You even less.

—No? Why?

—Emory wouldn't be caught dead in here. He doesn't like headshrinkers.

—Oh no?

Joey laughed; and gave a glimpse, unlike him—s shyness mingled with awe.

—Well, a beautiful one he might. He'd try to get you on Freud's couch.

—Down there with him—said Lydia, face flushed.—A lady's man.

They stood up: the well-dressed psychiatrist, and her client the athlete, in a t-shirt.

Joey said:

—I feel a little better now.

And then, before Lydia Falliere knew it, he had embraced her. They were cheek to cheek nicely. There was an electric spark, as from a rug, in the first instant of their contact.

These traumatic phenomena repeat compulsively until insight begins piercing through to freedom—and furthers the trajectory from passivity . . . to mastery. Pathognomic of PTSD they offer, considered universally, a 'raccourci' or foreshortened view. Passage from childhood dependence to mature adulthood: the price. (For: 'Oedipus On My Couch')

Gracious as ever—trying not ˙ to look ruffled—the doctor had ushered him out. Boundary #1: never countertransfer romantically.

Chapter Sixteen

I

Carlyne stared out the trailer window at the big German shepherd named Dirk. If ever there was a vicious dog, this one was it. And he was her guardian.

Early mornings Melchior drove his van down the gravel driveway and off to the tobacco factory. And his woman in the trailer lot three miles outside Mebane breathed a sigh of relief. First she gave the child her breast. Then she cleared away the mess and washed dishes, swept the floor, dusted, tossed out beer cans and cigarette butts from the carousal the night before.

At eleven months the tiny girl Rhoda Strong was okay. All normal as far as Carlyne could tell: Rhody smiled, babbled; she turned to her mother's voice. Her weight was about 20 pounds. Only thing: she was often whiny, if not crying, and choleric. The country boy Melchior did not help things when he came back full up to here with his boss's lip, and the day at work.

The brawny tobacco processor was a bit too nervous some evenings and quick on the trigger till he got his 6-pack. And then he could be even quicker, depending. At times Carlyne didn't mind, almost, when he hit her and then made love like a factory on speed-up. She knew he was doing it because deep down he felt he was beneath her. And hey a little sentiment makes the world go round. Also he was sorry the next day. He loved her in his way, if you can call that love.

But of the baby he felt jealous. And she rarely let him handle her.

Now, looking out the window, Joey Gilbert's wife felt the irony of her situation. She was living in a trailer again like that summer in the Minor Leagues when she didn't take to it. She said to herself: this is good for me; this is what the likes of me deserves . . . But there was another voice in her which said something different as she paused staring out at Melchior's vicious dog. This was the voice of Carlyne the Lumbee's nature: stubborn, restless, it wouldn't quit. This was the voice of her character, which would out, and dog or no dog.

For today she meant to get away.

II

After all Melchior had his own cross to bear. He wasn't the worst by far and he loved her to death and was afraid she would try to leave him. In his fits of jealousy he called her a whore and said he saved her from every Joe Blow on East Main. So she owed him right much! Not that she didn't put out for him too; but she had a self-willed style of whoopdedoo which made him wonder. She could seem pretty distracted while in the act. This was food for thought. When the thing had ended, and he lay back and scratched his belly, he couldn't quite tell what her mood was or what to say. So he either tried to keep things light, or got himself all in a huff.

And yet she seemed to look for a good beating now and again. Why? Well, she had her little secret, or big secret, and the man knew what it was, though she didn't know he knew.

Mornings on his radio Melchior listened to the Country Boy, and in the evening it was romantic songs from Charlotte. But above all things, except one, he liked baseball. It could be midnight after he guzzled his brew and had a good bout of roust-'em-out sex—the rabid fan tuned in a game on the staticky radio from Chicago or St. Louie. He knew a team by its announcer's voice and its beer commercials: the Ozarks, land of sky-blue waters.

He used to take time off from the tobacco factory and drive his van on campus and watch the best college ballplayer he ever saw. He loved it when Joey Gilbert dove and speared a bullet down third, or poled a towering fly over the high wall of shrubbery in left. Shirtless, all brawny shoulders and overalls, Melchior talked it up and felt like a real man when a coed gave him a tumble on the grassy bank behind the first base dugout. Then that summer he had kept up on pro stats in the *Herald Sun* from the third baseman's first year in the Minors.

Then it made him wonder when Joey hung up his spikes—after a cup of coffee in New York—to go shoot communists in Vietnam, and get shot back at. But he would wonder more when he learned that each Saturday he made fast and furious sex at 20 bucks a coup with his #1 idol's wife: whom he knew not as Carlyne but as 'Tray'.

Once or twice Tray heard her husband's name when the redneck chatted between the orgasms he paid for like piecework. But in those first visits on Lamonde he went away when he was told: when she gave the breast to Rhoda in the alcove. Oh, he wasn't the worst of 'em, not by a long shot. Maybe she was worse in her way than he was. It was only jealousy made the poor guy mean and ornery. What he could not swallow was the idea Tray had other clients, because you know he was simply nuts over his tawny squaw with her deep blue eyes like an Ozark lake and her strong bosomy body. He even got used to the baby as long as the tiny tot didn't give him no jive or shit up the place in her crib or have one of her asthma attacks when she started wheezing like a little blue devil.

Yep, he spent a C-note one or two nights on Tray when he was the first slugger to clout five homers in a box score. But Tray said no thanks to a package deal: one fee includes romantic sunrise. All in all this relationship was costing him more than marriage though it wracked his nerves a little less. He was paying her top Durham rates yet at times she couldn't stand the sight of his face and said: Look, get your ass out. He surely took it amiss when she would not say his name, kiss him on the lips, have dinner with him and see a movie at the Criterion like normal couples.

—Normal? Us?—Tray laughed and hurt his feelings.

—Now listen, Baby, I mean it. You and Smelly come out and live in my trailer in Mebane. Save you rent money.

—You mean save *you* rent money.

—I cain't have you walking no street, now can I? You got some strange cusses in this town. Other night last row of the Criterion I sat down next to a big blond. Bit young, aincha' Sonny? she says. So I felt between her legs, and lo! it was a hardass.

—Lovely.

—Look, Tray, I guess I love ya'. Come live with me in Mebane.

She gave him a wry look, which hurt, 'cause a man didn't say I love you to every whore he met and besides he spent more hard-earned cash on her than he did alimony payments sent to his ex-wife every month.

Tray sure could put on airs for a prostitute. She could talk country and she could talk educated, but mostly she didn't seem to care a damn for him or herself either, but only the child. Boy if she kept needling him he would surely smack her one day.

—Thanks but no thanks—she said, wearily.

—Think it over, I'll take care of yuh. We could be happy.

—Happy?

Her laugh stung him.

III

Unlike most folks Tray didn't cater to radio or TV. Wittily Melchior said she didn't need no boob tube 'cause she had such big boobs. Once in a while she brought out some old school book or other and read a little.

—What's that? he asked.

—Russian novel.

—Oh yeah? Well I ain't got no use for no Rooskies.

Melchior had a small battery radio clipped on his cowboy belt; it had an earplug so he could play it at work. One night as Tray rose from bed with a sigh and moved toward the alcove and Baby Two-Shoes, he took the portable radio from his Farmer John overalls and turned the dial. He tuned for a late-inning game, but the Midwestern stadiums lay dark and silent by this hour and you can't ever get the West Coast. There was country music on WWVA in Wheeling, West Virginia, 'Fräulein, Fräulein . . .' Melchior listened to the song, and belched; but then rose on one elbow.

—Say there.

—What?

He sat forward.

—Honey, listen here.

The edge to his voice drew her gaze. Unsatisfied customer? It was her occupational hazard. In the middle drawer of the night table behind tampax and tissues was the sheath knife.

Child to the breast she peered from the alcove.

—What?

—Just heard a news flash. Somebody I knew died . . . I used to take off work and drive on campus to watch him play third. Man, could he hit.

—Third base?

Melchior chuckled.

—He paid the tab.

—What's his name?

—Porbubbly you don't know it. Baseball aincher' game, even if'n you got curves. Ha ha.—He leered at her: the flesh taut on her cream-colored nightgown, digging into those big teats now the brat was fed. Hair up tight in a bun; perfume and touch of lipstick; she must need an extra twenty. Yup, it was time to shell out another twenty.—Too bad, too bad. That guy had promise. So do you, honey; it's a shame, a knockout like you living this way. Come with me to Mebane.

She said again:

—The name.

—Huh? Oh, it's nothing. But he was some ballplayer. Each year in late March the parent club comes through here headed north; but those boys so good they don't seem human. Them's the Bigs, baby, and you's the Bigs, ha ha. Come out to Mebane, we'll be two pigs in a trough.

—Tell me his name.

—Huh? Oh, Joey Gilbert.

—Ah.

—People round here remember him. Say, where you from? You never tell me.

She turned her back to him since her face had begun to twitch.

—Ah.

—Baby, you look all shook. There's a fan in you after all, deep down. Well, if I ain't a tinhorned lizard.

—Turn off the light.

—Say what?

—Off. It hurts my eyes.—Her voice trembled.—I've got a bottle of brandy: we'll drink to Joey the third baseman.

IV

That night she made love like a wild animal in a trap. Very drunk she sang a pop tune but then doubled over and groaned. Melchior wondered should he drive her to emergency. What a time for an appendicitis! But again she clawed him and made guttural sounds and almost turned him off with her humping even more lewd than his own.

He couldn't believe the sudden change in her so he said Joey Gilbert's name again for the hell of it to see her reaction. Phew! Did this honky Durham girl have a crush on the pride of ACC baseball? Now for the first time with her Melchior felt himself in the cockpit: when she got so wild she forgot to use it like a cash register.

In the deep night she dug her nails in his skin and raised her leg over his thigh and clutched at his sweaty neck and made him work, baw'! Why, she should have been paying him for it! But then she grew quiet and gulped more brandy and hiccupped. She rolled over, away from him, and started to cry.

The big man lay wide-eyed on his back and wondered why she let him stay there and even got her mind off his wallet. It was good Rhody slept through the ruckus. For who could have coped if she woke up and gave her creasy wail and flailed for the tit or had her damned asthma attack? Not Melchior, no way! You crazy, hoss? A real man leaves the dirty diapers and such truck, piss all over creation and caca and upchuck, to the little woman.

At eight a.m. he went out and called in sick from a pay phone and came back to stay with her. What was going on? A nervous breakdown? It weren't no easy life walking the street: all on 'em nuts more or less, except high-class call girls. So he supposed.

He lay beside her listening to his transistor as ol' Country Boy read an ad for Kroger's out there on Hillsboro Road and then came a Garth Sprung tune and then awhile later more about Joey Gilbert in the news from Vietnam.

Finally he did oblige himself to go and take a dish cloth to Rhody's rear end. By 9 a.m. left to her own devices, good gracious! she lay in a shitty mess. How could you be such a little tyke and pollute the atmosphere that way? Melchior held his breath, head up in a dignified pose, while swabbing off her pink rashy rump. She kicked a little bit and was just beginning to pitch a fit for Tray's squirty milk. Well, she knew what was good.

The man worked his nostrils and thought: Lordy, can I do this? I must be in lu-u-u-uv.

V

But a minute later the grin faded from Melchior's dimpled cheek.

As Tray lay asleep he poked around for some formula and clean baby clothes. The room on Lamonde looked sad by morning light—on this street a stone's toss from the tobacco factory where he spent his days no longer so dreary since he met this alley cat.

His big calloused hands rummaged among pink outfits with a cotton lace fringe. He tried one of Rhoda's stubby shoes on his thumb. There was a coquettish little bonnet with strings. Baby Buntling.

But his finger touched on—what beneath the clothes? Was it the child's birth certificate?

Maybe he could learn Tray's real name and where she came from. He pulled out a document in gothic lettering. Ah, so the uppity woman has her high school diploma which he never got.

> The Faculty and Trustees recognize
> the successful completion of studies
> required by the
> College of Arts and Sciences
> and confers upon
> Carlyne Locklear Gilbert
> the degree of
> Bachelor of Arts

Carefully he read the official signatures: Board of Trustees Chairman, University President, Undergraduate Dean, Secretary of the University. There was a seal too: a flaming cross in a landscape.

Melchior stared at the diploma framed in glass. A Latin inscription ringed the seal: Eruditio et Religio.

Since boyhood he had seen the well-fed kids stroll from campus into the seedy town where he lived. They went to the College Shoppe for their madras shirts and the Carolina or Criterion for a movie date with a coed he could never hope to say hi to. He saw their sports cars, Austin-Healy and MG-B; they were Phis and ATOs who liked to talk shit on benches outside their frat houses and have parties where the Rot Guts played and go for pitchers of beer at the Rathskeller in Chapel Hill. Then it was Myrtle Beach for a week when school let out in June. Oh, he had seen them for a long time and heard their laughter like sour apples. He imagined life after college graduation: well-paid jobs in Raleigh and Richmond. Why, in two weeks seated at a desk where they pushed a pen and talked bull on the phone, they made his factory pay for three months. Blasé, spoiled, they took life for granted.

Not that Melchior took all this amiss. Hey, people on TV were the same way. But he did know their chitchat weighed like chaff except when it came to money. And given the chance he would act more manly than these creatures with clay feet. Yet he envied and even respected them—but now lookee here: one on'm turned into a proper whore.

He put Carlyne Gilbert's college diploma back in the drawer.

That day she woke up toward noon.

The burly man snoozed in the worn armchair. Rhoda lay in his lap: her pink curly head in his meaty hand that never quite looked clean. Ad for matrimonial happiness.

He opened his eyes and saw the woman looking rumpled like her nightgown.

—C'mon, Honey, I'll take you and Rhody to my trailer in Mebane. You cain't stay this way no longer. I know you ain't no whoah-h.

She stared at him. It was grief, and she was like a wounded animal, lame. Hadn't even asked him to pay for the three orgasms while she drank and laughed and sat on him.

—Come, Hon'. You'll love it out there. It's nachur'.

After a moment he rose and let her take the girl as he set about to clear out the drawers and do up her stuff. He was a man in control.

VI

It hadn't been easy living with him. She came near braining him when he went on—too insecure!—about 'unedjacated Injun' and 'tobaccy face' and 'Cher'kee slut'. Sometimes she thought over the idea of suicide. She liked to. But Rhoda Strong's clamor and needs held her back so far.

The child made Carlyne think of herself abandoned, that morning long ago, and she was alone in the world. And the day came when she tried to replace her father by an athletic demigod with dark eyes and a kind smile. It was her very own manly ideal. For sure he could satisfy her every need and whim. What say? Not quite? Then who else could she idealize? Her wise, learned, famous father-in-law. Hm. That hadn't worked too well either, and so now here she was with her ideal Melchior, who could glug jug, belch loud, fart tart, feel and squeal, brawl and squall.

But now it was time to leave this Eden.

The first hurdle was Dirk, the guard dog.

VII

She stood at the sink and wiped off dishes, one by one, with a dishcloth. She took her time, looking out at the yard. Through the window she could see the German shepherd asleep twenty feet from the trailer. Quiet now, soothed by the sunlight, the attack dog would eat a child if given the chance. A trainer had taught the big sleek animal to go for the throat with its fangs—and mangle anyone within range besides its master. This meant her too if she tried to go outside—stepped out for a breath of air. The watchdog's chain ran to the trailer door. It was like Melchior's sick jealousy.

For weeks she had the worst sort of cabin fever. Life was a misery in here with him. At times she did want to kill herself, but it made her head spin to think how quickly this man would unload the child one way or another. He watched his mindless TV shows like a drug. He swore more and more and insulted her. He got rough. His soul was so sloppy—who could ever tidy it up?

But even all that wouldn't have gotten her on the move—by itself. After all she had no money. She wasn't fit for normal life anymore. Broken in spirit. She only had one resource left: the street. So maybe she did belong here: a prisoner who couldn't open the door without a killer dog's slaver in her face.

What a gray furry beast it was—perfect symbol of the male when he didn't get his way. And it hated her with all the rage of a cast-off favorite.

But asleep now, abeyant.

What to do?

What brought Carlyne back among the living? Hatred of Melchior, his fists?

No.

One Saturday afternoon in April he was watching a Major League game on TV. It was in New York. When a camera panned the home dugout, Carlyne gave a lurch.

Of course Melchior knew about Joey Gilbert being alive and returning to baseball. Till then Tray hadn't heard the news, but it had to happen sooner or later.

That afternoon the network cameras showed viewers the unshaven face with black hair in a tangle at nape and cap. Those features, a cross between Zeus and a hippie, were out of place in a sports setting to put it mildly.

And now Carlyne, who thought her husband died in Vietnam, saw him.

The zoom lens didn't linger on Joey Gilbert. And there was no comment. The upbeat announcer took no notice. Ostracized, in silence; fined by the Commissioner for his unpatriotic act of not putting cap to heart for the Star-Spangled Banner—why was he here in a baseball dugout and not in a doorway on the Bowery? Just look at the guy. One sensed his contempt for the chuckleheads seated away from him along the bench: pinch batters, utility infielders, tomorrow's starter busy at a chart, veteran coaches, deadpan manager. Look at him, and then look at the baby-faced boys married to their high school sweethearts. They wore crew-cuts, and made horny remarks. What did they know besides slug-ging percentages and RBIs, scouting reports on a hitter's weak-ness, or relief pitcher's stuff? But he was like the news story said: a man back from the grave, who knew its secrets.

Then Carlyne in front of a TV in a place called Mebane had a shock—not just to see him, but also to see him *that way*. And what did she feel? Pity: as if he was her son. And remorse: to see her work, and what it did to a man. Yes she saw the work of a master. What had she done to the man who loved her so? It stunned her.

What power she must have even now over him. How he needed her. For one person only in the wide world he gazed into a network TV camera. Well, he should have been in a hospital gown, not a baseball uniform. He belonged in a nuthouse. But the New York team's owner had to compete for publicity this year with such things as protest marches, and the Chicago Eight trial: join the conspiracy! Baseball was upstaged by the Easter G.I.-ci-vilian demonstrations and Spring Actions against the war where a hundred thousand marched through New York City in the rain, and the Crazies paraded pig heads on poles. The political events cast a shadow over leaping grabs against the wall, and bottom of the ninth roundtrippers.

VIII

So Carlyne saw her own despair in Joey's eyes. He was a man alone out there. He was like Henry Berry Lowry.

Behind her a beer can crunched. Phizzz! Melchior swore as he crushed the can in his fist and beer foamed up. It splattered the TV screen. He was the boss in his own trailer, goddamn it; and if you don't like it, cunt—then you can't leave!

Now she knew. That was the afternoon of recognition.

Also, he knew her secret. Knew her name. Sure, he had seen the diploma in her suitcase. On to her all these months; but she hadn't known he knew.

Then he yanked out the plug of the set. Melch belched, and stuck out his beer belly with pomp, and grabbed up his boots. Go outside and harass the ferocious dog? Fuss under the hood of a jalopy?

—I'm sick of this shit!

He looked like a ruffled cock. But it was all a fake. Upset, shook up, gonna' lose her.

He glimpsed Carlyne who stared at the gray screen.

—What? she said.

—TV sucks!

—You don't say.

She almost laughed. Television was his church, his pew and his pulpit.

—I'll hurt you—he pointed at her—bitch!

Then he hefted the set toward the door. Comical with the bulky appliance in his arms, he turned back.

Grimly, she said:

—Take care: your hernia.

Now this wasn't funny. The man snarled like his dog:

—I mean it, Red. Don't you ever . . . cross me.

Despite everything she laughed at the shit-eating look he had. Horse out of barn door. Now he'd lug the thing out to his tool shed and watch it there: cursing the world and himself for being such a big fool. For now he'd be lonely. Like most TV addicts he preferred to share his living death with someone.

IX

Another moment she stood at the sink and slowly washed off last night's dishes. In the pane of the slightly open window her face had a hard country look. An unsutured scar marred her brow. She wasn't pretty. Bruises dotted her body. The man had a few too. How he kept after her last night into the wee hours, slid down and mush-mushed her shapely buttocks, obstreperously. Pretty soon it would be her rear he went for. Tongue probed. Teeth bit flesh. Lick it, slurp, burrow in her thighs. He had a whiny tone. Sweet nothings. Then said he meant to dress her up real fancy some night and go shake a leg in that juke joint on the highway this side of Raleigh. She'd be the Queen of Route 70.

After round-the-world he snuggled up in a pillowtalk frame of mind. Poor panda, unpampered by life, uncouth as hell.

—You sure quiet.

—Grateful, she said.

—You 'n yer' words.

He looked up at her. She always surprised him. He never surprised her.

—Keep still.

—Momma, le's me and you get hitched. I mean it. Mebbe' I could relax then.

—Sorry.

—You too good for me, Red?

—No, I just don't go in for polygamy.

—Pigallome?

—Precisely.

Drunk, he sighed, because he knew.

—Well, gimme' a buss, sweetie.

Like a prostitute she wouldn't kiss his lips. One of his beefs against her.

Joey was back. She was quiet now; she didn't flutter in her cage. No, she brooded in silence and sought a way out. One thing was the watchdog. Two: no money. Three the long walk to Mebane center for a train or bus. Four: what about Rhody, food, a place to sleep? Five: where to?

Still she had to go. Why? Not because a hillbilly battered her up. Not even because her husband came back from the dead to walk this bitter earth. Him she had zero hope ever to see again. No, but . . . it was her people; it was her ancestors hunted down in the Carolina swamps. Eyes transfigured by the tribal past they still wanted to be free. They didn't give in.

Through the week she tried to plan. She couldn't decide. At night when her mood quieted down she had a look at the burly tobacco processor, who was also looking her over, squint-eyed. But even as she waited, in her thoughts, Carlyne handled him like a master. Her extra flesh since she gave birth played to his most extravagant desires. For a few more nights she'd respond to his caresses.

—You're too nice—he said—too smooth. Like a cat.

—Miao.

She purred.

—It ain't us, said Melchior. You mean to leave.

—Sure—her voice fell.—Over your watchdog's dead body.

Back from the factory he stayed outside more among his rusted chassis, auto parts, the bricks he picked somewhere, an old Thunderbird with a For Sale sign.

Then, this morning when he went off to work, she decided. Now or never. And no matter what! Time to go.

As usual she was impulsive, but so what? Today she would get on her way again while her jailor put in his shift at the plant. Goodbye to you.

Sometimes at lunch break he drove out here from Durham to check up on things. His jealousy and his absolute lack of tact, savoir vivre, cast a shadow over any sunlight there could have been in their relations. Not once had he invited a co-worker for supper and a friendly game of 7-card stud. She was his secret; she was his joy, plaything, housemaid, nursemaid, hope, despair, his dream of a better future and his nightmare in the present; his heaven, and his hell. Also they didn't talk. To her questions about his outside life, family background, first wife and a daughter, he answered curtly if at all.

—Shut it.

He was not courteous; a limited man, mean at times, gruff, but not all bad.

Time to go. On my journey now, as Lumbees used to sing at prayer meeting in the long house, during Carlyne's girlhood. Go where? To her doom? Alright to her doom then, but sho' nuf' gone from this living hell in a trailer in Mebane.

Why not to her people then? Yes, down Lumberton way. Under Lovedy's wing she and Rhoda could breathe freely again and have a chance. Folks, the elders, got a certain look when they recalled Selva Locklear courted by a special judge, the Kinstonian Vick. Yo' ar'n! And so Selva's child and grandchild might make a new start down home? It would be a simple life. Live poor; go to work in Pembroke as a waitress maybe, a cashier. On the main drag a minute's walk from the junction there was a home style restaurant: Town & Country. Still open?

It was time to start leading a quiet decent life, because this was her nature—not the ugliness of streetwalking; and not the bad dream of life among the Gilberts.

At the kitchen sink a moment longer she held up a dish and daydreamed of a swim in the cold, clean, tannin-dark Lumbee River. Down there, in the southeastern part of the state, there's a country road which runs among the trees . . .

X

She packed a few basic items and got Rhoda ready.

And now for the dog. Put out beer on a plate? Drug the beast?

Carlyne opened the trailer door, and a whiff of freedom made her giddy. But the guard dog bounded toward her in a clink-clink of its chains. Sun gleamed on its dark fur. She closed the screen, and it leapt on the steps. The weapon of its white teeth snapped in a frenzy.

It snarled and barked some more. On its hind legs, eye to eye with her, it clawed at the aluminum. Dirk was a killer. Beer wouldn't faze him. The pink spotted gums ran saliva. The long tongue flung around. Good, she thought, you and I know the score; in a minute we'll see. No mush-mushy stuff between us at least; no lovey-dovey show to be put on. It's a war. Good.

The dog's eyes had a murky fury as it leapt up and fell back. It wanted her, and scraped paws on the screen as its fur bristled.

Carlyne breathed deep and felt hatred and said low:

—You want to play?

She turned away and from the refrigerator took a tenderloin steak. She went to the back of the trailer and shut the bedroom door. The baby was upset by the commotion and lay crying in her crib.

The German shepherd huffed and puffed at the screen door. It smelled the steak. It poked its snout and reared with a paw clawing the air and drooled.

On the kitchen wall hung a rack with knives. Carlyne chose one and touched the blade to her thumb. She stabbed the meat, slid open the sink window, and hooted the big dog around to the yard side.

—Dirk! Heu! Come, boy! Here!

It scampered round, barking. It snarled and whined beside itself and jumped at the sill and the steak which Carlyne held to the window laughing. Terrible and comical the black muzzle trimmed with tan snapped at it, or her. She could glimpse its tonsils as it fell back. Dirk leapt, snapped, writhed away. Had to have that red meat.

She tossed out the raw strip over its head and in mid leap the powerful dog twisted fluid as a diver, gnashed the treat in its ivory fangs, champed a grip. It settled on the grass to eat, and the pink tip of its penis was unsheathed.

Then anger welled up in Carlyne. What kind of love was it that made a man sick an attack dog on his beloved if she tried to go out or budge an inch from his clutches? Submit, little woman, and that's it. Tell me, why the hell should there be equality for the sorry likes of you? Ha! You have your own ideas and a say in things? Tell me another one. You are my maid, my cook, and my private whore. Keep that in mind. I've got you where I want you, so anything goes!

There were codeine tablets in the medicine cabinet. She could doctor a piece of meat, gouge in pills like garlic, and hope to lull Dirk that way. Why not? Wouldn't the strong drug put the animal to sleep?

She wasn't sure. Anyway it would take too long. The time was near ten a.m., and she must get a move on. She had to leave this hole in her life. So long. Get out of my way, says life, if you know what's good for you—and passes by.

First teach this Melchior fellow a little lesson.

XI

As Dirk wolfed the juicy meat, Carlyne opened the trailer door, and stepped outside. Grasped in her left hand behind her back was a carving knife. Rolled on her right forearm was a face towel.

Down the tin steps from the mobile home and into Melchior's junk domain she went, slowly, step by step. She braced herself as her heart pounded. Well, she and Rhoda might have made a dash for safety out of Dirk's reach and into the road. Maybe, maybe not; and she helpless with Rhoda in her arms . . . It wasn't the way to do things.

Out back the savage dog went wild over the choice strip of t-bone. Oh, he was good now for a few seconds. The steak hopped off the ground like a live thing caught in Dirk's jaws. Ravenously Dirk growled and snapped, ripped the limp prey, which didn't resist.

But the dog went stiff, ears up, alerted. Fur bristled. For here coming toward him was a meal even more succulent; it would take a whole hour, after the kill, to chew and swallow such a morsel.

Dirk looked up at her, and back to his bone shiny with saliva. There was a gruesome humor. Two in the bush? Wasn't he just the male?

But the chain clinked as the dog sprang. She saw the teeth bared wide like a projectile headed right for her. This beast was its master's alter ego—Melchior underfed it, whipped it silly, jeered at its pained howl.

Carlyne set herself as it hurtled forward and sprang high off the ground gnashing for her neck. A moment ago she might have poisoned, scalded, blinded this animal. No fuss: from the safety of the kitchen window. Why didn't she do it? Had they ever given her a break? Treated her fairly? But the hatred and the roused beast in her wanted to see blood flow and even if it meant hers too.

Now there were no more nice words, no more prissy Gilbert notions or talk about the great man. This was a poor dumb animal not a great man; but maybe they were the same. Only the animal wasn't a seducer; it was more honest. It didn't sell you a bill of goods and raise your expectations and fill your mind, your heart, full of the poison of hope.

Dirk came on and attacked high. She gave him her right arm wrapped in the towel. And as the German shepherd lunged, not barking but just breathing with all his might, she too drove forward with the knife and cried out staggering back on impact. But she didn't fall.

She jerked the carving knife up under the snout smudged a reddish brown from the steak. With all her soul she drove the blade deep and gave it another thrust up, up, till her fist was in black fur beneath the collar. And the knife tip came out at the back of Dirk's neck. She jerked it around, again, again, nearly losing her balance in the big dog's rippling onslaught, which didn't go slack despite the knife in its neck.

At close quarters the dog humped on its hind legs. Inside the coppery neck she worked the bloody steel, and the animal fell heavily down and jolted her back. Still it snapped. But by now the eyes were not the same, and Dirk was at heaven's steaks. Even in death it knew only to attack, kill, eat.

On one knee now and splotched with blood and the dog's spittle Carlyne had her shoulder to the furry warm bulk. She kept on with the knife, jabbing with all her strength, and didn't know she was shrieking right in its red eyes. That is, she too was an animal in those instants, and knew nothing.

And then the head lolled, gory, on her breast as though it would suck. The steel tip picked up a glint of sunlight at the furry ridge behind its perked ears. Dirk gave a gurgled squeal, whining, unable to breathe. And once more the German shepherd raised and rotated its head a little. The dusky eyes quivered at the corners and rolled up.

On his flank and spread beneath her Dirk made his last tries to rise. He might have been one of her lovers. Carlyne yanked out the knife with a spurt of blood and then with both hands and a throaty scream drove it into the filmed eye, on to the brain.

There was blood all over—the ground, the dog's matted fur, her. She gave her own low snarl and looked around. Blood soaked the face towel and purled on her forearm and stained her blouse. Go in and change—hurry! No time; he'll be home from the factory soon. What time could it be? Did this with Dirk take a minute or an hour? Hurry! Time is running out: the brief instants of freedom.

Tissue and gristle hung exposed from the dog's minced skin.

Carlyne felt nauseous.

A third time, beside herself, she struck the enemy who was down and defenseless. Above the soft pale underbelly where the hair parted she stuck the carving knife into the heart.

To break the silence, to hear a voice, perhaps, she said aloud:

—Turn about . . . is fair play.

Rhoda cried, exasperated, inside the trailer. Rhody was calling her.

The dog Dirk lay still. Its hind legs twitched.

XII

Carlyne stood up and backed off shakily. She was coming to herself again and felt her stomach upset. In a sweat with a sickened feeling she looked over her work. A bird chirped into the silence and calm around the trailer. What gloomy weeks and months she had spent here with never a friendly visit, never a distraction. Really can a woman ever find peace in herself if she is dependent on a man?

She turned away and with her arm held up went inside. At the sink she let cold water run over the chewed flesh with its shreds and necklace of tooth marks. The sunlit trees in the window revolved upward, out of kilter, and she held on trying not to faint.

—No, no.

Not now, she could not; please . . . not faint! It was 10:24 on the kitchen clock, so a kind of lifetime had passed in a quarter hour.

At noon or before, anytime, the man could come up the drive in his van. The minutes were precious. Quickly she rummaged and found what she needed.

She poured iodine over the shredded skin, gasped, cried out, then bowed her head to throw up in the sink.

With this she felt better and taped gauze plus a clean washcloth on the forearm. It throbbed; it needed treatment, stitches. Was a vein open? Would she lose too much blood?

She moved about getting ready as her body sort of told the pain and her mind the fear after the fact. What have I done? Where to now, dear? I am alone. Who is to blame? She gave a shiver.

Brusquely she changed clothes and brushed her hair.

XIII

Out the door she went dizzily with Rhoda on her good arm. She almost fell forward on the steps. She didn't have a penny to her name. Where to? Her people? South to Lumberton? Aunt Lovedy would always take her in. But how could she find the highway?

Over her shoulder she had a last glimpse at Dirk the dog, her keeper. The head was jolted back at the death spasms. The fur was streaked in the sun. He lay in a heap, looking smaller. He lay still now.

Carlyne walked a back road. How far was the route south toward Sanford and Fayetteville? She needed a lift and pretty soon. She kept looking back because if she saw that van, his van, coming toward her, she would run in among the trees. She would take to the forest rather than go back to that life with him again. She couldn't take it anymore!

On the road with its tar soft in patches in summer she walked. Briskly she went. For a moment she thought of what Joey Gilbert would do if he ever knew what she had done, what she had become. Did she fear Melchior's meaty fists and his violence? That was child's play beside what her husband would do to her. For he would love her, and that was the worst.

Hell, don't think, girl. Scoot and be free. Even if it's a fake freedom, not real. Hitchhike out West? If it wasn't for the child she would have done away with herself a long time ago. Don't look back, just go on. Joey hadn't died but she had, and so never mind, go away, for good. Start again? One or two will still want you. Ha ha ha . . . If the dreadful truth was ever known it would be time to go in a room, lock the door, and hang herself.

XIV

She waved at a car, and it pulled over. The driver wasn't a man, thankfully, but a prim young woman.

—Could you take me to the highway?

—85?

—I guess.—Carlyne's voice trembled.—I don't know. South.

Her lips had trouble with the words. She breathed and spoke in starts. When the woman asked her something, she shook her head and tried not to cry.

The other, so neatly dressed and not long out of high school, looked across at her.

Then there were trees and a highway divider and the sough of cars at high speed on the Durham-Raleigh approaches. A transport van sang on its way past. This was Interstate 85, east.

—Don't you need help? Let me take you to my house, or a hospital.

—No. Thank you.

—But your blouse. Look!

Blood oozed through the white fabric and dripped on her jeans. Christ, was it an artery?

Carlyne warbled:

—I don't have time.

With tears in her eyes she touched the prim young woman's arm and left the car and began to walk down the ramp.

The other called:

—Do you have money?

—Just drive away. Thanks!

From the bottom of the entry ramp she went on walking.

She made signs to the cars going by too fast to react in time and stop on the highway shoulder.

Carlyne went on. She would no longer consent to be a prisoner of her guilt in someone's dreary trailer. She and her child had to live one way or another, and even if it meant the swamps. It was the pride in her blood, and Rhody's too; it was the pride and rebellion of their ancestors.

North, said a road sign. Was it north they were going? Then north, so be it, if fate was heading her that way. She wanted to escape and get away, but now in her heart it seemed she was only getting closer. So, so . . . For a long time each turning in the road only took her the opposite way from the one she wanted. But she just went: whether or not she knew what was working inside her in these instants, what vital force was driving her along.

The wide world stood before her like a blur. From here she might journey south into Robeson County, the past, or north toward Henderson and the Virginia state line.

So fate led her north. The coils of her fate, and not only hers, were tightening.

With every step Carlyne made she might still think she was going away from her fate, since she never intended to see her husband again.

If she went to Lovedy's in Pembroke then he would come and find her there.

But every step was only getting her, and them, closer.

Chapter Seventeen

I

—And on the field when your mind wanders—?
The psychiatrist paused as her patient brooded in the recliner.
—I told you: I don't know.
—It's Carlyne in your thoughts.
—Maybe. No.
—It was your father and his plan for Lemon.
—No, not this time.
Lydia waited a moment. Then asked:
—Has their been any word from the detective agency?
—Only their bill.
—Sorry. I feel responsible since I gave you the number.
—No need. Let's see what comes of it.
Eerily, for a long minute, he gazed in space. She thought over the next question. She was probing.
How much longer could he hold out? If there was no talk then there was no cure. They both needed to know the whole story. From day to day his club wanted a quickie cure to this 'adult situational crisis', and they were paying for it. Her fees were as handsome as she was. So scientific method and preparation risked getting swept up in the whirlwind of a pennant race. In the Major Leagues there was pressure to perform. On the psychiatrist's divan there could be none. If the New York team's front office got

antsy and tried to hurry things then Lydia Falliere would have to
refuse their money and do things her way—slow, analytic, as she
put controls in place to probe deeper.

Lately there was a tension in the sessions. She knew there was
a clear and present danger he could bring Vietnam and its violence home to her quiet office.

—On third when you have a lapse: is it . . . the war?

—Yes and no, different.

—How yes and no?

—Sports are war without bullets.

He gave a shrug.

She prodded.

—It's late innings of a one-run ballgame, and the fans are carried away. Does this in itself affect you?

—Sure. Like . . . oh, if you have heat there will be fire. I guess
the excitement can flip me out but sometimes yes, sometimes no,
I don't know why.

—Are you more likely in the late innings to be startled by the
crack of the bat? Do the cries and cheers get to you more?

Gracefully she moved to an armchair nearer the recliner. Maybe
this was the word for her: grace. Her movements had a music.
She knew he liked to watch her. Perhaps she had more power as
a woman than as psychiatrist, since by now she was half carried
away by her own desire; and waded in amid the treacherous currents of the countertransference. Love is love, she said, laughing
to herself, but it wasn't that funny. In her married life she had had
too little of life's part of passion. Now if she had such an appetite
then why scrimp at least in her mind? She was an emotional and
vital woman in full maturity. Hers was not the medical mentality:
life in a test tube.

—Ump's call: stee'!—She mimicked it with a laugh.—A helicopter flies over. A truck backfires in the street outside the stadium. Or roll of thunder high overhead. This has no effect?

He gave a laugh too, sort of, watching her. She had become
important to him: say the big sister he never had.

—It has more effect when I see you sitting in a box seat there by
our bench. I think: what brought the learned scientist out to the
ballgame? Could it be . . .? No, she is too beautiful and wise and
. . . something . . . to pay any attention to a poor fellow like me.
Outside her work. Anyway she's too old.

—That's true.

—No, it's . . . a lot of times it's just anger I feel, which gets my eye off the ball. You know: these tyrants with their arrogance who sent us the young people over there, and for what? I wish they'd get some too so I think the higher they rise the harder they fall . . . like that. Out on third. But they're in charge and who'll ever get us out of this fix? God, you say? Since time began the power boys have made a mockery of God, and God never did a blessed thing to them in return. So count him out. In their madness they just keep shitting on all that's sacred. And so they're in the wrong and that only makes them angrier and even more violent and after Vietnam it'll be some other small country but next time they'll try to pick one that can't defend itself so well . . . And so I think: if things are done their way, and if they have all the honor: then what good is my love, my sacred dance so to speak, I mean if their lies win the prize? Am I the only sucker who doesn't know the score? Or are we, maybe, as a people? Out on third base I'm thinking even while I stare home for the catcher's sign, it's for us too, thinking: why, why did fate or my nasty luck send me and my pure motives so far away to fight for a band of lying hypocrites who want to control the world as my brother says . . .? The good oldtime American way is dead and done with if it ever did mean anything: not God, but the godly way of life, the truth we should live for. Something like that, Doctor.

Bemused by his speech he looked around at her. Lord, what fun it was to look at her, and talk to her.

II

Against Lydia's better judgment she went to watch him play again at the owner's invitation. It took her breath away: not the game really, a mechanical conflict with only a phony sensibility: winning and losing, an abstract objectivity. She didn't care much for baseball as such, all that derring-do for dollars. But Joey Gilbert's presence on the field was a kind of wonder to her. And she felt jealous which was good too having to share him. In her life she wasn't the jealous type, rather generous and open than envious; but here the multitude loved her love-object too and felt his fascination. This was a thrill, and it shook Lydia. Also exciting was the way he took her so in stride. Inside her office they were just two people, a man and a woman.

To be sure she knew from the past what could lurk behind his casual interview tone: namely a powerful affect, which was suppressed. Violent nightmares by night and then by day any slight rubbing the wrong way could lead to a fight to the finish. He was mild-mannered, and he was lethal. She had read a PTSD case that showed the patient's homicidal/sexual fantasies about the therapist. As he opened up to her more then watch out—she would have one sort of power, and he had another.

The sessions went on around the same themes: still prepping, still marking out terrain.

—I see things.

—What things?

—Well, I shouldn't see them, you know. Nobody should.

—How do you mean?

—I could laugh about it because the others care so much but I hardly give a damn if we win or lose. On the field I'm busy thinking . . .

Now from the recliner he stared at her because he saw things, you know, and his look then sent a tingle up Lydia Falliere's spine. It touched her depths. It massaged the organ of her loneliness, and it was also sexual, oh yes.

Last week he had told her a dream. A U.S. soldier was taken alive by VC and strung on a pole like a hog carcass and paraded through a village. The G.I. was cursed by a long line of faces, and spat on, but not struck. And then they gave him a birthday party.

—Did he feel guilty?

—Like slitting his wrists in a tub, for a relief. Maybe then he could get it on again.

—Get it on.

—Arousal, you know.

In the silence of her plush consultation room they heard the rumor of the street nineteen storeys down below. The ocean stir of Manhattan mingled with their attentive breaths. Her eyes asked a question beyond the one at hand.

—Has this to do with why you lapsed in the eighth last night? Afraid if you . . . if you tried to make love to your wife, you couldn't?

—The soldier in the dream was me, or I had his feelings. I was wounded. They . . . one of the villagers, a girl named Moonlight, took icing from my birthday cake and spread it on the wound.

—Did you like it?

—Yes and no.

—Yes?

—Yes because she was very pretty.

—And no?

—No because . . . no because we were related . . . and I wanted to do something. She held up a gob of icing which had blood on it, and smiled. She wanted me to taste it, the decoration, but I . . . I . . .

—What?

—I was so afraid.

III

—I keep seeing things.

—Can you describe them?

—No. I don't want to.

—Why?

—Better not, that's all. Just . . . better.

—You relive the village?

He looked up at her, past her. He blinked.

—Why talk about it?

—You . . . must. Sooner or later. To me.

—It isn't nice. You'll lose respect for me, if you have any.

—I do. I won't lose it.

Danger signal. Fear makes for guilt—guilt more fear. By respect he meant: decorum, their controls? Could we control the fear? Or—

—You would, he said.

—No.

Her voice was low, a hypnosis. She thought: by the bedside of the person we love—we love even the odor of their sickness. It too may be sexual, deeply. But the beloved worries: ah, lose respect?

—I did, and you would.
—No. To me. Go on.
—I can't.
—But you must.
—Oh.
—On third base you go to the village. You see the hell.
—Hell is just a word.

Lydia tensed in her chair by the recliner. Her heart was beating quicker. Now for his run? This is what they paid her for: the cool head at the key moment.

—Trust is another.
—N-no—he looked away.—I won't put this on you.
—But it's the deal, and I agreed. I took an oath.
—It's too much.

She gave him a sad smile, but firm. More and more this was her mask for the world: sad, and firm. She said:
—I'll risk it if you will.

IV

Joey sighed. Make no mistake: that was anguish in his dark eyes as he glimpsed her. Gone now the self-assured air and devil-may-care shrug of the big athlete. A ripple passed over his hard-edged suntanned features; it was the facial tic he brought home from Vietnam.

—It . . . It is . . . it.
—What?
—Xo Man. Again and again I see it in my dreams, like I did in real life. No, different . . . but it's the horror. And I'm there and I can't budge. I sit on the ground but the others run around on a rampage. And last night I saw it too out at my position in the eighth. The same thing came over me, Xo Man, the horror. How could I pay attention to their goddamned sports with that going on?
—What did you see?
—No, you won't like it.
—Let me worry about that. Tell.
—I won't. I care what you think.

—Ah, so it's only a question of face?

—I . . . I care about you.—His voice sounded strangled, as he blurted this.—I don't want to hurt you.

—I'm up to it if you are. We'll see it through together.

—No. I'm afraid.

—Ah ha. So the big boy is afraid.

He shot a glance up at her. This talk was not like her. It was un-psychiatrist-like to challenge and push him like this. But even as she sat there waiting, Lydia's mind was doing its thing, or its theory. *The suicidal mode is an outgrowth of reaction formation in early childhood when the tender psyche was faced with a defeat in parental relationship . . . Later on quantity of reaction formation turns into (umschlägt) quality of suicidal impulse . . . or neurotically into greed . . .* As she waited staring at him, thinking, Joey Gilbert looked back: not at her face, eyes, the distinguished intellectual with her books and honorary degrees, but frankly at her body, at her breasts, at her thighs beneath the fine material. In those instants it was Lydia's flesh that seemed to breathe life and concern for him and much, much more. He noted her neck and strand of blue pearls and felt his desire for her surge even as his thoughts flew apart in fragments and were back at Xo Man—*your neck, vampire . . . identify with my victim . . . punish myself in another . . .* With a grimace he looked her up and down again. He clutched his head with two hands and shook it a little, taking a deep breath. Was he losing control?

Her hands were folded. The fingers were long and ringless as if she was too elegant to wear a ring. Maybe she was a bit vain? The East Side psychiatrist wore a business suit of the finest tailoring. There was lace at the collar of her beige blouse with some brocade over her petite breasts: breasts so unlike Carlyne, but like his mother. Her features too had Anne Gilbert's wistful concern.

Joey breathed deeply.

—Doctor, you won't enjoy this.

—It doesn't matter. Please go on, I'm here to listen to you.

—You want to tour Nam, the sights and sounds?

—With you, yes, if you want.

Then the psychiatrist gave a grin that seemed to mock him, offhand, and cocky. She seemed to goad him: who's the jock here, you or me?

In the window was a sunlit day in early summer: Fifth Avenue and Central Park, blue sky dappled with clouds. *The reaction*

*formation becomes the pasteboard on which the suffering person tries
to build and live—stands or falls on that intricate defense mechanism
which is his or her spirit . . . So if it is threatened then life is threatened;
and the psyche cannot stand for it to be questioned much less put in
jeopardy . . .* Lydia stood up. She looked down at him a moment,
and he up at her, there by his head, in a sexual way; and there was
only their breathing in the air-conditioned room. Then she turned
from him and went to open the window.

V

Joey went into it without a prologue. He spoke low in an eerie
monotone:

—I saw and didn't see our catcher's knee dip so I'd be in on the
sign and the home plate ump hunched under his chest protector
and there was sort of a flick in my left eye as their second hitter
squared to bunt on the 2-1 . . . I saw hootches set back among
clumps of bamboo and it was so vivid, so real this time not a bad
dream. I walked on and sniffed the waterlogged earth of Vietnam
and heard snorts of pigs, swill-thrills as medic Artus called them,
the little piggies oink-oinking over our C-rat cans; and there were
the clucks and peck-peck of poultry. We ambled into Xo Man and
you asked for it Doctor and now you're going to get it. We weren't
told to seal and search this ville and so Six had cut us some slack
at exactly the wrong time. Good people here we come, we are the
Death Platoon so give us your dull peasant stares like so much
thatch.

I saw huts and a dirt square and a big old banyan tree like elephant trunks stuck in the ground. It's the scene I see in my dreams
but . . . hard to describe . . . outlined so sharply it is painful and
not distorted like a dream. There's a sense of death in the wings
as some black crows caw in a Kapok tree and mama-sans go along
yoked to shoulder poles with breadfruit and durian and manioc.

"G.I. numbah one!"

"One! one!" It's a playable pop off first on the 2-2 and our
shortstop holds up his index for the outfielders: "Two more and
it's party time in Midtown!"

A flock of wild geese soars in wedge formation over the ville and Chi-Bar says that's the NVA Air Force. With a finger Private Thingum wipes a spec of bird doodoo from his frizzy cheek.

"Sistah! One dollah!" Now a kid comes hopping up alongside with his laughter, crooked teeth. "Fuckee G.I. you numbah ten fuckee! Ha ha!" Out at third I hear his voice again and it is *so real* as he grins and beckons us ahead to enjoy his sister and gang-bang sister-san or so we think. I smell the fish scent from the hootches and nuoc mam brine used to season every dish. I'd go buy some in Chinatown 'cause it's delicious but I can't stand the sight of an Oriental. I smell the rice and cereal scent in the burg and look! Look at 'im! A sleek rat goes wriggling up the reed thatch of a hootch.—

In the recliner Joey sat a notch forward and pointed: he saw the rat.

—What then? said Lydia.

—To the last detail, you know, it happens again. I think my head is ready to split just as their third hitter steps in, a righty pull hitter. It's coming my way maybe in the key moment of this game. But where am I?

—Xo Man, said Lydia. Intrusive imagery, a flashback. But why in late innings of a tight game? Does the tension bring it on?

—It's too much.

—So you lose control?

—I'm a madman.

—No, that's a label.

—But I see them. There's Izard again and Kid Ringwood from Carlyne's neck o' the woods down in Carolina. They stand looking at me on the other side where the dead stare across at life.

VI

Now they were in the zone. And whether he played inspired third base trying to deny Vietnam or else brought back the war here in her office: it was a struggle for insight even as, under psychic duress, he began to lose control. Lose it he must in order to regain a livable hold.

At length his defenses gave way. He decompensated. And into that vortex he drew his therapist.

Lines said by Jocasta, the hero's wife, in the *Oedipus* came to Lydia's thoughts: 'The mind of Oedipus with its hurt is too in an upheaval to judge recent events in the light of the past. He stands in a trance before anyone who talks of fear. So I will take gifts of garlands and incense to the temples, O Lycean Apollo, I know what my science is worth and so I turn to you for help. Purify us, deliver us from this curse; now we shrink from the sight of this man struck dumb with wonder as he seeks to find a way . . .'

The verses ran through her memory since she knew the thing was on the march and it had been coming and it was at hand. His run—his breakdown when she could only try to keep her head and hope help came from the gods.

Of course it wasn't always this way. The present case was far more dangerous and explosive—more likely a tragedy than other sports cases on her calendar which were like comedies. For instance a patient in his forties called his sister at two a.m. to talk 'one last time before suicide'. And the reason? It seems parental favoritism had kept him from his destiny as a winner of big tennis tournaments. In another case a middle-aged man was contesting his deceased mother's will. In visits to Lydia he ranted on and on his hatred for a born-again Christian older brother. But then the former halfback in high school talked obsessively about golf and his upcoming debut on the senior tour despite alcoholism which he denied. Golf was the last stand of this man's dignity—how sadly the lone ego has come down from its windmills and demon enchanters.

Such bizarre flowers grew in the swamp, thought Lydia. Sports were an American Utopia. Not realism and hard work, not struggle for change; but a collective neurosis gilded each and every day by the mass media with its sham pride and its glamor, for profit.

Both the above cases had passive-aggressive traits and were less likely to abreact violently than a Joey Gilbert. In those sessions she could improvise and work theoretically as she brought her gnomic concepts and symptomatology to the test. But here she was going full tilt into the abreactive zone by a big uncontrollable patient's side, and so the clinical terms took on a vital life. Here phrases like cognitive disruption, isomorphic episode, emotional anesthesia, dysphoric-disassociative states; also her own PTSD-Scale derived from the PERI (Psychiatric Epidemiology Research Instrument) with its list of symptoms: guilt, demoralization, somatic disturbance, distrust, impotence, suicidal ideation—here the lingo had life-and-death overtones as in Joey Gilbert word became flesh. Not ten-gallon phraseology, but electric reality charged Lydia's inner office now and sent them reeling into a vortex.

Last evening a slant of light over the Park at twilight told her the facts of the matter. The excitement of his visits was due to a strange otherness, quite exotic, and she had fallen in love with him. Once in life was it given the lucky souls—to go the whole route for another person. And then the smart ones went for it: they risked social status, financial livelihood, life if necessary. Was Lydia Falliere in love with a psychotic? So far she saw none of the inherited predisposition, or formative early trauma, said (by Freud) to be the basis for later jolts to become pathogenic—in Joey's case attacks of hysterical paralysis—via a causative chain. A memory served as impetus for the attack, namely the hallucinatory reexperience of a scene which was key to the outbreak of illness. But could a war memory be a primary site? Wouldn't it be a repression of an early childhood event that was far less accessible?

For a breathless moment, on the brink, the patient was silent. But she felt he or his gut had turned a corner, and he would tell her all he could—not tell but show, do. Here came his *attitudes passionelles*, right at her.

VII

—*Banh troi! Banh duc!*—Joey mimicked a street vendor, and he chewed.—Mm! Sticky rice cake, tastes good. *Gio cha! Gio cha!* Sausage for Bufillu.

"One dollah shoeshine. One! One dollah!" Voices, smells, so clear. Weird bird chirps, frog peepeeps, click . . . click: what's that? Across the dirt square a boy's smiling by his shoeshine box. Xo Man—Joey's voice went low, spooked—it's Xo Man . . .

"You fuckee G.I.! Numbah ten fuckee G.I."

I call across: You guys spread ranks. Don't stay by that vendor.—

—Why? said Lydia.

—Wait. —Joey's face bristled; he leaned forward in the recliner.—No takers for shoeshine boy in the jungle? For sister-san, yes, a dollar a pop. Vaney-Vane! Riii-i-ip! Vane tears the tea vendor's blouse and spills her counter and cute bowls, plaaah, in the dirt. She has dark frail shoulders.

—And what then?

—They look angry, but they're afraid to say so. The vendor screws her eyes and gives the talkeetalk. I don't like it: there's too much movement. You there: fug off . . . Villagers bustle about while a few mama- and papa-sans squat on cane matting like a stage set. Glum. Neutral eyes. VC? Pity for the torn blouse: I feel it, she is a tea vendor with her dignity. And Sistah-san's fake satin bodice, one dollah! And the crab soup smell I remember. Wild tamarind and pawpaw. And Carlyne ten thousand miles away, safe in my father's house . . . A moment longer I stand around, but I want to shake a leg, move out. Strange this loneliness.— Joey's eyes, boyish, hurt, met the physician's.—Baseball too, you know, loneliness.

His voice trailed off.

—What then?

—On your toes, troops! Yah, le's hump! . . . The vendor gives a grin at the big black man spooning his pho soup; he helped her with Vane a moment ago. Hum. Quiet . . . why so quiet? A child is whimpering in a nearby hut. A cicada goes bzz-aa-a. Ringwood the Ringer fingerlicks ham 'n muds. But look . . . look.

—What?

Lydia sat forward as if she might see too.

—VC kid reaches down and slides a pencil from his shoeshine box. Now he runs. Skips away. Hey, wait up, kid! Naw, he trots away with a yip but leaves his box. Hm, what the—? Nobody in the dirt square, only us suckers. And tea vendor? Dollah-sistah? It's silent. Oh! the stillness of it, like a dream.

Joey shivered. Now his voice was low and very eerie, as though leaving her. Once on rounds through a locked ward Lydia heard a Vietnam vet give his words (she thought) the false wonder of war stories. For the hundredth time he told of revenge on the VC who— Was it to compensate for deep humiliation? And now Joey had the same nightmarish sensory tone, and the isomorphic detail.

Softly, she coaxed:

—Then?

—There was no more teenage whore. There were no fruit and vegetable sellers.—His glance shot around at her.—Bufillu? What—?!

He lurched from the recliner across the floor. His brow was beaded with sweat as he cried out and jerked his body around there at her feet on the rug. It was so sudden—his limbs flailing in the big blast.

—Izaaaaard!—Half up he swung backward hand to brow and screamed; the veins bulged on his forehead and neck.—Vane's eyes! Troupial call in the aaaaanngh! Ringwoodl Ooh! Ooh! Wipe 'em off! Red brains like fish eggs on my boot. Ringwoooooood!

VIII

Lydia held back and watched. She knew this was their chance and she had to let it come out and try to keep her head and stay out of harm's way. She was afraid; her nerves were on full alert. Her shoulders were shaking as she sat there, but still her brain theorized. Multiple identifications are packed away galvanic as the blast itself after it overwhelmed his psyche. Now he becomes the repressed event and scene. Mostly unaware? the repetitions, cf. stressor scale Axis IV, DSM-III-R: 5) severe stress, 6) extreme stress, 7) catastrophe.

—*Can bo! Can bo! Six, Beta-5, sniper fire 5 o'clock. Buh! B-buh! Ratatatata!*—On his feet in a daze he staggered about the consultation room with a demented glint in his eye and siren howl from his throat; he shook head to foot and fired off rounds at an unseen enemy.—*Can bo! Fuckemup!*

Lydia felt herself swept up in it as if gunshots impacted her eardrums.

—Oh!

—*Dong lai! Dong lai!*

Joey stomped wildly and fired his gun and gave outraged grunts; also animal sounds: a pig squealed in death; ducks quacked, flapped, enfiladed by his M-16. A water buffalo bellowed, pfoomph! burst into bits of blood and fur by a grenade.

—*Izaaaaard! Blair! Ben Bolt! Grease a chicken, Thingum! Ha ha ha! Cluck, cluck. Cluckemup!*

But then his wild hate-filled abreaction began to turn round the chair where Lydia sat trying to stay calm: like one more object of his lost objects. She was in the grisly scene with him and in his subconscious. Now his gun was a powerful sexual cathexis levelled in her direction.

—*Skol! Rape the gook girl in her hootch, Skoly-Skol!*

Hand to his eyes the G.I. shook his head perplexed by some idea—was it his wife again? The sight of her in his mind's eye tore apart his ego worn down by war on two fronts, Vietnam, and pro sports where a baseball was an anti-personnel grenade. Darkly, past fumes spuming up the thatch, he peered in at the truth. He made a pssss! sound and showed her the scene, and the spell was such she could smell the crisp acridity of torched hootch.

And now he stood over Lydia Falliere but he saw someone else. His big wiry frame writhed in the heat of palm leaves and the rushes ablaze of the zippoed huts. But then he turned away; drew back from her; strode a joyless lane.

Then in her soundproofed office with a window open high above the street he cried out:

—*Chi-Bar! No! No! . . . Six, Beta-5*—

Wide-eyed and frazzled Joey froze in his tracks.

Crouched at the low doorway of a hootch further on he began to weep with his hands to his face.

—*Chi-Baaaaar! 'Sssss.*—He showed smoke streaming up; he choked for breath and waved an arm as he went in a low doorway. He said:—*I'll save you, 'sssss.*

—It's the visitors' eighth! said Lydia. Two down!

She held up index and pinkie like the shortstop.

But Joey was in Xo Man where flames purled on the low thatched eaves and blent in with the twilight.

—This woman here—he said, his features distorted—these children: they don't look much like *can bo*. Communists? Cassava roots on a table. Tombigbee was right. Pumpkin leaves in a bundle. Friendlies. Mountain rice, ginger.

Joey writhed in the burning hootch of his memory.

He reached down and took Lydia's arm in his grip like steel with the adrenalin, the fear, hate. And now she knew something was going to happen, and fear lit her eyes. It was not nice, no, not in the least romantic: as sick things are not, but only like a lump of bad meat, with a smell. She knew this, but love is strange. Love goes for such scents.

Now she had better not resist or protest when he lifted and wrenched her against his chest and began the dance. If she drew away he would kill her like the woman in the hootch. But she did call out:

—Runners at second and third!

But her voice faltered.

He said in a broken tone:

—Carlyne, *can bo.*

IX

Even as he kissed the short hair over her temples Lydia was still thinking. It is fear of this which is behind the conformism of my colleagues. Now she accepted and tried to control his caresses as if they were childish. So the *petits collègues* won't admit a PTSD diagnosis? Then I'll write a piece for them and call it: 'The Subconscious Lie'.

Now Joey was the rapist and Joey was the savior. He found Lydia's that is Carlyne's that is the hootch woman's lips and bored in. It was not he but his tortured conscience that kissed her neck and kissed the fine lace of her blouse. With the only love he had he was kissing a violated girl; he was kissing a mother gunned down and fragged by his buddies in a montagnard village while he stood by and watched. He was the rapist and perhaps in his subconscious the object of rape as he raped to relive in a hopeless effort to make okay again this trauma done to nature and to the moral universe. He was trying but he still couldn't so he gave a whimper as his curly boyish head drooped to burrow in her breast, and kiss, kiss, kiss. She made a movement of resistance. And he countered, holding her in place. Brutal and pitiful with his face bathed in tears and sweat and his strength like a machine's he pulled her down onto the floor. And her skirt rode up over her stockings, the fatty thighs, as he wedged into position between her legs.

Not the first time, in her career as a healer, the gifted physician met a situation which was beyond her control. And it was decisive. Try for the intercom? There was a rescue button beneath her desk . . . He grappled her and yanked; he gouged her where she spread decomposed, loosed, under his physical size, in the inner office. Now was the time for the morbid sex of the schizophrenic. Coitus tristitia, this rich sweet jelly; and rancid. What if he impregnated her? Abort?

She didn't fear the man's desire. Now and again for a few years she had craved an abandonment of self amid the frenetic clinical round of her days, and single nights. And this desire had the twisted traits of an individualism, loneliness, which didn't care too much if it was pure. In her prime she had all a researcher could require, relative freedom, grants, a publisher. Her mother, Muriel, helped a governess with the three children, while Lydia went forth each day into the world of achievers. She wrote brilliantly; she went in front of audiences and the media; she headed a department in a hospital. Yet the mature and many-sided, the ripe personality seeks the creatural too, even deeper: more cultivated and more primitive. Genius seeks the species life, like homunculus. Lou Salomé seduces Freud's disciples: has them spank her. Thus Lydia didn't shy away from sex; she just couldn't find any which suited her.

But this wasn't sex. This was psychopathology.

—Joey?

She had her hand on the back of his neck. Her finger played in a ringlet of his hair.

X

In an instant he would unload not love into Lydia but rather his world of hurt and the traumatic guilt of Xo Man. He straddled his VC victim.

All her delicate probing for stressors while plying her analytic grid had come down to this. It was like foreplay for an abreaction. In this special case with her love and her more than concern she had cued a lethal reactivity in a patient: with their extended sessions, the two of them 'non-admissive' but emotionally starved and hyperstressed with sexual deprivation.

Maybe he knew it too? For a week he had beat a retreat. He missed an apointment and then brought her a blush and a rose. But on a Monday, open date for his team, they met for an extraordinary session in the Park, of unprecedented length, and then dined together in an East Side restaurant! Since then there was a phone call to her home in Scarsdale since she had given him the number. Not only he but she too had illogical moods, and got upset over a trifle, and the other liked it and apologized so tenderly. In a free moment the highbrow intellectual pored over box scores and looked at League leader lists. And certain words and phrases from the psychiatric jargon found their way into the bigtime jock's everyday speech!

Now with a hand on her neck, holding her down on the floor, he waved his free arm and called out orders:

—*Troupial, get Six on the hook! Dust 'em! Hose down time! Artus! Where's Artus?*

Lydia awaited her fate. She lay on her back with her long legs sprung from the rumpled business suit. All her tallish refined person was in disarray and at his mercy. A year after the actual events his subconscious still went among the flames of Xo Man. And still, incredible as it seemed, Lydia's mind worked overtime and sped over Kardmir's seminal study on postwar symptoms in World War I vets; on MacLean's postulate of 'primitive survival behavior' directed by the protean mammalian brain's limbic system: this neurological short circuit when triggered bypasses reflective thought and rational planification of the cerebral cortex. Coolly her head hypothesized even as her heart was in tumult and her bruised body began to arch and rock in a somber rapture beneath his thrust.

But he in his dream-like state was anguished in the act and swung his head to and fro. Now he was possessed by ghosts unlaid to rest of grunts in his squad. He cried out not in his voice but in theirs:

—*Oh my god not me not now!*

—Jo . . . oh!

—*Tombigbee, you quitter! Rock 'em in office hours!*

Above her his heavy breaths were a rasp. He held her head against the floor and wedged in for the insertion.

—*Bunt!*

But then he stopped.

—*Bunt down third!*

He drew up from her. He fixed his gaze on the wall behind her.

He began waving his free arm like a third base coach giving

the runner the go-ahead. And now Joey's features had the blank moonstruck look of his famous lapses.

—Jo?

—*Squeeze is on! Charge home plate, man! Go home!*

Frozen at his position he watched as the base paths emptied and runners crossed the plate. He was unable to perform. He couldn't make the play.

—*E-5 chokes in the clutch!*

The home plate ump, arms wide and palms down, bawled out:

—*Safe!*

Released from his grip now Lydia rose to one elbow.

Suddenly at point of entry he had gone limp. He was impotent with her: the usurper.

Unable to 'resolve his affective stressors in coitus' he hung his head, and looked like a very bad boy indeed.

Wild-eyed Joey gazed at her lying beneath him, so near, so far away. And she was the village woman with her children looking perforated by an awl: little red dots here and there. And then a grenade had been tossed in like an afterthought, and the frail torsos were gashed by shrapnel; they were mangled. In this instant Lydia was the Vietnamese woman in the hootch of death, and she was Carlyne wrapped with her child in a red embrace.

Pumpkin leaves, rice tin, tuber of ginger.

The third baseman's face was a tragic mask.

But then he laughed. It was the other dugout laughing in a chorus, and it was oh so strange. Laughter of death.

XI

Half in a dream now, on his way back to her, he said:

—I did save one.

—You did?

—I pulled him out.—Joey's face, neck, t-shirt were bathed in sweat; he gave a shiver taking in his surroundings; he said offhand:—It was a small boy with multiple wounds but alive somehow.

—Alive, said Lydia.

—I went in and got him. Took him to the medevac; though it's a no-no, you can't deal with them in a crisis.—Joey looked down at her beneath him: Lydia sprawled on the floor; and a furrow lined his brow.—Good heavens, what's been going on here?

—You had an attack.

—What have I done?

—You . . . lapsed at third.

—Bejeezus! Did I hurt you?

—Not at all, never mind.

—I didn't know it. Forgive me!

—No need.

He picked her up in his arms. Gently with his great strength he set her on her feet.

She glimpsed him, shyly too. The madman of a moment before was humble.

But still his thoughts were back there, at the scene.

—I had to do something, so I brought him out. You see we'd just lost Blair who was a bookworm like my brother.

—I see, said Lydia.

She met his gaze. She tried to smooth her skirt, and her nerves.

He shook his head. And now a question was in his eyes. Was she condemning him too? She wouldn't cut him off?

—You must think I'm crazy, he said.

—No, it's Xo Man.

—Not very nice over there.

—So I see. Not nice.

—But you know I feel—I feel—

—Sir?

—I feel better somehow. If you don't hate me.

—I don't hate you.

He shrugged. Boyish, he bowed to kiss her hand, thought better of it, and went out.

XII

Outside, along Fifth Avenue, in Central Park, a bright late morning in July seemed to brim over with life and sunlight. Peo-

ple strolled. People crossed at an intersection. People waited at a
bus stop. Yellow cabs fished for fares: one swerved with a honk
and squeal of brakes. Traffic moved on past the luxury hotels and
parade of shops. Inside the Park there were children exercising
their young limbs and high voices as they played in a playground.
Birds chirped, and bees buzzed. The day was hot and sunny but
not too humid for once. Further in, a horse-drawn carriage clip-
clopped on its sentimental journey past the zoo.

Big, wiry, supple in his sneaks, the third baseman stood before
a war memorial across from the doctor's office. He shook his head
at the sculpture and thought: That's not it. Then he thought: What
did I almost do in there? I'm crazy. And she . . . That woman . . .
Inside the Park he walked.

With a flush of pleasure unknown for a long, long time, Joey
Gilbert waved at some kids and did a sort of floppy dance for
them.

—Hey, you guys! Look! It's Joey! It's really Joey Gilbert!

—No way.

—Sure it is! I'd know 'im anywhere. Wanna' bet?

—Betcha' it ain't.

—Whatchoo' wanna' bet?

—Your packet o' Milk Duds for my Marzipan.

—I hate Marzipan!

They had seen the high voltage figure on their TV screens when
they should have been playing or reading a book. Yeah! Yeppa'!
Same one! Now he turned and threw up his arms at them with a
shy smile.

—It *is!* Joey-boy, you gonna' put one out o' there today?

—I'll try! I will if I can!

—Wow. He's big.

—Look at 'im.

—Why you always act so crazy, Joey?

—Guess I just am crazy. Can't help it. Ha ha!

—Is it fun?

—Naw.

His features were softened. But then his fine even teeth set in
the trademark grin as he greeted a business type, in a suit, walking to work in Midtown.

—How do. Late for work today, Sir?

Joey ran a little for the fun of it and then stopped to sign a few
autographs. He savored the free moment before he had to go out

there and do it again. He listened to a fan's words of wisdom about the opposing pitcher this afternoon and gave his opinion too. But now he had to git a move on or else catch a late fine. So the super-athlete trotted off toward Columbus Circle. But he whirled to wave bye bye; he kicked his legs in midair and let out a whoop as his mind toyed with a few new ideas. Say! It feels a little like this woman digs me. How about that! Poor crazy guy, and she— naw, don't believe it. She isn't that stupid. These women aren't stupid . . . Hey! I like being dug by somebody. Holy cow! Holy moly herb! Carlyne doesn't. That's for sure as hell. The swanky Lydia has a soft spot for me. But that other one, my wife who said adiós, she never did buy my act. Lydia's got legs. Whew! Those are some legs she's got on her, long ones. Like a spider waiting to getcha' . . . in all that web of sophistication of hers. Hm! She has personality. Well, whaddaya's say, sports fans? Maybe I'll just give her a ring later on for the fun of it. Ha ha. Ha ha ha ha ha! I'm Jo and she's The Doc and it's not so bad for once. Is it?

He skipped along like a kid and windmilled his arms and jabbed at a branch.

A private school class was playing soccer. One boy turned, and his arm went stiff like a pointer's tail.

—Gadzooks! It's World Serious!

—Eh?

—Cross my heart and hope to die. I'd know him anywhere.

—Zowwy!

—Boy, I wish I had his baseball card. It's hard to get! You got a Joey Gilbert? C'mon, I'll trade.

—No soap.

—Not for Harry the Hat Brecheen? Not for Lou Skizas from Easton, Texas?

—No deal, keep 'em.

—Oh! you Joey-babe. You gonna pound one out this af'?

He went gliding past on his long highpocket strides toward the entrance to the subway. Resplendent, joyous, the noontime sun sent down its rays through the peaceful trees; and it seemed life would have its loving way no matter how many hateful things were done to it by the savage creature called Man. Joey thought: Hey, I might fall in love with a maniac too if they paid me the rates she gets. Why else would she fancy a born loser, a goner? Maybe she's nuts also from an overdose of psychology: her 'ego-syntai' and her 'discrepant experience' . . . It'll be romance in the padded cell. Straitjacket sex. Live it up! The descendant of Pierre Janet, trailblazer in hypnosis, falls in love with the baseball bum. She has the seven-year jock itch.

Joey's mood soared when he thought such a woman might care for him. Why would she? Because he turned sports into a do-or-die conflict? Into a Vietnam? Because it was the eve of Doomsday yet he went on risking, affirming, prevailing?

Six at a time he took the concrete steps on his way to the train out to the stadium. Thought: Feels so cozy being with her, I could talk to her forever! When we take our sweet time, and mull over one thing or another . . . that's fun! Well, let's see. Maybe get together after the day game on Saturday? But will she trust me after what I just did? One thing about Lydia: she doesn't tell me to come here, come here, and then get away, get away. Come to think of it, I don't know if she could get enough of me! And there are no old stories about how my ancestors drove her ancestors off the land. That's a plus. And no Bangkok mysteries dressed up in a black negligée to seduce my young ass. No ulterior motives I can't quite grasp, and reasons to love me that aren't about me. I don't get no-shows and heartache from Lydia Falliere but only a calm, clear look, like an invitation . . .? Let's talk it over on Saturday night, alright? Do you forgive me . . . d'd'darling? Let's just focus on you and me and see what happens. Okay! It's a wonderful warm thing to be alive today . . . if only I didn't have to play baseball. Feels like an afternoon at a beach club when I was a teenager. Eternal summer.

—Oh ho!—he laughed out loud going through the turnstile, joining the crowd.—Fasten your seat belts. Hold on to your hats. It's time for a pennant race like when 'dem Bums beat damn Yanks and became World Champs.

XIII

On September 14th his team was back home after a tough swing through the Eastern cities. A day game got a late start due to rain.

Then tied in the sixth inning with runners on first and second and one away, Joey Gilbert stepped in. As usual he didn't take a practice cut, tap spikes, scratch bites, touch cup, transfer chaw after he spat, stare out as he measured his swing. None of this; it was unorthodox with him. The bat rested on his shoulder two, three pitches into the count until by some instinct he jolted in motion with the big hitch, the cock.

Look out! Ball way in: high hard one whisked his ear. He was the new League record holder in HBPs. But he didn't flinch. He didn't brush off dust after a sizzler put him on his back. He just got up again, and it was a staring match.

Week after week it was open season on his scalp—a few brushbacks per game as he bailed out at the last split second. All instinct he was, and stubbornness, and hate. His revenge was to hit, run, throw, slide, field, like a deranged demon. He grinned his steely grin and stuck a daisy in his cap. On third base one night a fan ran out on the field and handed him a raspberry creamsickle. With the thing in his mouth he made a five-three assist, and of course this made front-page photos the next day, instead of carnage in Vietnam. Once again the Commissioner barked but didn't bite.

Ball two. Slider low.

Into the last weeks of the season his batting average was over .400. He made plays in the field which energized his team and the stands.

Now a heckler yelled:

—Gilbert, yer' a manic-depressive!

2-1 pitch—

Hit 'im.

Joey didn't bat an eyelash when the ball caromed off his shoulder. He grinned, on the casual jaunt to first, and then made a display of rubbing.

Sacks filled.

—Ouch!—he said for the camera, and laughed.

Once, spiked during a tag at third, his forearm was spurting. He wiped blood on the runner's uniform and then dropped him in a brief scuffle.

—Violence is our national pastime—he told a reporter.—Baseball is boring.

He was unpitchable at the plate. No weakness. It was an enigma for scouts since there seemed to be no chink in the armor. HBPs only woke him up: brought him back from his war flashbacks. After an HBP he upset a pitcher's rhythm. As for his play at third base: spectacular, erratic; the lapses made it even more exciting. Much of the time he spent scanning the stands.

Bing! A bases-loaded single to right gave New York the lead.

XIV

So it stood into the last inning: a one-run edge.

Top half of the ninth, one down, two runners in scoring position—plip! Milwaukee sixth slot, a switch-hitter up left, lofted a sky-high pop off third. Up, up it towered twisting above the stands in shallow left field. Shortstop's ball; but he was at double play depth and shaded toward second.

Back went Joey, back, back he ran head down like he had eyes in the back of his skull, and, in a smooth ballet leap before jack-knifing the barrier and cracking his noggin on a box rail—made the grab. The packed crowd gave not applause but a gasp, a breathless sigh. There were no cheers, no chants after the amazing catch.

So it sounded shrill when a woman screamed.

While the coldcocked third baseman clutched the ball still in play in his mitt—the two runners tagged and zippedydoed. The lead run steamed round second with a whoop. Was it a 3-base sacrifice fly? The New York manager stood on the dugout steps writhing and groaning. What could he do? It was a live ball. The umpire couldn't call time.

But suddenly the injured fielder jumped to his feet. Was he playing possum? Wo there! Catch the runner in a mad dash from first to home on an infield pop-up?

Joey went racing up the concrete steps at field level. He turned his back on the scene where teammates were yelling themselves hoarse for him to throw the ball.

He ran. He ran as if his life depended on it. For there, like an apparition upstairs in the mezzanine aisle, stood a woman in a white top and bluejeans with a small child on her arm.

She had a transfigured air—staring down at the ballplayer who vaulted up toward her with long strides.

It was her.

In the instant before he conked out his eagle eye had seen Carlyne and the image was there like a flash when he came to. Big
Joey capless with blood on his curly hair went like a rocket past
box seats and up toward the mezzanine even as the New York
manager kicked the water cooler and shouted to throw the bleep-
ing ball before the go-ahead runner scored. This wasn't funny because the League lead was at stake. Far, far in the distance behind
him was the sound of Six's bark; but Joey leapt up toward her,
her. Cleats clicked. There was silence as the stadium watched the
chase.

It was a lull in crowd hysterics—no bedlam but only a big stillness as the tie-breaker crossed home on the sac fly. Fifty thousand
fans ignored this immense fact, upon which the League lead depended, in order to watch a soap opera.

Joey Gilbert flew out the field level gate. A minute later he burst
onto the mezzanine.

It might have been the Greek theater at Epidaurus as he hollered out to the hushed stadium:

—Carlyne, where are you? I need you!

Pouf! The woman in white had vanished into thin air. Was she
a ghost?

In anger and frustration he made a perfect peg home all the
way from the mezzanine. But it was five minutes too late. The
New York catcher rolled his eyes and threw up his arms.

—Way to hum that ol' pea! said a fan. What a gun!

But Joey just sat down and hung his head—with its hickory
and trickle of blood—among the quiet crowd.

Then with his fielder's glove over his face, hiding the pain, he
shook his head. Was it a nervous breakdown?

On September 14th New York fell a half game off the pace.

XV

On the front page of the morning newspapers were two photos. A Major League ballplayer sat with mitt over his face in the
stands among the spectators. A college student posed for her
yearbook picture.

HAVE YOU SEEN THE MYSTERY WOMAN?

Later that day the baseball player, yesterday's goat, phoned the detective agency he had hired.

—I said no publicity. Dammit, I'll sue you.

—We didn't give them anything. It wasn't us.

—Then where did they get the picture?

—Ask your people. This is our stock-in-trade: there's no breach.

—Come now. It's been almost four months, and you're stumped. I pay through the nose, and you break your security oath.

—I assure you, Mr. Gilbert, we did not. Why would we? We'd never risk our reputation by being indiscreet, and we didn't leak the photo.

—Then who—?

—Try to be patient. Hold on a little longer if you can. She is here: we'll find her now.

—Just—Joey hesitated—just look for a woman wearing a brooch . . .

Through the night he couldn't get to sleep. His wife was here in the City. And she came to the ballpark to watch him play. Herself. It was Carlyne. Yes.

Toward noon the club GM telephoned him.

—Your grandstand play will cost you 2500 dollars.

—Tst.

—It's not us. The League President's office sent word.

—If it was his wife he'd do the same thing.

The General Manager laughed.

—I'd like to give you time off. You could use it. But we need you in the lineup.

—I'll be there.

—Take a rest. We'll see you at six.

But he couldn't rest. From his East Side apartment he walked twenty blocks to the psychiatrist's office.

This wasn't his day, so he had to wait.

Then, on the recliner, he said:

—I saw her.

—So I notice. But tell me: how do you spot one person in such a crowd?

—She's my wife. She was in the stands with our baby. She was staring at me.

—She and fifty thousand others.

—Our time in Bangkok made me a father.

—Congratulations, said Lydia, softly.

—But why, Doctor? Please tell me why. Just drop the psychology and think like a woman for a moment. Does she enjoy torturing me?

Lydia frowned. Then her voice went low with a sort of catch in it.

—What are Carlyne's motives? You'd know that, Joey, better than I.

—I mean why did she fly to Thailand? And the next thing I know she's gone from the Rock Castle without saying where. Another thing: my father said she left in February, but Lemon told me it was January. Now why? Who is lying? Would my father lie?

—Maybe . . . your sister doesn't remember.

—One of them doesn't. But I think she does.

—Or he was in Washington, so he didn't know just when?

—She was made pregnant before she came to see me out there. In the fall that is. It was by Newell or for all I know by the old lecher Doan who hangs around . . . we thought for Lemon. Maybe he isn't particular. But the hospital records in Durham show my wife conceived in mid-September: unless the baby born in June was overdue, from my weekend leave before shipping out to Vietnam, or else two months premature, from Bangkok. But the baby's medical records say nothing about it.

In the air-conditioned office the doctor and the patient sat thinking in silence. The stir along Fifth Avenue sounded far off.

Joey shook his head.

Lydia said:

—People act irrationally through fear.

—Fear of what?

—You.

—But I love her! Any man would.

—Any man . . . Think a minute. What if something . . . difficult happened while you did your tour? You told me about your family.

—What does my family have to do with it?

—You paint Gilbert relations as a series of splits, like a family war. This one lives, and this one falls. Emory and Newell are like two killers who fight to the bitter end. Anne dies from cancer in her fifties. Lemon must marry an older man for reasons of state.

—What does that have to do with me and Carlyne?

He gestured.

—In her you were looking for a wholeness you never had in your family.

—A wife and kids like anybody else.

—But she has her own past. She has her own unmet needs, grief.

—Did she let me forget it?

—You heard her, Joey, but did you understand? What about *her* fears and conflicts? Did you feel them?

—I tried.

—You, Emory, Newell, you're winners. The way you describe your father, I mean his personality apart from your admiration and love for him: it sounds like he'll go to any length to win. And you too, Joey: you still mean to win the old war of your family needs. Make Mom love you. Make Dad love you. How? Through Carlyne? But maybe she can't face that. Maybe she can't afford to fight someone else's battles because she has her own.

—Somebody else's battles? We're married, we're one.

—Forgive me for saying so, but perhaps she couldn't face such a family as the Gilberts. Perhaps the last place she should have gone during your absence was the Rock Castle.

—She checked out on me. She left.

—She had a reason.

—Good, but now come back.

—Do you love her, Joey? Do you really want her back?

—Yes.

—Then learn that reason.

Lydia held his eye a long moment. Then she grinned, like him!

He looked down.

XVI

—You'll find her now. I can feel it.

—Can you?

Lydia laughed, but wistful.

—She loves and wants you so much, Joey, so much. She's near the campfire, but she's afraid.

—Of what?

—You. Gilberts. But let me ask you something.

Joey frowned.

—Go on.

—Did you ever leave her? Just go away without a word?

—No.

—Ah. I see.—Lydia gave a chuckle.—So you didn't fly away as far as possible from her, to the earth's confines, The Nam?

—To do my patriotic duty.

—Sure. But did you ask Carlyne first? Did she share in the decision?

—She pushed me to do it.

—Ah. She said get out of my sight. Go to Vietnam.

—N-no.

—The truth is that marriage is hard for two young people as different as you and she. And you could not be your usual self the winner. And so when the pressure was on, when it was really on, Joey, to stand up like a man and not like the golden boy out at third base . . . then you folded and ran away.

—Are you calling me a coward?

—Maybe that time. I don't know. I wasn't there. You decide.

—Oh.

—If so, then join the club. You're not the first child who tried to do a man's work as a husband, or the last.

Joey looked down.

—Alright already. I'm a child. I'm sorry. But now come back to me. Give me another chance.

Lydia nodded.

—She will. She can't run away from herself much longer.

He bowed, running his hand through his hair.

—I know it, Doc, she doesn't love me anymore.

Lydia laughed:

—Sure, sure. Take me out to the ballgame, a diehard fan.

—You like to make fun of your patients?

—No.

Silence.

Brow creased, boyish and slightly comical, he looked up at her:

—Got it all figured out, don't you?

—Not yet.

—It's quite impressive, really. But let me ask you one thing, Doctor.

—Sir?

—Did you divorce your hubby or did he chuck you?

—He chucked me.

—Why so? Your bed was more like a dissecting table? He got tired of the psych gobbledygook?

—Something like that.

—Well then . . . heal thyself.

—Touché.—The psychiatrist shook her head.—It doesn't help much to figure things out if you don't have the basics. In the end my husband and I didn't. So much for us. But you two love each other very deeply, Joey. Go ahead; go on out there and find her.

He gave a groan and, slowly, lifted his athlete's body from the recliner.

—Sorry. I didn't mean to insult you.

—All in fun.

—Spoken like a man.

Lydia watched him get up, and stand tall. Brow knit, she nodded:

—Good luck.

Joey grinned, cocky, a jock again:

—Don't worry. I'll find my wife.

Lydia's voice went low, a warble.

—I hope so. Forgive her.

Joey, on his way, stared back an instant. He muttered, as though he never heard the word before:

—Forgive? . . . Look, Ma, no hands.

Chapter Eighteen

I

The regular season ended with two teams locked in a first place tie. After 154 games they were even in the won-lost columns. So on a Tuesday evening in October the St. Louis club came to New York for a playoff game to decide the League championship. The winner would take on Baltimore in the World Series.

Inside the stadium, a bright green patch in the metropolitan area sprawl, the starting lineups were read over the P.A. system. One by one, as their names went wafting across the outfield, the players trotted from the dugout to form a row along the baselines. Applause rose and fell; it rose as the New York third sacker, League leader in four categories, came forth taking his time, at a walk.

Then a popular singer put her soul into the National Anthem, and there were more cheers. As she finished, hitting the high note, a peal of thunder rumbled in the distance out over the ocean.

On the nation's airwaves the cry of a hotdog vendor reached millions of fans from Montauk to Malibu, but it didn't make him a penny richer.

An ovation greeted the home team taking the field. First and third base coaches manned their posts, scuffed dust, tugged bill; they began fidgeting and giving their false signs.

The St. Louis leadoff hitter paused in the on-deck circle. He limbered up stretching his back muscles. He rubbed rosin on the bat handle. Then took a vicious cut.

The sell-out crowd awaited the New York ace from the home dugout along first. And here he came: the tall drink of water tugged his cap and shook his mitt as he strode over the lime. He looked big on the hill as he took a look around. By the rubber he dug with his cleats: worked at the mound for his toe-hold, kick and follow-through. The plate was so close on good days, but a mile away on bad. Then he took the first shiny white pellet of this money game and rubbed 'er up.

Now the eight warm-up tosses; and the 20-game winner turned his brawny back on the plate as, zip-zip-zip, the old pill flew round the infield—and then was lobbed, tenderly, by the third baseman to the big hurler.

Tonight the crew chief was the League's senior umpire. He bent down and brushed off the dish; then flexed his knees, hunched behind his chest protector, readied for the first pitch.

But he rose and held his mask by the strap a moment longer as the New York backstop loped out to the mound.

Then at last the ump, karst-browed, looking lockjawed after decades of arguments over close calls, flung up an arm and bawled:

—Play ball!

Baseball flowed out over the airwaves across the wide night of America.

II

In the small southern town there was a crowd gathered outside the Rock Castle. Some stood talking on the sidewalk and others were on the lawn while listening to the playoff game over a portable radio.

St. Louis went down 1-2-3 in the top half. Now it was the bottom of the first, two gone, Joey up.

—*Low bridge! Oh! He bails out as a high fastball sails in past his ear. Whoof! Ha ha! At the last instant Gilbert went sprawling on his belly across the plate. Plap! Well, fans, he learned that little maneuver*

*in The Nam. Incoming, troop! And look how he bounces back up again
and stares out at that big mound mauler who looks like he wants to eat
him!*

On the radio the distant crowd wavered in and out. Horse
laughs, cheers, catcalls made a breath of cosmos.

Outside the big granite mansion it was like a party as the people enjoyed themselves with beer or brown paper bag in hand.

Night had fallen. On the first floor a light shone: the desk lamp
in P. Laster Gilbert's den. And there sat P. Laster's son, the great
Emory Gilbert who came in a few hours ago from one of his lecture tours. He listened too.

—*The New York third hitter spits. His face is dusty after the knockdown pitch. Bat boy trots out to retrieve his helmet spun up along the 1st
base line. Gilbert is League leader for average, slugging percentage, tri-
ples, HBPs. He shakes his head a little. He blinks. Pfzuh, too much dust.
He spits, but doesn't brush himself off. No, sir. World Serious stands in,
stares out, grins. No score in the first. Two outs, none on.*

Emory turned down the sound, but the cheers and groans came
to him from outside. New York City and the nation were pulsat-
ing to his son's every move. There was a turbulent sense to it as if
anything might happen before this night was through.

III

On college campuses, at exclusive men's clubs no less than
packed union halls across the land, Emory Gilbert was the darling. They were eager to hear his ideas and be stirred up by his
idealistic verve, his grand if pedantic view of things, his grandiose nature on the scale of a Victor Hugo. Well, these days he was
still more a Bryan-type Liberal, but he was just so dynamic and
contradictory, like he had a devil in him. It was interesting!

From professional associations such as National Press Club to
branch libraries and the book clubs of our ladies—the lecture circuit gazed in awe as the great writer stood before them. He rarely
declined an engagement. From Emory the news media drew spice
for its nightly newscasts. And he was formidable at a round table
discussion.

A TV network featured the author in an hour-long special. He revisited his long series of literary works of the first order, and reviewed with some irony his recent bout of Presidential politics.

His life had been like a rocket with stages. And now he was a kind of spiritual leader for America; but not only. He spoke of starting a third major political Party, and he asked: Is there still enough health and vitality in this System to change things electorally? Can the voters take on the mighty corporations?

Now also he got carried away at times and told more truth than the good people were used to hearing. Due perhaps to the agitated national climate or to some sort of inner turmoil, he launched into dramatic new regions and surprised our silent majority. But pro or con, they enjoyed what made them feel alive again after the daily overdose of TV and good ol' Mid-American torpor. The great speaker pulled out the stops.

Now he was back home for a breather after all the excitement.

He sat at his father's old mahogany desk and listened to the New York announcer:

—It's the 2-2 . . . Oh! A low line drive foul right at the third base coach. Ow! My crotch! Down into the left field corner that line shot goes skidding on a single hop. What strength in his wrists, what a guy! He bites the dust beneath a beanball then it's up and at 'em. He turned on a belt-high curve and powered 'er a bit foul, like a blur.

Crowd noise was like ocean waves breaking along the beach of the Rockaways.

Raaaraaararaaaah.

But Emory thought of his lecture tour. He was no longer limited by a campaign strategy; and so he flirted with what may be much bigger. He said more or less what he wanted, and at times it was quite extravagant. His noble periods harked back to the brilliant liberal he once was, during the 'Thirties, in the vanguard of his generation.

Yes, he jolted 'em from the podium just as Joltin' Jo, Jr., was doing these days from home plate. Emory gave them what they craved whether moral outrage against the war; an apocalyptic vision of America; mankind's last stand led by a broad-based popular movement for reform and universal peace.

Was he a populist? You didn't feel that. You felt he was elitist—but just so swell, so good!

There were sniffles as the prophet went into his oratorical crescendo. Young women stared up at him with glazed eyes.

And then, one night, inspired out of his wits at a speech's climax in Minneapolis, he called for a Third Party which would be a principled, not loyal, opposition. What language! Utopian in tone, again, like Jennings Bryan:

—For what happens in our cities, our urban slums and ethnic ghettos with their 40 per 1000 infant mortality rate and their 75% high school dropout rate and their illiteracy hardly credible in history's richest nation? What happens in the industrial zones where millions remain unorganized, non-unionized, exploited every day and every hour by an ever more centralized exploiter class? What happens in the vast Third World-like sprawl with its segregation even yet and racial bigotry across the South and not only? Current poverty rates do this capitalist system no honor. Kids go malnourished and poorly clad and dys-educated by that drug television. Who reads? I mean really reads? And what books, what culture do we give them besides an escapist culture, a money culture, a cotton candy culture, a small stunted culture unwilling to confront big, critical problems such as our, humanity's, survival on the planet? . . .

"From year to year and from decade to decade the systemic decay goes marching on; it makes its way like maggots on an American flag. And every four years it's the usual comedy only with new faces for the network cameras. It's the same media field day as more conformists with nothing new to say run for United States President. One wins office, and the rest go back to a private life of VIP accomodations. I call it a no-lose situation as long as you don't make waves. But for us, for the people, it's a no-win.

"The bought-and-sold golden boys of electoral politics go back to their executive suites where they maneuver and raise funds and cultivate board members and wait for their time to moult from Party boss to national figure. But tell me, Citizens, does life get any better in the meantime? For our destitute families and our dispossessed millions? Do we mature as a people and begin to take ourselves in hand and plan for the future?

"On our own, now I ask you, do we begin to stand free and independent, truly free I mean, knowing and analyzing and changing reality? That's freedom! Not a blind instinctual illusion of freedom: just because each is left alone to pursue money and comfort while all of us without a historic plan are heading toward ruin. Humanity must come of age and learn to plan, and work together, or else self-destruct! Child grown to man must plan, and see the childish illusion of a creatural freedom for what it is, and begin to take stock of necessity. If not . . . if we do not take on the great problems of our era, which are do-or-die for humanity—then what? Then what?

"If we Democrats had been more aware of this; if we were more honest; if we took a consequential anti-war position instead of the line of least resistance, putting our own comfort and careers ahead of the Truth—then we would have beaten Nixon last November. But it still isn't too late. And so now I tell you: Bring the troops home! Bring the war home! Hell no, I won't go! Hell no, I won't go!"—

Tonight in the quiet den in the small southern town Emory remembered how he shouted out slogans and then turned abruptly from the microphone. And the standing crowd shouted and chanted in his wake, and then gave a long appreciative applause. And then there was more of: Hell no, we won't go! We won't fight for Texaco!

Whew! What a Schwung to that Emory Gilbert's social sermons.

What a man.

IV

—*Steeeerike three! Oh! oh! (Aaraarah.) A wicked slider low outside caught the trim! (Raararrhaaar.) Sit down! The heavy hitter gawked at the called third strike! Man oh man (haahraaaharraah) how these New York fans do not love it! But look how Gilbert will not move. He stays in the box with the lumber on his shoulder. What a mule! Ha ha ha! What's the mad guy doing now? Is it a protest? Is it a picket? Ha ha! There's a dreamy look on the third hitter's mug as now manager and trainer, also the third base coach go to the New York star and hold a psych consult alongside home. (Ahrrarraaahrahr.) How do you like them apples?! Was it a strikeout, or a psych out? Ha ha ha! Ump looks like he's got ants in his pants. Say there, Sigmund Freud, carry on your psychoanalysis during the seventh inning stretch . . . Well, it could affect World Series hopes when your best player has just had a schizophrenic episode. Ha ha ha. Or is it dementia praecox? Ha ha ha. Hey! Give that man a tranquillizer, a pat on the rump, and back at 'em, champ. This Miltown's for you!*

Emory had wished the Presidential fantasy world might never end. For if it did then he must come home and be alone with his soul. And so it was: one November night the bright lights went out. They lost. It was small wonder after the Chicago fiasco: as U.S. media portrayed the Democratic nominee as Candidate of the Cops, Dick Daley's man, an insensitive hardliner. On Vietnam, the key issue, he sat on the fence and did not risk a clear-cut position. Had Emory's boss had a positive influence on Party Platform debate over the war? No. But did the corporate networks ever take Nixon to task for his shuffle on troop withdrawal?

After Chicago many of the youth behind Eugene McCarthy were disillusioned and leaned toward the Left, or had thoughts of a Third Party. Then in the final weeks and the drive toward Election Day Emory spoke in public of the usual reform proposals picked to shreds by special interest groups and a mortgaged Congress. Much of his time was spent coordinating the brigade of consultants and advisers, public opinion specialists, pollsters, poll analysts, ad agencies, TV and radio producers, schedulers, advance men, state chairmen. Also he had to raise funds since his team ran up against financial difficulties: it costs money to make a king, and pay campaign expenses—from TV time and hired planes down to buttons, posters, t-shirts.

But Emory Gilbert spoke. Oh how he spoke from coast to coast in those days, Election '68. He addressed the nation at a crossroads. As ever his rhetorical flights were as sound as Cicero; though you didn't always know what he was saying. Just as the campaign lagged and flagged for lack of guts: so you never quite knew where the liberal stood. Only in his case you hardly cared because he wafted any audience aloft on wings of such a terrific lyricism.

At that time he held the line: our American way come what may; individual freedom whether for Wall Street magnate (give or take a few bank proposals) or a slum dweller. Both pay the same subway fare; neither sleeps legally beneath a bridge. He said he believed deeply in the Bill of Rights: Government spies, FBI snoops, wiretaps, steamy fingered tamperers of mail, agents provocateurs, political intrigues of all kinds aroused his moral ire.

As a campaigner he was a post-Enlightenment liberal. As a smalltown boy risen to the top he was free enterprise personified. Strictly anti-communist, his emotional emphasis was on Soviet abuses, not U.S. wars for the Third World's resources. Famous, wealthy, he would rather lose an election than make waves which divided the country, and stirred up the masses. He would certainly choose Richard Nixon over proletarian revolution.

Fully identified materially and spiritually with U.S and Western middle class values, parliamentary democracy, individual rights, comforts, privileges, he didn't care to undermine his own power. He knew which side his bread was buttered on.

And so, during the Campaign, he steered clear of any real commitment except to winning; of political conviction except the Democratic Party platform; of any social critique taken to its logical conclusion, which was socialism.

But this would change.

V

Into the final weeks of Campaign '68 his lofty Burkean discourse won the house hands down if not a ballot box victory. Some were sorry he hadn't gotten the Vice Presidential nod. Emory's sudden enormous popularity came ten days too late.

And then in high gear the Democratic campaign grew low on funds. Or the media committee had a half million dollar windfall yet could not buy TV time in New York or California since every precious second was bought up by local candidates.

Predawn game plans began his 18-hour day as he stumped the country. And nightly poll-watch and reassessment sessions ended it. He was exhausted and running on adrenalin. These heady times drowned out a still small voice he didn't want to hear.

It was a dizzy pace as Election Day drew near. Oh there were people, everywhere people, and how he loved them! How he revelled in his public persona reflected in their gaze. The great man! Those were wonderful ordinary hometown folks, like the ones down in Carolina who knew him when; and he was Emory Gilbert. Now it was they, so fine, so generous, who would sweep him on his Candidate's coattails into the Executive Office Building where all too human flesh took on the impermeability of stone. He was rather carried away by it all: a celebrity if there ever was one.

On all sides of the apogee there were staffers, volunteers, phone bankers, union activists—to canvas and educate and register voters. There were women and more women, like the down-front girls who stirred up the house when they shrieked, squealed, bleated, threw kisses to the father figure, the winner named Emory. Ah! How they admired him when he MC'd a huge rally and heaped praise on the next President of the United States.

And then came defeat. Fully 9% of the voters chose the Peace Candidate on an independent ticket. The result was a Republican victory.

Then there was the last luncheon, stunned, things at an end. High hopes and ambitions came undone.

—Vietnam beat us.

Too long, maybe a week too long, their man waffled on this critical issue. The eloquent Emory helped him do it. The Right held its breath while the Left kept crying out loud in the streets. You coward! Liberal opportunist! It was the way of spineless politicians since time began—the closer to power, the yellower. They were the long-as-it-doesn't-cost-me-anything liberals. But at the stroke of midnight Emory's Candidate woke up and played the trump card of Vietnam. He finally got the gumption to distance himself from LBJ, and came out clearly against the war.

It was too late.

The real anti-Vietnam War politician, perhaps, and potential Democratic winner had been Robert Kennedy.*

And then the roar and the foot-stomping receded to an echo. And whoosh went history's whisk broom. And all the staged joy and excitement were hushed for another four years while the loser smiled on camera and still savored his name in the news. The Dems made their peace and called it democracy.

And then silence.

Emory flew home to North Carolina after twelve months in the limelight. He had tasted the abundant fare at the banquet of power. For a year he flew high in the public eye, and then it was defeat, Nixon victorious.

Suddenly he found himself alone with his conscience in the silence of P. Laster's den.

---

*Thirty-eight years later the BBC would report Robert Kennedy may have been gunned down by CIA operatives while a hypnotized Sirhan Sirhan—who would always claim he didn't remember being there—created a robot-like diversion. In any event the fatal bullet came from behind, and only one inch away. Photos of the scene show three redeployed (from southeast Asia) CIA agents near the candidate who was to be assassinated.

VI

On the long sloping front lawn of the Rock Castle there must have been a hundred people. They drank beer and socialized. They sat on the grass listening to the playoff game. For the most part their voices were low and respectful, so Emory didn't mind; in fact, he'd go out there and join them in a few minutes. No one would be doing much sleeping for yet awhile.

All goose eggs in the third.

New York's wunderkinder had yet to get a hit, but they were staging a rally. Their pitcher drew a walk and was bunted on to second. Then a St. Louis miscue, a throw in the dirt, put runners at first and third with one gone, and Joey up.

In came the 1-1 delivery:

—Bawuh.

The crowd noise muffled the play-by-play announcer's voice and lent a sense of sound waves over great distances. It seemed the spheres hung on each pitch of this game to decide the Pennant.

Across the five boroughs of New York the packed bars were ready to erupt like jukeboxes at full blast.

Passersby, casual strangers asked one another the score and started up conversations. The nation's greatest city and all the other cities and towns buzzed and got worked up awaiting each pitch.

Now the home plate ump swayed and held up his count indicator. He swung his arms like an ape; then hunched over his chest protector: set for the next pitch.

The hitter waited on the 2-1. He had no stance but stood there with the bat on his shoulder. He didn't budge a muscle, twit an eyebrow. He just stared out at the righthanded fireballer the size of three Viet Cong.

A nation of TV sets focused on the crazy third baseman. All season the ex-squad leader left his mates in the lurch with bad lapses in the field: when he thought the hot corner was a Central Highlands foxhole. Or he left runners stranded when he got distracted in the batter's box.

But the clutch moment arrived, and he came through. This shell-shocked G.I. jumped all over one; he cranked her a country mile. And the center fielder raced back, back, and stared up at the stars. Kiss that sweet baby goodbye. After the bonehead play came the long ball. Joey Gilbert transcended. He dashed your hopes and kept them alive. O, ye (illegal bettors) of little faith.

—If Gilby hits for the collar, I'll moiduh 'im. I got a fin on this baby. Say . . . you got a stake too? Not in for your shoit, I hope!

Activity stopped across the sprawling metropolis as it did in the small southern town. In a 5-star hotel the desk clerks, bellhops and porters, the boutique keepers and the self-important door-man in top hat and tails, the hotel guests, tourists, diners, shop-pers—all stood with baited breath awaiting the 3-2.

—Ooh! Oooh-hooh!

The announcer was tense:

—*Fouled back . . . but what a cut it was. The big hitch, Joey Gilbert out of his catatonic trance . . . then bingo, swing for the downs. His wicked foul tip stuck in the screen behind home. Orthodontic surgery anyone?*

In the big murmur Emory imagined emotion ebbing and flow-ing across the City. He knew New York. Now from Battery Park to Spuyten Duyvil, from traffic gridlocks in Midtown to the broad avenues swarming with cabs, Queens Boulevard, the Grand Con-course; the Major Deegan and Pelham Parkway and the outer roadways with signs that read: New England; from the West Side wharves to Jamaica Bay squibbed with reflected lights of the Rockaways—everywhere, at the airports and bus terminals and Penn Station and Grand Central: the people awaited the payoff pitch. The wide night of baseball sent its signals across America—in Syosset and Little Neck; the length of Utopian Parkway, and Round Swamp Road; in Babylon and in Montauk. From the East-ern Seaboard to the Midwestern heartland, and from a freight-er's lone light in North Atlantic waters to the long Pacific Coast beaches flushed with sunset; and farther, far beyond: in the glar-ing noon of Vietnam where grunts tuned in to a former line dog's moment of glory better than a parade; and at a couple thousand U.S. military installations, like a global chorus of Armed Forces Radio—everywhere, everywhere in history's mightiest empire, it was:

—*Unwhoosh . . . ooschursh . . . whiishush . . . ehhreewhoarr . . .*

Tense as a raccoon who has stepped on a nail, the New York announcer called the play:

—*St. Louis ace rubs up the pellet. Stares in . . . Lifts cap. Wipes his sweaty brow with his red-sleeved forearm. He shakes off a sign. Now he's ready: steps up, toes the rubber. Nods at the lead runner inching off third. Big righthander comes set. Again he checks the baserunners at the corners. Now he rocks, kicks, delivers. Oh! It's a bullet—caught! Fielder dives headfirst and slaps the bag: out! A double play!*

"The St. Lou infielder went to his knees with the sheer force of that smash down third. You could not see it, fans! You had to look around. Was it a phantom? Or a schizoid phantasm? Ha ha ha! And the grab for dear life and he lunged and tagged the bag before the runner dove back. Boy oh boy! An unassisted DP quells New York's first rally as St. Louie lucks out in the third.

"But hold on—what? What's this? Look at Joey Gilbert crouched down along the third base line. After contact he ran not toward first but third! . . . Is it Wrong-Way Corrigan? . . . Now Gilbert on his knees waves an arm crazily, and it's: Hey! Once more, troops, into the brink! Ha ha ha! Look at 'im go! Like a spinning top! That nabbed liner was too much for the poor guy; something snapped! Now check this out! Look at the boy; he's firing off rounds, datdatda! datdatda from his M-16, an imaginary rifle! Wow, I'm glad it's not a real one: he just took aim at the press box. Joey Gilbert has gone loco, sports fans, completely berserk! Ha ha ha, I'll call the fire fight for you. Gilbert ducks his head. Gilbert gestures his men forward as he goes into combat crawl with his elbows in chalk twenty feet from home. Gilbert is shooting down fake Viet Cong with his fake gun, ha ha ha, this is really priceless! And listen to the capacity crowd laugh at his antics! (Haaaahroarrhaaahr!) Now the trainer trots on the field followed by the New York skipper. What's this! Gilbert takes aim and levels his barrel at his manager! Pah! Pah! Ha! Ha! He mows the man down, dat dat dat dat! Serves you right, old sourpuss. Always kicking the water cooler, big bully! Ha ha ha! Doesn't this crowd just love it? It's better than the King and His Court. Better than Tommy Byrne's behind-the-back pitch. (Aahhaaarhrtyyy . . . haarhhhaarrr!) Now Doc on his haunches tries to reason with him. War's over, Gilby. Wait! I think Doc is diagnosing. It's borderline schizophrenia, fans, with some good ol' pathological narcissism thrown in for good measure. Ha ha ha! But look! Look there! Gilbert has the shakes! He's trembling all over like it's an epileptic fit. Will he stay in the game? Can he play? Holy smoke! What a joke he's making out of Major League baseball!

"Hold on! What's that? Players are pouring out of both dugouts, and they look like they mean it! But why? Ha! It's the psych ward, sports fans! Hysteria is infectious, and Joeymania is on the march! Now look at 'em kneel and trade shots with their Louisville Sluggers as if these were semiautomatic rifles, and the base paths were trenches. Has everybody

gone crazy around here? Isn't there some money riding on this game tonight?

"*Ba ba bah! They're shooting each other, and they're falling—falling over and holding their ribs with laughter, dropping down dead with the giggles. The whole ballpark is in stitches! (Haaarrrhhhaaarharrahhh.) What a mad donnybrook; it's the new Major League make-believe. It's a case of mass hebephrenia, fans, as sides split here and there from laughing too hard. Joey Gilbert has just flipped out again, and turned this place into a circus.*

"*Say, is this lunatic making a mockery of our National Pastime? Could be he's unpatriotic! Maybe he's bitter about his time in Vietnam? But why take it out on baseball?*

"*Now look! He raises his submachinegun at the uproarious crowd, and fifty thousand fans laugh merrily. Bababadatdatdah! (Hhhaaaardyyhaarrhhaaaaarrrr.)*

"*Hey! On a hot night like this one, sports lovers, you know such jungle warfare can really work up a sweat and a big thirst. That's natural! Bartender, why not serve Joey a tall, cool, foamy, beaded to the brim glass of the world's best beer from the land of sky-blue waters? It's the Ozarks brew, sports enthusiasts, and it's the best on God's earth. Always good for what ails ya' and maybe even for a third baseman who's gone off his rocker. Mm, it's so good, I think I'll just go out and down a few after the game tonight—if you can call this a game! Why, this beer I'm talking to you about is so doggone great it just gives you a craving for the next one, and the next! You can never get enough of it. Mm-mm, try it and see, sports buffs. Spend your life thirsty. Hey! What the hell, you only live once. And this one is for you!*

VII

Between innings Maximilian Doan came up the front walk toward the Rock Castle. He passed by the mulling crowd with a hi here and there—then took the heavy stone steps onto the porch, and looked in the window of the den.

—Emory, old sport!

Max wore his colonial planter's garb which suited him to a tee. Safari helmet with chin strap, bush jacket, plaited khaki shorts, walking stick. His brown nylon stockings were tightly gartered on his blond calves.

—Hello, Max.

—I came to have a chat.

—So I see.

The distinguished visitor looked a little nervous, breathless, as he blinked with his eyelashes aflutter. Often he had this coquettish air when mentioning some high-level post he had held.

—Joey's knockin' 'em dead up there in New York.

Emory nodded.

—So he is.

—What a killer!

—I hope they win tonight.

—They will. Jojo's a chip off the old block, a winner. Like you two got your gusto for life from the same mother's milk.

—Hm.

—And Newell? Still in Berkeley? Not a jailbird yet, I hope. Ha ha.

—Not that I know of. Won't you come in, Max? Glass of pink lemonade?

—I'll stay out here. Air's so fragrant. If you asked me how a man my age can feel so brimful of life, so ready for more good fun, I'd only say: Dame Nature has a few tricks up her sleeve. Three wars, a dozen wounds both physical and, shall we say, sentimental? Nearly half a century of struggle to keep this world safe for decent folk like you and me to live in peace and freedom, and I still feel young as hell!

—You look fit.

—As a fiddle, sir. I'm rarin' to go. It's never too late to fall in love again and cherish some sweet girl.

Lemon Gilbert's suitor raised his head and sniffed with wide nostrils at the night air.

Sunday afternoon he had showed up and waited on the front porch with a bouquet of yellow roses. He was crisp and chivalrous in his blue seersucker suit with a vest despite the Indian summer heat. His regimental crew cut was silvery as mica on a rock. And he was polite: the semiretired General said 'Suh' to his future father-in-law. He spoke in a respectful tone, but he took straight aim:

—Suh! I wish . . . I make so bold as to request your lovely daughter's hand in marriage. Is that okay? Please talk to Elizabeth Mona on my behalf, and let me know her answer. Tell her there is a soldier who loves her and asks only to make her happy. I give her and you my word I will never let her down.

For some time Emory had expected such a formal proposal. But now their relations had taken a new turn. Max did not make himself at home inside the Rock Castle as before.

Now two days after the proposal he said:

—Have you asked her for me, Emory? What does she say?

—I'm trying, Max, but she's . . . Hold on a moment. If you want to wait, I'll go upstairs and speak with her. You deserve an answer. I'll see what I can do.

VIII

Lemon was in her bedroom listening to the Playoff Game on her radio. The crowd emotion sounded like ocean waves as St. Louis base runners took their leads at the corners with one away. It was a bad inning. New York had given up three runs, and a big hit could all but put the game away. Now the manager went to his bullpen, calling on a starter for long relief.

The din of distant battle rose and fell in the small radio on Lemon's night table. Then as the new pitcher strolled to the hill and took his warm-up tosses there was a break in the action. High drama turned, pzzzt! to a commercial jingle.

Lemon turned to her father's soft knock on the door.

—Yes?

—It's me. Can I come in?

And then he stood before her. His face was red: as reflected fire. Had he been drinking? He glanced past her.

—Couldn't this wait, Dad?

—It won't take long.

—Bishop Commynes come by tonight?

—No, he didn't.

There was a note in Emory's voice. He knew how to intimidate. He did it with Newell.

—Lemon, I've just been speaking with General Doan. He's downstairs now.

—Is he? How nice.

—What does that mean?

—Nothing—Lemon shrugged.

—I may not agree with Max, but I respect him. A good man.

—Good and old.

Emory's face flushed:

—Don't get pert.

—Yes . . . Suh.

—He's a highly respected friend; not to mention a top echelon Government official, U.S. Army brass, business executive. What . . . better companion could a woman ask for?

—Tst.—She turned her face aside with a gesture: supreme contempt. Her voice was fluty:—How about one not four times as old as she is? Look, Dad, I just can't seem to fall in love with his résumé.

—I said don't be sassy. I don't have time right now for impertinent remarks. This important man has shown regard for us, and for our family honor, by requesting your hand in marriage. At least be polite. And, Lemon, I don't see how we can refuse him.

—Why didn't he come talk to me first? Is this old China?

—Max comes from the old school. Nowadays you won't find his manners on every street corner. Anyway not in a field hand.

—What's that?

—Where did you go with that greaser boy today?

—Greaser?

Lemon's jaw dropped. For a second she stared and seemed to see through the father she loved. It made her cringe. Grimly she shook her head and frowned at the bedroom wall.

—You heard me. I won't have you going for jalopy rides with a seasonal worker.

—It was an innocent thing, five of us. And I like him. He doesn't give me a lot of randy vibes. And devious . . . hints.

Lemon gave a shiver.

—See here. A man of Max Doan's caliber doesn't have to hint. He's a bit brusque rather, a military man. But he respects you, and isn't likely to act like a teenager.

—Ah, a teenager.

—Yes, if you want to know. I think it's time you began to think of playing your part as a woman. I won't support you forever.

—No problem. I have Grandmother's inheritance.

—In trust. And for college.

—Dad, you and I both know Mom wanted her mother's estate to help us start out after college. The will says so.

—Now—

Emory, caught in a lie, turned fiery red.

Lemon felt a twinge of pity, but she kept on:

—So you don't want me in college, is that right? Joey and Newell could go, but I have to marry Doan. This fine high school we've got here, an assembly line for factory workers, was good enough for me.

Emory tried to control himself. In trying moments his southern accent came back to him.

—At your age I took life seriously.

—You hadn't met Mom yet.

—Be that as it may . . .—He took the plunge:—Look, girl, I've decided . . . It is decided.

—But it's madness. Are you out of your senses? I can't marry that man.

—Can and will. You'll marry Max Doan this fall when you turn eighteen.

—But I don't love him! Lord, is this real or a dream? Is it my father I'm talking to?

—You will love him. You'll learn.

—But he's too old. He has a crew cut.

The great man's features seemed to ignite. He erupted at his daughter:

—How much longer do you suppose I'll put up with your selfish—obstinate—little—

His big frame shook and seemed to explode at her with frustration, like a cannon being fired.

—Daddy.

—It is asinine! I won't have it!

—Dad.

She started to cry.

He looked away, exasperated.

Lemon missed her mother so—still. She was ten the year Anne died. And her older sister, Evelyne, also died that year, tragically.

Now Lemon looked away from her father. Crying, she stared out the window. Both her brothers were far away, and there was no one to support her. She remembered the terrible night up North when her sister died. That was a nightmare, and so was this.

Emory went on:

—I'll go downstairs and tell him. And we'll begin making preparations. We'll fix a date soon before the fall color ends. And then, not this year but in time, Max has agreed that you'll enroll at Greensboro College.

She gazed at him, her cheeks bathed in tears.

—Is it you, Dad? What is happening to you?

—Here, in the living room, Bishop Commynes will perform the marriage ceremony with a few close friends in attendance.

—If Mom knew about this, she'd—

—She would approve. Many women marry early. Your mother would tell you to accept this good man's proposal. Romantic love doesn't amount to much, and the time will come when you bless me and this decision. Max has social status, wealth, an older man's wisdom, and fond devotion. You don't know it now, but he will make you happy. A bit better than a field hand.

Lemon hung her head. She fought back the sobs.

—Oh.

Now Emory was calmer. He had gotten it out. He patted his younger daughter's shoulder.

—Go on now. It's time for bed. You'll find out about Joey's game in the morning . . . I won't tuck you in like I used to—he gave a laugh.—You've grown up so lovely, I know Anne would share my pride.

—Oh.

—Let me go to Max and tell him the good tidings. There, there, that a girl. I know you feel this deeply, like any milestone. If you'd refused, it would have broken my heart.

Lemon was unable to speak. She hid her face from him.

IX

She went to her bedroom window and stared out at the crowd gathered on the Rock Castle front lawn. In a tense moment of the game their voices were hushed. Only the radio was heard with its excited voice riding waves of crowd noise while calling the plays. New York was down by three runs, and its hopes of going to this year's World Series were fading.

Also fading were Lemon Gilbert's hopes to get a real education, have a career, live a full, productive, happy life by the side of a man she loved. Now she was engaged to a gentleman in his sixties by the name of Maximilian Doan, nicknamed Thanks-a-Million, and Thanks-a-Mill, because he was so cheap.

After a moment she saw her father and Doan appear on the front walk. Those were two tall impressive men, and they seemed to be stepping on her destiny, like an ant. They paused midway along the walk: talking about her. Then they went further on, down the long, slow incline toward the street, and the crowd of townsfolk began to take notice of them. There was applause. Lemon knew her father loved that: he never missed an opportunity to be recognized, applauded, adulated, like a peacock.

She thought: What to do? Could she refuse them? Run away? Did she dare? Go out West?

The thing she wanted most of all was to talk to Joey.

He was unavailable.

Just then the phone rang. She went out in the second floor hallway and picked up the receiver from a lowboy by the landing.

From the West Coast, collect of course, came Newell's voice—but low as could be, like a bass cantor. The boy was always fooling around.

—Hulloooah?

—That you, Nuper?

—Hey, kid sis'! Wah! Things don't look too good for the home team right now. Jojo's up against it. What do you think?

—Me too.

—What me too?

—Oh, Newby, if you knew what Dad's up to: what he's doing this very minute!

—I wouldn't be surprised. But prey tell.

—I think he's gone mad, Noogy. He wants me to marry Thanks-a-Million, and they're out on the lawn settling the details now. Setting a date.

—Wah.

—Our daddio is unbalanced, Nukey. All the media attention has turned him into a celebrity monster.

—'Where hidst thou when I laid the earth's foundations? He contendeth with the Almighty, and shall he instruct Him?'

Hippie chuckle.

—Oh, Noodle, don't hack around. This is my life they're playing with and I can't believe it.

—Take it easy, kid. I will exert my immense powers of insight and perspicuity, always well-grounded in reality, solid, to solve this problem.

—Stop joking! Dad's offering me up at the altar of his ambition.

—Saturn devours his children.

—That's right, and you're next! Pastor Commynes' pet idea these days is that you should be committed to a psych ward. You're a danger to yourself and others. I've heard them talking about it, Noose. I tried to call you. I wrote you a letter: did you get it?

—Pastor is right! Ha ha ha. Watch out, young genius, gare à toi! But I ask you, since I love deep considerations, and have an astounding capacity for fundamental insight . . .

He started singing in the phone. His voice gave an operatic roulade.

—Nupert! Have you been smoking pot again?

—I ask you: am I the man to let this happen? Will I walk quietly away from life's great struggles, with my tail between my legs? Will I let my inexhaustible perspicacity and sharpwittedness grow moldy on a psych ward?

—Tst.

Then he laughed—not a toneless chuckle, a fake, but the clear Homeric laughter of his boyhood.

—Don't worry, Lemming, I'll take care of it. Your problem is my problem: they're related. This suffering world's sisters and brothers are one in struggle, dear comrades.

—Oh, sure, only make things worse. Plus watch out: any day now they'll have you picked up and taken to some place they mentioned in Marin County.

—Marin?

—Wherever that is. I heard them say so.

—Well now they've got it figured out. Even made reservations.

Hippie chuckle.

Lemon gave a sigh.

—What can I do, Null? I don't want to marry Thanks-a-Mill.

—Really? But you could honeymoon romantically at the Anti-Guerrilla Warfare and Counterinsurgency Center in Puyallup, Washington.

—Oh foo.

Lemon shook her head.

The hippie offered his wisdom:

—All the petty tyrants think they're beyond good and evil. They flaunt their hubris like a fist in the face of a god. They have their quarter hour, and then what happens? For now if anybody dares tell them a thing or two, they get all dramatic and shout: Are you calling me a liar?

—You'd be surprised if you saw our pa. He goes in Granddaddy's den with his best friend Commynes, and comes out looking so wild-eyed.

—Could it be he did something bad, and the Devil is taking him to task?

—Oh, Nuradeen. I feel such pity for him. I love Dad, but he's breaking my heart.

—Ei, ei. Hypocrite liberal. He has a secret, namely that he's a coward. But he calls that cowardice: harmony. He wants the harmony of political forces: Capital, Labor, Government. Above all he doesn't want conflict, extremes: not fascism, and please God not a real socialism, workers rule. He's a wise middle of the roader taught by experience, yessir, the golden mean, nothing too much: while the world's children die of hunger, and Planet Earth is poisoned. Hey, Capital can have all the harmony it wants, though Emory may say: oh you bad, bad Capital. But let Labor reach out to cut a fairer slice for itself, of harmony's cake, and then the liberals say: hm. And they nod their heads, in sad approval, as the U.S. Government obeys its Corporate master's orders and sicks the National Guard on the striking workers. Better lock up the communist leaders! In the nearest FEMA concentration camp!

They fell silent, hanging onto the long distance connection another minute.

Outside the crowd was quiet listening to the game. The nation seemed to poise after the seventh inning stretch, and settle in for the stress and strain of late innings when anything can happen.

Lemon said:

—Dad looks desperate.

—Look, I'll talk to him. Somehow my deep connoisseurship of the human heart has made out that you don't wish to marry Old Crew Cut.

—What will you say?

—I will summon all my stupendous oratorical powers to make a dent in that thick skull of his.

—How, Knute?

—I know a way to get it called off. My deep-thinking oracle of a brain always finds the right word.

—Dad wants this thing for political connections. And he shall have it.

—Pytho proves more persuasive than pull.

—Oh, I don't think you better . . . Please don't meddle.

—I'll stop them.

—No, you'll make a mess and maybe ruin yourself. You don't know the ins and outs.

—Don't I? My dialectical gaiety knows all, sees all. My spirit has clout!

Hippie chuckle.

—Forget it, Newb. I'll marry Thanks-a-Mill.

—Outstanding!

—I don't mind.

—Sure, kid, sure you don't. That's rich.

At his flip tone Lemon tensed and drew herself up where she stood by the phone. Her upper lip trembled as she said:

—Look, brother, I live here, you don't. So please try to understand something. I care for Dad despite his faults. If I marry an old fart I don't love . . . then it doesn't concern you, but only myself and Doan. I feel pity for you sometimes, yes, you, because you've always had a harsh side. You have all things but one: tolerance. But I will block you from my life if you don't make a better effort now. Understand? Oh you can criticize people and society well enough, but I find you too one-sided, and you don't know how to forgive. Now you barge into a situation so cocksure, like some sort of savior. But you'll make the mess even worse. You should've stayed away. So go on: save the world, but not me! Ride off into the sunset with your high ideals. Around here you blurt out words that hurt people and don't even know what you're saying.

—What you imply doesn't jibe with my impeccable self-appreciation, striving ever to better myself for the sake of others. It overlooks my revolutionary humility, my adept critique and auto-critique!

—. . .

By the phone Lemon shook her head and fought back tears.

—Hey, you okay, L'il Sis'?

—No, and I'm not L'il Sis'. This mess, Dad's mess and my mess, has taken some time to create. It won't get solved by your high-flown talk. I know you, Newell. You'll try to help, but you'll only make things worse.

She put a hand to her forehead, like she might faint.

He waited a long moment—then said, in another tone:

—It's our mess.

—I know what you're thinking. You can't wait to say: Dad, if you make my sister marry this ogre, then . . . You'll defend your sister from the bully in the playground. I can already hear the threats back and forth, the name-calling.

—More.

Lemon gave her own little laugh. She had grown to woman-hood since her brother went away. She was matured past her seventeen years the way a young apple tree might be in blossom, but with blight.

She said:

—Other strange things are going on. It started during the campaign. The phone would ring. Who? I'd say hello. Nobody. Or low laughter, evil. Someone doesn't wish us well . . . Then the Democrats lost so I thought it would stop. No, it kept on. Emory goes out there, still a world-beater, but his mood has plunged since November. Like his grief and drinking after Mom's death. He looks drawn, tired, not good. It's in his eyes: a bad thing. He can't meet your gaze and wears dark glasses.

—He saw a ghost.

—I expect he'll start to drink again now. Late at night he paces the floor. I don't know why, but he goes up in the attic room where you used to study. And I hear him up there pacing to and fro.

—Is it a bird? Is it a plane? No, it's Captain Ahab.

—I think someone wants to destroy him, Newell.

—Too big for his britches!

—He is suffering from nervous exhaustion yet he travels around and makes his speeches. He comes alive in front of an audience. But then it's back to the Rock Castle again, and on edge, short-tempered, hard to get along with.

—Home again, home again. Well, he always was a prima donna. But now he's using you. He's hurting you.

—He can't help it. And I . . . I pity him so!

X

High in the night sky the same helicopter blinked its red tail-light and sent out aerial images of the ballpark nationwide. From afar the field was a bright, bright green in a shower of light: the infield and golden base paths, the grassy sheen of the outfield, and bleachers crammed with a colorful crowd. At this distance the big physically superb players were invisible, and their destinies dependent on a hidebound ball tiny as a molecule: just as the Earth itself was no more than a submicroscopic mote tossed like a wild throw, an error, E-5, into a somber universe.

In the chopper's camera the vibrant crowd focused to a blur beneath banks of incandescent lamps above the stands. A diamond set in the depths of night, the Major League stadium glittered in darkness offset by a million lesser lights across the Metropolitan Area. There was the mammoth waltz of bridges through the boroughs. There were the dark watery fields of New York Harbor and Arthur Kill, the broad Hudson flowing past Manhattan as it did the Catskills; and Jamaica Bay and the ocean beginning where the tiers of land left off.

Joey Gilbert, a few steps behind third top of the eighth, shook his glove between pitches and glanced up at the blinking red signal. Engine drone, the rotor rhythm made a basso continuo under the spectator noise; it took his mind off the play. His upward gaze was fixed as he counted blinks and felt a sudden urge to run for cover. The New York third baseman would probably be the League MVP if his team took this one-game playoff for the Pennant, but he was shaky now.

His nervous system was blasted by a year of counterinsurgency warfare in Southeast Asia, and then a long season of pro sports. So he was at the end of his tether, and he faltered. Since the first pitch all eyes had been on him. And there were St. Louis fans in the stands just waiting to jump all over Joey because they tasted blood and sensed his vulnerability. He was his team's hope and despair. And so rival fans laughed as loud as they could at the obstacle to a World Series bonanza for their city. They jeered him non-stop. Jubilantly they booed when he juggled a routine grounder in the 7th to set up a St. Louis insurance run.

5 to 1 now: call it a day. Ballgame. Yet it still wasn't enough. More runs were needed to put the icing on the cake. And so the out-of-towners hooted and booed him and went after this man in trouble. They laughed at his zombie stare, at his weird posture and gestures tonight. Cheeta-six, over! Ha ha ha. Movement out front, over! The hecklers shouted and called names until the base paths became a Calvary for the Congressional Medal of Honor recipient and winner of a hundred battles, if not the war. Reported killed in action he had risen up to fight another day. Play ball! And the dead walked.

But that's enough miracles. Tonight he would not win: somehow this was the general sentiment, even among hometowners; it was as if the nation wished his defeat. From the first inning when he went down on strikes to the third when he went scampering up the wrong baseline after his nabbed liner fizzled a rally—this didn't seem to be his night. And he did not like it, accept it; so he staged more of his insane antics, and elbow-crawled up the line, in some jungle firefight of the mind. Umpire! Please eject that maniac!

And then he made a pitiful goof-up afield: in the 7th when he booted a two-hopper any Peewee Leaguer could handle. Yes, even some New York fans had turned against Joey Gilbert and were ragging him from early on in the game. Many, many from behind home plate to the centerfield bleachers were laughing him out of town. And he was a man engaged in mortal combat with his soul, no less than with the opposing team. And in a moment he would break down mentally, and it would be for good.

Now into the 8th St. Louie hopes soared on flapping wings. They had a 4-run lead with their ace righthander on the mound. The crowd was quiet and just seemed to let it happen. Two more innings of three-up-three-down and then pop went the bubbly in the visitors' clubhouse.

One away in the top half. A second New York reliever was busy digging a hole for himself. First came a walk. Then a bouncer up the middle was backhanded by the second baseman. No play. Then—balk! The runners moved to second and third. An intentional pass loaded 'em up. Go for the twin kill.

One down, bases jammed: the infield was at double-play depth. And now the overflow crowd set up an earsplitting clamor of chants and taunts and stomping and hisses and shrill whistles. Here and there firecrackers pop-popped in the outfield bleachers, and pretty soon it would be time for the Fire Department to arrive.

The third baseman shook his head trying to focus, like a fighter on the ropes. Hey, they shoulda' stopped this fight in the third when he flipped his lid. C'mon, Skip, willya' bench this clown? And leave the water cooler alone: it's all Joey's fault, not the water cooler's. Yank 'im! He's goatsville! Naw, simmer down; you gotta' dance with the one what brung yu's.

The St. Louis 6th hitter stepped in. Play at any base. The New York hurler chose to come set for the 0-0 delivery.

Shortstop turned and held up a finger for the outfielders.

—One gone! Uno!

XI

Just then—as the St. Louis hitter twisted a foul pop back of first into the stands—Lemon Gilbert heard her father's heavy steps on the wide front stairway of the Rock Castle.

—I've got to go, Nuke. I've got to hang up.

—Wait, I'm not done yet.

—Here he comes. It's Dad—

Emory came up the landing. He looked distraught. He said to his daughter:

—Who's that you're talking to? Your Juanchi I suppose, the greaser.—He took the phone receiver from her.—Hello, who's this? Look here, I don't want—

—It's me, Dad.

—What?

—It's Newell. I'm glad I've got you on the phone. There's something I want to tell you.

—Don't bother.

—No, this is something you need to hear, and you're going to.

—I'm a busy man.

—Are you now. So driven by your principles you don't have a moment to spare? Well, watch out, you'll become a dull boy. But please tell me, Dad. As a man of principle, which you're always informing us you are: how can you sell your daughter down the river? Why do that? Does Max Doan know your secret? Or that devil Commynes knows and he wants to ruin you? Marriage by blackmail! Hand over the goods, friend, namely your daughter, or I'll cause a great scandal! Nice. Lemon lives happily ever after stowed away like a concubine up there on the Heights, and Emory the public figure pursues his career and Third Party aspirations. Is that it? A matter of careerism? Play ball, or your good friends veto your chances.

—America's chances.

—Yes, certainly, my fellow Americans. Hail to the Chief: it's another one like the other ones, who didn't chop down the cherry tree. All the corporate men, every last one Lincoln on down if you look a little more closely: they sold out the people. Liberal or conservative, but a coward.

—Not a coward, Newell. Courageous, but also wise. We're in a tight spot here, but there's no reason to commit suicide.

Newell chuckled.

—Fiddlesticks, Tricky Dick. Electoral politics makes cowards of us all.

—Is that what you had to tell me?

—No, Sir. It is this. I . . . I heard you on the stairs that night; it was the 19th of September, last year. I thought maybe there was a prowler in the house, so I came downstairs from the attic. I heard you, Father. I know what you did. I know the reality. So don't make yourself ridiculous by trying to deny. And now I do, yes, have an important thing to tell you. I think you'll find it significant. You see, I just can't see my little sister married to one of these GENRO types. When interviewed today Mrs. Lemon Doan told the press she supports her husband the elder statesman in his win-the-war and peace with honor position. Well then, Mrs. Doan, do you also approve current policy to limit scorched earth bombardment in Vietnam to the 20th parallel? Why of course Mrs. Thanks-a-Million supports her hawk hubby right or wrong.

—Look, I'm busy, boy, and this isn't funny. You go too far.

—I go too far! But not you of course. First you do that to . . . And now you want to screw Lemon too. Two strikes by my count. Steeerike two! cries the umpire, Fate.

—Lemon knows what she wants. And I've got to go.

—She—Newell gave a gasp, like a jolt.—Talk about opportunism.

By the phone Emory was red as a beet. He looked ready to combust.

—Talk about the easy cynicism of youth! To change this world for the better takes more than Marxian poetry, boy, more than half-digested rhetoric, and irresponsibility. More than what a hippie can come up with!

—Ei, ei. But if I say: look at our society, its media of ignorance, its cities flooded with drugs by the CIA, its massacres of the Black Panther Party, its illiteracy, its hospital closures, its labor unions a dead letter, its youth without hope, its conformism and all the good little boys and girls: then you'll sing your old nursery rhyme of democracy, and freedom to reform.

Emory shrugged:

—And the Left rants and raves.

—Right on.

—How soon these children forget the advantages heaped on them by a society they like to despise.

—Keep your privileges.

Emory laughed:

—Too late! I don't see you donating your share of your grandmother's inheritance to buy guns for the workers, like Marx did in '48. I don't see Newell Gilbert going class-consciously to work in a factory.

—Not my task.

—Newell, you make me laugh. Every year: first kid in Redemaine to collect the set of baseball cards. You stole from your parents to buy them. No other ten year-old in America bought them by the box in 1953.

—And redistributed them! Gave them to girls. Anyway that was childhood.

—We gave you everything you wanted: the first A-2000 mitt in the stores. We sent you to two of the finest private schools, and you were expelled.

—Matter of principle.

—And on to New Haven. And never a real day's work to help us. You know, I don't think you ever will grow up. You'll always pose as a revolutionary, as this, as that. Do something new till you get bored. Watch! The Marxist turns into his opposite. Why, at your age I had a higher degree, a profession, I was married. But you only put on airs. Well you'll make some proletarian, I can tell

you that. Namby-pambies of the world, unite! You have nothing
to lose but your stained undies.

Newell gave a laugh and said:

—Very funny. But I'll tell you something which isn't so funny.
Lemon says you've been getting anonymous phone calls. That
you seem to run scared for some reason. Is it threats? Harassment? Does someone outside the family know your little secret?

I didn't tell them. I never told anyone. I may be stupid, gullible,
idealistic, what have you, but I am not base. To your pink, rich
man's face I say we have our differences. I may not like you, as
my dad and as a person, but I haven't hated you. I hate the capitalist system, not its victims, poor imbeciles like you, or Tricky
Dick Nixon, same difference. No, I never told a soul. But listen
carefully, Father, because I mean this. If you don't drop your grotesque marriage plans for Lemon, I will send out press releases to
the four corners of the earth. And then, yes, you will be ruined.
I will tell the wide world your secret. Do you hear me? Does the
classical writer's brain of interest to science have room for this
little fact? It is finished, do you hear? You cannot do that horror to
my sister! You do it and you do it and maybe you don't know it,
but this time watch out, watch out!

—You draft dodger, you shirker, coward: who would believe
you? Anyway I don't know what you're talking about.

—You called me those names that night at your dinner party
two years ago. And they hurt. Well, I went into the lists, and I've
fought against your imperialist war. And what did you do, bigtime politician? You thought about how not to take a stand but
only make the other candidate look bad. Typical hack: I'm glad
you lost. Ha ha! Coward you! Unprincipled! At least Nixon will
polarize things. But you cared more about your 'commitment
men', your delegate hunts and brokers and machine politics as
usual, than the death of millions, U.S.-style, in Southeast Asia.
Ha! You call me a coward? Dukes up, sucker! Cowards support
U.S. foreign policy. Cowards destroy small countries: invoking
communism or terrorism to justify their genocidal war crimes.
Those are the cowards! Cowards in their shameful guilty hearts!
And they blame their victims, one way or another, calling them
racially inferior: oh, not openly like Hitler, the old American prag-
matism prevents such a mistake. I mean what the hell do we care
if a few more millions perish so long as we dominate markets

and get mineral and agricultural resources dirt cheap. You, the author, have a stake in this process, so you deny it! Just uphold the system come what may and a dozen honorary degrees from the finest universities will attest to your integrity. Lie well enough and they'll give you the Nobel Prize for Liars. You accused me of cowardice in front of others and I remember it but later that same night you did your filthiness some more and showed what a noble soul you are really. I happened to come downstairs and I heard what you were up to and it didn't sound like a prayer meeting.

—Liar.

—I wish I was lying.

—Say one more thing and I'll disown you.

—One more thing. So there. You've disowned me a hundred times. And don't threaten me, Dad, I don't like it.

—I do resent this, boy! Your mother and I worked ourselves to the bone so you could have every good thing in life. And what is our thanks?

—You must give up the scheme with Lemon. Or else.

—Shut up I said!

—It seems you fessed up. Confessed to someone. The wrong person! Was it a political associate? Astute move. You let the cat out of the bag, and then the nasty phone calls started. The coils of fate are closing in on you, like Oedipus. Now you're being told by your confidant, Commynes, or maybe Doan himself: Marry your tender daughter to a lecher. Or else! . . . Is that it? Is it?

—I can't listen to this. Goodbye.

—What a family. Leave the poor girl alone, I'm warning you! Tell the truth and I'll try to help you. We'll stand together. Let it go, Dad, give it up, it's a lie! Do your greatest deed. Turn, as they say, turn! Oh! How I wish I had a good humble father who told the truth and had principles! Went to jail for them, died for them, if necessary. How I would love him! But now . . . now all I can tell you is stop being so grandiose for once, and rejoin the human race.

—Goodbye to you.

—You sell your soul, and for what? You torture, you invade, you do any atrocity, leveling cities. And for what? The private property of the rich.

—Once again, goodbye. Now I disown you. I will call my attorney tomorrow and have him change my will. Don't call here again. Don't come here, or let me see you. If you do, I'll make a phone call and have you put away.

XII

The small red light of the media helicopter blinked high in the night sky. The dark water of the East River and Flushing Bay glimmered with city lights. There was a glum mood in the stadium; though the St. Louis hitter had flied to center and ended a rally that would have put the game away.

Now with three more outs, and behind three runs, New York needed a miracle. An unearned run in the eight had made the score 5-2.

The vendors went up and down the aisles:

—Get'tcha' cold beeuh!

—Hoddogs! Hot dough'ugs!

Radio and TV stations came back from their commercials.

The St. Louis mainstay looked in for the sign. He went into his windup.

The first batter, eighth man in the order, sent a dying quail into shallow right center. Oh! Grabbed by the second baseman sliding on his knees. One out.

Next a lefty pinch hitter sent a sharp grounder skidding in the hole past the diving first baseman's glove. One on, one out.

The leadoff hitter drew the count to 2-2 and then lofted a fly to left centerfield. And now New York was down to its last three strikes.

The big crowd rose to its feet. St. Louis was an out away from the National League Championship. The tall, dominant pitcher was in his rhythm and looked home free as he worked to put the wraps on this money game.

The second hitter in the lineup stood in. Switch-hitter up left. He held the bat over his head and then tapped the plate with it. He sketched his swing and went into his stance awaiting the pitch. But many an eye turned to the New York dugout where a big figure in a dusty uniform took his time at the bat rack, then crossed the top step, and strode slowly to the on-deck circle. The look of that man, dark, brooding, caused a ripple to pass through the stadium, a twinge of anticipation. But would he get his ups?

Strike one on the hitter. Groan. Oh, please God, let him reach base so that demon, Gilbert, can take his cuts. Ball low: 1-1. Joey stood motionless in the on-deck circle with a bat on his shoulder. He didn't go on one knee; he couldn't do anything normally. And did he stare daggers out at the League's premiere hurler who wanted him out on three pitches? No, he perused the stands.

For a moment the tall St. Louis righty looked past the batter's box at his rival for this year's MVP Award.

Then he peered in at his catcher. Shook off a sign, another. Now the set position, the pitch—ball two, a hair wide.

The catcher trotted out to the mound.

The ump leaned down and put his brush to home plate.

The pitcher toed the rubber, joined hands, offered. Called strike!

Now as one the stadium started shouting like this was a sex act and the next pitch was the climax. Both dugouts stood up. Through nine strong innings the St. Louis flamethrower had shown his great stuff. There were hard breaking pitches with pinpoint control. His fastball was smoke. The deafening roar did not faze the star performer as he gazed in for the 2-2, and then came set.

Eyes the runner. And the pitch.

It's a slow roller to the right side. Second baseman charges, scoops it barehanded and the toss—

Safe! Ooh! Ooh! Safe by a whisker!

The St. Louis manager charged out on the field and started leaping like a dervish around the first base umpire. He was beside himself at that call, cavorting, shouting, throwing down his cap and stomping on it. He might've had a wasp in his jock.

Suddenly the stands were mute. Now there was hope. Now there was a thrill. The equalizer strode up, cool, unhurried, staring darkly, like he had something else on his mind. Uh-oh. Beware that hope. What if he freaked out again and started acting like he was in Vietnam?

He took his place in the batter's box.

Two away. Runners at first and second. Walk the dangerous hitter? Go against the book? Unheard-of. The St. Louis manager must be thinking about it, but he couldn't do it. If he went out on that limb, he would take his job with him. No way he was going to load the bases and bring the winning run to the plate. Besides, Gilbert had nothing to show for his night, while the lefthanded cleanup hitter, 31 HRs and 103 RBIs on the year, had doubled and driven in a run with a sacrifice fly.

XIII

Joey Gilbert stood like a statue—less of a ballplayer than a soldier. But he grinned, as if he had a toothache.

The tie run was at the plate.

One of baseball's best pitchers, seventh lowest career ERA, fifth now in Ks, perennial 20-game winner, two-time Cy Young Award winner, was on the mound.

Crazy Gilbert was at the plate.

Two mean customers.

The crowd still stood, but it was quiet. The St. Louis hurler stretched a little. From the first pitch he had shown wicked stuff and whiffed eleven. Now he would proceed with caution: no point taking it to the clutch hitter with so much riding. He'd pitch away to Gilbert fanned twice tonight on sliders. Except for the hard-hit double play ball he'd had him in his pocket.

The big pitcher came set.

The batter stared out, mace calmly on his shoulder, New York's last chance. He never pumped. He had no stance. Also unlike others he didn't need to guess—such reflexes he had, honed in combat perhaps. Joey knew how to wait. So now he stared out past the pitcher at the night sky and glanced up at the chopper's red light.

—Stee-e-euh!

Groans. Oh, he's ahead of him. The fireballer was in fact going after this madman who just gazed out at the mound in a dream, it seemed, and didn't move the bat. So the idea wasn't to pitch around him.

—Bao-oh-wuh!

Slider below the knees. 1-1. Ump swayed and grunted like he had an ache. Then he straightened to shake out a kink, and hunched again.

The pitcher came set. Runners went into their leads.

—Stee-er-ahh!

The express train—pssst, over the century mark. And still Joey stood there and didn't bat an eyelash, much less the bat. Was he functional? Maybe he had a cardiac arrest, but he was so stubborn he wouldn't rub it. Stood there frozen as one of those blue popsickles he liked to suck in the dugout.

One more and it's over. One. And now the massive crowd on its feet was moaning in a chorus like this was the end of the world. One more strike stood between the City of New York with its hopes of World Series excitement and revenues—and disaster. So they were groaning, and swaying side to side. They bleated like a huge herd of sheep on the way to slaughter. Please, Jesus, oh please no strike three, oh, oh, thank you Jesus!

In a moment the town would shut down as a thick gloom settled over the neighborhoods.

The whole country, coast to coast, hung on the next pitch, and pitied the poor dizzy hitter who stared in space like a sacrifice led to the altar.

—Baw-roa-roar!

2-2! There was a pause. Nobody breathed. The fielders stayed half-crouched at their positions; they coiled. Fans howled. Police and park security braced for a riot if the game ended on a bad call or a close play.

The St. Louis outfielders squinted from the brims of their caps. They were played deep, a shade right. No gap in right-center since Joey went with the outside stuff, and rode it to the opposite field.

The 2-2:

—Ball thuh-reee!

Oh! High hard one hopped above the letters.

Count full with two out. Runners'll fly; they'll be off to the races on the 3-2. Crowd, city, nation waited for the payoff pitch.

Delirium.

XIV

The New York announcer called the play:

—*The string's run out now. 154 regular season games boil down to a pitch. The season hinges on this pitch. New York is three runs shy with two gone in the ninth and the 3-2 to Joey Gilbert just a wind-up away. Mighty Jo must make his move; he must put up or shut up; no bluffing the good stuff . . . And the St. Louie strikeout king, the Mississippi Steamer? Does he play things cute or is it sizzler city? Watch out if this pitch is too juicy, if he comes right down the pipe. For this is a game of inches.*

"*The runners move off the bases. Arms swinging they take their leads. They'll go with the 3-2. Pitcher steps off and rubs up. He flicks sweat from his brow. He spits. Blows on his fingertips. Now he steps up, and peers in; about ten feet tall. He has the sign, and here we go . . .*

"*Toes the rubber, comes set. Checks the lead runner edging off second. Nods at first, eyes second again; like a poker player, cards close to his breast. It's a wonder Gilbert doesn't step out. But he has not moved or given a sign of life in what must be five minutes.*

"*Now we're ready. It's the 3-2 delivery . . . The batter swings and lofts a high drive, fairly deep; it looks playable in straightaway center. This game should be on ice, it's all ov'—but wait it is sky-high; look how it carries! No can of corn, but a rainmaker, this one, high, high and deep . . . And the St. Louis center fielder drifting back, further back, on the warning track, he has time . . . Oh! Way back! Against the fence in dead center he times his leap and———oh! Oh-h-h!*

"*The towering flyball came straight down skimming off the wall an inch above his glove, ah! ha! Ball caroms off the wall or was it his shoulder and spins away; it shoots out toward right center twenty, thirty feet and rolls further and keeps rolling! Right fielder chases down the ball as the other shakes his head stunned there by the outfield wall. The ball must have hit his head! One run is home. The runner from first is rounding third and he'll score.*

"*Here's the right fielder's throw in to the cutoff man. It's a triple for Joey Gilbert the League leader in———no! Oh! oh! Here he comes on his way with the tying run! Look at him fly as he rounds third through the base coach's signal. Look at him go! He's a bazooka! And here comes the second baseman's peg from shallow right and it's a bullet on target. And the ball, and the runner———*

"*Holy crow! The tie run comes exploding into home and the catcher slaps on the tag and he's———it's———he's———and he's . . . What is it? Is he out? Is he safe? The ball! The ball squirted up from the catcher's mitt. And he's in there! Safe! The call is safe!*

"*Oh, he looks hurt, friend. Their catcher dipsy-do'd, thar' she blew'd, cut in two'd—he's crumpled up by home plate. Oooh. Coldcocked. Bring out a stretcher. Got your health insurance card handy?*

"Oh the hit he had put on him . . . But maybe we'll be needing two stretchers. It seems the New York pilot has had a cataleptic fit on the dugout steps.

"It is twelve midnight on the dot in the city that never sleeps. And all is not well. Ha ha ha.

"Joey Gilbert has blasted an inside-the-park homerun. And the score now stands deadlocked at 5 to 5. We have a brand spanking new ballgame!

"Oh, pardner! Will you please pass me the ammonium carbonates?"—

XV

At home in Scarsdale, in her bedroom, Lydia Falliere worked while listening to the Playoff Game. Tomorrow's agenda was full, but she wouldn't go to sleep before she knew the outcome.

Now the game—and her patient's ordeal—went into extra innings.

At all hours, in therapy sessions, on rounds at the hospital, and while writing and studying, she thought of him. These were vital thoughts with a yearning for life, and this was love. But she was also trying to figure out his wife's strange behavior—the secret, and the fear, lurking in his own questions about Carlyne.

For instance: what was the 'ulterior motive' he sensed when she went to be with him for his R & R in Bangkok? And why upon return did she leave? Why did she run away from the house of her in-laws in the small southern town—in January as Lemon said, and the landlady in Durham concurred; not in February as Emory told Joey? And she left no word, and no one knew her address until Joey went there and found out. Why was Carlyne Gilbert so secretive? She went away in January because . . . she was pregnant? And it was beginning to show?

She was seduced by her brother-in-law, the hippie? Or by the semi-retired Army General named Max Doan, who was a lecher?

What happened last fall at the Rock Castle after Joey went away?

Lydia turned off the desk lamp and went to stand by the window. She looked out at the residential streets quiet and empty de-

spite delirious excitement in the great nearby City. After midnight
the air was sweet and dewy in the shrubs and gardens. There was
a fresh scent of kids going back to school; and of summer's end;
and the autumn leaves soon to paint the suburban community a
gamut of reddish ochres.

A night bug gave its cumbrous buzz. A moth plunked on the
screen. Then a strange sound: some burrower lowing amid the
damp soil? Also a katydid lingered in a tree across the way: it
fiddled with halts now, singing the decline of another year.

For a long moment Lydia paused in thought as an electric
storm rolled and echoed in the sky westward. The night grew
quieter between the peals of thunder.

How about that. Through the aeons the mysterious earth had
produced contradictory Man. And now the psychiatrist was
stumped by the Sphinx-enigma of Carlyne Gilbert? Who was she
and why did she act that way?

Lydia turned from the night of fragrant trees back to her work-
table where she switched on the light. In a folder was her article
called 'Oedipus on My Couch'; and beside it the thin volume of an
Oxford Classical Text. She flipped to a passage annotated in blue
pen during her student days in Paris, while writing a Doctorat
d'Université on Freud and philology, and since then revisited
many times. The pages were dog-eared and yellow at the edges.

Lydia read: *'The Sphinx of spangled chants'* (crafty, riddling; enig-
matic songs—ποικιλῳδὸς) *compelled us to look before our feet'* (follow our noses) *'and leave alone'* (neglecting: μεθέντας) *'the unseen'*
(unknown, inscrutable, hidden, secret).

She interpreted. She jotted notes:

—Social forces, struggles, deform our everyday awareness.
This leads to a false consciousness which has its counterparts in
the dialectics of the unhealthy psyche. It is stumped by a riddle
because it dares not look to the base where an answer awaits. The
rationalization factor in psychoanalysis is thus like a key mode of
bourgeois ideology which it reflects; namely, we, the privileged,
live off others, and try to hide it. False relation to the base.

"Primary defense reaction = bourgeois law?

"Obsessional neurosis = fetishism?

"Capitalist media (voluntary censorship) = repression, sup-
pression, 'screen memories'.

"Conversion, or somatic innervation = racism.

"Projection = blame we cast on otherness, the alien, our victim who, at the base, does our work for us (basic needs); we project our guilt on the other.

"Hysteria, 'disease of the past' = hunt, war material, reemerging. All violence?

"Breuer's 'hypnoid condition' (states of exhaustion or exultation when symptoms originate) = . . . patriotism!"—

Lydia laughed.

—Competition starts with birth, if not conception. We compete for material and emotional security.

"The Sphinx-like contest of success has our false consciousness (culture) spangled all over it, brightly obscure, carefully hiding the inner workings, the pathology.

"Things are not what they seem. The appearance (fetish) denies the reality. Surface phenomena, the things we see, diverge antithetically from the dynamic depths.

"Fetish is fixed, forever. Life is movement, dialectical, passes. Fetish-America, you say one thing, you are another."—

Emory and Joey were achievers. Both were eminently successful men in society's eyes. But they had depths. There was a Gilbert mystery. What was it?

Carlyne went away from them without a word. Like an act of anger: she didn't say goodbye. Why?

Anne Gilbert, Joey's mother, died in her fifties of cancer. An older daughter died tragically one night while a senior in high school.

The younger son, Newell, saw through the glittery enchantment of the Sphinx. He lit out on his own. He wasn't having any: not playing that game.

Why? What did he know?

A secret lurked beneath the surface.

XVI

Crowd noise from the radio on Lydia's night table seemed to ebb and flow like an ocean at night, as the game went into the eleventh inning. A chill came in the bedroom window; so she pulled her bathrobe about her and lay in bed unable to sleep.

Light on again: Lydia leafed through the thin volume in Greek, and her eye fell on verse 924. Long ago she made a note in tiny script in the margin: 'pivotal scene'. She read.

A messenger came from Corinth looking for King Oedipus. Here is his palace, stranger, and this woman is the mother of his children. 'Then may she be blessed forever, being a perfect wife.' Note the great primitive dialectics of Sophocles: on the surface Jocasta bore his four children and is happy; in the depths, due to their history unknown as yet: she is his mother, and happiness will soon be disaster. In the recognition (anagnorisis) quantity turns into quality; in the reversal (peripeteia) things turn into their opposites for Oedipus and family. A few verses more and the happy wife will be a suicide. Her husband finally seeing the truth will put out his eyes with her brooch.

The messenger tells Jocasta the people of Corinth want Oedipus for their king since King Polybus has died. 'Go tell Oedipus,' she says. 'O oracles of the gods: where does this leave you?' For the oracle said Oedipus would kill his father, and he thinks Polybus was his father. Now Oedipus, who must suspect the truth, comes out and says in a clatter of monosyllables: 'Who is the man and what does he have to say?'

And now comes the elation before catastrophe, like a terminal patient's upswing in the hours or days before death. 'So my father has gone to Hades with those worthless oracles. But needn't I still fear for my mother's bed?' For the oracle had said he would sleep with his mother.

Then Jocasta: 'What has a man to fear since fate or luck (τύχης) leads him on and can't be foreseen? Live and let live without fear. *Many men have dreamed they slept with their mother.*'

In dreaming they do it, but they do not know it. Six are present, said Freud, when two make love: the lovers and their parents. So we see the son is there in bed with his mother, and the daughter with her father, in terms of their unconscious drives.

The dialectics of the Greeks embodies a drive in a masked character and lets it act. The myth breaks down reality into its components. And so they do it.

But since then we have lived 2500 years of history, and our dialectics are historical. We do it too. We seem to know not as myth but as historic reality the interpenetration of those opposites, son with mother, daughter with father . . . father with daughter . . .

Lydia closed her eyes a moment. We seem to know . . .

By now it was after one a.m. Joey Gilbert had led off the twelfth inning and grounded out to short.

She read on.

The messenger from Corinth was a meddling sort. He had good news for them, and of course he wanted his reward. Now he said: 'Who is this woman you're afraid of?'—'It is Merope, wife of Polybus. Once Apollo told me I would have sex with my mother. So I fled Corinth and came here to live in exile.'—'Then,' says the messenger, 'have no fear because Polybus was not related to you.'

Shudder. Oedipus' sense of deliverance is turning to anguish as the messenger tells how he as a shepherd got an infant from another herdsman in the wooded clefts of Mt. Cithaeron and took him to King Polybus to raise. The baby's feet were pierced and pinned together which is how he got his name: Oedipus— swollen foot, with a pun on 'knowing'.

Shudder. That herdsman came from Laïus: King Laïus who was later killed at a crossroads about the time Oedipus, a young man then, having been to Delphi and heard the terrible oracle, was going away from Corinth and shunning Polybus and Merope forever and making his way to Thebes.

And he came to the same crossroads in Phokis where roads from Delphi and Daulis meet. And he killed a man and his driver there. And then he went on to Thebes where he solved the Sphinx's riddle and married the queen of the late Laïus.

'Is this herdsman still alive? Can I see him?'

'Don't bother with it,' says Jocasta; for now she knows. 'It is foolishness.'

But Oedipus insists, and he says:

'With such signs as these I will know the secret of my birth, come what may.'

And so it was that a man killed his father and made love to his mother. And, wonder to tell: it seems he was all men. Only they don't know it. But he found out.

He was all men because man's subconscious is the micro substratum of our macro history as a species. And that macro history reacts no less on our unconscious needs and strivings: according to the law of interdependence of movement.

Nothing is separate for the fathers and mothers and daughters and sons. And every generation does just as Oedipus: it wants the land; it wants to control the production of basic necessities and wealth.

But so far we still haven't learned to work together, negotiate, plan; only the roughest sketches. So far we are still raping the land and the means of production and the life force and psyches of others and our own personhood in so doing—no less than Laïus did it to Chrysippus.

And so the curse was laid on the line of Labdacides by the boy's father Pelops who had his own fill of violence and so he didn't mind fomenting more.

Oedipus heard a gong in the messenger's words. Then in terror he waited. He turned to the coming of the herdsman who had gotten him as a baby from Laïus. He was the seeker. He must know.

Today we are waiting. Have we, humanity, heard a gong?

XVII

At P. Laster's old third floor office inside the First National City bank building, Emory Gilbert sat with his childhood friend Paul Commynes. It was past 2 a.m. The Playoff Game was in the fourteenth inning.

Commynes said:

—Tomorrow I will phone the contact, and he'll get the Berkeley police into action. I made a number of calls. I did the research and know about the commitment process now.

Emory shook his head:

—Paul, I'm not sure.

—Don't worry. They are ready and waiting for you to give the word. I call, and they go to the house on Hillgard and take the hippie into custody.

—Ah. And then?

—I'll tell you. I found out all about it for you. Off he goes to a special examiner: M.D. at a local health facility under contract to handle such cases.

—My son a case.

—It's routine. They run a cursory check to see if he's a 'danger to self and others'. Any symptoms of mental illness, which there will be, Newell's next stop is a State Hospital.

—Marin County.

—Marin.

—And then?

In the dark office lit only by the pink glow from a neon sign across the wide lot—POLICE—Emory looked away.

—The next day a doctor examines him on the same two issues: dangerousness and emotional disturbance. He says yes. And then your son gets treatment prior to a hearing within the week.

Emory sat forward.

—Hearing? This must be kept from the press.

—No problem. They understand you're a concerned parent.

—Concerned. I had my son put away.

—A due process right applies here. Since the State of California is taking away Newell Gilbert's liberty, he has the right to a commitment hearing. A lawyer is present.

—He'll hire a lawyer?

—Well, the State provides free legal defense in such cases. It's from an Office of Special Counsel, in the Courts Administrative Office. Most people in his position can't afford an attorney.

—He has money from my mother-in-law's will, and a little from Anne too, if he hasn't spent it all.

—But listen. It's a ruse, or fake 'due process' as a rule, since public defenders are overloaded with cases and can't dig very deep. Of course Newell could contact an activist lawyer, some Peacenik zealot, but it won't help.

Emory frowned:

—Why not?

—Wait. They take the patient before a District Level judge, a lower judge in the State system. The burden of proof in such cases is on the State. It must establish by clear and convincing evidence the two points of danger to self and others, and lunacy.

—So it's a lawyer comrade: someone in his camp. He'll get off scot-free, and then what?

Bishop Commynes laughed low. His face looked bathed in a pink halo as he played God. It was he who incited Emory Gilbert to marry his daughter to Doan. And it was he who played on his best friend's fear, and tortured him week after week, until he had him on the verge of confining his son in a State asylum for life. He was the great man's closest friend; and he hated him with a hate that was cold, mechanical: a daily aggravation and torture in small ways, anonymous calls, playing on his nerves, spying on him, snooping around the Rock Castle. What a Satanic mission. What an abominable envy. And the son of P. Laster would always be sincerely grateful. He would never know who destroyed him. And that was fitting. After all who was it, if not himself?

—Not so fast.—The Bishop laughed easily.—So the State examines the patient and also witnesses on behalf of the petitioner which is you. Then the lawyer for the respondent, Newell, uses his right to cross-examine the State's witnesses: namely the same doctor who did the State Hospital exam. Then the boy has a chance to present his own version.

—Uh-oh. He'll buffalo them.

—Ha ha. Not this time. For a good hour the Trotskyist harangue will resound through the courtroom. 1905, and the Saint Petersburg Soviet replayed ... He's a danger to self and others! Even if our influence hadn't rigged it from the beginning ... such an outburst could bring a charge of high treason, a real prison. We'll save him from himself.

Emory glanced down. He couldn't sustain the churchman's gaze.

—And after Newell's speech?

—Well, then the verdict. It's up to the Judge. Out? Or in?

—Tell me again. How will he decide?

—As I said you need clear and convincing evidence. 'Preponderance' means 51% on one side: say a standard tort case, like a fender-bender. Then comes clear and convincing, as you know, a higher burden of evidence; but your guess is as good as mine what that means. And the highest degree, proof beyond a reasonable doubt, is what holds in a criminal case. But for Newell it's the murky middle region.

—So a judgment call. Not: has he already done something?

—With a liberty interest at stake it takes more than preponderance but less than reasonable doubt.

—Poor boy.

—Poor you, poor us!

Commynes laughed softly.

Emory raised hand to brow:

—So my son wastes his life in an insane asylum. And I did this. I put the knife to his neck after he threatened me and said he would slander me to the press. I cannot accept this or let it happen: not for my sake personally, but for the great cause I uphold, which is world peace. But now I say: Please, Lord, I cannot carry through this sacrifice. Let the sword fall on my neck. Let me perish instead.

Bishop Commynes leered in the pink light:

—No, Sir. When the time comes, you'll handle the low-level magistrate official charged with our petition; though it doesn't take much weight thrown around on his level. And anyone can lie and sign an affadavit to the effect that John Doe made suicidal statements; or else said Doe just shot out his TV set and barricaded his front lawn; he's hollering and waving his gun at the neighbors. Our peon will take the safe course and sign the order against Newell not only because Emory Gilbert wowed him with a phone call, but also he's got nothing to lose. Also if he doesn't sign then he may look bad: if he fails to hospitalize, and the said Newell goes out and takes over Jack London Square and fires off the first shots of World Revolution with his cap gun or maybe a real gun. Anyway, Newell has a safeguard: the hair-trigger magistrate signs the order, but two physicians have to see your son within twenty-four hours. There will be two exams of Newell-Trotsky and his delusional system. Then even a third within ten days: a State institution doctor does the first interview which is anywhere near meaningful. Though in this case it won't take a med school to see a poor soul gone bonkers.

—No.

—Oh, we'll need you to call a Democratic Party contact out there: once we know the District Court judge assigned to Newell's case. Find some friend, corporate lawyer or whomever, who plays golf with that judge and will make sure he sees the case in our light. It'll be good if you put the Party machinery in motion around this. You're so good at that, Emory; you could snow-job the Devil himself.

—Or herself.

—Ha ha. I admire you.

—But is this legal? Tampering . . .

—All quite illegal! But it works. And in a case like this, with national security at stake, the end justifies the means. Our friend the golfer must have ex parte discussions re Newell with that District Court judge.

—It is illegal.

—But all for the cause of world peace, as you said, and also your son's best interests. He needs help. Yes, yes, a judge, a referee, isn't supposed to discuss a case without both sides present. But the famous Emory Gilbert has a long arm, and a persuasive tongue. That's as it should be. You must let them know your son has been troubled since he was a kid. Got kicked out of prep schools, and then acted up at Yale; and now his bi-polar disorder has him thinking he's America's answer to the founder of the Red Army. Well, we'll contact a colleague who owes you a favor, and he'll build up prejudice and inflame Newell's judge to put him away for life. The judge must know the things you said: how this boy has a delusional paranoia with regard to his family and has threatened a slander campaign to ruin his father.

—It's sad—said Emory, lips pale.

—But you must also talk to the Assistant Attorney General and give him the facts. It will all be quite informal, and him a young guy, head turned by your call.

—He'll believe me?

—He won't know if we told him the truth. And it doesn't matter. What matters is the star-struck prosecutor, wowed by Emory Gilbert, is whetted up in our favor.

—In or out? said Emory.

—In.

XVIII

Suddenly the portable radio on P. Laster's desk erupted. Crowd noise had been sluggish into the fifteenth inning, as relief pitchers set down hitters. And it was the middle of the night. But now, in the bottom of the 15th, the New York third baseman had hooked a homerun around the left field foul pole. And so it was over: 6-5, the final score. The St. Louis players could go home, but the New York club would take a ride to Baltimore for the Series opener on Friday.

And then it was strange. The radio grew quiet. A stillness came over the stadium in New York as Joey Gilbert, after touching home, went into a victory lap by himself around the outfield.

Emory and Paul listened to the big hush over the radio.

And then there was a sort of laughter, lone, eerie, like the mew of a seagull that got into the PA system.

It was over.

Emory turned off the radio, gave a yawn, and said:

—How long will he stay in?

—A first-time commitment is ninety days. The judge pronounces: I impose a commitment order for the maximum period.

—Three months.

—Well, I was told they usually do thirty days to start with. But Newell could be treated as a special case.

—Could they release him for any reason?

—Two weeks after the court rules, not sooner: if his treatment team thinks his medication is doing the trick, and that he's no longer a danger to self or others, they can do a discharge. And the judge never knows. But if they still think the person is a menace, then within a week after the original order expires, the patient returns to court for a recommitment hearing. And then our judge can give the hippie a 180-day confinement.

—So we'll need to cultivate a hospital administrator too.

—Yes, or the attending physician. I'll find out their names, and you can call.

—What happens after the new six-month period?

—The renewal process can go on indefinitely. Twenty or thirty years.

—So someone can be shut up for life on a pretext.

—It doesn't matter how shabbily. And as we know domestic relations can get pretty shabby. It's not hard to put away someone you love, or an inconvenient relative.

Emory shook his head:

—Like a family purge.

—Sure. Get rid of your mother-in-law finally. But the problem is that, in a State-run mental institution, they move them out quick unless someone at the other end is footing the bill. No money? Hm, the patient shows marked improvement lately. Functional on lithium? Newell walks, if Papa won't pay for his stay.

—How much?

—A lot. But you say he's got money from Anne's mother?

—He does.

—Use that. I'll call Marin and get an idea of the cost. Of course they could discharge him on an outpatient commitment to a nearby community health center. Once off the locked ward he must report on schedule for therapy sessions, shots, meds. Heard the voices lately? Ah, so you got a gun and made a plan to attack the town hall? Then back in, comrade. More intensive treatment is in order. Patient needs shock therapy; and if that doesn't calm him down, then a frontal lobotomy.

—He'll make for Canada.

—Could.

Emory thought a moment.

—Or here.

XIX

It was past three a.m. In the dark office Emory's face was a mask of anguish. His perspiration picked up a pink tinge from the neon sign over the police station.

Bishop Commynes had done his homework. And now it was like a Devil's catechism, as he tortured his childhood friend with all the zeal of a savage monomania. Vengeance is mine, thought the clergyman who would be God; and this long session was the thing itself.

Commynes gave a low laugh. Right now he looked rather happy and pleased with life:

—Their court-appointed lawyer won't go out and talk with a lot of people. He won't try to find out if the detainee is mentally stable. But Newell's activist lawyer will. And he'll call here: maybe talk to Lemon.

—She'll vouch for her brother.

—He could contact Joey if Newell gave him the number in Manhattan. But it seems Joey may need his own longterm care, inside, not out, before the chickens come home to roost, and he hurts someone he loves.

Commynes eyed his victim to see the effect of this comment.

Emory went pale and said in a strangled tone:

—What does that mean?

But the pastor passed over this question.

—Will Newell's attorney bother with that cuckoo's nest in the Berkeley Hills? Will he speak with his client's so-called Peace Committee? No doubt. An assigned lawyer from an office near the State Hospital in Marin County, where he helps service one of California's catchment areas, has little time for field trips. His case load is backed up. Also, this is a case with instructions from a high place: no need to work too hard finding out the truth . . . On the other hand, Newell's lawyer will do the footwork, but it won't stand up in court. The same doctor picked to examine Newell within ten days will walk across the street to the courthouse and swear: 'I find Mr. Newell Gilbert ill, and dangerous to himself and others'. Whereupon the respondent, your son, if I know him, will stand up and say: 'This doctor, this courtroom, this society, this economic system, are the sick ones! I smell a capitalist rat! Or is it my old man I whiff: the incorruptible leader of our liberal opposition? You can silence me in a padded cell since I know a certain fact which would ruin him. It's a family secret. This wise parent wants his son shut up so the beans won't be spilt. But you see I wouldn't tell anyway: I'm not a tittle-tattle! . . .' Thus Newell, more or less. And the Judge says: 'Out with it then'. That's if he replies. And then Newell: 'Sorry, Your Honor Sir. It's none of your business. Lock me up and throw away the key, but I won't rat even on a rat. No, I don't squeal. And no tumbledown judicial system, symptom of bourgeois decadence, can make me eat cheeze. Matter of principle, Sir . . .' And so on, and so forth. The boy rants, raves, and gives the whole Leftist spiel again. And the poor Judge feels sorry he asked. And then there is silence, as Newell stands there looking down from the height of principle. But maybe no one took him seriously about the family secret . . . And then, well, you tell me whether the upright Judge believes irresponsible Hippie, or state-paid Doctor. 'Paranoid delusions! Megalomania! Projections used as defense mechanisms! Dangerous to self and others. In.'

Emory, somber, looked down.

—Noble boy.

Commynes said:

—Will he protect the person trying to take away his freedom?

—He doesn't care if I live or die. But he loves his brother. He'll keep quiet for Jojo.

—If not for arrogance. Look how pure I am. History will absolve me.

Emory said:

—Won't anyone find a conflict of interest when I, the petitioner, begin to pay Newell's bills after his savings run out?

—Then you can say: Look, I'm not obliged to meet my son's debts. He's an adult. But add up his bill year after year: he'll owe the State of California a fortune. And then he's broke when he comes out someday.

—True. We're not heartless.

Bishop laughed:

—At last Newell comes out into the sunshine, a bit shaky, calmer now. He's a middle-age fellow with some gray hair. Still needs supervision? Look at him: run down by the long confinement, and brutal treatment of his zoo-keepers. They wound the radical extremist in a wet ice-pack each time he protested the fascist system of Big Nurse and Uncouth Orderly. But now here he comes: discharged, out, after forty years of therapy. And he owes his jailors a half million dollars into the bargain. Hey, says Dad, I'm a good sport, I'll pay. I know I don't have to, but call it a personal gesture. Sure, I'll help the poor boy. Send me your monthly bill for services rendered.

—He's my son, said Emory, pale.

—There you go. You'll pay with pleasure. And if you pay, it's an incentive for them to keep him in.

—Just pay the money.

—That's right, and he'll be safe. Public mental facilities always need funds. There won't be any haste to waltz Newell out the door, and he really will have gone mad. Often, I was told, the judge's decision rides not so much on dangerousness as on an alternative placement if nobody can pay. Newell may need to stay there, but they'll put him on the street if there's no money.

—You mean once his funds run out . . . if I don't take over.

Commynes said with a grim humor:

—Look at the upright public servants . . . our judges. Look how arbitrary they are: all ready to lie under oath, to commit perjury, or at least act wishy-washy on this thing called dangerousness. And it happens, so I was told, just about every time they hold this kind of court proceedings.

Emory was in pain. He looked bad, old, in that lurid light, as the early hours turned toward dawn. He shook his head, and said:

—It's Joey who belongs in an institution. He's the one who needs help, not Newell. You know, at times my mind plays a strange trick, and I think Newell is the only healthy one among us.

—So healthy he'll destroy you, if you let him.

—Then why not yet? He's had his chances. I attack him, and he protects me.

—Like you said: Joey. But now he'll choose. Now he'll try to get his sister out of a tight fix.

Commynes laughed.

For a long moment Emory stared into the night beyond the window screen.

—You think they'll buy our story? Lock him up?

—Of course. The little District Court judge will be thrilled by his connection with power. They'll do as we say. Trot out National security issues if necessary. If you leave this terrorist on the loose, who knows what he'll do? The National Security State has such an awesome power to buzz around in people's ears. Look, folks. This guy Newell Gilbert, the hippie radical over there in Berkeley, you know: he needs to be kept away from his playmates. He's gotten himself into some shady goings-on, I'm afraid; he's a subversive. Now as the war rages in Vietnam, and there's violence in the streets here at home: better put bad elements like him away . . . And they will. For a long time. Be sure of it. Your moral authority, the eminent dad in deep distress over his son, will seal Newell's doom. And your phone call to the California Governor and also the FEMA chief will bowl over the small-bore bureaucrats out there. He's a helpful fellow, that Governor, he'll go far. Bit of a chameleon . . . Well, he's an actor. And, anyway, who can afford to have principles in our day and age?

—Amen—said Emory, in a whisper.

But Bishop Paul Jezreel Commynes gave a hearty laugh:

—It seems we'll never lack for heroes, in the land of the free, and the home of the brave.

XX

Dawn approached. Joey Gilbert unlocked the door of his apartment in the East 80s. He didn't have the strength to get undressed. He lay down on the living room rug and closed his eyes.

The phone rang. At this hour? He reached to an end table for the receiver.

—Who?

—It's us. Are you ready?

The detective agency.

—You've found her?

—Yes.

—Where?

—We'll come by for you. We'll take you.

There was a twenty-minute wait. And then they sped uptown beneath the 125th Street Bridge onto Harlem River Drive. The private eye had radio contact with a partner on the scene.

Joey stared ahead. He wasn't tired anymore. He didn't feel his extreme fatigue after a week of bad if any sleep caused by the Pennant race, and nightmares the moment he did drop off.

—A Cuban exile took her in. He's a dentist. Uses the ground floor pad for his illegal practice.

—Where did he find her? On the street?

—We don't know that.

—Is she alone in there? Now?

—N-no.

—With the dentist?

—At night he goes to Jersey. Wife and kids.

—So she's . . . receiving visitors?

—There's a child with her. And . . . yes, she receives visitors.

At Audubon and West 174th, across from a Spanish grocery, the detective pulled over. He parked.

—I'll take it from here, said Joey.

—Hold on. Over there's my partner.

From a car on the other side, by the bodega, the partner gave them a glimpse.

—Where is she? said Joey.

—First floor. The windows left of the entry.

It was the third tenement from the corner. The stoop with its few steps and landing was lit by a corner streetlight.

—You say she isn't alone?

—No.

—Who with?

—She went in with a man—he looked at his wristwatch—forty . . . nine minutes ago.

—Not the Cuban?

—No.

Joey frowned.

—So she lives here. She turns tricks . . . I knew that.

—Sorry.

—Don't be. How did you find her?

—She was in the crowd at the game on Sunday. We picked her up in binoculars, and followed her here.

—Forty-eight hours, and you didn't tell me?

—We had to be sure. Stake out the place.

Joey gave a little laugh:

—You talked to the Front Office.

—No.

—The General Manager told you to hold off until after tonight's game.

—No, sir.

Calmly Joey opened the car door.

—I'll do the rest.

—Better if we stick around.

—Send me a final bill. Your job is finished.

—This is a rough neighborhood. Who knows what sort of guy she has in there with her.

Joey stared across the front seat at the detective.

—So you have been talking to them. And they told you to keep an eye on me and look out for their property. Tell me: are you on their payroll?

The private eye gave a low laugh:

—Who? Us?

—Isn't that sort of illegal? Break trust with a client?

—We didn't do it.

—Thanks for your help. Now get out of here.

—As you wish. You know, I've followed baseball since I was a kid, and I've seen the great ones play. You're like them, and you're just beginning. Be a shame if you got hurt. This league—he scanned the deserted street—plays by other rules.

—Send me your bill.—Joey opened the car door carefully.—You're lucky I can't be bothered to sue you. First you talk to the press—

—Never!

—They got a picture. You leaked it.

—It wasn't from us. You're unfair.

—Go.

—The papers protect their sources. If you want, we could try and find out.

—No, that's enough. Just clear out. Your partner too.

After the two cars drove off, he stood there thinking what to do.

He glanced about for a place to wait.

Dawn approached.

XXI

He crossed to the other side and took his post on a stoop. The air was cool, and he was in a t-shirt. A few cars passed along Audubon as first light played in the cornices of five- and six-storey tenements. He listened: crouched out of view, looked and listened, like a LURP. Sooner or later she would have to come out and buy food; she and the child would need this or that from the store across the street.

The minutes passed, and his heart pounded. She was in there with another man: a stranger. Jealous yearning, and anger. The question of who fathered her child seemed answered: any man.

Expectation, anguish: she was here, a few feet away from him. It was her. She was in there, and she was . . . working . . . as a whore. Well, he knew this. And she wasn't a high-priced call girl either; or like those at the bars of the better hotels, on sale for a C-note. No. She was a streetwalker. Common variety. She'd rather sell herself in public than go side by side with the Major League MVP? Then what was she doing in New York?

He stared at the stoop, at the windows. He felt like storming the place. A bad tactic. No key; couldn't get in; just alert them, her, with his pounding, banging, if the door didn't give. Wait. Surprise was his best ally and tactic.

After five now; the sky was lightening. The adrenalin flowed, but he drooped with such exhaustion, it was hard to keep his mind in gear.

Over the rooftops of Washington Heights there was a red glow.

XXII

Suddenly he heard a woman's voice. It was hard-edged—raised in anger.

Her voice. The southern accent with a quaint note: the Lumbee. But that tone he had never heard from her.

Jolted alert he rose up on the stoop where he waited. There was a scuffle going on. Would it spill out on the street? The voices were ugly, the man's and the woman's; it was the gutter.

The woman came stumbling out backward and tripped: almost falling backward down the concrete steps. She was trying to stop the other from leaving as he, a heavyset man, pushed forward at her, and had a thought to tuck in his shirttails.

He hit her; tried to buck her aside.

She hit back.

—Bitch, out of my way!

—Pay the overtime!

—You wanna' get messed up good? Well looky here! It's Jane's pimp waiting outside all night while John fucks out her brains. Pleased to meet ya'!

—I said pay the second time, and I mean it!

Now Joey stood by the curb in full view, and the customer was in a flurry to leave.

Carlyne's features looked older in the predawn light. Make no mistake: it was her alright; but hardened, coarse, like she lived a lifetime in months. Fallen. But right now she looked more pitiful, in her defiance.

—No! No! No!

She glanced around and saw Joey. In horror she turned away,

and she was no longer thinking about the money owed to her. Again, for an instant, she stared; then did an about-face and lunged for the door.

Joey leapt forward. With a growl he took the steps. A body punch made the fleshy customer double over, coughing for breath, drooling. But he was left alone now and he dragged himself off without looking back at the whore and her pimp.

In a fury she tried to close the door and get away from the other rushing at her. With all her strength she slammed the door on his arm and glared through the chink. She was like a panicked animal. Death seemed to stare at her through the door still ajar.

Then he tore it open with such a force it left one hinge.

But she wrenched away with a gasp and jerked convulsively from his grip. He bounded forward. He was on her. She scratched his face and dug in her nails, but he had her. No one was around to see them; but neighbors must have been woken by what sounded like a rape in progress. She flailed, lashed out, kicked, wriggled as he grabbed at her upper arm and shoulders and clutched her neck.

And then in the dark hallway he slapped her very hard. He hit her with his flat hand, and Carlyne's head snapped back, and that was it. She went limp in his arms.

Joey stood there holding her to him, against his body, with one hand on the wall to steady them.

It was a year and nine months since he had seen her, and held her this way in the airport in Bangkok.

From inside the apartment came a thin babble:
—Abooja-booja-boojah-beek!
Her child.

Then Carlyne came to and went wild again. Much worse it was than with the John. But she didn't cry out now; she only hit him, his chest, his face. She beat his face with her fists, and his blood flowed, but he stared down in her eyes, and took it; only bobbing to protect his own eyes. She was hysterical. Hissed at him, choked. Then a ripple went over her body. Her face was gleaming with spittle, hair wild, her blue eyes terrified.

For a long moment he just hung onto her in a strange silence while she hammered away at him and whimpered. Then he got her pinned between his body and the wall, so she couldn't run away from him any longer, not now anyway. Still, still she grappled and tried to squirm away, but it was no use. He was too strong. She gave low bestial sounds and wheezed for breath after the hail of blows she dealt him.

And then he held his wife in his arms. Her hands pounded his back a little more, but his were firm on her nape and shoulder blades. He closed his eyes and rocked. Now he didn't care where she'd been or what she'd done or how she looked. He only cared about her matted hair on his neck and cheek making him sneeze, and the smell of her sweat more sacred than any incense, and all of her, there, against him.

He leaned eyes closed and breathed her in, like that day a lifetime ago in Bangkok Airport, after he thought he had lost her forever.

—Beeja-beeeja-chat! Adabeech!

Chapter Nineteen

I

May 1970

Carlyne Gilbert bowed her head after falling to one knee in the backyard of the Rock Castle. She gasped for air, and her body shook. A small sound, like a question, came from her throat.

The back door slammed to. A kitchen window banged shut.

He was in there. She was out here.

She looked up with glazed eyes at the big eerie mansion. Her breast heaved . . . What to do? Joey was inside. *He knew.* The thing she had feared every day and every hour since her reunion with him—he was in there, with *it.*

He was her husband, and Rhoda was her child. They were inside. She was out.

Carlyne rose trembling from the back walk. He had launched her through the kitchen door and then wiped his rough farmer's hands, and said:

—Scat.

She stared up at their bedroom window. Around the side a shutter was closed with a will. Bang—end of discussion. Now he would lock up the place; he'd batten down the hatches and turn his father's house into a military fortress and defy the world.

Stunned, in the calm sunlit afternoon, she cried out:

—Joey, listen to me!

—Go to hell.

—I'll come inside if I have to break in the door.

—And then I'll break your skull . . . Clear out!

—I'll go but let me take Rhody.

—I said get the hell out of here! You're no mother, you're a slut!

—Give her to me and we'll leave. You don't want us anymore.

Carlyne's body was sobbing. Her eyes were dry.

—Damn you. I never should've trusted you.

—Jo, I love you! Jo—

Her voice broke.

His grim laughter rang through the big empty rooms:

—Strike three, out!

—Please. Oh . . .

He flung open a second-storey window.

—You see this, bitch?

—No.

He pointed a semiautomatic rifle down at her.

—Now I'll give you sixty seconds to scram. Rid me of your presence. If you don't then I'll shoot you down like a skunk at the garbage. First you and then myself.

—But Rhody, Jo . . . our child.

She looked up at him as she backed away—now, yes, tears on her cheeks—along the walkway.

—Our child?—He gave the same bad laugh.—You mean Daddy's little joy?

—Don't . . . Let me come in. I don't care if you shoot me.

He pointed the M-16. He aimed, and his voice quivered:

—Don't you now, you incestuous whore? Say one more word. Say one more, and you'll get your wish.

She almost said okay—she just didn't care if she died. She deserved to. But he had said: then myself. And his mind no longer belonged to him where he stood, so alone, a dark figure framed in the window casement.

He would probably finish the job by shooting Rhoda—who *didn't* deserve to die. Include the child in his sick self-pity. Well, maybe the parents did deserve it: he for what he did in the war, she for what she did at home, and turned into. But was a little girl to blame for what went on?

In this instant Carlyne loved the two of them so much. She loved and wanted Joey with all her being—more than ever now that he knew.

So she thought of the psychiatrist whom she admired and feared. What would Lydia Falliere tell her to do right now?

Retreat.

So she turned and ran.

II

Fifty yards back of the Rock Castle there was a garage with pickup truck and two cars. A tractor was parked outside. Further on stood the barn, a silo, barnyard with hen coop, and old farm outbuildings cleaned out by Joey last fall and made fit for use. In the bright sun Carlyne walked with her head up, still in his sites, across the grassy back plot with its tall oaks newly in leaf and the remains of Wilhelmina's old rock garden and fish pond which he meant to put back in order too.

She felt his dark glare at her back. And so she tried to control her steps and look steady, calm. He was poised and ready for action in an upper storey window; and Dr. Lydia had told her something like this could happen if he got a bad jolt—did she *know* too?—and felt he had to take on the world. He hefted his weapon with safety off and in this moment of recognition he wanted to destroy not only her and himself but all reality. Oh yes, he'd shoot his wife and fire a bullet in her brain, very neat, and then done. But it wasn't him, said Lydia; it was his sickness, the demon he brought home like a parasite from Vietnam.

Carlyne went on past the garage. Then, round the side, the instant she was beyond his line of fire, she stooped and took off her sandals and began to run. And now she was a Lumbee girl again on a farm—oh! she could run.

She lit out with all her might toward a pay phone, if only it worked, by one of the vacant storefronts up town.

Carlyne went running barefoot through the fields. She was shin deep in a cover crop Joey planted over wide fertile acreage tilled for the first time in decades. She took the long way to town because she knew what was happening to them must be kept a secret. And so she ran until her sides ached and then kept on running and the idea of her daughter back there in the Rock Castle and her husband in a blind suicidal rage made her run like the wind. She might sell herself on the street and want to die, but now she had the survival instinct of a frightened doe bounding across the swamplands of southeastern Carolina. And by her side was the outlaw Henry Berry Lowry, her ancestor. She took the furrows with an ache in her gut and her breast ready to burst; but there was a glimmer of hope in her dark blue eyes. Now it was out. Now he knew. If they could just get through this crisis somehow . . . and she knew he loved her. But to come out alive together she felt they needed Lydia Falliere's help.

And above all nobody in this town must know. But somebody did know and whoever it was did not wish them well—and had sent a sort of hate signal which had blasted at least for now their struggle for happiness. After all the suffering they had begun to get along and show promise as a couple.

When the ordeal of baseball ended, Joey was still in his moods. That big stress was over, but he kept having nightmares, sudden attacks of panic he didn't understand, and flashbacks of combat. All day in the fields he wore out his sickness, and took out the hate and his mean streak when the thing came over him, on the sea of weeds which was P. Laster's farm left fallow for half a century. Nature has tangles as stubborn as a man's. And in physical pain and toil Joey felt relief from the mental. He kept working the land in winter, storm and sleet; in fact he liked that best. He went out there—what else could he do? Take out his violent fits on the wife he loved so much?

He set himself the task of clearing this rich acreage for vegetable and tobacco plantings, and also the hay, silage and pasture crops Emory once talked about but more as a nostalgia for his boyhood. Joey planned improved forages, fescue and ladino clover mixture, alfalfa, orchardgrass, bluegrass swaying all day in a breeze from the Yadkin River.

But then came the bombshell. She still wasn't quite certain what it was—somebody told Joey the basics, she thought it must have been by letter; but maybe a phone call? or even some clue he came across around the house? And so now her husband's mind was not his own anymore.

The main thing—thought Carlyne as she ran along—was to survive the first onslaught. If only he didn't do anything while she was running to call for help: while she was away from the Rock Castle. But she did have to get away from there and out of his sight. That was for sure.

Reach Lydia in New York. The psychiatrist was trained for this; she knew techniques to handle a crisis. Tell her: the truth has become known, it is out, and this is the worst. I know you love Joey too, and among my reasons to suffer has been jealousy. But I don't care. I just want to save my husband and daughter if it means I have to die in the process. Now the battle is engaged. Now this is out in the open. Can you help us? Can you . . . come here and help?

Help.

III

On the far side of the town cemetery with its brick wall and ivy Carlyne came in from the fields. She tried to look calm and walked along with her head high. Quickly she moved through the graveyard with its rows of stones for Confederate soldiers, some unknown, dated 1861–1865. She hit the sidewalk and went a few blocks lined with furniture showrooms fronting the raised train tracks. How run down it all looked except for the well-kept grassy embankment where the long freight trains rumbled through without stopping. How empty the town was.

Down an alley she broke into a run again: across back lots with their weedy lading platforms, and trails of reddish vine on the frittering brick walls.

Into the town center came Carlyne Gilbert smoothing her dark hair. She flicked a blade of winter rye, whisked seeds and grass from her bluejeans. She looked wild with a fierce glint in her eye—another Rhoda Strong Lowry come to spring her man out of jail. But this was harder: she had to save him not from the law but from himself.

A few men up town on errands this warm, slow-moving afternoon in the South took a look at her as she passed by. She was a sight to see, Joey Gilbert's wife, her black hair looking wild like a rooster tail. They watched her go to the public telephone and hunch over it dialling a number.

Just then a mile-long freight train came up from the east. It rumbled and clattered over the main intersection while she tried to get through and hear and make herself heard.

—Oh, come on!

Disheveled, deeply shaken, but ready to fight to the last, Carlyne put a finger in one ear as she spoke into the receiver.

And then the long distance call was over. And she put the phone carefully on its hook, and turned around. She took a deep breath and looked down the street—out the main road where it ran a quarter mile to the Rock Castle.

What to do now? She couldn't do anything but wait. She couldn't go back there, and set him off . . . Alright then: wait. And she thought: wherever you go, husband, but by your side. Like it or not, you and I live or die together.

Midafternoon was past. In a few hours night would fall.

Still by the pay phone Carlyne looked round the other way: at the main intersection and the tracks. And there by the bank building she saw a lone man in a dark suit with a clerical collar. He was staring at her. Oh, oh, what a loneliness there was in those eyes. It made her shudder.

IV

A week after the World Series ended, Joey Gilbert told his team's General Manager he would not be back in the spring. That was it. Better quit while he was ahead because his nerves couldn't take another season of baseball.

This was a shocker. Across the country it made the front page. No signal, no discussion. Decision final. He couldn't wait awhile and let New York enjoy the euphoria of its victory. I quit, and that's it.

Major League baseball might feel the loss of such an exciting player, but there was also a sigh of relief. And in the sports pages and the words of columnists there was a sense the big boys, corporate sponsors, wanted him gone. They wished Joey Gilbert well and quoted his letter of resignation. 'I cannot be the kind of family man I want to be and play baseball everyday. My plan is to become a farmer in partnership with my father in North Carolina. This fall I will enroll at N.C. State for courses in agriculture.'

Thus a stroke of the pen and the future Hall of Famer was only a southern farmer. He had no regrets, and he expressed no thanks to his team or the League, the great game of baseball. The system, capital, would miss Joey as a source of profits; but top brass were leery of such gate receipts. The man was a liability: for one thing a living reminder of Vietnam, and U.S. inability to get its way with a smaller country—like tiny Nicaragua back in the 'Thirties.

Who'd miss the talented but erratic third baseman most were the fans in this great sports junky of a nation: where stimulation is the name of the game, and each thrill must outdo the last.

New York won its World Series victory in six games. But there was a sort of bad aftertaste. When the last out was made, Joey Gilbert just stood at third base. No victory lap this time, as after the Playoff Game. What's more he didn't go wild and jump around like an overgrown child; he wouldn't run to the mound and play leapfrog with the pitcher and catcher and show the jubilation of a winner. None of that; instead, he waved off his teammates and walked over to the enemy dugout. There he met chilly stares though a few did shake his hand.

The League Office fines players for fraternization. It is not seen as *bon ton*. It is no lesson for today's youth.

Communists fraternize. We are free: to win, beat the other, and rejoice.

Joey was a great player, let none say nay: first to hit .400 since Williams. But, you know, he sort of didn't play fair. He went to war out there.

And so the League said goodbye to the wild child who was not one of theirs. Maybe he was a flash in the pan. He didn't win either League or Series MVP: the sportswriters wouldn't vote for him. He didn't even get Rookie of the Year in this his first full season. It seems the millions in profits, the capacity crowds and concession stand revenues, the TV ratings and the rest were due to some other factor, not Joey Gilbert. If anything, he hurt our National Pastime: made fun of it, then snubbed it. In the end he rubbed just about everyone the wrong way; and especially the important ones, the executives. From Saigon to Midtown Manhattan this grunt had no use for desk jockeys.

So they denied him.

In Baltimore he put on a display at third base and at the plate to astonish the most blasé.

Then back in New York he asked his wife:

—Can't we get out of here? I hate it.

She laughed. Carlyne's face lit up, and she let herself laugh:

—You mean I'll have to say goodbye to Lydia Falliere, your true love?

—She may be my true love, but you're the love of my life.

And he picked Carlyne up, and swung her around.

Now there was a joy. Now there was hope in her heart. She kept it down; she didn't show it.

—Where to, Jo?

—Let's go down South. We'll drive to North Carolina: you, me, and Rhoda. I'll phone Dad and get him to let me start up the farm. We'll be happy, my darling. Let's pack up and go out for dinner and a walk in the Park. We'll leave tomorrow!

—Alright.

—Are you with me?

—Yes.

—Oh—he rubbed his hands—I bet you I'll take to farming. I could grow things, and I'll be good at it. Revive the old Gilbert spread from the Rock Castle out to the river. Make things hop!

She had a catch in her throat:

—I'll help you.

—Will you? Will you, my darling? Support me, stand behind me? Then I'm the luckiest man alive.

The daughter of Tuscarora and Cheraw, farmers long before this republic existed, said quietly:

—And I'm the happiest woman.

V

Well, she earned it. Her life since being reunited with Joey had been a hell—a hell with hope, which may be worse.

Only once was she able to talk in person with Lydia Falliere, the formidable rival. With her husband at the stadium practicing, the off day before the Series came for its third game to New York,

Carlyne put Rhody in a stroller and walked to the career woman's Fifth Avenue office. It was a golden afternoon in early October.

She was afraid to go in there. She hadn't even called first. But then she did go in, and Lydia was on hand seeing patients. Carlyne spent two hours in the waiting room; but then they were able to visit and have supper together which the psychiatrist had sent to her office.

Joey's wife was ushered by the receptionist into the wainscoted inner office with its desk lamp aura, bookshelves of fine collected editions; its framed academic degrees, scientific awards and prizes, original paintings. While Lydia was in another room tending to something, Carlyne had a look around. She loved books too, the good books, but it wasn't her fate to read many of them.

Then in came Dr. Falliere. She was taller than Carlyne, handsome, very elegant, yet she didn't look so terrible. She curtsied, and had a friendliness between women. Lydia smiled and apologized. And there was something about her: maybe a bit vain, yes, Carlyne could see she was; but also modest, or at least very courteous. The doctor gazed with a sort of awe at Joey Gilbert's wife, and invited her to sit—as a few more notes had to be made in a case folder. Ever a whit harried, Lydia smiled as she jotted: not wanting to lose an insight . . . And then she let the pen fall, and stared an instant longer at what she had written.

Carlyne watched her. Rhody was napping in the stroller.

Yes, the doctor's frank handshake and pleasant curtsy put Carlyne at ease, and made her feel a twinge of shame at her jealousy.

And then for a moment the two women looked in one another's eyes.

They settled in by the window overlooking the Park. Lydia worked the blinds to let in some light.

Little Rhoda in the stroller murmured from sleep like a chick.

Carlyne wasn't much for smalltalk. She never had been, and now less. She groped for a start:

—My husband, I . . . I don't quite know how to say this.

Lydia waited. It was disarming the way she kept silent with a kind smile, and sat slightly forward to hear. In an instant Carlyne's feared rival became her only friend in the big City, her only ally for a long time. And she yearned to tell her things, the hard, bad things, the secret she had never told anyone. But she couldn't.

When she too fell silent, Lydia helped with a question about this or that, the child's health, their life together in New York, their plans. After ten minutes or so Carlyne was back at it, like a patient, speaking from her pain. Lydia took the sudden attempt at intimacy as a tribute.

—We don't, you know, he—

Carlyne got up and took the child starting to stir from the stroller. She placed the little girl on her lap and bowed her cheek to Rhoda's forehead. She frowned, pressed her lips, shook her head.

—Go on.

—What a life, Doctor. They say war is hell, but I wish I could go and fight. It would be a distraction . . . When Jo . . . Joey . . . when he found me, I wanted to tell him so much. I mean everything. Well let us two stand at the altar of Truth and be remarried. Let us begin again. But . . . but I just can't tell him.

—Maybe he knows already. He forgives.

—He doesn't know . . . the worst. Oh what came after, that yes, but—

—After?

Lydia had a way of letting the silence settle in. And that was a good way because it affirmed what was said, as she took this seriously and thought it over. Then the silence itself seemed to follow up with a question, and set the stage for more, maybe deeper, delving. But she needed to speak too: so this young woman who didn't look so young, and talked about the altar of Truth with a rough southern accent, wouldn't feel strange or think she was being laughed at.

—Oh I told him all about it. Yes, I did. I said: don't love me, Jo. I can't stand it. Go find a woman suited to you, someone much better than me, like that Lydia of yours. You see, Doctor, I have sold my body a hundred times to the first comer. I have done such things with my mouth, I have no right to coo my baby, or kiss the sole of my husband's foot. That's right. I've been sick and had disease in me . . . Well, this I told him, and he took me to see the gynecologist, your friend. Thank you for that and for helping my husband . . .—Carlyne bowed low, shaking her head, pressing her cheek to Rhoda's dozing head.—I've told him other things too; though he knows them in the main from how he found me, a hooker. But it doesn't matter how much I tell him, Doctor, because you can't go halfway down the aisle to the altar of Truth, you have to go all the way, or don't even bother. And then he sees I look like a goner, and he puts his big arm round my shoulder and says: 'Hey, Babe, cool off. What do you think? I'm just so glad I'm with you.' This is what he says. And I could tell ten other worse things or a hundred since he thinks he's to blame, leaving me for Vietnam, and for starters he doesn't want any Mother Mary in heaven for his girl but only Carlyne the Lumbee Indian, hooker or no hooker. That's what he says. And pats me on the back a little, softly, like he was afraid to touch me because I'm so holy, you know, or I might vanish at the touch and go away again, leave him, you know . . . In his dark eyes there's a twinkle, like a naughty boy in there who wants to trust, something like that. I haven't seen it in a long time, and it hurts me, it hurts. 'Anyway, don't worry,' he laughs, 'you're a spotless madonna compared to me because where I've been and what I've done are in another category. And when I think of the time you'll have with your crazy husband before we get old and maybe calm down a little: don't worry, kid, you'll have a chance to redeem your sins. Just don't give up on it', laughing again, kissing my hair, 'and I don't want to see your head drooping 'cause I'm the happiest madman there ever was and I love you, my darling, I do!' So you see, Doctor, there it is. And I have to listen to this and know all along he's playing straight with me but I can't with him: can't tell him the main thing, the main thing of all, since it would put an end to us. And if we can't talk about it then we'll never get free of it. Never. I could confess to him a hundred or a thousand times, but his forgiveness still wouldn't work because I haven't said the one thing more damning than all the others combined. The original sin must stay a secret. And he, thank God, does not know it. And I can't tell him, not him or anyone, yourself included. So don't ask!

Carlyne stood up.

Rhoda, jolted, awoke and began to squirm.

Carlyne drove herself to the limit, and it made her features quiver. But no tears.

What did Lydia do? She stood up and took a menu from her desk drawer.

—Let's order dinner.

When that was done they settled in again by the window. All Lydia's bearing seemed to say: don't worry, you can talk. So she asked a lighter question or two, and put in a comment of her own, quite personal. And before Carlyne knew it they were back in the thick of things.

—Jo has a bad dream. Same one: when the team loses, when something doesn't go his way, watch out. Any sort of bad thing and then, late at night, our bedroom is a free fire zone. I'm the enemy.

—Affective stress—said Lydia.—Tell me the dream.

—Joey feels . . . like he killed one of his squad mates. His name is Kevin Blair, a bookish kid like Newell, my brother-in-law. Blair died in combat. Or no, he turned up missing at dawn when they broke camp, and later on they found him stuck up on a tree, what was left of him. But when Jo has this dream, it happens after . . . I can't.

Carlyne, agitated, looked down.

Lydia paused a moment; then said:

—A recurrent dream. And then?

—There's only one place I feel safe anymore. That's the stadium, and I hate going to his games . . . By his side in bed our heaven becomes a hell. I'm afraid to go to sleep with him in such a state, so I snooze during the day. I'm done in, I'm scared. I'm risking my own life and the child's every time my head touches the pillow. Rhody's quiet in her crib across the hall. Joey's breathing regular: his pinkie sort of playing on my haunch, touching me, like he's afraid I'll go away again. Vanish into thin air like Blair.

—Or else he will—said Lydia—into his dreams.

—Making sure I'm still there . . . Don't worry, honey, I am. I'm lying awake at 3 a.m. with eyes wide open, waiting for the sun to come up. Then . . . I just can't help it anymore, so tired, I drift off . . . But not for long. Jo? That you? My eyelids open a slit, then real wide. No, please, Jo! No! Before I know it he's kneeling over me and crushing my arm.—Carlyne rolled up a sleeve to show the bruised arm.—He's rolling his eyes and grinding his teeth. It might be funny but the look on him is terrifying. Wild eyes, gasping for air, hair frazzled. They turned him into a monster over there . . . I wish the club would make him cut that hair, but what do they care? His wildness is a box office draw to them: the madder the better.

—You saw in the sports section about Samson at third?

—No.

Carlyne shook her head. She breathed in starts.

—What then? said Lydia.

—Huh? Well I react. It's my nature I guess: you get beat up by life and it becomes a reflex. I can't take that on my back. Okay, go loco, flip out. But what if he kills Rhoda in one of his nightmares? This is real life, not memories of the Central Highlands. Why hurt her? What sin did she ever commit? One punch and it's good night, little baby, you don't get to have a life. Hey! Mister Joey! Wake up, dear! On the bed I lurch forward. I jump from sleep to self-defense. I pound him, I beat his ugly mug!

—And then?

—How would you like to fall asleep every night so afraid? It gives new meaning to the prayer: if I die before I wake.

—What do you do then?

Carlyne swayed side to side with the baby in her arms.

—He has me by the throat. What a grip! War training: strangle you one-handed. But I don't scream. Oh no; and have this crap all over the front page? No, I just grunt in his face and jerk a forearm at his big sourpuss. I hiss at him: get the hell off, you prick.

—Does he wake up then?

—Not yet. He wants to cream my ass, like a VC woman he stabbed to death on the trail one night. Oh, he told me all about it in Bangkok: the way he 'greased the gook', a VC cadre on recon. That's why I won't let any weapons in the house if I can help it. But I think he has some in storage down South. I found invoices for a lot of money: itemized only by model numbers. Maybe he's a gun freak. I know he dreams about hand grenades 'cause he'll jolt awake wide-eyed, over me: one hand on my chest, the other lobbing a grenade and urging his men forward. Later I tell him, and he feels foolish and hangs his head like a puppy dog. But I can't do a thing with him when he's in his dreams.

—And when he attacks you? What then?

—Huh? Oh, I yank out his curly hair and push him right off the bed. Down onto the floor we go in a heap and we roll around awhile. I light into him, I hit him pretty hard. He seems to like that: still in a state, you know. My darling! My pet! And I cuff the dazed motherfucker like he was one of the Johns I pick up, giving me trouble. I slap his ass silly, trying to bring him back from the deep end, you know. Then he twitches his nose and talks some shit in my ear, still out of it, the big fool. And then all at once I have him, yes, my sweet, sweet child, my loving boy. I kiss his battered face, I caress him and he goes limp and starts to whimper like a child in my arms. And now I'll tell you a weird thing, Doc-

tor. I can't hardly explain it. Would you believe that I have fallen
in love with my husband?

—Will wonders never cease?

—Please, Ma'am, you who are the scientist: look into this and
make a report. It is amazing: I love someone. And it's my husband of all people.

The food came. Lydia set a nice table for them with a candle.

She gave a concerned look at Joey Gilbert's wife who was the
focus of TV cameras: this Carlyne who sat statuesque in her slacks
and blouse among the anxious players' wives. Photographers
went for the hint of disdain on her lips, and the contrast: bored
by the game. Quite photogenic: the proud eyebrows, the sheen of
her raven hair in braids: the hard note to her features. In the field
box Carlyne Gilbert sat quietly; she invited no chitchat; but she
did arouse a voyeur instinct. The other wives raised braceleted
arms, and cried out at clutch plays and big hits, in the crescendo
of suspense. Carlyne, the sphinx, waited in silence for the game
to end.

And then in the early hours, after his ordeal on the field, Joey
drifted asleep by her side. And then it came again: the moment he
let go, a nightmare had him. It was terror. And so the long season
he had played third base with little rest. It made him an inspired
player, fueled by subconscious, but he also had the lapses.

Two nights before Carlyne visited the doctor, her husband
had jolted awake, eyes wide in stark terror, drawing himself up
against the bedstead. She was awake; she lived on alert.

She described it to Lydia:

"—Jo? That you?

"—. . .

"—What did you see?

"—No!

"—Go on. Tell me.

"His voice flies up, boyish. His gaze seems to swim, but he's
trying to shake it off. He hasn't attacked me.

"—It's him again!

"—Him?

"Joey catches his breath. Trouble breathing.

"—After we killed them!

"—Them?

"—VC. They were!

"I can feel his distance, like a brink. I tug at him, gently, from the edge of the bed.

"—You?

"—I led them. Grenade in a hootch. Slam open the door, pah! pah! Smoke. Spray 'em, M-16.

"He grinds his teeth, staring at me.

"—You threw it?

"—Not me!

"—Only saw?

"—I watched. I watched.

"—You thought: no good.

"—Mama, kids. Stick-limbs. Blood all over the hut. Oh, there they go again, flames, crackle.

"Slowly, he shakes his head. He is there again, in it.

"—You ran to stop them.

"—Ran?

"—Halt! you cried. Did you? Halt!

"—No! No!

"I'm trying to hold his gaze. Get him back, keep him. But it is in my eyes I guess he sees the VC hamlet, the woman, the flames.

"—No what, Jo?

"—Don't kill! Don't kill! Kill!

"—You don't want this. You didn't order it.

"Out of breath he says:

"—They grease . . . us. Ambush . . . Blair.

"—Pay them back?

"—*Can bo!*

"In anguish his head slumps on my shoulder. He's sobbing. Since we got back together, I feel like I'm his mother, at times.

"—I did it, he says. I killed. And now, as you see, I can't make love.

"—You will.

"—I want you so.

"I wait. I'm trying to act helpful like his Lydia, so I ask:

"—You said *him?* You saw *him* in the dream?

"—Yes.

"—Enemy? VC?

"—. . .

"—Tell me, Jo. Go on.

"—We march. We leave the dead ville. Smoke pouring up through the trees. Behind us it's just . . . psssss. Out there, where we're going, it's distant ridges, in a haze. Spidery branches.

"—Spidery?

"—Stripped trees, in the sunset.

"—They caught fire?

"—No, it's herbicide. Klik or two now from the hamlet. Lopped limbs. Jut up.

"—And then?

"—Tree trunk carbonized. Shiny. Defoliants we use: kill everything green.

"Doctor, that's how in the late night silence I coax him. I took a psych minor in college; but no method like you, it's only instinct. Feeling around . . . That's what I do. Try to have Jo get out the bad thing, the real bad one.

"—Tree trunk?

"—Along the road. Sunset over there, in the broken boughs.

"He's heaving for breath in my arms. We're getting close now, close. He heaves, gives a gasp. Then grins up at me, so strange. My fingers entwine his hair. I want him.

"—Shhh.

"Suddenly he sits up, shouts, bloodcurdling:

"—Crucify the grunt! Revenge, O Christ! It's for the children, and I have to watch this all my life!

"—No.

"—Even out on third I see the big horror bird. Well out there I'm alive anyway, not impotent; it's only a game. But the way I feel I'd toss a Series ring in the trash with all my fruit salad.

"—Salad?

"—Medals.

"I cradle his curly head. I coax him down, I want him down, at my breast and . . . Why? I can't describe my feeling, but you know it.

"—Yes, my darling, my darling . . . it's alright.

"Dry eyed, he just can't cry. Like me: the two of us with bad stuff in us we can't digest. But a sob grumbles in his throat, like thunder over the grandstand.

"He's lying back with his head on my breast. His sweat flows cold; shoulders a little trembly. Can't stand the idea of what he'll see, if he looks. And I share his anguish because I know what we'll see, if we look . . . Then he goes on:

"—It's like Bufillu says. I don't care what gives with this goddamned planet on its way through space. Lot of ridiculous little creatures, human beings, all shook up about their hopes and
dreams. No, I'd wash my hands of it. But the children, it's those
kids, I can't forget.

"—I know, Jo.

The two women ate supper together, and they talked.

Rhoda in her stroller finger-fed bites of the good food too.

Mostly it was Carlyne who talked. It felt like in her life she
never told so much to anyone. And it helped, yes; no doubt it
made her feel better. But it couldn't have the desired effect since
she was not able to say the main thing on her mind—no; not to
Lydia Falliere, and not to a soul on earth.

But she went on, trying anyway.

—So we try again, Doctor . . . I razz the Big Leaguer without
pity and tell him he better get off his ass and produce. Maybe not
a good tactic? Well then I tickle him. I goose him. You don't know
how badly I want a second pregnancy. Well, that may be out, after what I've done with my body. Yet I think it's almost a life and
death matter for us . . . But the man can't do it, or he won't. The
war did that to him. And then I believe he's thinking of you, his
Lydia, I know he does. Why would he want to father a child on a
whore like me, a sewer? And I know he loves you by the way he
says your name sometimes; it's so . . . so nice. He doesn't say my
name in such a tone. Never did. But probably my time has passed
now. It's you he admires, and needs to live. Next stage.

—No, Carlyne. You're wrong there. You're his wife, and he is
deeply in love with you. A writer once said, Tolstoy—

—Oh, I like Russian novels.

—Said he didn't go around gushing how he loved his wife, or
his right arm. But try to take either one away from him!—Lydia
laughed.—I wish a man loved me like that.

—Joey loves you.

—Maybe. I hope so. But you're his wife, and you give him destiny. Oh, I could love just about any country better than this one,
this monster; but my destiny is here. Moreover, I happen to know
he adores you; he's told me. So please be clear: I give him, and
you, my support and friendship, all the help I have to give, at any
time. Just ask!

Lydia laughed brightly.

—He adores me? Ha ha, that's a good one. Why do I go around needy all day and tortured by desire for him the way he used to be for me? It's a hell for us, a sexual inferno, I sizzle on a spit! At night I tease him and egg him on, but it's no use; he just sighs and turns over; can't get it up! And I'm jealous now. Never in my life been jealous; but I'm in such a state, Doctor, you've got to help me, I'm jealous of you! I don't want to share my husband, such as he is, with any psychiatrist! Please, Dr. F., I beg of you: let me have my hubby back! Let him go. But first make him able to do it again! Ow, ow, it hurts when I laugh . . . Look, don't they pay you good money for that? How much do you want? Ha ha ha, forgive me for laughing, I'm just a poor vulgar girl from down South, the former streetwalker. But the team is paying you a fortune for your services; now use your science or your black magic, I don't care which: my man must learn to do his duty again. I am dying for the League's top slugging percentage to hit an inside-the-park homerun or at least a single. 'Cause if not and pretty quick . . . then no joy in Mudville. We all lose. Oh! I just want so badly to conceive by him, my husband, by Jo! Is that a sin?

Carlyne ranted: tears in her eyes from laughing, crying, like a patient.

—I'll try to help you.

VI

The psychiatrist did as she said. They didn't meet again, but there were phone calls.

Lydia knew a few tricks of the trade that were not like Carlyne's.

And then after the Series ended the young couple went back to North Carolina where Lydia referred them to a colleague of hers in Greensboro. But they stayed in touch.

One night Carlyne called Scarsdale for more advice. She felt calmer now that her husband was away from baseball and Lydia Falliere's divan.

She told the older woman:

—Two nights ago I went all out. We ate at a swanky French restaurant and had a 7-course meal, the works. I slipped him a mickey like you said, zinc powder and whatnot. And I talked to him about a little brother for . . . our daughter.

—What did he say?

—You know Joey. He loves kids. You should see him with Rhody when they play. What a kick! The big gorilla stoops at the knees and holds her hands so she can walk. And she totters forward and sort of throws out her legs, the little floozy. She's drunk on life.

—What age?

—Sixteen months—no, thirteen months now, that's it.

—She babbles? Indicates her needs?

—Well, it's a lot of boojaboojabee. But she can pick up things and stand on her own. Crawls better than walks; but she'll tramp across the rug with her hands in Dada's hairy ones, booyeh-booyeh, adabadaba! It hurts me, Doctor, hurts me to watch them having so much fun. He acts silly and plays on the floor, and she climbs on him and yanks his beard, ouch! Say she waves away her bottle, he'll drink from the nipple, the big clown, and then Rhody leers at him. And he'll change her diaper too! When it's playtime he follows her under the furniture, an obstacle course around the room; they get in all kinds of mischief. What she likes so much is he gives her freedom, out of the stroller; he's not like her hen of a ma, but he is there ready to catch her like a play at third if she falls forward. Jo lets 'er run till she gets near an electric socket. Beebahbeebahbeebahbeek! They're just so happy together, Doctor, so good and natural. It hurts, it kills me.

—Hurts to see how much your husband loves his daughter?

Carlyne paused.

—Just his . . . his illness. And our troubles . . . you know, not being able . . . Will we ever have a child and a normal family life?

Silence.

From far away Lydia said:

—Go on. Tell me more.

—About what?

—Zinc powder.

—Oh, that. We gave it the old college try. Home from the rich meal I took a hot shower and slipped into a black negligée. Strand of pearls, my belated anniversary gift, over the lacy bust. I put on perfume and had a seductive simper. C'mon now, bench warmer, time to see some action. If you choke in the clutch this time, I'll . . . I'll go to the tattoo shop and get a black widow spider on my mons

veneris. Okay! says the boy; he goes in for that sort of stuff, you
know, the foreplay . . . Then Muscles lay quietly by my side. He's
so glad not to have to play baseball. He gives me a nudge, and
holds me close, and we talk a lot of rot you know in low voices,
both tipsy. But it was taking too long so I said: Batter up! and then
I tickle and bully him. Well after the whacks I've had, welts on my
body, cut on my forehead, I don't tend to play pattycakes. Give
the bast'uds some back. A knee on his shoulder, I said I'd . . . ha ha
ha, and then bowed down and bit his lip till it bled. We're a pair
of big cats mauling each other and biting. I slapped him good. I
pinched his pecker like it was a bedbug. Come come!

Lydia said:

—That's right.

—Then I told him to wait. I better close Rhody's door across the
hall. Then back at it: I prod and tweak him and my laugh doesn't
sound like church bells. But I move to the far edge of our kingsize
bed and heckle him. Boo! Hiss! In a slump, slugger? Can't get
your licks? No clutch ribbies? Hey, just make contact and meet
the ball. You know, it's time for you to snap to, big stiff! . . . Now
provoked by my catcalls he rolls over and the idea is to take me.
Hit away! Connect for the long ball! Ha-ha . . . I dig my nails in
his ribs but then push the big sucker away. Time out, Ump! Step
out of the box . . . I strain and stretch so the black silk is tight,
tight over my bulging breasts. Oh the straps cut my flesh swollen
with desire for him and with rich French cuisine. I have that big
sleek panther in a frenzy; he's on fire to mount his dame. But still
I push him away, resist his thrusts, jab his pectorals, and make
catty little mews. Now burn 'er right in. Bases loaded, he's hitting
away. It's time to unfasten your seat belts, fans, we're going into
the bottom half! So in a rage of lust he grabs my body fat hard,
hard, and shakes me out like I was trousers for him to put on.
And by now my guts feel like an oven, I want him all, all 6 feet 2
inches of him, all in me, O Jo! So I squirm, I wriggle a little like I
don't wish to be spit lengthwise on his . . . his long . . . you know,
and roasted slow on his fire. What a hypocrite I am. Oh no, Jo, you
can't . . . now I told you not . . . oh! This game is being played under protest, as my body quivers into position, and I'm wide open
for him, and completely in the male's control. Sure, sure, honey,
tell me another one. I am hypnotized as he hovers on the verge
of insertion and comes boring through the sheer black negligée.
I think his explosive passion will blow us both sky-high. We'll

go corkscrewing upward through the ceiling of the Rock Castle which is granite . . . For this isn't play anymore. This is a war. And then . . . and then—

Carlyne breathed in the phone.

Lydia waited a few seconds. She said:

—And then?

—He can't do it. I told you he can't. Short end of the box score.

—What does he say?

—I say: Jo, you okay? But he stares over my head, and mumbles.

—Eerie tone?

—Yes, like it was someone else.

Lydia said:

—The mystified voice goes with PTSD. Avoidance mechanism. He can't relate to key factors of the traumatic experience. But what does he say?

—He's in The Nam . . . 'I had them move out southwest. Our faces glowed red, and we felt the heat on our backs. Up the dirt road from Xo Man it was Tombigbee waiting for us. To our left were blue ridges in the mist. Wild dogs barked. Green and purple, the brief sunset, as night comes on . . .'

—Same thing again.

—But then he sees—

—Blair?

—Everything stops. Jo's body goes stiff on top of me, and he throws out his arms.

—Like Blair impaled on the charred tree.

—You know, Doctor, a woman may shake with orgasms when a man plays dead on her chest. But this is different. I know what this is: plain sickness.

—The dreams your husband is having . . . He has described them in his sessions with me. A VC fighter comes at him out of the dark, but Joey can't react. He shoots and misses. He is overpowered. The enemy leaps down from a tree on top of him. He hits, hits up with his rifle butt, but the other is a leech on his skin. Or Joey has only his bare hands to go against a bayonette . . . In his dreams of combat it's the same thing in many forms. No outcome; it 'ends before anything happens'. Also, he feels unclean after a firefight; and the uncleanness is due partly to the excitement, which is sexual, to do with it. He says: 'To kill makes you unclean and sets you apart'. And this cut-off sense, this apartness was there in another dream. When a mortar landed by his foxhole and buried him alive, he screamed and tried to fight his way out.

Carlyne's voice wavered:

—I called tonight to tell you one thing. I have lost my husband. I don't know if I can save him, or myself. I mean to. But if not . . . when the time comes, and my day is over, please, you take him. I know you love him too. I know that: don't deny it. Anyway you never have. So I say if I fail him again, then you cure him, you keep him. After all he deserves to live and be happy.

—Dear, I won't take your husband. I'll help both of you.

—I know, I know. But just listen to me. In this I may know more than you. Joey loves you: it's a different love, I think better, higher. He and I belong to an earlier time; we didn't know ourselves or one another. But now we do. We mean well, but we're still not right. How could we be? So when he and I just can't make it any longer . . . then you take care of him, you cherish him. Believe me, I never deserved any Joey Gilbert for a husband, and I haven't been up to it. Things happened to me in the past. I'm a bad character . . . yes, yes, I am . . . don't say anything because you don't know about it. Why do you think Jojo went to Vietnam in the first place? It was because he found himself married to a stray dog who would bite off his hand if he tried to pet it. But I'm learning, I'm getting the hang of this. Maybe too late! Which is where you come in.

—Not too late, said Lydia. Call if you need me.

Carlyne's voice seemed to contort:

—If you knew . . . if you knew you wouldn't want to talk to me. I tell you I don't have a right to him, and I can't stand this guilt. It's the worst! The worst! The worst!

VII

When Joey threw his wife out of the Rock Castle and took little Rhoda hostage, his father was living in Washington, D.C. Emory had bought a brownstone in Georgetown after accepting a guest lectureship there. He worked on a new book and went on his speaking tours. There was a new woman by his side and talk of marriage; she was duly blue-blooded and -stocking'd, something of a cultural figure in her own right with her grandfather on a postage stamp. The society columns said she had entered the great man's life with all her charm and vital energy—in her late thirties—and a sense of humor.

When the Gilbert family crisis began, Lemon Gilbert was finishing her freshman year in college. Her dad did not have it in his heart to make her marry General Doan; it may have been her tears, it may have been Newell's threats; or perhaps a frown Joey gave him when their paths crossed: a new note in their relations. In any case Emory, true liberal in this as all else, didn't find the grit to carry through such a plan; it was not a Doan deal.

And so the Rock Castle was empty when Joey and Carlyne came south in the fall of '69 eager for a life of honest toil, a return to the land. They settled in with the small girl named Rhoda Strong. And together for a few months they knew a kind of happiness even despite Carlyne's moods and Joey's bad nights. From dawn to dusk that man hitched his demon to a plough, and wore out his pain, and self-torture.

Cindy Phillips, the family's faithful servant for forty minus one years, came back to help them. She didn't want to. She said she was getting old, and she was. She was enjoying life as a grandmother, and also a great grandmother. But she came to the Rock Castle part-time for a few hours because she loved Carlyne, and she couldn't say no to Jojo whom she'd known from the crib. Oh! Such things she had seen happen in this erratic Gilbert clan, the adults and the young'uns. What a scene was sure to occur when the passionately jealous Wilhelmina pitched one of her fits! The whole town said Wilhelmina's moonshine tippling made her lose control: as she stewed over some peccadillo new or old of the town's holiest sinner, namely her husband P. Laster, the radio preacher. Well, they were an ambitous bunch, the Gilberts. And they got themselves in a scrape now and again because they could do it: with all the airs they put on.

Three days a week Cindy came to the Rock Castle to help out in the kitchen and show the young couple a thing or two about keeping house. But she said it was the last year. She did it more for Carlyne who was like a niece to her. Cindy passed for wise; she knew how to weigh this against that and the other thing. She remembered when Carlyne went away after New Year's of '68, and the trip to Bangkok. And she watched her now: how she was brave, and pitched in and shared her husband's work all day, and had joy and sadness in her eyes. No saint, that one, but she had character. How low she could talk sometimes, lawdy! And how high she could do.

VIII

Emory always hoped his younger son would help revive the Gilbert farmlands. He didn't think of Jojo, the ballplayer, in this respect. During his stay here Newell took a theoretical interest in farming, as he did everything else; but there was no getting him to pick up a hoe when his hands were full of Hegel. The one thing he and Emory agreed on was that their fertile acreage far out to the Yadkin River could produce well and maybe have a bonanza.

Joey spent a few boyhood summers tramping around this farm. Those were good times, age eight, nine . . . so he knew something about it; or let's say he had a bit of the farmer in his blood. His ancestors were farmers, and preachers. Now he planned more emphasis than his forbears ever placed on labor-intensive, but high value per acre, tobacco, both burley and flue-cured. From boyhood he recalled area growers prepping the plant bed sites in the fall; but he wasn't here in those cold February days when farmhands seeded the beds and covered them with plastic. It was in late April when the men transplanted flue-cured tobacco seed-lings to the fields, and later in May the burley crop. In July after a 10-week maturation period the fieldworkers topped the blos-soms and removed the lateral shoots which were called suckers. While in Vietnam Joey thought of all this with nostalgia. There were twenty or so salable leaves per stalk ripening from green to yellow in the southern summer. And then came the harvest and placement in racks for the cure—a bright golden color 'fixed' on the leaves tied in great sheets of 180 pounds each for the sale.

In thought sometimes, like a coach going over his roster, he would take care to assign staggered vegetable plantings for the non-tobacco fields. In the cooler months collards, mustard greens, asparagus, cabbage, beets, broccoli . . . In his mind Joey tended to them like his children, and Carlyne was by his side: during long humps across the hostile land where he had been sent not to make healthy things to eat but war on the people.

In camp at night Joey fantasized his wife's loveliness but also the family they would raise together along with bumper crops of corn and cucumbers, eggplants, snapbeans, peas. Yes; he had farming in his blood and so he cultivated things in his thoughts; and he saw in his mind's eye the tender plants flower and ripen, as the warm months were filled with a steady activity. The long fertile rows went out to the river: rows of nutritious sweet potatoes which were his second crop after tobacco. There were abundant harvests of squash, okra, cantaloupes, watermelons. With seasonal labor contracted from Puerto Rico or Mexico he might make a go: if he was tough enough, efficient, and didn't get too moralistic about the effects of tobacco on human beings. Maybe later drop the money crop? But now, besides Carlyne's support, he needed a firm and reliable foreman: this he knew from chatting with other Piedmont farmers.

The foreman would be himself, at least for starters, working there with them like they were his squad. And he wouldn't drive them to the limit while pinching pennies and squeezing every cent he could out of them. No. Make sure they had money to send back home to their families. And he would be the leader, and work as hard as they did. And smart, educated Carlyne would help with the accounts, and phone calls: all the entrepreneurial side.

The old Gilbert farm lain fallow for decades might produce beautifully. Again and again as he plodded kliks south of Buon Me Thuot or waited for the day of discharge in the RevDev ville, Joey's thoughts went back to farming in North Carolina and the fields of golden tobacco: the bright leaf turned yellow from the bottom up when they cropped off the ripe ones and strung up the bundles on 'sticks'; when they took the sticks into hot 160°-heated barns where the stems dried, and the tobacco 'killed out', cured. And then straight it went to the grader bench, as in long ago days of his boyhood . . . North Carolina produced two-thirds of the nation's flue-cured tobacco, and ranked first in yam production. But yams were good for you, and tobacco was not. Tobacco gave pleasure though . . . hm. While overseas Joey had thought and thought: what to do when he got home and found his wife, and went to the Rock Castle and set to working the land.

Newell couldn't see himself as any foreman over Chicano
fieldworkers. But Joey would take to it. Newell scoffed at money-
grubbing and pointed out the economic contradictions of exploit-
ing immigrant labor. The hippie launched into a diatribe to agitate his backward father; he shot off salvos from Preobrazhensky
about Tsarism and the Russian peasantry.

But Joey just thought about how he and Carlyne might make
a go of it.

IX

Newell had gone underground.

He slipped from view when he heard what his dad was up to.
He didn't feel he needed locking up in a psych ward for his own
and society's well-being.

Newell wrote his brother an epistle on farming which shows
the man of letters *en herbe:*

> *'Somewhere on Earth?*
> *January 1970.*

Salve, Gladiator.

Retarius, naked with net and trident, went up against the
heavily armored Mirmillo whose helmet is fish-crested. Heu.

I read with relish (from my Francefarter, on a pun) of your
World Series victory and then unsportsmanlike conduct. Rome
grants you no Triumph, but I commend you on your broken oath:
the *auctora mentum gladiatorum* which Marcus Aurelius would
abolish. To Tartarus with the oblong shield, the visored helmet and
short sword, proh!

O Spartacus: wage your Servile War, if you must. Thracian and
Samnite, Celt, Germanic renegade, condemned criminal and slave,
comrades! Turn your curved scimitar and shield on the savage
beast, Capital.

Heu.

Meanwhile, Cincinnatus (not Reds, but Lucius Quinctius) cries
out like a home plate ump: Pitch hay!

The ancients hated pro baseball; that is to say, occupations, trade. Agriculture they held in high esteem: *No Roman citizen permitted to earn a living as tradesman or artisan.* (Dionysius of Halicarnassus, Roman Antiquities, Bk. IV, Ch. 25.) The basis of plebs as a class of sodbreakers is indicated in their quiritary property.

Antiquity saw husbandry as the proper job for a free man, and the school of soldiers. It was on farms that the nation's ancestral stock sustained itself; whereas alien merchants and dealers settled in the cities; they were drifters bent on gain. The freedmen who were dollar-slaves, not the citizens, amassed riches.

And today?

Giant agribusiness—monopolies—gobble up small farmers despite the myth of free competition.

Four firms sell 90% of breakfast cereals. Twenty supermarket chains sell 40% of all food. Two huge companies share 50% of U.S. grain exports, which is a lot since U.S. exports 36% of wheat traded worldwide, 64% of corn, barley, sorghum, and oats; 40% of soybeans, 17% of rice. Those two set prices and have a virtual monopoly control.

Good luck!

Local yokel, you sit down for Sunday dinner, and say the blessing. Thank ITT for providing your Smithfield ham. Thank Greyhound Corporation for the turkey, Dow Chemical for the succulent lettuce, Boeing Company for potatoes, Tenneco for fresh fruits and vegetables. It's American Brands applesauce, Coca-Cola and RC Cola fruit juices . . . Say there, Farmer Brown, dig in!

On the supply side, you must buy farm implements and fertilizers from monopolies such as International Harvester: at fixed prices no matter what the current demand. Yet a depressed economy will lower your profits: even as middlemen, canners, packers and distributors controlled by conglomerates, jack up their take to 60¢ on the food dollar, and retail mark-ups rise while you go bankrupt.

Good deal!

There are 2/3^{rds} less farms in the U.S. since 1945, though land in tillage is the same.

Three packers slaughter over 80% of U.S. beef.

2% of farms, the huge ones, sell 50% of all produce sold; while 73% of farms, smaller ones, do 9%.

The average farm gets only 14% of its income from the farm. 22% of farm households live below the poverty line.

Carry on, gladiator. You offered your blood to the Coliseum sand, in Etrurian funeral games, but Fate saved you for the filthy pigsty of business.

If you get up early enough in the morning, and go to bed late enough at night, then you may make money—if your hoe strikes oil on your land.

Our forefathers were farmers from N.A. Gilbert down to the gentleman farmer P. Laster with his red tractor parked outside First National City Bank building up town.

Well, go hog wild. Reclaim the land, but please don't exploit or mistreat the seasonal workers, like Juanchi who had the bad luck to be in love with Massa's daughter.

Best regards to Carlyne, and to Rhoda whom I haven't met yet, and to our sister Lemon at college.

Vale faveque,

Son of Fulvius
(whose father had him put
to death for joining the
revolt of Catiline).

P.S.—I pursue my studies while living on a crust. Anger macro and micro: ira facit poetam, heu.

X

Joey took to the hard work. He throve on it. Physical pain relieved the mental, as he yoked his post-traumatic stress to the gruelling round. Also, he dug into his own funds after signing a partnership agreement with his father.

In April he began to hire farmhands and put in crops. The former squad leader toiled like an ox alongside Mexican field workers. He was so gung-ho, he left them behind and didn't notice. But he treated the men with respect, and paid better rates than competitors.

Once the land was cleared, they sowed the far fields. The long seeded furrows ran perpendicular to the river; it was a pretty sight. Through the strenuous day Joey had a curt word here and there; he didn't spoil them; but Carlyne did. For she was playing her role as farmer's wife to a tee. And the thermos and snacks she brought them at ten, then again at three, hit the spot on cold early spring days while they worked planting collards, mustard greens, asparagus. With Cindy's help she got up the legendary meals that are proper to a farm. And, as a young homemaker under Cindy Phillips' guidance she kept the Rock Castle clean and tidy, and made it good living. In her heart of hearts she only wanted to raise kids and take in stray pets for the next fifty years or so. Despite her trials, the ordeal in bed at night, she kept a pleasant disposition.

Joey went to consult with other Davidson County farmers. They talked crops and fertilizers, machinery, markets. He was learning fast from the older, established men aided over the years by the banker P. Laster. He met farmers' sons who were more active now than their dads. And then after getting advice he entered contractual agreements with produce and grain distributors, and tended to a hundred other business details, along with Carlyne. It was all new to them.

Up North playing baseball he liked to get up late. But down here he was riding his tractor around the small southern town at daybreak, and taking care of many things to do with the new life.

Carlyne had a good hand, clear and neat, as she learned to keep account books and files for the various aspects of a farm. She wrote out the weekly payrolls. In those weeks as she gained in authority she became a lady: still a mite rough round the edges, and apt to swear if you didn't mind your manners, but softer and more gracious.

She showed no end of patience toward Jo and the men. When they tracked in mud, she could fold her arms across her chest, and tap a foot with a show of sternness. But it was half in mockery at herself playing the mistress.

Yes, she was taking heart. It was hard, and she didn't get much sleep. But hope was seeping in.

Joey and Carlyne walked out together in the gathering twilight. They strolled along the dusty farm roads as the evening shadows drew over the land. They went amid the calm rustle of a field of oats; it was good to look at crops growing in long furrows to the river.

Back in the Rock Castle Cindy was getting Rhoda ready for bed. But out here the young couple walked hand in hand, like a pair of shy teenagers, acting like nothing had ever happened. Maybe they gave a laugh at this or that; though the light at dusk, and river breeze across the fields, and the quiet before night came on, and a few stars twinkling in the eastern sky—all had a kind of solemnity.

XI

Then, one early morning, Joey Gilbert kissed his wife's cheek, and walked out into the warm sunlight. He didn't come home for lunch. For thirty hours he was not seen by anyone including the field hands who went to a sector and worked on their own.

Carlyne was going through hell. She didn't know what to do, and she didn't dare call or tell anyone. Max Doan? Bishop Commynes? It wasn't likely she would turn to either of them.

She was alone. Not quite ready to bother Lydia in New York, she went about her day in a trance of anxiety. Carlyne gave the hired men their meals, talked over the day's task, and told them what to do while making up a story about Joey. Then she waited out the hours.

Where had he gone? And why? What was happening—to go away like this? Not a word, not a sign, so suddenly! Was it a bad relapse of the PTSD? Or a new, more advanced stage? A psychosis declaring itself?

Should she call in the town police? . . . Carlyne wrung her hands and went from worry to anger and suspicion to a rage like that of the jealous Wilhelmina who once ruled the roost here. Ah! So the bum ran off to Manhattan on me, and into the waiting arms of his refined Lydia? Couldn't even leave his lawful wife a note to let her know he was skipping out. Alright, so it didn't work out for us again last night; I guess I was jeering you pretty bad, poking your ribs and whatnot; but is that any reason to go flying off like a bat out of hell?

Did I do something wrong, Jo? Has something gone wrong that I don't know about? I'm sorry! Only please come back, come home, my darling, and take me out of this anguish.

She remembered how her ancestor Henry Berry Lowry vanished one day, went away, out of sight of men's eyes, and was never seen again.

XII

After breakfast Joey had gone out into the warm, sunny spring day, and found a wilted rose taped to the windshield of his tractor. The red rose had a note with it: a folded card with no return address, and not signed. The few typed lines had an official air. He read them. Then he got down from the John Deere.

He sat in his truck a moment, rereading the anonymous letter:

'Go ask Cindy Phillips who is the biological father of your child. Ask her about the second key. Then go to P. Laster's office in the bank building, and look in the bottom drawer on the left of his desk.'

Slowly Joey drove his van down the driveway in back of the Rock Castle. He didn't feel like himself after the first jolt. But he kept his presence of mind, and he was thinking: this anonymous letter can't be so anonymous—to know about Cindy and some sort of second key and to know of Granddaddy's office up town and his desk . . . Slowly, still in first gear, Joey turned left at the foot of the sloping driveway. He went to the corner and pulled out into the main street, then right down a gradual hill half a mile to where the more well-off black families had their homes.

Cindy's descendants were playing on the lawn, and she was inside. She always had a smile for Joey, but this one was blent with a note of concern. She invited him in, and they settled in the living room.

—You okay, Mister Jo?

She picked that up from Carlyne: Mister Jo. The womenfolk were pleased with him. And during these months at the Rock Castle she had been happy in Carlyne's and his happiness. It was an act of kindness on her part, and not only, to come out of retirement and go there part-time and help them.

—No.

—Why not?

Joey sat in silence a moment: staring at her so she didn't want to hold his gaze. He was stunned. He was strange.

—Look at me now, and answer.

Cindy's eyes narrowed, just a bit.

—What is this tone, Sir?

—How long have you worked for us?

—Since 1930.

—And you've always been faithful. That's what the Gilberts say: faithful Cindy.

Brow knit, she said softly:

—I've tried to help.

—Be faithful now, please, and tell me the truth.

—What truth?

She looked at him—the tic on his cheek. And sort of hunched, stricken, he was, like a fox dragging a trap. His dark eyes might roll up, if he let them.

—Were you at the Rock Castle when Carlyne came to live there?

—Of course. You know that.

—And what were you doing?

—Cooking meals for you Gilberts, cleaning house.

—Were you close to my wife?

—Oh, yes. You know I love Carlyne. And she always wanted to help me.

—Did you work at night too? Were you at the Rock Castle in the evening?

—S-sometimes. Why, Jo?

—Only this . . . that . . .

From the side pocket of his olive drab jacket Joey took the wilted rose with the folded card. In his fist he crushed the rose and tossed it in a wastepaper basket. He handed her the note. He waited as she read. Then asked:

—What about the second key?

—I don't know what he means.

—He? Who is he?

—I don't know.

—Listen to me, Cindy, now listen—

Joey sat forward. There was that about him, a threatening thing in his posture, and words, which made her say:

—What have I done wrong?

His stare seemed to nail her to a stake. Children's voices came from the yard, but he didn't hear them. He said low, in a tone like a warning:

—Nothing. But now I mean to know. And you are going to tell me. Tell it: the second key.

Her gaze fell. She shook her head:

—I do know who this note is from. I think so. It's that sick man, who snoops in other people's business.

—What man?

—Pastor Commynes. He's your father's childhood friend and acts like his friend now. Listens to his high affairs and such, I guess his secrets. But he hates the Gilberts. Hates you, all of you. But Emory doesn't know, or won't see it.

—Hates why?

—Because of P. Laster's . . . because of . . . Look, the whole town knows this, Jojo, but maybe you don't know it.

—What?

—Your grandfather was Paulie Commynes' biological father, like this note says here. And he's carried that around with him all his life. And he still wants revenge!

—Revenge for what?

—For his own birth, if that's what it is. He felt humiliated or something to have P. Laster as his father.

—Being a bastard.

—Well not exactly. He had a legal father too, but the man went away. It was in the first year of P. Laster's marriage to Wilhelmina. So . . .

—So what?

—I can see why, maybe.

—How do you know all this? Did my grandparents tell you?

—No, boy. I'm the hired help. You don't tell such things to a colored woman who comes to make your beds.

—Then how do you know?

—I know because I had to listen to their arguments for over thirty years. Mama Gilbert pitched him many a fit, and she got good and drunk on her moonshine from the still she kept down cellar, and those two had violent arguments, bad ones. Once a year your grandfather went and got himself checked in the hospital for a rest. In the end he died of a stroke, as you know.

Joey did know, but his thoughts were only half there. He sat looking jolted. His eyes did roll up now.

Again the silence came over them, but it was like a voice shouting, with a menace in it.

XIII

Now he came back to her. He said:

—Now listen, Cindy, and I mean it. You say my father doesn't know? Well I'm tired of not knowing what means most to me. And now I will know, because you're going to tell me, or else. Did Carlyne, when she was here, ever sleep with my brother?

—Oh no, Mister Jo. God forbid! She loved Newell.

—They were often together. Long talks, long walks out to the river.

—That's true. But not . . . never.

—Lemon told me they went places, in the woods—

—But not in her room, not the guest bedroom, she saw to it! No, you're on the wrong track there. And I'm in a way to know it.

—How?

—We talked. Women talk. Cooking, doing chores. Carlyne helped me, said she liked it; the Rock Castle was her house too. No, Sir! She and Newell would never . . . She told me what he said: it was a promise. And Newell may be a crazy guy, but he's funny about promises, he keeps them. And that way he made her feel at ease; she loved and trusted him for it. I know this is true because she said so, and the way she said so, confiding in me. No, Jo. No man made love to Carlyne while she was here, and I am sure.

—Prove it. Tell me about the second key.

—Second key? . . . Oh. Well, you know, there was men about the place. And she trusted her brother-in-law but she didn't trust Master Doan for all he's in his sixties. Plus she was afraid of that strange Commynes, so starchy but eyes like a devil, on her. And then, you know, Carlyne being beautiful she got to not going up town since more than once some man took a notion and touched her, brushed against her, even followed her home. She got to only going out if she was escorted by one of her menfolk, Emory or Newell. Carlyne is modest, and careful. She is. Your wife loves you, Joey. Respect her, take care of her. I never saw a woman more careful about such things.

—The second key.

—Ah. There were men around. Doan and Commynes stayed late chatting in Granddaddy's den. Doan slept overnight sometimes when Emory was away: as a favor, you know. Kind of keeping an eye out; but I don't trust him either, the way he ogles Lemon. Well, Carlyne would lock her bedroom door at night when she turned in. Nobody else had the key.

—Nobody had it . . . Where'd she get it?

—Why, your daddy gave it to her. Had an extra one made for her.

—No one had the key except Carlyne and my father?

—Only those two. So you see your fears are groundless. Only Emory had that key. I know because he and I had a good laugh about it one morning when I was making Carlyne's bed and found a key in the sheets. She was so careful she would sleep with that thing.

—She . . . she needed it to lock herself in?—Joey was pale as a sheet.—Was it her key or my father's you found?

—Hers.

—I see.

—Not Newell nor anybody else made love to your wife.

—How did Pastor know about it . . . to write this note?

—Your dad must have told him. He tells him a lot of things during their late night talks. And that man saves 'em up, and waits.

Joey sat deep in thought. He stared past her.

There were birds chirping, and the children's voices at play. Lint sifted, peacefully, in a column of golden sunlight from the living room window.

Joey gave a shiver. He was white as a ghost. And what he did

next came straight from Vietnam: from Phoenix Program operatives at work in the villages getting names of VC cadre and sympathizers, by guile, or by force. He knew of CIA-AID tactics, and
the intelligence platoons. Now he took out that bag of tricks and
used one on Cindy.

From the vest of his military surplus jacket with its pockets
he drew a gun: .45-caliber service revolver. And he pointed it at
Cindy Phillips' forehead, and said nothing.

She began to tremble, and said:

—Are you going to shoot an old woman?

—Yes, if you don't tell me the truth. And not only you.

—Who?

—Your great grandchildren out there, one by one, then you,
and then myself.

—Oh, don't.

—I've been kept in the dark by everybody for over two years:
since October '67 when I was overseas and my wife stopped writing and I didn't know why. Now I'm tired of it. Now you tell me:
who screwed my wife at the Rock Castle? Who is the real father
of Rhoda?

Cindy sat in silence. She looked at him, and shook. Couldn't
she talk?

He helped her. He stood up, went over by the window, and took
aim. Still she didn't speak. And he cocked the pistol—cli-ick!

Then she said, in a broken voice, like hiccups:

—If only I had died that night.

—That'll come soon enough if you don't tell the truth.

—I'll die even sooner if I talk.

—Stop stalling. Out with it, that's all.

—I don't . . . I can't let you hurt them.

—Now I'll count to five, and then I'll start shooting. One . . .
two . . . three . . . four . . .

—No! No!—She stood up.—I'll tell you, Mister, but don't ask
me! It's awful, it's too awful.

He lowered the gun. But she only shook her head.

He aimed it again, squinting.

—Four and a half. Like rabbits. Don't make me ask you
again—

—Oh! oh! This is the worst. This is the most terrible thing for
me to say.

—And me to hear. But say it now. Don't wait! Four and three-quarters . . . I'm pulling the trigger—

—Okay! No! I'll say it! No, Joey, no! . . . It . . . it was Emory, he's the one. Your father went in to Carlyne. He had her.

XIV

Joey walked out of the house and got in his van. He turned over the ignition, and he was thinking: so it's clear now. And Rhody doesn't look like me; she has the lighter features of . . . I thought like Newell, but even more like Emory. Ah, so that's why Carlyne said she left the Rock Castle in February, lying about it, and my father lied too in agreement with her. She really left in early January, like Cindy and Lemon said, telling the truth. She had to go since the pregnancy was beginning to show: the child conceived not in December with me in Bangkok, but last fall, in September, *with my father* . . .—And he repeated the words in his mind:—*with my father.*

He drove to the First National City Bank building. It was closed for business since five years ago. Emory Gilbert still occupied his father's office.

Joey had the key to P. Laster's old third floor office with him. And, after nodding to a security guard, he took the steps.

Inside the executive suite of the deceased bank director there was a musty smell, dust, books and file folders, papers. But it was tinged with something else. He knew that acrid odor. What was it? Where did it come from? It was familiar, as death in life . . . The place had been closed, the windows shut for months. With Emory away in D.C. nobody used these rooms, and Cindy didn't come to clean them.

In the inner room was P. Laster's desk.

Joey Gilbert went to it and opened the bottom door on the left—as the anonymous note said. As he did so the scent was a bit keener; it came from here. Inside he found a crumpled brown paper bag.

And in the bag—what? a dead rat?

A piece of note paper fell out: nice stationery, which Joey gave his wife before he went away to war. On the fine paper with a tracery of flowers and stems intertwined, he read a few lines of handwriting:

> 'This is me. This is what you did to me, Father—your daughter-in-law, who believed in you. Look at your work. I return your brooch to you.'

Carlyne wrote that. No mistake: it was her handwriting.

Joey held up the paper bag and looked in it. There was something dark inside with an odor, a distant sort of tinge. It was a dry smell now, as of something long after, not the full putrid smell of a rotten thing. The decay was done, but the bad scent still tinged the stuffy air in the office.

And then with two fingers he pulled that object out.

It was hair.

It was long, jet black hair with a sheen to it, and streaks of blood turned to a powder. Vietnamese hair: it was from the young woman cadre of the Chignon Battalion—the one Joey killed on the trail that night. And he gave it like an Indian scalp to Carlyne in Bangkok. Merry Christmas. What ever possessed him to do that? Anger at her . . . And she didn't throw his trophy down the toilet in the Hotel Victoria, but instead brought it back here and made use of it in her own way. She too gave it as a Christmas present: to another man.

The wrinkled paper bag might have been thrown in the trash basket and then taken out again. By Commynes?

Joey glanced at the note again. *This is me* . . . He gazed as if from afar at the rich shiny black hair on the desk before him: the chignon with its bloodstains turned to dust. *Look at your work.*

He picked it up and held it a moment in his fingers. He dropped it on the blotter, but picked it up again. He could tell the cameo brooch—ah! his father's gift—the brooch had been used as a hairpin, by Carlyne, for this strange still life. But it was gone now.

XV

Back in the pickup truck Joey drove from the wide parking lot, past the police station, and on around through the old center of town. Slowly he went by those storefronts like a cluster of moldy grapes. At the main intersection he turned left and rode alongside the raised train tracks past blocks of red-brick furniture plant and on to the cemetery with its low wall.

It was noontime, and the factory hooter gave its shrill blast, sending the workers to lunch. Joey Gilbert didn't hear it. He only drove: not knowing where to go—not the Rock Castle, not yet. He didn't want or dare to see his wife. He was numbed by the shame and grief; but he was still himself, and afraid he would go too far, and hurt her badly. He feared to confront Carlyne at home now—and shoot her and the child, conducting his own Phoenix Program to root out traitors. And he just kept thinking, his head in a daze: *With my father! . . . See your work, Father? . . .* The truth was a blinding blur.

So he decided not to head straight for the Rock Castle.

He drove out toward the river and an old swimming hole where he used to go as a boy. The truck raised dust along a farm road amid fragrant newly cultivated fields far out by the Yadkin. It all looked so neat, so good. Man's toil.

Many summers ago as boys they used to swing on a rope tied to a bough over the sunlit stream. Now he had a coil of rope in the back, and he wanted to hang himself from that overhanging bough. That was a good idea, and apropos—enough of this: be done with this foolishness. Let his wife and father and the others go on with their life of lies if that's what they liked. *With my father.*

Through the night he sat staring at the darkness: like that night along a highway in . . . was it Mississippi? when he was en route to Bufillu, coming home from the war where he left his peace and his mind. Now like a perimeter guard pinned in by enemy fire, he saw no way out. Only lies, lies coiled on lies like the barbed wire round a strategic hamlet.

Joey waited, in a daze, in the onset of grief trauma.

Out there by himself in the long hours before dawn, he thought, and thought. *See your work? . . .* And he was hanging on. His mind was trying not to give way.

XVI

Dr. Falliere's secretary was still finding the quickest flight, and then transferring appointments to a standby physician, and notifying the hospital—as the psychiatrist rushed to LaGuardia and boarded a plane for Greensboro.

Dressed in a gray-blue business suit, a beige tan blouse with lace fringe at the collar, but no necklace, Lydia ran from the airline counter to the gate where crew members waited for this last passenger on a special order.

Then the airplane lifted high over Manhattan and sailed out on its course southward down the coast. To her left was blue sea. To her right lay the land in a golden mist . . . Delaware, Pennsylvania extending off into the western day. Towns dotted the landscape going a deeper green. Way down there some lights twinkled. A twilit river wended its way through blue hills maybe near Harrisburg in the distance.

The seat belt sign was off, and Lydia settled in. She said no to a cocktail but asked about dinner, and tried to relax. Night was starting to fall as they passed over the nation's capital looking like spokes, she thought, in the wheel of world history.

And she thought: freedom—consciousness of necessity. The fight to make life nicer . . . Last summer she went out to watch this man she loved do battle on a baseball diamond as the hero in a myth. Charcot's 'grande hystérie' was a sign of the times: namely a retreat. But Joey Gilbert seemed to come home carrying the war and its guilt on his lone shoulders. In just about every case when Vietnam with its flashbacks, nightmares, and kinesthetic delusions were too much for a vet's coping mechanisms, when they resulted in PTSD: then the victim suffered from estrangement, loss of capacity, a weakened interest in meaningful activity. Yet Joey went out and made war some more and had one of the great seasons. He played out his drama before packed stadiums. And while his team won the Pennant and then World Series, he bled inwardly. He took on the world, and carried his personal campaign forward, ever forward. He felt like death warmed over, but he had no choice.

In a mountain village a bomb in a shoeshine box blew G.I.s to bits. A woman and her children died in a torched hootch. A bookish buck private ended up spit naked, arms wide, on a charred bough; he seemed to soar like a Winged Victory over a joyless road southwest of the horror of Xo Man. By a midnight trail a female VC cadre gushed blood in her LURP killer's arms. Through the streets of Saigon Joey carried his buddy ruined from the waist down on the night of Tet. A bunch of pitiful, gullible young men died in a minefield out past the perimeter of the model hamlet they were trying to build.

And after that he trotted out to his position. He was plopped down at third base by the Freedom Bird, an eagle or a vulture, which brought home the Joeys, the Bufillus, and the unviewable Blairs, in its talons. At his position the magnificent athlete shook his glove at intrusive images from that other world. On third he saw such things and felt them, and him, steeped in guilt, in shame, in too much shame for a nation, let alone one man whose best hope was to forget. Though America might use the National Pastime as a collective avoidance phenomenon, a 'grande hystérie', with a built-in affective stress response . . .: Joey Gilbert remembered Vietnam. He was branded by the imprint of what he had done there: those war crimes seared in his marrow.

And so Carlyne had it right—how could he love her or anyone else when he hated and feared himself?

Would a day come, thought Lydia, when the man, and the nation, must face facts? and atone for them?

Their hard work in therapy sessions had lessened the guilt reaction to his traumatic combat experience, and the residual fear. Fear fosters guilt and guilt fear; and paranoia; but also a pleasurable sense in the possession of weapons. For a season he had played ball as a risk-related behavior, as a war. This gave him release and a grim pleasure. Each night he raped his own psyche, so to say, in atonement for what he and the others had done in Vietnam: raping the land.

Lydia had tried her best to change things for Joey. But his past actions were likely to determine his present course. An ignorance of reality, of historic necessity, is condemned to repeat. Only necessity conscious of itself is free to strive for change.

Joey didn't know it, but in this hour he was seeking a way out, tragic if need be, and a catharsis. Even so America, after the primary trauma of New World conquest, and the genocide of indigenous peoples, could find no way out besides more conquest, more

violence: the national violence of slavery, the international violence of U.S. imperialism paving the way for capitalist globalization. With such a force of ascendant bourgeoisie behind it, history's most colossal productive forces and internal market; with the
absence of any feudal background, any pre-bourgeois giddiness,
and thus a total indifference to the human element as casualty
in the worldwide war of competition;—the day was near, maybe
it was at hand, when America would astound the earth with its
energy and violence, and make the Europeans for all their wars
look like children.

And so the agony went on: the micro-agony of a Joey Gilbert,
the macro-agony of a United States. It was a long one.

The ballplayer's conquest and superstardom were the effects of
such blind forces: a reaction formation after war in Vietnam traumatized him. This system, thought Lydia, sanctions and rewards
its civilized conquerors, its corporate leaders and Presidents, its
politicians, its judges . . . academics and cultural figures, celebri-
ties. They wear blue suits, but their abreactive violence against
the weaker ones, people and nations, is a reaction formation built
into the reality of empire. So the master becomes a moral slave.
And no true culture, no science serving man, thrives in such a
land.

She recalled a Post-World War II case study of traumatic shock.
A certain soldier's physical aggressivity when he returned to civilian life was correlated with 'family frustration and deprivation
in childhood: a lifelong inability to express justified anger toward
parents'.

Happiness is the struggle to make life better.

Unhappiness is unconscious denial. It is submission.

XVII

Night marched on the land. There was a crisis underway, out
there in the darkness. So far only a few knew it.

Greensboro in ten minutes. Lydia's pulse raced. In normal
times this man wired her—and now? She tried to compose her
thoughts and settle on a plan. Get to him: inside the Rock Castle.
That was the main thing. And then? Then . . . we'll see.

So the famous father who was trusted and idealized by the dutiful son—so Emory Gilbert actually slept with Joey's wife? And now Joey found out about it? This could make a boy lose his inhibitory illusions. First he gave up his health and mental stability for the sake of a fiasco. And now this was his reward.

Well the older ones sent the younger generation to a faroff war. They were afraid of them. King Laïus in the tragedy meant to 'expose' his son Oedipus on Mount Cithaeron where the wolves would devour the infant. For an oracle told Laïus his son would kill him and marry his wife. But Laïus didn't want that; he wanted to live and enjoy the good things himself. And the same for the older ones in America, the corporate men: they wanted the land, they wanted its good things, they wanted Jocasta. For what is an oracle? It is the truth coming out somehow, devious and unclear, like the future unfolding from the human heart of things. Now the winds of change were blowing in America, winds of social conscience, winds of socialism to sweep away the old life under tragic capitalism with its threat to the planet and its Vietnams . . . But the older generation couldn't admit that, let that happen, so they ate up the younger, ate their own children. And their old way of life poisoned Earth and all the life, all the youth, all the beauty on it. This was a case of the old raping the young, Laïus raping Chrysippus; the great Emory Gilbert taking his son's wife for himself, for his own needs, while the son was sent away by the system Emory played for all it was worth . . . to die in the Central Highlands.

As the plane lost altitude toward a landing, Lydia thought of Joey in crisis. What did it mean for his superego? The tenuous social restraints they had worked so hard together to shore up—more or less out the window? He could do anything now.

Armed to the teeth he had taken a child hostage: his daughter and not his daughter. So it might turn into another Xo Man. It was a perfect metaphor for war. For his war experience.

To kill the enemy was okay. Medals were awarded for killing Vietnamese children. It roused a U.S. serviceman and no doubt it roused a nation to drop bombs on foreign cities, Hiroshima and Nagasaki, Hanoi and Haifong. Who's next? But in the last analysis those were self-destructive acts. If we destroy the future, we destroy ourselves.

And so it was that Joey Gilbert began his headlong gambit to resolve an impossible situation. For, subconsciously, he 'deserved to die for what he had done'; he had to be punished on a par with Xo Man. But not only him. And he didn't mean to go alone.

While the plane descended in the evening above North Carolina, Lydia's ears rang. On a whim she had brought the thin volume from her night table. And now, in these moments before she too went into combat, she opened it. Her eyes fell on a tragic chorus from the *Oedipus*:

> *Ioh! Human generations,*
> *I account you as though*
> *you hadn't lived.*
> *What man, what man hasn't*
> *for his greatest joy*
> *a shadow of joy that fades?*
> *By your example, O wretched Oedipus,*
> *I may not call mankind blessed.*
>
> *He aimed as high as possible*
> *and had a chance for the best success.*
> *He destroyed, O Zeus, the Sphinx,*
> *the talon'd prophetess,*
> *and rose up like a human rampart*
> *to defend the land against death.*
>
> *Then you were our king*
> *receiving supreme honors,*
> *master of great Thebes.*
> *And now who is the most suffering?*
> *Who has a worse curse,*
> *whose hardships can compare*
> *with such a reversal of life?*
>
> *Ioh! Illustrious figure, Oedipus:*
> *to go up in a same nuptial harbor*
> *it befell the son and the father?*
> *How could, how could the furrows,*
> *O wretch, of your father bear you*
> *in silence for so long?*

Like it or not you are caught
by all-seeing time, which judges
the unholy marriage and the seminal son.
Ioh Laïus' son, if only,
if only we had never known you.

Like a dirge the cry pours out
of my mouth. Truly it is you
who let me breathe
and also closed my eyes.

XVIII

The plane touched down. Lydia rushed through the terminal to a cabstand. She told a driver the name of a town thirty miles away.

There were dark streets, trees, then highway as she rode toward the meeting place of her mission as a medical doctor and a woman.

—Go as fast as you can.

Along the divided highway with its signs lit up by headlights the taxi went racing. And Lydia Falliere's heartbeat raced. In these instants she seemed to let go of her PTSD studies and daring book in progress, her scientific mind with its theoretical constructs and life of inquiry. She was a human being now in the deepest sense, a woman going to support and try to save the man she loved; and all her science was in her nerves. Still she tried to think. She had to think how to do it. Get in the house; get inside; that was all she knew.

Here was the exit ramp. So a few minutes more. And she thought: Joey came this way, twenty months ago, and he was home from the war—only to find a new war.

There were fast food places, a few gas stations. There was the usual commercial clutter which told no tale of the reality: the fuse of a potent bomb lit and hissing on a nearby street in this small southern town.

She passed the raised tracks and the long blocks of factory

plant. Old two-storey structures seemed to cower by the deserted sidewalks.

At the main intersection was a monumental chair: the emblem of this furniture town. It looked like a huge spider in the lamplight. And, further on, a low-eaved train depot huddled among the shadows.

—Let me out here, said Lydia.

Then she stepped into the silence that was more than silence. At half past nine there was no traffic here by the main intersection: what looked like a crossroads of yesteryear. There was not a soul in sight, and no sign of Carlyne Gilbert.

XIX

But she was there. She had waited out the hours on the wood platform of the old depot. And now she saw the cab come up. And Joey's psychiatrist, tallish, elegant as ever, with only an attaché case in her hand, got out like a hired gun into the lazy town on a quiet evening in springtime.

Carlyne slipped from the shadows and went to meet her. She spoke her name. The two women shook hands, and their eyes met a moment by lamplight from the intersection.

Side by side they started on the quarter mile walk to the Rock Castle. Should she take her through the fields to ensure secrecy? Lydia wore stockings and a business suit—better use a shortcut through the back streets. It wouldn't do to lead Dr. Falliere out into the fields . . . She didn't ask her.

Down a narrow alley between two stores they made their way.

—So sorry to trouble you. And so grateful.

—No need. Tell me what's going on.

—Well I was angry when he came in the house after two days gone awol. Then I saw his eyes . . . He told me he was going for a walk in the fields for an hour, and when he got back I'd better not be there. I asked him what it was about and where he'd been. When I reached to take his hand, he grabbed my arm and wrenched me to the floor. He called me a slut and said: What did you do? With his other hand he shoved a paper in my face, anonymous letter, and then a note I once wrote . . . he found it in Emory's office up town. And so I knew he knew: that I, and his father, had been lovers. I tried to defend myself and said I had no choice, a . . . a half-truth. He said: Sure, sure, you rotten whore, you had a choice! . . . How so? I cried at him. It's Emory's house; it was 2 a.m.; what do you want me to do? Call Newell for help? Call the Fire Department? . . . He gnashed his teeth and grabbed my blouse and shook me around . . . winding me. Don't talk back! He was using my breasts for a punching bag. Curse! he shouted. Slime! . . . Don't, Jo, I said. Liar! Harlot, goddamn you. And he spat on me. I writhed in his grip and tried to yank myself away and upstairs Rhoda started crying. Hold it, Jo, please . . . our daughter . . . Ha ha ha! he laughed like a madman and spat again. He kept holding me down beneath him, but I'd had about enough of that . . . Then, on my feet, I tried to hold my ground, stay inside, you know, as he dragged and manhandled me through the back porch. He threw me out on the brick walk leading to the garage and farm buildings. Joey! I cried at him on one knee, listen to me! . . . No, he said, that's it.

They walked down a back alley in the darkness.

Then Lydia gave a start. Further on she saw a man, just a pair of eyes at first: he waited at the end of the narrow passageway between two commercial buildings. It was a somber contour— tinged with pink by the police sign across the wide lot behind P. Laster's bank building.

—Hello, Mrs. Gilbert. How are you tonight?

—Hi.

—Have a visitor, do you? Out for a walk?

—Good friend from New York come to visit.

—I see. Showing your house guest the sites.

His eyes seemed to pool the gloom tinged orange-pink by that neon sign: POLICE. He took in the other woman with her short hair and intellectual air. And she looked at him. For an instant they sort of took one another's measure.

—You have a good night, Reverend.

They could feel his gaze on their backs as they walked on.

The old aristocratic sector was five minutes from up town.

—Local clergy? said Lydia.

—A sick man. He's a town joke, if it was funny. Satan cult, and so forth. I think he's the one who left the anonymous note.

—Why?

—Because he is P. Laster's bastard. He's Emory's half brother, and full of hate for Gilberts, and desire for revenge.

—That's what I call piety.

The two women walked out of the town toward the Rock Castle.

XX

On the long sloping front lawn and around the house the tall oaks rustled. Lydia looked up at the great granite facade of the old Gilbert place looming in darkness. Set back from the road, its angle turret and high parapeted balcony seemed to tilt forward over the slow gradient of the walk. It hulked up, and up, into the night sky, like it might have a great fall.

In the silence with no cars passing, and no lights about the place, there was an ominous sense. The window casements had a way of looking down at the everyday goings-on of the town.

Carlyne frowned:

—I hope he's been feeding Rhody.

Beside her Lydia's brow was knit, but she didn't frown. There was an air about this manor house built in stone—as if it didn't care a whit for her science and her treatment techniques. What big and very, very difficult situation had taken generations to come to a crisis behind those massive walls? It was larger than life, like in tragedy. Before the porch stood an ancient oak with tree-sized runners from its gray roots and trunk.

—I have to go in there, she said.

—Here's my key.

—Better if he opens. But alright . . . You'll hear me telling him why I'm here, what I'm doing.

—I tried to phone. He's not picking up.

—While I try to get inside to him, you go behind the house and wait. No one must see you; it's too bad that other one saw us.

—If there's movement, if Jo's surprised, he could shoot.

—I know. He'll have guns.

—An arsenal. Could be. Trucks have come here with crates. He says it's farm equipment, but he has them brought in a Dutch door on the side of the house. There's a circular room he keeps locked beneath the turret.

—Explosives?

—Who knows. He's had money to spend with the World Series check.

—You don't have the key?

—No.

XXI

Lydia made her way up the long front walk. Her first steps were not so sure; but on she went, nearing the wide front porch. Now she could see the old place looked neglected; it was dark, but there was a sense of decay—in the window embrasures, in the gables high overhead.

Step by step she drew closer. Day after day he was in her thoughts: now she braced for their first meeting since last October. She spent her life amid the family conflicts of others, but it seemed all her fine-tuned methodology was not worth a sigh.

Go up the porch steps, and open the heavy oak door. Gain entry.

A twig snapped beneath her feet. To her right the huge oak stood with its trunk gaping: hollowed out by disease. Could it have died? Its leaves still murmured of life; its hoary bark with a profusion of ivy and other growths was like a patriarch with eros.

Lydia's heightened senses had a poignant sharpness: far from Manhattan, in a fragrant May night in the South.

Onto the wide front porch she went with its Romanesque arches. This house had pretense, a false grandeur, hubris. She took a deep breath and rang the bell.

By the front door she listened. Inside it was quiet. There was a grandfather clock in the front hall. Tick . . . tock.

When the doorbell chime drew no response, she said:

—Joey? It's Lydia. I'm here. I think we need to talk. Are you okay?

More silence: it lasted ten, fifteen seconds, as she cleared her throat for another try.

Then his voice. Just inside the door:

—I'm not talking anymore.

—I know, I understand. But still we should put our heads together. Don't shut me out, Joey. Let me be part of what you're
going through.

—Did my wife call you? To come all the way down here? That's
typical. She makes an unholy mess, and asks you to come clean
up the filth.

—You've never shut us out, Joey. It's your nature to let people
in. I admire you.

—You admire a donkey.

Lydia paused. She might have to can the psychiatrist crap, as
he would say, and try it a different way. Now there was no use for
scruples—he must be saved from himself. She could seduce him;
she could play the trump of her womanhood. And never mind
about his wife, either, who would have to understand. Extreme
measures for extreme situations. Yes; give herself to the man who
was in an agony of impotence. He felt the world was against
him, and first of all himself: ever since his combat experience and
the things he did during the war, which he couldn't get over, or
forgive.

Now Lydia Falliere was ready. She would sacrifice herself if
necessary, like the time he nearly raped her during a session;
though it wasn't the idea.

Her voice was low. Luckily there were no close neighbors.

—You know what I feel about you. I feel the thing your squad
felt during the worst times in the bush. When you're hurting, you
play your best for others' sake. That's why we love you so.

—A fool's game. Love is fine for donkeys.

—Then I'm a donkey, because I love you.

—Fool loves fool.

—You're the furthest thing from a fool. You deserve love. And I
would do anything for you to live and be strong and happy.

—Don't make me laugh.

—You told me as a child you felt shut out in your family. You
were hurting, but you kept on and you said yes, yes, I want to
live, I want love. You worked through all that pain on your own.
You didn't want to give in to anger at Newell, your brother, who
was your mom's favorite.

—I could stand that, but not this.

—This too. You can stand this because you have me now. I am yours and it's for life, Joey. I'm with you.

There was silence as he thought about this. Her tone, the words she said took him aback, a new element.
—Anyway . . .
—What?
—It's not revenge I want, but . . .
—What? Tell me.
—I don't know. I want the past not to exist.
—We can understand it, and use it to change the present.
—I don't see how. Filth is filth.
—You know it's not that simple. Much is healthy and hopeful: about you and your family too. We'll ally ourselves with the good part, and work to heal you and better the situation. It is possible.
—You're dreaming.
—No, I'm hoping. Together, yes, we can make a new start. Decide, Joey, live. Life will be so good. Don't cash in your chips when the game is just beginning. That's not your way.
There was a pause. Then beyond the door his voice sounded boyish:
—Bring my father here. I want a talk with him.
—We will. We'll bring Emory to you. He must be suffering too: think what he must feel—
—Feel! That's rich.
At mention of Emory there was such a tension. It was beyond measure, and ready to erupt. Lydia spoke to it:
—He'll have to look his acts in the face. We need to worry about ourselves . . . and the worst is over now; the thing is known. Our job is to get through this difficult moment together.
—I know what I have to do.
By the door Lydia was quiet. It would be a mistake if her tone pleaded, or offered a nuance of resistance. She took the plunge and said:
—It's chilly out here. Can I come in?
—Why? So I can hear more of that stuff? A walking psych book! Him, you, Newell: all the eggheads ready to change the world with blah-blah. So long as it doesn't cost them anything.
She thought: good, let him talk, and disburden. But he stopped. So she said, quietly:

—I came here.

—It's no skin off your asses, just mine and Bufillu's. Wow, freedom and democracy: just kill enough of the little fuckers, then
they'll be free. The honchos like my old man go on TV and feel
good about themselves. But the grunt gone mad gets stashed
away somewhere safe. Comes home with cancer from Agent Orange, and they tell him it must be a mistake. Believe in a lie all
your life, and die a sucker.

He laughed low.

Lydia leaned forward to hear the words sounding sort of
spooked inside the door. Then she said:

—There's nobody here but us. We'll have to sink or swim together. I'm not talking like an intellectual now; I'm here and I'm
in it with you. I wish you'd invite me in. But, if not, I have a key,
and I mean to use it. I didn't come here from New York to stand
out in the cold.

—No, sir.

—Also, please know I'm not doing this as a doctor, but as a
woman. You see, I need you to be alive. I need to love a live Joey
Gilbert, if you don't mind.

—No one comes in. Don't try it. I have a gun.

—I know you have a gun, but I am coming in. Shoot me if you
have to. Then you'll at least know this life isn't all bad, if someone
loved you that way: until the end . . . Now I'm putting the key in,
Jo. I'm inserting it.

He said:

—You open that door, and . . . I'm sorry, but I'll blow your head
off.

She heard a small sort of sob. She said:

—Go ahead. You've been provoked. You have good reason.

—I mean it. Don't open.

—Go on, Jo. Shoot. This little fucker forgives you.

She turned the key. C-c-click.

XXII

When Lydia Falliere pushed forward the front door of the Rock
Castle, it gave a whine in the quiet night.

Inside, in the front hall, he stood pointing a semiautomatic rifle at her. He meant to make his last stand—but backing off, at sight of this woman more terrible than a VC, because she loved him. Right now he was no longer the glorious baseball star, but a guiltsick, confused, enraged war veteran with an M-16 in his hand, and fear on his face.

To open a door: was it the last act of her life? She thought: This is his League I'm playing in; be cocky and brash? And so she said, softly, and maybe it saved her:

—Here I am, troop. Blow my egghead off.

He was back in his survival mindset. Kill, kill. This instant he could be hallucinating the violent images he saw nearly three years ago when a helicopter pilot read enemy activity on the ground and told greenhorn replacement troops to run like hell and stay low and not feel unduly concerned by loss of bladder or bowel control.

The front door stuck a bit, but then opened further. It was her turn now. The elegant woman went into combat. She did this not because she hated but because she loved; not for someone else's interests but for her own.

Joey had painted his face like a LURP. The two eyes met hers. It was the 100-yard stare. Yes, he was afraid; she could see the fear clear as day behind his green and black facial paint, as he made a retreat up the wide carpeted stairway. Then he took a half-crouched position with his assault rifle aimed at her. Dressed in his jungle fatigues, and the gnarled muddy boots he wore home and kept as a memento; his face painted up for a search and de-stroy mission in the small southern town; Joey waited. He was alone. He was a LURP behind enemy lines, and this enemy was the most terrible—for she was in his blood, and if he hurt her then what name could he call her to make it okay? A gook?

Staring at her from his position on the stairs, he looked . . . what? Mad, macabre. What a jolt he had taken, the final blow. And now his eyes were filled with a depthless darkness after the recognition scene, the tragic anagnorisis: like the eyes of Oedipus spurting blood on his beard after he put them out with his wife-mother's brooch. And it wasn't only one who came to ruin; it was the ruin of two, the man and the woman . . . But in Joey Gilbert's case the end hadn't come yet. It took a lot to break him. Another would have folded long before this. Three weeks ago Lydia was called for a consult when a returned vet in Maryland threw furniture and television out an upstairs window, smashed things up, and smeared blood from his gashed arm on the bathroom mirror. Then he shot at neighbors and the police: all without an apparent precipitating stressor.

In the darkness the clock ticked.

—Alright, stop there.

On the bottom step she looked up and ran a hand through her short curly hair. In these moments her features had an aura: a person triumphantly in love, at last able to give herself fully, in conscience. She paused to let him get used to her. She said:

—Hello.

Then, for a good minute, he didn't answer. He sited her down the barrel of his gun held in one hand.

At last he said:

—Well, you've got some balls on you.

Lydia knelt on the steps to catch her breath.

XXIII

Tick, tock. A car passed in the street outside.

—How've you been?

—In the pink. Just keep away from me.

His voice croaked.

—But the child, Jo? Is she okay?

—Rhody stays here.

—I know. But have you fed her?

—Do you hear her crying?

Lydia nodded. Getting inside was a victory, and so was staying there: minute after minute. Carlyne would just have to wait outside, all night if necessary; it was time to have faith. Besides the three of them nobody else knew of this standoff. Right?

—How do you feel? she said. Do you have pain?

—Stage Four.

His voice was distant, like a pebble tossed in an empty tank.

—No, she said. It's Three. The crucial stage: if we can get through this . . .

The four stages: a diagnostic indicator which they used half in jest during their New York sessions. Three, not Four—there was still a prognosis; you could still bet on Joey Gilbert. He hadn't entered the irreversible Stage Four. That was a place no one came back from. That was a Cu Chi tunnel system of the psyche: there no more sunlight, for a G.I.

No, thought Lydia. Time of faith.

XXIV

Above all she needed to make him talk. Relate. And gain time.

—Tell me again, she said. In Stage One—

—Forget it, he said.

She paused a few seconds, but insisted.

—Stage One, remember? I didn't know until you told me. A virgin to combat experience; the loneliness, the shock after your first firefight. The squad learns about death. It's a war, it is real.

—Ben Bolt.

His voice had a little quiver. Of hope? In the final stage, no hope.

—The grief, sorrow, pain come in waves, in Stage One. You feel afraid.

—Numbed out—he said, and looked away from her. Was she hypnotizing him? Using her power, there at the foot of the steps, to subjugate him?—Numb.

—There is terror—she said, low—and atrocity.

—It's a butchery. Children.

—Remember? We use, we say the words to see a thing clearly—

—And understand it.

—By understanding, we begin to—

—Master it, change it.

This was the therapeutic responsory of their work the past summer.

—In the initial stage—she said—there is denial. There are diversionary thought patterns. Men take to alcohol and drugs to get them through. The hope system is wounded.

—First casualty of the war.

—But it's not the *you* in you, the survival—

—No, he said, not yet.

—And Stage Two?

—Combat. Into it: routine.

—Combat highly charged?

—Yes.

—Erotic?

—That too.

Sexually aroused in retrospect, perhaps, behind his mask of sadness—he looked down where she was edging a little closer, step by step, wanting so to be by his side, touch him, and knowing he saw. It was like the way kids play a game of 'red light'. In a minute she would reach up and brush him with her finger: put a fingertip to his stubbly chin, like a supplicant. Let me, let me. On the steps Lydia's skirt rode over her knees: rode up on her long shapely legs which had a life of their own. Her legs . . . He glimpsed them—like a sleek animal there on the plush carpeted stairs.

—So it's sexual?

—Yes.

—How so? How do you feel?

—I'm excited. I'm high on it.

—Sadistic?

—Yes. Waiting for Charlie. Here he comes.

—He comes?

—It's him, the tick. Here he comes over the wire; he owns it. Sappers, packing a punch like VC boom-de-boom girls, only they don't act so sweet.

—So it's war as a sex act, a consummation . . . And then Stage Three?

—I'm hardcore. I'm battle-tested.

—But the *you*-you still hasn't died.

—Not yet! But there's a world of hurt, and I have to deal with it. No wonder they hate us! And, you know, they act like it.

He looked around, wondering, as if it was news to him.

—And that's you, Jo, at this moment. You're in Three.

—No. I'm in Four. It's a fact, and this is living death.

Lydia laughed, low:

—You've got some balls on you . . . I happen to know you say Four so you can play possum, and not have to deal with it. When there's no hope, then . . .

—Why should I deal with it? Please tell me that, Doc, I want to know. Why the hell should I?

—To do the great thing, which would be like you. To struggle for love. Give love for hate.

He sneered:

—Those are nice words. How I do detest them. I thank you for your fine sentiments, worthy of Jesus. Tfui! They turn out fakes, sooner or later.

Joey spat over the banister.

—I didn't say turn the other cheek.

—That's what I heard. The headshrinker kisses the booboo and makes it better with her lingo. As usual it's the miracle of inter-pretation: costing her patients a pretty penny, but her nothing. And she'll deny me thrice before the cock crows. Like the others.

—What others, Jo?

—Well our CO for one, the holier-than-thou platoon leader. He liked to spout Bible versets, and he was good at it. But we needed a man, not a picture of piety. First time a crunch came, the FNG lieutenant brought us in at a bad angle: smack into an L-shaped ambush, VC specialty. The stupid gung-ho officer used his point-man as a probe, and Ben Bolt got an RPG right between the eyes. And for a few seconds I saw Ben Bolt up ahead there with his head a red mist in the sunlight. I can't get over that. It was death at the penny arcade. Hey! Give that man a fart sack and a ticket home. Minus his head. And all because of West Point kiddy corps, who had religion, and a ribbon to pin on his chest so he could feel good about himself.

—That didn't help Ben Bolt.

—No, it didn't.

—Do you see him in dreams?

—Him, Blair . . . I see the woman in the burning hootch. I see her children. But I swear to you: let our brave Secretary of Defense go fight the next one. A grunt goes overseas and fights for dear life and then comes home to find those closest to him have denied him, motherfucked him, literally, while he was away. That's his thanks, and . . . and . . .

—What?

—Baby killer.

—No.

—Maybe he deserves it—Joey's features contorted—maybe he did it.

—I don't accept that. You love children, and you never hurt one.

—I did! I did . . . I did.

Lydia was midway on the stairs by now. She had to touch him, take his hand; he had to let her.

His eyes glistened.

—I won't fight for them again. It's just money and selfishness. They put one over on the people. Let Mr. President lead our Senators and Congressmen into battle in their blue suits, if they love freedom and democracy so much. Let them get blown to bits for once instead of Ben Bolt or Billy Ringwood. I found out about that pack of liars too late.

—It's not too late.

She edged closer to him, up, up. A few more steps and she would take him in her arms and hold him and soothe him.

—I know what I've done. So please, dear, no more phony talk of love for hate, redemption of sins, and whatnot. There will be no forgiveness for my sorry likes. The average Joe lives a lie anyway; it's Stage Two across America with people denying and living comfortably while the wide world can go hang. That's what my brother says, and he says the two things are connected. Well, his words seem righter than I thought, some of them, even if his life is fluff. What he doesn't know, or feel, in his blood like me, is that good men, valid people, are dying in Vietnam. You know, I'll bet it's not only there.

—Live for them. Live for the valid people. Then it won't matter about the lies and Stage Two denial. Then you'll have a reason to live. The right reason to fight.

Joey looked down at her and said:

—Why did you come here?

—To be with you.

—Don't soft-soap me.

—I came here as a woman, Joey, on my own account. You're married to Carlyne, but I love you too. I'm allowed to love whom I please, if it's real. If the man I love is in trouble, I go to him.

—So it's your duty, type thing.

—My responsibility but not only. A woman has more than her duty to do, much, much more.

XXV

She edged nearer, and he peered down at her from behind his facial paint. Lydia's gaze on the dark stairs spoke not of psychiatry, the thousand-dollar insights of an hour spent together; not of hours but rather of years and decades;—of a life for a life. In her eyes was a frank desire: the sexual arousal of combat, the exhilaration of risk.

—Much more? he said.

—I love you, as your equal. I want you, here and now, but I also have to play fair . . . I never met your father, and I can't judge him. It's too bad he had to do that. He made a very grave mistake, yes. And he made her . . . if it wasn't outright rape. And she has paid for his mistake the way few of us have to pay. Remember, she lost her parents in childhood. She was still a girl, though more seductive than most women, when she went looking for a surrogate father in a jock.

—You use my words against me.

—For you, not against. Don't blame her, Jo. Don't blame Carlyne. It isn't good to blame victims. Listen, you never . . .?

She had crept up the steps to him, and he knew it and let her. His dark eyes shone under the greasy makeup. Grim, bespattered like the day he came home from the war, he looked at her and waited. His boots which had been through Xo Man, the Tet Offensive, an overrun RevDev hamlet and a minefield, then AWOL flight over the red earth of Vietnam . . . his boots were like a last obstacle between them: where they rested on the plush stairway.

Now Lydia Falliere was into her new role, and she yearned to heal herself. Not analyzing anymore but in a transport, she rose up and touched his curly beard, and then bowed to put her lips to his fist tight on the weapon. She strained further up against him and kissed his lean painted jaw, and her lips found his lips. Her sensual fingers seemed to charm a snake, as they lured his grip from the oiled gunbarrel and led him to her silken blouse. She guided his large calloused hands to the lace round her breasts. Now she would go in Stage Four with him if she had to, the land of the living dead, and bring him back. For herself she did this, too. It was a long, long time since she gave herself, and received in turn, and had her fair share of rapture.

She murmured:
—I want you.
He whimpered:
—You can't take my gun.
She sighed, touching him. She stroked him.
—I want you to have it.

Their legs entwined at the top of the stairs. He clutched the heavy submachinegun even as their bodies strained for each other and lulled thoughts which were too much for his mind a moment ago. He was timid with her, hesitant. He followed her lead but made love one-handed since the other still clung to his gun. A soldier's gun came first; but was he a soldier, or a lover?

They rocked together as she drew him over her and prodded him. Let it go, Jo, said her hands and kisses, let it go . . . Lydia positioned herself and groaned beneath his big, powerful body. The tailored business suit was drawn over her thighs as she gave herself up to him and there would be no impotency this time, no images of death and disaster. All open, all desire for life, all fertile with future she urged the chosen male partner onward and up into her. She wanted this man so, this one, in her deepest being. Too late for another child? No. Despite her age she would welcome a baby by him to cherish no matter what else might happen.

—I'm yours, Jo. Take me. You decide for us.

She cradled his head. She kissed him, pecked; spread her hand on his chest. Then her fingertips caressed the vein like a rope on his neck as he poised rigid at the instant of entry and she arched over him and now . . . now . . . here . . . it's . . .

But suddenly he jerked back from her.

He shot a glance over his shoulder and down the dark stairs.

XXVI

Eyes glinting like an eagle's he swung around.
—What, Jo?
On the wide stairway Joey drew away from Lydia, pushing her from his field of vision, as he pointed the rifle at the front door.
—They sent you here!

There was a patrol car out there in the street, at the end of the walk. The staticky radio carried in the silence.

And now there was the burst of a siren. A second squad car was on its way from the police station up town.

Outside the house a red light swiveled; it flickered in the front windows. Who had called them? Could Carlyne have done such a stupid thing? Crouched for an hour out there in the shrubs, and jealous?

—They didn't send me, said Lydia.

—Go on—said Joey, coldly—Clear out.

—I didn't call them, and do not think so. That's the last thing I wanted, and I told your wife not to.

—I don't believe you.

—They'd have got here sooner, no? . . . The sick man who sent you the anonymous letter, the devil's clergy . . . we met him in town on our way here. He hates your family, and he probably sicked the police on us now.

But Joey wasn't listening. He was all combat reflex thinking what to do.

—I said get out of here. You're in my way.

Lydia shook her head, getting herself together.

—I'll go deal with them. Then I'll come back to you.

Joey said:

—No, I'll handle this. You go to New York where you belong.

—I belong here with you.—She stood up, smoothing her skirt.—I'll go make them leave.

—Affirmative, Sarge. You and my loving wife set this up.

—Oh, Joey. Tst.

—Then why did they come here?

—You're so excited, you're not paying attention. It may have been that man: the minister who looks deranged. It seems he wants to destroy Emory. Or, if he thinks someone is happy, like you and Carlyne lately, he just can't stand the sight.

Joey thought a moment.

—Anyway it's too late. Thanks for trying; I'll have to see this through by myself. The child stays.

Slowly, reluctantly, Lydia moved down the stairs away from him. It was not a bright idea to leave him in here alone. That wasn't why she came. But what else could she do? Once outside she might not get back in again, yet she had no choice. He put it to her, and now she had to prove she hadn't called them: that she wanted them gone too. Also, he told her to go, and this wasn't the moment to thwart him.

So Lydia tucked her blouse and ran a hand through her hair. She felt his gun pointed at her: trained on the front door as she neared it.

In the foyer she turned and looked up at him in the shadows. Joey Gilbert was a powder keg ready to detonate, and now here came the law. Now he would entrench and make his preparations. It would be a hostage standoff. If they wouldn't go away, then a major crisis. And then . . .?

For another few seconds she stood there, looking at him. She lingered, and seemed to see a dark figure far out on the perimeter. In her mind she was crying and protesting: poor boy, I love you, I need *you* so. If it's Stage Four then let's spend it together . . . But her lips only said:

—Give me a chance.

XXVII

Going against her instinct Lydia pushed open the heavy front door. She went out on the porch and down the steps. The important thing was to present an unruffled exterior. Officers, why the sirens and red lights?

Just then a third squad car pulled up and parked by the curb. It came rushing on the scene. Well, they must know about Joey Gilbert's condition even if they never heard the acronym PTSD. So why turn out in force and set up a conflict?

She tried to compose her thoughts. Someone called them, and she didn't think it was Carlyne. The churchman then? The bastard spent his life envying the legitimate son . . . Talk about small-town misery.

Head high she went down the walk toward them. She was a picture of professional dignity as she drew near the half dozen patrolmen who spoke low, and looked at her.

—Good evening, officers.

—Miss, some problem in there?

The southern accent was like a slur. As one they took in the elegant woman whose cheeks and beige blouse were smeared with an oily substance.

—No problem. What brings you here?

One took out a pad:

—Your name, please?

—Lydia Falliere.

One clicked on a flashlight at her:

—You the plumber?

—Friend of the family.

—What's the grease?

—Oh. A little repair job.

—Why're you out here, and not him?

—He's putting his daughter to bed.

—We don't see any lights, not one. Why no lights?

—Dinner by candlelight.

—And the squa—and his wife?

—Carlyne went for a walk.

—Kind o' late, ain't it?

She said softly:

—Not so late.

The flashlight stayed on her:

—Now tell us more. Whatcha' got on your face there? Looks like war paint.

Lydia put a finger to her cheek. With a little laugh she said:

—After supper he got me helping him with one of the tractors. Can't get it going. Thanks so much for your concern, officers, but we don't need you. All is well.

The light went over her blouse, skirt:

—Looks like paint on her clothes, greenish.

—Maybe they playin' cowboys 'n Injuns.

—Say, what y'all up to in there? Skirt's rumpled too.

They shared a glance.

—It's what I said.—Lydia returned their stares.—We're thankful you're on the case, watching over the public safety. Now all the best to you, really: have a good evening.

—Public safety . . .

She turned from them to go back up the walk.

But just then Carlyne came across the lawn in the shadows. Her features were drawn, as she frowned at the gathering. The flashlight left Lydia and lingered on the full, voluptuous blouse and bluejeans of Joey Gilbert's wife.

One patrolman gave a low whistle, and said:

—It's the redskin.

—Back from her walk in the dark.

Carlyne stared past the flashlight, and didn't blink.

—What can we do for you? My husband asked me to see what it is you need.

Behind her was the granite mansion with its massive facade, porch, balcony. It rose high above the long incline of the front lawn and appeared to lean forward and try to overhear. In those instants an eerie glow played on the conical turret, the Romanesque arches of the front porch, the parapeted balcony and high gables . . . In there, as the two women knew, Joey Gilbert waited behind the blinds with his M-16 cocked and pointed at the meeting on the sidewalk. The group of policemen paused another minute, grim with their little quips, officious: filled with the self-importance of this small town which kept them busy. They had no warrant or they would have showed it. Now it was time to run along, but they had a notion to stay.

The squad car lights rotated: red, white, red. The strong flashlight shot past Carlyne at the porch and front door and den windows.

—Dark inside, no lights. Why?

—Looks like somethin' fishy goin' on.

—Please ask Mr. Gilbert to step out here a minute. That way we'll resolve this.

Carlyne said:

—He's in bed by now.

—She said he was working on his tractor.

—Or putting the child to bed, wasn't it?

—Look, ladies, as soon as he gives the all-clear, then we can leave. No problem.

Carlyne met Lydia's eye. She said:

—Alright we'll tell him, but he may refuse.

—Why so?

—He's in one of his moods. It's hard enough for us as it is. You know he's got a condition from the war, and your being here just gets him stirred up. I'm asking you to go along now, please, and we'll give a signal if we need you. You're only making things more difficult.

—We got a call.

—Did you? said Carlyne. Join the club. Joey Gilbert gets crank calls all day long.

—The caller said there's trouble. Joey may've barricaded himself inside there with the child.

—Who's the informant? Who said so?

—We can't tell you that.

—Well he doesn't know—said Carlyne.—We know. If what he said was the case then we'd be the first to ask for your help.

—Joey has hardware, guns.

—Respect our rights—said Carlyne more firmly.—Or I'll go inside and call a lawyer.

—He's armed to the hilt and could be a danger. So we're told.

—Hunting rifles. We're licensed for any guns we own, like everybody else in town. Now I'm asking you politely to leave, and I'm also telling you. Why do you come snooping around here? Because he's a famous ballplayer? Now he's a farmer, and a law-abiding resident of this town.

—We got a call, and we respond. It's our job.

For a moment the police ignored the two women, as their gazes conferred. And then there was the instant of relaxed attention before they turned and made to leave.

XXVIII

But suddenly a cry rang out from the Rock Castle—inside the house, through an open window? or among the shadowy shrubs about the porch? It was loud, like a man who has reached his limit, and he better be obeyed. A world of anger burst forth in a curse. It charged the quiet night.

—All of you get off my property! Do you hear me? You've got sixty seconds to get the hell out of here!

Carlyne and Lydia didn't budge. But the six men in uniform spun and ducked behind the squad cars parked at angles to the curb.

—I see you . . . you bitch! Out there with the police! Go ahead, you get lost too!

One of the patrolmen, kneeling for cover, spoke into a radio.

Another said:

—You women move back! That's an order.

But the two women stood there, facing the house, their tallish figures outlined in the turning red lights.

Carlyne yelled:

—C'mon, Jojo! Enough already with the war games! Me 'n Lydia are coming in now. It's time to go to bed!

But the tinny war zone static of 2-way radios had taken hold, and fastened onto the calm southern evening. Another squad car and a police van pulled to a halt some hundred yards from the scene, in the direction of up town. And then the first ones screeched from the curb and backed out of harm's way; they scampered to join the others.

And now a hostage crisis was on the march. It could go far.

Voices spoke low over radios. The call went out to State Troopers.

And then came an event that sealed it. A first shot rang out. It sounded like a pistol shot, but not from the Rock Castle. Dat-da! One, two gunshots, loud in the sudden hush with only a child crying now; and not that close by. Did Joey Gilbert fire into the air as a warning to them? He wasn't playing war games?

But it sounded like the shots came from a different angle: on the other side, across the street where a neighboring estate stood back among tall trees and a sprawl of lawn.

Carlyne and Lydia held their ground, though they knew it was too late now. The thing was under way.

Chapter Twenty

I

While the town police backed off, and dug in, there were State Troopers arriving on the scene. In the quiet out-of-the-way town a hostage situation was declaring itself which could be of national interest. And so word also went out to the press. The two shots from a revolver were as if heard around the world; they set off a communications landslide. There were urgent phone calls to nearby Greensboro, and to Raleigh. There were calls to U.S. Government lines which never slept in the nation's capital.

That same evening Emory Gilbert was giving a speech in Evanston, Illinois. Ten months after his Party's defeat in 1968 Presidential elections, he was still going out there to revive the excitement. He could do it. He addressed state leaders; he gave an elocution at this or that Women's Club; he was on the circuit for commencement addresses at universities. Such engagements were more than echoes of his fling in the grand arena; though they couldn't have the dizzy intensity of a campaign. Part of him did yearn for the elegant exclusivity of thousand-a-plate dinners, the cachet of a black tie reception, and romance of a dress ball in the Rotunda. Fondly, oh yes, he thought back on strategy sessions at dawn in a close to the vest fervor. How to get out the vote? What tack with labor and our disenchanted farmers? How to reassure the major donors and yet address the 'youthquake' of 14 million new and idealistic voters? What tasks for the Women's Committee? Time and again as Campaign pointman Emory had turned a phrase, stunning yet media-safe, to get past the issue of Vietnam which was like a mine-field. Career politicians were unable to maintain a credible stance on the war, and they wilted in the glare of camera lights. But the great Emory Gilbert, author of literary classics, heavyweight of the human spirit, said nothing and made you buy it.

Then defeat. Overnight the excitement died away, but still he gazed back at his lost paradise of network media attention day after day. And he issued forth like Don Quijote's second foray and rousted 'em out some more. He could still have his thrills: on condition that he move further Left, and make ever more auda-cious speeches, and yes finally start to take a position and say something. Now he had one foot in the Establishment and the other in the Anti-War Movement. For he either had to be a dis-sident and oppose Government policy in Vietnam and at home, or else bore everyone in the hall to tears and find himself tossed in the dustbin of history.

And so he spoke to packed audiences and stirred up another kind of excitement than that of electoral politics. In his way, on the new platform, he took things to a higher level. In tremendous speeches he began challenging America to end its wars abroad and begin to build a more just society here at home. He reasoned, pleaded, warned; he put the verve of Pindar into a popular cause. He would never lift a finger to organize and build a vanguard Party, but his 3-hour addresses verged on the sublime. He could animate a capacity crowd out of its mind, and himself along with.

But each time the rapture, the divine moments of self-forget came to an end—then he was back in his Georgetown headquar-ters and a prey to spells of depression. Well he rested and consorted with the latest in a long line by this time of gracious ladies and zesty sexual partners. He worked on his current opus and spoke with his agent about the next round of speaking engagements.

For the present he could only keep on beating the world and seeking to achieve an even more glorious success than the one before. Till the day he died it seemed his ambitious mother, Wil-helmina, would be driving him on to greater heights, and depths. There she was like a specter whipping him up to more efforts for the redemption of old Gilbert sins. And time and again, no matter how immensely successful he was, he couldn't forget much less redeem his sins. And so he found himself alone again, uprooted away from the Rock Castle; and, despite a lot of women around him saying the contrary—at times it all seemed in vain.

II

As Left opposition to the Vietnam War factionalized, and self-destructed, the Anti-War Movement was recast in broader coalitions. The more centrist peace groups were able to capture media attention and put on much larger demonstrations. And in this phase the liberal Emory Gilbert was one of the principle spokespersons.

Turbulent months had followed the First Counterinaugural—Counterin*hog*ural, said Yippies and their offshoots, The Crazies—and then Chicago Eight conspiracy trial indictments. There were the spring 1969 anti-war actions when Yippies brandished pig heads on poles in New York and elsewhere; and Parade Committee organizers invited Joey Gilbert to join an active duty G.I. contingent by the speakers stand; but his club's front office dismissed the idea.

New radical groups were born such as G.I.s United Against the Vietnam War. And then a group of activist soldiers, the Fort Jackson Eight, were put in stockade or under barracks arrest. Also, Weatherman 'action-factions' were in the news as they tried to inspire the nation's youth by taking on the police. All in all those were unstable days and weeks, as Rumor, fleet-winged, head hidden high amid the clouds, told of revolutionary stirrings across the land.

Meanwhile, Students for a Democratic Society (SDS) did itself in—with help. The national group turned from its often highly effective student base, and proposed a chain of 'radical territories' on campuses across the country; SDS planned what loomed as a fiasco called the Days of Rage. Thus the Left was getting nudged toward the margin as the comrades went back for more in the Chicago streets.

Within SDS the Revolutionary Youth Movement (RYM became RYM-II in opposition to Weatherman terrorism) vyed with Progressive Labor for control. Slogans clashed: *Mao-Mao-Mao Tse Tung* versus *Ho-Ho-Ho Chi Minh*. There was endless debate but no clear analysis. The activists took to invective and name-calling—filthy bourgeois!—as SDS chapters fell apart just as had the Berkeley Peace Committee. In each case they had help from FBI agents and paid informers sent in to cripple the New Left. Some independent SDS chapters became free-lancing local groupuscules, which were harmless enough; or else they affiliated with the Student Mobilization Committee and other national organizations.

Liberals took over the Anti-War Movement. And Emory Gilbert's oratory played a role. He called all people of conscience into the streets for an October 15th Vietnam Moratorium. And this event had a semiofficial character: school administrations, city councils endorsed it; local politicians agreed to speak at anti-war activities in many cities, colleges and universities. The demonstrations and rallies were mostly moderate in temper: as mayors spoke out, and movie stars chaired the platform. The New Mobe organized it with a coalition of 84 diverse groups, including American Friends Service Committee, Teamsters, Amalgamated Meatcutters and Butchers. The Communist and Socialist Worker Parties kept their hand in the game; they stayed, but the forecast looked bleak for the Weathermen who had cut themselves off from the mainstream.

III

Tonight in Evanston he was in fine fettle, and he spoke stirringly, but not recklessly. Emory Gilbert evaded the idea he might spearhead a major Third Party drive. As ever he flirted with a more direct appeal to the masses; but he also turned pale at his own power when it seemed his words might spark a popular uprising, and the bounding uncontrollable flood of Revolution.

Grandiose at the podium his voice soared and he gestured.

There was a scuffle by the door at the back of the hall.

Someone began to chant and then others took it up:

—Cambodia! Cambodia! Cambodia!

While security guards showed a Trotskyist from YSA the way to the exit, a Weather Underground chant went rippling through the audience:

—Turn New York into Saigon!

In recent months there had been a few signs of this. Bombs went off in Manhattan: at the house of a judge assigned to a Black Panther trial; at a townhouse on West 11th Street where a Weather cell was making explosives; then at certain corporate offices in days that followed.

The Vietnam War went on. 472,000 U.S. soldiers were still in-country at the end of 1969. Bomb tonnage expended, and Vietnamese killed (also G.I.s), exceeded '67. It went on; and never mind Tricky Dick's announcement of troop cutbacks, and so-called Vietnamization of the war.

Emory was soul-tired, but the crowd response was like wind rippling in the wings of his rhetoric. It reminded of his son Joey the year before: the athlete on a tear though he goes out there exhausted day after day. Tonight, as often, the event turned out different than what he and host campus groups expected. From city to city all sectors came out to hear him speak, and for different reasons. But since most were worried about the Nixon Administration's handling of the Vietnam issue, he got swept up in their emotion, and outdid himself. The liberal was propelled forward by the interaction of his own contradictions with our society's.

Depending on circumstances this speaker might dampen all the militancy in the hall, or stir it up to a chorus of rabid foot-stamping and chants. He could analyze reality with a scalpel, like in his books, and this was helpful; or serve up a visionary mish-mash cum U.S. utopia, and this was not. He taught them, an educator of the nation; and he raved: as well as the New Year's Gang member (Weather kin) ejected from the hall a moment ago. For some things change less the more they change. And this man was an opportunist to the core: Left opportunist now, Right opportunist the next time—depending on this or that, maybe the day's newspaper headlines—; social chauvinist, apologist for capital, false leader who led the way forward despite his cringings. The goal was to wow big crowds, engrave his name in posterity, impress some woman—perhaps not in that order. It seemed Emory Gilbert was the cause he believed in, if he even did: this kindly man, and literary genius, and driven maniac. He let you down at the key moment. But then a packed gathering carried the keynote speaker away, and once again his oratory was a tremendous thing, and together crowd and celebrity fanned the Vietnam Era fires.

Many of those who came to hear him had bused across country
to huge 1969 Movement events: to the spring anti-war actions,
and G.I.-civilian demos. On April 5th a hundred thousand had
marched in New York City despite the rain, 30 thousand in Chicago, 40 thousand the next day in San Francisco, thousands in
Atlanta, Los Angeles and elsewhere. Then came the Days of Rage.
Then multi-faceted actions nationwide for the Vietnam Moratorium. Voices were raised in protest by the hundreds of thousands.
Then came the March Against Death and November 15th mobilization in Washington, D.C.: where the people numbered a quarter
million or more amid flags, banners, peace signs along Pennsylvania Avenue on a bright, clear, cold day. The activists and center-
Left elements in Emory's audience had faced tear gas cartridges
late that afternoon—as police charged over the hill of the Washington Monument toward bonfires where demonstrators tried to
get warm and waited for return buses.

The big liberal never got tear-gassed: unless that time in the
swell setting at Chicago. In his life he hadn't spent a day in jail.
But he did get carried along with the tide of history.

Usually he steered clear of sensitive Third Party talk: sensitive
only because he if anyone in the U.S. might make it work; he was
compared sometimes to Henry George. Instead, he gave them
more word wizardry. But suddenly the elements seemed to fly
apart—life erupted, and came crashing over his pitiful need to
evade the truth and with it his own power. The militants on hand
goaded and pushed him; they gave him de facto leadership on a
platter—as a kind of Gene McCarthy to the Nth power, and heir to
discontent. And then Emory got into the swing. The inexhaustible
supply of lofty chatter and sublime gab burst forth in the flames
and heat of a sacred fire. He no longer played it safe:

—Do you remember how, after the March Against Death, while
untolled numbers in Southeast Asia were dying, dying . . . how
Richard Nixon emulated Marie Antoinette for political astuteness
when he said: 'It's a fine afternoon to watch a football game . . .'?

Here came an interpolation of five minutes on the uses and
abuses of American sports.

Shouts from the crowd left hanging:

—To the point! The point!

—Cambodia! Cambodia!

—Shake 'em and bake 'em!

—What were you saying about Spiro's insults?

—Tell us! Tell us!

—Speak out! Say it loud and clear!

—Yes, yes, the Vice President has the gall to dismiss us anti-war activists as 'effete snobs' and 'rotten apples'. Say, did he mean me by that? Ha ha ha! Always these politicians, conformist to the rotten core, talk down to the people like we were children . . . And they lie! Oh! Disparage the dissident intellectual's integrity and courage. In the eyes of those with a vested interest in the status quo, no matter how bad it is, the one who tells the truth and fights for it will always be an irresponsible adolescent!

IV

A few nights ago, April 30th, President Nixon went on TV to go public with what amounted to an invasion of Cambodia. It stunned the nation when he said:

—In cooperation with the armed forces of South Vietnam we have launched attacks this week to clean out major enemy sanctuaries on the Cambodia-Vietnam border. This does not constitute an invasion into Cambodia.

The President said there were clandestine headquarters kept by South Vietnamese communist forces inside Cambodian territory. So this move was meant to shorten the war; although some 3,630 secret B-52 air strikes against insurgent bases on Cambodian soil over the past fourteen months did not seem to achieve this effect.

In Nixon's speech the ever broader sectors committed to a de-escalation of the war saw only betrayal and more military buildup. Victory was not on the horizon. Even the U.S. Senate now demanded all contingents of our military be withdrawn from positions inside Cambodia.

And yet even now Emory Gilbert did not want to talk about it. He didn't like the idea of this country's first general student strike ever. SDS might disintegrate, but Cambodia helped regroup the Left remnants with student liberals and more mainstream anti-war elements. In the works at this hour was the shutting down of business as usual at over five hundred campuses, some briefly, others for the rest of the school year.

Still Emory (Emeritus, as some called him in the Movement)
held back. At first he seemed to see, feel, abhor not death and destruction and genocide Made in America and exported to towns
and villages across Southeast Asia, but rather a lot of outside agitators with no respect for Ivy League tradition and the academic
prestige which he believed in deeply—he the small-town product, the provincial who gained success and fame.

In tonight's address, on the campus of Northwestern, he went
on:

—Since the Foreign Relations hearings last November, and the
President's Vietnamization order to General Abrams, I've considered this current Administration in default on its campaign promises. 'Positive reaction' does not mean a step toward ceasefire.
The terms 'ceasefire' and 'standfast' are mutually exclusive in this
instance. And so I believe a time will come, and it approaches,
when the younger more progressive forces in our country start
trying to build a broad-based Third Party with vital ties to the
grassroots: the new electoral Party required by history and our
nation's destiny.

—Do it! Do it!

—Now! Now!

—Not only electoral!

—Take our destiny in our own hands!

—Peace now! Peace now!

—Out now! Out now! Out now!

—Free Panthers! Off pigs!

And Emory, at the microphone, into the explosion of slogans:

—Over forty thousand American soldiers have fallen to date in
the jungles and paddy fields of Vietnam . . .

In droves they came to hear him speak in the hope something
concrete would come of it. The masses seemed ready for action,
and Emory Gilbert worked them up some more, but then he let
them down. Mostly he analyzed the situation brilliantly and
then grew lyrical instead of taking the lead. He did an egg dance
around the question of leadership, and: what is to be done? Always and ever he shied away from political action apart from the
Democratic Party. He recognized and despised the irrationality
of the United States Government which would end up jeopardiz-
ing not only life in Vietnam but across the planet. But he dove for
cover when someone said there was only one means to put an
end to that madness: namely a great popular movement on the

march toward socialism, and with a centralized leadership that meant business.

In general these days his audiences gave him a more seasoned and thoughtful applause. Some there were, yes, who taunted him, and said it was high time for Dumbo to fly in the circus. At dramatic moments, like this one due to Nixon's stunner, Emory was pushed to take a stance which went against his nature. At his age he wasn't going to reverse the moral and political course of his entire career. An inspired ambiguity had worked so well. And it was fun! For anything truly confrontational in this national writer you had to look back thirty years to the prewar period: when he showed such promise as a vanguard intellectual. But in his case, as always when there are political stakes, the red-baiters came out from the woodwork. They went after him. And he had a career to build, not blight by Marxism, and a family to provide for. And so he retreated. He found a refuge in literary form—way above the fray of political principle where reputations get tainted, and success stories wind up in ostracism, and the high riders like him are relegated to the usual fight for survival.

This evening, as in the 1968 Presidential Campaign, he felt buoyed up by a large exuberant gathering. And he was making news with words. And all on hand from the podium to the excited crowd to the picketers outside the main entry, far Left elements: all had a sense of America on the eve.

A twilight seemed to gleam on the old unconscious life.

But was it the twilight before dawn? Or nightfall?

V

What happened next was a surprise—to put it mildly.

His behavior perplexed the spectators since no one knew the why or wherefore.

First, a moment before something stopped the show: this darling of the mainstream astounded everyone by his sudden radicalism. The finale of the Evanston speech was a tempestuous indignation and a powerful incitement to act. It was so uncharacteristic of the man, as he went further and further, and drew his conclusions at the brink. Activists, concerned citizens, community groups, Elks and Rotary—every forum from factory shops to the Chamber of Commerce must begin to form up in soviet-like groups, he said, and think, study the national problematic, discuss things seriously. Come out! It was the historic duty of the local PTA to wake up and begin to participate. It was the time of honor, it was the time of principle, it was the time of protest. Resist! Resist the U.S. Government's global policy for the sake of corporate profits while the world's children get starved out and die.

Thus Emory: sounding like his hippie son, his opposite. At last in his public life, just as in his unbridled sensuality, once he got started, he went all the way.

Bring home the troops! Let them fight here at home: put their fists in the dyke against this sudden deluge of narcotics in our inner cities. Drug abuse, he now knew, was a planned and coordinated CIA policy—to destabilize domestically, to etherize discontent and depoliticize the slums. Let the people devour each other! Drugs made the so-called Great Society a mockery, as the Americans were brainwashed by that even more potent drug of TV. Who is free if they do not know the score?

Return our boys to us! Let them fight a just war over here, a civil war against corporate greed, boardroom hegemony: not filthy imperialist wars versus the poor and underdeveloped nations!

For a minute Emory, red in the face, waved his arm like a poster of Lenin. Turn war of aggression into a domestic war! He pounded the lectern and then—horrible to see!—shook a pink fist. His deep doctoral voice soared round the rapt hall:

—Historically . . . throughout modern times the industrial powers have kept down the weaker Third World countries like Vietnam. The idea is to keep them on their knees in order to exploit them maximally. The mighty transnationals rape a vulnerable nation's mineral and agricultural resources. Dominate their markets. Ensure their cost-cheap labor force is a slave to capital. And this goes on: across Asia, Africa, Latin America. Stymy any real competitive industry, any home market besides the subservient comprador sort totally dependent on the outside, on the industrialized center, on Wall Street, on the international lenders.

"And so decade after decade the great Western democracies with ours now in the lead have oppressed the smaller nations to the south and showed them no mercy, none, ever, despite the myth of our benign relations and aid to them and despite all the sham Alliances for Progress which are more of the same disguised exploitation.

"See, we extract fabulous wealth without pause. We usurp their national patrimonies. CIA-AID, the U.S. diplomatic corps in conjunction with the oligarchic government and military of a given nation, our own military if necessary: all means are used to enslave while keeping order. We are the masters of state terrorism. We make a science of violence. We repress any homegrown resistance. No matter what the cost!

"Well, what better use for the dollars of U.S. taxpayers? Suckers, we do it in your name. No matter how much death is in the world historic recipe of the American Century. All our so very humanitarian acts of genocide we call a glorious crusade for freedom and against the worldwide communist-terrorist conspiracy to overthrow our honest, our noble, our fair American way of life and our time-honored American values and our sacrosanct American liberty and justice and our American God made manifest by such good works and pious actions around the globe.

"All the while, every day and every hour, we suck the life blood out of the world's children. We, you and I, pillage and plunder the wide world with perfect legality, we think. Sleep well! Thank you. We keep this earth's workers producing for us at starvation wages. Hey you, manual worker, uneducated native, you there, cheap life! You say you don't like it? Hell, we can get ten more where you came from, and a hundred and a million, and the kids are even cheaper to feed. Millions will take your place gladly, submissively, on the speeded-up assembly line of the global economy: from the acreage of banana plantations to the hotels and restaurants and the brothels and dives also staffed by children.

"Ah, you say you don't like it? You grumble among one another and get up a good anger? You murmur at the unfairness? You combine illegally—because, you know, labor unions are really trusts—you call a strike? You stage an action? Oh! You red commie terrorist! Will you never learn your lesson? We'll disappear your family, we'll torture you to death! Cheap life!"—

Beside himself, shaken by the sermon he was giving, Emory paused.

Pale lips pressed tight together, an exalted glint in his eye, he looked over the hall.

—So you see, dear sisters and brothers, it goes on. I believe it may be human history's most sordid chapter before it ends, if it ever does, and that's saying something. Maybe the planet will have to end first.

"Make no mistake: this is our own United States I am talking about. This country we've loved and believed in since childhood days of pledging allegiance to the flag, and crediting by and large what our media and history books tell us . . . it is not doing right. And that is the understatement of the millenium."—

There was a silence filled with pathos. He made this different vision of America seem so real.

He thought another moment, and then seemed to sum up:

—I speak to you as a U.S. citizen tonight. Oh, not as a Marxist. I'm no revolutionary. Too old for those new tricks. I still uphold our society's positive side as a light to the world. I've no interest in tarnishing our cherished American values. That's not what I came out here to do tonight.

"Just call me a human being trying to make some sense of all this—this American chaos, this wrong stuff.

"I just can't see why a super-wealthy tiny minority should rule and possess and control so much while the vast majority go hungry and helpless and illiterate.

"And then if you tell them this, the super-rich and the corporations who are doing it, they will call you undemocratic! For a long time they've been saying the have-nots must not be permitted to tyrannize over the haves! Oh, we have a long history of such reasoning around here. And since corporate interests control the courts and legislatures, the media and educational system at all levels, and public opinion generally, they get away with it! They know it, and they do it!

"Well, die any way you like, or live for all I care, but leave me alone to enjoy my wealth amassed by hook or by crook.

"For this is the private property of the rich, my friend, and it is sacred."—

VI

Emory stopped. He looked left as a figure lurked in the wings, and then came out on the stage toward him.

One of the organizers of this event stood there with a message in his hand. Emergency?

Distracted from his train of thought, Emory still spoke into the microphone:

—Therefore the task of the activists at this critical juncture . . .

People waited quietly while the other held out a memo.

At the podium the speaker grew pale. Again his voice tried to resume its flight, but faltered. His élan, courage, his rousing spirit came from the roused assembly; they interpenetrated; they educated one another. It seemed their response made him more than he was: more than a man who poses, and sops up photo ops. For the major media loved him too. He was safe, and he upstaged the serious ones of the opposition: the real leadership.

Emory Gilbert paused in the amazed silence to read the memo he was handed. *'Your son Joey in hostage standoff. State and local authorities on scene. Return at once. Commynes.'*

In the wide hall you could have heard a pin drop. The speaker's hand trembled as he held the piece of note paper. It was like bad news expected and feared for a long time; and when it comes, the effect is not less, but more.

He turned back to them:

—There is a crisis in my family. My son Joey is in trouble. I have to go home now . . . My agenda has me in Madison tomorrow evening, but the way things look, I don't know if I'll make it. (Emory glanced away, as though another jolt might come. Then he spoke.) Let me leave you with this. I believe the time has come for a new kind of politics. Not like me, oh no. First off we'll need young'uns, as we say down South: new life ready and able to take the knocks, stand the hardships, much better than I ever could. I'm an old softy as you must have guessed by now. But there must be another thing about them. Let's see: how to say it? They . . . they don't take off the mask. That's it. What they do, they do for others. It's not for publicity, money, career. They don't want to be praised. Can't use it! What they must do is clear the way for a new, a just society good for children and adults. They live for that; they die for it if they have to, but they hate that idea, because life only started, I mean really came alive, once they got on this new course. In a mask, yes, since the new way will only get its true start, its difficult beginning, away from the public eye . . . So not like me, dear friends, please. Not my kind at all. Young, I said; though it's not about how old you are. I say we need a new kind of men and women, and they'll have what is needed to see it through to the end. And they'll keep on the mask until the task is complete, which may not be tomorrow. Masked so the corporate boys won't know them, can't find them, buy them, coopt, suborn. This is the only way to win.

Emory Gilbert stood before them. Just a moment ago he was so exalted, but now he had a wilted air. He looked out at them a minute longer before leaving the stage.

There were first smatterings of applause. Then more, thoughtful: like a gentle rain. They knew or felt his limits. This man would never lead them in a real beginning, far from it: he'd break your heart instead. But they forgave him because he was just so gifted, and he did give of what he had. He was a link, if a weak one, in a process no one knew quite yet. For a season his ambition and vanity ran tangent to the national life. And now, this transitional role ended, he was ready to leave the platform.

But he turned back. He didn't want to end this way: with a whimper. And so he brought down his fist on the lectern and summoned a few more words trying to shake up the hall:

—Come forward, I say! Come forward, all of you, the best young and progressive forces! Wage a great campaign for social justice in America. Don't be afraid! Militants! If Government won't look to the needs of the people, then the people must organize and see to their own government! Not in the staid and superannuated politics of yesterday, all moss-grown with special interest and gross corruption, like fungus between the lines of the Constitution! Only we, dear friends, we, my sisters and brothers, we, comrades, we the people have hope and truth on our side. We stand or fall on our own: young at heart, principled, progressive, determined, revolutionary!

VII

Now, okay, he was ready. He gave a wave and a smile as he turned to leave. And the applause grew.

It grew. It lauded his words, and showed a new resolve. For President Nixon never did mean to wind down the military effort in Southeast Asia. His intent was to escalate it deviously. 'Vietnamization' only meant expending Vietnamese and not American lives.

But now, in the same way as applause for Emory grew stronger: now there would be an upsurge of movement against the war. From it might emerge a more fundamental opposition to Washington's policies both foreign and domestic. Maybe a Third Party; but it seemed Emory Gilbert was not meant to lead this—at least not until he took care of a family crisis, something about his baseball player son, Joey, who was troubled as everybody knew.

Now there were mass meetings and rallies planned and in progress on a hundred campuses. Protest Nixon's crimes in Cambodia! Anti-war actions were going on at Princeton after students and faculty met to strike the college. In New Haven, where a Black Panther trial had drawn protesters; in New York, in the Chicago area, and out on the West Coast; also in a northern Ohio community called Kent State, like so many others—an American public ever slow to rouse was seeing through the politicians and feeling shocked by the lies.

When the great writer walked off the stage, he looked tired. Well, he would rebound and reschedule the Madison speech once his problems were resolved. But he did seem spent: as if his day was ended.

In these hours the political situation was exploding across the country.

Emory Gilbert had a haggard air.

But after he departed the applause grew stronger, stronger.

For two years he had put on one hell of a performance.

They stood up. They clapped harder, harder.

It was a prolonged ovation. For him?

Farewell!

VIII

At the airport Emory waited for a flight to North Carolina. He was shaken. His nerves were in a bad way after Paul Commynes' telegram; he wanted a drink of liquor. But he knew what this meant for him—there was disaster in the first glass. Yet such a thirst he had, such a deep down need to sip, perchance to beam. Not a shot glass then? Not a thimble? Where's the harm? It could relax him to leave this lonely VIP Room and go in the bar and have a drink.

There was a spasm of . . . like a relapse of grief for his wife. He yearned for the good Anne Gilbert and wondered how he would make it through this night without her.

With trembling fingers he dialed Commynes' number, but the good friend did not answer. He was out there on the scene; indeed it was his cup of tea. He was with them at the Rock Castle. Perhaps he had gone in and gained access to Joey? Yes, that's it: Paulie Commynes always worshiped the Gilberts; and now he would do his best to pay the debt to P. Laster, his mentor, and help to resolve the crisis? . . . Of course that's where he was right now: using his pastoral care training to defuse the situation. An anguished Emory felt such tenderness and gratitude toward his childhood friend, he could have kissed him. Now he placed his hope in the wise, benevolent churchman.

Then he thought a bit more; rang up long distance information; and a moment later reached the police station across the wide back lot behind his father's bank. An officer took his call.

—Yes, Sir. You should come here at once.

—That urgent?

—Joey has your granddaughter in there. He's holding her hostage.

—And Carlyne?

—She's outside.

IX

At the gate he awaited his boarding call.

Tense, throat dry with anxiety, he was burning for a drink. Why not wander back past the airline counters and take a seat in the lounge? Have a look around: maybe find a ground hostess off duty at midnight? Why go rushing to the Rock Castle when there was probably nothing he could do? Better if he went home tomorrow when he felt rested . . . and he would feel rested if he found a woman and engaged in the excesses he liked to use as antidote for frayed nerves and his banquet circuit exhaustion.

These past thirty months, since he got started, he had carried his sexual adventurism further and further. After fifty years of frustration he had learned how to let out the throttle of desire. Late nights on the road he entered a fantasy realm so fraught with erotic pathology, the most experienced call girl had a right to a wage differential.

But he couldn't do it tonight. It wouldn't work unless he drank because his nervous system was in an uproar. And why? Maybe his son was waiting for him at the Rock Castle. And if he didn't go there and face him—then what was this brave posturing and playing the national figure all about? Was he Emory Gilbert the coward?

He knew what he had to do, and it wasn't find a woman.

Commynes' note gave him such a charge; he could only ask himself over and over: Does Jojo know? Could he? Who told him? What is happening? Why not try to find out right now? Give him a buzz and ask him! . . .

By the telephone Emory stood pondering: What is the extent of my liability? Does this standoff have anything to do with me and Carlyne? Am I implicated? Is . . . is that why he's holding Rhoda? . . . And my career? How much has Joey or possibly Carlyne said to anyone? Will it be in tomorrow's headlines? Our media is a past master at slander and would destroy me with gusto. I need to know a few things so I can gauge the situation before showing up at the scene before all those cameras. And there's only one way to do this—phone him. Get through, if possible, to Joey.

X

Twice he dialed the number—his own—but he was so jumpy his finger got it wrong. He tried to calm down and told himself a sane Joey would answer the phone, and cry into his ear, and ask the father he loved for help.

Then Emory got an operator and gave her the number.

Ring, ring, ri'————click. Someone picked up, but no hello. Silence.

—Jo? It's me . . . it's your father.

A child was babbling in the background. That was Rhoda. Up so late?

—. . .

Swoosh of long distance calls.

—Son? Are you there?

There was a siren out in the night.

Then a hoarse laughter, devilish; it jolted him.

—No, a ghost.

—Son, I . . . Jo, is that you? Emory here.

—Son? That's a negative, Sir! No one by that name.

Again the low, demonic laugh—not unlike laughter he heard in anonymous calls, a form of intimidation.

Now there was a toothy whistle: like a mortar, it seemed to whine in, falling. A small explosion followed, in the receiver.

—Jo, listen to me—

—No Joe Schmo, no such rank. Poom!

—Are you okay?

—Tip-top, Sir! Colonel Ringknocker, Sir! Strak.

—Can you just tell me what's going on, Son? I don't—

Suddenly Joey turned and shouted out the window:

—Don't you come in here! Gook girl! No boom-de-boom inside the wire!

—Hold on—

—I'll zap ya'! Grease 'er, Skoly-Skol! Go get 'er! Little Pu's a sapper if I ever saw one.

Joey hissed in the receiver and made war sounds. Rhoda babbled in the background and seemed contented.

Outside a siren was loud and near the Rock Castle. Then it trailed away in a moan.

Emory heard the tinny stitch of two-way radios, men's voices, static. The area was being turned into a war zone? Above all he had to stay calm; it was the moment to use his old paternal authority and talk things over with his elder son who really may be going crazy. But by the phone Emory's handsome face turned yellowish when he heard Joey flying into what sounded like a maniacal rage. And so he sought an exit:

—My flight's leaving shortly. Son? Listen to me. Pull yourself together, Jojo, stop shouting. I have to hang up now, I'll see you in the morning. Can you hear—?

—Division Headquarters on the double! This soldier reports: body count outstanding, Sir! Au Co the canteen queen, Chi-Nguyet also called Yangtse, and La Cai or Well-Run-Dry as Hole calls her with sincere affection: they can come in and liven up the barracks. Also Dzit the Slit, who makes beds and then unmakes them.—Joey turned and screamed out the window:—Contagious bitches! Stand clear! Ooh-ooh! The power these gook women have: before you know it you're walking down the aisle with Dreaded-Sea-Fish!

He yelled at the top of his lungs and then mumbled something pitifully under his breath. A second mortar fell shrill in Emory's ear—and then reascended weirdly in a whistled rendition of *Taps*.

—Jo, I—

—These women give us a world of hurt if we love them. Ha ha ha. My darling, you gentle creature, let me protect you.—Joey's voice was a murmur which faded . . . and then exploded:—Kill! Kill! Kill!

Emory winced. He drew back from the battle cry in the phone. Was that kill-kill meant for him?

—Please try to steady yourself. We always talked man to man.

—Ay-ay, thumper man, M79. I know the deal, so you can chuck the fatherly tone.

—I'm trying to help.

—You don't say! SOS Division, call air support! Six, I'm AWOL: can't take Hanoi Hannah's propaganda. Court-martial me, Sir, lock me up, I'm a swinging duck! Ha ha ha, Loseby!!! Grunt loves Betty.

—You're not making sense, Jo. You're talking riddles.

—Sphinx riddle! And our guys die. I'll clear up this mess, Top, then inspection. Walk the walk, you 'n me need a wee bit of parley-voo. Affirmative! Take care, Sir! NVA surrounding the compound: not impressed by your résumé, Sir! Grease your distinguished tykey ass, Sir!

Emory spoke with a tremor:

—I've got to go. They just gave the boarding call. But I tell you this, Jojo: try not to lose respect for me. All our lives we've had a good relationship; it wouldn't do to lose respect. Has something gone wrong with you and Carlyne? Or the farm?

—I know who stole Tootie's boots. It was Graves Registration detail.

There was a pause. Silence between them.

Rhody chirped. There was the hush of the late hour . . . but not only. He could hear activity, like a crowd astir outside the house?

—Son, if you love your wife, then forgive her. Forgive us if . . . we've been in any way insensitive.

—Ha ha, that's rich. Insensitive yet: Miss Nuoc Mam of 1967. Roundeye non-hacker! With a brooch, in a hootch, for a smooch.

—What? I've got to go.

—Go then, my good rat. Skin 'n charbroil the little buggers: tastes like chicken.

—Paul Commynes sent me an emergency telegram. He says you've taken a hostage.

—Wisembroder on the burr! Ooh! Robidou caught it too!

—I hear Rhody playing. Don't hurt her, Joey, she's innocent.

—Why, yes, fine advice. Drill sergeant's bastard, a pink bundle of cuteness. Don't worry, I'll change Little Miss Zippo Hootch's diaper before I die. She'll make it out.

—We're not perfect, but we love you.

—Tst, you love . . . I'm sure you'd never hurt anyone. Look what you did, Father, look at your work.—But he turned away and shouted, a war whoop.—Payback, Ben Bolt! Mosey Rink, FNGs XII and XIII, Cherry Kool-Aids! Payback, Oakleigh! Horse Shue! Skiball! Mad Medic Artus!

—Oh, Jo—

The phone slammed down at the other end.

XI

WORLD SERIES HERO IN BIZARRE HOSTAGE SHOOTOUT

Joey Gilbert on Rampage Sequesters Small Daughter

VIETNAM COMES HOME TO HAUNT
A SOUTHERN TOWN

Toward dawn, inside Greensboro Airport terminal, Emory paused at a newsstand to read the headlines.

Overnight the story hit the wire services. It was on the front page of every paper. And Emory Gilbert thought of a plot to assassinate his character and ruin him politically. This was no accident: they meant to humble him, tame him at the crux moment? Also use Joey to divert attention from Nixon's Cambodia invasion, and the protest actions from Maine to California?

'Former baseball star and Vietnam veteran Joey Gilbert has ejected his wife from the mansion owned by his father where they are living. Authorities on the scene say he has taken his two year-old child hostage.

At shortly before 10:30 p.m. last night Joey opened fire on local police from a window in the old Gilbert place, as townspeople call it, located a quarter mile from the downtown sector.

Through the late hours the scene became a state of siege as law enforcement agents entrenched behind a perimeter of official vehicles in the mile-square area which is cordoned off.

Last night Achilles' wrath erupted in a small town of the North Carolina Piedmont region . . .'

XII

In early morning on Saturday, May 2nd, Emory rode the thirty miles to the hometown which had watched his rise to prominence with admiring eyes. Here his forefathers had lived and worked the soil and waged their struggles. Here he first saw the light and found nurture and spent his childhood and boyhood. And here he came to visit with Anne and the children from summer to summer through the 'Forties and 'Fifties. Then in later years he came home to retire; but world history gave him a nod, and he went away again.

This time coming back there was a tragic sense. And he thought: will my road end here?

Once, his alcoholism shocked and saddened P. Laster and Wilhelmina in their twilight; even as the local newspaper featured him on its front page. Now, on his way toward a meeting with his 'armed and dangerous' older son, he craved a drink worse than sinners roasting in hell.

The newspapers said Joey Gilbert, who suffered from a mental condition—called 'Vietnam Syndrome' by his New York-based psychiatrist—had demanded to see his father in person as first condition for laying down his arms.

The taxi drove on down the highway in the dawn light.

Nearing his sleepy hometown the roads grew active. Official vehicles, marked or unmarked, were converging like the nation's eyes on the spectacular crisis.

Where State Troopers manned a roadblock out on the Old National Highway, at the town limits, Emory Gilbert told them his name.

And then they rushed him away in a squad car with bursts from its siren.

XIII

They took him to a mobile command post inside the restricted zone, a few hundred yards from the Rock Castle on the up town side. It stood screened from the onetime infantryman's field of fire by parked vans and also the tall trees.

Alongside an armored personnel carrier, one of three plus a dozen other military vehicles, and two tanks—a State Intelligence agent greeted the father of the distraught war veteran. The FBI joined them: a hostage rescue team coordinator. Also there was an Internal Revenue Service operative from its ATF Division.

Radios spluttered through the armed camp. Men spoke in tense voices. Some were uniformed, but most were not. One sprinted across an open sniper-zone space beyond the delimited command area. The scene looked, sounded and smelled like a war zone due to the tanks, APCs, two-way communications; the protocol in force among all those present; the Red Cross unit and ambulances.

Quickly in predawn hours a first team of four FBI snipers had arrived and gained positions around the Rock Castle. Two sat atop diagonally situated manor houses within visible but somewhat distant range. And two were in Gilbert farm outbuildings behind the target structure itself.

During the 'Thirties a new National Firearms Act required registration of machineguns, silencers, sawed-off shotguns. All were illegal to possess unless on file with the Bureau of Prohibition, or, by 1970, the IRS's Alcohol Tobacco and Firearms Division. Accumulation of such weapons if unreported was a Federal violation.

Joey Gilbert had licenses for his guns, at least as far as anyone knew; and so the hostage situation fell under State jurisdiction. But he also had explosives, and who knew what else: an arsenal of stockpiled war materièl purportedly. And this, though denied by his wife, provided a pretext for bringing Federal contingents on the scene. This highly visible case involved not one but two notorious players, and thus drew FBI agents plus a first ATF investigative group diverted from moonshine revenuing which was still carried out, in North Carolina, on the threshold of the 'Seventies.

XIV

News teams, television crews, reporters flocked to the drama of human interest and presented their credentials. They came from the outer checkpoints and sped to a press office set up in the lobby of First National City Bank building. This Doric temple for the transactions of American bankers had a squat, frumpy Greek Revival facade duly adorned with pillars and lions.

In those first hours as the sensational story began to unfold, there were correspondents arriving from far places. They chomped at the bit; they wanted access to the principles—the battered wife, the controversial psychiatrist with her Post Traumatic Stress Disorder theories, the man himself barricaded inside the gothic mansion of his ancestors: this Rock Castle turned into a fortress for a Vietnam War vet's last stand. The bevy of aggressive journalists demanded a statement from Joey Gilbert hunkered down inside the house. There was a court order not to seek any direct contact or dial the Gilbert's phone number. So in the meantime they interviewed townsfolk, local merchants, the police officers first on the premises yesterday evening.

For security reasons no one including law enforcement personnel was permitted beyond a high sniper screen on the inner perimeter erected by FBI combat engineers helicoptered in before daybreak. The media was penned in from the scene and limited in its movement, but it didn't waste any time. Since this was a national story there was no end to the inquiries and follow-up phone calls. Old friends and acquaintances of the Gilbert clan were unearthed. So much gossip hit the fan, it seemed this leading family was a Twentieth Century scandal. All sorts of smut and bitter stuff came to the surface in the flotsam and jetsam of local history; and for a few days it clogged up our print and electronic media. Plenty was critical, much was silly; all had the effect of trimming the great Emory Gilbert down to size. If the TV and radio networks and news services and major daily newspapers were right then it would be hard to have more vices than the successor to Eugene McCarthy as father figure of the ranks of anti-Vietnam War activists. Emory was dissected in public: his background, family, comings and goings in the town which knew him when. To put it more graphically: he stood before the nation with his pants down.

But not only Emory. Even a Rock Castle ghost got trotted out. She was the adulterous wife of the baseball player's great uncle. Town folklore said old Dr. Gilbert murdered his wife after he caught her in flagrante delicto with the town Police Chief at the time. It seems the Chief had said the General Practitioner brewed moonshine liquor in a circular 'turret room' down cellar, where Wilhelmina later had her still; and the lawman came round to explore . . . The story had variants; at any rate, the wife vanished. Maybe her spirit haunted the subterranean rooms of the Rock Castle: its mysterious trap doors and twisting stairways leading to who knew what sort of vaulted ancestral chambers, if not dungeons.

Also, if this wasn't enough, it seems Emory's father the prominent banker, radio preacher, and First Citizen: Mayor P. Laster Gilbert had sired a wood's colt at the turn of the century. And with P. Laster as mentor that boy went far; he grew up to become a ruthless financier whose pile rivalled the pyramids. At the acme of a fabulous career in banking Paul Commynes was the pivotal figure who ushered in the big national chains and ruined most of the local merchants—the same men who were his Masonic brothers and connived with him through the years as business cronies. Oh well, it had to happen sooner or later; at least so P. Laster thought perhaps as he watched his oldest friends sink in ruin—they were devoured by the monster he himself had created in more ways than one. P. Laster shook his head and sat back and watched it come to pass.

But note the irony: an entire section of up town was financed jointly long ago by Commynes' *United Commercial* and the big boy *First National City* whose branch head was P. Laster Gilbert. And now that part of town was a cemetery of small businesses whose midwife long ago became their gravedigger.

And then after Commynes' wife died violently he had his road to Damascus, changed his ways, and became a Protestant minister and then Bishop of the Southeastern Conference. He fell and was redeemed. But what redemption, unless at the Green Stamp showroom, for this old dreary town center?

An aged pioneer here, a living archives with white stringy hair and eyes like a buzzard, went on network news after the standoff began:

—Why of course Paul Gilbert, that's P. Laster, gave Paulie Commynes his start in life no less than in business. Any damn fool knows that! We all grew up with the idea, and Wilhelmina drove him plum crazy for it too: that and his great love the prostitute called Cherokee. Try to imagine being henpecked for sixty years! And she threw fits!

There were more juicy anecdotes. And who could know and begin to describe—unless a vengeful god—the effect of all this talk on the sick soul of that wood's colt himself, Paul Jezreel Commynes. His glands gushed poisonous gall in normal times: if we are to judge by his stiff-necked posture and bilious mien, and his deep eyes gleaming with the campfires of hell. His saintliness must have suffered from the publicity. But vengeance may yet be his, and someone will have to pay.

One other P. Laster story, discrediting the Gilberts, bears mentioning. It is the night when a rookie patrolman caught town leaders up in P. Laster's office—in closed committee with the tall gorgeous Cherokee, an itinerant worker in the field of sex. And on the morrow P. Laster himself suggested the young lawman might have fallen down the elevator shaft there in the bank. And lo! What do you know? There he was: when a search party went looking for his body.

But how to suspect much less arraign for murder the Radio Sunday School preacher and town's First Citizen?

Of course our major media felt no such scruples. They were rabid to capitalize on one scandal after the next. The power boys, the network producers came here to this backwater rather than Providence, R.I., where four thousand students filled the quad at Brown University and agreed on a campus-wide strike and shutdown of classes. Down with year-end exams! Down with the grading system and academic credits their parents had paid for— as long as U.S. planes were scorching the earth of Southeast Asia and bombing cities out of existence. Nor did the media moguls focus on Berkeley where 5000 protesters met at Sproul Plaza and proposed the university as an anti-war center.

Instead, the lavish packagers of glitz flew South and from hour to hour elaborated their hard-hitting news segments, their action-packed coverage of a family's troubles. There was all a tragicomic Gilbert past to be unravelled. There were lovers who had a star-crossed destiny. There was high drama unfolding in a small southern town; and it had not only human interest, unsparing exposé, high emotion, but also fateful overtones for the nation. What passion! What human grandeur crashing down into the sordid depths! What a falling off was there! What primetime suspense and, oh yes, what popularity ratings.

Without respite, without pity, the camera lenses zoomed in on three, four, five human lives going awry. They shot them, they riddled them with their own kind of bullets, in the free fire zone of U.S. media.

XV

Inside a command trailer an FBI higher-up along with a few others briefed Emory on current strategy and the gamut of possible tactics. Still early in the crisis they ruled out a frontal assault led by tanks converted to hurl in tear gas; though a tear gas specialist was waiting in the wings. The problem was the child.

So far negotiations had gotten nowhere. The man inside had run amok in a siege mentality. But he kept to a hard line. There must be no contact with his wife whom he would shoot to kill if she came in his sight. And there would be no dealings with the authorities since in his view they were worthy of no one's trust.

Any direct military action against the house had to imperil little Rhoda. But news outlets counterbalanced this factor by portraying Joey Gilbert as out of control and too distraught to have a thought for his daughter's basic needs. So the team on the scene, which was becoming a small army by this time, was torn between two courses. Who could know if he had changed her diaper or even fed her since the siege began? The media didn't say Joey was a savage barbarian who was the last man you would want for your father, but they implied it.

Also he was in and out of a psychotic state which besides his violence in the crisis, scurrying to ready his defense, did not bode well for good parenting. What if—while moving from room to room in the Rock Castle: assembling heavier guns, setting up emplacements—what if he lost patience and began taking out frustration on a child? Everybody knows how willful and hyperactive toddlers can be—how they run a blue streak here and there, and make a mess all over creation, annoying their parents. What if he abused her? Then send in the tanks? The forces of order would have their justification for attacking.

In vain did both the hostage taker's wife and his psychiatrist spurn the idea of Joey Gilbert as a child abuser. It went out as fact: upheld by Government experts and the considered opinion of a few paid consultants.

There was a sense of prior coordination between news producers and on- or off-site command centers. And this pervaded coverage of the delicate and maybe politically explosive situation.

Until now there had not been a Saigon-style press conference, a Five O'clock Follies. But if they couldn't control the march of events over there, and how these were seen by the public, then they meant to do so here.

If Joey had on a television, and if he watched for signs of his plight from network programming: then the moral climate which the media created, as a backdrop for Government action and use of deadly force, could only heighten the tension. There was a deep hatred emanating from within the granite walls of the Rock Castle. Or so you felt.

And thus it was that as the hours dragged on a peaceful solution to the crisis seemed to recede. Who wanted peace? Not the State, and not the man at bay. So it appeared.

The problem was getting the child out of the house before the onslaught came.

XVI

Inside the command trailer Emory Gilbert seemed to enter a stage set. He felt what they said to him was scripted beforehand. They wanted his rubber stamp on their decisions, and that's all; he was to have no real say in what happened. The Government team did not mean to work with him in any equal way; they lent an ear when he talked, all he wanted, but they weren't sharing much of what they had with him: the facts as they saw them. This he gathered from their comportment around him, and their protocol. It just wasn't his role to make the decisions here; but only give his nod publicly, say a few bowwow words for the cameras, and have faith in the forces of order. If the layman knew what was good for him, he would go with the flow and say yes to steps taken on behalf of his family. This was no time for heroics. For once in his life Emory had better cool it; no showing off!

—I need to talk with my son. I called him from Evanston last night, and we spoke at length. Now I have things to ask and tell him. They're important.

—For example?

—Well, you see, he has always looked up to me. He loves his dad, and I'm the one with the authority to smooth this over. Not you. Why are there so many guns all over the place? Why snipers on the rooftops? Please put me through to Joey, and I'll work this out with a father's kindness, and wisdom. What we don't need is State and Federal security forces huddling with Military Intelligence to come up with a plan for a three-pronged surprise attack.

—At present we can't sanction any contact with the house.

—But why? You'll end up doing things the hard way when I might get it done with words. Let me restore harmony my way. All your guns can't do that.

—Professor, the situation is simply too volatile. No one's able to predict his reaction. He's said once he'll shoot you on sight. Other times he says something else: that he wants to see you, talk to you. But we just can't trust him at this point; he's sick; he's not in his right mind now. So I'm sure you can see why we won't let you go out there or even talk to him on the phone. It's for the child's sake. But why would he say he wants to shoot you? Can you tell us that? This would be your duty at the moment: to tell us what you know, what we need to know.

Emory's face, usually so rosy from rich food and desserts, was now apt to go very pale. In these hours he was not fit for a magazine cover—upset, frustrated by bureaucratic hindrance. He cared deeply for his son and wanted to go to him, but his features blanched with fear at the mere idea. He kicked against the constraints yet felt a keen relief in letting the professionals decide. They were highly trained to do this work.

—Please tell Joey then. Say I came here and I mean to see him through this. He is my son, and I love him.

—We know you do, but such a call is unfeasible at present. For starters the phone is off the hook. For that we can thank the reporters who get in our way.

—Have the operator break in. The line can be kept open.

—Not if he ignores us . . . Our advice to you is just stand by. For now rely on us. We have long experience in these things, and we know how to go about it.

Taken off the hook Emory bucked with frustration even as he breathed a sigh of relief. Really he dreaded more than death any direct role in negotiations. He must put on a good show, and the G-men seemed to see that and let him rant. But physical courage was not Emory's forte. He drew back readily enough, and yet it rankled. An FBI station chief oozed the same duplicity as the State

Department in its Vietnam policy. Lies were a style, a political way of life—lies in the grand style in the Oval Office, the upper echelons, lies with a big L in public life; and lies of the same kind, constant lies, with a small l, if you like, here in this tawdry show. Those lies were System.

The Civil Servants in charge were less interesting than a character in one of Emory Gilbert's novels. Not life, free will, conscience: their words and acts were like plastic artifacts produced with high finish by a System bent only on its own self-preservation. The rest can go hang. These men were polite enough; they shook hands and called you sir; but their responses were like catchwords of the living dead. The Federal and State agents—as Emory could see by the light of his own vital interest—were like cogs in a vast implacable machine. Yes, they spoke and moved like part of a script. But Joey's lines were not written in. So the outcome was unknown.

Emory sensed they wanted this impasse. They did not want a bloodless outcome. Why? Could there be orders from on high to this effect? Did they not like the idea of Joey Gilbert, flashy Vietnam veteran, locked up in a prison ward as he awaited a politically charged trial? Then watch out: he'd become a symbol, be a rallying point for the Anti-War Movement; he would garner international support. No; they would kill him if they could do it plausibly, like Che Guevara in Bolivia. Joey must not look like a sincere man up against an irrational system.

Emory sensed this. And he felt the Feds meant to draw out this hostage crisis and had orders to that effect. It was all a display: their concern, their deliberations. It was manipulated and fake: the way they were handling the hostage deadlock. For one thing Joey never said he was taking his daughter hostage; and now if he did so it was to save his own life. Could it be the people involved, Joey, Carlyne, Rhoda, Emory Gilbert as well, were of no importance except as pawns?

So he felt. But would he do anything about it?

He loved his firstborn son, but he loved himself more. He must live and have more life and more—more wealth and celebrity, more honors for the lionized author; more good life, a lot more, and sex! More women like dessert portions set before him.

And so, without realizing it perhaps, he too looked for Joey's blood to flow. He chose what for him was the lesser of two evils.

And then, if he made it through, if his fame and his moral integrity were kept from becoming carrion for the vultures of the media—then, perhaps, after the *sparagma,* the catastrophe in this Greek tragedy—he would welcome the silence.

The rest would be history, but without the key to history.

XVII

In a steady voice, a tone filled with conviction, he said to them:

—Gentlemen, I urge you, no, I insist that you put me through to my son. We'll settle this together.

His charm, his gracious smile under duress didn't make a dint in the armor. And he didn't want it to—since any talk he had with Jojo would be taped, and there's no telling what the boy might say.

—The Bureau cannot recommend such a course. Please, Sir, do have patience. And trust our expertees in this. Our best ally is time.

—I'm thinking of the little girl.

—Don't worry, we have her situation in mind. Let's give her father some time to think and realize what he has done. When the reality hits home, when he sees what sort of forces he is up against; then the sleeplessness and nervous tension will make him think twice. He's under inhuman strain in there.

—I don't think he'll give in.

—Trust us. We've been here before, so many times. He'll come to doubt the wisdom of his ways.

—And if not?

—He'll have no choice but to seek terms and surrender.

Emory gazed in space a moment. He was exhausted. He said in a softer accent:

—I can't speak to my son?

The operative smiled:

—We can't recommend it. Not at this stage. Wait.

XVIII

A State Trooper in riding breeches ushered Carlyne Gilbert into the command center.

She had a wild exotic air about her, hair frazzled, dark blue eyes like a tigress whose cubs are in trouble. By contrast with the uniformed officer, like a blue and black cutout with his official buttons and silver badge, she looked even more out of control. Black hair awry, surly features, she didn't try to hide her hatred right now. She saw how these men made things worse and turned a family matter into a powder keg. She and Lydia might have defused it quietly; but no, they had to get in the act.

Now she came in the command trailer like gangbusters. She glared at the FBI agent in charge, and swooped down on her father-in-law.

—Joey wants to see you.

—I asked to speak with him. They won't let me.

—Not call; you have to go out there. When all this started, before these idiots showed up and screwed us over, he asked for you to come talk in person. Now if you care about him, us, if you care about anything besides your high and mighty self, then you have to risk it. Just go on up the front walk and through the door. I think he would listen to you. If you said you were sorry, and meant it, then all this could blow over.

The chief FBI agent straightened. He stepped forward:

—Not so fast. We cannot sanction any such meeting at the present time. It could sabotage all our efforts. So not yet: no meeting yet. Also, Joey Gilbert is heavily armed and very dangerous. He's opened fire once and may do so again. No; you'll have to wait awhile; settle in with the rest of us. It would be a blunder, and maybe fatal, to send anyone out there now. We know from psych consults he has a 'negative fixation' on his father; this may be a case of patromania.

—Lydia Falliere said no such thing.

—Our expert said it. Ours. And objective. Joey's doctor may say what she pleases, but she has no mandate here.

—Your expert? Carlyne sneered. Ha ha ha, that's funny. He knows shit like you do. He's an outsider a thousand miles away from the situation. Never even met us yet gives his official diagnosis. So-and-so has a problem with authority? Oh, then he must hate his dad. You buy opinions to suit you.

When Carlyne erupted inside the trailer, Emory drew back from her. Inwardly he cringed. Look, Father, look at your work ... Now the two partners in sin stood before the law, and they looked at one another. It seemed she might strike; she had him in the 'meshes of her robe'. And so he saw calamity, and wanted to stay out of her way. But where could he hide? Behind the FBI?

She had him in the toils. But he must play her along, and let her hope he would do all in his power to save Joey. If not she could reveal their secret, and say right out the real reason behind this madness. With a word she could destroy him.

He held out a hand to her, as if reciting:

—We'll save him.

But she didn't take that hand. She looked at it with contempt for his cowardice which was clear as day. She just wanted to save her husband now; and she would use any means; she would not stop at any sacrifice.

FBI turned away from her passion, and toward Emory:

—We couldn't answer for your life if you went to the house.

Carlyne ranted:

—And if you don't, Mister, if you listen to these imbeciles then kiss your son's life goodbye! And not only his but your daugh'— but your granddaughter's also. Maybe you don't care about her and wouldn't mind if she died?

Again the FBI agent in charge urged a saner approach:

—You'll both help us negotiate when the time comes, but from here. No going out. We will open the phone lines to you at the proper time. But to go out and get in his sites, expose your lives ... no, we can't permit this.

XIX

Carlyne attacked.

—His son is in trouble, you robot. Do you have ears? Does anything at all get through your metal skull? Or don't robots become fathers and love their sons?

—I have two daughters—said the agent.

—Girl robots! Well, you have no say in this, do you hear? It is this man's business, like it or not, and mine. I'll see to it! This is our flesh and blood on the line, not some tin robot's.

Emory raised a hand:

—Carlyne—

—Listen, Father. I call you Father because I know you're going to act like one. Together we must go to him. Go out there and walk right up and knock on the front door. You have to give him a chance! We can talk sense into Jojo and save him, but why do they stop us? He's shown us the way. After all he is true, he doesn't lie, and he doesn't betray his friends. Am I right? But he does want them to meet him half way . . . Well, if they have something on their consciences, then let them come clean, out with it. He'll forgive, and we'll start over. We'll be a family this time. Alright? Alright, Father?

—I . . .

—Please, Emory, let's go to him! Won't you go with me? I could still love you so . . . I know we can become a real family, and forgive. All forgiven, Father. Let's go now. Let's, please!

The FBI agent stared at Carlyne. When she finished, he said calmly:

—You shan't go anywhere. For your husband's sake and your own, you'll do as we say.

She fluttered a hand in his face, and shouted:

—For my husband's sake! We had this settled quietly when Lydia went inside, but these jokers came and blew the lid off. What a sorry crew you are. You've done your level best to turn a husband-wife quarrel into a tragedy. And why? To get yourself promoted to Chief of Robot Staff? Or grub more money and buy a new oilcan. Maybe you want to prove what bad apples these Vietnam vets are after they let us down over there. Is that it? Such an upright and just war! But the drug addict grunts couldn't get the job done. Now they're feeling guilty because they let America down; so they commit suicide right and left, ay-ay, Sir! The parts all fit, don't they, Mr. Erector Set? Washington isn't to blame for the campaign of mass murder. No, Joey Gilbert is!

In the command trailer her eyes threw sparks.

Again Emory held out a hand:

—Girl—

But the anguish, the sleepless nights and tension were too much. Her voice broke. She gave a dry sob, but this didn't stop her. Words jerky, the tirade went on:

—Just make amends . . . by your actions. Help us turn things around, a new life, in the open, no more denial! And no need even to forgive or thank one another in family.—She sniffled; she heaved, catching her breath.—But you have to choose! Do you want our respect, our love, or is it only high posts and empty distinctions you care about? Make up your mind. The U.S. Presidency is an embarrassment to anyone with a conscience. Is it these clowns you love more than us? FBI All-Stars intent on ruining our lives? Is it? You'd better decide soon, Father: either a principled life, with honor, or more of this filth, more greed, more war. Which'll it be? . . . Oh, yes. Don't shake your head at me and look superior, as if I need pity. I know what's going on here; I know what they're up to. They want their way, and no matter the lies and violence. Baby must have his bottle! They wear blue suits, but they're a bunch of wild animals, and they don't care about our pain . . . So I ask you one last time, dear: is it them you're with, or us? Them? Or us?

He stared at her. He gave a small laugh.

—It's not so simple.

—It is! It's only too simple! Basic as ABC . . . We either awake from this nightmare, and get free together, or else no one does. That's all. Not us, friend? Then not you either . . . But once you come out there with me, Emory, once we go to him . . . then, yes, we'll be on our way again. Positive this time; and nothing can stop us. These robots won't be able to do anything about it: squirt more oil, it won't help. But you have to decide now; we don't have all night. Do we or don't we make a final try? I'm only asking you to carry your own weight in this, and do your fair share. Nothing more. And so I beg you, and we will love and admire you so . . . but please, my dear Father, please pluck up your courage now. Use your influence with them if you have any. I doubt it. But one way or another we have to fulfill our duty by Joey, and you and I both know what we owe him. If only we can survive this . . . and take a first step toward sanity as a family, and love!

Emory frowned. The noble brow looked sort of threadbare, as if the pain showed through.

Again it was the same:

—You oversimplify.
—That a fact? she said.
—Young people always do.
He gave a gesture.

In an agony she had pleaded and done her best with him. At this stage Carlyne would say or do anything to save her husband. For an instant she looked at him with tenderness, but her eyes also said: you got us into this, now get us out, or else.

After the outburst came a pause. And into this silence flowed the truth. She knew he would never take a stand on his son's behalf. Newell always said this: at the key moment the liberal runs. There was no point in blaming a U.S. President any more than you would an animal. But the liberal knows, and does nothing.

XX

Then she said the kind of thing Emory didn't want to hear.
—You got us into this, Casanova, now get us out.
—I . . .
He stared at her.
She spat her last words at him:
—Get us out!
She darted glances, right, left. Her tiger eyes flashed. For a minute she lingered, and her gaze went from one to the other: three Government agents, and a State Trooper; and then this one, her partner in sin. She looked at the G-men dressed in necktie and business attire, but made from steel plate—sectioned and fit by the bureaucracy to a finished design. In their bland manner was a technological infallibility.

Carlyne moved toward the door, but she glanced back. These men would not help her. And Lydia couldn't help either: the doctor did her best, but now they had her off the case. Anyway more than science was needed here; it would take a miracle to save Joey Gilbert.

Then she thought of Newell. In despair, at a loss what to do next, her hope went out to the hippie living underground somewhere in America. He had no address and could not be contacted, but he must know what was happening to his brother. Today Newell's eyes like everybody else's were focused on the Rock Castle.

Once—it was late summer of '67—they went for a walk in the fields after supper. They held hands like brother and sister as they went along the farm road out toward the river in twilight. And he told her not to worry about anything. More than once he said this to her: Don't worry about anything; while he spent his days and nights studying, and thinking of the world's injustices.

That evening her brother-in-law said to her:

—Many men find you supremely desirable, as you know. And you are intelligent, well educated. I note a masculine force in your feminine beauty, according to the dialectics of our species sexuality. It is this, plus an exotic touch, of the demonic, which makes us biped beasts drool at you, and butt our horns around, and kick, in a wild rut! Yet, though I may share such sentiments, you have nothing to fear from me. Please don't worry! I love my brother, and I wouldn't betray him. So I care for you in a better way than the studs. I know there are a few in this town who long to have you, subject you to their mediocrity, and crumple up your loveliness like a fast food bag. But my uncommonly acute perspicuity, my profound connoisseurship of the human heart, my truly oracular brain (Newell broke into an operatic roulade, like a bird's pure trill across the fields; he was enchanted with himself in these instants); my highly developed sympathy for humankind, minus the 20% who control 80% of the planet's resources while the rest of the people can die for all they care; my good-natured kindness has let me in on your little secret, Carlyne: namely that you are good, besides being a beauty and very clever. And so you see I want your and Joey's happiness. And what I say, I do.

"Yes, dear, I am not like the machos. Tell me: why this craze to subjugate? Why grind a good woman under one's heal? She will not be good after that. Just look at all these macho men: how they fawn, grin, bring flowers, sigh, whine, beg, badger, swagger, and ache to procreate! Before long they are hugging, kissing, feeling up, pawing, mauling, mounting. Yank panties, grab ass! Hump and bump! Yay, and so get off rocks at last, and grunt hourrah . . . Afterward they snore, and soon want more. At breakfast see them stretch and yawn, eat for three, curse easy as you please, belch. And then it's time to hang out, shoot the shit and watch TV, talk a lot of rot until they stink up the place. And then, perhaps, there's nothing better to do than batter the little woman.

"But that is not my way, and I would rather die than act so low. Newell Gilbert the hippie, outcast and social deviant, has other fish to fry. I am a sincere man, and I insist on a pure life with a clean place to work, and relate. In this spirit I've found the way for us to love, Carlyne, or let's say communicate. Better qualify the term love, it's such a buzzword, like Marxism.

"I guess for me those two terms form a dialectics: Marxism and love, science and goodness. You need both. One isn't enough. Marx was good, principled to the end, but not all Marxists. So with those two I mean to take on reality honestly, all of it, or as much as I can, no matter how difficult and hateful some is, how bad. And I will be happy: because I am struggling for the people. Which people? you say. History will draw that line, not I; it is called a barricade.

"After the long dark night of Capital, and a murky twilight of early socialist attempts, beloved sister: Look! Our vision in joyous struggle with reality begins to mature. See there? On the horizon there is a true and sunlit Socialism: a society where women and men can begin to realize themselves fully. There is hope for the children. We have fought so hard, and suffered so much, but now we are winning. It was a close call for the planet and for humanity; but now we are not only surviving but also loving one another, struggle teaches this, and living on a higher level . . ."—

That was Newell. He would do something about this mess if he could. And he was just crazy enough to find a way. But he was not on the scene; he was still out on the West Coast deep in his studies, as far as anyone knew, and maybe didn't even see a newspaper.

Carlyne shook her head: it was hard to imagine Newell as a factor in this crisis.

XXI

Through the long afternoon and into a second evening the Rock Castle braced to meet its fate. There was a mood of dread to the patriarchal oak with its great hollow trunk in front of the granite mansion. There was such loneliness on the long front porch, in the deep-niched windows. Everyday life had fled from the entresol and graduated gables and the carven chimney. Now the decorative battlements had been turned into real emplacements with merlon and crenel holding Joey Gilbert's loaded guns. And all the while the old Gilbert place was sited by a hundred Government snipers. The round angle tower with a turret on its brow was like a menace to law and order and good people everywhere in these hours filled with the threat of terror. All the stonework and embossed ornamentation, crockets and finials, spire with its golden ball: all this Old World frippery so ridiculous in a small southern town only served to heighten the tension and give it a sense of mystery.

A helicopter sidled high in the sky on recon or a media sortie. Then silence.

Who would have dreamed, in this quietude punctuated by the chirp of a cricket, that a small army, a motorized base camp had been set up just out of sight past the shrubs and tall trees? Who would guess there was a no-man's-land on the up town side?

In these day's history's most powerful nation was being convulsed by crises at home and abroad. Yet it turned its eyes to this one-factory town in the Southland.

Again the chopper passed over high in the twilight.

Then nothing stirred. The leaves of the hoary oak gave a rustle, like a shrug, as though they had seen everything.

XXII

More personnel were flown in. A top FBI negotiator and a Justice Department official were among them; also more medical staff. There were food caterers from Winston-Salem. A team of psychologists arrived along with a 'psycholinguist'; and there were attorneys, more reporters and media, plus the U.S. Congressman from the district.

All had questions. All sought to go on camera and speak as if they knew.

Night and day the TV networks were having a field day with this big-name athlete scandal bonanza. It preempted regular programming. Shock waves seemed to emanate from the great macabre mansion—shock and sadness to family members involved, but a feast in time of plague for media who flocked around giving shrill squawks.

FBI and IRS-ATF operatives were in contact with the U.S. Attorney General.

Questions, questions, urgent questions.

Was there imminent danger for the two year-old daughter?

Had the deranged G.I. amassed the kind of weaponry over this past winter which could put a town at risk? News outlets reported ten thousand ammunition rounds for his semiautomatic rifles; also anti-tank weaponry, an RPG-7; a 7.62 mm machinegun. The press sent out the most amazing detailed accounts of this lone man's military capability. Where did they get their information? Official sources?

It was said the psycho ex-soldier was using the tense deadlocked hours to assemble an arsenal: howitzer, 8-inch gun, 175 mm with appurtenant devices, installation equipment. Vietnam had come home. It was a one-man army. Did he have napalm? Did he have general purpose bombs, rocket launchers, artillery rounds, 20 mm strafer explosives? Stand back: it was time to cleanse this burg of rednecks.

XXIII

That night the militarized encampment swarmed with agents in helmets, body armor, green flight suits. Helicopters landed in the wide lot behind the bank building. G-men moved about in the pink glow of the neon sign above the police station.

How much longer could this go on?

When would an armed contingent move out behind tanks and advance across the wide sloping front lawn of the Rock Castle in the darkness of night? When would they spray the house with tear gas and pepperfoggers?

Would such an action prove fatal to a small child?

How long could the authorities allow this berserk individual to flaunt the law?

When would hostage rescue team sharpshooters, good for a quarter inch target at 250 meters, get the go-ahead to wound and disable? Agency rules of engagement forbade direct fire without a recognizable danger to the hostage, or else a shot taken at an agent.

The psychologists said the mind of Joey Gilbert, a well-armed infantry combatant, had sunk in dementia and paranoiac ideations. It was a revenge obsession due to symbolic loss of manhood in battle. They addressed a news conference dubbed by one correspondent and veteran of Saigon press briefings: The Psychotic Follies.

On Watts line from the Bay Area, now Brigadier General Daniel Pricecroft spoke with command center about the former squad leader and survivor of a hundred fire fights. Pricecroft offered his services in a humanitarian capacity; and, as an afterthought, he mentioned the name of Emmet Bufillu.

—It was a rare friendship, he said. Each saved the other's life.

XXIV

Snipers poised. At ten angles around the Rock Castle, they waited, in position. Through high-powered lenses they tried for a siting of the former jungle warrior and counterinsurgency expert.

Special agents waited in the wings. These had capacity to storm the house once FBI on the ground decided: and if the Attorney General and perhaps the White House in this instance were in agreement.

As fatigue grew there was more frustration among law enforcement officers.

The deadly force option could not be ruled out.

Much was at stake. The country, stunned coast to coast by student strikes, and an ROTC building burned to the ground at Kent State, in Ohio, looked on as the Government sought a way to contain one man. It seemed like a key moment in the nation's history.

Hour after hour the impasse went on. With all that firepower aimed at a single target, the authorities, specialists, officials on the scene played down the possibility of violence. Still the casual observer sensed a perplexity. No one, not a foot soldier and not President Richard M. Nixon, must thumb his nose at the Law of the Land.

Beneath the calm professional exterior there was a tension. It rose toward the limit as, at any instant after night fell, an attack might begin. And no one could know the price in human lives. Intelligence services worked to establish just what weaponry that furious man had at his disposal. Who didn't recall the astounding performance Joey Gilbert put on last fall in the League Playoff Game and then the World Series? TV networks spliced baseball footage with scenes from Vietnam. What jumped out at the viewer was the war mentality. Kill.

Local and State Police were evacuating residential areas nearer the standoff; though there were differing projections as to the Rock Castle artillery capability. By daybreak tomorrow thousands would be billeted to school facilities across Davidson County: all those who had no relatives to stay with or other sanctuary.

Meanwhile, the chief FBI negotiator was urging Emory Gilbert to endorse a combined assault if one had to take place. Among the 'pro' factors was a deteriorization of sanitary conditions. Also, the agent said child abuse had been detected by a listening device of the latest sophistication. It seemed Rhoda cried periodically and then stopped with a suddenness. Was he gagging her? Was he hitting her?

—Sir, this may be our best chance. It may prove to be the way to go for the little girl's sake as well as your son's.

They wanted to issue a public statement. The father gives his consent to the use of military means.

Would there be an all-out attack at dawn?

Child welfare workers came on the scene. The regional coordinator led a group from Charlotte to advise and support the hostage rescue team; also to help a distressed grandfather.

At this stage Emory Gilbert looked so worn down, and willing to play ball with the devil himself if he could just make it through this—he probably would have approved any measure, no matter how drastic, except for one fact.

Earlier, in the command trailer, his daughter-in-law whispered in his ear:

—If you say yes to a direct attack, you'll live to regret it. If we go down, you go down.

Chapter Twenty-One

I

Wisteria these first May days perfumed the southern university where Joey Gilbert met and courted his wife one springtime in the mid-'Sixties. On Women's Campus in front of the domed Jeffersonian auditorium there were coeds speaking out against the war. They read statements and led chants. Press were on hand. Here, as across the land where students gathered, the quad was filled with the sounds of protest. After the President's revelations on Cambodia there just wasn't so much interest in school routine. Classroom business as usual seemed a mockery at such a time.

In a tense atmosphere the academic schedule did stay the course. Semester review and pre-exam study week went ahead. But the clarion call for more mass slaughter in democracy's name; the blatant transgression of last year's solemn campaign promises; the fateful lies of those in power—stirred up our young people and made them look for an outlet. It was too crude and baldfaced: the way men like Tricky Dick posed as the epitome of wisdom and sincerity, yet it was all about selfishness and greed.

Many students carried on of course. But others put their belief in quality-point ratios and class position, GREs and grad school applications, on hold. There was something more urgent to be done.

Then came more bad news. Then came more duplicity in high places. It seems that at this noble institution of higher learning, no less than at the much publicized Berkeley, the university was passing along names of campus activists to the FBI. And this was common practice. The school administrators ratted on the students. Alma Mater informed on her own.

Well, what else is new? Do you know what kind of money endowed this school to begin with?

Disaffection grew.

II

From her second-storey window Lemon Gilbert heard the rally being staged by her dorm mates and friends. One read Nixon's words into a microphone, and the potent sound system made year-end exam study hard even in the reading room of the library. Lemon couldn't hope to study. She was in anguish, and unable to take part in the scene outside. If she went and joined them, the press would be all over Joey Gilbert's sister. This she couldn't face for the moment.

—'*Our third choice is to go to the trouble's center. Clean out North Vietnamese and Viet Cong occupied territories. These sanctuaries serve as bases for attacks on both Cambodia and South Vietnam . . .*'

Lemon lay propped on pillows with her eyes closed and a textbook spread on her lap. There was also an unfolded letter: a few pages in Spanish about life in San Pedro de la Cueva, a village in northwest Mexico where the seasonal worker Juanchi lived with his family. A tear rolled along Lemon's fresh cheek.

—'*Now, faced with three options, I have made a decision . . .*'

Earlier her father telephoned. Under no circumstances must she catch a bus and come home, which would interrupt her studying for final examinations. That was an order. But as the hours passed she met her brother's crisis at every turn. Radio and TV stations were giving the 'Rock Castle crisis' frequent updates. At first reporters and press of all stripes, whether or not accredited, were trying to gain access to her floor with cameras. The first ones made it inside and up to her floor and upset her. Two campus police were placed downstairs by the entry. Now a dorm mate had to bring her food; she didn't want to go out when everyone was staring at Joey Gilbert's little sister.

—'*Tonight I again warn the North Vietnamese. If they continue to escalate the war while the United States withdraws its forces . . .*'

And then she had to deal with her dad's call. There was a maudlin note in Emory's voice though he tried to stay upbeat. It made Lemon think of the time before her mother succumbed to cancer; and then came months of grief made worse by his alcoholism; then the decision to retire and move South to his childhood home.

—Don't worry, girl. Nothing will happen to Jojo, we'll see to that. You just stay put and do your work.

But would he? Would their father make very sure Joey got out alive? And Rhoda? His words slurred with fatigue, or he was drinking again. She could hear a police radio sputtering in the background. And this brought home the reality her brother was living through, and she gave a shiver.

She felt a misery of inaction. Her voice trembled with grief and sleeplessness as she told him:

—Jo's in bad trouble this time. We've got to do something.

—'*The action I announce tonight puts North Vietnam's leaders on notice. We will remain patient and work for peace, conciliatory at the conference table, but we will not accept humiliation.*'

There were boos, catcalls, whistles across the grassy quadrangle scented with lilacs and wisteria. The slogans arose spontaneously, the shouting in chorus. Liar! Killer of children! Tricky Dick!

Her brother's life was in danger. What could she do? Was there a way to rescue him? Now Joey hated Carlyne and would not let her come near him. He threw her out of the house, said press reports; he took their daughter hostage. He cursed his wife in public. The idea of this made Lemon want to start crying again.

Maybe Newell could've talked sense into their older brother. But Studiosus was living underground since Dad tried to have him put away in a mental hospital. He might not even know about this . . . But yes—thought Lemon—he was on his way to the Rock Castle fast as he could get there because right now it was the only thing to do. If not, then he wasn't her brother . . . But he was far away, still in California, at last sighting; he probably had a long way to travel.

Well and what about herself? What was Joey's sister doing to help? Ah, their father told her to stay put where she was, stay away from the Rock Castle . . . and she must obey? She loved her father—but did she still respect him, after all that Max Doan business, and after . . .? Did Emory have the moral authority to tell her what to do? Whose decision was it—what she did or didn't do during this time of family crisis? His? Or hers?

What about the New York psychiatrist? Joey admired this woman, Lydia; he said the best things about her. If there was anyone who could turn things around, then wasn't it Dr. Falliere? Lemon knew from news reports she was on the scene. But the FBI was keeping tight control of things over there. The authorities didn't seem likely to let any free-lancer have a show. The controversial Lydia was under wraps; she had been inside shortly after the crisis declared itself—but would she be able to get back in?

And so the hostage standoff went forward on its own momentum. Where? Those in charge seemed to favor a military solution; that was the tenor of reports; like Nixon in Cambodia. Kill all, destroy all. If it resists, flatten it: never mind any Joey or Rhoda inside a Rock Castle. In the news tomorrow there would be some pathos and fine words. The civilian deaths would be swept under the rug of a ten-dollar phrase. By then the person Lemon loved most on earth, after her mother, who passed away—her brother Joey would have perished. His life would be over, his great abilities gone in large part to waste.

Stay there, said Emory. Do not come home. And did he have the right to say this to her, and make it a fact? Had he earned that right by his own bravery and behavior as a father? Had he been honest? Caring for his children, Jojo, Newell, herself? Was Emory brave—would he act with courage and principle, as Newell always said, taunting him, now that the chips were down? Would he be able to intervene? Would he get the job done: the job of being a father and acting uprightly? Weren't those the minimum requirements of a man?

Since the mad thing began, like an ancient tragedy being turned into a soap opera, or maybe vice versa; since the Gilbert family madness hit the fan, it had been a constant—Look! There she goes, Joey Gilbert's sister! In the cafeteria, by the Student Union mailboxes, along East Campus walkways, or in the library, it was: What? Is she still here? Gee, you're here, you haven't gone there? . . . What's happening? What's the latest? Shouldn't you go be near your brother . . .?

Lemon heard them. She nodded; though mostly they just looked at her, and didn't say anything—to her.

She felt responsible, and tragic. Always, since a young age, since her older sister Evelyne died: she felt herself a kind of moon to Anne Gilbert's sun . . . when it came to her two big bruvvers. Newell liked to call her: Little Mother.

Now, as the siege dragged on, the hours were like an agony.

Could she stay here in her room? Could she just stay here on campus and cram for exams like her father ordered?

Lemon's first year in college had been one of growth and personal discovery. Not that her required freshman courses were any great shakes. But she was off on her own at an intellectual center after the recess period of high school. She loved to read and study beyond the curriculum; but such things as tests and grades were seen in another light now.

—'*If the enemy responds to our offers of peaceful negotiations with increased attacks, more attempts to defeat and humiliate us, we shall respond accordingly.*'

III

In the morning she lay in bed unable to rise for breakfast and her morning schedule. She felt sick. At any instant the phone would ring, and her father's voice would say gravely: Come home, it is over. Okay now, all clear, you may come when it's too late. Time to go to church and pray over the dead. Okay, it's safe now, you can catch a bus. The time of grief; the time of a lot of postmortem sentiment after *you did nothing* to change the situation and save the person you loved when you had the chance. Is that love? No, don't hold life sacred and try to save it—everybody take the easy way out, the line of least resistance now. And then go home and worship death instead: at the funeral of Joey and Rhoda Gilbert. That's easier.

It was a cruel thing to hear these men talking on the radio about her brother's life as a series of 'tactical options'. So calmly they said the words: a 'tank assault with tear gas . . . to storm the house and overwhelm the target'. If not then they could only try, 'beg' as a Government psychiatrist said, 'to relate on equal terms with a megalomaniacal war veteran in shell shock two years after his service . . . an acute psychoneurotic with borderline schizophrenic traits . . . given to fits of hysteria.'

Somehow the whole thing and all this chatter of 'little Rhoda Gilbert's welfare' sounded so disgustingly hypocritical to Lemon, like an echo of Nixon's address to the nation the other night. It was a big lie! These were real people they were dealing with, but all they could see in it was a 'tactical option' and a media event. Her brother and niece were inside the besieged Rock Castle ready to die; this wasn't about some technocrat's jargon and his 'model'. Get out now! Leave my brother alone! Joey would never harm a child; *you're* the ones who hurt children! . . .

Lemon wanted to cry, and she did start crying when she thought of some TV footage she saw. The former Minor League third baseman was dripping Vietnamese kids from his shoulders, back and hips, as he carried nine of them on a bet across the dirt square in a Central Highlands village. She knew him. She knew he helped save her day after day from Newell's teasing and roughhousing during their childhood. For a time she would just fall down and moan when Newby got home from school and came in the living room like a rhinocerous: big bully that he was. In Jo's absence The Nooper brought her down and piled on after the tackle as he whistled shrilly through his teeth and cried out:

—Fifteen yards! Unnecessary roughness! Ha ha ha!

Emory yelled at him and it meant nothing. But if Jujube was on hand, and saw him get carried away like that, then watch out. He wouldn't try it.

Now it sounded to her like the authorities were shuffling. They took advantage of the hostage situation and used it for their own purposes. Lemon thought so. She wasn't sure why, but the whole thing seemed wrong to her, fishy.

At midmorning her dad called. His voice was slurred, exhausted, bad.

—Don't worry. We'll get Jojo out of there.

—I'm trying to call him. I can't get through.

—Don't even try! That's against the law.

—Dad—

—Just have faith, Lisa. Stay put and study; earn high grades and make us proud.

—I'm sure Joey will be proud of my high grades.

She detested it when her father called her Lisa.

—He'll be okay. He's been in rough scrapes before.

Dozens of times since first hearing the news Lemon had dialled the Rock Castle number. Always busy.

—Dad, are you in contact at least? Will you have him call me?

—I can't. No one's allowed to talk to him. They control the lines.

—But why? That's crazy. We need to talk!

—Not now, Lisa, unwise.

—I'll come to him. Then—

—You will not! I said no on that and I mean no. They'd detain you at the checkpoints anyway. You'd only be taken in custody instead of spending the time studying for finals. And then what? We waste a semester's tuition money, and for what? No, I said stay there, and that's an order.

Unless something was done soon it would be good night, Joey Gilbert. In an hour, in a day—then the attack on the Rock Castle. Then too late.

No way to save him from a hundred miles away.

If the job was left to Government security forces, FBI, a Military Intelligence unit now at the site, it might not get done.

IV

Emory's call shook Lemon. It gave her a foreboding, and made her feel hopeless.

When they said goodbye, she had a jolt. Even as they hung up she was deciding. And the moment she decided and rose from bed to dress and get ready: then the anguish, the dread turned to something else. All her pessimism and annoyance at her dad fled like an evil spirit from her seventeen year-old limbs. Then she was ready and no matter how dangerous it was—no matter what! She did up her hair and put on a pair of sunglasses.

In bluejeans and a gray sweater, her light-brown hair pinned under a beret, Lemon Gilbert went out in the sunny May morning.

Bright leaf aroma filled the town; it'll kill ya' but it sure smells good. Along East Main she breathed in the pungent tobacco smell

and moved with a will toward Five Points and the seedy Durham
bus terminal with its greasy spoon.

At a few minutes past noon she boarded.

V

Along the highway west there were overpasses, Old Mount
Church Road; there were fields in cultivation, and stretches of
forest with tall Carolina pines. There were bridges, road signs,
exit ramps with motels and gas stations; more fields, some hilly
pastureland with livestock, and horses. Here and there a river or
a blue lake shimmered in the sunshine.

On the bus someone had a radio. Over it came the voices of a
press conference. A woman was being interviewed, a psychiatrist.
Lydia.

She spoke of the hostage crisis, retracing its development, and
said she blamed Government and law enforcement agencies for
making a mountain out of a mole hill. She rejected the official diagnosis of Joey Gilbert given by a team of psychiatrists.

A reporter asked:

—Do you consider Gilbert dangerous?

—Provoke someone long enough and they may explode. That's
true. But who is the dangerous one, provoked or provoker?

—Is he a traitor to our nation? Or merely a criminal, as many
believe, in open defiance of the law?

—This depends on your point of view. He served his country
well in Vietnam. He risked his life everyday, and then came home
to find apathy and ingratitude if not hostility. He was sent to do
a job and went there and followed orders, trying his best to do it.
Then he returned and was blamed, and people called him names,
after he gave his all. How would you feel?

—He referred to the President of the United States as a REMF
hyena. Care to comment?

—Why don't you explain REMF for the audience?

—I'm told the first two letters stand for rear echelon.

—Well then that much of it is true.

—Dr. Falliere, the FBI is alleging a large arms cache inside the
Rock Castle. I'll quote: '. . . firearms, machinegun possession,

gunpowder crates, TNT, hand grenades, assorted rifle parts and magazines . . . illegal semiautomatic to fully automatic weapons conversion . . . chemicals explosive when combined'. Is this a correct assessment in your opinion?

Cameras clicked in the background.

—Unless . . . there is a breakthrough soon . . . you may expect a fullscale coordinated operation against the house. Government representatives on the scene have set the stage for a military solution, and they have their reasons for wanting one—

—Elaborate?

—I mean as a show of force in a critical period, as a lesson to rebels; but above all maybe as a diversion. What may happen, and soon, is . . . not a non-lethal tear gas assault. I can tell you that a proud, categorical Joey Gilbert isn't playing around at this point. And he may have his own perhaps subconscious motives for welcoming such an attack on the Rock Castle. In any event he will fight if need be, and he is ready to die.

—And the child?

—Precisely, the child. But why get excited, gentlemen? There are Vietnamese children dying like flies, but you don't seem too worked up. Their life is cheap life, as the 5-Star General remarks, the man who is their flyswatter. Look, as you know, our Clark Kents care more about conforming and keeping their jobs, than mangled kids. It's only when we can't seem to win, and our own young people come back in body bags, that you may take note. So I find your question a bit bigoted. Your corporate employers show no such concern for the 250 million child laborers in factories, sweatshops, etc., worldwide: who don't play, don't study, who have no fresh air or drinkable water but only 16-hour shifts. Or they work as prostitutes . . . 325 million children do not go to school. Do you know that? Come now, you don't feel their pain at all; it isn't fit to print. Unlike celebrity gossip. But let one child come along who suits your program, a Rhoda Gilbert, and then you all stand up and take notice on cue, like a chorus line of elephants in tutus. Then you get excited.

Background laughter: as if what she said didn't count.

One asked in a more relaxed tone:

—Doctor, do you have a book about Joey Gilbert in progress? Does all this add up to a lucrative contract for you?

—Soon I'll publish a monograph on PTSD, Post-Traumatic Stress Syndrome, in Vietnam veterans. It's been a taboo subject till now among our psychiatric confrèrie; so it isn't lucrative, or likely to endear me. Conclusions emerge about guilt, I mean our collective guilt, our guilt as a nation, and about aggressivity. You see we live in an empire. Our country is the most powerful empire in history. So we . . . this affects the way we think and live.

—To return to Joey Gilbert, Doctor.

—Yes: unconsciously he seeks to expiate his guilt, I think. Three years ago he was idealistic, a patriot; and he joined the effort to pacify and control a small country. Over there he saw things which didn't jibe with his ideals, including a woman and her kids die bloodily. This changed him. You might say the scene imprinted itself on his psyche, his life. Now he wants to trade places with them and step into the shoes of his victims.

—Why?

—He . . . the guilt is too much. He has a wish to die as they did when his squad raged through a village and he couldn't stop the massacre. In a real sense, a few days ago, he went in his own peasant hut which could now be set on fire. He regresses: he steps back in time to replay both killer and victim roles.

—How so?

Lydia cleared her throat. She paused for a sip of water.

—As . . . as killer he tries to repeat the traumatic event. A village called Xo Man has stayed in his subconscious; it is a big chunk of horror, in there, and it causes him more pain than he can stand. This is because he is good, gentlemen, he cares and feels for others. But it costs him to feel responsible, and there are outbursts of violence when he just can't keep it in anymore. When we can't, let's say . . . accept, digest an experience: when we deny it . . . then the thing lives on in us like an alien force. It can grow into a monstrous thing, a kind of psychic tumor. It haunts and possesses us, if you will. But Joey is also a big healthy man, a strong one, and so he doesn't give in. He won't throw up his hands and say: God help me, for I cannot. No; he still wants to win, wants love—

—And that's where you come in?

—Do you love him, Doctor?

—. . . wants happiness, wants to reconcile and make things be okay. But he can't. He is a killer unable to admit it, and he revisits the scene at Xo Man again and again subconsciously, in his dreams, in hallucinations . . . and now in a real-life setting as he tries to revive the past and maybe remake it and do the impossible. He would try to reprocess the fear and guilt and the reality.

He would try to reestablish the status quo ante . . . But that can't be done. Can't there be some moral sanction for his actions? A political rationale: patriotism? The fight for a noble cause, freedom and democracy? The bloody crèche in the hootch in Xo Man tells him all this is a tragic farce. Moreover, our own people, our society has finally begun to see through the lie and can't believe it any more than he can. But he did it, he's a killer, he's guilty and deep down he knows this even if he refuses to submit to the evidence. What? Joey Gilbert confess to the most horrific action one can imagine? Complicity in a child's murder? Never. He cannot accept this; he won't relate to it; but what he will do, driven unconsciously, is try to expiate it and restore the natural order, so to speak, by his own death. So the Rock Castle becomes the Xo Man hootch. And he is punished. And then, and only then, in death, is he free from the unthinkable, the guilt . . . Again and again Joey has repeated the disaster: in fire fights over there (by the way this explains many G.I.s' opting for a second tour); in his mad baseball days here; in his dreams, as I said, and intrusive images. But it's no use. Violence gives a temporary vent, but the pain and the guilt come back. His system can't forget what he did in Vietnam and put it behind him and move on. There is fixation. There is no hope. And do you know what? Sometimes I think Joey Gilbert is America. Oh, he is far in the vanguard. But such convulsions will keep occurring here. They will spread. For ten years or a hundred they will go on, violence and guilt and more violence, in a spiralling cycle, until the whole thing comes crashing down like the Rock Castle may do tonight or tomorrow.

Chorus of questions, like protests. A reporter asked:

—Doesn't the Veterans Administration exist for such cases? Why all the fuss after all? He could drive to Fayetteville and have himself admitted and get the treatment he needs. No?

Lydia laughed low.

—First you're not listening to me. And second the VA hasn't begun to admit the existence of Joey Gilbert's illness, which is PTSD. That would cost too much, on various levels. My colleagues in psychiatry don't accept the diagnosis yet either. But VA issues apart: he doesn't see himself as sick exactly, not a mental patient. He's proud. And he stands guard over his manhood, and repels such notions. He'll battle that enemy, namely himself, and protect his dominant position, his potency and control, to the bitter end. What else are we all about? But meanwhile his pain gets worse, and it is unendurable, it goes . . . beyond. His ego remains rock hard. Does it? A matter of dignity. He may be desensitized and intractable; he reflects our arrogant society, our American hubris. What do you think? Is it too late for him to change, and for us? Will Joey Gilbert never know himself: any more than this rich, poor, shallow, tragic nation will know itself? Can the sick soul gain insight, and begin to talk to the old school male, the corporate, military ego? I fear not. There will be no easy way for Joey, and none for us either. Maybe it's only broken down slowly like Rome, only disintegrated from within and eaten up by its patricians, that the United States will find an end to its misery, which is the world's. Who knows? But as for that man out there, barricaded inside the house of his fathers, the Rock Castle, he is not so patient and passive as that. He wants an outcome now. Make it right or die trying. The time is up and he can't take the pain any longer, but he won't surrender. On his feet, actively, he must set right what he did and atone somehow. Well, it's his despair. He murdered tenderness back there at a joyless crossroads in the Central Highlands. Now it's too late. But the soldier must still try to rescue the maimed and bloody little boy stuck to the dead mother. And that boy's name is Joey Gilbert.

A few called out questions.

—Are you a cynic, Doctor? Why such a poor prognosis?

Then a woman from one of the wire services:

—Can he go it alone? Without anybody's help? He deserves better!

Cameras clicked.

Lydia caught her breath. She sighed into the microphones.

—Like anyone else I . . . It's a shame really. The other night, just as we were reaching a decision for him to accept longterm treatment, the police showed up. I'm not sure why they came. There was no disturbance and nobody was breaking the law. But some meddler called the station. So just as, finally, Joey hung on the verge and wanted so much, so much to ask for help . . . they chose that moment to barge in and make a mess of things.

—What can we expect in the next twenty-four hours?

—Do you have any predictions, Doctor, for the outcome of the siege?

—Joey's psyche is crying for release as the sickness nears its crisis. An open conflict like this, even if it's one man against an army, comes as a relief after what he's been through.

—Why not commit suicide and get it over with?

—A question of manhood. A man doesn't quit. And he's not a destroyer; he came to save.

—Save?

—Save Vietnam, or so they told him. Let's not forget that. This includes the children. But I would say he still has hope; that is, his subconscious is hoping, even if he doesn't think there's any. If he can make it through this, then there will be a new start for him, a new life.

—Will there be no negotiations then? Is there no peaceful settlement on the horizon?

Click, click.

—You tell me. The ancients had physician-seers: iatromantis, they called Apollo, Aesculapius. We don't have them. I've tried to explain the situation to you, but crudely, and certain factors I may not reveal. There is a strong determinism at work here. A freer man would decide consciously and work to change things. This one fights on blindly in a way his fixation dictates. Also: to me there seems to be no intent on the Government's part to settle this peacefully. They've done nothing toward that end and everything to the contrary. Why? I ask you why do they want bloodshed? Here, in Vietnam . . . and now watch out: on our campuses as well, blood could flow.

—Why is this, Doctor? You tell us.

Lydia gave a sort of laugh:

—If you don't know, I can't tell you. I think the basic reasons may be economic, don't you?

Pause. A moment's lull.

A woman reporter toward the back asked:

—There are rumors you're in love with Joey Gilbert. Won't you comment? Maybe set the record straight?

—Yes, I love and admire him, as a friend.

—Could you save him if you went to the Rock Castle?

—I don't know if I could still persuade him to go in for treatment. At the start of all this, yes, he'd listen to me. But now Government forces have created a war zone. They've barricaded the town and set up roadblocks. So I can't get close. Yes, I love him, and I love Carlyne, too. But what I love most of all is the truth. And the truth is that all this is unlawful, just as our presence in Vietnam is unlawful. Those first squad cars to arrive on the scene were a provocation.

—Was it a mistake for you to leave the house, Doctor?

—He thought I called them. He no longer trusted me or wanted me in there.

—And his wife: what does he feel about her?

—He loves her. If they could just be left alone to work it out . . .

—And your plans, Dr. Falliere? What will you do now?

—I'll continue the struggle. I'll stay here until it's over. And what about your plans? Wouldn't it be better if you focused on the unwinnable war we're waging in Southeast Asia, and the student protests across this country over Cambodia? Do you think it is wise for you to turn everything you touch into the usual media manipulation?

VI

At the turnoff ramp where Interstate 85 exited to the Old National Highway, Lemon told the bus driver to let her off a hundred yards further. Then she got out, had a look around, and made for the border of woods by the road shoulder. By skirting the exit she managed to elude a police checkpoint at the base of the curving ramp.

She made her way on foot into the town. At once she saw unusual activity: squad cars and official vehicles, media vans. As she went along she saw people standing and talking on their front lawns. It was a holiday atmosphere for those not evacuated from zones deemed at risk. The lazy small-town pace had been sprung by events at the Rock Castle.

By a railroad underpass named after Paul Commynes, the financier, State Troopers manned a roadblock to divert traffic from the old business center. On seeing them Lemon turned and made her way along a residential street. Then she doubled around on her way up town. She knew shortcuts.

So far her disguise, beret and sunglasses, did the trick; no one had called her name. Eyes and thoughts were all on the scene at the nearby Rock Castle. Everywhere talk, talk, excited voices; she never saw such a thing here. What a trip to be from the third baseman's hometown!

Where Tasty Baker's glazed doughnuts and cakes embalmed the defunct town center, Lemon took right and then left down an alley which was once busy with deliveries, long ago, when she was a child. Then she crossed a lot behind the old Palace Theater beside Rosa's Five & Dime.

Breathless she paused on the main street and took a look around. It was an armed camp. Men in bulletproof vests carried assault rifles. Canine gas masks grinned at the young woman as she passed by. All over the place were police, law enforcement officials, TV crews, men in dark suits despite the heat, medical teams, more State Highway Patrol.

Beneath a metal awning the County Sheriff gestured into a news camera and shared his views on the matter.

Lemon glanced here and there. They were too busy to pay her any notice, so she drifted in the stir of people with a purpose: the street swarming with out-of-towners, uniformed and plain-clothes cops and backup personnel, reporters. She blent in; she had a purpose too. Do what she must, but reach her brother.

Then across the street she saw a Max Doan in full regalia. The grayish blond gentleman was jaunty as ever with medals galore on his broad chest. He stood there like a figure in a movie set. She heard him say to someone:

—Where is Emory?

—Must be at forward command.

Lemon turned away. She kept walking.

Out along the old main drag, a few hundred yards, stood the Rock Castle set back from the road among the tall trees. No one dared to go near it now. But she would. Quickly, let's go, before Thanks-a-Million with his boyish snub nose and eyes like grape-shot came marching after her and went on his knees in no-man's-land to ask for her hand in marriage.

VII

A ten-foot high sniper screen protected the forward area on the north edge of up town. There were four armored personnel carriers parked just this side. Behind the APCs where lateral movement became more secure was the tactical operations center; and from here, during the night, a state-level Emergency Response Unit had deployed round the target house in tandem with FBI sharpshooters and Hostage Rescue Team members. They made a tight ring around the Rock Castle.

For a moment Lemon hung back by the official vehicles. To look like she belonged here she jotted a few notes on a pad and made a show of calm while drawing closer to the sniper screen.

Then she crouched between two APCs and scooted ... She darted past a State Trooper posted behind overlapping sections of the high barrier. Taken by surprise he swung back and grabbed at her sleeve, but she yanked free and made a dash for it.

—Hey! What the—Come back here! Halt! Halt!

Joey Gilbert's sister burst out alone into the vacant terrain between the heavily armed, high-tech encampment behind her, and her father's house also a military fortress.

She heard them shouting.

—Halt! You'll be killed!

—Stop! Halt! Halt!

Lightly she ran. And her heart jumped. Yes, she must get to her poor bruvver, he was upset! Talk to him, soothe him. If anyone could coax some good old horse sense into Juniper ... then she was the one. Not all these men in blue looking like a herd of stuck pigs. They had enough firepower to raze a city, but she knew a better way.

—Joey! It's me, you kid! You baby-boy! Don't shoot up your li'l sis' who loves ya'.

In full view now she called out in order to break the silence and let him know that she was here, that she was coming in to him, and wouldn't take no for an answer. It was a bit like one of the puppet shows she used to put on in her bedroom upstairs.

—I've got my key to the front door, Joker! Stand back! Make way! Here I come.

She took off her sunglasses, and waved her arms, for him to see. She ran fast but then, curiously, began to canter like a horse. This was from her old schoolgirl obsession with horses. She sort of came loping up the long front walk toward the great old oak with the hollow trunk. She passed it, looking around.

Quietly she had slipped through the maze of their checkpoints and their protocol and run out past the barricades. And now no doubt it was a media event, and all the cameras were on her.

But no one followed her out there into the zone of high risk: not her father, not her chronic suitor Doan who was such a war hero, and not the forces of law and order who didn't dare show their faces out here, but could only come sneaking after dark.

She left them all starting with Emory back there behind her, rather far behind, with egg on their faces.

VIII

Head up Lemon waved her arms some more and then glanced over her shoulder as she took the last ten yards. Still no movement this side of the encampment. She was all by herself, though the nation watched. But behind her she heard the murmurous stir of them, their flurries of communications and male voices tinny amid the radio static, like a swarm of gnats.

High above her the Rock Castle seemed to lean forward to hear all that activity as well.

On the front porch she paused a moment and, shoulders heaving, gasped for breath. She knocked softly. No sound inside, no response. Were they alright in there? He hadn't . . .? No, he couldn't . . . that wasn't Jojo.

Then she took her key and put it in the heavy front door.

It opened slowly.

Cre-e-eak.

—Joji?

She saw the front hall table where his letters home from Vietnam once lay waiting in a little pile, day after day, to be opened.

Silence. Such a silence there was in the big empty rooms.

Were Joey and Rhoda okay?

Before her rose the wide carpeted staircase. To her right was P. Laster's old smoky den; and, further on beside the stairwell, the guest bedroom where Carlyne had stayed in her husband's absence.

Lemon glanced left at the rarely used living room, and she couldn't believe her eyes. This Georgian décor of the last elegance was cluttered with weapons: a machinegun on a tripod, a row of semiautomatic rifles lined along the front wall. Ammunition crates and war materièl lay spread out across the Persian rug. There were web belts, helmet and flak jacket; there were revolvers. Joey Gilbert was readying his emplacements for the final battle, and the place smelled of metal and oil. He was going to die, but he didn't mean to do it alone.

What struck her also was the tictoc . . . tic . . . toc of the grandfather clock which held forth ever since her summer visits here in childhood, and it hadn't stopped. Amazing; time went on.

But it only heightened the silence. And there was such a silence.

Wait. Suddenly she heard a small childish sound. Lips slurped: a child sucking. Now swallow.

—Jo? You in here? Jocose?

There was a small cry from another room. The blinds were drawn, and the lights were off. Lemon paused on the threshold. She stared in at the two of them. What a sight!

Inside that cave with grimy beard and scraggled hair sat a green-faced madman. He was two white eyes grinning at her from beneath the facial paint. Grin, yes, but ah! the glint in those deep eyes: the sadness, the outrage. It was her older brother alright, but he looked like a severed head in the depths of a well.

In one hand he held a big greasy M-16; though it was almost amusing that he didn't bother to man the defenses, the windows, as a visitor came in.

In the other hand he had a pink baby spoon. Apricots. There was the fruity tang of baby food in the air, puree of apricots. The scent seemed to dance like a butterfly above the scene with its ominous smells, oily weapons.

Joey fed Rhody seated on his knee. He held the pudgy little girl in the crook of his arm, and for a moment she chewed thoughtfully with her curly head resting on the gun barrel.

Rhody drooled her food and gave a smirk. She had a laugh and spit some out. Take that! It was fun to spit mush on Joey's big, rough, hairy hand. Then she ate a little more from the spoon, puckering contentedly. Good girl. But she tongued out another mouthful and tried the little laugh again. Joey, a bit impatient since this wasn't supposed to be play, rolled up his eyes in the LURP mask. Bad girl.

Lemon gazed in the dark sleepless eyes of her brother. She looked for the old Joji in there, the fair-minded, the nice one who saved her many a time from Newell's teasing.

Boldly she stepped in Granddaddy's den, and gave her own little giggle for the fun of it.

—Papa Jo, can I have some?

She went up to him, bowed over them, and put her cheek to his painted face. He stared straight ahead and said nothing and let her. With a hand on his shoulder she hugged him and tugged his sleeve.

—Darn you.

Then Lemon began to tremble and cry a little.

She put her head to his mad head and mumbled something about how she loved him.

IX

Newell Gilbert was hitchhiking east.

As he talked to his rides about the great issues of the day, about the Vietnam War, and student strikes and actions on a hundred campuses; as he walked the highways with a duffel bag slung over his shoulder, Newell watched the American landscape pass by.

But it wasn't going by fast enough, and he was afraid he would get to the Rock Castle too late. So his plan was to make it out of California before having money wired to him; then catch a flight to North Carolina. He didn't know where he would go to an airport: maybe Salt Lake City, depending on the rides.

After he got word that his father meant to confine him to a State mental hospital, he left Hillgard Street and went across the Bay to live underground. He didn't want money sent to him in this state where there could be a warrant out for his arrest. So he had to get away—and with luck not be hauled in for thumbing rides—before the funds were sent for a plane ticket.

As soon as he saw the headlines about his brother, he hit the road, and the first night saw him in Tahoe. The next day beyond Carson City he hung a right on 95 toward the juncture with Route 66, and twelve hours later he was in Kingman, Arizona. After a few lifts he walked the highway all night and crossed over the Little Colorado at dawn.

On past Petrified Forest and the Continental Divide, across the Rio Grande River in Albuquerque, he hitched his way. Then three long rides through Oklahoma and Arkansas brought him into Memphis.

Driving on through the wide night of America he slept and dreamed and awoke to think things over.

The decade was at its close: a special time in the nation's history. A need to look into ourselves and talk about things came due in families, on campuses, in the streets. It was a sort of Revolution that went on amid the idealism of youth; it had aspects of class struggle but still amorphous—not bitter and pervasive, not yet. The ideas of students and Leftists were in play. But only the profound economic interests of the workers, farmers, ever broader sectors locked in a life-and-death struggle against Capital, would take things to the end.

This was not the same as the Red Family and Blue Fairyland, Beats and anti-HUAC demonstrators, Civil Rights sit-ins, the Free Speech Movement, the Vietnam Day Committee, hippies and 'New York types' as local police termed them, the *Barb* and KPFA, Truth Radio, free schools, study groups, off-campus communes, professional collectives, dropouts and visionaries, trashings, barricades for a day. All these were good; they were what was possible for awhile, a delirium, a vision. But their time had passed.

In one night in Berkeley he had seen more radicalism, more kaleidoscopic counterculture, more dope smoked and free love made, more political and spiritual discussions, than in most pre-'Sixties lifetimes.

But then what?

There was a place called People's Park. Newell joined the Berkeley Freemen one Sunday morning and helped turn a plot of urban blight into Utopia Now. It was on vacant ground between Dwight and Haste: behind Telegraph Avenue away from the cafés, repertory cinemas, funky shops, classic bookstores, dope dispensaries, preter-hip posters, bikists, rock music, and all that leafleted landscape of hippiedom.

And here the people worked on People's Park. During the Great French Revolution the Parisians came out in a similar spirit and got the terrain ready for their Fête de la Fédération. What a relief for Newell Gilbert and what fun after the sectarian hell of Left politics in the U.S.

Some area merchants put up the cash. Soon truckloads of plants and sod came to the scene. Longhairs and straights were developing their powers of sacrifice and construction—to quote El Che—in an attempt at a token socialism.

Together they built a park. Tenured academics, solid citizens, bourgeoisie rubbed shoulders with the comrades, and some stone cold freaks. A playground was made for children. Flower and vegetable gardens were planted, and striplings of symbolic significance. From bouillebaisse vats were ladled bowls of Saint-Antoine stew, named after the famous workers' quarter in Paris; while joints passed from hand to hand. And so it was that human liberation seemed like a Sunday picnic.

In People's Park the people talked over many things such as Primitive Communism, the Red Man and Seventeenth Century Digger, and humanity's edenic dream of a great good place.

The first night everybody danced around a bonfire. But fire trucks and uniformed men came to put it out.

—Comrades! Comrade Police Officers!

—Come join us! We've got the good stuff!

—Outstanding!

Sunday was Commune Day, and the masses came out gaily to plant, till, break bread, roll joints, dance, critique all things human not alien, gush, hallucinate, talk, love, talk some more.

Then one day the police came out too. They were sicked on People's Park by California's right-wing governor. There were issues to do with the university since it owned the land. It seems the authorities of U. Cal. at Berkeley did not see People's Park as a project they could support.

On a bright day in mid-May of '69 the cops bulldozed the gardens, put up a fence, and sealed off the area. A crowd marched down there behind the Park creators and tried to take it back. They threw rocks and they breathed in tear gas. Jump suits appeared: special units. It was the Blue Meanies, namely the Alameda County Sheriff's deputies.

There were shots. Police sprayed the people with buckshot. People fell. Among the fifty injured was a young artist blinded for life by birdshot. And one died.

That night the governor ordered 3000 armed National Guardsmen into the town. So People's Park went from Free Territory in America to fixed bayonets along the cordoned streets, as the right to assembly was suspended. Martial law, curfew, in Berkeley.

A local cop held his gun to a handcuffed activist's temple, cocked it, and said:

—Now you will sing the Star-Stangled Banner.
In the aftermath a large campus rally got tear-gassed.
The hospital and nearby schools were also sprayed with tear gas from a helicopter.

More marches and rallies took place as the summer of '69 wore on, but People's Park stayed closed.
When Newell went to places where the Anti-War Movement met and debated on what was to be done, he listened to the talk and came away in a lonely reverie. He felt a yearning for nature.
He wanted culture and deep studies. He wanted personal adventure: to grow. He still lent a hand and helped staff an anti-war office, but he thought of going to Europe for a year, maybe longer, and studying languages, filling notebooks as he tried to understand economics, and history. It wasn't enough to declare South Campus and Telegraph a liberated zone, and think up ways to aggravate Lynch'em Johnson and his successor Nix'em. History had to come home to America; and then there had to be a historic plan, and men and women willing to begin implementing it.

X

—I turn here, buddih.
Newell opened his eyes.
—Carolina soon?
—Yessih. Keep on Crossville up t'hyir. Crab Orchard intih Knoxville 'n 'a state line.
—Well, Sir, we disagree about politics. But thanks for the ride, and good luck to you!
—You too, boy. Nivir mit uh hippie 'ifore, real 'un. Nut suh' bad's ah thoat.
—When the time comes, I guess you'll come around. When it's your family that's suffering, you'll see this scoundrelly System for what it is. In the meantime my words are just words. Right?
—Ah giss'. Hayell! I'll nurt' unihstan' no comoonism, free liv' 'n sich. Most times ah jis' lit things pass me by, peac'ble lak. M' wahf's blather 'niff 'n it fer one man! Her-her-her' . . . But some

on'm feels raht diffrunt 'n you bitter watch yer tongue roun' t'hyir. We ain't no Reds. 'N you goll on git uh hyearcit 'fore some on'm dizz it fer ya'.

—Right on, Sir! Bye now.

He got out at the exit ramp and walked on. Was there time? Would he make it to the Rock Castle before Government forces stormed the place? After all he hadn't bothered to stop and take a plane. That was iffy and would take a day or two: to get the money transferred.

XI

In a restaurant by the highway he went in for a meal and a look at the headlines.

536 college campuses had struck across the land.

Even a castrated U.S. Senate, minus its war powers since Vietnam, sang a falsetto demand for troop withdrawal from Cambodia and an end to air bombardment by July.

In Santa Barbara, in Buffalo, in Seattle, the students were rioting. Young people threw arson bombs, stood up to police fire and took casualities. After disturbances at Kent State the past couple days a righteous Ohio governor called the protestors 'worse than Brown Shirts and night riders and vigilantes'.

The pithy Vice President Agnew said: 'Next time a student mob waves its non-negotiable demands and pitches rocks: imagine they're wearing brown shirts and act accordingly'.

Hm! All those fascists against U.S. genocide in Vietnam.

And then, from the summit, Tricky Dick spoke the historic words:

—These bums, ya' know, blowin' up the campuses.

KENT STATE ROTC OFFICES BURNED TO GROUND

PRINCETON STUDENTS AND FACULTY SHUT DOWN CAMPUS

In New Haven demonstrators at the Black Panther trial were calling for 'immediate withdrawal' plus a nationwide school stoppage to end academic complicity with the war. At Brandeis acitivists had set up a National Strike Information Center.

DIAMOND DEMON JOEY GILBERT SAID TO HAVE AN ARSENAL IN HOSTAGE STANDOFF

Newell thought: so he knows.

Hurry now. Get to him somehow. Arrive in time!

He went up to people and asked them for rides. He wasn't shy now. He sped. His thoughts weren't on problems of political economy.

Over and over he thought: *Joey knows.*

Hold on, brother, I'll think what to do . . . Go public with the facts! Joey Gilbert took Rhoda hostage to make a point. And right now he is waiting, waiting for his father to come forward and confess to adultery, to incest! Well, don't hold your breath. The day Emory sacrifices himself for one of his children or anyone else . . . it may be too late.

But once a scandal erupts, and everyone knows, then the hostage scenario becomes irrelevant. Doesn't it? Joey relents because his point has been made? No, no . . . that's idealism. What I have to do now is get inside the Rock Castle, decoy him, conk him on the head, and drag him out of there for his own good.

How to do it? How to get to him?

Just hold on, boy. Last it out another day, and tomorrow night we'll talk. We'll talk, and I'll act.

In the front seat Newell tried to make conversation with the driver as they sped along the highway. But he thought, thought, thought: Will I be in time? Ah ha, so you found out somehow. The chickens came home to roost. Alright then, all will know it. But hold on, Jojo, just hold your horses, old man. Nothing rash.

I'm coming!

XII

Inside the Rock Castle the soldier looked amphibious. Like a reptile his painted face emerged from the jungle fatigues. There was a bad thing in his eyes, a sick thing; and looking at him Lemon's face showed pity and maybe a hint of aversion. Life was falling apart in here, but she had her new college life and studies, a world between girlhood and adulthood to enjoy.

Her brother's eyes had an ominous glint and a fixity. Only see this through, his look seemed to say, and then I'm finished with all of you.

—Jobe, you're tired and fed up!

He shrugged. All day his mind drifted in and out. He was ranting to himself amid the spells of madness and hallucinatory fits. Or he shouted out for Troupial to call in air support on a bluebird chirping outside the front window. Super-strak! he barked. And little Rhoda, if she was in the room with him, said: Suwuwak! Grim, tight-lipped, he was getting ready for combat, and he gave orders to Rhody as he once had to Izard, Thingum, FNG-IX. On the double, Sir! Ay-ay! But the main thing on his mind now was to get her out of here.

On the perimeter he took catnaps. At 0630 when the threat of a predawn attack had passed, he was able to liberate three hours' sleep from the enemy. But he woke up jolted by a horrific dream.

Again he went about preparing for his last battle, making trips to and from his crates down in the subbasement. Then he saw to Rhody's needs which seemed to bring him to his senses for a minute.

All the while he was mumbling incoherent phrases.

—I'll have the perch with fish-cress . . . Homesick for Vietnam? Well good for you! . . . Won't you please grease my wife? said the drum and fife. With a satchel charge, since her ass is large.

There was hysteria as the day wore on, but it came and went like a tornado on a sunny day. No matter what he went through: still his youth and vital strength met it head on and tried to get used to it, digest it, bit by bit. The effect of all this was just too much. Yet he still had his willpower, an athlete's tenacity, also his immense personal courage; and these had him feeling his way

back from the brink. He groped among his 'objects', as Lydia
would say, the stuff of his 'reality principle'.

And, as he went about putting last touches to the Rock Castle
defenses; as he worked in a clear way and knew just what he was
doing and why, in full connaissance de cause; as he got things
ready and made his preparations for Armageddon—the grisly
LURP took a moment to change Rhoda's diaper.

XIII

Now he gazed at Lemon who stood there before him. His sister was the one person left besides Rhoda he didn't mistrust or
suspect of being a spy. He blinked at her with a candid amazement. But her presence only served to show how far, far out he
had gone. It was painful. It hurt him. He felt so cut off and alone.
Right now he was halfway across the earth waging war, and in an
hour, in a day he would torch the hootch of his own poor muti-
lated self.

Lemon frowned with a tear in her eye. And she smiled.

—Joeykins, you look too pooped to pop.

—Yessir.

—Rhody okay?

He grunted. The camouflage paint looked wild as he rolled his
eyes at the ceiling:

—Sarge, why don't you ask her if she needs sick bay?

—No, I can see she's fine.

He leaned over the small girl in his lap:

—At ease.

She reached up and yanked his beard:

—Dog-gie!

—When you leave, you're going to take her out. But do me one
favor—his face scowled beneath the paint—don't give her to that
whore.

—Jojo, don't throw stones at Carlyne. She loves you so.

—I know how she loves me. You don't know it.

—Are you sure?

—When you leave in a few minutes, you'll take Rhoda and also
a message for the friendlies.

—No, I'm staying with you. You'll be safer.

—I won't: with you and her in my way. I said it, and you git.

Again Joey's eyes, set in the black and green paint, rolled up. But he started to talk and tell her things. So alone since the siege began, he just needed to gab a bit like anyone else. So he told his younger sister the kind of thing he might say to Lydia. With a sigh he murmured strangely:

—Over and over again I see a guy from my squad, Ben Bolt, run a few more steps . . . floosh! And then I'm in that ville and Ringwood is staring at me, and guess what? It's time to say goodbye. The whole stupid thing comes over me like it was going on right this moment.—Joey whined.—Or I have to watch Blair spitted naked on a defoliated tree, and his hand points down at me and I seem to see Newell. Ha! That's a good one. Those VC are a bunch of fun-loving fellows: they left on his granny glasses. Look! Look how he stares down right at me! But I guess death must be nearsighted: it stares through a pair of eyeglasses down at the grunts. Wow! Catch the boy's act: soaring spread-eagle up there with the tip of a charred bough in his mouth, like a snake's tongue.

—That's horrible.

—Affirmative. And I have to see it.

He grinned. But Lemon frowned and bowed her head. Joey's eyes were deep and dreamy as he nodded a little and put a finger to his hairline, and scratched.

Lemon seemed to know by instinct he had to get some big thing out—some big big thing next to which she was a mere tiny dot, and maybe he too.

So she said softly:

—Go on, Jo. What more?

For a minute his head hung down on his neck. He was all greasepaint and matted curls like some kind of jungle vine. And then he peered up at her with his two eyewhites very weird in the penumbra of the den.

—You know, I loved that man since I saw the light.

—Who?

—I was a good boy who believes in his dad. And this helped me a lot: to have faith in him, in someone; and over in Vietnam too. Righteous father, like our righteous and all-seeing God way up in the sky: he will make things okay for us, you know . . . Dad and I never even argued, not once. I felt no need to say nay to pa-

ternal authority any more than I did God or Uncle Sam. Heck no.
And Newell had a way of pissing me off: I thought he liked to get
a rise out of people and be the center of attention. Well maybe he
did . . . But the time came when I started seeing through this mys-
tical father type of thing. It took me long enough, too long. I had
to go to Vietnam. But one day God, Jesus as anything more than a
man, patriotism: it all came a cropper. At some point you get tired
of praying and waving Old Glory when real life is shitting in its
pants. Then high heaven begins to stink too, and if God Almighty
lives up there then he doesn't have fussy tastes. (Joey paused; he
thought.) After that I came back home and played some ball to
take the edge off. But I just couldn't believe this sense I had, this
feeling of . . . disbelief! I trotted out to third base like I'd never
been away . . . and what did I find there? I found more of the
same old bullshit, myself the . . . what? Nothing real at all. I mean
no real dignity, no identity; but only a kind of whore with nothing on my wife the whore except glamor which was my whore's-
makeup and more money than she got for her cheap tricks. What
is a whore? Just a show of love, a love without substance, nothing
more. In my case it was like making love when you're dry, no love
to it at all. I hated my year in the Big Leagues from start to finish.
When it ended they stuck a World Series ring on my finger and
called me a champ. But they wouldn't give me the MVP . . . As
for Carlyne, my loving wife, she deserves the MVP award for the
venereal disease league. Number 1 in filth and misery and selling
herself on the street.

XIV

Sun lowered through trees on the street side, the huge old oak
whose trunk was like a gray mountain cliff with a cave: outside
the den window beyond the porch.

Joey droned on as sunlight lit the blinds and sent a thin line of
gold light over the rug.

Rhoda, restless, worked her arms with a laugh and gave a few
swift kicks at the strong limbs that held her. So Joey leaned the
M-16 against the wall and turned her over like a sack of seed in

his large knotty hand. Rhody shrieked as he bounced her up and
down on his knee.

—Geeyap, horsy!

She tilted, tottered; she chuckled bumping along. But Lemon
was afraid the child might fall in that breakneck ride, and sat
forward.

Joey jostled her some more and said:

—Poor kid wasn't too lucky with her parents.

Lemon gave a gesture:

—I don't understand, Jody. Why . . .?

—Why what?

In the cozy den she nodded at sun-filled curtains, and silence
outside.

—All this . . . hate.

He glimpsed here and there, forgetting about Rhoda. He was
eerie:

—You know . . . They come and haunt me: when I'm asleep,
awake. Bufillu shot in the spine . . . he wants to take his own life
when his wife goes out to buy groceries. Loseby, Izard, Skol are
posted to their folks' front door in fart sacks. Courtesy of the U.S.
Army. Others . . . they were called Sumter, Fern, Tommy Lerch,
Manito; one was my good man Clement; they all cut it more or
less, they hacked after all. Now give 'em a marble monument
with their name. Isn't it pretty? Isn't it nice? . . . You know it gets
my goat. All my life I felt a . . . a kind of anger. You call it hate?
. . . Okay, if you say so. I could never give it a name, or explain
it . . . just a distant sense, an otherness type thing. On a baseball
diamond I got it off, not all; mostly it was turned inward on myself. It messed around with my well-being I guess and my self-
esteem. Athletic success might serve to rid me of the uneasy feeling, but by college I think sports were starting to get on my nerves.
I couldn't admit it of course. I just felt I needed more stimulation,
sort of, a higher high. I got married which was a downer. Don't
be in any hurry to get married. Often as not it's a bill of goods;
and for Carlyne and me it wasn't what it was cracked up to be.
Then I went to war, and maybe there I was beginning to realize
my potential for anger. Yes, call it hate if you like. But I think only
now in these next few hours when they try to come in here: only
this time will I get down to business and hate all the way. I had a
vocation for hatred, but it wasn't the Vietnamese, it was . . .

—What, Jo?

—Not any person. I never hated a person. I don't hate Dad and Carlyne, out there, though they are with them, traitors, and against me. No, it's what happened that I detest so much, and the reasons why, if I even knew them . . . But now it's almost over, the wondering why. All my life I've been fighting in a fog, and I couldn't see the enemy clearly; but I knew he was there, hating too, hating first! . . . And now when he comes with his tanks . . . don't worry, I've got RPG-9s for those tanks . . . when he rumbles up the front lawn out there in front of a few dozen infantry then I'll at least get the feel: this is it, this is it at last, the enemy. So let's have at it . . . all the way. And there will be something in that. I'll go out fighting at least. If I can just get Rhoda out of here and off my hands.

—But it's no good, Jojo. We need you. You're too important. You can't just go off half-cocked like that. You have to live a long time still and help and fight for the people you love and even those you don't love. You don't have the right to take your life in your hands. Nobody does. It's too selfish!

—Be so kind as to name a person who deserves my love, besides you.

—Rhoda.

In his lap Rhoda made spastic movements. She strained to get away from his ugly mug and his grubby mitts. She did this the instant he turned from playing with her to more serious matters. So he lifted her, face down like a cat, and then set her right side up on the rug. He put her there sort of like a wind-up toy, and let her go.

Zoom—there she went straight for an electric socket. Across the Persian carpet she strode like a chubby juggernaut. She tripped, lunged into Auntie's arms with a laugh. Lemon tickled her and she giggled and squirmed. She said:

—Cheesy.

Joey said:

—I told her what a cheesy crew they make out there. Always going where they're not wanted, the Rock Castle or Vietnam. And they don't even know why: sold a bill of goods. Hey, what do they care, long as they share in the goods . . . But, you know, it's a funny place, The Nam . . . I remember blank peasant faces by the roadside, mama- and papa-sans and phony smiles of kids when the G.I.s came tramping through the hamlets. Those are hungry little tykes and they dig ham 'n mothuhjumpuhs, as we called them, C-rats. Why I don't mind if I do. Kids with a grin like a crumpled tin can . . . But you never saw such an odium as there was over there. Vast, it was, impersonal. Look at the heroes, those butchers, moving through Pinkville while a lot of glum masks watch them pass by. Go away! No, sir, not yet. We must kill, kill, act like men, and then deny it. We must win! Torch 'em, and give them a new RevDev ville. Thank you, ma'am. And still you know we wouldn't have questioned; still we'd deny it all ad infinitum, so long as we had good reason, a cause; and mine wasn't so-called freedom anymore but only Carlyne. She was my cause; but it was the last, because one by one the great reasons had got peeled away from the mind of the overgrown boy which I was. And when the final layer of that onion was peeled away, just the other day when I found out a little fact about our family . . . then I stood naked as Kevin Blair with a charred tree limb stuck so far up his ass it came out his mouth. Hey, what's the boy doing up there? Maybe he's showing off. Think so? He forgot to wear his flak mesh, like a fig leaf . . . And Carlyne too, the person I put before myself: she was naked then in the same way, when I found out about them, and she was not beautiful. Well, it wasn't the first time she tasted the apple, oh no; she's known for a long time what I just got wind of. But she pretended not to, with me at least . . . Well, that's funny, almost. I was the last one to know. Every one of you knew, and Cindy too. I was the only sucker who didn't know.

Rhody, ever so restless cooped up in here, grappled free from Lemon's embrace and scooted away again.

—Cheesigee! . . . Beeja.

At the rug's edge she fell. Bumped her noggin, but no matter. Back up again: beeline for the den entry.

Joey in two strides overtook her.

—I know they have snipers posted, and I know where. One's waiting in the silo, others in the farm outbuildings, and across the way at our neighbors'. Sharpshooters sit all day and wait for the order to shoot. But I've got them in my field glasses, so it won't be that easy. I'm dropping with sleepiness but I have to stay on the ball, keep me and her away from the windows, while I gauge angles. What a drag this all is when you think about it. I could be farming.

XV

Lemon could see her presence settled him. Since she came in he was growing calmer by degrees, still exalted, but more coherent. There was always a shy tenderness between them, ever since childhood; she had a special place for her older brother, and she would stand by him as he did her. She knew his apartness and his need, because their mom favored Newell, and it was too obvious; and Emory loved his oldest daughter best, Evelyne, or Lady as he called her, who died in high school. But nothing shook Joey's trust in his little sister, and today was proof. So she must put it to use.

—Look, Joji, there's one way to get back at them. We can come out winners if you, Rhody and I leave here together. We have to go out the front door, and walk out there side by side in the sunshine.

—That's what you'll do in a minute, and take her with you if you don't mind.

—You too.

—Not me. I'm not going to them, and I'm not asking them for anything.

—If I take Rhoda they won't have to worry about how it looks anymore. They'll attack and go for the kill.

—No matter, let them. Then we'll see.

She stared at her brother. She was feeling very, very sorry for him a moment before; he looked so downcast, and broken, where he sat in his mad costume. And now? When he said 'Let them', he looked almost happy.

—It doesn't matter to you maybe, but it matters to me, us. And . . . say what you like, Jonas, it matters most of all to Carlyne, who loves you truly and puts you before herself!

—She can go to hell.

—You're unfair. I never knew my good Jo to be unfair.

—You don't know what she did.

—I beg your pardon. You yourself just said we all knew, and me too. I'm in this family, and I know what happened, what Dad did to her. The big famous baby couldn't help himself; he thought he was too big to spank, but he's being spanked for it now. As for Carlyne, I think she is . . . she had no choice. House guest living

at his expense, loving and admiring him like everybody else; she
was vulnerable. Dad I forgive and I don't care if he deserves it.
You know he did one or two things and made a few sacrifices for
us when we were growing up, all those years up North.

—Like what? Mom did.

—He provided. You think it's child's play being a husband and
father?—Lemon gave a laugh.—I know all about it . . . And . . .
and anytime one of us was sick in the guest bedroom downstairs,
remember?—you moaning and groaning with your bad stomach,
New with his nosebleeds all day, which Mom couldn't deal with:
Dad brought home some little gift from the office, or not little, a
fine toy . . . and it was everyday, because he loved us in his way.
But mainly I forgive him for the simple reason that life has to go
on, Jodhpur. Why carry the poison around inside? Spit it out! Spit
it up to Lydia, whom *you* love and wouldn't mind making love
to, oh yes, I know how that stands too, I do! So go on then, if *you*
must. But live! Get if off your chest, and proceed . . . Oh, I so want
you to forgive Dad and Carlyne. It's for the future, Joli, because
I just can't afford to lose a swell bruvver like yourself, a sweet
one. Please put away your gun now, and let's walk out there with
Rhody on your shoulders, and say: Howdy do, Tex Ritter.

—No, sir. Not me.

He gave a strange wistful smile.

—But why? Don't you want to live?

—Not like this. I'm sick of it.

—Then work to change it, but don't give up this way. That's
for cowards.

—I'm not giving up. This is a hurdle and I'll try to get past it.
If not, I did my best . . . But the hurdle is there, and the cowardly
thing would be to say it isn't.

His lips quivered with the paint, like a night crawler.

—Stubborn, perverse! Are you a man or a mule?

—I'm a man whose wife doesn't love him and never did. Say
what you like: is she in here with me now? No, you are. End of
story.

—But you threw her out!

—And good riddance. I'm tired of playing God. See how I
broke those eggs, Daddy, can you put them together again? She
never gave a single inch, not since our courtship: a day by the
Lumbee River when she arm-twisted me into what I wanted anyway, marriage with her. Well, I gave her what I had, it's not a lot I

grant you, bumbling jock; but she played games and aggravated me to death. What is it with these women anyway? Are they insecure? Just look at the way she . . . the way she does up her hair and wears her clothes, it's not frank, not truthful. But I'm to blame of course because after she hypnotizes me by dangling it in front of me I'm not as sensitive as I should be to her needs. Well at long last I saw behind that little relationship. Too bad it's too late. She only had to crook her little finger and say: you, boy, come here. And I'd come. But no; instead she put my heart through the wringer as well and made sure she kept me hanging on and in her power . . . Lord, what a way to be. Where do these women get such a bag of tricks? Where do they learn it?

—From these men.

—And she wonders why I went away!

—No, just when you're coming back.

—Ah, that so. Well, fug 'er, 'cause this time I'm not.

They fell silent in the quiet late afternoon.

Outside the window nature went its way with the same small buzzings and warblings for a million years. Naive nature; it had no idea the face of things might change in a few minutes, at least here at the Gilbert residence.

Rhoda on the loose was still fascinated by the electrical outlet. So Lemon dragged her away, back onto the rug. Rhoda spent ten seconds with a children's book, but then got involved with a heavy glass ashtray used as a doorstop. She stared at it, rubbed it, nudged it a little. She gave a laugh and looked up at Joey.

He gazed at her, the dynamo.

—Wait a sec'.

—What, Jo?

He rose, hefting the oily semiautomatic rifle in one hand. He took his grungy camouflage cap and put it on his sister's pert curly head.

—Watch the kid. Stay here: don't either of you leave the room.

Then he went in the guest bedroom. Lemon heard him turn on the shower.

With an eye on Rhody engaged in play she thought about the family. When Lemon came to the age of reason she was the child of two aging parents. Anne was in decline. Emory was still his energetic and gallant self, and yet not himself, drinking too much. This meant she looked more to the two brothers she admired so:

Newell for free spirit, and ready wit, an aggressive mind; but Joey on a deeper level for quiet character, a deep stubbornness at times. And so when springtime came here in North Carolina, she liked to take walks in the woods where she sensed their childhood. It was in the many tender hues and tints of springtime, in the pinkish tans, in the mist of sallow green shoots arisen from the earth in early April . . . all nature taking wing in a bird's song, in a man's. How she loved this older brother and how she wanted to stay in here by his side until the end if need be.

On her young head Joey's sweaty combat cap had the heavy, much-used feel to it of adult things, like a Big Leaguer's glove. The heft of it made her feel inadequate; a sort of emblem.

In his absence she was suddenly very nervous, afraid of the creepy situation: all those big men out there getting ready to lower the boom.

But she wanted to stay.

When he came back, the paint was gone from his face. Clean, almost fresh, now he wore swim trunks and a t-shirt.

He looked more relaxed.

—You'll come out now, won't you?

—I can't.

—But you won't win, dear. There's an army of them.

—Who's talking about winning? They won't win either.

She gestured.

—It's a law and order bedlam up town. The big men just want one thing: to move in, strike the Rock Castle, use what they have. Try it out!

—I've got an idea what they have from TV. Yes they've got weapons, a world of them, but what else?

—You'll die, Jojo.

—Not alone.

—But you'll kill people.

—I'll kill a few killers. I won't turn my guns on the town, as they're saying. I wish I could kill all the creeps in blue suits who sent us to that death trap in Vietnam. If I had my way, they wouldn't do it again.

Lemon's face rumpled as she kept back tears.

—Your wife loves you so.

—She has a funny way of showing it.

—What if you talked to Dad?

—I'm waiting. I'd say there's as much chance of his coming up that walk to have a chat with me, as there is of snow today.

—What if he came clean and said he was sorry?

—Let him tell the world he's sorry. What he did is an offense to nature, to the human race. I'm not Rhoda's father, I'm her brother. I might as well be . . . Carlyne's son, not her husband.

He gave a shiver.

—But if he does confess . . . then will you come out? If he confesses his sin publicly?

—Go tell him to do it.

—Why don't you, Jo? You tell them. Say that's why you're doing this.

He gave a little laugh.

—It's not just that. Let Johnson and Nixon say they're sorry. Let Kennedy come back from the grave and tell the people he, or the big corporations, the contract-boys who made him, never should have started this unholy war. But the world will die before a U.S. President ever tells the truth about politics, or gives a sign he has a conscience.

He shrugged.

Lemon stared at him.

—You look impish, Jo. Almost happy-go-lucky, like Newell.

—This farce will soon be over. Once you take Rhody out of here then I'll have a free hand.

—I won't take her. But . . . I guess I'm supposed to go and tell Dad what you said. I don't want to leave you . . . It could be I'm the only one who can make him spill the beans.

—Wait up. Just what did I say?

—If he confesses, you'll come out.

—Ha ha, hold your horses! Not quite! . . . I said that he must walk up the front walk, and knock on the door. Like you did. But you're a man, Lemon the man. He's just one more lowdown, lying, yellowbelly blue-suiter.—Joey laughed.—He's a REMF. Yes, now go out and tell him I said that. I'm waiting for him. Come on, honcho, if you've got the balls. First we talk. Then I decide, not you. My turn.

—You always idealized him. Now you fly to the opposite pole.

—Shit ideals.

Lemon cast about:

—He didn't want to hurt you. You know him: he's a child when it comes to some things.

—Like my wife.

—He couldn't help himself.

—And I can't help myself.

—You know what a clown he can be, always calling this or the other one a great man, but he means himself.

—I didn't know, but now I do.

—Forgive him.

Again Joey shrugged.

—Him maybe, if it even mattered. But not . . . all of them. They come here to face me down, as if I was in the wrong. What a crew they are, forever sticking their nose in other people's business. And my father's in cahoots with them.

—Never mind them. They have their punishment.

—Which is?

—To be themselves.

—That may be, but I have to mind them. They hurt others, including me! They sent me to Vietnam, and they made me . . . You know sometimes I really do want to destroy myself just to show them and be rid of them.

—Do you think they'd care, Jo, or even think about it except to gloat? You can't change people, or punish them, except maybe the two or three who love you. I think if you saw Carlyne again, you'd see you've punished one person, at least, enough. I think in her way she's been fighting for you a long time. But you don't see it.

—I see she doesn't give me what I need. Right now she'd say anything because she has a guilty conscience.

—That's unfair.

—Listen, I doubted myself until I couldn't live with it. I hope you never know such a pain of inadequacy. She called me a jock and turned her face from my kisses. So then I saw sports in a different light, okay. But how do you change your life? She razzed baseball and she razzed me. Don't think I exaggerate . . . Then I went away to war. I thought a soldier, after he fought for his country, might find favor in her eyes. Well, she came to me in Bangkok, and it seemed my tactic had worked. But she was still a she-devil. She seduced me to make me think I sired her brat, and to falsify dates. She told Emory to tell me she left the Rock Castle in February, but she left a month earlier since the pregnancy, by him, was starting to show.

Joey shook his head. A tear rolled on his lean cheek bronzed by days in the fields. There was still a tear in him, but it couldn't change the set look of his jaw, the sharp premature lines on his forehead. He brushed his hair and beard neatly after a shower, but the M-16 was across his lap.

—Rhody's not a brat. And your wife was just doing what she could.

—She lied. That's all. Now I know it, and I know why. Finito the mystery.

With a finger he flicked the tear.

Lemon's voice went low:

—Dad took her. Don't you see? He went in to her.

—She let him. I know her. She wanted him.

—No. Or maybe part of her, but it's more complicated. You're a cool guy and I love you better than animal crackers, but there are things you don't understand.

XVI

For a long moment neither spoke. Lemon looked like the strain was getting to her. She might break down and start crying.

She lowered her head, and her thin shoulders shook a little. In the quiet house the child fussed over a doll, and said: poopoo. Rhoda played her whimsical game in the time before baby talk went beyond two-word phrases.

An insect buzzed up the screen going a deeper gold as the afternoon began to wane. Birds sang away in the trees outside the window.

In the distance, but not far, there was the stir of men, vehicles, two-way radios.

Joey Gilbert, his lips pressed and pale, bowed his head. He swayed slightly like the warm breeze in the drapes.

Lemon said softly:

—Carlyne loathes herself, and loves you.

—Who says?

He had such a bitter look.

—Why throw it away? Put down your gun. The war's over.

—It's not, by a long shot.

—Let's go outside now. We three, side by side. They won't shoot us, and you'll go for the treatment you need.

—From them? They'll lock me up and throw away the. key.

—Dr. Falliere won't let them. We'll all be fighting for you.

—She's a blue-suiter like the rest.

—Really? I don't think so.

—She called the cops.

—Oh, Jo. I don't think so. On the bus coming here I heard a radio interview. She said it was the cops that caused all this.

—Somebody told them. Who?

—The sick savior, Commynes. Or maybe my ex-fiancé, Thanks-a-Million; he's out there with them, having a fine old time.

—Or Carlyne.

—Never. C'mon, Jo.

His brow creased as he seemed to reconsider. Then he mumbled:

—No, sir. I'll not give up. I can't see myself with a frontal lobotomy.

—Nobody's gotten hurt. It's not too late to settle.

—You want me to give up? Trust them? Then do as I said: go find our father. Tell him to do what you did, or lead him by the hand . . . Hold on, I'll be right back.

The shiny black gun in one hand, the giggling girl in the other, he left Granddaddy's den and went up the stairs.

After a few minutes he came back with Rhoda dressed in a dainty pink outfit. She looked around contented. She was clean and peaceful on his brawny arm.

—Doo da.

—Changed the diaper.—He grinned.—Now take her out of this madhouse before it explodes.

—I don't think I will, Joey.

—I mean it. Here, take her.

He held out the child.

Rhoda said:

—Momma come?

Lemon gestured at the window.

—If you're alone in here, they'll launch an assault.

—Good. Tell them there's a dress reception for them at the Rock Castle. It is catered by their friends the arms manufacturers.

—You want to die?

—I don't, but worse options exist.

—What do you want?

He laughed.

—If I said it, you wouldn't believe me.

—What?

—Honor.

—But you've got it. We admire you.

—You admire a baby killer.

He managed another laugh as the pain shimmered across his taut cheekbones.

—Let it go. It's not your fault.

—I said take the baby. Now I mean it. Here—

—I'm staying.

Lemon shook her head. She sat there hunched and stubborn.

He leaned and gripped her arm.

—You're going.

—No.

He stood her up, placed the child on her shoulder, and moved them from the study into the front hall.

—Go on. Go! Tell Dad.

The strength in his big steely hand, the way he manhandled her, made Lemon bow her head and cry. Tears dripped from her eyes like juice from a sliced fruit.

—What if I don't see you again?

He pushed her and the child forward. He patted her rump like a rookie's.

—Don't worry, kid.

By the front door she fought back tears. She put Rhoda down and turned to hug her brother. Then, for a sniffly moment, she held him close and rubbed his broad back.

—But what if I don't, Jo?

Her cheeks streamed as she held onto him.

He was reaching to open the door.

Shaken by sobs Lemon pushed him away and moved un-steadily out the door.

—Wait, he said. Rhody—!

Too late. And he couldn't show himself. Lemon had her back to him as she tottered toward the porch steps. She only said:

—Bye, Jove.

From the threshold Rhoda looked up at him.
She held out her arms to be picked up.
—Momma?
Exasperated, he reached with his gun barrel to shut the heavy front door.

XVII

The sun hung on the summits. Its bright rays slanted past the rustling treetops across the way; it glared off a blossoming magnolia like diamonds on a matronly breast.

All waited. All felt a foreboding at the approaches of night.

The warm breeze seemed pensive as it moved through the leaves and new grass and visited the gardens of May.

The silence belied a hundred guns and powerful rifles sited on the Rock Castle entry where the young woman stood in a daze. She wore bluejeans and a gray sweater; her thick braid was coming undone. On all sides there were unseen monitors which followed her unsure movements.

She looked shaken. She raised a hand to the sunny blur.

Then she left the front porch of the Rock Castle and slowly made her way down the long front walk. Lemon Gilbert frowned. She stumbled on a crack in the cement, almost losing her balance.

At the end of the walk she turned left and came shuffling along the sidewalk toward up town. She made her way back toward the sniper screen and the armed encampment behind it. In that no-man's-land beamed to every state in the nation she put a finger to her eye and tried to compose her features. Thirty steps from the high screen she paused, and gazed over her shoulder at the great stone mansion. She stood there a moment wavering. For it was still her choice, and she could go back to him if he would let her in. But the instant she went in the compound, then that was it. The old town center was Government territory, and there was no leeway.

She walked a few more steps. She hesitated: fixed by network TV cameras though unaware.

If she went back there he would just make her bring out the girl—strap Rhoda to her, and this time there would be no slipping away.

XVIII

They were waiting for her.

The instant she stepped past the barrier it was a whirlwind of dark-suited men and photo flashes in her face. The G-men, the State Bureau of Investigation men, Troopers, soldiers—they looked grave. They asked her to step this way, please.

More agents, more police officers plus the media horde mulled outside the First National City Bank building, as Lemon Gilbert looking frail and unsteady was hustled beyond the glass entry.

In a ground floor conference room, cleaned up and dusted for the occasion after a decade in disuse, the interrogation began. The younger sister sat there, forlorn and alone, while they fired off their questions: FBI, SBI, Justice Department official, State Attorney General's envoy, Federal psychiatric team leader plus associate, local Police Chief whom she knew. They looked at her as if she had had her fling, and it was time to pay the band.

In vain she asked to see her father, and said it was important, and asked again instead of answering them.

How would she describe her brother? What was his mood, his mental state, his physical appearance? What did he tell her? More details! What rooms was he using, and where did he put in the time? Had she seen many firearms? What kind of guns did he have? Describe them. Describe, please. What was he doing all day, and how about the child? What condition was Rhoda in? Was there milk? Was there baby food? Were there clean diapers? Was he taking the trouble to feed and bathe his daughter? And the guns? The guns? Where had he positioned his guns, automatic weapons, machineguns? Be more informative about this because it's for your brother's own good. Be specific. Details. What military preparations was he making and in which rooms? What had he said to her? What had they talked about together? He did have automatic weapons, right? Did she see a tripod? What was Joey's mood? What were his thoughts? And intentions? Was there any mention of explosives? Any big elaborate firearms that he had to assemble? Artillery? . . . When did he sleep? Where did he eat? Which bathroom did he use? Was the child crying a lot? How was the two-year old Rhoda reacting to all this? How many guns did he have? Were there guns stored down cellar? Did she see crates?

For a good hour they coaxed Lemon, urged her, reasoned with her, browbeat her—barraged her. They kept up the tension. They spread out floor plans on the conference table and with a pointer tried to walk her through each room. How had he marshalled his defenses and deployed the arsenal which FBI reports said he had?

Also what information had he obtained about the Government presence and capability, facing off with him, a few hundred meters down the road? What did he know from television? Did Joey have any other source of info or contact with the outside? Did he complain? What was his tone? Did he resent the blocked communications and control exercised over his telephone?

Did he ever get angry? Did he fly into a fit at the restriction of his liberty—or was he calm, in control?

Through all this onslaught of questions, and silences as they leaned on her to answer, Lemon Gilbert stared down at the table. She shook her head, and her shoulders trembled, as she tried to stay in control. At moments she wept.

Then, when they seemed done with drumming their questions at her; then, after a full minute when nobody moved or spoke and you could have heard a pin drop in the conference room—she looked up at them and said:

—My brother . . . didn't ask for this. But he is waiting for you, and he will fight. There is a child with him. You know that. If you go there, you will kill that child . . . Now I want to see my father. In private. That's all.

XIX

The double door swung open.

Two agents ushered in Emory Gilbert followed by his entourage.

She glanced up and gave a shudder—at his exalted stare, red face. His eyebrows seemed to swoop like the wings of a scavenger bird over what looked like the death agony of his productive life.

Alongside him was another dreadful sight. General Max Doan was not a sight for sore eyes in this setting. Dress uniform, chestful of medals, he beamed with pride, gallantry, and his blond crew cut. Where did he get the impulse to look like that when right before his eyes there were people in crisis and fighting for their lives? Was he trying to impress his girl?

As for Bishop Commynes: the churchman's dark eyes followed every move of his childhood friend, his best friend in life going under—with a fiendish glee.

Emory wasn't drunk. No. His head was up as he said quietly to his daughter:

—You okay?

She gazed up at him, and his aspect was too much for her. She looked down again, her cheeks streaked with tears. In the old days up North her father would have railed at her for not obeying. Now he was beaten down and disgusted by this police action with its rules of engagement, investigation and conduct; by all the law and order men who heard every word that was said only in terms of their intelligence needs. Now Emory didn't call her a damn fool and slam her solo attempt to save her brother. That would have been easier for her to take than the way he looked, and the way his two closest friends looked—the one all spruced up for a tragedy; the other a picture of schadenfreude while his childhood playmate become such a famous man drew nearer and nearer to the abyss, and got ready, at Commynes' prompting, to self-destruct in public. What an abominable envy! What poison in Paulie Commynes' heart these many years. And what was he bent on doing now, as the great man became putty in his hands, and he saw a way to cap his long campaign, and ruin Emory utterly . . .?

Lemon made an effort, looked up at them, and said:

—Dad, he needs us. He says you must come talk with him in person. I'll go with you, and Carlyne will. We'll go out there together. They can't stop us if you say yes.

The roomful of stonefaced men waited quietly. Then one and the other emitted a: 'We cannot advise . . . we could not sanction . . . we won't permit . . .' There were wise words from the FBI, the Justice Department official, IRS-ATF now on hand, State Attorney General's representative, State Intelligence agent, town Police Chief, and eminent psych consultant plus colleague.

Lemon fought back her tears, but she seemed on the verge of nervous collapse. Now more than anything else maybe it was Max Doan's presence that caused her to feel panic, and brought her to the point of bleating out sobs like a child in front of them. When she saw that man, she just wanted to run far away; but with her luck Emory no longer able would probably make him her legal guardian. So she tried to pull herself together and block the sobs. She must convince her father to go out there. She had a mission; though now again she sensed the big, uncontrollable thing, the enormity she had felt when inside the house with her brother.

She glanced up blurry-eyed at her father ready to crumble while he put on a show of false grandeur, the caring parent. And then she scanned the row of bland automatons in the conference room. Lemon felt so ashamed for him and filled with such pity— she wished she had never come back to them but had stayed inside the Rock Castle. There it was hopeless, like the world getting ready to end in violence. But it was honest at least. It was clean after all, like Rhody in pink after her bath, and Joey telling the truth as he saw it. There her life, along with the child's, might have added weight to the scales on the side of a peaceful solution.

Lemon looked away from them. She closed her eyes.

XX

All were quiet in the room once used for bankers confabs.

But they heard a commotion outside.

A woman raised her voice demanding to come in. Her words flew through the wide ground floor area once busy with tellers and townspeople, bank transactions and typists, but now a financial morgue since the day this branch of First National City closed its doors for business.

Suddenly the door flung open.

In plunged Joey Gilbert's wife, wild-eyed, black hair awry, hands aflutter over her head, palms outward, in a crazy gesture.

She cried out to Lemon:

—You got to him? What did he say? He wants to see his father, right? Come out! Come out, wherever you are! Ha ha ha!

—Oh no! Oh no you don't! I can't go there, they won't let me!

Emory's voice flew into action. No, he wasn't done quite yet, as the two shouted at each other, and made an operatic duet. The doctoral tone wanted to drown her out and override her words by sheer volume. The shrill female flung her arms in a frenzy. She shrieked. And he was afraid of what she might say, as the lawmen stood staring at them. She was already hinting at it!

The stolid G-men let it happen—hoping for an intelligence breakthrough. They waited blank faced in their fine suits and maroon and blue striped ties: no less in costume than Doan or the Police Chief.

—Ha! ha!—Carlyne cried out.—You coward! With all your high-flown claptrap you're just a windbag! Or should I put a worse name on it?

—Don't insult me and don't try to cow me! We all know you'd say any nonsense right now, but you better calm down!

She shook a finger at him, and her eyes bulged. She swung into them:

—The mess of you aren't worth my husband's little toenail! Pack of liars, shufflers, oink-oink you selfish pigs! And you, Sir, my esteemed father-in-law, are one of them!

Face beet red Emory bawled and blustered at her:

—This isn't the way to save Joey!

—Well you're not going to do anything, except try to cover your ass! All the big men: each has his own agenda, but the truth can go hang.

—Please control yourself, Carlyne, and lower your voice.

Her gaze flushed hate at him. And he knew fateful words hung on the tip of her tongue. If driven to it, and she was getting there, just weighing the effect on all of them and the impact, she would say ugly words about ugly things. She would spew forth their shame in public.

—I've waited and been patient because I believed you would come forward on your own, and do your duty to history, as you're so fond of saying. But the time is passing and your time with it, Sir, and I will not keep my own counsel forever. There are lives in the balance here, and the great man's vanity is not our first priority!

Lemon, her frail shoulders shaken by sobs, hung her head and swayed a little. Inside the Rock Castle, under the gun, she had looked danger in the face and kept her wits. But in here she sat small, a teenage girl in a naughty world, lost.

The law enforcement agents kept silent and were pleased to

listen. Solemnly they refrained from comment as they watched the scene, and made mental notes to be jotted later in their case folders—for practical use or as testimony by court-subpoena'd witnesses. Down the road all this might have the most complex legal ramifications depending on the outcome.

Only the town Police Chief sketched a smirk at the local gentry's carryings-on.

The forensic psychologist raised a knowing eyebrow.

But the others kept a professional silence and let the confrontation unfold. They showed the aplomb of the career criminologist.

XXI

Amid the excitement, as the in-laws ruckused with no holds barred, the door opened again, slowly.

A face peeped in. It looked out of place here, to say the least.

This was Cindy Phillips, the longtime house servant at the Rock Castle. The past couple days the great grandmother in her late sixties had been cleaning and dusting P. Laster's old bank building, just as she used to do. Cindy was the likely choice since she still came once a week as a town employee to vacuum an office suite used by the Chamber of Commerce.

Well for forty years she had heard their quarrels, bitter ones, and even been appealed to by Wilhelmina who liked to holler with pain at the good P. Laster, that Sunday school preacher, that righteous Job of a man who had concubines around town and even consorted with a notorious harlot called Cherokee.

Now Cindy made to come in the conference room.

One of the officials gave a little wave: do not enter. But she cast a glimpse at Lemon Gilbert broken up where she sat at the long oval table. Lemon was Cindy's precious ever since a little girl.

And so the dignified older woman came in anyway which amazed the Police Chief. But she had known that dignitary as a snotnosed pug too, and maybe she thought he never did grow up much.

She went to the teenage daughter of her strange employers and put an arm around Lemon's shoulders wracked by sobs.

The other two, Emory and Carlyne, had paused in their volley for the moment. They stood across from one another sort of looking abeyant, and growling beneath their breath.

Cindy soothed:

—Now girl, now girl.

She took a seat. She rested her body gotten on in years after all the work it had done for others. And she stared up at the row of tall self-important men. She saw P. Laster Gilbert's son, the star of this town gone up North for a career so brilliant nobody around here could get over it. And look at him now, the higher they rise, the harder they fall. He was fighting for his survival; and his face was so flushed and worked up, it looked like it might explode, fly to bits, after eating six gooey desserts. Well, sir, that's what comes from being too big for your britches. So arrogant these Gilbert men! No fear of God in 'em, thought Cindy.

And who were they but a bunch of parvenus like all the other European descendants, white people, in America.

And there was Emory's daughter-in-law looking fit to be tied, and maybe she had a right. Maybe Carlyne should act up and fling the angry words and even a good round curse or two because maybe they hadn't treated her too well in this family. Not spoiled, this one, oh no. Well what do you expect? She could try to pass and go to one of their fancy colleges and like that but she was still a colored woman. She weren't too likely to receive the royal treatment around here, now was she?

Cindy, a devout Baptist and churchgoer, shook her head.

Around the room there were the authorities—looking wooden, taking it all in, as the girl wept, and those other two stared daggers at one another.

But the servant with rag and duster in hand sat staring into space. She had seen a thing or two in nearly seventy years on this earth, but these goings-on of late just did beat all. Cindy's face had aged under the burden of personal worries, but her brow was calm now because nothing the white folks did would surprise her.

By contrast to them she had a dignity. And so she stared straight ahead with a pity not for anyone in particular but for things in general.

Her arm was around the girl to comfort her. And, in the momentary silence, she moaned to herself and rocked a little and gave a headshake.

—My, my, my.

Chapter Twenty-Two

I

And now Carlyne Gilbert knew that if she didn't go to the Rock Castle, and stand by her husband, then he would die. If she did not save him somehow despite himself and despite his hatred for her and despite everything else, then he had no chance. She was his last chance.

Not Lydia Falliere and not Emory, not Newell who was far away and not anyone, least of all the police, could do this for him. Only she could. And it was time.

In the command trailer, in the bank building, throughout the military compound: she felt their fate tightening like coils around them and she sensed an inevitability. All the elements were conspiring for Joey Gilbert's destruction.

The various law enforcement agencies on the case from Police Chief and County Sheriff up to the U.S. Attorney General's office and even the White House perhaps: all, all were probably as driven by circumstances, at different levels, as she herself. A lone individual was defying and embarrassing the United States Government before the eyes of the nation, the eyes of the entire world by now; and this at a time when political pressure boiled over after President Nixon's revelations on bombing raids and military escalation in Southeast Asia.

So Joey Gilbert became a sign of the times. He was a figurehead of civil unrest across the land. And he was adamant. He would not be moved. He would not negotiate except maybe with his father, as though this latter had offended him in some way.

And so the third baseman could perish as a signal to campus protesters around the country. He might die by a sharpshooter's bullet; or by door gunner fire from a dawn helicopter raid like those on villages in Vietnam; or by a tank assault up the long front lawn glacis: as task force attackers scrambled onto the porch and fought a bloody battle in the front hall.

But before it was ended the Rock Castle defender would detonate his explosives. And then the huge shadowy mansion would burst into the air with its hundred tons of granite, and go up in a conflagration.

After that Time would be the only caretaker. As the decades created their legend, Time would sift the ashes of the sparagma, the convulsive rending at the end of this tragedy—and try to find out the secret, and the reason why.

But Carlyne knew she must go to him before this came to pass.

What could she do now that he hated her?

She could talk and try to persuade. She could try even at this late date to seduce him. Or perhaps she could mother the poor boy and let him rest his head on her lap while she sang a lullaby as old as the hurts of earth's children.

But if none of this worked then maybe she knew another way.

It was up to her.

II

Her conference room theatrics had a dual purpose. Work on Emory: twist his arm to enter the fray on Joey's side. But also throw her police surveillant off the track and make him think she was too upset mentally and physically to have a plan, and say one thing and do another.

So when her part was over she said she had stomach cramps and made her way for the ladies room.

While a State Trooper stood posted in the hallway outside the first-floor rest rooms, Carlyne got the window open, lifted herself over the sill, and jumped down.

She slipped into an alley between two vacant stores which faced the railroad tracks.

Night was falling. She flew along knowing she had only minutes to escape them. They'd be right on her trail.

She went sprinting past the low-eaved depot—then broke into a run up the grassy embankment and crossed over the train tracks. This way she might outflank police barricades on the edge of the old town turned into an armed encampment.

Carlyne knew the way. She made for the fields.

She stooped and took off her sandals and ran. Even now they must know of her getaway. Already they had sent out pursuers, maybe with dogs though she hadn't seen any in the compound. They would post an all-points bulletin for her capture. And once they laid hands on her this time, it was all over. Then forget it. She'd be led like an animal on a leash to a cell in the town lockup. Then not a peep. No more movement for her until the crisis ended. A punishment worse than torture.

Over her left shoulder she saw the high water tower with its vertical steps and two red lights high in the sky growing darker.

At the western rim of the cemetery, on a block of furniture factory plant, there were officers talking by a squad car. They were State Highway Patrol.

Carlyne hefted herself over the stone barrier. And then she went among moss-grown headstones toward the far side which bordered on the wide Gilbert farmlands. Ouch! She stubbed her toe on a grass-covered lot marker. Lucky in her headlong rush if she hadn't broken a bone . . . she limped away, and went on.

She trotted along and thought of the best way to get to him. The Rock Castle was built on a slope. And, on the lower level, a Dutch door on the far side opened to the cellar laundry room: the 'hatch' they called it. There she might break a pane with a rock, and gain entry. He would hear her of course, and come to meet the intruder. She must call out his name and hope he didn't shoot.

On that lower level was a hive of rooms used for experiments, it was said, by Dr. Gilbert, Joey's great uncle, the M.D. accused of murdering his wife long ago. Also in the turret room Wilhelmina had kept her still for brewing moonshine liquor.

This week in a magazine article the FBI alleged munitions and war materièl amassed in fantastic amounts and stockpiled, in those subterranean rooms, by the Vietnam veteran who had now run amok. There was more than one machinegun; also a grenade launcher, plastic explosives, Claymore mines, asphyxiation bombs, an anti-tank weapon; it was a long list. Through the winter yes Carlyne had seen truckers pull up the back driveway and unload crates she took for farm equipment, seed and fertilizer, new machines. Some of it came inside the Rock Castle; some stayed out there, in the barn, silo, outbuildings, shed.

In a fluid motion, like a kid up a pole, Carlyne shimmied the wire fence on the outer side of the cemetery, but caught her blouse on the way down. She put her finger to the tear by her breast and touched warm blood where the skin was broken. Fingertips to lips she tasted it, but ran on, like a grazed deer out into the dark fields.

III

Behind her the factory town gave off a glow and murmur of a crowd stirring, vehicles in motion, as night came on.

But out here there was only night with its stars over the land. From a ways now she glanced back at the red watertower beacons.

Suddenly across the darkened farmlands she saw the Rock Castle seem to burst into flames.

—Not yet! she gasped. Turn them off!

The old mansion in its grove of tall trees was like a baseball stadium lit up for a night game. The authorities had got floodlights positioned about the place, and they turned them on and off through the night. Mostly on: to monitor the scene, and work on the hostage taker's nerves. No doubt they also needed darkness for the maneuvering of operatives and resupplying their emplacements. Never stay calm; never let the enemy alone; always, in this case, advance and ready the climax while playing on the embattled G.I.'s resolve. Here it was take the initiative, and gain the advantage.

The cut bled warm under Carlyne's blouse. She didn't give it a thought but only flew along and hurdled the low furrows cleared by Joey and the men after decades of lying fallow. Now there were no more tall weeds, no thickets of volunteer trees, from here to the river. What a fine start they had made at reviving the old Gilbert spread. What a crying shame all this had to happen. Joey threw himself into the long day's work with an abandon; he bought or leased the needed machinery and equipment, hired farm workers, and had a third of the total acreage under cultivation with another third due by mid-June: soybeans, corn for silage, hay crops, fescue, orchard grass, clover, alfalfa; he also wanted to plant a horticultural sector and was talking about cotton too.

New life. Hope in the daily grind together, and a blessed day off on Sunday. Then he gave himself to his family. There were good times together. There was love.

And now this.

IV

Toward the illumined mansion she ran low with an eye on the border of fields and a hand to the damp earth. A hundred yards from the barn she drew up.

Out here one night Bishop Commynes came to startle her as she took a moment by herself. He tossed a pebble at her and quoted a Bible verset with a laugh. And then she knew her secret was known.

Now she knelt on a dirt road between two sectors. Soil clung to her bloodstained fingers. So with her wrist she brushed back her hair.

And she too had taken to farm life. She felt it in her blood, her ancestors' blood: those men and women of the fertile soil for centuries in southeastern Carolina. Oh how she had wanted to see the child happy in school and watch Rhody's normal growth and development, and their own as well. The bad days were a thing of the past—more than enough of adventure and baseball and life like a guerrilla war. She just wanted the everyday problems of a happy family; and more children, by Joey, eleven of them. And they might yet have that together, a productive life side by side, if she could just make it inside to him and hold him in her arms and not let go.

Ghostly in the bright floodlights with its steep gables and somber contours and spire, the Rock Castle rose amid the incandescent trees.

In a moment she must make her run for it and surprise his and their watchful defenses by a hell-for-leather dash that would get her in. And all the violence of her past life, her fights as a prostitute and battle with Dirk the dog and survival tactics she had to use with a mentally ill Joey since they got reunited—all of it was like preparation for this.

What if after the siege began he had made his own late-night forays to lay a minefield in the backyard? That was possible: for a LURP used to making sorties out past a pattern of defensive-mines. Maybe he had ordered anti-personnel mines with the rest of his arsenal. An FBI list, fanciful in the extreme for a civilian to possess, was printed in this morning's newspapers.

Alright then a minefield. You have to be lucky too: to win.

Carlyne knelt and surveyed the scene. House, trees, farm buildings glistened; it was a lurid glare, like sin. By this act she meant to salvage her own honor if nothing else. When she faced death for her husband's sake, it must be seen she was not the kind for so much debasement. Worse than the idea of death, she hated this separation from the one she now knew she loved: this banishment from him in disgrace, away from her place in life.

For another moment she paused and felt an exultation. Free now—to act and have her chance. And the truth would be known to him, that she loved him, in spite of what she did.

The worst was over. Let's face the future knowing the truth, the bad but also the good. The good and the bad! They were related, even part of one another; they went together.

Okay, she would let him punish her to the full extent, any way he wanted; but he would not expel her again. She belonged in there and she had rights. She was earning them.

Yes, she welcomed his anger because she loved him and wanted all between them out in the open. But she had also learned by now, the hard way, to protect herself when the male got carried away and went too far.

It was her part in life to see her family through and work to deserve their love. As for him—whether or not he ever wanted her again, and treated her as an equal, she meant to make him know and respect her. That would happen, like it or not!

Ruthless with herself no less than others, Carlyne didn't think in these instants of tripping a mine in the backyard or failing in any way. Right and left she had made blunders, but she couldn't help it and never intended to.

Now here we go—like her ancestor Henry Berry Lowry who was a man, and his wife Rhoda Strong who was a woman: both just wanting to be left alone to live and love in this misbegotten America. They were hounded down by the right respectable racist society of their day into the swamps. They were called outlaws when they only wanted their land back, their birthright on this earth, and for the self-righteous white man to stop robbing everybody blind.

On hands and knees in her own swamp now Carlyne Gilbert took a deep breath and leaned forward and got ready to make her run.

V

But she crept closer. Within striking distance now, and they couldn't stop her because they were afraid to show themselves. They could only shoot her—as a way to save her, no doubt, and their operation.

Beyond the barn spread a field neatly cleared and ready for seeders; but it wasn't the time for seeders. There at the edge she crouched, studying the terrain, and gazed up at the mansion alit like some old castle in a fable.

She must reach the postern door on the basement level and get inside. Then move quickly across the spacious cellar past its washroom area, and boiler, on her way upstairs. Announce herself loud and clear so he wouldn't open fire.

And she thought: if he still wants me, he'll make a lot of noise and blow off steam, like men do. Or else play coy and sulk awhile, but then start to soften.

And Carlyne remembered the first time they ever made love, their wedding night. Her arm went up around him and seemed to say: Oh, for so long, my darling, I wanted to do this, and give myself to the man I love; now please tell me it's true and I haven't done the wrong thing.

She rose up and began to run. She went sprinting out from the shadows into the zone of floodlights. One shot from a sniper would set off the battle for the Rock Castle and they would all die. A strand of black hair came loose and streamed out as she hurled herself forward at the side door.

By this time Government forces may have been expecting her. How long was it since her evasion from the bank building? There must be a general alert.

The night was filled with encoded messages as she erupted in full view of the monitors in Central Command. The silent community of sniper nests and forward observers, listening posts, all those posted in among the shrubs and trees of the target house or further out where they lurked in the neighbors' eaves—all awaited the signal to open fire. They went tense as a pointer gundog when they saw her. In any case there would be no orders to pursue her into the glaring field of fire.

Down the embankment on the far side she flew. But she tripped and fell hard. Stunned, she lay still a few seconds, then got up holding her shoulder, and walked forward shaking her head.

She limped as she ran a few more steps to the door.

Her voice was low:

—Jo?

Carlyne knocked and waited a moment.

No response.

Then louder:

—Joey, I'm coming in. Will you open for me?—She tapped on the casement window pane.—Jo? I won't say please, I live here.

Why wait? She knew the answer.

She raised her fist and put it through the glass of that Dutch door which opened in two parts.

Then reaching in she scraped and cut her arm clutching for the knob.

VI

Still it was quiet. Her violence was the only sign of life.

Inside the big silent house she went trying to catch her breath.

Her hand stung. The flesh of her soft underarm felt mushy: shredded by the cemetery fence.

She was in.

—Jo? Where are you, my darling?

Then she saw him. He was there by the basement stairs; he was waiting for her. And he looked afraid.

Joey looked bad: just two deep mournful eyes, like slits in the camouflage paint back on him since Lemon came out. Was he deranged by the days and nights of crisis? No one all alone like he was could take that inhuman tension.

For the moment he did not seem to be in a lucid interval, as when his younger sister came in here. The grunt cut a grim figure, standing in his jungle fatigues, frozen with hate.

In a low brusque voice he told her, like she was a troop:

—Come over here.

She went. She drew near him.

—Joey, forgive me. I love you so mu'—

His fist lashed out. He struck her————so killer hard, it made a crunch as Carlyne's neck snapped, and her head flapped back.

She crumpled senseless at his feet.

VII

He bent to pick her up like a cat run over in the road.

Upright, he held and pressed her, a floppy doll, against his chest. He propped her lolling nape with his two fingers like he would a newborn baby's. In his mind's eye as he did so there was Ben Bolt stalking forward headless up the sunlit trail.

Blood ran from Carlyne's hand, arm, and her mouth now. She leaked blood. Her heavy head with the thick black hair come undone wobbled and fell off the prop of his hand.

The mouth was open and rasping for air. The punched left eye had flown off at an angle.

In his massive Xo Man brutality he hauled her like one more fart sack up the narrow basement steps. Her temple banged on the doorjamb as he carried her out onto the first floor of the Rock Castle.

Then up the plush carpeted stairway he went with her.

And on, beyond the landing, upstairs into the master bedroom where the child was sleeping quietly.

When he looked at her helpless in his arms, his face contorted with who knows what rage, hate, self-hate.

—On your knees, you gook whore. I swear this is for Blair.

He slung her down on the floor.

In his mind the botany student Kevin Blair—spread-eagle, stark naked, his being all butt-fucked by the branch of a tree burnt by herbicide—soared over the road leading from Xo Man in the twilight.

VIII

She listened to her brain. To the rhythm of her heart it rang, gong, gong, like a hammer on the side of a tin cistern.

Her face was to the floor in a pool of blood and spittle. She lifted an arm the way a crushed insect might move its feeler, and reached to touch her shattered cheek. She was beginning to think again.

Was her neck broken? With one finger she tested the sensation in her face. It felt numb. Was she going into shock?

Carlyne lay on the floor drooling blood and mucus. She coughed a little. She brought up a blood clot with more of the sputum. Was she finished?

—Jo?

For a long, long moment he stared down at his wife sprawled before him. And the sight must have begun bringing him to his senses because he said:

—Is this where you two did it together? Let's see, I guess if Rhoda is my sister, that makes you my mother. As for my father, he's . . . he's not my father.

Strangely, she grabbed at her hair, and some came out in her fist. She gurgled:

—No. Not here. I didn't go to him. He came to me.

—Ah. In the guest bedroom then you ruined the two of us. But you couldn't leave it at that and go away. You had to come to me in Bangkok, so you could lie later and say it was my baby.

—Yes. I was scared.

—You were pregnant when you came. I know you'd never have made the trip for me.

—No, yes.

—You lied. And you lied when you acted like you loved me.

—No, I loved you.

On the floor, at his feet, she gave a hiccup.

—You loved me so much that you and he hoped I would die in Vietnam, and then you'd be off the hook. Have a fine old time then. Clear sailing to cohabit . . . What a noble man my father is, what a grand gesture worthy of him: to take in his dead son's wife as a charity case. Make her his housekeeper. Why, he's a regular Thomas Jefferson, sleeping with one of his slave women. But meanwhile you were both green with fear I'd come home.

—I . . . came here—

Carlyne tried to raise herself. She turned a little on one knee. From her cheek hung a web of shiny mucus.

—But I didn't die, not physically at least.

Her teeth chattered.

—I . . . l'loved you then, J'Jo . . . and I love you n'now. O'only then I d'didn't know it . . . so.

—That's why you indulged in incest and then went and whored yourself on the streets in Durham so my wife became a goddamned prostitute. You told me you did. Will you deny it now?

—No.

She lifted her face to him. One side was discolored to a bluish pulp lit up by the field of bright light outside. Blood oozed from her mouth onto her chin; and her good eye, glazed over with tears, shone in the shimmer of the drawn blinds. The other was afloat, out there, on its own.

—But that still wasn't enough. You had to come and find me in New York. Better if you hadn't.

—I wanted you.

—Oh, did you? You didn't want me when I was a bum in the Minors. You didn't stand by me then. You had no faith in Joey Gilbert the big goon back then. But a Major Leaguer's wife, why yes, that's a bit different, fancy hotels and glamor. You as much as sent me away to Vietnam, but when my luck changed you wanted part of the action. Hey, success is success, even in baseball, and that's when you wanted me, not before. Didn't you?

—That's w'wrong. I said I wished't you hadn't enl'enlisted.

She spluttered. She was holding her head and trying to get up but she couldn't.

—In New York you said you were bad and told me the filth you'd done, some of it, and you didn't deserve me. I loved you so much nothing mattered anymore, I only wanted you in my arms. But you were careful not to tell me the clincher. And maybe that was the only thing I couldn't have digested. I don't care if you're a piece of snatch in a cathouse or a leper with syphilis. But let's leave dear old Dad out of it if you don't mind.

—I made a mistake.

She was bleeding from her gums, nostrils, the burst eye. She tried to lift up her head and look at him.

He was sitting on his haunches a few feet away from her—always with an eye on the front or side window, and with M-16 in hand. So his gaze was averted. He didn't want to see her. He gave a low laugh:

—Mistake? You? . . . No, I don't think so: the devil doesn't make mistakes. Since our picnic that afternoon by the Lumbee River, you were calculating, you were twisting me around your finger. No; I was the mistaken one when I believed in you. I just loved you more and more and blamed only myself. And all the while you lied, you lied.

—I lied.

—I never turned you out, but you turned me out.

—You are good.

At this he gave the bad laugh, and spat.

—I'm good. You don't say. I'm not worth shit and never was. The only difference is: then I didn't know the score, now I do.

—I'm sorry.

He stared down at her—the woman groveling, shivering, slavering blood on herself.

Outside it was quiet. When they stopped talking, a silence that was more than silence seemed to flow into the room.

Still she hadn't quit. She worked her head, turning it with her hand, giving a little cry. She gazed up at him eerily, as if seeing him for the first time. One eye sparkled. The other was bruised shut.

He glanced back at her, and then away, and said:

—Well, at least you won't look so pretty.

—That's true.

Then he rose and went to the front window for a look past the blinds.

—After awhile they may turn off the lights for resupply. They won't attack with a child in here, it's bad press. But tomorrow you're taking her out of here if I have to strap both of you on a wheelbarrow.

He took his finger from window blinds lit up by the lights flooding the front lawn.

And spat.

IX

An hour passed, and another.

Then on schedule the powerful floodlights went out. Joey was all motion then: downstairs to turn on porch and back lights, up again to peer out the bedroom window facing the front; then to another room for a look-see at the farm buildings.

Carlyne lay balled up on the rug.

When the grounds lit up in a blast, he came back and sat in a chair by the dresser.

Outside the light was so intense, he could see their photo from Bangkok framed on the night table: a young couple smiling in the sunlight.

He lay back his head, closed his eyes in the shimmery darkness of the bedroom, and said:

—Why did you come here? For Rhoda, right?

—No.

—You wanted to save the child you had with him. Well, you will.

—No.

—They sent you.

—Tst.

Curled up on the floor, she trembled. Going into shock?

The minutes passed.

At length she spoke, very weak, low:

—I came for myself.

—Yourself? You're not going to tell me you feel guilty.

—I don't feel guilt.

—Why then? It's to try and save the girl.

—No.

—Well then I give up.

She paused, a long moment, as if getting strength, and then said:

—I came to die with you.

He thought this over, and then rose and went to stand by the window again.

With a finger he drew back the blind for a peek at the front lawn.

—I'm afraid you won't get your wish. In a few hours you're clearing out with Rhody.

With an effort she said:

—You decide.

Nauseous, she made a sound in her throat, heaved, and retched weakly on the rug.

X

After awhile the child began to cry in her crib. It was a singsong lament at first, but then louder. Carlyne lay in the same posture, drawn in herself, shivering. Her teeth chattered.

But when Joey got back from going downstairs for baby food, the situation was changed. He stopped on the threshold with a stare. It was stunning. Carlyne sat up, cross-legged on the floor, with her daughter on her lap.

The tiny girl gazed up at the terrible face. For a minute it fascinated her, but she gave a little whimper, and snuggled to the breast.

Joey turned from that sight. He had to keep up his sentry duty, here, there, at the forward positions, at the rear guard. Never for a second did the M-16 leave his hand, as he resisted sleep.

It was late when, seated quietly by the north window, he felt a tug on his boot. As dawn drew near he was trying not to sleep, and he must not, but the need was too much.

There was something down there, in the punji pit, and it was stirring; it was still alive. It pulled his big toe.

—Do what? he mumbled.

He gave a start, waking to the same heavy silence.

Rhoda was back in the crib asleep.

Carlyne had been unable to remain upright and lay on her side now with the bad eye up. In pain she groaned, and she was holding onto his foot. Her body shook a little. She had inched nearer and taken his gnarled jungle boot in her two hands, and was putting her head on the leather like a pillow.

He said:

—What now?

Her body gave a tremor on the rug beneath him.

He sighed, stood up, gave a stretch and a yawn.

Then he moved his boot, and her head went on the rug. He nudged her away.

Frowning, he stared down at her. He stepped over her, went to their bed, and pulled off the bedspread. This he folded and draped over the feverish woman lying on the floor.

But she touched him again. She put her head to his boot as she lay trembling. In the deep night she seemed to seek him where he sat at his post. She breathed unevenly with a wheeze. Was she finished? She hung on to his boot.

Later, he reached down and picked her up by the arms. In the crook of his elbow he held her blurry splotched face and looked it over. Carlyne needed help. On one side the features were dreadfully swollen, deformed, the ruined eye bloated purple. Was she in shock? In a coma? The sight made him soften, but he didn't know what to do. There was no corpsman on hand—Artus who went crazy at Xo Man, strapped in restraints with a wild laughter for the dustoff.

Maybe Tootie the RevDev medic? Greased in a minefield.

She groaned when he moved her. But the good eye was on him. It stared at him. It met his gaze. It asked a question.

On one knee alongside his wife, he held her up, and she winced.

Joey put his arms around Carlyne, his stubbly cheek to her soft cheek, with a hand in her tangled hair. She was very warm. He held her as he did that afternoon long ago by the Lumbee River when they rode there on his motorcycle from college. He hugged her as he had in the Bangkok hotel room when she came to him, a soldier who needed to touch his wife. Joey drew her to his chest the way he had that time with such a full desire for her, such a passion the night he found her turning tricks in a tenement in upper Manhattan.

He took her to bed, and held her.

Through the early hours they stayed there side by side: in the big oak bed where P. Laster and Wilhelmina once slept and came together despite everything, their lifelong feuding; and where Emory slept alone after his return South.

For a long time Joey and Carlyne, the one wrecked mentally, the other physically, held one another close, not finished yet.

Their limbs, their pores stuck together with her Xo Man blood, as the first light of dawn appeared in the window.

—Mister Jo—she whispered.

Chapter
Twenty-Three

I

On Tuesday, May 5th, the sun rose over the river and newly cultivated Gilbert farm acreage. Long slanting rays shot past the treeline two miles east where the Yadkin River flowed, and flushed the upper storeys of the besieged mansion. At six a.m. the Rock Castle with its rusticated stone, steep gables and high angle turret with spire and ball, was painted a reddish gold in its grove of patriarchal oaks.

Inside, in the upstairs bedroom, Joey Gilbert picked up the phone receiver. There was a closed circuit now, and he could speak only to them and anyone they might allow through.

—I want you to send Lydia Falliere here.

An FBI negotiator said:

—For what reason, Sir?

—My wife has a high fever.

—Hold on.

Put on hold he waited thirty seconds.

—Well?

—We can send someone.

—Dr. Falliere. No one else.

On hold again: while they talked. So he put down the phone and went to the bedroom window. He stood there as the minutes ticked past on the grandfather clock downstairs, tic . . . toc . . .

with a sort of mocking note. He looked for Lydia's tallish figure
to emerge in the morning sunlight and shadows, moving through
no-man's-land this side of the high sniper screen toward the long
front walk sloping slightly upward.

She didn't come. A half hour passed.

He glimpsed Carlyne on the bed. Her face was very bloated.
She was silent except for her rough breathing.

He picked up the receiver again and said:

—You're not sending her.

The voice at the other end was polite: with its educated jingo
twang, like they all had:

—Sir, we can't do it.

—Why not? I'll let her take out my wife and the child.

Put on hold—a minute passed, tic . . . toc . . .

—We can send a medical team if you come out first. You must
be unarmed. They will bring what your wife and child need and
take them to the hospital.

—No—said Joey, and mimicked him—we can't do it.

II

At shortly before nine a.m. he tried again with them. This time
a new FBI negotiator wanted to talk all about it and started asking questions about what had gone on during the night and why
his wife needed help. He knew they were trying to get him to talk
on tape. Also he seemed to hear they wanted an end to this, and
pretty soon; it might not go on too much longer. There was an
edge to the businesslike voice. Of course this siege was costing
the U.S. taxpayer a pretty penny, as one man thought he could
engage the U.S. Government in a standoff.

—You haven't sent Dr. Falliere to help us.

—We can't.

—Then forget it.

He hung up.

On the bed Carlyne was burning up with fever. Through the
night she had drifted to and from consciousness. Now gently he
applied a fresh compress to the bruised and swollen forehead.
Her eyebrow quivered.

Then he knelt by the bedside and held her limp hand.

She rasped small breaths, groaned a moment, and then mumbled. She was delirious:

—If . . . knowed 'er before. Heeezr. Look! Mama, the trees at Fair Bluff. So long, I.

She worked her lips. One side of her face was softened, but the other looked terrible, a greenish yellow.

—Playzarr. Btees . . . scute.

In one blow last night to her head he had dealt out his jealousy and disbelief.

At instants she opened her good eye and had something like a grin.

—Want my room. Fitz'ugh? Thisinnamrunn. Homago, vet lamb.

He bowed, and put his forehead to her hand, and rubbed.

III

As noon passed she lay quietly. He had fed and changed the girl, and now sat in the armchair for a moment's pause from sentry duty at the windows. Rhody played and chirped cheerily; she kept active in her playpen.

It jolted him from his thoughts when Carlyne said:

—Mister Joey?

He stood up and went to the bed.

—Can you stand?

It cost her to talk:

—P'p . . . help me try.

He supported her head and, slowly, began to lift her. He put an arm under her shoulders, neck, slid the other under her thighs.

Joey raised his wife off the mattress as Rhoda watched them leave the bedroom.

On the stairs he said:

—I want you to do as I say.

—Yessir.

She felt hot in his arms. She gave a whimper. On the stairs he said:

—I hurt you.

She said softly:

—I love you still.

Joey choked on the words:

—I care for you too.

She closed her eye, as the lid pressed a tear onto her cheek.

—Then let's go out there.

In the front hall he set her on her feet. He held her up, against him.

—Can you stand?

—Yes.

He eased his hold, and she tottered with a hand to the front hall table. Her thoughts seemed to whirr in the dark whorl of her hair.

—I want you to take the child.

—No, Mister. I won't.

—I'll come in a few minutes.

—Tst. I know you won't.

—I'll go get Rhoda. You're taking her out of here.

—Together, or no.

—You two first, then me.

—No.

—Do what I say.

—Hold me, my darling. I'm dizzy.

—Give me a sec'. I'm going to fetch Rhody.

—I'll fall.

He turned from her and took the stairs:

—Wait—

Her voice broke:

—I need you, Jo.

IV

Left alone Carlyne steadied herself. She grew more alert as she watched him go up the wide staircase, in long strides, as if to his destiny.

The game hadn't ended yet, and it wasn't hopeless. She knew she shouldn't leave him alone in here, but he was making her go. What then? When all else failed only a two year-old girl would be able to save Joey Gilbert? But now he meant to send the girl away too, and then they would be free to attack. He wanted the two of them out so he'd be free to fight an army and die. He was in the shoes of Henry Berry Lowry, though a white man. Never mind the color—what does a man do who is a man? Sit back and twiddle his thumbs?

She could take her daughter to safety, but forget about seeing her husband alive again. This she knew from the mood up town. They wanted to strike. They didn't want a peaceful settlement. It was a political thing based on the needs of the moment. There was nothing human, moral, about it—except in their tales to the media.

Oh! How Joey had loved her and gone about his chores only a few days ago: seen to the busy rounds and strenuous farm work they were doing together. How he came to her in the kitchen with his little quips and his kisses. Why not? Sometimes he just took to the wife's presence and her simple words, her company, her caresses after the long day of backbreaking work with the men in the fields. Joey Gilbert was a born farmer. He acted like one. Even his stress symptoms were less frequent. The war wounds had finally begun to heal. Had they? For a brief few weeks at the end they found a down-to-earth contentment in one another.

V

She heard his steps moving about upstairs to get Rhoda ready. They were resolute steps and beneath them the floorboards creaked; the ancient foundations of the Rock Castle gave a sigh.

Carlyne took a shaky step past the mahogany table. She knew this siege had nearly come to its finale. Such tension couldn't last much longer. Through the day? Another night? So if she went through the door alone she would be risking Rhody's life. But he wouldn't come with her, so she had to do it.

There was one more thing she knew, but she wasn't saying. And it looked like this thing was the one chance for the three of them to survive after all. It was her trump card, but to play it she needed to go out there by herself. So be it.

He came down the stairs quickly toward her.

On his arm he held Rhoda dressed up in pink Sunday-go-to-meetin'.

—Here we are! Baby, go on with your ma. Scram. Ha ha.

Carlyne saw no other way. It had to be her plan. His wouldn't work.

And so as he came down the stairs she summoned her strength and opened the heavy front door. She stepped over the threshold and went out where he could not follow—out into the bright May sunlight riddled with the sites of a hundred high-powered rifles.

—Wait! Hey, what—? Not you too!

She moved from the dim foyer out onto the porch. And then strangely, like a creature from another sphere, she turned and beckoned him. And still she was backing away, a bit further, nearing the half dozen stone steps down to the walk.

—Come, Jojo. Come out here with me.

—Careful! The steps!

She paused. She stood there outlined above the wide green lawn filled with sunlight.

Carlyne gave her husband a smile. She was gruesome, and beautiful, and her face with its tragedy and comedy, the comedy of love, was meant to haunt him then and stay in his mind.

—Come, young'un. Just come.

—Dear, I can't. I'd have to leave my gun.

He stood there with the restless kid in his arms, anguish on his lean sweaty face, as he hung back from the threshold. She could see him seem to writhe inwardly as he held back in the shadows from their field of fire.

She made her maimed face smile eerily. She was still so gorgeously statuesque as she floated away from him, like an image in a dream, and beckoned him to follow.

—Come, my darling. Bring Rhody, and let's go face them together. We've paid for our mistakes.

Joey squinted out at her. His lonely eyes were hungry for the bright warmth of our human life. Twice he had lost her, but he didn't give up and accept his loss. And now a third time she was going away—or he was, and for good.

He stood there holding the toddler who pushed at the big oaf's arms and squawked:

—Put down!

—Huh?

He looked at Rhody, thinking, and then set her upright, and gave her rump a little pat:

—Go Mummy.

But she turned back. She pushed past him and yelled:

—Doll-bubba.

She wanted the doll she had left upstairs. Strong-willed like her parents, she'd go up and get it.

Joey caught Rhoda and turned her back toward the door. She tried to twist away and would not do what he wanted. He put her on course again, but she bucked and fell on her duff. Then she kicked at his shin with her little saddle shoes.

But she got up and made another try to get away. How could she leave Doll Baby behind? Once more she squirmed from his grip, saying words she heard somewhere, which enchanted her:

—You dope!

Joey hung away from the doorway.

Carlyne watched them another moment, and then turned and went slowly down the stone steps. Too late then, too late.

He stared forth into the glare; stared at her back, and blinked.

But then he raised a hand and ran it through his curly head.

Flashback?

—No, no . . .!

Joey began to tremble and in his sudden trance he had a hang-dog air. In that instant his wife whom he had maimed with his own hand was the Xo Man mother of his nightmares.

—Come, Jo. Come to me.

Weirdly, seeming to ripple like fumes off the walk, she invited him. She beckoned him into the blinding sunlight—into her torched hootch!

VI

When the front door opened, a hundred guns took aim. From M-60 turrets positioned along the road up town to snipers surrounding the house—all had a wounded Carlyne Gilbert fixed in the cross hairs of their sites. She swayed on the front walk and took a few steps and stopped. She looked behind her and made a wan gesture.

Until now rules of safety had preempted rules of engagement. This meant no deadly force would be used unless there was an aggressive act from the Rock Castle. If so, it would controvert the

order, and call forth fullscale retaliation by an elite Delta Force
unit which was now on the scene.

Non-deadly firepower, a Hostage Rescue Team water cannon
for example, had no chance of getting close enough to be effective.
Also the presence of a child meant no anaesthetic gases could be
sprayed. So a combined tank and tear gas assault probably moved
up on the list of plausible responses as the standoff wore on.

But one thing seemed ever clearer as debate continued in the
command trailer, and beyond, and the minutes ticked away. Time
had almost run out for the former star athlete—this man who
was heavily armed and bitterly defiant inside his granite fortress.
Even today's news coverage had a tenor to it, a pathos designed
to convey as much, and prepare the public. Joey Gilbert could not
count on the forbearance of the U.S. Government indefinitely.

In special bulletins, in on-site reportage there was a shudder
which the nation felt as a man got ready to meet his fate in a blaze
of sunlight. He was alone. He had contempt for the law no less
than for death, but no one seemed to know the motive really, beyond labelling it sickness, any more than they knew what was
going on inside the house. They only knew what they were told:
namely that Joey Gilbert was crazy, and that he was estranged
from his wife. This vagueness heightened the dread of it all, and
the awe.

Not a few pundits weighed in with statements to the press.
A Johns Hopkins specialist in psychiatry, who was also a Men-
ninger Institute trustee, had been contracted as a Government
consultant; in other words, his task was to provide theoretical basis for any official action. He said on primetime TV:

—The great ballplayer is an eternal child, *puer eternis,* on fields
of resplendent green. So he shows a deep identification with children victimized by war, and perhaps by his own participation. He
feels guilty, but it is misplaced guilt because unable to relate non-
combatant casualties to the cause he fought for, which is freedom.
His, let's say, childishness prevents this. And so, by an inexorable
law of the subconscious, he seeks to bring about his own death.
And he really does victimize a child this time: the little girl named
Rhoda, his own daughter.

On the steps of the bank building Dr. Lydia Falliere gave her
view as part of the same TV news segment:

—Quite poetic. But I'm afraid the Government expert is singing his own denial. In general our doctors are bowing to Estab-

lishment control when they deny the fact of Post-Traumatic Stress symptoms. They won't diagnose PTSD because then it would have to be treated. If it exists, we must tend to it. And this takes an investment on several levels. This means a values realignment on our part. And it means risk.

The Johns Hopkins department head came back on camera and called Dr. Falliere 'the quixotic PTSD standard-bearer'.

—She has written a book on a nonexistent subject.

Lydia laughed and quoted a dismissal long ago of Freud's ideas. Then she said:

—I'm pleased to tilt with the learned colleague, but there are no windmills in Vietnam. What Joey Gilbert found there is, yes, the guilt and shame of a military aggression. What he seeks now is a way out: not death, not comorbidity but life and human empowerment. Somehow I don't think my opponent in debate today has delved as deeply into what may be called Vietnam Syndrome as he has into Victorian verse.

VII

Now Justice Department staff, IRS-ATF, FBI and State Bureau of Investigation agents, Highway Patrol detachments, the North Carolina Attorney General on the scene, Hostage Rescue Team operatives, military in combat fatigues with grenades and CS tear gas canisters hung on their belts, local police and detectives, County Sheriff's office personnel, Government contracted forensic psychologists and other specialists, medical teams, food caterers, sanitation crews, the town Mayor Newton R. Lott, the highly visible U.S. Congressman from the district:—now all watched on the many monitors as Carlyne Gilbert tottered along the Rock Castle's front walk with a lost air.

In the sunlight she came forward for the world to see. Her face had been beaten a pulpy blue; it looked lopsided; it did not argue her husband's tender concern for her and his contrition. Inside his stone bunker Joey Gilbert was ready to meet them with an arsenal, and he challenged them to attack. And now the living image of a badly battered wife went out over the television networks and served to justify and force that attack. By doing what he did

Joey gave his enemies a propaganda coup. Millions spent on public relations could not have done it better. For what must be happening to the little girl in there? What must her life be like?

Now the nation turned its gaze from student demonstrations. The TV channels went to the small southern town where a family drama was nearing its climax.

Snipers stared through their sites surveilling the window embrasures. This round-the-clock alert made all law enforcement officials tense on the trigger finger.

At present no negotiations were underway. The Vietnam veteran either showed contempt or else he was hallucinating when efforts were made to talk with him on the closed-circuit telephone. He growled and gritted his teeth into the receiver. He told the caller who knows what sort of stuff, and said he didn't speak to lickspittles. Then, before slamming down the phone, he said:

—Send me a man.

VIII

Thus every telescopic lens had focused on the old oak door when it opened, and Carlyne Gilbert came out. Ethereally, in a sort of gray-blue haze, she stood looking here and there.

The sight of this young woman, who had some kind of courage, stunned everyone. There was a lot of blood on her blouse. She could faint at any moment on the front walk. Swooning upright she touched a fingertip to her bulbous brow, and her eye, which looked cyanotic. And all who saw her could only think:

—This can't go on.

Someone had to act. Someone must put an end to a public display that had become a national embarrassment even being shown overseas. Cry, America.

Carlyne swayed. She came down the walk a few steps at the time, trying to stay on her feet, in the sunlight. She peered round at the door still open behind her.

But she turned and said:

—Jojo?

He had drawn back. He wanted to die his way, blazing away at them, not by a sharpshooter's bullet. He was waiting. Let them stage their combined frontal assault with tanks and infantry. It will look pretty childish: all that military might coming up the front lawn like the postman. He was waiting for them. But if the cowards opted for aerial bombardment like on a Vietnamese village without electricity or a flush toilet: then he was ready. He had a Cu Chi tunnel system dug out in the subbasement.

Along the walk Carlyne paused in her slow unearthly movements. She was a target as well. For what if there was a suicide bomb strapped to her body? What if explosives enough to blow away a building at one hundred yards had been tied on her by the deranged ex-soldier who was her husband?

She came forth: her beaten face, her black hair in a whorl, her womanly figure. She had a tragic aura.

Carlyne took a few more steps down the slow incline in front of the Rock Castle. Nearing the edge, almost to the sidewalk, she turned to gaze with her good eye at the high sniper screen this side of town. She stared out at the military compound hidden from his view by the trees.

Then she swung back again.

She pointed up town and said as loudly as her burst face let her do, into the silence and the heat:

—All quiet for now. They have tanks.

He heard her. From inside came his voice:

—I know what they've got. You come take the baby.

Hand to her brow in the blinding sun Carlyne appeared to study the scene. Then she stepped off the walk, looked for a good spot on the grass, and sat down on the Rock Castle lawn.

—No, Sir. Think I'll stay right here awhile. I'll watch.

IX

At the same time Joey's wife took a seat on the grass to watch what would happen, her brother-in-law was making his way hitchhiking across Tennessee. It took him forever to get through Memphis; and then to do so he took a ride on Route 70 as far as Brownsville. But this got him off Highway 40, and so he found himself catching short hops from town to town, Humboldt, Milan, trying to get back on the Interstate. It was frustrating because time was of the essence. Yet he didn't want to risk saying he was Joey Gilbert's brother and ask a driver to go out of the way and bring him to the ramp onto 40 toward North Carolina.

From hour to hour the situation at the Rock Castle could explode. But he was not far away—if only he got lucky with a good ride: say to Winston-Salem.

Coming across country Newell saw a newspaper here and there, and he was struck by the size of demonstrations against Nixon's Cambodia policy. Eighteen ROTC buildings had been bombed or burned. There were now National Guard units on twenty-one campuses in sixteen states. The militant protests were drawing more and more middle class elements into their midst. Everywhere were marches and rallies.

But another headline also expressed the angry mood across the nation:

CAROLINA TOWN A WAR ZONE

U.S. ATTORNEY GENERAL UNDER PRESSURE TO RESOLVE HOSTAGE CRISIS

In one front-page article after another the point was driven home. Time had almost run out for Joey Gilbert. Not too many hours remained until the decisive assault took place. From state to state news coverage sang the same refrain: the patience of Federal authorities had nearly come to an end. Since the decorated soldier and former baseball player was breaking the law, he must lay down his arms and surrender. And he must do it soon.

Then came an article on the military aspect with an incredible list of weapons allegedly in the hostage taker's possession. Joey Gilbert had: three AK submachineguns and two M-16s; one M-40 anti-tank weapon; hand grenades in quantity; a CM-79 grenade launcher, a thumper; plastic explosives, unknown amount; C-4 with blasting caps; Claymore mines; two XM-203s; M-67 frags; some 800 high-explosive and illumination rounds; a 4.2-inch 'four-deuce' mortar . . .; two BAR (Browning automatic) weapons; a PRC-25 radio; a Xenon searchlight; a gross of B-3 C-rations; iodine pills to sterilize water; standard infantryman's issue: steel helmet, flak jacket, lightweight jungle boots, full-webbing, spare ammunition bandolier, an E-tool. He also had a 9-gauge riot shotgun; an M-2 carbine with paratrooper (folding) stock; a Polish K-54 pistol; and a water bottle.

All this and no doubt more, said Government sources, the highly paid star of a World Series had ordered from suppliers since last November. Was it possible? A mortar into the bargain? ... He thumbed his nose not only at the authorities but also at Federal firearms regulations.

X

Every minute counted now. Newell knew: if he meant to save his brother, he had to get to him today. He guessed the assault wouldn't come in broad daylight but rather after dark, or at dawn tomorrow. He could make it in time—and then there was the problem of getting into the house, knocking Joey out with a piece of lead pipe when his back was turned. He could get there before the onslaught; but the problem was he got stuck on 70, Dickson, White Bluff . . . coming into Nashville. At Dickson he was so near Interstate 40, five miles or so; but he didn't have money to pay someone to take him there. And if he said his name and asked for help, then watch out: he would alert the world to his presence, and local police or Tennessee State Troopers could come looking for him.

It was an explosive moment across the nation. Now a dozen sharpshooters awaited the order to lodge a bullet in Joey Gilbert's brain, and end a standoff that had gone on too long.

And now, in Washington, D.C., and across the country: not only anti-war lobbyists but a thousand lawyers, thirty-three university heads, a hundred corporate executives, also doctors' groups, eminent professionals in every field raised their voices against the genocide in Southeast Asia. It also had gone on too long. Over two hundred State Department employees, among them fifty Foreign Service officers, had put their signatures to a formal declaration disavowing the current Administration policy. Moderates were up in arms. Even the so-called silent majority gave its seismic rumble ... All over America from coast to coast the social order was being disrupted by dramatic street actions. It almost seemed the very fabric of U.S. Government was about to rend asunder.

Nixon chose this moment to talk about 'those bums blowing up the campuses, ya' know'.

Meanwhile the media scapegoated the Vietnam vet who held his small daughter hostage. An elite force lurked in readiness to storm the Rock Castle. They would come with the darkness, Emergency Response Unit, Hostage Rescue Team, snipers. They were in their positions behind the high screen or amid the trees and farm outbuildings where Joey Gilbert couldn't see them. Could one man withstand an army?

No. It all ended simply—in minutes, in an hour or two. Shots, then silence.

For some, relief.

For others, grief.

For Newell Gilbert, as he stared at the junction of Route 70 and Interstate 40 west of Nashville, there was only tense anticipation and a sense of helplessness.

XI

Midafternoon saw him east of Nashville finally and speeding along the superhighway past New Middleton, Boma, Cookeville.

Near Mayland and halfway to Knoxville, he got in a truck with a day game on the radio, and the day's newspaper folded on the front seat.

—Mind if I have a look?

—Sure thing.

FOUR DIE AT KENT STATE UNDER NATIONAL GUARD FIRE

—Wow, look at this.

—Yep. Country's going nuts.

Newell read.

For a few days, since Nixon's speech, Kent town's main street had been filled with demonstrations. Both the Ohio governor and Vice President Agnew fanned the flames with remarks against student protests.

On May 2nd, after ROTC headquarters got burned, the local mayor requested National Guard support. Then, on Monday the 4th, Kent State students rang their 'Victory Bell' for a rally planned days in advance and endorsed by many faculty members.

At the last minute campus police went around with bullhorns saying the rally had been forbidden by a General of the National Guard:

—You may not assemble!

A crowd of shirt-sleeved students had gathered round their bell mounted on the Commons. Others were still in class and not aware of the banishment order.

A Guard officer said to an educator on the scene:

—These students will now learn about law and order.

An organizer on hand called for the campus to go on strike.

Then a State Trooper came through with a bullhorn:

—You must leave this illegal gathering!

Between five hundred and a thousand students had converged on the Victory Bell. And now, across the grassy Commons, the National Guardsmen came on, advancing toward them. Some demonstrators threw rocks. The Guard was ordered to load and lock its rifles. No one thought these troops had real bullets. Live ammunition was restricted in many states since the 1967 bloodletting in Detroit by National Guards.

Then the students faced some hundred Guardsmen who were toward the athletic field's chain link fence. The unit began its march up Blanket Hill where a few protesters razzed and hooted at them from seventy yards or so away. But they were not surrounded; their uniformed ranks had space on all sides and an unobstructed route back to ROTC headquarters.

Some helmeted Guardsmen trailed on the right flank. These stopped suddenly, wheeled almost completely around, and faced off with students on the south side of Taylor Hall. They leveled their rifles to a ready position.

A shot rang out.

Someone yelled:

—They only have blanks!

Students began running in retreat up the grassy incline.

Then came a deafening barrage.

The shots went on. Dirt flew in faces. There were thuds; there was splintered wood. Bullets whizzed and gouged around and stuck in a tree trunk. Rounds hit cars in the parking lot, shattered windshields, dented fenders. The people ran.

A girl screamed:

—Not blanks! . . . Not blanks!

Some fled across the lot. Others bowed, choked, and vomited from tear gas in the air. For an endless eight seconds the semiautomatic weapons crackled as twenty-eight soldiers fired like redcoats in a line at unarmed students. Some shot in the air.

One protester in full flight gave a jolt and fell dead.

Another collapsed and tried to rise. He was hit.

There was a pause. Then came more shots. Blood lust.

More cries—students got up and looked around.

One girl lay on the ground, and her face was very pale. She held her stomach.

Some moved, and some didn't.

—Get an ambulance! Get an ambulance!

Panic. Someone was crying, sobbing, hysterical. Another leaned down trying to raise a limp body—forehead covered with blood.

Screams.

—Dead! I knew it! . . . Dead!

When the smoke from M-1s cleared: four students lay lifeless on the ground. Four were shot to death. Nine were seriously injured; one paralyzed for life. None had made any action or threat against the Guard. All got hit between 265 and 390 feet away.

The newspaper Newell Gilbert was reading printed claims by Guardsmen that they were shot at. But eyewitness testimony said this wasn't true. There was no evidence of sniper fire on the Kent State campus.

Among those shot some hadn't come to demonstrate but were only walking across the parking lot at the wrong moment.

The parents of the murdered students gave interviews.

One, Arthur Krause, said:

—Have we come so far a young girl gets shot because she disagrees deeply with her Government?

Nixon stood by the National Guard action. He did not accept criticism of it.

The dead were:

Allison Krause, 19; Jeff Miller, 20; Sandra Lee Scheuer, 20; Bill Shroeder, 19, who was on ROTC scholarship at Kent State.

For a long time Newell stared at the highway . . . Grossville . . . Ozone . . . he read the signs. He asked the truck driver:

—How much further to the Carolina line?

—Another seventy to Knoxville. Then figure forty or so from there.

—What do you think about the students getting killed?

—Beats me. Maybe they deserved it.

On the dashboard clock it was quarter of four, as they rode toward Knoxville, listening to the late innings of a baseball game.

XII

None came out for Carlyne Gilbert foundering on the lawn as the hot sun beat down. Sunstroke might send her into a coma if the bad head injury didn't. She was out there suffering, maybe dying, for the world to see. She might have made it back to the porch, and the shade, but then Joey would have pushed Rhody out to her, and this she couldn't permit. Dr. Falliere would surely have come out for her, or Lemon Gilbert, but now no one could hope to get past police barricades. Now the Rock Castle was sealed off tight.

Maximum security had clamped down the compound, and nobody else was going to cross any lines. Everywhere were marshalls with special armbands, everywhere men in gas masks and police and State Troopers, and agents in civilian clothes. The defunct town center teemed with people again: like Everybody's Day in the fall when people hit the streets to buy things at the vendors' stalls, and the old'uns thought back with nostalgia on a time when their town had a vital life.

Now storefronts clustered by the railroad tracks gazed dumbly at all the high-tech bustle. The ghosts of Harvell's Drugs, Haight Furniture, Tomlinson's Grocery, Robby's Hardware, Sink Appliances, and City Shoe, looked on with a pang at this visitation from the four corners of the world. They could have done some good business, if it wasn't another age.

But beyond the high screen at the commercial district's edge—was only silence. Not a soul went out for Carlyne Gilbert.

Into the late afternoon she sat motionless in the heat, as police monitors amid shrubs across the street zoomed on her profile.

She put a distracted hand to her hair; she swayed a little, and
her head dipped, and came up again. Then as the sun bore down
she slumped to one side on the grass. One side of her face was so
swollen it looked like it might burst. In trouble, maybe unable to
stand up again, badly dehydrated, she cupped her hands over the
wound on fire. She curled her limbs to give the pitiless sun less
surface. She sweated.

None came. Who dared come out into the no-man's-land? Not
the authorities, and not a Red Cross team.

At this point it might have seemed negotiations could begin.
That was a sad spectacle, and the hardest of men should soften.
But no. While both sides temporized, Carlyne drifted into shock.

An FBI spokesman told the press:

—We have advised Mr. Gilbert he must lay down his arms and
come out, with his hands held high, before a medical team can
go out and tend to his wife. If not, then security considerations
prohibit. The ball is in his court for now.

So she lay out there alone. She was abandoned, an orphan
again, like her years at the institution down in La Grange.

Unable to rise, she waited. She made a sorry sight with her
white blouse splotched by blood and her long hair undone from
the bun, and muddy jeans. She looked like a wilted gardenia.

But then she surprised everyone. As dusk came on, she lifted
herself up, slowly, first to her knees, then on her feet swaying side
to side.

She began moving back up the front walk toward the house.
From lack of strength, from dangerous dehydration after lying
unable to move in the intense heat of the sun all afternoon, she
went to her knees. She advanced on all fours a little ways. And
then she crawled, she dragged herself along the cement walk; but
then got up again for another stage in this journey of a few dozen
yards. And it went on: up, down, on all fours, up again, while
everybody watched. It was dramatic. It was an event, as Carlyne
Gilbert, probably with heatstroke, drew near the front porch of
the Rock Castle, and then stopped and looked right.

Some twenty feet from the steps she went across the lawn to
the huge old oak tree and sat down with her back propped to the
trunk away from the house.

Maybe ten minutes later a thermos bottle, and then a plastic
bag, fell on the grass ten feet or so from her after being tossed
from a second storey window.

XIII

Night fell.

The darkness came on with a silence accented by the absence of traffic. Still the rumorous stir came from up town, but far away, like the dead congregating; while around the old mansion were the settlings and random sounds of bird or insect on an evening in May. High atop the steep conical roof of the granite angle turret sat its spire with the golden ball glinting red in the fading light of sunset.

Then for a last few moments the Rock Castle appeared to pose— massive, towering, nostalgiac as it sat there in a dream of moats and lofty towers, barbicans and machicolations above its Roman arched front porch, and crenelated balcony. Behind the great stone facade leaning slightly forward as though to intimidate and brave the world, there were twisting back stairs, trap doors, hidden passages leading to vaulted chambers where spirits sat conversing in the sculpted oak chairs. The tremendous thickness of the walls concealed old secrets. In the upper storeys was a stonework made finer by the passing of time round the high-niched windows, with their embroidered caps. But in the basement and subbasement there were long unvisited rooms, dungeons perhaps; and who knew what had gone on down there through the years, through the decades, centuries.

Night enfolded the contours of the Gilbert place where they rose up among the summits of the tall oaks. At any moment the floodlights could come on; although the hours till midnight, and longer, could also pass without them. Or they might burst on like an explosion and then go off again a short while later. The bright lights were being used as part of psy.-war, and apart from other strategic concerns, on or off, depending. Among the calm settlings, a nocturnal bird's call, a burrower's lowing, a breeze stirring in shrubs and trees—was that a click of gear? Someone scurried to a more forward position? No one doubted that for days the deployment had gone forward: the preparation for an all-out assault on the house. Now were the authorities gaining time while last-minute details got put in place? Perhaps a tunnel was being dug for a sudden entry? With the political stakes so high anything was possible. The way things were going in Vietnam, and here at home with the tragedy of Kent State, the current U.S. Administration could use a victory which put it in a good light. But there would be bad press if the little girl got hurt.

What was that? In the shadows! Was someone running between two tree trunks? . . .

Then, at a few minutes past eleven p.m., there was a loud noise inside the house. It was a hammering: knock, knock, knock. Why? What was going on? Was the hostage taker making something? His own coffin maybe?

As the hours passed, one a.m., two a.m., a question hung on the fragrant night air laden with dew. And this was: would the attack come at dawn?

XIV

Dawn came, and there was no attack. But there was something else—more surprising.

All through the day before, Carlyne Gilbert lay on the grass in the hot sun. Like a wounded animal she rose on one elbow and then fell back again; she tried to sit upright but went on her side curling in a ball. She had a high fever, and only her long black hair as shield from the rays of the sun beating down. But then in late afternoon she rallied and managed to rise, onto her feet, and drag herself slowly, in stages, up the front walk and across the grass to the ancient oak tree some twenty feet in front of the porch.

Now she was gone.

By the first light of the new day it was clear for all to see. At some point during the night Carlyne had gone somewhere. Did she take herself off, out of sight, to lick her wounds and die? Was she back inside the house with her husband?

Had the Feds after all sent a team for her—in the dark of night during a spell when the floodlights were off? Joey would have known it. Easily he would have seen their dark figures on the front lawn, and heard them. He didn't sleep, he did not dare to catnap at night.

In any event she was not there. Where was she?

As the sun rose on another day of siege, this was the question on everybody's mind:

—What happened to Joey Gilbert's wife? She vanished into thin air.

XV

But that wasn't all.

There was another story already known in the armed encampment up town—seen at once by anyone glimpsing the front page headlines of the nation's morning papers.

EMORY GILBERT IN ADULTEROUS LIAISON WITH DAUGHTER-IN-LAW

And so there it was: out in the open for the wide world to know. Who told the press? The sordid story was emblazoned on page one: upstaging the aftermath of the Kent State massacre. It must have come from someone on the inside: such were the dates and details. Quite bizarre the whole thing was, and a gossip columnist's dream. The great writer was biological father to the little girl being held hostage in the Rock Castle by his son. Ah so. This went a long way toward explaining the affair.

Today the name of a prince of Twentieth Century literature was sunk in opprobrium. He was seen as a classical American writer. And he was the darling of the 1968 Presidential Campaign, more popular than his own candidate.

But now it would be hard to find a word to describe him. In any case he had turned into his far opposite. Yes, the bigger they are, the harder they fall—especially when such a load of vanity is being carried about, in the eyes of the world, on such feet of clay.

This morning in May 1970 the U.S. press was absolutely merciless in discrediting, destroying, breaking the big man who for a moment in the nation's history had meant to spearhead a real, competitive Third Party, based on humanitarian not business principles, to take on the Republicans and the Democrats.

They did it to him. They got the job done.

XVI

Rhoda Gilbert sat in her high chair. In her slurry southern accent she said:

—Lemmih' go, dope!

All she ever wanted was to run all over creation making a mess. She was too big for the chair and kicked at the foot rest and tossed finger food overboard from the tray. She laughed at that, and tried out another new word:

—Stinky.

Rhody strained against the fastened straps and tried to climb out. She clanked her spoon, drooled apricot baby food with delight, spit it forth in a shower, smirked.

She laughed and gave her dada the evil eye.

—Papi! I wanna' . . . ooounh! oounph!

She grunted and half stood. She leaned, tilting the chair forward. Soon she would be a barefoot farm girl, scourge of a few dozen chickens: that is, if she lived through this, if any of them did. She rarely cried, only if she stubbed her toe.

—Momma git!

Joey looked out the window at where his wife curled like a fetus yesterday. He stared at the sunlit grass. Where was she? For him as everybody else it was a mystery. The Red Cross hadn't dared come for her. And he couldn't see how the Feds came that close to get her during the night. He would have known. Through the day she had lain out there, scorched, in delirium, raising an arm at the sun.

Last night it dawned on Joey what she had tried to do for him. He remembered her smashing the glass of the Dutch door downstairs after she broke through their lines. She came in to him lit up by her action—with a grin like his when he played his best baseball, only more positive, more human: about something.

This astounded him.

He didn't want to think of what he had done to her.

But he didn't want to be saved. And drag out a ruined life? In prison the rest of his days. Re-up for a second tour in this hell?

Through the blinds he peered into the morning sunlight, and shook his head. For an instant he felt strange again and feared a nervous attack: the hallucinations. Then his mind could lose control once and for all, going, going . . . he would no longer have a say in what he did. Then he saw Ben Bolt again, punji-staked Slidell, Horse Shue and E-4 Loseby on the bridge at Phu Bai. Then he saw Ringwood, Izard, FNG-IX blown to bits in Xo Man. Eat shit and die.

Alongside the front window Joey grimaced in the sunlight. Beyond the trees, he knew from TV images, the small southern town looked like a mini-Da Nang.

—Okay—he said to himself.—You win. But where are you?

XVII

Grimly, M-16 in hand, he went to the night table, the telephone. For a minute he thought over a call to the enemy. He was worried about his wife and wanted to know if they had her. Had an emergency medical team come during the night to save Carlyne? No; not without his knowing. And he knew like everyone else, from hearing a radio report, those two news items: the woman's unknown whereabouts unless, they asked, she was back in the Rock Castle? and the fall of Emory Gilbert.

An idea had camped out in his mind since the standoff began; but really much longer; perhaps since arrival in Oakland two years ago when she hadn't shown up to meet him home from the war. That idea was suicide.

Just as he reached to pick up the receiver, the phone rang. It startled him. Had to be them. So he gave a sigh and picked it up.

At the other end he heard:

—Hey, man.

—Who?

—It's your old partner in crime.

—Emmet?

The grunt gave a laugh:

—What gives with you?

Joey paused.

—Nuttin' much . . . How'd you get through?

—They called me. It was set up by our Colonel Pisscroft, you know, old boy from Division Headquarters.

—Ringknocker … But you better sanitize your language. They're listening.

—Ha ha. They gonna' send me to The Nam?

—I wouldn't put it past their asses. Well, Private Bufillu, what's the scoop?

—Same ol' shit, Jo. No change except my diapers. Each day I wake up to a wheelchair, poor paraplegic type thing. They carried the All-State tight end from Atmore off the field of life on a stretcher. Hey, I ain't feelin' too sorry for myself anymore. No suicidal ideations, as they say. Ha ha. Still it's a beeboppin' bitch.

—How's Nora?

—She's solid. She says hi. You know, I don't deserve her. I try not to aggravate her too much … Say, I saw yours on my TV screen all day yesterday. You could see her pores, sweat. No good, brother, it's messed up. Where is she? In there with you, Jo?

—No questions, Emmet. And I have to go.

—Where you goin'?

—Nowhere fast. But while we chat those assholes might attack.

Bufillu said low:

—Well, bye bye, World Serious.

—S'long, Bud.

—Give 'em hell, partner. John Wayne type thing, in reverse.

Joey went to hang up but hefted the receiver. His voice had a tremor:

—Take care. Sorry it had to end this way.

—Sure—said Bufillu.—I understand. Do the same thing in your shoes. Feel sorry for your wife though. Stag night.

—I know.

—Well …—Bufillu paused.—Some times we had, Tet 'n all, whatcha' think?

—Some times.

—Last time I done do'd it, night o' Tet. Outstanding.

—I'm sorry, Emmet.

—Hey, not your fault. Not any'uns. That's war … make a mistake, and pay. Shoulda' kep' 'er in my pants, l'il bait bug. Only rig'll hook not only the fish but the fisher and land 'im too. Ha ha. Hey, you know what I like? Fishing. They come for me early, and we go in the Gulf down there off Pensacola. 'fore summer's out we'll go deep-sea fishing. Wanna' come?

—Love to.

—Bring Carlyne too, she 'n Nora'd hit it off. You know yesterday I could see the beauty spot on her neck; they had it zoomed so. Guess they could grease you with one shot if they wanted.

—Not unless they can see through granite.

There was a pause. Joey Gilbert listened to the peaceful day in faroff Atmore, Alabama. He saw Bufillu's front porch and the ruffled window curtains. Spanish moss hung from the trees, and life was sweet after all. Warm breeze wafted a cereal scent from fields across the way, and birds were chirping for all they were worth. A katydid fiddled even now into the receiver. Afternoon, blue sky overhead . . . deep South. Later on Bufillu's calm, steady wife would start supper.

—Yep, Jo. We saved one another's hides, didn't we? Took turns at it. Xo Man, Saigon, some kicks. Absolutely, and positutely, as Six used to say. Wonder where his ass got to by now . . . Hey, you rescued my flabby ass again that time you stayed an extra day on your way home. So I owe you one. Wish I knew a few wise words to save your scrawny butt just now.

—Save 'em.

Bufillu chuckled into the receiver.

—Say, you know what my wife calls me? I mean my nickname since I became a basket case? Sweetcups. Pretty appropriate, wouldn't you say? She's a sweetheart, strong too. Helps me up, bathes my backside, works like a mule all day. I guess you'll be helpin' Carlyne if you both make it through. No, she dweren't lookin' too good out there. But I think, my opinion type of thing, for what it's worthless . . . is you better hang in there, Mister Jo. Things change, the worst passes. She'll be needin' ya'. Ain't finished witcha'. And this life we got here beats military scrip even if it is a—

—A beeboppin' bitch. Thanks ever so . . . but . . .

Bufillu waited a moment. Then he said:

—I caught the gossip about your dad on TV this morning, on *Wake Up America*. So you hate her so much you don't care if either of you dies?

—I don't hate her.

—Hate the Government then? The cops?

—I only pity ignorance.

—Well what then, kid? Why the vaudeville?

—Look, you know the reason. Maybe Sweetcups forgot, old Mr. Goodlife strapped in his wheelchair. But Private Bufillu hasn't. As for me, I can't forget it since these imbeciles won't let me. You say: don't do this crazy stunt. I say: okay, let them call off their dogs and leave us alone. We'll pick up the pieces and try to live. That's all. But if they don't, then a few shitkickers are going to die with me.

—That's an affirmative. But you said there was a reason. What is it?

—They want my . . . As foolish as it sounds, they want to take my honor. That's why. That's what I hate.

—But who is they? Is it your wife? the police? the Pentagon?

—Who? I don't know who. Life started this. Long before Carlyne or my old man. For better or worse this life has no plan worth a shit. Boocoo messiness like you said. But sooner or later the mess needs cleaning up, or at least an outlet. So some madman like me puts on a show.

—I don't follow you.

—In my skin you would. And you said so: you'd do what I have to do, when we hang up. End this farce, and fuggit.

—Then we'd better not hang up! Ha ha.

—It's getting to be an expensive call, Pardner. And I don't know if our Government will reimburse you.

—Shucks, the VA?

—Time to go, my good man. Tell your wife hi for me.

—Look, you told me I had to live for my family. Alright, I'm doing it. Why not you?

—They'll be okay.

—Ah ha! You can preach, but when it's your turn you don't practice. Okay with you gone, Jo? Your wife looks real nice in the family photos they showed on TV. Child too, right lively, a smarty pants. She deserves her chance. Shee! . . . Why not grin 'n bear it a while longer for them, type thing?

—Because in my case that means giving up. No, Emmet, you carry on and live for others, I can't do it with honor. I can only go down fighting . . . with honor. I will say this though, and then so long. I had something good in me. I was more than a ballplayer at least before Vietnam. I might even've been a man, a person people needed and depended on. But the good thing had no chance around here. Nothing for it to do! Charity? . . . give me a break. Well, I didn't know my own worth I guess. Didn't know myself; so I went off half-cocked to The Nam, which was a sucker play. Why did I go there? Because Carlyne couldn't understand my boyish love? she wanted a man? Here then, Honey, enjoy your anniversary gift. I'm home, a war veteran, and a man. Unfortunately she could've used the boy a little more: not the man who knew, but could not do. Guess how long, troop, since I went all the way with my wife?

—. . .

—We got our sweet asses lopped, mopped and diddlybopped over there. Well, you saw me in combat, and I saw you. We two at least know what our country lost for no worthwhile reason. And would you believe it? America doesn't care. Stepmother America doesn't give a flying leap what happens to her best sons and daughters fighting for the world's worst cause: the private property of the rich, as my hippie brother says. Well good, she says, good for your sorry ass, if you're stupid enough to believe what I say. And so she throws away her necessary men on the junk pile. Hate is what she really needs, hate and hate and more hate! Gimme more bankers, gimme more o' these politicians, gimme more idiot functionaries like those out there beyond the trees, and more conformist reporters. Gimme more hate! See how, every day and every way, America throws her good money after bad? But the essential thing is missing. The real day doesn't come. A nation's growth is stunted. So we miss the boat. Necessary men? That's a laugh. Apparently not so necessary, after all.

—Don't give it up. There's other boats.

—Missed! Time to go, Emmet. Take care.

—But you're still young. In your twenties! And we need you: squad leader, World Serious.

—I'm no leader. I'm the third baseman who pays the tab.

—Okay. Just a friend then. I, we need a friend. I never met anybody like you.

—Got to split, Bufillu, now. It's no good. Any instant those rascals'll come bursting through the front door, and me on the phone, away from my post. Don't scope the burr, and they'll know it, remember? Shit tactics. In a minute I'll have 'em all around me, a room to room firefight here in the house. And the kid still on my hands.

—Hang on another day.

—They're using you as always. It's a diversion. Sayonara.

—Take your time, man. Why the rush?

—I got a hot date. Bye bye!

Joey laughed. His voice brightened. Bosom Bud calls for chat. Decision made at last. Thanks, Pal, what a relief.

—Wait up, Jo.

—Nope. Bye now. Check your buns later.

But the brother wouldn't say goodbye. He hemmed and hawed and stalled around. Why?

Bufillu said:

—Feels like I had the opposite effect of the one intended.

—Thanks anyway, cám ồn ông.

—Tried to help, and did a booboo.

—Not at all. But I will hang up now.

—Don't go just yet.

—Bye, Uncle.

—Wait.

—Fate can't wait. Got to split.

—Hey, man—

XVIII

At once the phone rang again. He picked it up and said:

—This you? Then listen. In one hour I'm sending Rhoda out to you in a baby carriage. You send someone to take her to cover, I'll hold my fire. I'll get her to the end of the walk: you must not come up the front walk. Don't place a foot on it, or I'll open fire. She cannot stay in here because I am not giving up to you. Once she's safe, you yellow liars, then let's to it. Le's goo.

Alone now. The pain was over, the indecision. No more visits, and no phone calls. Just his luck if his brother arrived; but no, Newell couldn't get through.

Time to start.

Was he right? Did he have it right? This didn't matter. The pain hadn't left him since he touched soil Stateside that day. But now it was gone, and something like an inner joy surged up and recalled the best times—at third base, and by Carlyne's side. But now was even better, hope or no hope. Now for a moment he sensed an inner completeness that was new to him. On the verge of action, in an action far different from Vietnam, or baseball, he felt a kind of assuredness that was like his birthright.

First he had to get Rhoda as far as possible from harm's way. If they had come and gotten Carlyne during the night, then they would send someone out now for the little girl so their hands would no longer be tied, and they could strike. But they might think he was using her for a decoy.

Carlyne's public agony had made the Government look bad. His good faith in getting Rhoda out would do the same. So they would have to come for her. Poor kid—he had no choice but to roll her out there alone, on her own, to go toward her fate. But once she was down the steps . . . and on the front lawn—if she died it could do some public relations damage to the powers that be.

Bad business? Hopeless? Another bad war?

Alright then fight the bad fight. Die if necessary, but with some sort of dignity.

Hey, you don't like it? Then (gesture) ya'.

XIX

Now the old grin was on Joey Gilbert—hard, metallic, as if cut in his skin by the burin of an engraver.

Time to begin.

First the bathroom. He showered and hummed the song which they, the grunts, used to hear over Armed Forces Radio. Those were sunny days, never a drop of rain, in Southern California.

He put on clean fatigues and brushed off his combat boots. He sat at Carlyne's cosmetics table making himself up again. Then, looking duly strak in his camouflage paint, he went to Rhody. Oh! Did she love it and screech with pleasure when Dada picked her up in his great arms and waltzed her with a laugh around the room and ended that scandalous inactivity of playpen and high chair which she couldn't stand!

—Baby, let's take a ride.

—Sunday ride, Poppa?

—Righto. Drive in the country.

—See them fields?

—You got it.—He laughed.—Affirmative, troop.

Little Rhody doted on nobody 'cept when she got the blues then maybe her Momma. But she surely took an interest in this huge, stern Dada. And now she dangled face down delighted as she kicked her stumpy legs—wriggling under his arm, laughing. She chirped, babbled, sang a few toneless bars from the musical score of her childhood.

Then he held her in one hand against his broad soldier's chest like a piece of ordnance.

A greenish drop of sweat fell from his lean jaw onto her pink dress as he tickled her neck and said:

—Goochie-goochie.

Rhody squirmed, laughed some more, and stared up into his painted devil's face. This was the most fun she'd had in a week.

—Gnyuh-nyuh.

Downstairs in the basement a large antique baby carriage had gathered dust for years. Last night he was working on it when there was hammering heard inside the Rock Castle. Its black hood arched like a cat's spine over the frame with a silver-plated base and spoked wheels. It was a Gilbert heirloom complete with coat of arms; and the thing had taken him, sister Evelyne, Newell, later Lemon on many a stroll up town during summer visits to their grandparents in the 'Forties and 'Fifties.

Rhoda watched as he worked to reinforce a wood crossbar he had added beneath the frame. Then he went to get a rod and reel plus tackle box from the laundry room.

Joey came back and crouched by the carriage. Then he stood and tilted it far sideways to test the makeshift anti-roll bar. He stared at Rhoda, seated in there, on her level; and thought it over another moment; and then said:

—Time to shove off. Hump de hump, leathernecks.

Up the cellar stairs he hauled carriage, gear, little girl. On the back porch he positioned her on the plush interior, coffin-like with ruffled cushions, and fixed the straps round her waist and chubby legs. He took cord from a hip pocket to try and secure more tightly her tender and fidgety person. He talked to her man to man as he had with Tootie, Sumter, Chingi, Tommy Lerch in the moments before they went in the minefield.

—I'll leave your hands free. Good, sit forward. Let them see you. Hopefully they won't think you're a bomb, which you are.— He chuckled and made to rub his face in hers but remembered the paint.—Daddy's little bombshell.

She squirmed in the carriage and said:

—Mommy outside?

—That's an affirmative. She's on the perimeter waiting for us to move . . . Now when you see somebody, no matter who it is, when you get there then say: Help me! Help! Go ahead, let's hear it. What are you going to say?

—The Moms. Git!

—Not git. I said: help!

—Der George—Rhody laughed—der George.

—Kid, you got to obey orders for once.

—Giddyap! Horsey, gip! Ha ha ha!

A week ago she had charmed them with this riding motion, reins held high, as she rode her Dada's back across the rug.

—Hell . . . Do what I say. Cry: help!

—Hell!—She tried out the word.—Hell!

—Not hell. I said: help. P-p.

—Hell. P-p.

—Good. Now let's get this show on the road.

—Show on the road?

In the kitchen he rummaged a few minutes and then put a lunch box in the carriage beside her.

She touched the animal crackers design on the tin cover.

—Case you get hungry or thirsty outside. Look: water bottle in there. Okay, now we got to git. You ready?

—Dada.

—Ready, set, go?

Rhody looked down at her strapped legs. Brow knit, she thought it over a moment. Then her face lit up:

—Gyap!

She rode the carriage. It squeaked in the silence.

Joey nodded.

—Strak. Time to move out, troops.

XX

The antique baby buggy creaked in the hallway: past the stairs that led down to the basement; on past the guest bedroom, wide stairway, living room entry.

He parked her by the front hall table.

—At ease.

Then, in P. Laster's gloomy den, he took a piece of stationery from the desk drawer and began his scrawl beneath Emory's elegant letterhead:

IN THE EVENT OF MY DEATH

I give all my money and worldly goods, with one exception, to Carlyne Locklear Gilbert.

The exception is I give seven thousand five hundred dollars to Cindy Phillips who was our house servant for a good forty years and served the family through thick and thin though we should have been cleaning up after ourselves.

If my wife dies also and can't make a will, then our money and possessions shall go to Rhoda Strong Gilbert who is our daughter.

But in this event I leave $5000 each to Newell and Elisabeth Mona Gilbert because I love them.

My father I disown. I bequeath to him my ghost. May it haunt him.

I want Dr. Lydia Falliere to adapt Rhoda legally and bring her up if my wife proves medically unable. I don't want Rhoda to grow up an orphan.

Joseph L. Gilbert

XXI

This note he signed, folded in an envelope, and put inside the lunch box next to the child.

—We go, Da?

—You go, I stay.

—See you later.—She frowned.—You come too?

—Later.
—You too!
She kicked.
—Nope.
—Sappy doag . . .—said Rhody, her Carolina accent deep, back-woods, like Carlyne sometimes.—Go, Da. Dope!
She chanted like when she banged her spoon on the high chair tray. Her leg movement was limited by the straps, but she kicked her saddle shoes from the ankle.
—Stop.
—Dope, dope, dope! Da de da!
—Remember what I said. Help! Help me! . . . like that. Okay? Say it.
—I want Dolly. I want Doll Baby to ride!
Joey's eyes rolled up. He gave a sigh:
—Do what? Geez, not again.
Rhody tried to kick:
—Go get her, dope! Oh, the l'il precious—
Now she started with the fake crying. She hammed it up and glanced teary-eyed at her bad, bad Dada who would even think of leaving Doll-bubba inside the Rock Castle when they were go-ing outside to play.
He glimpsed the ceiling. Today she wasn't cutting him any slack, that's for sure. And there wasn't any more time for daw-dling; they must hurry. He had things to do and he had to get ready because now there was a feeling in the air, in the silence—a pre-attack sense, the brink before action. If he wasn't careful, if he let himself be distracted by her whims, requests, then first thing you know he'd have them all around him. And then she died also.
He shrugged.
—Okay. Doll Baby. But then that's it. Then you're boonie-bound, troop, and no more insubordination.
—Hell! she cried. Help Dada!
In a few long strides Stretch reached the landing. His combat boots squished on the carpeted stairs plush as elephant grass. Again he sighed with pre-combat butterflies. It was time and past time to get this act in gear.
He had thought over the scheme to evacuate the child before Rock Castle grounds became a free fire zone. Very lucid in these instants and his decision firm, he didn't trust Rhoda's stumpy legs

to take the porch steps on their own. Not long enough yet—she could trip forward and break her head on the stone. So he had debated: devise a ramp? Or push the carriage the few feet of porch and then onto the steps, unreeling her slowly down . . .?

In the bedroom he snatched up Rhody's doll.

Down the stairs he vaulted with a hand on the banister: the way they did as boys to Wilhelmina's horror. And she looked at them and said: Do what?

—Here, kid, Doll Baby. Hope you're happy now.

—Aw, she's precious!

Rhody squeezed the doll.

—Time to hit the trail.

—You ride, Daddy.

—No. Move out, meet your maker.

—You ride?

—That's a negative, it's too small for me. And zip the lip: I'm in charge here.

—Blah-blah.

—What's that? You want your slack ass in stockade?

—Yerass.

—Ah! You hear that? Latrine duty, grunt. Peel taters. G.I. party.

—Blah de blah.

The child looked so serious it made Joey want to laugh or cry. So he threw back his head and laughed like a pure gurgling stream. For a minute there was no grimness in his painted face as he nuzzled the little girl and kissed her a bushel and a peck and she cackled.

—You blah-blah your CO. That is not an outstanding tactic. I'll have your grunty little ass court-martialed for that.

Rhody giggled. Then, hesitant, she looked up:

—You go Mommy?

Joey drew up the hood. He grooved it halfway.

—Serve you as roll bar. Try not to exceed the speed limit.

She held her red-haired doll close.

—Doagy, woo-oo.

Then he rolled the high carriage toward the front door.

A moment longer he paused with his hand on the knob. He knew their sniper nests; he knew the precise angles of fire, and what he had to do.

He bowed to kiss Rhoda's cheek and spoke low:

—Good luck to you, kid.

The small girl looked lost then. By now she knew something was up, and frowned at him:
—You go, Daddy?

XXII

It was a few minutes past two p.m. as men spied from foxholes and advanced posts dug in a wide circle round the Rock Castle. Sniper aeries poised at their sites amid the tall trees, Gilbert farm outbuildings, the eaves of the mansion within range across the way. Up town the Government command center and siege compound watched every slightest movement on a few dozen closed circuit monitors. On the hour there were updates so the nation could see the scene and follow events at the Rock Castle. At any moment there was a special news bulletin over network television.

Now suddenly a flurry of messages sped in code. Camera lenses zoomed in from their careful distance. The heavy oak door of Joey Gilbert's fortress opened a peg and then further as though by itself. Was this a new development? A decisive turn in the affair? Now special reports flew out over the airwaves in the hushed yet upbeat tone of a tennis match.

The front entry yawned open and . . . a—a what? It was a baby carriage . . . Going for an afternoon stroll? Set high on its spoked wheels the old carriage bumped once, again over the threshold. The thing must be self-powered as it inched forward and then paused above the half dozen stone steps.

On all sides there were murmurings.

Newscasters, law enforcement officials riveted to monitors, Hostage Rescue Team members in advanced positions: all asked what was happening. The tone was urgent since little or nothing would be needed to send up the tinderbox.

—How—? What's in there?
—What's it contain?
—Something pink!
—Raggedy Anne stuffed with *plastic* explosive?
—But he said—
—The girl—

—And the range?

—So a remote-controlled bomb?

—It's a trick!

—Ingenious!

—Shoot it?

It came.

The front wheels took the top step. The hood bucked down and tottered; it hung there.

—He called and said he was sending out the child.

—Is it her? Is it—?

—Ready or not here she comes! . . .

Held by high-test twine, or an invisible wire from the shadowy foyer, it hung over the edge. The hood was drawn up halfway. What sort of ploy was this? . . . But they could see her. They saw Rhoda Gilbert as a rosy face peeped out: a flash between the black rim and heraldic emblem etched in gold.

The fancy carriage took the second step. Then, on the third it skewed and tilted dangerously—held up by a bar attached to the frame.

From afar all watched as the carriage was tugged at and maneuvered by a line, perhaps two lines, from back inside the Rock Castle. On course once more it plumped down, finally, onto the cement walk, and was ready to roll forward.

Now were the terse directives issuing forth from central command. Like flocks of winged words were the whisperings among FBI agents and other operatives, military advisers, state and local officers, elected officials on the scene, specialists, support personnel. There were rapid-fire messages amid static.

—Advise possible bomb planted in the baby carriage.

—Radius?

—All forward positions could be threatened.

Once off the bottom step, and straightened, the front and rear wheels, slowly, began to roll. Like a hearse from the old days, the black carriage looked stately, solemn, as it came forward. Stuck in a crack it was reeled back a step, shaken a little, nudged till it went on down the slow gradient.

The carriage moved toward the sidewalk and main road from town. It was past halfway by now. The effect was rather bizarre, all those eyes fastened on a baby carriage, in the sudden hush.

On it came.

And on came the urgent radio messages relayed to and fro.

Tinny over the two-ways the voices of men went banking round the armed encampment. Was there a bomb, *plastic* explosive, in that baby carriage? A hundred kilos of it he was said to have amassed this past winter during his Hot Stove League psychosis. A wild guess? There were fabulous quantities of high explosives stowed in the Rock Castle subbasement?

And as wasps dart in frenzy around some threat nearing their hive, and they gyrate in every direction and are lashed to a fury by the hostile presence; as they buzz closer and look to fasten on with their stingers and inflict death with their sting: so now the low tense voices crisscrossed between the positions, and spoke in code.

On it came.

XXIII

From one side of the foyer Joey knelt working two strings attached to the baby carriage. He jiggled and kept it rolling forward slowly on the front walk. He had got it started with the fishing rod: nudging, pushing it out to the steps as he risked showing them his extended arm. Once on the sloping walk he had to keep tacking with the two lines, working it side to side, drawing it back when it halted on the cement joinings.

Then he looked up. He shot a glimpse beyond the carriage.

There was someone in a blue suit walking along the sidewalk: just coming in view this side of trees and shrubs on the up town side. One of them—he thought;—so they had the heart to send an escort for her . . . It means they must want their hands free too: to end it too. But could it be? . . . Whoever that was he didn't look much like a law enforcement official. Was it a politician: the U.S. Congressman from the district? Maybe a childcare worker? One of the psychiatric consultants on the scene? The tall dignified figure looked unsure and tripped a little.

But the man . . . the man had an air about him which was anything but professional. He went slow, arms by his sides, with a fateful note as he reached the front walk of the Rock Castle. He seemed more intent on his thoughts than his steps.

For a few seconds Joey's attention was divided what with getting the carriage to move on. So he still hadn't given the other a good look. Now he did. And the sight jolted him. He crouched lower, staring like a scared animal from the dim foyer out at the sunlight.

For that person, appearing distracted, as he came nearer—head high but at the same time stricken: with a bad thing in his gaze, like grief, with a sort of tragic halo—that person was the one most dear to him, worthy of love and trust, all his life until a few days ago when he became the enemy, a stranger. Into Joey's mind came an image: a cloud he once saw out the airplane window the day he was coming home from Vietnam; how it changed and became a different shape and color, but was still the same cloud . . . And so it seemed like two men walking toward their fate: two far opposites in the same person. But how much living and struggling it took for the second one to come out and be known, like friction making fire. And yet he was there all the while, waiting for his day.

Now Emory's majestic head did not look so bright and full of life as during these past two years when he was playing the role of great man ever in the public eye. Now it bore the weight of the ages, like the conscience of Western man as he came forward with a ponderous gait and might have been taking his last walk on earth. There was just such a gravity in those slow steps, but at the same time—what? It could not be said there was joy, the elation of deliverance: freeing himself at last from the intolerable guilt he had denied and carried around so long . . . No; not that. For this was a terrible thing he had to do, perhaps his last act as a man. And yet there was something like that: say a note of triumph over his cowardice, a joy in tragedy if it were possible, because here he was after all, come out to face the music.

In these instants there was such a poor fellow in the great Emory Gilbert, such a deep need and fear, a note of the creatural. But there was also something grand like a character in one of his best books. Was he still playing a part? Yes and no—yes since he had become his own creation; no since this wasn't a book, this was real.

At a glance Joey felt all this. But he thought: did they send him? Is he here to take Rhoda away? Well, that's fitting.

From the shadowy foyer he called out to him:

—What are you doing here? Come to fetch Rhody?

—No.

—What then? Did they send you here?

—I came on my own. Though I had help. And they, as you put it, were willing enough for their own reasons.

—Help?

—Y-yes, you see, your father couldn't make up his mind by himself. Too yellow for that. Needed a little coaxing.

—From?

—It's Commynes' idea. I'm out here in effect because he made me. He always said I had to go public. I wouldn't do it. So he went and told the press what I did to Carlyne, and you; he took it in his head to confess for me, to the world. Said it was the only way *we* could save my soul for all eternity. This past year or so I'd refused to do it on political grounds; it was political suicide; so he took the step for me. In his concern, in his piety, my best friend looked after my soul for me. I guess you know the story is in all today's newspapers. Front page, across the nation. Ruin. I'm finished. Emory Gilbert is history, but not quite yet. I'll have some sort of resurrection, if it kills me. It's a moral victory, coming out here to you, whom I've offended.

—Reverend Commynes did that?

—My closest friend ever since we were children . . . or at least my soul's. You know, I think Paul Commynes is the real madman among us. Why else would he pose as my savior while he aimed to destroy me? I think for fifty years he waited and looked for a way to do that. And all along I didn't see it. He was the one I went to in my weakness. When I couldn't take the self-torture anymore, I went to him, I made the devil my confessor. Such a babe in arms I've been: I let him. Never saw what he was doing when he made me force my daughter toward marriage with a man four times her age. He had my mind so tied up in knots I tried to have my own son locked up for life in a mental asylum. Luckily Newell got away; if I know him, he is on his way here, right now. If one of us Gilbert males is sane, healthy in his instincts, then it is him. I see that now, and the rest, when it is too late to make amends. I did it. I did that! So now you see me here before you. You too can see, Jojo: what I am, what I've become . . . a monster. The opposite of what I wanted, and believed!

XXIV

Halfway down the walk Rhoda sat babbling in the baby carriage. But there was an accent of impatience to it since she stopped moving and wasn't riding for fun anymore.

Emory fell silent where he stood up the walk from her not ten yards from the steps. It was curious the way he stared at the house of his father and forefathers, and also the tall oak to his right and the blue sky overhead: as though he was looking at these things for the last time.

Joey said, not loud, into the silence:

—Why did Commynes do it?

—That's what I'm just now understanding. He's P. Laster's bastard . . . I never put that name on it . . . and filled with hate for the legitimate one, his brother. My father sired Paulie on Martha Commynes one night over in Skeeter Hawk . . . The Lord is long-suffering, but he does not clear the guilty. He visits the fathers' iniquity upon the children into the third or fourth generation. That's the Book of Numbers, XIV, 18, chapter and verse. But it is also the curse of the Labdacides: Oedipus and his sons punished for the bad behavior of Oedipus' father, Laïus, who was punished as well.

—Halt there! It's far enough. Don't come any closer. How did you get them to let you come out here? You're taking Rhoda back.

—No, I'm not. As for them . . . they won't be sorry if something happens to me now. You can't make speeches like the ones I've made lately and think they won't take notice. I mean at the highest level. They don't like this talk about a Third Party by someone who might have the moral authority to get it started.

—Even if you're finished, as you say?

—I'm finished, but not quite yet.

—I said no closer! Don't get in my field of vision.

—I want to see you. Your face.

—Why?

—I want to look in your eyes and tell you that you're my son and I love you. Also there's something I want to show you.

—Never mind, I can do without seeing it. I've seen enough because of you.

—But you need to, and you will.

—I'm warning you. I don't want to shoot my own father, but I'll do it. Just clear out of here and take Rhody with you. Go on!

—I can't do that.

—But you're in the way here! What are you doing? This is not about your pretty talk, all your literature and your 'moral authority', and then you stick a knife in your son's back, who believed in you! Now I said turn around and go away and I mean it. If there's any decency left in you then take *your* bastard along with you. So I won't have her on my hands, and I can at least make war in peace!

—This is the crossroads.

—What the hell does that mean? Do you think this is a theater? Git! Git along with you! Goodbye.

—One more thing, Joey. And then I'll go away if I'm able.

—Well what is it then? C'mon! Make it snappy.

—It's too late to confess what I did. You already know. I was too big a coward to come clean when it counted.

—That's true. But you know what? I think it makes no difference, and neither do you.

—I won't say I'm sorry.

—Well, good! That's honorable at least. For once you didn't dress up your lie: like one of your fancy women.

—I . . . I don't regret what Carlyne and I did. Maybe I'm just a pagan. I am. But I wanted to live and I had to live . . . What I hate myself for is all the trouble I caused you and her. I didn't mean that, I didn't . . . but I deserve . . . if not to die, then worse than that, because of it.

—Bravo. Now goodbye to you. We're done.

—Not quite. Do you see this?

—Forget it.

—I can't. This brooch, Joey, you know what it is?

—Yes, yes, I know about the goddamned brooch. You gave it to Carlyne. She brought it to Bangkok and wanted to give it to me, but I didn't take it. And now . . . You know, I think that's your worst sin. How could you let that devil in on our secrets? He's used them to destroy us.

—I trusted him.

—What a fool . . . not to get rid of such stuff.

—I know, but . . . I didn't want to. I just valued it, anything, about . . . I wouldn't have hurt her for the world.

—Tst. I'm sure, I'm sure. But this . . . this life is a war, and you don't know that. You'll go to your death trusting and spouting high-flown phrases.

Joey stared out at his father in the silence.

Further down the walk Rhoda was quiet now. Maybe she drifted off, napping.

Joey was still letting out the string, as though his instinct told him: get her away.

Emory went on. Growing maudlin? What was the point—and would the comedy ever end?

—I worked like no one on earth all my adult life: to achieve something in the cultural field, and serve humanity. And now that work, I believe important to our people, has been smeared with filth. Will it be discredited, lost? There are powerful political forces taking advantage of this. They've buried me alive, but they also want to stigmatize my books. I can't let that happen.

—What's that to me?

—Only this . . .

There was a pause. Emory stood not ten steps from the front porch by now. All the while Joey knelt manipulating the two rolls of twine and moving the baby carriage along further, on further toward the sidewalk.

Then Emory held Carlyne's brooch up a moment for his son to see: the fine cameo work of a tribal woman in profile on a brown-ish red background.

Emory took the gold clasp with a glint of sun in his two fingers, opened it carefully, looked at it, as if he was about to give a demonstration.

And then, closing his hand on the brooch, he plunged the clasp in his eye.

As he did so he gave a roar—and stuck the long pin of Car-lyne's brooch into his other eye.

Blood spurted on his face. Blood gushed on his neck and shirt. In an instant his eyes were put out by the brooch, two red pools, as his blood came welling forth. But he wasn't done, and jabbed it in again, and again. Still on his feet, he swayed, punching in the pin, roaring each time.

—My eyes won't look at the suffering I've caused! No more! Darkness! No more seeing what I never should have seen, know-ing what I should not have known!

The blood poured out in a dark stream from Emory Gilbert's

face and onto his clothes, dropped to the cement walk. He stood there shaking, groaning, choking over a few more words.

—I thought I was happy and free, I was just one more unconscious animal. So pleased with myself and fame and now what is it all but a curse, but death and shame? I should never criticize anyone or even see the light of day! I am all that is worst on earth without exception.

He moaned and cried out like an agonizing lion as he went to one knee in the pool of blood at his feet.

XXV

As he went down on one knee, and then fell heavily on his side, Joey watched him.

Suddenly it wasn't the stranger, the hated one, he had seen coming along the sidewalk. All at once it was his father again: the man he spent his boyhood loving and believing in.

And so he couldn't help himself. He went out to him.

This jolt after all the others was too much. It was the crowning blow. He lost control and acted on his impulse; he sprang forward from the vestibule of the Rock Castle into the open and the sunlight.

—Father!

Emory was mumbling on the ground. He kept talking like he had all his life; even now the words had the Emory ring to them, like lofty lines from a play. He whimpered:

—Now darkness . . . the hateful cloud comes over me . . . and life's over? Jojo, I think I hit my brain . . . with the brooch. It prickles . . . stabbing, like the memory of what I did.

—I'll get you inside. We'll call them. I'll give in now and they'll send an ambulance.

—Friend . . . is that still you by my side . . . taking care of a blind man? I know your voice.

—I'm picking you up.

With the M-16 in one hand Joey bent over his father to take hold of him under the arms. The army surrounding the front yard did not open fire. It wouldn't be good publicity if they began shooting from all sides at Joey Gilbert trying to rescue his father.

Emory was raving, or, perhaps, even in his agony reciting poetry. Joey went on one knee to lever the heavy frame splotched with blood up from the walk. Under the dead weight he staggered a first step, then another, with his back to the Rock Castle entry.

—It's Apollo, my friends! Apollo did these things; the god gave us this pain! But I put out my eyes when nothing worth seeing was left for me.

Joey with his father over his shoulder backed away, another step, another, up the walk toward the front steps. As he went he cast rapid glances: here, there, at the tree summits, and beyond the long sloping lawn, across the road. With one hand he pointed his submachinegun and with the other steadied the heavy burden on his shoulder.

And Emory chortled in his throat, groaned:

—That's true! . . . Get me away from here quick. Out of life's sight . . . the great man . . . most hated of all by the gods! I should've died a long time ago so I wouldn't hurt the people I loved most. Not debauched my daughter . . . destroyed my son.

And then with Joey taking the steps, slowly, stooping half over and feeling his way with one hand up toward the porch—a shot rang out. Was it from his gun? Did he trip on one of the stone steps? Was it his semiautomatic weapon discharging by mistake? Or did the bullet come from the other side? A sniper perched in the trees, or across the way? On his back Emory's body gave a little lurch as if hit.

Joey swung back, and he knew where they were. He knew their positions after the days and nights of keeping a lookout and watching for a slightest sign. And so now he fired off a first volley. And a sniper fell, hanging, holding momently from bough to bough—then down along the trunk onto the grass across the street.

There was a flurry of shots—many, all sides.

Joey fired off rounds back at them, and he felt his father's body take hits, jolting, on his shoulder, as it shielded him.

Was he hit himself? He went plunging, diving inside the door: far enough to slam it closed.

He dropped his father in the front hall and drew deeper into the house.

Emory still had a few more words, though no one heard them. He murmured to himself:

—They wanted me dead. They sent me out here to die. But I have made it so my works will live.

Chapter Twenty-Four

I

Dat tda! tdat tdaaa datatatatatd! From the first volleys the grunt gauged angles. .50 caliber MG ... where? Suddenly: *tup! tup!* sniper activity, four, five of them. *Buh-thuiit! buh-thuittt!* More nourished fire, incoming! They had a LAW—using a light anti-tank weapon against the house. There was a crash—glass shattering in back. The attack was on.

He knew he must fight in the dark without battalion intelligence, an S-2 to intercept radio messages and get enemy positions: when orders came from the tac-op center, and the monotone became a rasp. Alone Joey scampered between his loopholes. By now every opening was taking such a volume; it was enemy fire across the spectrum. Pinned in, then hold off. He had prepared for this—so wait ... Now: pop! He worked a sniper nest. Pop! At nine o'clock a man fell in stages, like a stunned monkey, from the upper limbs. Poppop! He finished him.

Explosion out back—emplacement set up beyond the barnyard. They had a 3.5-inch rocket launcher; weapon used to blow open houses in Hué City: like an old bazooka. Then they tossed in grenades. So none must get close enough. Good night once they entered and fought him hand to hand between the rooms. Poppop-pop! In the deafening roar of a hundred detonations he scurried front to rear defending the house. Keep 'em out!

A tank appeared. The huge green beetle poked its nose through the trees on the up town side; it maneuvered its cannon. From the front—a piano alcove on the angle turret's ground floor serving as revetment for his B-40—Joey fired, and missed. But the tank backtracked.

Guns blazed. Lodged in eaves of the mansion across the way, perched in a hayloft over the barnyard out back, on the advance between tree trunks and farm outbuildings, Government forces kept up a steady hail of fire. Projectiles chipped chunks and charred the Rock Castle facade. 7.62 mm, 20 mm slammed in against the granite and ignited great hives of sparks.

The lone fighter inside moved here, there; he manned the entire perimeter.

He shouted out to them:

—Toy soldiers! That the best you can do?

He ranted and didn't hear his own voice. He taunted them, and thought only one thing could end it for the impregnable fortress: an air raid, a 500-pound bomb dropped from the sky. Then the end. Or a CBU-55 asphyxiation bomb: suffocate all life within a 750-foot radius.

From among the trees across the street an M-60 was sustaining its fire. Joey put out rounds, pop, pop; I don't mind the barrage, boys, but keep your distance!

One of their sharpshooters stood erect, tottered, and fell three storeys from manor house eaves above the machinegun position.

Window panes burst in and, flung against the far wall, tinkled. Suddenly there were rocket explosions whirling shrapnel through the south casements into the elegant Georgian rooms.

Uh! Joey groaned and crouched down. Hit? Where?

Sickened, he felt fluid beneath his fatigues. He thought of Kevin Blair. The kid fought pretty well in soiled undies.

II

Plup! Mortar rounds? Plup! On the roof! Burn him out? Certain mortar increments cause inextinguishable fires. Well then you asked for it . . . Dizzied, in a trance, Joey knelt by a back window. Beside the steep driveway a baby-faced soldier wielded a blooper, M-79 grenade launcher. Pop! Got'm. Pop! The boy cried out and dropped his weapon. What a surprise. Ah! You mean this is real? This is me?

Mad minutes, shrieks, shrill whistles as rounds cascaded against the Rock Castle: 105 mm mortars on target. The heat was growing extreme inside the stone mansion. Joey ran low to and from his defensive positions amid enfiladed machinegun fire. But he was thinking the ammo dump down cellar might blow if it caught fire and began to cook off.

Hit again! This time in the neck. Deep? A graze? His blood was flowing but he still leapt here, there, a dervish. Pop! Out back toward the seasonal workers' quarters he saw a team approach with a flamethrower, XM-191. He knew about it: similar to a LAW, its half-size bazooka tube sent 66 mm projectiles a 300-meter range and produced monstrous fireballs, thirty meters in diameter, on impact. But it was rarely used in Vietnam since any obstruction within the foreground, say the first 30 meters, charred its operators. So they were using him as a test ground for the improved weapon? Pop! Phwooooshwooooshhh! An incendiary charge came in. Flames raged up in the back porch and kitchen.

Rounds rained in the windows. Artillery shells screamed in exploding. The ground floor was filled with blunt-nosed missiles from an M-79 grenade launcher; the six-ounce rounds burst into 300 fragments and sliced the air at five thousand feet per second, like furies; they point-detonated in the living room, in P. Laster's cozy den, in the guest bedroom where Carlyne stayed while her husband fought for his life in a faroff land.

The battle went on. Outside the windows the gray-blue smoke gushed up and drew a premature twilight over the wide manorial grounds and farmstead out behind the Rock Castle. Steadily the sniper fire crackled at all o'clocks with pinpoint accuracy past the burnt-out embrasures, finding a slightest crevice or interstice, Joey's loopholes. Wounded a third time, on the right side and maybe more seriously, the grunt still flung himself from one position to another: those frontal and rear emplacements unaffected by flames.

His grin was the invincible grin of the winner; it looked carved in granite, set forever. But not like Vietnam, and not like baseball— it showed a kind of joy in this combat. He wasn't grim in these instants. The agony was over of having to see his wife out on the front lawn: the woman he loved and had hurt so bad. Now that anguish was over; she was out of sight and she must be safe. So there was nothing more to decide, and he was free to fight them.

But he was losing blood. And his mind began to waver, in and out.

III

He jungle-crawled across the master bedroom carpet and called for RTO Troupial. Behind him Bufillu moaned and begged for a medic; his back was on fire.

Joey smelled waterlogged earth, fish scents; he heard frantic clucks, pecks, snorts. He saw abandoned huts on the dirt square and a banyan tree like a cathedral organ. Some crows flew over a kapok tree. The mama-sans had beat it fast with their breadfruit, manioc and durian. The people went poof!

Wild men raced M-16s ablaze among the hootches. Gray smoke plumed thatch. A howl went up as villagers died, women, children, the old: those not in on the secret. There was hysterical laughter amid the crisp acrid fumes. A kid's voice sang out:

—One dollah shoeshine, ha ha ha! G. I. Fuckah!

In a narrow lane, Skoly-Skol, talented pointman, crouched and watched.

Chi-Bar, Thingum ran about yelling wildly:

—Dong hai!

—Didi! didi!

Jumbled voices. Punctured pigs squealed.

Joey shook his bloody head. His mind had to stay clear.

He knew what he had to do. Across the second floor hallway he slid on knees and one hand into Lemon's old room. Beside it was a bathroom; and, through an inner door, a low ceiling'd utility room ran fifteen feet to a large bay window, or oriel. Above a parapet it projected, semi-hexagonal, supported by corbels; it was picturesque in contrast to the everyday interior. And here, drawn back at an angle, protected by thick stone wall, he had his 4.2-inch Four Deuce set up. Now he targeted the enemy's military compound, the police station, the First National City Bank building within range.

They used mortars. He too would use a mortar.

Out the window he saw the baby carriage: it sat there amidst a battle. It looked like a wounded insect, slightly tilted, its hood frayed, at the end of the walk. He couldn't tell if Rhoda was still in it, sitting there exposed in the middle of the bombardment and retaliation. If so, it would affect her hearing, at very least. Had central command up town given the order to come take her away? Or would Government forces send in a round and take her out so they could say he did it?

—DASC 0-1 FACS (static) I repeat . . . coordinates hot pad alert, prep LZ 'legs'. In trouble as always, you slackers?

Tinny PRC-25, in and out:

—1st Brigade 101st Airborne, hose 'em!

—Hose down those mudderlubbers, Spooky!

—Three 7.62 MGs miniguns a hundred rounds per second—

—I had my KBAs today.

—20 mike-mike kill ratio suspiciously low . . . troop!

—Don't shoot! Chieu hoi!

—Ha ha! S-5 Civil Affairs builds ville. S-3 Operations razes ville. Hoi chanh.

—Sir! A good time was had by all, Sir!

Joey crouched by the mortar. Behind him flames were coming up from the floorboards in Lemon's room. Supply lines were cut, and there would be no retreat. The smoke threatened to overwhelm him and do what an army couldn't. *Tatatatata! Dat! dat!* Fuckemup, Sir! Can bo! Pfoowooshf! He pumped a mortar out over the old town center: the vacant stores huddled in a row alongside the raised tracks. Pfwoofthsh! There was a momentary lull amid the havoc and thousand-gun rant and the sirens.

IV

Up ahead he saw Highway 4 between My-Tho and Saigon.

It was a ghost village of clay and bamboo with leaflets strewn everywhere. *'We must destroy the VC to have peace and prosperity.'* Planes had sprayed the fields with a blue and yellow powder. They turned the crops to a gray dust.

Where the flames were getting hold of his little sister's room behind him: it was Xo Man in his mind. Men swore, whooped, poured submachinegun fire into a hootch.

—I dedicate this to Kevin Blair!

—Ben Bolt! Ben Bolt!

—This is for Slidell, you commie dinks!

Caught up and tossed like a rag doll Troupial laughed and spat.

—It's fun! Have a blast!

A wisp of gray hair was seen in a doorway.

—Chau an, Pappy!

—Chi-Bar, outstanding! Ooh! Sister-san's loving it, ha ha ha!

—Why fight this two-bit war on VC terms? Why not nuke every last one of their slanty asses?

—Six, Beta-5. Six, Beta-5.

The girl gave a dry whimper.

—Give Chi-Bar a "V" for valor, Sir! One hefty orgasm confirmed, Sir!

Rotor wash fanned smoke. In the dust-sting a hootch roof spiralled up, torched. On his shoulder he carried Ringwood's gristle and shredded flesh.

—Bop and mop! Dong hai!

They fired desperation rounds at an unseen enemy. Ouch! Ouch! Cuff on fire. Talk about hotfoot! Ringwood, out at home. Reckon he played some ball down there in southeastern Carolina; but he's hung 'em up now. Izaaaard! Can bo. Claymores strung along concertina slow up VC sapper patrols at night. Check your local classifieds: one high school sweetheart, avlbl. *Ratatat-tatd! Dtat-ata!* Ya' bastuds: do that to me? Thrwoofshthf! I gave my all . . . Can the pathos, grunt. *Rata! ratd-tdat-datdat!* Save your gripes.

V

Face grimy, blood on greasepaint, he went on. Flames hissed in the great heat. A chopper ventured closer in. Pop! Direct hit on the back porch, crashing in. Granite rumbled as it collapsed. Pop! pop! He watched the helicopter gain altitude as plaster dust showered down in his eyes. His ears rang. In this instant he heard a thin chatter of two gibbons in the evening silence. Three idiots make one wise man, they said. But one whitefaced monkey is worth three professors. Noble ape. Red brains like fish roe on Bufillu's boot. Pitiful whore sistah' in her fake satin bodice. Scents: crab soup, wild tamarind, pawpaw. Shake down the superflux to us gooks. But you, Sir, you numbah' 10 fuckee United States President, Sir, go home.

M-16 in hand he stood in the eternal silence before a hootch. The woman's hair was a fine black sheen like Carlyne's, and the poor children were wide-eyed. Her man was off with the ARVN fighting Viet Cong somewhere. She was a friendly, but the horror was on the march.

Ghost landscape. It was his AWOL flight to Saigon. Bomb craters dotted the roads. White psy.-war leaflets looked like birds sprayed with herbicide. Long tracts were dioxened. Trees were blackened in the hail of general purpose bombs, H&I bombs, prep and destruction bombs, defensive concentration bombs, WA bombs, TOT bombs.

—'sssssss . . . sssss.

Flames hissed. Ville fumed. The Rock Castle burned and shook.

He brushed back his greasy hair with bloody hands. Now a head wound? He sent forth M-16 rounds. Once again he unleashed the mortar.

A first F-4D Phantom screamed over. He heard it distantly. Now payback for the insolent Four-Deuce rounds lobbed on top of them up town. Now they wanted an end to this embarrassment dragged out for days while the nation watched. Now they would have their way, and fast. One man cannot fight an army.

Flames purled. Flames spread from roof to thatched roof in Xo Man hamlet where the mad minutes had almost ended. Why, Carlyne? Why did you do it? Lust, my dear. But adultery? And in the family—betrayed by family! This is the thing I can't take . . . Beaucoup pain. He stared in at the woman and her children. Their limbs were entwined, their lost gazes . . . implored? Cheap life!—chirped the gibbon. Hmph, still not dead? They waited. They were humble, a tenderness in their features. Wide-eyed kids, trusting, to the end.

The G.I.s grouped behind their squad leader: Troupial, medic Artus, Thingum with a smirk and chicken feather on his lip, cagey Skol. They were lucky guys. They survived the shoeshine blast.

World Serious peered in. He levelled his gun. Curious, he felt no emotion in these moments. Cassava roots on a table. A bundle of pumpkin leaves. Some mountain rice in a tin. Ginger rootstalks.

Gently, he pressed his trigger finger, there, on the death imprint.

He squeezed . . . and shattered the Xo Man silence————

VI

There was a huge shriek as a second Phantom flew over low. This time the pass was lower. Then the explosion shook earth.

Fire danced in the shock waves. Fire sprung from the floor-boards, whoosh, whoo-oo-o-oshhh! He felt himself swept up at the ceiling just as the frail woman lurched and fell sideways try-ing to shield her children with her body. He heard the girl gasp as bullets pierced her flesh like a ruby necklace. Carlyne! He saw the pale virgin skin split open, *datdatda-da!* Then they jerked back, grappled a last instant together, and fell onto the dirt floor. They clung there, stuck in a mass, at the conqueror's feet. Mother, chil-dren, in death.

Brought back to his senses for an instant by the inhuman heat, he screamed, and fired off an M-16 volley.

Rooted there in Xo Man, stunned by the sudden silence, he blinked at his victims.

Then he heard eerie words. Dr. Falliere spoke in a mystified tone:

—Avoidance mechanism . . . Inability to relate key factors in a traumatic experience.

They moved out southwest, and their faces glowed red.

On their backs they felt the heat from Xo Man in flames.

Up the dirt road Tombigbee, the Arizona Navajo, was waiting. He didn't say anything—just stared down at the heroes. On the left were blue ridges in a mist. In the distance was a howl of wild dogs. Gray-blue smoke billowed up to the rear, in the sunset turn-ing from green to purple, as night came on.

Later, after dark, they heard tamtams from a Rhadé tribal vil-lage. Out on third base he heard those same tamtams, ball two to the fifth hitter, a free pass? Load 'em up? By the bag he tapped his mitt. There was a glow of firelight in the ARVN scout's gaze. Moonlight shone through the tropical forest.

Strike one, outside corner: wicked stuff caught the trim. No letter today; not a signal in weeks from his wife disloyal like Ben Bolt's. To me you did this, my darling, when I was giving my all? Tomorrow new guys were due—replace Izard, Ringwood, Vane, FNG-IX, Chi-Bar. Too bad for Bufillu if he had to come back. Ball three—

Shaken, ruined as a combat unit the grunts spread and set up a perimeter. Their nerves were shot. Morale at zero. In the trees a monkey screeched like a high laugh.

Thingum said:

—They got Kevin.

Since sunrise their minds were on Blair. Had the botanist wandered out alone to gather samples? Guys break down. Go nuts.

Next day the VC were ready for them. Oh yes, it was a stage set. Round a bend on the dusty road a few kliks southwest from Xo Man, there in a defoliated stretch—

—Blair!

Couldn't miss him: in a tree, grunt brochette. Au point.

Oh! the frenzy of it seeing him like that.

—Bunt! Bunt down third!

—Call Six. Probably he's a bomb too.

They gaped. A shoeshine bomb. Now this.

—Damn it all, Kevin, goddamn it!

The third baseman stood in a daze. The ball rolled inside the chalk. Runner crossed home.

Why, my darling? Such desire you put in me to play my role as husband and father. Such love I had for you: the tension was too much, once we met. That night I went to find you in Women's Campus Library, remember? I was so afraid I might ever hurt you, confuse you. The love just overwhelmed me, adrenaline, lifelong.

VII

Still alive, Joey crouched by the mortar. He sent another round out over the small southern town where his forefathers were born and lived and worked.

A star shot far, far out in the infinite darkness dotted by lights. Joey's jawbone worked like a fish gill. His eyes were burning. He heard a blast, whoo-o-oosh! In his brain an intergalactic wind made ripples over a vast miasma. He had a taste of putrefied self as the great whoosh rolled on toward——

—I went and killed them for your sake, you REMF mother-fuckers! Now I'm talking to you!

The phoenix bird, said Blair, on the beach at Nha Trang; it symbolizes fidelity. It hops among the ancient *tung* trees, coc! with its guttural cry. The phoenix bird doesn't grow old since it gives of itself freely. The male broods the eggs.

—*I, Joey Gilbert, murdered them! A soldier reports! I'm the one!*

Twilight trail. Three corpses, Lerch, Sumter, Chingi.

They rose up, slowly. Click, click. One said: You live, we die; now why is that?

It was a hundred-gun salute. The echoes flew up, up, away.

There was a wild all-out shout from inside the house in flames:

—*I died for you, America, Sir!*

Silent, reposeful was the Annamese Mountain range. In the distance of deep blue haze Truong Son drew into itself.

Then he said something else. Oh, that one was close. A few more minutes, seconds, and life would be over. Was it for nothing? An accident? . . . Another bomb came— Hand on fire? Touch my face . . . Didn't pay that seed debt yet . . . Does it really never rain in sunny California? By the Lumbee River, Carlyne . . . Fire, eyebrows, eyelids, in my eyes. No sense now. Death, any instant. Yes, life's over, as my dad said. Can't stand up. I don't think. Count squad, count 'em . . . one, two . . . The day up North we rough-housed: I told Newell, Don't tease her, a bully picks on little ones . . . Strak, only burns. Like Xo Man . . . saved by Bufillu. Doesn't hurt: when it breaks the register. Dry mouth, such thirst, hard to breathe . . . suffocating . . . Light flashes, mortar? Their cannonade? What do they have out there? . . . This pressure is too much . . . I . . . the best fertilizer . . . my darling . . . I can't anymore—

VIII

But he wasn't alone. Behind him in the doorway a figure seemed to rise up from the smoke and flames taking hold through the house. It was Carlyne.

She stood there filthy from head to foot as if she had been burrowing underground. She looked ghostly, covered with cobwebs from wherever she had been, getting in the house. She was enwound with soot and spider webs: crawling with the nastiness of the Rock Castle's underground rooms.

Half her face was purple, terribly bruised and swollen; it was like nothing human. Her hair and eyebrows were singed away. One eye socket was closed tight, and so she turned her head and seemed to bore in with the other.

She stood on the threshold a moment in the great rant of guns and ordnance detonating around the house.

And then she came forward.

She moved on her husband sitting with his back turned by the artillery piece.

In her hand was a rolling pin. In the terrific heat a blue flame penetrated the floorboards from below and purled up along the door frame to the lintel. Carlyne held the wood cylinder by one of its handles, but the look on her face wasn't about rolling out dough. She had the mask of the warrior made more grim by her necrotic features, better than war paint; though she did no dance, and gave no war cry advancing on her husband from behind. She was as fearful as everyone else was—as the army of men encircling the Rock Castle and still not daring to storm the place and come in for him. And she knew, as they did, that at any moment the massive stone structure might blow sky-high from the ammunition bin in the cellar.

Her idea was to hit him hard and knock him out, but not kill him. So she came forth and struck not with a metal implement or a length of lead piping, but with Cindy's rolling pin which she took from the pantry downstairs. She knew where it was.

Across the utility room in three catlike strides she was on him and swiped Joey hard on the side of his head. It might have taken less; he was all but finished anyway, with multiple wounds, and weak from loss of blood. Down he went without a fight to one side, but not quite out. So she hit him again and then stomped him down with her foot. She stood over him ready to crown him a third time if he asked for it; but no, now he would be good.

Bending down she turned him around and began dragging him backwards by the legs over the threshold the way she came.

In the second floor bathroom she paused to wet two washcloths to use for the smoke which could kill them if nothing else did. She dragged him further, feet first, out onto the landing above the wide stairway. And then down the stairs they went with his legs around her waist, like he was a wheelbarrow. His head bumped from step to step going down, but it was the plush carpet.

At the foot of the stairs she saw her father-in-law lying in the front foyer. She cried to him:

—Emory!

His clothes were on fire. Flames were consuming the blue suit he wore and the flesh beneath it. Was it too late to save him? The bright red of his bloody face had a bluish tinge: seared like meat being broiled. Was he dead already? She paused at the foot of the stairs gazing at him, but there wasn't a second to spare.

And then he raised one hand a little: not the arm or wrist but the fingers. He seemed to gesture her onward and tell her to forget him. Go on, go your way . . . Or else it was a nervous tremor, in the first spell of death, as the hand which had written books now gave its last little sign of life.

His noble face was all a porridge of blood. His neck and hands had a gray-blue tinge of cyanosis in the light of his body on fire and the living room furniture in flames and the mansion of his ancestors now become his funeral pyre.

IX

The smoke gushed up, and it was too much. She rubbed the wet washcloths over their faces and went on. Back past the guest bedroom she dragged her husband; and across from the entry to the back porch she took the steps which led down to the basement.

In the cellar on the left was the old playroom which they were planning to fix up for Rhoda. On the right was the entry to the laundry and boiler room: where he met her the night before last, and knocked her senseless. And in there, besides the Dutch door leading out to the yard at the north side of the house, were two more doors. One, further in and toward the back, led down to the subbasement where Joey stored his crates. Now a number of these lay open down here as well as in the rooms upstairs, and they invited the flames. Others remained in the passageway and storage space at the foot of those old steps.

The third door went into the turret room, and this is the one she opened.

It was a round unfurnished room, just cement walls and floor, where a young Negro slave woman was said to have been lodged, or kept, in the mid-Nineteenth Century before the Civil War; and where Wilhelmina had her moonshine still during the Prohibition years and after.

Now it was a crescendo of gunfire and artillery rounds pounding the granite fortress from 360° as well as the air. In a minute, in seconds a shell would find its way to a crate of Joey's ordnance, and the whole place would begin to blow in stages.

Into the turret room went Carlyne pulling her husband behind her. It was dark in there, but she knew where she was going. This was the way she came.

An oblong, curving slab of concrete had been removed and stood leaning against the wall. Where the block was before now stood the opening to an underground passage. And this mole's tunnel through the earth, big enough for a human being to crawl, led among the root system of the huge old oak on the front lawn and then up, to its base. There it became more roomy and even had steps to go up into the hollowed out trunk where Joey and Newell built their tree fort as boys. And so when Carlyne disappeared last night, in a period after Government forces turned off their floodlights, it was into the gaping hole of the tree trunk she climbed, summoning all the strength in her injured and traumatized body. And then she made her way down into the underground passage, as her brother-in-law once showed her; and she fought to clear the way those fifteen or twenty yards into the turret room. She was a ghostly sight by the time she got done, spitting out spiders and many-legged insects, with cobwebs and disgusting mold all over her clothes and flesh from head to foot. And now she had to go that way again and take him with her, hoping they would be far enough away to survive the great explosion when it came.

She grappled him up in her arms. She worked to get the two of them into that narrow passage leading through the earth. Now on her knees she yanked and pulled and struggled with his 220-pound body as they went down the underground tunnel leading from the turret room beneath the Rock Castle to the secular oak out front. On and on she lugged him, straining with all the force in her back and young limbs, on and on. This she did: eight, ten yards, crawling, tugging her husband after her, crying out with the effort. Foot by foot and yard by yard as the precious seconds ticked past they made their way in the darkness inhabited by spiders and crawling with larvae and no doubt snakes and who knew what else. It was a long, long time since the two brothers played down here as boys. No one knew who had dug out this passage or when. It must date from an age ago, and be part of the Rock Castle mystique, days of slavery, concubinage, who knew what other family scandals embedded in the Gilbert past.

On they went as Carlyne pushed and pulled her husband toward the root system of the old oak whose trunk couldn't be spanned by a class of kids from the one-room schoolhouse holding hands, so they said in the old days.

She kept on. And the movements of the two of them, inching along, took on a sexual rhythm, propulsion, groaning.

It would not be much longer now before the fire spread and was everywhere and got hold of one of those crates and then one went up and another and the whole thing went up in a climax of flames and blown-up stone and earth and a cloud of smoke pluming into the sky.

But if she could get them to the opening like a landing deep under the tree before that happened, then they might get lucky. They might not be trapped underground when the chunks of stone rained down and the earth pressed in on them. Then they might survive the collapse, for what that was worth, in the state they were both in—if the oak tree itself weighing many, many tons didn't plunge in on them and crush them to death.

She brought him almost there: not quite under the tree. And she knew they had better stay down in the earth beneath the tree. Don't go up. They won't keep on forever like this, fighting against a phantom. So wait it out.

Carlyne heard the pandemonium going on above the ground: the rabid savagery of U.S. Government forces in a coordinated attack against a single man defending a house like a fortress. She asked herself if Rhody could still be alive outside in the baby carriage at the end of the walk—as a jet plane came screaming over the Rock Castle and dropped a bomb on it which shook the earth where they lay in one another's arms.

Earth trembled: as if going into its throes.

Were they far enough away from the center of the catastrophe when it came? Would the soil and great roots of the oak support them? Or would they die down here in the dark together?

Earth shook.

The end was coming. It wouldn't be much longer now.

As they waited Carlyne knew the one last thing she could do and had to do for him. She knew it because since they got together again thanks to him that night seven months ago, she had understood something about him. Despite his sickness, despite his violence, despite the hate which was the other side of his love—she believed in him. For the thing she understood was in her too, and maybe in all people if they understood themselves.

And so she maneuvered around in the narrow slot they shared beneath the earth. And she got on top of him and lay there trying to shield him with her body in case the ground caved in. This could save him. In anticipation of the hundred-hundred ton mansion blowing to bits and flinging slabs of granite at the sky in a radius from the main road out front to the wide fields in back, the Rock Castle in the absolute frenzy of its σπᾰραγμός—she spread her body out on top of him hoping that if one of them had to die then it would be her.

She believed in him.

X

A third Phantom jet shrieked over—the pass, then a pause, a curious vacuum as the Rock Castle began to blow with a rumbling explosion in its entrails. More black smoke billowed and spewed up darkening the sky. Joey Gilbert's ammo dump of hand grenades, mortar rounds, *plastic* and other explosives, began to ignite—and then hurled up a thousand-foot fireball like the one at Khe Sanh caused by 90 mm high explosive, 106 mm Beehive,

90 mm canister ammunition. It was like a small atomic bomb in the twilight.

Gables, battlements, the incinerated interior went whirling up like a funnel or a huge tourbillion and then began to rain back down. Within the long smoke trails fiery sheets rippled like banners. The torched boughs of trees round the house took more hits and shook accusatory fingers.

Still the semiautomatic bursts continued. It was an infectious going for the kill from sniper lairs and emplacements further off from the demolished house. The furnace heat spurred the mad minutes.

No fire truck came on the scene, and there were no sirens now. Neither fire fighters nor medical personnel hurried to the disaster. It would have been a mockery—except for the child left to her luck at the end of the walk.

There were more explosives. There was more curtain fire from Hostage Rescue Team marksmen, and six tanks now ventured in closer. The elite Delta Force unit was sneaking out into this theater of war in its grand finale.

But then there came what seemed like silence.

Beneath smoke columns the gutted structure with its truncated storeys crackled, and seethed.

A moment later the great hollow oak split down its trunk and fell sideways with a long roll of thunder. The roots like writhing dragons went jutting up in a dense cloud of dust.

And then there was another sound. It was human.

A first few figures emerged from behind the high sniper screen and the APCs used as barricades. They moved cautiously forward past the tanks. But then they paused.

The small girl strapped in her baby carriage toppled into the street after it sped over the curb propelled by the blast—the child bawled and groped to get out.

Lydia Falliere appeared. In the shock of the aftermath she broke through police lines and ran out arms raised into the zone of chaos. After-blast danger existed, in a big way; but the doctor came running along the sidewalk with her arms raised—to see if anyone was still living.

The charred house burned. It sizzled. A crossbeam fell.

A first few photographers peeped out and snapped pictures to send around the world—alongside images from the campus of Kent State.

Little Rhoda hollered and worked her limbs in the overturned carriage.

Lydia got to her and began undoing the straps and fastenings Joey had made.

The ruins of the old mansion smoked and sent up new spears of flame. A portion of thick wall over the first floor study grumbled and fell in on itself.

Overhead was a dark cloud of ash and sparks.

Half the angle turret stood erect but sheared lengthwise, jagged and blackened, minus its spire and golden ball blasted into the next county.

Of course there were horrific photos. One was syndicated in the nation's newspapers under the caption:

AMERICA'S WRATH

In St. Louis, in Cincinnati, in Chicago there were day games underway. The players ran here and there on the bright green grass limed with basepaths beneath a blue sky.

The fans cheered. There was a slick 6-4-3 double play. There was a rundown between second and third: put on the tag, ou-u-u-t! There was a line drive homerun which hooked into the bleachers past the left field foul pole.

Chapter Twenty-Five

I

Two years later, on a day in early summer, Newell Gilbert said so long to his last ride and began walking into town from the Interstate Highway. The air smelled so familiar. A freight train went whistling in the distance; and suddenly Newell was a boy again on a summer day in the South, and the boxcars were clanging past: Santa Fe, Southern Pacific, Great Northern, Norfolk & Western. The long heartline trains chugged, smoked, and thumbed a royal nose at the quaint old business clusters of their crossings, the abandoned showrooms and secondhand stores.

A heatwave had its grip on the Piedmont region. The sun beat down on blocks of red-brick factory plant, on the cemetery across the street with its mausoleums of past factory owners, and plot for Confederate soldiers. There were new signs of life in a few of the stores—Family Bible & Getwell Card Emporium; also Religious Goods, Inc.; and a thrift shop and three or four pawnbrokers. A night light in the lobby of First National City was left on during the day. There were two large gashes in the classical revival facade of that building which no civic-minded party had come forward to restore. Tourists who came to view them could have a soda at the new café next door with its antiques and curios for sale, and bluegrass music on weekends.

Newell walked through the center and remembered the old names: Rose's Five & Dime, Robby's Hardware, Sink Appliances, Haight Furniture; the three movie theaters, Palace, State, Davidson. A day came when P. Laster Gilbert's protégé, Paul J.—some said J. stood for Judas—Commynes gave a kiss of death to the town where he was born and raised. His last act as a businessman was to open the door to the national chain stores, paving the way for shopping plazas and malls.

In a reverie the heir to the Rock Castle walked along the main street past his grandfather's bank. He went down a narrow alley beneath boarded second-storey windows. He saw weed-grown lots and brick walls covered with vines, old lading platforms. On a weekday during business hours there weren't many people around.

II

After a meal at the old diner, down from the depot, Newell walked out from the center.

A high fence enclosed the grounds of the Rock Castle. So he went in back and found a way to climb over it with his knapsack.

As dusk began to settle over the old Gilbert place he couldn't believe his eyes. He had seen the sight before. Who hadn't? . . . Not an hour after the great battle ended, one man against an army, he came on the scene by way of the Yadkin River in a motorboat. He made his approach running across the Gilbert farmlands, but by then it was the aftermath. He got here too late.

Now he recalled watching from the boat he had rented in the next town up river. He saw the sky flicker over the combat zone. Orange tracer bullets arced to and from the dome of smoke over the Rock Castle. Phantom jets roared in: their bombardment mixed in the din of tank and mortar fire. The riverbank seemed to shake as the combined assault shrieked and thundered.

Then Newell watched a fireball rise up in the premature twilight. There were more explosions; they came in a succession as the subcellar ammo dump ignited in sections. He was watching from the river as the battle of the Rock Castle went into its mighty climax.

And then, after a few more detonations like afterthoughts, sniper and M-16 rounds expended from nervous energy—then there was silence.

It was a good idea he had: to make his approach by water. But too late. The last stretch of his journey, the 250 miles from Knoxville to Winston-Salem, took him a full day to hitchhike.

Now he couldn't believe his eyes, as the peaceful evening settled over the scene. The immense framework was blasted and torn apart with jagged slabs of it still erect. Walls, hallways, rooms lay in a mass of charred and jumbled stone. The gray cinder crunched underfoot.

But he had to be careful. The balanced fragments of stone could displace, cave in; there were holes and craters underfoot. Tracts of ashes padded down by the rains and the dewy nights had a bad odor grown more faint with time. Beneath what once were floorboards went a dark descent. And unexploded ordnance?

The back porch was grown over with a grayish moss. There were tall weeds where the elegant rooms once were with their Georgian décor. Again he thought of the long smoke trails rising into the sunset—shots, salvos, sirens were at last quiet.

TV ran Vietnam footage that night. And there was more on Kent State. *Only blanks!* a voice cried, as dirt pelted the faces of demonstrators. Then there was Carlyne Gilbert sitting stone-faced among the other players' wives; she watched the game from a field box under the mezzanine with its World Series bunting.

III

Morning sun shone through the leafy ruins. The hippie blinked, yawned loudly, chuckled, and flung out his arms. After the voyage he slept well.

A bird chirped gaily in a gashed embrasure. Dew glistened in Cindy's kitchen.

He gave a nod at the ashes and hoisted himself back over the tall board fence. But he glanced back and saw, amid the gray earth and cinder, a small object. It was Carlyne's cameo brooch of a proud tribal woman in profile with a feather in her headdress. It too was burnt gray, ashen, but still intact, with its clasp bent back from the base. Newell jumped down; he picked the brooch up and put it in his pocket.

Up town he went in the old diner and had breakfast. Then he walked from the lonely town with its boarded stores and long cemetery wall across from the furniture factory. He went to his father's grave.

As he sat there he heard the chirpy voices of some kids playing in the neighborhood. He read the dates on his family headstones, P. Laster, Wilhelmina, a few others, and now Emory.

A faint breeze came from the river and the wide Gilbert farmlands left fallow again since there was no one to work them. The children played, and the birds sang. Newell thought of his father: that contradictory man.

He thought of his father's liberal ideals: prosperity for all who were able to get it, like he was; but at the same time a free and unfettered exploitation of the weak by the strong, of the worker by Capital. It didn't matter how genial Emory had been: his liberalism always ended up by serving Capital, big bourgeoisie, and seemed a pretext for taking an ever bigger share. In the beginning this was a guise of individual freedom, but more and more it became a way to trick the workers and dispossessed: look, you can be rich too . . . What was the credo of a ruling class could be made by the left liberal Emory Gilbert's poetry and eloquence to seem like it was good for all the people. His books could please everyone on the spectrum from radical to reactionary since they had that opportunism about them: just as democracy in our age is a rallying cry for the Right, the Western democracies a last bastion of reaction; and at the same time democracy is an ideal of the Left. Liberalism in the writings and public life of Emory Gilbert had such charms—love of humanity, populism, freethinking, utopianism—no wonder it could seduce all strata of society once given a platform.

He was a seducer.

His practice was not as his preaching.

When put to it, nose to the grindstone of Truth, he became evasive. He did not want conflict since he might lose—lose all that he had. In evading any notion of class struggle he flew high and far to the realm of 'spirit', mysticism: away from the real, if you please, away from the economic and social forces which were in conflict.

Reason, progress, brotherly love, belief in the future: these fine words were always on his lips. Mind, education, enlightenment, compassion, religion—yes, yes, he said he was for all that, but what did it cost him? Where was his post? Was there ever such a phrasemaker?

Newell always thought of him as a 'long-as-it-doesn't-cost-me-anything-liberal', and now wondered if that was fair.

Emory's emphasis was on the form: in the fine and finished form of a book or a speech. Except toward the end of his life, he played approach-avoidance with the content. With great skill he used literary form, the moral authority of his art which was hard to combat, to put the best face on the interests of a dominant class to which he belonged. Thus he was much loved as its mouthpiece, its megaphone. Spurred on by the incentives that social class could give, he became its major writer. He was the closest thing it had to a prophet. America: bourgeoisie in its last ascendance.

So his liberalism reflected the mood and situation of the American middle class. He was like a people's tribune; and since he was nothing if not pragmatic, his politics had zigzags. He wavered, he was fickle, he contradicted himself with pleasure and panache; he had how many 'honorable turnarounds'. But all through his career he was loyal to the U.S. Constitution, a moderate at heart, taking his stand on private property, as it does. He was a belle-tristic enlightener.

At times he might sound like a young radical, and this gave him great appeal among young people. But he went only so far, and then drew back. He would veer sharply to the right in time of crisis and heightened social contradictions—as Victor Hugo did in 1848; or as Emory Gilbert did during the McCarthy Era, sobering up. He feared communism. He would have come out sharply against any workers uprising. The 'Sixties Movement was not the Paris Commune, barricades in the streets; so he used it to play a role.

And then he could work for a Presidential candidate who was opportunist to the core: just as Hugo supported Napoleon III. While these bourgeois limits were imposed on his life force and his literature, they also kept him from being truly great and thereby tailored his literary works to the taste of the general public, who loved him in the era before television.

Toward the end he might call himself socialist; but it was a vogue. His method remained that of a liberal: enlightenment, persuasion. What could it ever do? What did it do besides serve as a buffer, and draw off forces from the real opposition?

At the end he had the world vision of a radical petit bourgeois whose heroic period in history was over. Now he would avoid struggle, in the decisive moments, at all cost.

For Emory the deal was peaceful evolution, progress, the triumph of the 'spirit', passivity. Or he might suddenly become grandiose, in a militant masquerade, a towering rage which also helped the public give vent to its frustration. He was a past master at manipulating public opinion in an optimistic mode, since 'the good must triumph' . . . But as to any real engaging of the battle . . . no, sir. When it came to that he expressed a profound pessimism.

His triumphalism was a liberal's wishful thinking. And so his literary works have a stylized quality, with much hyperbole, studied contrasts, caricature; also pages blazing with an incandescent poetry. Those fireworks had an incredible success in America.

He tried to make heroes of the Democratic Party. Good luck!

As someone who wanted love, unity, fraternity, but not conflict, not political reality: he was like a cultural demigod. He was the national writer, a literary Czar.

And he was a peacock: vain as all getout. Emory Gilbert was a megalomaniac with a touching naïveté. He had the acrid smell of self of the best of our cultural figures. Not much character, no real principle; and when the chips are down, they back off, like a liberal politican accused of being soft on communism.

He supported lost causes when they were good and lost: when it was safe, the way Hugo supported the Paris Commune when it was dead and gone. Hey, no skin off his ass then.

Risk was a sort of game he played: for the sake of publicity.

History was a flirtation.

He dreamed of glory, and he could make you dream of it.

He loved pleasure and personal development.

He believed in God.

He made the liberal's progress from aristocrat to democrat. But any real fighter for the rights of workers and the dispossessed, he would disown. The moment it got serious, violent in the streets, like a Latin American country let's say: then he would call any real leader, who meant it, to the end, a demagogue.

There was so much fantasy in his books and revolt against convention. He was such a maestro of romanticism and the romantic release of emotions. Extravagance, individualism, egotism, power to preach and play on people's feelings—all this was Emory Gilbert.

His works didn't set in motion and reveal the inner workings of life under capitalism; they didn't have the rich realism adequate to a picture of the national life like Tolstoy; instead, they had a calculated exaggeration and fantasy aided by flamboyant rhetoric, like Victor Hugo.

Flamboyant—that was Emory Gilbert.

Grandiosity, richness of images, unparalleled language with the rhetoric of a soaring eagle—it was puffed up at its worst, but a wonder at his best.

He was tall, handsome, majestic in later age, a lion. But lions are not brave. Lions are scavengers.

He was an artist of contrasts and a man of contrasts. Gothic, simple; aristocratic, plebeian; cosmic, petty; bulky, cumbersome, pompous, but with an effort at development and completeness.

What writer could equal him at times for bad taste? Wordiness? For impulsive mistakes? For dangerous illusions? Yet he had grandeur. He was an American fetish.

His hope after all was groundless—thought Newell finally—it was the false hope of the liberal. It was based on a system of illusions: starting with the illusion that phrases could get the job done.

Much, much must be forgiven Emory Gilbert. And much can, because he was so gifted; and because his works might, the best things, still prove useful, though in another way than they were intended—when the real day comes.

IV

The next morning Newell paid another call on the diner, and then turned his steps toward the highway. But by the old depot his gaze fell on the home of Bishop Commynes across the tracks. It was a picturesque place with its three-sided veranda.

Newell crossed over the railroad embankment and took the steps onto 'Paradise Porch'.

The doorbell was solemn, low-toned, like a knell.

The churchman came to the door. He looked older with his features a bit crimped beneath makeup. Newell noted the hair dyed jet black, the pencilled eyebrows, the feminine lips. Did he use a touch of rouge too? For all his ecclesiastical distinction Paul Commynes had a note of the worn-out whore. Emblem, thought Newell, of the Church?

Bishop's brother Jake Commynes, pawnbroker in town for half a century, had grown rich too nickle-and-diming the townspeople.

Truly they were a 'par nobile fratrum'.

—Hello, Newell.

—Sir. Care for a chat?

—By all means, come in. I noticed you were in town. Seen the lawyer, have you? Looking after your affairs?

In the early years of the century the Colonel's House was one of the best known brothels in the Southeast. Now it needed a paint job, but the interior was handcrafted quite finely. Tiger Oak Salon, Cherry Wood Solarium, paneling, library cabinets: these were signs of the southern gentleman's good taste and good living. Here were Confederate pretentions to the neo-Hellenism of a hundred years past.

Now a sunlit column with lint like angelic hosts came in the wide east window hung with sheer linen curtains. Late morning in this matt décor had a musty shut-off scent.

Newell paused by the marble hearth. A bas-relief had a Latin inscription from Ovid's *Artis Amatoriae*.

He gazed at old master reproductions on the papered walls. Here were snakes and Eves, trees of knowledge, *Espulsiones*, and the Evil One, the Prince of Devils, Belial himself. The town knew Bishop Commynes had a Satan cult.

Now he gave his guest a tour.

There was a Botticelli parchment drawing, pen over silverpoint, from *Inferno XII*; also Orcagna's *Prince of this World*, and Sodoma's *Tempter*. In the silence you seemed to hear wild squawks from sinners jumbled nude, flesh unseamed, head to privates. There were a lot of sadistic demons: a Van Eyck *Last Judgment*, triptych wing; Dürer, Bosch, Goya. The erotic sadomasochism of Christianity never occurred to Newell, the graduate student in art history, until now as he paused before a Crucifixion by Grünewald.

The conscience of Western man was being flayed here on the walls of the Colonel's House. In the Satanic chapel of the downstairs den Michelangelo's *Giudizio Universale* had pride of place.

Unlike a few business magnates Commynes knew his collection; though he possessed no originals. There was a copy of Brueghel's *Triumph of Death* over the living room mantelpiece. Oh, those were sinful multitudes—stick figures crucified in the distance; men and women lynched, put to the rack, flung by the shovelful into fiery crematories. Human beings were gobbled by dogs all gullet and ribcage; they were peeled, pecked, ripped, tossed, slung, drawn and quartered. There was a cart loaded up with skulls. Lower right were courtly lovers: at her breast he plays the lute while behind them a skeleton strums, waits. Smoke gushed in a burnished landscape, by a gray sea, beneath an apocalyptic sky. It was the teleological chaos of the Dark Prince and his legions at play.

Newell smiled, but he couldn't laugh. It seemed clear who would have the last laugh here. On a stand Bernini's Saint Theresa was in her ecstasy. The sculptor who did this copy had her hand under her robe; and it was well rendered: spiritual orgasm half rapture, half smirk.

—Reverend, do saints masturbate?

—You never know, Newell. Renaissance and Baroque poets likened Cupid to Satan. For example, Federico dell'Amba: *l'Amore del Diavol tien semblanza* . . .

—The Devil has a southern accent?

Commynes laughed.

—A Giottesque allegory at Assisi, and Piero's Cupid in Arezzo, show Amor's close affinity with Satan. In the one, Love with a demon's talons gets chased from Chastity Tower by a skeleton with scythe. In the other, Cupid is half turned into a devil and wears the scalps of victims on a belt.

V

In the library there was a shelf labeled: SATAN. It had the usual mail-order editions of gilt-bound classics: Milton; Dante and *Faust* in translation, etc.; other tomes with something to do with Lucifer, Mephistopheles, Serpent, Dragon, Baal-Zebub, Asmodeus; or a pagan prototype, Homer and Virgil.

There was a rack of theological tracts, monographs, *Satan Through the Centuries*, which Bishop probably leafed through while watching TV.

His bookcases were filled with vulgarity: such was his fixation on the Devil. But let's not forget Empedocles the wonder-doctor and self-styled god; and Pythagorus who was 'God's son' and thaumaturge; also Apollonius of Tyana, the 'pagan Jesus'; and then Simon Magus, Cyprian of Antiochia, Theophilus of Adana, on and on—they were kin to Satan along with Anthemios. They were led astray from the true way: like Faust and other more modern examples.

Among Bishop's treasures were rare tracts on the medieval devil-pact, and Theophilus. He had books on this aspect of Luther: his 'personal demon', his belief in the Pope as carnal Anti-Christ. And here was Klingsor, the devil's son from the Arthurian saga; and Herzog Robert, another son of a devil. And Popes! Sylvester II, Gregor VII, Paul II, Alexander VI—all suspected of hell-pacts, and diplomatic relations with the Devil. Eternally damned? Well, good for them; at least they wouldn't bore themselves to death in heaven.

Then came Neo-Platonic doctrine: the Jewish Kabbala. Under the heading of black magic: the learned Abbot Johannes Trithemius, Agrippa of Nettesheim, Theophrastus Bombastus Paracelsus of Hohenheim.

Also the Krakau, Toledo, and Salamanca schools . . .

Paul Commynes was a universal man when it came to sin.

VI

—Why all this, Pastor? Do you worship the 'God of this world'?

Bishop's eyelids fluttered. His tone was affected, with a sibilance:

—Satan cult harks back to antiquity. From long ago, Newell, long . . . the human spirit cringes beneath his tendonous black wing. Later, as you may know, the service became a revolt against Christianity; its blasphemous ritual was meant to desecrate the Christian rite. The ascent of Satanism really began in the Twelfth Century; it found its full expression in the Black Mass. But demon adoration, its extent and influence, remains shrouded in mystery to our day . . .—Bishop's eyes went wide.—Obscure, as a soul's abandon; secret, as a dreadful act of pleasure; it haunts our deca-

dent age. We know Satanism came back with a vengeance under
Louis XIV.

Newell stared at him. The widower half mad with loneliness
gave a discourse in his drawing room. Outside were the silent
trees, the dead town.

—Reverend, did Antichrist tell you to destroy my family? To
write anonymous letters? Twist my father's arm so he went to his
death a bit early?

—The term Antichrist doesn't apply to Satan.

—Grand Master of the Sabbat then. Did he 'enter into you', like
Judas, and make you get your stigmatizing mitts into my father?

—More like Ananias.

Commynes gave a dry laugh.

—But why do that, Sir? Because of something that happened
one night in Skeeter Hawk a long time ago?

—I never made Emory do anything. He was free.

—Sure, America is a free country. Even its devils are free. But
you told the press. Don't shake your head: we know you did. You
created a scandal, and that sent my father into despair, and he
went out.

—He had to. And I had to. I couldn't let him throw away his
soul. He sinned, and he must pay.

—Tell me: who were you in cahoots with? Did Church and
State put their heads together? Did you decide it would be best if
Emory Gilbert sacrificed his life at the Rock Castle?

Bishop Commynes laughed again, low.

—Newell, you're a beginner at this business. You may make
some progress, the hard way I'm afraid, but you won't win. Only
man's soul can ever win, not his body, earthly life.

—Sure, sure. Long as it's someone else's body. Why, you old
whore, you're as stuffed full of good life as the established church.
It seems Jesus can save everybody but himself.

Bishop blinked. But unperturbed:

—What I did may seem like evil, but it resulted in good. We
could not have posterity thinking Emory Gilbert was an unre-
demptive sinner who went to bed with his daughter-in-law . . .
now could we? And what if he didn't get up the guts to go out
that day? Do you want the great man to be remembered as a
chicken?

—You stupid old man. You just wanted revenge on your half-brother who was an obsession for you, the object of your envy, a monomania. When I think about it, I could almost lose my cool.

—And take revenge?

—On you? Don't flatter yourself. You're not worth it: just one more Jesus freak, or Satan freak; maybe it's the same. All the while you sin in thought and deed, like sin was going out of style.

Commynes' eyes twinkled.

—Ha, ha, ha—he laughed to himself, pleased with the jest.

Newell said slowly, as if savoring the words:

—Actually you're a bastard runt from Skeeter Hawk who went far. You became a Savings & Loan sharper. You're Jake the pawnbroker's noble brother, and it shows. By the way: did Dewy Spivey take revenge on you by blowing up your wife? Or was that Beelzebub doing good again, saving Claire from her earthly life with *you*?

—Kind of you to ask.

—Tsk, tsk. Little Paulie got born a bastard. Well, take it out on life then. But don't forget to sugarcoat it with a lot of religion and self-righteousness. And, if that wasn't enough, the little bastard must play God. You incited my father to marry his daughter to a pedophile four times her age. And have me put away in an insane asylum: when you are the insane one. Really with a friend like you who needs enemies?

—Got it all figured out, have you?

—Yes. We grow up with the religious sickness. Pauliekins is chosen, of course, saved. So it doesn't matter what he does. Why, I think he must be perfect, don't you? And not the fornicator P. Laster but God Almighty is the real father. It's a fact! And yet, would you believe it, behind the emotional defenses of religion there is stagnation, dammed up, cut off from the flow where life renews. Metaphysics, never dialectics. And so a poisonous energy builds up: hate . . . Could it be God is Hate? You for one are a rather violent Christian, you know. But what else is new? Say! You know what? I think maybe you loved P. Laster's legal son as much as you envied and hated him.

Silence.

Unfazed by this Bishop Commynes gloated. His deep eyes stared at the guest.

—Go on.

Newell shrugged:

—No, that's enough.

—Well, then the rebuttal. You're a Gilbert male, Newell, and as far as I can tell you shouldn't be throwing any stones.

—Don't prevaricate, Pastor. You screwed your best friend. Thou hast killed. As for stones: Carlyne once told me how you were in the fields together one night, and you stared at her chest by starlight, and then tossed a pebble at her. Are you without sin?

—No.

—Then why ape God?

—I don't.

—Satan then?

Urbanely Commynes nodded:

—If you will.

Newell hissed at him:

—Snake, your sick imaginings destroyed lives … your superstition!

—Prove it.

—Superstition.

The reverend recited:

—'Where didst lurk and cower when I laid earth's foundations? Declare, if thou hast understanding.'

—You can find anything in that Bible of yours. Our corporate rulers swear by it.

—Or in Marx. Your totalitarian dictators swear by it.

—Which ones?

—Lenin.

—Wrong again. He lived by reality and struggled to find a way. He died in his early fifties for his pains.

—Lenin would damn us all.

—Give us a chance, you mean, not illusions. The time hadn't come. Western Europe failed. It was the first great attempt at socialism, so we can survive as a species on this planet. But it was also early, crude, and it had to be. Socialism will take a thousand years to construct, but we don't have that long. Still the people's struggle has hope despite all; whereas you benighted ones with your Abaddons, or Apollyons, you choose the name, your Satans, have only despair.

—There will be no socialism, Newell. Human nature makes the price too high. Revolutionary periods turn to darkness and terror.

—Terrorized and distorted by the old order! Of course the saintly United States of America never did a sin: never invaded a smaller country for its resources and bombed it back into the Stone Age.

Commynes flushed with pleasure. This visit was making his day. Soulfully he said:

—Do you fear death, Newell?

—I'm too young. Not death, and not the Wicked One. I only fear . . . compromise.

—Then don't get married, son.

—I've always felt life has such beauty because we die . . . But give me time. If I live long enough, in this society, I'll start running scared too. I'll obsess about my health, bank accounts, insurance. I'll go to church!

Newell laughed.

Bishop said:

—You're a cynic.

—Not you though: after you and Max Doan the pedophile conspired to wreck my family. By the way, someone told me yesterday Thanks-a-Million got in a scrape with his pedophilia. Some parent complained, but he got it smoothed over.

Bishop Commynes shrugged. Still his dark eyes gloated:

—Youth is cruel.

—No, Reverend. Age is. The old way is.

But suddenly there was an eruption in the quiet room where they sat talking. So deep in conversation, they hadn't noticed the approach of a freight train. And now it roared through, rattling the windows of the Colonel's House. It clanged on past the sleepy southern town without a nod in the bright noontime.

Newell rose to go. With a headshake he stood by that marble fireplace which had an erotic bas-relief and Latin inscription from Ovid's *Artis Amatoriae*.

Outside, the irregular three-sided veranda seemed in contrast to Commynes probity and moral sobriety. The town knew it as Paradise Porch. In sad decay now, its boards warped and perhaps rotting underneath: it once creaked with rockers and hempen hammocks, a railroad swing for Cupid to rest a moment after strenuous efforts, shooting his full quiver. On midsummer nights a fragrant breeze played in the ruffled curtains—as it had long ago for the benefit of the Colonel's visitors.

VII

It was time to leave.

Newell Gilbert with his backpack, a few books and a change of clothes, walked the Old National Highway out to the entrance of Interstate 85.

Hot evening in store. And another scorcher was forecast for tomorrow. A tar melter.

Out on the highway he held up his thumb to the drivers passing by. Sooner or later one would stop and give him a ride.

He was on his way now.

The long tractor trailers went whining into the distance—round a bend, over a hill. As evening came on their taillights shone. They rolled along the divided highway on the way northward.

Chapter Twenty-Six

I

In late spring the following year Lemon Gilbert, a college senior days away from graduation, came out of her student house on Women's Campus. On the lawn before the auditorium Lydia Falliere knelt to explain something for a little girl. Rhody, a doll's suitcase in one hand, listened but then saw Lemon and ran across the grass with her arms held out.

—Four goes on five—she said.

—Does it? said Lemon. Well, can you tell me why ten was so afraid?

—N-no.

—Seven eight nine.

Eyes wide, Rhody stared up at her aunt.

—. . . Oh.

—What do you have there?

—Daisy's suitcase.

—Can't Daisy carry it herself?

—She's just a doll.

—I see. Where is she now?

—In the car.

—Won't she be hot in the car?

—N-no—Rhody thought it over.—I have brothers.

—Do you? How many?

—Two.—She held up three fingers.—Big ones.

—I see, said Aunt Lemon. Do you like them?

—Of course!—Rhody turned to Lydia. Shaking her head at Aunt's questions, she said:—Daisy won't be hot.

II

They rode south for two hours in the rented car. They went on beyond Fayetteville, then west from Lumberton twenty minutes to Pembroke, which was Lumbee country.

Dial's was a wood structure on State Road 1158; it sat in the shade across from some wheat and tobacco acreage.

Getting out of the car they stretched. Rhoda looked at a large web-footed bird: a gannet took flight and went soaring off above a chicken and hog cooperative they had driven past.

Pine forest, oak and gum trees were in the summery air.

The three ladies went inside the spacious old country home. Rhoda stared up at a man dressed formally in black. He spoke quietly and ushered them into a room where chairs were lined in a few rows.

In the aura of light from the half closed blinds stood an open coffin.

Lydia picked up Rhoda and Daisy. And then with Lemon they drew closer and stood alongside.

—Mommy? said the little girl, and glanced from the mask-like tallowy face back at Lydia.

—It's your mother, Carlyne.

—I see. But . . . I want you for my mother.

—Alright, but Carlyne is too.

—Awright.

This past March they had gone to her at Lovedy Locklear's home, her aunt, where she lived the last three years. They had seen her and visited though she lay unable to speak anymore, and her bed was already turned to the east which was an old custom. Then she gazed up and seemed to bless them with her dark blue eyes like a mountain lake. Then there was a yearning in those eyes; she just wanted to see her husband again, so much.

But now her waxen cheek had a touch of yellow and white from the daffodils which were in clusters above her head. A sweetness played in Carlyne's features; a sense of life lingered. Her breast still had a proud fullness in the simple and girlish gray dress she wore.

—Remember her, said Lydia. She was great.

—She was?

—She loved, and suffered.

—Suffered?

Sometimes Rhoda didn't catch what you said the first time; you had to repeat it.

—She had courage, and she didn't give up.

—I love Daisy.

—That's good, said Lydia, and bowed to kiss Rhody's temple.

In the last months a roughness had come over Carlyne's features; as though, once the mind was growing less active, the ordering intelligence lost its hold. So her personality seemed to wane except at moments: when she made an effort to focus on things outside herself. For a long time after the Rock Castle tragedy she was still alive, but she was . . . unviewable, emotionally, and her mind had been affected. But then serenity seemed to descend upon her—maybe it was like the great spirit of the indigenous tribes who loved and were loved by this fertile land . . . but then got penned up in a sordid reservation like a pitiful game preserve for human beings.

Now, however, she looked younger, fuller, despite her pale features, where she lay in silence. The left brow and cheekbone were relaxed, and no longer so distorted. And death brought a strange, a sweet sort of release, as it may sometimes, to certain people.

—I live with you—said Rhoda, with a nod.

—You do.

From her perch on Lydia's arm, so she could see into the casket, Rhody reached and tugged a thoughtful Lemon's sleeve.

—I live in Scarsdale. I have two sis' . . . wait. I have two brothers and one sister.—She held up four fingers.—You have to take a plane, and a special car.

—Do you? said Aunt.

Rhoda looked at Carlyne, and then in Lydia's eyes.

—I live with you.

—Yes.

She mused a moment, and said seriously:

—Long time.

—Of course. Till you grow up and go to college.

—College?

—So you can study, and become great too.

Rhody looked at her mother again.

—I don't wanna'.

—Well, a college in New York maybe so we can still live together. How's that?

—Awright.

Then silence. For awhile they stood there alongside Carlyne
and thought about her.

Lemon had a notion and stepped around to open a window.
A thrush was warbling in the warm day outside. A soft breeze
rustled in the tall pines out back of the funeral parlor. Sunlight
and trees and the river not far off gave a sweet scent to the air.

III

Family members began to arrive. Lovedy came in with an older
man named Daystar. Then more, husbands and wives with their
children: they were Lumbee. A group of them had stayed awake
until dawn: the second night's wake, or the 'settin' up'. The men
talked by the fireplace and chewed tobacco; they ate country food
as the hours passed. One or another went out for a drink by the
woodpile. But the women stayed by Carlyne where she waited to
go get herself funeralized out there at Burnt Swamp Baptist.

In June 1970 Lydia came and saw to Carlyne's transfer from
the Davidson County hospital to her tribal family in Pembroke.
Aunt Lovedy and the others wanted this and said: 'She ar'n'. And
Carlyne wanted the move; she was no longer able to take care of
Rhoda or herself. From the blow she took resulted chronic subdu-
ral hematoma: the nerves, blood vessels, tissue around the brain
were torn, shorn, ruptured. She bled intracranially. Fluid built up
(edema), and this caused pressure like a growth mass within the
skull. She had impaired motor skills, apraxia, inattention, now
and again an airy sort of euphoria. As time went on she could still
grasp word and context meanings, and knew how she wanted to
respond. But it grew harder and harder for her to say it, and she
used ever more expletives (Broca's aphasia).

Then Carlyne seemed to hear the siren song of her people, her origins, the land. Long ago, in Kinston, her mother learned to speak and act like gentry; but she was always seeking out this or that tribal woman in Lenoir County. She needed to talk. Selva and Carlyne came home to Pembroke for summer visits without Judge Vick. They arrived at the Depot where trains stopped in those days, beside Buie's Store; in the same passenger car with boys coming home from World War II, far places on their lips, Midway and Bataan. The long coal and freight trains left behind wood boxes and suitcases, and snatched a mailbag from the hooked pole, there at the famous intersection: longest stretch of straight track in the nation.

Those weeks after her married life ended Carlyne lay there. After the great effort to save her husband and herself came numbness; then sorrow, a pain so hard to feel and live with everyday. She was like an orphan child again. She couldn't see to her own needs anymore, and she felt so alone, so alone.

She lay in bed dreaming back on a house daubin' to get up four walls for someone; on the barn raisings, and corn shuckings, and quilting parties of her girlhood. The ladies met at each others' homes in Brooks Settlement around their frames; they made quilts for the elderly, or a young woman engaged to be married. You couldn't buy work like that in a store. Or, in the evenings by a kerosene lamp, they husked corn before the trip to X-Way and other gristmills where the corn got ground into meal for the staple bread eaten everyday. Extra ears they took from the corn crib and put in burlap sacks for the old'uns to feed their chickens and hogs. Later on, burnt cornstalks lit up the sky, and the ashes returned to earth.

Alongside them, a little girl, she had got in wild fruit and vegetables for jellies and preserves to be put in pies or on bread and biscuits during the winter months. Long ago, a long time, she went to visit her relatives and heard their words about how to get by in poor Robeson County. Smoke rose from the clay and corn pipes of the elders. Aromatic tobacco spiralled up with thankful words for the Great Spirit.

At night the rain beat down. It leaked in log and stick dwellings after the long day's field work to harvest crops. The uncles and cousins made trips to the river and got pelts, raccoon, otter, mink, beaver, muskrat, to sell to itinerant traders from up North.

Carlyne sipped persimmon beer the old folks brewed, and

helped pick sassafras roots to make tea. Out back there were sweet potatoes 'hilled' under earth or fine straw with a hole so you could retrieve them. Then came baked turnovers or potato cakes for the evening meal.

Once each summer she saw ocean beaches when the elders went for fish to salt down in brine as a winter food source: mostly mullet, gutted, beheaded, scales left on to preserve the flesh.

The children wove sweet straw and pine needles into baskets and round boxes with lids; these they presented the elders at Christmas season. Used tobacco string she helped collect and weave into doilies and tablecloths, or simple wall hangings, after being dyed to different colors with tree bark and berry stains. Old clothes the people tore in strips to make rugs against the cold weather.

These things she remembered, while she lay there, those days and weeks. She was in a twilight. She liked to think of her childhood then—a hog killing, the 300 pound hogs gambrel'd and dressed; or a wood sawing. There would be a fodder pulling in the hot August days. Once she went to the yearly ritual of 'school breaking': when the one-room schoolhouse recessed for summer, and the long table got heaped with chicken 'n pastry, salted fish, homemade biscuits, collards, grits, cornmeal, blackeyed peas; and the principal said a blessing too long for a good appetite.

There had been such hope at the Rock Castle in the weeks and months before the roof fell in. And then all went up in smoke. And in its place came loss, numbness, a pain so hard to face. And so she thought of her mother, and of Lovedy and other Lumbee women, overdressed in their frumpy outfits. The men, the fathers came staggering home from their meetings—'sad' after whacks at the jimmyjohn jug, or forays into the swamp for a swig or two of home-brewed stumphole. Leave for tomorrow the struggle to keep a last overtaxed parcel of ancestral land. Tomorrow the ten cents per hour to pick cotton, or twenty-cent work at the tobacco market.

How many times a young Lumbee woman boarded the train with her newly wed husband and went away . . . From Pembroke Junction they headed North toward the new life together. They went into the white man's world of bright lights and a fast pace, Baltimore, New York.

But someday they came home. Relatives and loved ones would see a girl through the pain which was too much for one. There

were remedies. There were 'polsters' handed down from ancestors in another age.

Lying there on her back Carlyne yearned to get up with family again. She thought of meeting the new ones born after she
and Selva no longer went home. She could get herself 'smudged':
made pure in the Purification Ceremony. And then, at her death,
there would be the same tribal burial that was handed down long
generations.

—Yo' ar'n—said Lovedy, and all the cousins and the in-laws
said it too, the Locklears, Jacobs, Brooks, Lowrys, Oxendines.

She couldn't bring back the past or her mother.

But she wanted so to go home.

IV

Inside Dial's the silence was turning into a stir. Family arrived
for a last look at the deceased where she lay, neat in her gray
dress, within the coffin of fine heart pine timber. The warm summery day also came in the viewing room and lit, for a moment, on
Carlyne Gilbert's forehead and high cheekbones.

In spite of all she had been through her features still kept a hint
of girlhood. She seemed to be thinking—almost home now; time
to pause and remember other warm days scented with jasmine:
when that boy played third base at the university. And then the
boy struggled by her side, and far away at the war, and then home
again—to become a man. It is difficult to become a man. It is difficult to learn to love someone . . . Almost there now—said her
expression—a few more minutes, is all, for the sake of the living.

Rhody had wanted down from Lydia's arms. Now she reached
and tapped her aunt's arm a few times:

—Hey . . . hey.

—Huh? said Lemon.

—I saw a gumball machine.

—Did you?

—Yes.

—Wow. Where was it?

—In the airport, on the way.

—And did you try one?

—Huh? No.
—No? Why not?
Rhoda was solemn. She shook her head.
—Gumballs break jaws.
—Do they really?
—Yes.
—That's good thinking. But I've heard they taste okay.
—I had a redhot once.
—Did you? A redhot. How was that?
—Hot.
—Was it red too?
—Huh? Yes.
Lemon blinked at the tears in her eyes, and shook her head a little, as she stared out the sunlit window.

V

The crowd outside was quite large by now. People filed slowly past the bier, sharing the sorrow.

Carlyne's black hair, combed straight back, highlighted the Oriental cast to her features.

The funeral was getting some media attention. It came at a time of growing tribal consciousness. The first Lumbee homecoming had taken place in 1970. And then, last year, the pan-tribal Pow-wow Movement came to Pembroke, and ingathered many thousands from the 49,000 of total estimated Lumbee. A great pow-wow was held at the longhouse.

Now it took time for all the visitors to pass by this dignified young woman who had departed from life. She achieved her bachelor's degree at an elite school. She attracted national attention as the wife of a pro ballplayer.

The funeral cortège to Burnt Swamp Baptist Church went on for a mile. The long line of cars moved slowly behind a black Buick with daughter and sister-in-law, Aunt Lovedy, and the New York doctor. A thousand pairs of headlights burned in the afternoon sunlight.

VI

There's a country road runs down there in the southeastern part of the state: some eighty miles from the coast as the crow flies. Along the road, near old Scuffletown between Moss Neck and Lumberton, a splintered sign stands half hidden amid the trees. It has an Indian chieftain in full regalia pointing down toward the river, who knows why anymore; and he smiles from the faded billboard which is part fallen away.

It's farm country round here. The wheat is harvested by July; the cotton's up eighteen inches to two feet, and tobacco runs higher than a man's head, if it rains right. There is a rich velvet smell, left over from last year's bright leaf crop, and this blends with the salt breath blown inland from the ocean. You could say it's a little like certain coastal stretches in Vietnam: where a dense tree cover turns the steamy sunlight of the fields to a diaphanous gold.

Now the people moved in silence, two and three abreast, along the path. As on the day eight years before when Carlyne brought her college beau down here to court and take a swim—the Lumbee River flowed its old brownish mauve hue from tannin in the trees. Its strong deep movement was kept hidden beneath a quiet surface. There were fish lazing visibly in their clean cold beds along the edge. A snowbird sang on an overhanging branch, and insects buzzed around.

The long line of mourners paused from their talk as they followed the closed coffin further into the forest toward the Scuffletown burial grounds. The path led a quarter mile along the riverbank; and then, where a landing once stood in the time before motors and paved roads—when this river was the lifeblood to a woodland community—they turned left and made their way on a slow incline. Here and there was a clearing grown over. A boarded cabin still stood with rotted steps and porch. There were signs of life long ago, as the procession made its way from the stream, and up the long slope.

Then from a grassy prominence they looked out on miles of Robeson County forest and farmland: west toward Maxton (Shoe Heel) and Laurinburg, east past Lumberton toward Elizabethtown and the Bladen Lakes region.

They arrived at a Locklear family plot. There was an open grave beside that of Selva Locklear, 1908-1955.

Alongside Selva was a headstone for the circuit court judge who had been buried elsewhere. He had liked everyday life by her side: even if it wasn't what you'd call proper for a Kinstonian.

Hon. Fitzhugh Foster Vick
1887–1953
(Lenoir County)

VII

In the cemetery a bluebird sang, and wildflowers blossomed at the edge of surrounding forest.

A minister read Scripture. The crowd stood silently to hear the sacred words being read.

Then they joined in a hymn 'lined out' for them by one of the elders. The people sang a hymn for their sister Carlyne's soul.

Sweet Carolina air, a serene spot in the woods; inviting scent of the pine trees and the river . . . Lydia stood with Lemon and Rhoda by the casket ready for lowering.

An elder, the man named Daystar, stepped forward and said a few words:

—Our sister gave much in her short life. She gave, and she suffered. As an orphan, a student, a wife and mother . . . she lived more in her twenty-eight years than many live in eighty. Here we return her mortal remains to the earth that bore and nourished her, as it does us all. That she may find peace in this place we invoke the soil, the rolling river, and the big mysterious sky. We call on the tribal spirit of our human life together, and we say: O eternal nature, receive her, treat her kindly. To you the children of time come home. And we say: go gentle with her, memory. She did the best she could. She loved and struggled in her brave way. We are all one big family, and so we owe a debt of love to our sister Carlyne Locklear Gilbert.

The coffin was lowered. One by one starting with Rhoda shown what to do by Lydia the nearest of kin took a handful of earth and tossed it on the coffin cover. Then Lovedy did the same, then Lemon, others.

Among the crowd in the old tribal cemetery the people turned to one another and hugged, and wiped a tear. For miles around the vista of land was a greenish brown in the clear light.

—This is for your mother, said Lydia.

In a shoal high overhead were alto-cumulus clouds going their way. The little girl frowned, nodded, as Lydia leaned and said a few words to her there by the grave.

—She was gweat, said Rhody.

First on the edges and then from the center the crowd began its descent back to the river and country road where cars were waiting in a long line. They moved off through the trees. Nobody spoke much now. You could hear the meaning in a bird's chirping, a wisp among the leaves, the silent stream flowing on.

Family and close friends lingered a few more moments. It was after four p.m. when they too turned and went down the hill toward their day with a sigh amid the routine and more pressing concerns.

As the late afternoon waned a breath of warm Gulf Stream air whispered in the trees. Birds, catbirds and jays, a yellow wing and a redbird, flew among their haunts and sang a little as dusk came on. Small animals peered out. A fox squirrel sniffed here and there. A raccoon nosed about after so much ruckus. Phee, phee! Too many humans, what a strange smell they have!

As night fell the sun went gold, crimson, then a mystic purple. This bluff above the river was a good lookout point for sunsets. A trail of mist was rising where the Lumbee River brooded, dark, impetuous in places, among the swamps and woodlands. It was Drowning Creek upstream; it became Little Pee Dee in South Carolina; it confluenced with the Pee Dee merged into Yadkin below the Uharie mouth further north. And so Lumbee and Yadkin, Carlyne's river and Joey's river, flowed together to Winyah Bay and the ocean. How many struggles they witnessed along the way and as promptly forgot.

Venus looked out and winked, pinkish, from her balcony in the sky. A night breeze murmured in the summits of the trees. Some small animal poked and fidgeted around the fresh mound of earth.

The newcomer lay in her simple gray dress, in the cold coffin, away from human eyes.

Carlyne slept in the burial ground of her ancestors beneath the stars.

VIII

At close of day they drove toward the coast. White Lake, Tomahawk, Tin City, Chinquapin. For a long time, along the road, they didn't speak. Rhoda slumbered quietly in the backseat.

They digested the rich Lumbee fellowship and food. It was a warm interest; it was a right hearty welcome for Carlyne's daughter, sister-in-law, and doctor friend. Yo' ar'n.

After awhile Lemon said:

—I find it strange.

—What?

—It'd be nice if Newell was with us.

—You miss him.

—Oh, yes and no with Old Obnoxious. I miss Joey more.

Lydia thought a moment.

—I've only had one talk with Newell. I liked him. But more than anything he gives a sense of . . . not distance, so much, as singlemindedness. He's the stuff Robespierres are made of, and yet it's clear he loves fun and to joke around.

—Family's his weakest suit—said Lemon.—Never worth much to any of us.

Lydia gave a little laugh:

—Maybe the weakest suit of us all . . . How many times in my work I've had to try and activate the volcano of families, of primary relationships. I need to put safeguards in place before I start drawing forth those old emotions. Say good wholesome water to douse the spontaneous combustion . . . I know it may sound awful, but maybe it's time civilization thought of moving beyond the nuclear family.—Lydia chuckled.—With Joey I was probing for some early trauma predisposing to a more acute PTSD. As his sister would you remember something . . .?

—How do you mean?

—Well, did your parents support him?

—I think Mom went a bit overboard favoring Newell. He just took up so much space.

—And your father?

—He liked Evelyne best, my older sister, but he liked Joey too. They didn't argue.

—Then there was no mystery, or let's say . . . an unfairness hidden in the mists of childhood?

Lemon considered.

—At one stage . . . You know, it's a long time since I thought about this. But at times Joey got on himself, and then he wondered aloud if he was adopted . . . the way kids say 'retarded' nowadays. When he messed up, or things didn't go his way, he ran himself down.

—Any possible truth to it?

—No, I don't think so.

—Or illegitimate?

Lemon thought a moment.

—He didn't look or act much like us. But I never heard that.

—The papers would exist, said Lydia.

—Where?

—In New England, or down here.

—I don't believe it.

The psychiatrist smiled:

—Well, it's just a theory. Maybe he was Thetis-born . . . Anyway I found no such dislocation in childhood. I only know he played with a lot of pain after Vietnam. He had acute symptoms, estrangement, diminished interest; he was a volcano ready to erupt. But unlike others he could turn the hyperalertness, his 'exaggerated startle effect', to account on a baseball diamond. Now I think about him everyday. The guilt he carried around, the flashbacks, sleep disturbance, the awful nightmares: how do you become an All-Star with that in your system?

Lemon frowned:

—Does All-Star matter?

—Well, for him it did. Combat high to forget. But also I think a matter of dignity. He lost in Vietnam.

—But he needed a hospital, not the hot corner.

—True. He was stubborn. He wouldn't go in; he had his super season to see through. You know I . . . it's hard to admit this, Lemon, but at times I feel like I let him down.

—We all did.

—No, but I failed myself. You see, I . . . well, never mind.

The two women fell silent.

Then Lemon said:

—I'll tell you one thing about Joey. When he was young, he spent a lot of time alone. I mean out of the house he was a regular Spring Glen boy. But many times he stayed by himself. And among us, at home, he was often like a loner.

IX

Lydia drove.

The dark trees flew by in the twilight.

—One day Carlyne came to my office. She was battered and bruised from the night before. So bad I sent her for X-rays. There was a cracked rib, but she waved this off. Didn't need a prescription; only wanted to ask me one thing: 'Why do you call my husband an exception, not normal, but maybe better than normal . . .?' So I started lecturing her: we come into this world, and we face difficulties, in the form of other people, their needs, weaknesses, expectations. Science can't quantify the severity of it, but people react differently. Some can't face facts, having no power or strength of will to change them; so they turn away and pretend, they deny, they make a bad compromise with reality. But when this is done, a door shuts; and behind it, even if it has a silver plaque, there is no air, no health, no movement, growth, development. Door shut on talent, on new life, on vital seeking the truth, on real sympathy for others. And so we go about in a bad silence. And we are highly respectable and civilized. Case closed. Or is it?

—Is it? said Lemon.

—Later on we start our own family. And sooner than later we produce splits, let's say compartments of loneliness. These seem to be passed on: at least I think so, and I spend my life exploring them. We put up partitions to shut out those we love, and those we don't.

—That's sad.

—At the same time we are . . . you name it: God's elect, patriots, great if only . . . But all the while the door to reality and fresh life stays locked tight until a crisis arrives. Is it too late? For the genius in us, yes, it is . . . Well, I believe Joey suffered some such split. But he kept on, no complaints about his broken ankle, the quiet type.

—Loner.

—Pierre Janet, the psychiatric forerunner, liked to release pathological memories by hypnosis. Janet said: change the way we *see* the traumatic event. It really happened differently. In essence he was urging a compromise; he wanted to rewrite history, you might say. It did not come to pass that way . . . But we today, the best of us, insist on the reality: relive it, consciously, know it, analyze it, work through and change it. Go with the mental set, cognitive structures and effective controls, to this end. When I called Carlyne's husband a miracle, I was placing hope in his courage to confront the past: that 'mystery' as it bears on the present. But before this could happen they came South to live. Then there was the anonymous letter setting off a crisis. Instead of controls, the police came into it. And then came destruction. But despite splits, exclusions, Vietnams, I could feel the positive force in Joey Gilbert: active in *me*, like humanity's. I believe in it because I feel it and have seen it: that we can meet life face to face and know it and change it to survive. I need that belief and that struggle to live. So in his way Joey Gilbert set an example.

The two women fell silent.

Rhoda slept as they passed through Jacksonville, and drove toward the Carolina coast.

At Cape Carteret they went over the bridge. Lights were reflecting from across the dark bay.

In the backseat Rhody awoke, stretched, and sat up. She cried a little, rubbing her eyes, and then asked one of her questions, in a peeping tone, even as she yawned.

After a few minutes Lydia pulled in at a motel by the ocean.

The surf rumbled in at night beyond a wide terrain of dunes.

X

The next morning after breakfast they walked down to the beach. The sun was warm. There was a salt seaweed smell with the scent of a driftwood fire. At sight of a girl waving her arms, a few stout sea gulls took wing and rode the seabreeze, mewing.

White breakers curled in over a sandbar offshore. The long aquamarine waves were in a tender mood today. On a pleasure cruise to this far shore they came caressing the garlands of algae and kelp, rockweed and dulse left by the tide. The waves crested and rolled in easily over the golden beach.

Rhody showed a restraint which was unlike her. First she shooed the gulls and scolded them, pointing her finger. But then she paused to stare at the ocean. She ran forward a few steps, but then turned and gazed back at Lydia. She stooped, still prudent not to soil her clean shorts, but that wouldn't last long, and then took off her shoes. A minute later she was crouching by the rainbowy arc of the surf with a palm to the foam.

Pretty girl, she had her mother's ruddy complexion and blue eyes. Sometimes she brooded, and sometimes she cooed. Now the surf seethed in about her bare feet and made her squeal. Down the beach there was a thump, thump, like thunder in the water when it pounded the sand and scraped over pebbles and went sucking its way back in the undertow.

XI

Delighted and into the swing of things Rhoda played while the grownups were talking.

Lemon said:

—I remember once, up North, in our childhood home . . . It was long about my eighth year. Joey and Newell were in high school. In those days Nunu could not lay eyes on his kid sister, me that is, without throwing a crushing tackle there in the living room which was his stadium. Splat! Down I went. Bring on the stretchers. Well, it got so I just gave a groan and fell on the rug the minute I saw him. He played too rough. One of those guys who don't know their own strength, at least when it came to me. Mom was worried he might go too far, you know, twist back my legs and not realize it. I don't know why I sort of . . . liked the attention.

—Women—said Lydia, with a laugh.

—Well, this one time he came forward at me half crouched, like a linebacker, and he had a mean look in his eye. Hard day at school? I guess it was the fed up look Dad had for him. Brace yourself for a cruncher, kid, a cross-body block. I was quaking in my boots. I shook like I had to pee, whined, dropped on my knees. Don't do it, Nooligan! Unnecessary roughness! Then I started to holler because he looked like Bronco Nagurski, brow knit and bearing down.

—Uh-oh.

—But just then Joey came down the stairs. It was rare for him to be home in the afternoon; he had baseball practice, and did weight lifting in the off season. Also, Juju got part-time jobs, rather than take money from Mom and Dad. He soda-jerked at Floriani's pharmacy, and liked to joke around there: dishing out a cone that was too big and then watching while a little kid's face and hands got all smeared with black raspberry.

—And clothes—said Lydia.

—For awhile he drove an ice cream truck, too. Used to gather a group of peewees up at Lavater Field and and make 'em a deal: who catches this pop-up gets a free popsicle! Then he threw the ball way up there, so high, it fell down on a kid's noggin and bounced up ten feet again. Little fellow starts to bawl, and Joey forces a popsicle into his hand.

—For being game.

—But as for Neuro, forget it. He'd never get a paper route, or deign to do a chore for Dad. No way! In high school he worked in a pizzeria for awhile: got a girl, and needed cash. But in general he only worked when he felt like it, and then like crazy; he'd do a month's homework in one night. Had a phase when he stole money from our parents: up early, sneak in and steal a twenty off Daddio's dresser . . . When they found out, he went under *their* bed and cried and carried on all afternoon.

—Shrewd tactic.

—Anyway they gave what he asked for. Neuter was spoiled rotten by Mom. And he just went on racking up their cars, and en-

joying the excitement of public high school, friends and frat parties, you know, after he got kicked out of a couple of prep schools.
But Jojo was the quiet type, went his own way, worked for his
money.

—Two brothers.

—So there he stood, Jody I mean, on the landing. Maybe Anne
had said a word to him, 'cause she knew Knute Rockne listened
to nobody except his older brother. You had to beat it into him.
But there you have our mother . . . Once a boy up the street had
a nervous breakdown, you know, big deal in those days, unmen-
tionable in the 'Fifties, like cancer.

—Uptight outa' sight.

—That's it. So Mom staged wild scenes between Dad and Neutral; they screamed at each other over the kitchen table. It was
scary. Tears, cries in the night. You hate me! Serve humanity! . . .
Ha ha, seems like comedy now. I came sneaking downstairs in
my pajamas as those titans battled it out. I remember Ma Newell's
(Joey called him Ma after some old football player) Ma's high-
pitched wail: You don't love me! Dad's baritone: Finest education available! Strive nobly! Do better than your best! . . . Newell
stamped his foot at that, and spat on the floor. Dance jitterbug!
Be happy! Tool around! At which Dad went red as a beet and
lost his temper. He browbeat the boy awfully, but he couldn't
tame him, finish him off. I think Mom wouldn't let him go for
the jugular. She set up those crazy scenes. But Emory's nerves
couldn't take it anymore, so he sent The Nuisance away to boarding school. Farmed out his son, and called it the finest education
available.

—At least Newell didn't have a nervous breakdown—said
Lydia.

—Are you kidding? Nature doesn't have nervous breakdowns.

XII

The two women walked along more compact sand just above
the surf. Nearby Rhody nosed about; she poked the dried shell of
a horseshoe crab with a stick. The morning sun was a wide shimmery field across the water to the horizon.

—So Joey got involved that time . . . when Newell picked on you?

—38! 71! 64! Hut-hut! He jumped all the way from the landing like they did as kids, and slid on the rug. As Ma Newell came on with a snort to flatten his little sister, Jojo bounded down, man, he threw a vicious tackle on the tackler. And the house shook. What a play! He laid him out on the living room rug, man. Hut! Hut! Joey rolled up a towel he had in his hand, and handed it off to me with a bark. Bootleg 32! Hup! 17! 89! Hike! hike! hike! Then he led the interference. From room to room we ran the broken field, first him then me behind. He yelled out: She's over the thirty! She's to the forty! She's at midfield! She's into enemy territory!

—Wrong-way Corrigan was a woman.

—No, ma'am, Right-way! Nubile sat in a daze with the wind knocked out of him; he was stunned at this betrayal between hard-asses, you know. After a moment he jumped back up and was a tackler in hot pursuit, as we headed for paydirt. He never gives in, no way! Like a bulldog. And now my big sister, called 'Report Card', left her homework and ran along with us from the kitchen to the dining room. I stayed behind my blockers and gave a hip fake and a straight-arm while our old lickspittle cocker spaniel, Sandy, came yapping after us and got into the act.

—A collective effort.

—Phew. Joeykins cried out. She's past the thirty, she's to the twenty, fans! Look at 'er shed tacklers! And then on upstairs we went charging through the old house on Santa Fe, in Redemaine. I stiff-armed Sandy who was jumping up and growling for the first time in ten years. Mom had a whistle and blew it in the upstairs hallway, but luckily Dad hadn't come home yet from the office . . . often so distracted, and bad tempered. One time he came in the house and started to throw things around like a wild man and mimic Newell. What a riot!

—Outside: urbane, witty—said Lydia—like my ex-husband. But he lacked humor en famille.

—Well, Emory had his own kind of humor. Pop's corn, he called it. Couldn't fly a kite without using more and more string, all the string he could find, and then cut it loose. He made a big drama out of it as the kite flew skyward. Or ironic: got all indignant, nose bent out of shape when we went to gamble at a county fair one time, called the Bazaar; then happy as a kid when we came back winners. I guess he just wanted to stay home and work.

—So did you make the TD?

—I hit paydirt. But as I crossed the ten chugging for the end zone, Newell the deep safety came on to make a last-ditch tackle. Whoomph! Joey flattened him, baw, he knocked him for a loop! It could have put a blocking sled in the infirmary. He knocked the living daylights out of Newberg. And then the two of them went rolling higgledy-piggledy down the stairs with Joey calling back: TD! It's a touchdown! The longest run from scrimmage by a woman in gridiron history! No flags, no clips. Take that, Franky Albert! Put that in your pipe and smoke it, Y.A. Tittle!

—Good Lord.

—At the foot of the stairs Newby sat in shock. Joey really had floored him, like he meant it! Nothing of the sort ever happened before. Strong, more than strong, Jojo didn't throw his weight around, but maybe he was doing Mom a favor. I remember them on the front hall rug, as they caught their breath. Newell wheezing, stunned, with his lesson. Anne, Evelyne and I peered down from the landing a little worried about Nutrient's health. And then, I'll never forget it, I can hear it now. Joey gave a chuckle and said to him: 'Don't pick on little kids, Bud, or girls. Bullies do that'. You see, Joey didn't say much. He didn't tell people things.

—About bullies, said Lydia.

—Then he got up. Put Null on two feet with a pat on the rump, and sent him on his way in a daze. With a lesson. So it ended, but . . .

—What?

—Well, for a minute, Joey played parent. And Newell stopped teasing me so hard. He did it, but softer, more brotherly.

—Didn't go for the jugular.

—He was thickheaded, still is. But I guess he finally understood.

XIII

They stared out across the water. Rhody, a sandman by now and wet through, stooped to pick up a shell for her red plastic bucket, and her room in Scarsdale. Then she sat at the foamy fringe and made happy little gestures.

Along the beach a few kids played and chattered.

Unhurried, the breakers came in, crescendoed, and pounded down on the runneling undertow. As a rider doffs his hat a wave tossed up its spume and then dismounted, after the long journey.

Far off the coast a tanker was headed south in a sunlit mist.

Kwup! kukkuk . . . A sea gull veered and hovered.

The midmorning was all asparkle like a royal way across the blue water. Rhody played house in the sand with a glance at other children running here and there—darting forward to shake their arms at the waves, crying out. They squealed with delight. Kids squeal at the beach.

Lemon stared at the slow progress of the tanker against the horizon. With a frown she said:

—Mom told us to do our best.

—Did she? said Lydia.

After a moment Lemon's words had a ripple, a bit like the surf:

—Her motto. I guess, after all, we're trying. We're doing our best.

Awhile longer the two women stood there, looking out at the emerald sea, and the eternal summer.

XIV

Later in the day Lydia and Rhoda waited by an embarcation gate inside Raleigh-Durham Airport.

An hour earlier they had dropped Lemon off at her student house, so Aunt could study for final exams. There were hugs and bye-byes. There was the happy prospect of being together in New York next fall when Lemon started graduate school. But first came her commencement exercises, and then summer in Europe with a friend, touring with a backpack, staying at youth hostels.

Now while Rhoda sat quietly with her nose in a children's book, Lydia gazed toward a distant place. It was a country with a strange landscape: the Eden deep in the psyche, shared by two people. Oh, she never hoped to possess Joey Gilbert; he wasn't hers; but she only wanted to love him and be so glad, so glad he lived and breathed and had his moments of triumph. O the joy of it when a person one loves is happy . . . And everyday she thought of him, and he was part of her enduring ideals and goals in life and her personal hopes and fears.

Well, she had fallen in love. And for us, also, says the poet: one time, once, and not again. And this completed Lydia. As a sincere artist in highest prime lives mainly for those creative means and powers brought to full expression, in control, a complete worker: so Lydia Falliere was living for her profession. It was self-realization on condition she give up very much, and not have a social life in the usual sense. But this wasn't so hard because she still had hope, and her heart was alive.

Certainly her patients benefited from such professional dedication, and objectivity. Also, her trailblazing PTSD study, *Vietnam Syndrome*, and then two other books, *Oedipus On My Couch*, and *Psychiatric Tragedy*, were very, very good and had sold through editions.

With the three children by her marriage well on their way in life, Lydia took a late mother's pleasure in the eager, active nature of Rhoda Strong. They loved and struggled together, the first grader and the intellectual M.D., like two friends. Legal adoption would follow once Carlyne's will probated.

—Ready to go?
—Weady.

Rhody closed her book. She smiled up at the tall elegant woman with dark eyes, short black hair, features with a Latin cast, as the two got to their feet and made to go.

—Here, take your ticket.
—You hold it—said the girl.

She reached and took Lydia's free hand.

—Okay.
—But when will I see Auntie again?
—I told you: in a few months, in the fall.
—Few months? Oh . . . But not Carlyne.
—Not Carlyne. But we'll remember her, Mommy.
—Remember her? Okay . . . She was gweat.
—Yes—said Lydia, a tear in her eye, severe.—She was.

Chapter
Twenty-Seven

I

April 1975

Dawn approached in Quang Ninh Province. Pinkish blue air sifted the coastal humidity. Along Bach Dang River the silent figures moved with rifles high.

On the outskirts of Cam Phe a shadowy unit slipped past outlined by low craggy hills.

Deep in the southern plains three women, in black, crossed a plank over a canal.

In Vietnam twilight gleamed.

Nha Trang. Gao trees. Birds sang. By the shore frogs croaked among the combretum shrubs. Password? *Trieng,* phoenix.

In Hué City a man waited beneath the royal poincianas. He rolled a cigarette. Lotus embalmed the quarter.

Now it was time to finish with them. Now it was time to begin. The NLF scouts rose from their hammocks. Explosions, gunfire were in the area.

Regional liberation forces ate their rice rations on the march. They advanced.

In Saigon a gray-headed man entered a waterside structure on the Thi Nghe River. A few minutes before daybreak he came out and looked around.

II

On the Caravelle Hotel terrace the international press, TV crews with their tripods, relayed images to a waiting world. Through the night there was heavy fighting round the South Vietnamese capital. Tan Son Nhut Airport was under attack.

Route 4: cut off by liberation forces. Smaller outposts in the suburbs: wiped out. The 232nd Force moved on Saigon from the southwest. Tanks, amphibious vehicles; cat-tracked 122 mm self-propelled and 85 mm low-trajectory and 130 mm artillery; anti-aircraft battalions; the 3rd, 5th, 8th, 9th Infantry Divisions and 16th 24th, 88th independent regiments: all went forward, all were gaining their appointed positions.

Operation Ho Chi Minh.

Total liberation.

Throughout Saigon the special action and sapper units deployed. Crack commandos, shrewd, courageous, absolutely dedicated. Group 429 was to attack enemy artillery emplacements in Saigon Wards Eight and Nine.

At 5 p.m. on April 26th the final battle, after centuries of popular resistance, had begun. It was a five-pronged assault. Crush the enemy's defensive positions. Encircle, split, destroy.

In Bien Hoa there was combat for seven hours without a lull. Revolutionary heroism.

III

A panicked exodus began. U.S. personnel and supporters—fleeing.

Route 1 northward, Route 4 to Mekong, Route 15 to Vung Tao: all were cut off, controlled. Bien Hoa Airfield was now closed. On the U.S. Embassy roof and elsewhere an auction was in progress for helicopter evacuation seats.

Yesterday the former Vice President and current Air Force Marshall Nguyen Cao Ky talked about the 'cowards that run away with Americans'. Today he ran.

Throughout the Saigon-Gia Dinh Special Defense Sector, in Precincts 1, 2, 5, 6, 7, 10, 11, 13, the people came out to support the regular forces. The five prongs advanced, advanced. NLF flags flew.

Sapper units captured Rach Chiec, Rach Cat and Ghenh Bridges, also the Saigon River Highway Bridge. They were welcoming the liberations forces who entered.

Explosions shook the city. Huge smoke pillars rose.

The northwest prong attacked and captured Tan Son Nhut and Thieu's General Staff offices. Western prong tank forces overran 25th Division Headquarters at Dung Du, former U.S. 'Tropical Lightning' base.

They came. Fierce combat was taking place at the gateway to national liberation. There were more tank battles, more artillery duels. Puppet regime planes whirled overhead and dove, bombed, strafed, like wasps being driven from the hive.

At No Hai, at the Army Motorized Units School in Nuoi Trong: there were counterattacks. Eastern front: the Armored Vehicles Depot fell.

On the eve, Ho Chi Minh Campaign tactical center swarmed with activity. Everywhere flashlights, lamps, headlights, maps, nonstop telephone communications:

—Forward, comrades! Total victory!

IV

From thirteen tall buildings the panicked exodus went on, Americans and their collaborators.

Commando units advanced. Tough, yet flexible, like bamboo. Men and women with strong nerves, clear goals, a scientific outlook, they advanced. They waged short no-quarter battles: along Highway 13; from Cat Lai naval base on the Dong Nai River to the Saigon waterfront: at the big Ha Tien cement factory twelve miles east. From the four corners of the world: have-nots besiege haves. The people fight their oppressors.

Everywhere local NLF forces rose up to attack the foreign occupier, as they had invader armies of the past: the Mongolian Empire, the Chinese down the centuries, the French colonialists in modern times, the Japanese aggressors, and for these past twelve years the most powerful and savagely destructive nation in human history.

Puppet Battalion 327 on guard at Sang Bridge, in the western outskirts, fell to Hoa Lu regiment. Binh Gia regiment destroyed enemy positions at the 5-way Van Lom Crossroads. At the key Bay Hien intersection, where seven roads met a mile from the heart of Saigon, the battle lasted forty minutes; it was a paroxysm in the fighting; many died.

Exploded, in those instants, the myth of U.S. invincibility— with its technological superiority and local pro-imperialist power structures, its administration and military crucial to neocolonialist war and pacification efforts. Now the Americans ran. Their mystique vanished before the eyes of a stunned Western press corps, TV crews: before the world's eyes.

V

Dawn, April 30th, broke clear and cool.

The five-pronged Liberation Army made a star with Saigon in the center.

The U.S. quislings convoked their ministers to a 10 a.m. meeting inside Independence Palace. It was too late. At 9:25 the news had arrived: four divisions lost, the 5th, 18th, 22nd, 25th.

The gentlemen asked for a ceasefire.

Word went among the popular forces as they advanced:

—No ceasefire! It is a once in a thousand-year chance!

They entered Saigon.

And the people went with them, ushering them in. The *people* poured out in the streets to greet the liberators. And together they went marching past government buildings which were vacant now. And the red flags and banners made a forest *en marche* down the homestretch toward the workers power, and the socialist reconstruction. And many laughed out loud and shook their fists at those offices fled from in a stampede by the herd of corrupt lackeys and U.S. collaborationists. What inane dunces to betray your own people. Thrice you deny Uncle Ho? Now the cock has crowed. You served the murderer Uncle Sam? Now go along.

The people carried flags and beat on drums and hollow wooden fish. The people manned the megaphones and took it upon themselves to neutralize certain spies and traitors. They disarmed enemy soldiers. They were there to escort Uncle Ho's battalions into the city.

The people! The people!

We showed what we could do
at Dien Bien Phu.

They brought out food and drink for the fighters.

They gave directions.

From Thong Nhat, the central boulevard, a first tank ploughed its way through the high ornate Independence Palace gate.

There on the steps Big Minh, the firefly President, surrendered.

Fifty-five days and nights of battle: the Ho Chi Minh Campaign.

Total victory. Saigon liberated. At 11:30 a.m. the revolutionary flag flew from Independence Palace where various troop-wing contingents met and embraced. Peace with justice: a true peace after thirty years of war.

What a clear, beautiful, jubilant morning it was. Peace! Fragrant peace, radiant peace!

Hanoi also overflowed its streets, and waved flags, and threw flowers. Heroic Hanoi, Uncle Ho's home, sang, and breathed in the purified air, the sweet, sweet air of reunification.

Across united Vietnam the people danced and sang. The mountains, rivers, paddy fields, coastal plains, Mekong, the islands: *O unity, O peace.*

And Vietnam wept for her two million dead, for the martyrs inconsolably precious, every one. Vietnam wept for her children.

Monstrous tiger-caged Paolo Condor, where CIA-trained and AID-funded torturers held their orgies—wept.

The Vietnamese people cried. And they exulted. They took pride in their great, heroic, their immense achievement. Such a contribution to world history: this prototypical victory over impossible odds; a model for future U.S. defeats by popular movements—resisting the aggressor, invader, occupier, exploiter.

Yes, it was a great spring victory for all progressive forces. It was a reverse for U.S.-led reaction worldwide.

Pride, excitement, victory songs, tumultuous joy, hugs.

Tears.

All were tired, but nobody slept. All danced, sang, wept.

Saigon's million-strong puppet army collapsed.

A Huey gunship maneuvered with its glare of identification lights. The last panic-stricken U.S. personnel scooted; they flew as best they could, like flapping chickens with their expensive luggage—across the Embassy lawn. The evacuees proceeded to the UH-1E rooftop pad, or a CH-53 lift-off in the courtyard.

Massive crowds moved along Independence Avenue.

Saigon fell.

Ho Chi Minh City rose from its ashes. Phoenix! Symbol of fidelity.

From the placards held high Uncle Ho's kindly arm beckoned. Come, everyone, toward the future! In the North the bell still echoed through his house on stilts by the side of the pond. News from the front! Victory day! With his gaiety, and a keen affection, Uncle invited earth's peoples to win their liberation as Vietnam had done, and take their place at the festive table of brotherhood, which is socialist.

Next task, comandante!

Onward, comrades: till the bugle call of total victory.

VI

The helicopter lifted up and away over the green-brown paddy fields. These were the final hours of Western military presence in Vietnam. Now it is the hour of the masses: the ancient coolies and city workers trampled underfoot for centuries, until today. Now is the hour of the peasantry exploited by taxation and exorbitant land rents, serfdom, slavery in the countryside, huge plantation tracts under absentee ownership while the toilers, the actual producers faced starvation daily: like human beasts put to the plough a thousand years by usurpers in faroff places. And this still exists, comrade, yes, today, across the earth; but not in Vietnam.

In Vietnam the people took up arms. From scratch they started, picking up a club, fashioning a bamboo spear, getting their hands on a crossbow, then a musket or flintlock. In Vietnam they formed defense units. They set up small arsenals and studied homemade grenade manufacture. For years there were scarce raw materials, few machines, no technical cadres. But in 1941 the Vietminh Resistance was born. Then mass organizations began to link up whole regions soon inaccessible to the French despite their fine rifles, or the Japanese.

Look, the tanks!

The tanks advance along Independence Avenue!

At 12:15 p.m. on April 30th, 1975, a Provisional Revolutionary Government representative announced over the radio:

—*Saigon has won its total liberation. We accept the unconditional surrender.*

Two thousand years. Struggle to the death. Mongols, Chinese, Japanese, French, Americans.

Chào cô, goodbye.

—*There is nothing more precious*—the PRG spokesman quoted Ho—*than independence and freedom.*

Saigon streets filled with people. Armored vehicles at the Presidential Palace. Desperate flight of the occupiers and their cronies; and others with their heads turned by news of a bloodbath that never happened.

A helicopter went toppling into the sea sideways—like a huge locust from the locust plague of imperialism feeding on the Third World. Rotors submerged, the chopper fell down, floundered.

Girls in the *ao dai* danced on a platform stage before the National Theater in Hanoi.

A helicopter went soaring above the long rice fields glimmering in twilight. It followed along the Mekong tributaries toward Vung Tao and the coast.

Sampans, fishing smacks, earthen junks with their lug sails furled up—peacefully the boats were anchored by the shore at nightfall. The waves plashed. The rigging creaked.

Twenty centuries of struggle.

Now calm.

VII

Calm of victory.

How different from the silence of defeat, in many places, still, across the earth.

And so it ended: after fifty-five days and nights of military movement and frenzied battles. Some four thousand U.S. planes were shot down and 300 ships sunk or ruined, U.S. naval vessels. 6500 U.S. military vehicles of all types, 660 artillery pieces, 275,000 other weapons captured. Of 680,000 South Vietnamese (ARVN) troops engaged: 21,000 were killed and wounded, 231,000 captured or surrendered. Eleven ARVN infantry divisions were destroyed, and eight independent regiments. 216 Civil Guard and regional troop battalions: destroyed. Twelve armored regiments, 800 tanks and armored cars, 35 artillery battalions, over 700 artillery pieces, three air divisions, 1200 naval vessels and river patrol boats, a thousand more sundry aircraft: destroyed.

Who paid for all that waste, the entropy of world history?

The gullible Americans with their tax dollars.

The humble, heroic Vietnamese with their lives.

There was no bloodbath. The Western press said there was: they trumpeted it. But there wasn't.

If I wanted a character reference on you: would I ask your worst enemy?

For a long time no one will call Vietnam a socialist paradise: after what the U.S.A. did to it. 100,000 tons of chemical products were used against a country the size of New Mexico. 80 million liters of herbicides, 21 million gallons of Agent Orange were dropped on Vietnam. Tell me now: were these weapons of mass destruction? Generations of Vietnames will suffer the effects: cancer and other diseases, birth defects, molar pregnancies.

And how many Vietnamese, how many children will suffer horrible deaths and maiming from unexploded ordnance left behind, like a testament, by the American war effort? Of course the U.S. refuses to have anything to do with cleaning it up.

But even all this will not dim the Great Spring Victory, or be a blight on the national life.

A socialist revolution teaches its people to read, and gives them healthcare, and struggles to relieve poverty. It develops the nation. It industrializes.

The wide night spread away as far as the dawn.
Tomorrow brooded.
Tomorrow was on its way with a lot of warm sunlight and shades of green the length and breadth of Vietnam. There is the green tinged lightly gold of the sugarcane fields. There is the tender green of the rice in summer, and deeper green of bamboo hedges. Filao pines are an emerald tint here and there, like the offshore waters. In the villages and rice paddies and forests of Vietnam there is a rich gamut of green.
For now the waves rustled at night. They rolled in along the coast from far out in the East China Sea (East Sea) and beyond. Murmurous, the tide came in, and seemed to say:
—Why try to limit life?

Epilogue

Years later—many years—on a hot day in summer, a man stood by Carlyne Gilbert's grave in Scuffletown Cemetery. His hair was cut close with a touch of gray in it. He wore bluejeans, a blue work shirt; he needed a shave unless he meant to grow a beard.

He sat down by the grassy plot and had a look out at the view of Robeson County farmlands and distant stretches of forest. His big frame now in its forties, with a sense of exertion in the wiry limbs, was a little tired because he had come a long way.

He had come from Kentucky where he spent seventeen years in a Federal prison. He was let out three days ago.

There is no need to go into the Gilbert case in detail. After the hostage crisis at the Rock Castle he was flown to a prison hospital. Some months later he made his appearance at the Federal Middle District Court in Greensboro; and there, with Dr. Lydia Falliere in attendance, he based his plea on traumatic stress disorder. There was no trial. He was sentenced to life in prison without parole.

In the correctional facility he was permitted visits but no physical contact with his visitors. Now and again his brother or sister came to see him and speak with him through a screen. He never saw his wife again. She couldn't make the trip. Like two orphaned children unable to take care of themselves, they were separated. A note, a letter came from her in Aunt Lovedy's hand: just a few words about this or that. And: I love you, Jo. For two years he wrote his wife letters filled with love for her, sort of like he did in Vietnam, but not so wild.

Once a month for seventeen years, usually on Sunday, Dr. Falliere came to visit him at the prison. She got there in the afternoon
and flew back to New York the same evening. Often she brought
Rhoda with her. By her side was the pretty girl, a bit of a tomboy,
growing up. And she brought him books; but the bindings had to
be stripped off from hard-cover editions.

On his third hearing as he tried for a pardon, he got one.
The Governor of North Carolina commuted the sentence of the
decorated war veteran—citing good behavior in prison, and remorse. Probably the public image of the professional athlete was
a factor.

Through the day Joey had the graveyard to himself. He sat
leaning on Carlyne's headstone and thinking about her past,
which was like a part of him. The things she told him were different now. He remembered what she said about this or that event
in the longhouse which she as a girl had helped to construct. He
thought of this as if he was there with her the summer they built
it—cutting and stripping bark from young pine trees, and daub-
ing clay between logs to keep out the wet and cold . . . And then
there were chants, drumbeats, toe and heal dances, songs and the
rattle of gourds when the people celebrated completion of this
place meant to gather folks in and give them a tribal self-respect
. . . Joey also thought of the struggle of her ancestors: Henry Berry
Lowry and the group of men living out in the swamps, fighting
against injustice.

Sitting there he recalled the old-time customs still a part of the
life of her people—pole and rain dances, quilting parties, school
breakings, corn shuckings, fodder pullings, hog dressings, tobacco croppings. There were the drives to market with farm produce and the fall powwows. There were the settin' up wakes for
folks who departed, and Sunday visits to this cemetery and the
other out there along Route 710, over the bridge.

In his mind he passed in review the brutal treatment that was
done to her people, such a big part of their history: the restaurant
and movie segregation; the land grabs by the white man which
went on into the 1960s. He read many books while in prison on
the fate of the indigenous tribes. There was so much selfishness,
so much violence. And for what?

Well, Carlyne learned to talk two ways. She spent her life in
the world of the white man. But she knew she was still Little

Blue Smoke—as a Piscattaway chief once called her, admiring the blue-eyed schoolgirl and her braids. If you were a Cherokee, if you were Tuscarora, or Cheraw . . . then sometimes you longed to go home.

For a long time Joey sat by Carlyne's grave thinking. And it seemed like her past was his too: as if it was inside him, and he was in her skin.

Then he stood up, stretched his arms at the sky with a yawp, and turned with a last look to walk back down the trail toward the riverbank.

He spent last night by her side.

Now the second afternoon had begun to wane. There was a gold dusky light, a tobacco fields hue inland from the Carolina coastline; it hung above the reddish brown Lumbee.

Joey took off his work shirt and bluejeans and pushed off into the dark river. Was this where the grown-ups warned the kids not to come? Was it not a good spot for a swim?

Water rattlers with a deadly stinger in the tail were a sort of pasty color on top. And copperbelly mocassins . . . watch out!

He lay on his back, and turned over, and swam a few strokes in the cold, pure water.

Now where to, Joey Gilbert? He wanted to go spend a moment on the campus where they were young and courted. It was too late for the springtime fragrance, magnolias in blossom, wisteria. But he could walk across the campus with its Classical and Georgian Revival buildings, its sense of the Old South.

*
*   *
*

Now it has been many more years since the two days Joey sat by his wife's grave; then went for a swim in the river; and then walked out to the highway wondering which direction to take.

Of course there have been stories and rumors about him. He was working on an oil rig in the Gulf of Mexico; he was a fisherman in Iceland. He was a drifter hitching rides around the country and riding boxcars.

Here and there a word in the media had him picketing with striking workers out West somewhere. Further afield might seem

MANIFEST OEDIPUS

a rumor that he had gone to fight as an internationalist along-side the MPLA in Angola: or, quite recently, that he was helping with the national sports program in Venezuela. More likely, at least closer to home, were sitings of the ex-baseball player in a small town in Alabama where he was said to be studying political economy in a hut out back of a war buddy's house; or serving as interim principal of a grade school on a Reservation near Tuba City, Arizona; or back east walking along the Shenandoah River where he had been to see the parents of a fallen G.I. who was in his squad in Vietnam.

It is said people in Scarsdale have seen him around town; though he doesn't seem to have become a member of the PTA yet.

And once he was spotted in Central Park with a boy of five or six who was holding his hand.

Be all this as it may, he is probably still out there looking for something: just as he was from the moment he left baseball the first time—before that he was *nature*—and went away to war; just as he was the night in Berkeley when despite himself he read his brother's article on Vietnam's greatest leader; just as he was in sessions at Lydia's office, probing his soul; just as he was in the days of his crisis, and then the long years in prison, study-ing, talking, thinking:—all the time he was the seeker, he was the man of struggle. So much, so much he always wanted to stay put somewhere and try to be happy; but he had to keep going on and looking for himself, looking for a way to live. It was like he had a curse on him, and maybe his curse is our curse too. We are innocent if we did not know, if we were only trying to get on with our lives. Oedipus didn't know; he became a man of destiny when he learned, and had to see it through . . . And Joey Gilbert's life would also seem to say this: we have no other course but to see the reality through, if we mean to survive as a people, as a species.

We must come to terms with Oedipus if we mean to triumph.

If not, we will be doomed by our guilt.

Oedipus is the great symbol of life's movement: form (father) renewed, content (mother) reengaged. This is the dialectics at the heart of life. And its contradictory movement tells us that until man learns to plan better—wins that socialist right—the world will be brutal and violent.

Can humanity live that way?

Now I see him striding on the horizon of America. He is seeking the truth no matter how terrible it may be. He is calling us forth to our great struggle as a people.

He is calling us forward.

Ho Chi Minh City
New York City
1981–2007